STAR TREK®

IMZADI FOREVER

STAR TREK®

IMZADI FOREVER

Peter David

Based on
Star Trek: The Next Generation®
created by Gene Roddenberry

A special signature edition of
Star Trek: The Next Generation—Imzadi
and *Star Trek: The Next Generation—Triangle: Imzadi II*

POCKET BOOKS
New York London Toronto Sydney Singapore

POCKET BOOKS, a division of Simon & Schuster, Inc.
1230 Avenue of the Americas, New York, NY 10020

ISBN: 0-7434-8510-6

First Pocket Books trade paperback edition December 2003

10 9 8 7 6 5 4 3 2 1

Manufactured in the United States of America

These titles were previously published individually by Pocket Books.

For information regarding special discounts for bulk purchases, please contact
Simon & Schuster Special Sales at 1-800-456-6798 or business@simonandschuster.com

Introduction

I had no idea when I was writing it that *Imzadi* was going to be the most popular book I ever produced. All I knew was that I'd been given the mandate by then-editor Kevin Ryan to write the story of how William Riker and Deanna Troi first hooked up.

Frankly, I was just excited about the prospect of writing it. *Star Trek* has a great mythic, epic feel to it, and being allowed to explore such defining territory was a terrific opportunity. However, I didn't just want to write a flashback story. I wanted to do something vast, sprawling. So *Imzadi* covers Riker and Troi's past, "present," and possible future—with a tip of the hat to Harlan Ellison, whose original concept for "City on the Edge of Forever" was that Kirk was willing to let the universe unravel in order to save Edith Keeler, and it was the emotionless Spock who made sure she died. I dropped an elderly, embittered Riker into Kirk's position, Data into Spock's, and the story practically wrote itself.

The impact it had and continues to have to this day amazes me. One couple told me that they used Riker's poem for their wedding vows. A couple of squealing teenaged female *Imzadi* fans, upon realizing who I was, actually jumped me in a parking lot as if I were a rock star while my horrified eldest daughter looked on.

Imzadi II was a bit more problematic. If *Imzadi* was a snapshot of the happily married writer I was at the time I wrote it—producing a novel of depthless romance—*Imzadi II* came after my marriage went south. It presented the more dour message that things don't always work out the way you plan. That what gives a story a happy ending is that you choose to conclude it where you do . . . because any story continued long enough always ends sadly, in tears and loss. On the upside, it also presented the idea that when things don't work out, it doesn't necessarily mean the end of one's ability to love, even though sometimes it may feel like it. The human (or, for that matter, Klingon) capacity for resilience and seeking out new companionship is nigh infinite. It's reflected both in the lives of the *Enterprise* crew and in my own moving on to a second—and quite happy, thank you—marriage. If Riker, Worf, and Troi could rebound from romantic setbacks, so could I. And so can you, if you're reading this and are in the throes of a busted relationship.

I am pleased and proud that Pocket is putting out this fancy-shmancy edition of these two novels. I doubt there'll be a third, since the rest of Riker and Troi's relationship is being chronicled elsewhere.

I further wish to acknowledge: John Ordover, who oversaw *Imzadi II,* and Margaret Clark, who is seeing this edition through to fruition; the ever-cooperative Paula Bloch at Paramount; Ron[ald D.] Moore, who took it upon himself to assure me that the similarities between *The Next Generation*'s then-forthcoming final episode and elements of *Imzadi* were purely coincidence; and Jonathan

Frakes, who did a sensational job reading the audio version of my adaptation of *Imzadi*.

And since the first book was dedicated to my first wife, and the second book to my second wife, Kathleen, so let this edition be dedicated to the thousands of fans who have supported the two books and have taken the time to let me know how much the novels meant to them. I write all my books from the heart, but I suppose that when it's a book *about* the heart, it's more obvious. So a shout-out to romantics everywhere or, as Anna sang in *The King and I,* "Be brave, young lovers, and follow your star."

Peter David
Long Island, New York
September 2003

IMZADI

The events take place during 2366,
just prior to Commander Riker assuming
command of the *Enterprise* during the Borg
invasion of Sector 001.

THE END

One

"Let's get the hell out of here."

A gentle, eerie howling was in the air, which seemed to be permeated with the haunting and lonely cries of souls that had existed or might never exist or might be in some state of limbo in between.

In the distance was the city. Its name was unknown and would forever remain so. The air was dark and filled with a sense that a storm might break at any moment. It was that way all the time. The storm never did break. It just threatened to do so. The very withholding of the actual event implied that, should that storm ever arrive, it might very well bring with it enough power to wash away all vestiges of that remarkable intangible called reality.

None of that mattered to the man who was the leader. The man in the greenish yellow shirt, whose mind was elsewhere and elsewhen. Behind him stood his friends, his crew. They waited patiently. For a moment it appeared that he was wondering just how long they would be capable of waiting. What were the limits of their patience? The limits of their confidence in the man who was their captain?

But it was clear that he was not going to test those limits. A man who had been driven to go out and explore new places, discover new frontiers . . . this man had finally found a place filled with potentially endless vistas of exploration. Anywhere, anywhen. And his response was not to embrace it. No, all he wanted to do was leave it behind, to get as far away from it as possible.

"Let's get the hell out of here." The words hung there a moment, startling in their vehemence, in the longing and resignation and overall sense of *Oh, God, I can't stand it anymore, get me away from here, away to a place where I don't have to think or feel, to a place where I can just be numb.*

The crew took several small steps closer to each other. To a degree it was out of reflex, to make sure that they would be well within range of the transporter effect. But there was something else as well this time. It was an unspoken desire to try to lend support by dint of the fact that they were *there* for him. There was nothing they could say or do. Indeed, they didn't even fully understand what was going through the captain's mind.

They did not yet know the sacrifices their commanding officer had made. Did not know that, in the best tradition of romance, he had found a part of his soul existing in a woman and had been drawn to her. And then had lost that part of his soul, which he hadn't fully realized he was missing in the first place. Lost it beneath the screeching of tires, under a truck's wheels . . .

Not just the wheel of a truck. A wheel of history, an unrelenting, unyielding cog that had ground up his love and his soul and spit them both out, bloodied and battered . . . and broken.

Yes, that was the difference that the crew sensed this time in their captain. Many a time had he been battered . . . but as the old saying went, "Battered but unbowed." This time, though . . . he was bowed.

They got the hell out of there.

And Commodore Data watched them go.

She was simply called Mary Mac. Her last name actually began with a sound approximating "Mac," but the rest was a major tongue twister. As a result, the other scientists addressed her as "Mary Mac."

Mary Mac was extremely peculiar. For one thing, she was an Orion. This in itself was not particularly unusual. She was, however, fully clothed. This *was* unusual, as the vast majority of Orion women existed purely to be the sex toys of men in general and Orion men in particular. They were known as vicious and deadly fighters and radiated sex the way suns radiated heat . . . and indeed, some thought, a bit more intensely.

Mary Mac's skin was green, as was standard for an Orion woman. In every other aspect, however, she was markedly different from the rest of her kind. She wore loose-fitting clothes . . . deliberately loose so as to do nothing that could potentially emphasize the formidable curves of her body. Because she liked her arms unencumbered, her tunic was short sleeved, although an off-the-shoulder cape was draped stylishly around her. She had long, jet-black hair, but rather than hanging saucily around her shoulders, it was delicately and elaborately braided . . . certainly not an ugly hairstyle, but hardly one that would inflame the senses.

Most incredibly . . . she wore glasses. They had a slight tint and huge frames.

Nobody wore glasses. They were considered to be phenomenally out-of-date as well as unattractive.

Which is why she wore them.

Mary Mac regretted, every so often, that she felt a need to "dress down," as it were, so that she could operate within society. She was, however, used to it. There were precious few prejudices that one had to deal with in the day-to-day operations of the United Federation of Planets, but one of the few remaining was that all Orion women were nothing but animalistic sex kittens. It was an understandable notion because that description did indeed fit virtually all Orion women, including most of the ones whom Mary Mac had ever met.

It did not, however, fit her, and if she had to go to extremes to get her point across, well . . . then so be it. Her "look" had gotten her quite far. It had, in fact, been something of a plus. People would be interested and amused by her as she would discuss some involved or arcane bit of scientific lore . . . interested because usually they'd never heard an Orion woman put together a sentence of more than five or so words, and amused because they'd smugly be waiting for her to revert to type any moment. She never did, of course. She'd trained too long and too hard to allow that to happen. As a result she was always a bit of a surprise, and throughout the galaxy, people loved to be surprised.

Which is why Mary Mac had worked her way up through the ranks and eventually landed the assignment of project administrator on Forever World.

The planet did not have an official name. Somehow it had seemed presumptuous for any mere mortal to give it one . . . somewhat like painting a mustache on the face of God. It had simply been nicknamed Forever World, and that was what had stuck.

She passed her associate coordinator, Harry, who didn't seem to notice her. A muscular and dark-hued terran, Harry's attention was fully on a set of equations or some other bit of scientific data on a palm-sized computer padd. "Hi, Harry," she said to him as he walked past. He waved distractedly and continued on his way. He had probably already forgotten that he'd been addressed at all, much less by Mary Mac.

Mary Mac made her way across the compound, nodding or conversing briefly with other scientists on the project. One of the odder aspects of conversation on the Forever World was that one tended to speak in a hushed voice. There was no particular reason for it. It certainly wasn't mandated by law or tradition. But somehow, particularly when one was standing outside and the eerie howling filled one's ears and one's soul, the speaking voice tended to drop to a soft tone that could best be described as "subdued" . . . and perhaps even a bit fearful. Mary had once commented that it always seemed as if the cosmos was hanging on your every word here. It was an assessment that had been generally agreed with.

The gravel crunched under Mary Mac's boots as she got to the other side of the compound and headed toward the reason for the perpetual presence of a half dozen or so scientists on the Forever World.

Just ahead of her was the only other constant noise that existed aside from the mournful sigh of the wind, and that was a steady, constant hum of a force field. She stepped over a rise, and as always, there it was.

As always was not a term used lightly, or incorrectly. As near as anyone could tell, the Guardian of Forever had always been there, and would most likely always be there.

The force field that had been erected around it was ostensibly to protect the unique archaeological discovery from any potential ravagers. But in point of fact, it was there for a subtly different reason. Namely, to protect life (as it was known) from itself.

Erected just outside the force field was a free-standing platform about two meters tall. An array of readouts charted the energy fluxes that surged around the Guardian of Forever within the force field. There were, in addition, two small lights, one brightly glowing red, the other pulsing a very soft green.

To the right of the platform was a large screen. It offered, in essence, a taped delay. When a request for a period was made on the Guardian, it ran so quickly that the best anyone could hope to perceive was fleeting images. But the screen would then capture those images and play specifically requested moments in a more accessible fashion.

At this particular moment, the Guardian had finished yet another run-through of a particular era. It was now silent, displaying nothing, waiting with its infinite patience for the next request from an audience.

Standing outside the field, staring at the Guardian, was an android. Playing out on the screen, having been recorded moments before for replay, was a scene very familiar to Mary Mac.

She stopped and simply took in for a moment the irony of the situation. On one level, what she was seeing was one machine watching another. But neither of them were simple machines. Both of them had sentience, which raised them from the level of machine to the status of . . . something else. Something unclassifiable.

The very thought of something that could not easily be labeled or pigeonholed was anathema to Mary Mac, and yet at the same time the existence of such things was a pleasant reminder that no one could ever fully know every wrinkle that the universe had to offer . . . and that, therefore, a scientist's work would never, ever, be finished.

Her first inclination had been to think of the android, despite the rank of commodore, as an "it." Just as she had thought of the Guardian as an "it" before coming to the Forever World. However, shortly after she'd met Commodore Data, she'd found herself forced to revise her opinion and mentally elevate the commodore to a "he." As for the Guardian, she was still trying to get that sorted out. The best she could come up with at the moment was a "whatever." Or perhaps, more accurately, a "whenever."

Data stood there, his back to Mary Mac, hands draped just below the base of his spine. The stark black and green lines of his uniform, with the silver trim on the arms and trouser cuffs, seemed to shimmer in the perpetual twilight of the horizon. His attention shifted momentarily from the Guardian to the scene being replayed on the screen.

Mary Mac heard a familiar voice, a voice filled with resolve and yet hidden trauma. And the voice said, "Let's get the hell out of here."

She smiled and called out, "That figures."

Data turned and looked at her, his face calm and composed as always. His gold skin glittered in the half light. "Pardon?"

She pointed at the Guardian. "That moment. It's one of the most popular."

Data nodded slowly and looked back. On the screen, the crew of explorers was drawing closer to its leader and then, moments later, shimmered out of existence. "That's not surprising, I suppose," said Data. "Although there are many moments from history that would be far more impressive in their scope, the history of James Kirk and the crew of *Enterprise* would certainly hold some degree of fascination. People would probably feel more empathy toward someone who is closer to their own frame of reference. What I find interesting is how primitive the transporter technology was."

Mary Mac looked at him in surprise. "You know, Commodore, I've seen so many people watch this moment. The story of Kirk's ordeal with the Guardian, and what he sacrificed for the sake of history . . . it's become so well known. One of the few modern-day legends we have. And I've seen so many reactions, ranging from hysterics to mourning. I've never heard anyone just comment on the technology . . . especially not when they're seeing it for the first time."

Data glanced at the screen. "It's not the first time. It's the second."

"When did you see it before?"

"When it was displayed on the Guardian, one point three minutes ago."

She blinked in surprise. "You were able to make out something that played on the Guardian himself?"

"Of course. The image feed may be rapid for you, but for me it's relatively sluggish. Still, I wished to see it on the replay screen in the event that I missed some sort of nuance. But I didn't."

She shook her head. "You are a rather different customer than we usually get around here, Commodore, I must admit. Most people don't quite know how to react when they see their ancestors brought to life, or shadows of life"—she gestured to the Guardian—"before their very eyes."

"Understandable," said Data. "However, the difference is . . . I have no ancestors."

"You were made. Other androids existed before you, even if not in direct lineage. If they're not ancestors, what would you call them?"

He considered it a moment. "Precedents," he decided.

She smiled broadly and clapped him on the back. "Come on. We have dinner up back at the compound. We'd be honored if you joined us."

"I'd like to touch it."

Her hand stayed on his back, but her expression slid into a puzzled frown. "Touch what?"

"The Guardian of Forever."

"Whatever for?"

He looked at her in such a way, with his gold-pupiled eyes, that Mary Mac felt a slight chill. The same sort that she had felt when she first stood in the presence of the Guardian.

As if he had been reading her mind, Data said, "To be honest . . . I'm not entirely sure. The Guardian and I . . . we are rarities in the universe. We are each one of a kind." He shifted his gaze to the Guardian. "For a brief time I had a brother . . . but he's gone now, although part of him"—he tapped his forehead for a moment—"remains with me. For an even briefer time—forty-two years ago, to be exact—I had a daughter . . . but she was barely here long enough to establish her presence. I sense in the Guardian a kindred spirit." He looked back at Mary Mac. "Would you consider that funny, Doctor? The notion that something inhuman would try to lay claim to something as human as a spirit?"

"No," she said quietly. "No, I wouldn't think that's funny at all. But . . . look. Getting within range of the Guardian . . . it's not exactly regulations. In fact, it's *against* regulations."

"I am very aware of all Starfleet regulations, Dr. Mac. My programming makes me incapable of violating them. What is prohibited is unauthorized use of the Guardian, especially for the intention of altering or changing time lines. I don't wish to use it. I simply want to . . ."

He paused, and for someone as clearly articulate as Data, it seemed very odd for him to be pausing, trying to find the right words. "To connect with it," he said finally.

She studied him for a moment, then showed her white teeth. "All right, Commodore. Although frankly, I'm taking a big chance here of getting my ass handed to me."

Data frowned and looked at her buttocks, but she quickly made a dismissive wave. "Not literally."

She stretched out an arm and placed her palm flat against the control padd that stood outside the Guardian. As she did so, Data looked with curiosity at her upper arm. "How did you acquire that bruise, Doctor? It's very peculiar."

She glanced at where he was looking. Sure enough, there was a small abrasion on her upper right arm, perfectly round and about as large as if one made a circle from the thumb and forefinger. "I don't know," she said in mild surprise. "Must have banged it against something."

She dismissed it mentally and looked back at the control platform. A thin beam of red light shot out from it and scanned her right eye, feeding the retinal pattern into the compound's central data banks. It came back with a Priority Alpha clearance. A moment later the force field faded, the steady hum of the generators disappearing. Now there was nothing but the crying of the wind.

Commodore Data slowly walked forward, approaching the Guardian with as close to trepidation as he could possibly come. He stopped several feet away. "Who are you?" he asked.

The vast, round portal flickered as a voice spoke with a booming, all-encompassing vastness that seemed to come from everywhere at once. **"I am the Guardian of Forever."**

"Are you a Guardian in the sense of a preserver? Or a Guardian in the sense of a protector?"

"Both . . . and neither."

Data cocked his head slightly. Mary Mac, for her part, had quietly activated her wrist recorder. Any direct communication with the Guardian could result in some unexpected new insight. She had conversed with the vast portal on a number of different occasions, and every time there was some new nuance to its replies.

"How is such a self-contradictory assessment possible?" Data asked.

"Since I am possible . . . then all is possible."

Data considered this a moment. "Are you saying that you are the keeper of time and protect it from trespass . . . but since every man's fate is in his own hands, you really cannot protect it from those who wish to affect it."

"All living beings affect the flow of what is. I am but one portal through time. There is an infinity of others."

This response brought a startled glance from Mary Mac. Data didn't turn his attention from the Guardian.

"Are you saying there are others like yourself?"

"Of course. In every moment of time that there is . . . then I am there. As you exist within all the moments of your lifetime. But you exist in the individual moments. I exist in all."

"Holy Kolker," whispered Mary Mac.

"You transcend all boundaries of time and space?" asked Data.

"No. I do not transcend them."

"What, then?"

"I define them."

Data looked back at Mary Mac. It was a curiously human move. It was almost as if Data wanted to reassure himself that she was still there. Then he looked again at the Guardian.

"May I touch you?" asked Data.

"You have free will. Do as you wish."

Data paused, then walked up to the rocklike surface of the Guardian. Without hesitation, he placed his gold palm against it.

The lights throbbed beneath his hand. From the chill that cut through the air, he had expected that the Guardian would feel cool, even cold. Instead it pulsed with an odd sort of warmth. Data lifted his hand for a moment and could feel no heat being radiated from the Guardian's surface. But when he placed his hand against it again, there it was, entirely self-contained.

"Very curious," he said.

He stayed that way for a long moment, then stepped back. "I would like to talk again at some other point."

"All will occur," replied the Guardian.

Data turned and walked back to Mary Mac. She watched him with curiosity. Anyone . . . "normal," for want of a better word . . . would have walked away while glancing repeatedly over his shoulder at the Guardian. But Commodore Data, having decided to take his leave, was now completely focused on the next order of business.

"Thank you for the opportunity," said Data.

Mary Mac inclined her chin slightly toward the Guardian. "Did you understand any of that?"

"I have an interpretation that I believe to be fairly accurate. I'd be most interested in comparing my conjectures with those of the other members of your research team."

"Hey, that's what you're here for. To check up on us and keep Starfleet apprised of our progress. The invitation to dinner is still open."

"Thank you. I'll just check with my ship first. . . . Commodore Data to *Enterprise.*"

Mary Mac stood and watched him as he held a conversation with thin air.

"Good. I will be remaining on the planet surface several more hours. Be sure to keep the ship sufficiently outside the range of the temporal distortions, since we're uncertain of the effect long-term exposure could have. . . . I'll want Science Officer Blair joining me. . . . Very well, then, as soon as he's completed them. . . . Thank you, Lieutenant Commander. Commodore out."

He turned and looked back at Mary Mac, who shook her head. "I can't get over that," she said. "That comm-chip implant so that you can hear each other inside your heads."

"A two-second procedure to install. Inserted with a hypo spray. Impossible to lose, so we can remain in touch with each other at all times. Plus increased privacy for communications. Had I wished to, Doctor, I could simply have whispered my replies and you would not have been able to hear any of it. However, there was nothing particularly confidential about this communiqué."

"What's it like?" Mary Mac looked skyward as if she could detect it with the unaided eye. "The *Enterprise,* I mean."

"The *Enterprise?*" Data paused. "In many ways, the *Enterprise* 1701-F is similar to the 1701-D upon which I first served. It is larger, more powerful, more maneuverable. Crew complement of two thousand twenty-three people."

"And you're in command."

He nodded slightly. "There is that, of course. And yet, in some ways . . . I find myself thinking of the past, more and more often. I suppose, as one acquires more memories, that is natural."

"Yes. It is. Certainly—just like yourself—not without precedent."

Two

There was nothing desirable about Starbase 86.

It was far removed from the more frequently traveled space lanes. Visitors were rare, commerce even rarer. The facilities were not exactly top of the line.

Starbases served a variety of functions: ship repair, stopping point, rest and relaxation, observation of the territory around them. At its most basic, a starbase was a signpost of the United Federation of Planets that said, "We are here. We are thinking about you and are here to help you."

Starbase 86 filled all of those requirements . . . adequately. Nothing more than that, and nothing less. It was simply good enough.

Once upon a time, the commanding officer of Starbase 86—and since the term *86* meant something had been killed, the starbase had been nicknamed "Starbase Dead End"—would never have settled for good enough. In fact, he had lived his life by the axiom "Good enough never is."

But that viewpoint had been held a long, long time ago, by a man who was somewhat different from 86's current CO. A lifetime ago, in fact. Someone else's lifetime.

He stared out the viewport of his office, watching the lights of stars that, because of the time required for light to travel, might have been extinguished years ago. How odd, he mused, to be looking at something that was no longer there. And yet it had reality. Every sense that was available to him told him that the stars were still there. But that didn't mean anything.

"Sometimes," he said to no one in particular, "seeing isn't believing."

There was a chime at the door. He made no move to answer it at first. What was the point? What was the rush? If he didn't respond now, sooner or later the buzz would just sound again. And again. Things happened whether he wanted them to or not. That was a hard lesson that he had also learned.

Sure enough, the chime repeated. This time it was accompanied by a worried "Admiral? Admiral Riker? Are you okay?"

Riker permitted a small smile to tug at the edges of his bearded mouth. The voice was unmistakably that of his second-in-command, Lieutenant Dexter. Dexter always sounded a bit apprehensive, and Riker knew precisely why. Dexter was something of a hypochondriac—not to the point where it interfered with his ability to function, certainly, but he was preoccupied with medical well-being. Not just his own, either, but that of everyone around him.

As a result, Dexter was always clucking after Riker, inquiring after Riker's health, and generally making a polite but determined nuisance of himself. In a way, Riker supposed that it was something of a blessing. Certainly Riker himself didn't care all that much about his well-being. He was seventy-three years old, and although he wouldn't refuse the idea of seventy-four and onward beyond that, neither did he particularly welcome it. It would simply happen or it wouldn't. The rest was of little consequence.

The longer Riker didn't respond, the more apprehensive Dexter would get. Probably the lieutenant was already conjuring up images of an unconscious or even worse, a dead Riker, sprawled out on his desk or under it. He even knew precisely what Dexter would do upon finding a deceased commanding officer. Dexter would undoubtedly drop to his knees and proceed to lecture the corpse.

"I told you you weren't taking good enough care of yourself," he'd say, shaking his thin blond head. "I told you that you should take more of an interest in yourself and the running of the starbase. But would you listen to me? No. You wouldn't. And now look at you, with the average life span being 114 years, and here you are, barely half that, dead as a burned-out star."

"Come in, Lieutenant," said Riker.

Dexter entered before Riker finished the last syllable in *lieutenant.* He coughed nervously. "Did I catch you at a bad time?"

Riker spread his wrinkled hands broadly. "I have nothing but time." Then he pointed off to the side. "See there? Loads of time."

What he was pointing at was virtually the only thing he took any pride in at all: a large, ornate grandfather clock, Swiss construction, made in the early twentieth century. It had been fully restored and was in perfect working order. It stood in one of the corners of Riker's fairly austere office, and its pendulum swung slowly, back and forth, back and forth. Each swing was accompanied by a resonant ticktock.

The sound affected different people in different ways. Riker found the noise calming, even reassuring. Dexter—Riker could tell—thought it was damned distracting. The lieutenant would cast repeated, annoyed glances at the clockpiece whenever he was in Riker's office.

"Yes, sir. Loads of time. As you say, sir." Dexter fingered his thinning hair nervously. "There's some, um, matters to bring to your attention."

Riker sat down behind his desk and half-swiveled the chair so he could stare out at the stars. Rarely did he look at Dexter anymore. He had in the beginning, back when he'd taken on the command of the starbase three years ago. Dexter had been one of the few humans he ever spoke with. He'd considered that a blessing. Now he was bored.

Riker's head settled into his hands. His beard, mostly gray but with a few strands of brown still peppering it, felt brittle against his palms. He raised one hand and ran it experimentally through his gray hair. Strands came out between his fingers, more strands every day, it seemed. He could have treatment done to prevent it, of course. But what was the point? Whom was he trying to impress? Dexter? Surely not. Himself? Hardly.

"The surveying ship *Chance* will be coming in next week," Dexter said, consulting a small computer padd in the palm of his hand. Mostly it was there for security; Dexter's remarkable memory enabled him to recall all information almost instantaneously. But he was anal retentive enough to want to have the printed confirmation in front of him, just in case. "They had a synthesizer malfunction and will be putting in for new supplies and synthesizer repair."

Riker nodded. "Make sure our food stores are adequately stocked to resupply."

It was purely a cosmetic order. He knew damned well that Dexter would already have attended to that. But it was something to do other than just sit and nod his head as if it were going to fall off.

"Yes, sir," said Dexter neutrally, as if Riker's order were a novel idea. "Also, a communiqué from Starfleet. They complained that we were not processing our forms 1021-JKQ rapidly enough."

Riker raised an eyebrow in mild amusement. Amazing how much gravity Dexter could attach to something that Riker considered so utterly trivial. "Not fast enough?"

"No, sir."

"How much faster do they want it?"

Dexter blinked owlishly. "They are supposed to be filed within forty-eight hours of departure of any ship that's Constellation class or larger."

"And we've been taking . . . ?"

Nervously clearing his throat, Dexter tapped his computer padd and said, "We've been averaging three weeks."

Riker stared at Dexter gravely. "My God. This could spell the end of the Federation as we know it. And I'll have to live with that knowledge for the rest of my life."

Dexter blew air impatiently out between his colorless lips. "It's not a laughing matter, Admiral."

"I don't recall hearing laughter, Lieutenant. Not even so much as a mild guffaw. It may have been a while since I laughed, Mr. Dexter, but I do distinctly recall what it sounded like."

"You weren't laughing per se, sir, but you most definitely were making light of the situation."

Riker leaned forward, his fingers interlaced. "If I don't speed up the processing, Dexter . . . what are they going to do to me? Transfer me? To someplace worse than this? We both know there *is* no place worse than this."

Dexter shuddered slightly.

"You know I'm right," Riker said mirthlessly. "And you know what else?" He leaned back in the chair, putting his hands behind his head. "I wouldn't have it any other way. I'm right where I want to be, Dexter. Right where I want to be."

They stared at each other for a few moments. "Anything else?" Riker said.

Dexter cleared his throat again and then said, "There was a communiqué for you of a somewhat personal nature."

At that, Riker frowned. "What was it?"

"Well, sir, I never go prying—"

"Of course you do," said Riker, his voice cracking with impatience. "Don't shadow-dance with me, Dexter. I know damned well you have your finger in every pie that comes through this armpit of the galaxy. Now what's happening?"

"Well, sir . . . the communiqué was from Betazed."

Riker was silent for a long moment. "Betazed?"

"Yes, sir."

Riker drummed for a few seconds on the armrest of his chair. When he spoke, he was looking away from Dexter. "It's from her, isn't it?"

"Yes, sir."

"Is she all right?"

Dexter's lips thinned even more, which one would have thought was impossible. He took a breath and said, "No, sir. She's dying, sir."

Riker said nothing at first. Then, finally: "And?"

"She's calling for you."

"Is she? Yes . . . she would, wouldn't she." He considered it a moment. "There's no way I can get there in time."

"Betazed officials have already spoken with Starfleet command. She is quite influential, you know."

"Yes, I know. Believe me, I know. And what did Starfleet say?"

"The starship *Hood* is in this sector. They had not originally planned to put in here, but we are not significantly out of their way. And Betazed is situated only a few parsecs from *Hood*'s destination."

"How very convenient." Riker frowned for a moment. "*Hood* is Crusher's ship, isn't it?"

"Captain Crusher, yes, sir."

"Um-hmm. Old ghosts, Dexter."

"Pardon?"

"Old ghosts. They're coming back to haunt me." Now Riker shifted his drumming to the desktop. "Old ghosts want to see me. Old ghosts are going to transport me." He paused. "I don't suppose I have the option of not seeing her."

"Of course you have that option, sir," replied Dexter stiffly. "This is merely a request, not an order."

"A request." Once more Riker ran his fingers through his gray hair. "How much time until *Hood* gets here?"

"ETA is fourteen thirty hours, sir."

"All right. Radio Betazed that I'll be there as fast as I can. Tell *Hood* that I'll be ready for them when they get here." Riker rose to his feet and fixed Dexter with a stare. "Anything else?"

"No, sir. It's just that . . ."

Riker could barely contain his impatience. "What? . . . What?"

"I just want to say that I think it's good of you that you're going, sir. You've, um . . ." He harrumphed and continued, "You've spoken of her in the past. It's clear that this will be very difficult for you."

"I've done more difficult things than this, Lieutenant," said Riker stiffly. Then he hesitated and added softly, "But not much more."

He came around his desk and headed for the door. And then Dexter said, "Why do you think she wants to see you, sir?"

Riker paused in the doorway. The door had already slid open, waiting for him. But when he didn't pass through, it slid softly shut again. "Why do *you* think?"

Dexter, after brief consideration, said, "Perhaps, sir, she wants to make amends with you."

"Amends?" Riker said the word with amazement, as if it were the first time he'd ever heard it. "Amends? Lieutenant . . . you don't know her very well."

"It's possible, sir," Dexter persisted. "When people are dying, they tend to see things in a different light."

"You have a lot of personal experience with death, Lieutenant?"

Dexter ignored the verbal jab. "It's possible that she wants to settle loose ends, as it were. Close accounts. It's possible, sir . . . that she wants to forgive you."

Slowly Riker shook his head. "Why should she, Lieutenant . . . when I haven't forgiven myself?"

And Riker walked out of his office, leaving Dexter alone with the steady heartbeat ticking of the grandfather clock.

Three

The structures in which the scientists of the Forever World lived were, at best, functional. But then, these people did not seem to Data the type to care overmuch about physical needs. If what they had served their basic requirements, then they seemed content.

Data looked around the table that served as the communal eating place for the scientists. In every locale on the *Enterprise* that was designed for group consumption of food, Data had always been struck by the steady stream of chatter that had accompanied the act. Indeed, eating a meal seemed as much a social occasion as anything else. Such socializing did not appear to augment the replenishing of the body's stores of nutrition. It was, however, customary. Or so Data had been led to believe.

It was not the case here, however. The six scientists who were grouped around the table ate quietly. Talk was at a minimum, and anything said was merely along the lines of some functional request such as "Pass the salt."

Seated next to Data was science officer Blair. Blair was tough to miss in any situation—a head taller than Data, and covered from head to toe with thick, brown fur. His jaw jutted out and his eyes were so small that they were almost impossible to spot. His Starfleet uniform was specially tailored to accommodate his height and bulk. The others at the table had to crowd a bit closer to each other in order to provide room for Blair.

Thus far there had only been one entrée into conversation. Data had glanced around and said, "My records indicated there were seven of you."

Mary Mac pursed her lips and then sighed. "There were. Recent defection—Mar Loc. He took off the other day—haven't seen him since. You'll have to update your records. To be honest . . . we lose people all the time."

"Why?"

"It's not easy to take this place, Commodore," said Harry as he put food out on the table. Around the table, heads bobbed up and down in agreement. "You have the constant wind. You have the solitude. And with the Guardian out there . . ." He paused, trying to find the words. "You feel . . . you feel like you're staring into a mirror from hell. And it's only so long before you see something staring back out at you. Some reflection that you don't necessarily like. At which point . . . it's time to get out. Or you can lose your mind."

"We've had that happen from time to time as well," said Mary Mac darkly. Again there were nods.

The scientists volunteered no further conversation, and once the food was put out, from then on the only sounds that could be heard were the clinking of eating utensils on plates, soft noises of mastication, and of course, the wind . . . the ever-present, ever-haunting wind.

"Is it always this quiet?" Blair finally asked.

The sound of his hushed question was almost deafening in the relative stillness. The scientists stopped and looked at each other with an air of polite puzzlement.

Mary Mac, who was seated next to Blair, leaned forward on one arm. "It's not just quiet. We're working."

Blair looked at Data. "Working on what?" asked the commodore.

"Our thoughts," said Harry. "Our observations. Every night we record our conclusions in our logs, and every morning we group together and discuss them."

"As part of the Federation's annual evaluation of your work," said Data politely, "I'd be very interested in reading them. If, that is, you wouldn't consider that an intrusion."

The scientists looked at each other and there seemed to be an unspoken, uniform shrug. "No problem with that, Commodore," said Mary Mac.

"What sort of observations do you make?" Blair asked.

Mary Mac glanced around the table. Clearly, both through Federation designation and natural ability, she was the spokesperson for the group. "We make observations on society. On history. Most of us here are social scientists, Commodore . . . Lieutenant," she added, with a polite nod to Blair. "We make studies of the histories of different societies and from that draw conclusions about not only that society's past, but the circumstances that brought them to their present and, most likely, are aiming them toward their future."

Harry now spoke up. "Just an example. Two planets, Gamma Delta and Gamma Origii, had been at war off and on for hundreds of years. Even though they, as a society, had evolved in their perceptions and attitudes, there was still a centuries-old tradition of hatred between the two. Our studies here at the Forever World uncovered the real origins, long forgotten, of the anger between the two worlds."

"That being?" prompted Blair.

Harry endeavored to keep a straight face as he said, "A d'clat belonging to the emperor of Gamma Delta consumed a markill that was much beloved by the empress of Gamma Origii."

Blair looked in confusion from Harry to Data. Data, with just the faintest hint of a smile, said, "A d'clat is a large, caninelike animal, known to be quite fierce and to reach lengths of three meters. A markill is small, somewhat feline, and usually very docile."

Understanding spread across Blair's face. "You mean the guy's dog ate her pet cat?"

"That is essentially correct."

"And *that* led to centuries of hostilities?"

"The incident led to bad feelings," corrected Mary Mac, sounding a bit pedantic. "The bad feelings led to the hostilities. By the time the modern era was reached, the reasons for the hostilities had long been forgotten; only the anger remained."

"How did the two planets react when they learned of the root cause for their antagonism?" asked Data.

Mary Mac could not hide her amusement. "The heads of the two worlds met and with great pomp and circumstance signed into law new, strict regulations about leashing d'clats. A newborn markill was then presented to the present leader of Gamma Origii. Frankly, they were all a bit embarrassed about it and were happy for the opportunity to put it all behind them."

"Well, that's excellent," said Blair. "That's just excellent."

Then he paused, and Mary Mac picked up on the fact that something else was on his mind. "Yes, Lieutenant?" she asked.

"I was just wondering . . . are you ever tempted? To go back, I mean?"

"No," said Mary Mac with such speed and firmness that it was a bit startling.

"What, never?"

"No. Nor are any of us." She looked at her companions for confirmation, and almost as one, they nodded.

"Why wouldn't you want to?"

"Because that is not a responsibility that we would want. It's . . . it's too much. You'd have to be . . . I don't know . . . bigger than life to take on that challenge. I'll pass, thanks."

"If you shun the responsibility, why does anyone have access to the Guardian at all?" asked Data.

"We need access when we want to talk to it," said Mary Mac. "For some reason it won't address us if we speak from outside the force field. The Guardian doesn't acknowledge us unless there're no barriers between us. When we do converse with it directly, we do so with the utmost caution." She put down her eating utensil. "Your conversation was fairly interesting, Commodore. What did you make of it?"

"It would seem to confirm, on the face of it, that which we had always known. That time is fluid. Although"—he paused only a moment, considering the possibilities—"there is another interpretation. And that is that all times coexist."

"You mean parallel universes," said Mary Mac. It was clear from the speed with which she picked up on what he was saying that it was something she'd already given thought.

"It's something that has been considered," said Data. "That parallel universes are, in fact, alternative time tracks. There was a fascinating paper done recently, expanding upon a notion expressed in, of all things, a newly recovered twentieth-century piece of fiction."

"The Niven Doctrine," Blair said. "I was in the audience when it was presented. Shook up quite a few people."

"Alternative time lines," said Mary Mac, nodding. "The scene you were watching, Commodore—the experiences of Captain Kirk—certainly is one of the better-known instances."

"There have been others documented," said Data. "There was Captain Kirk's experience with an alternative time line that resulted in a parallel universe with an aggressive, warlike Federation. There was another situation that I myself was involved with, the full details of which I didn't learn until some years after the fact."

"You, Commodore?" asked Mary Mac. "What was it?"

"It involved a . . . memorable young woman. Her name was Natasha Yar, although she was more popularly known as Tasha." Data's face, as always, was the picture of composure. But Blair, from his long experience with his commanding officer, could tell that the memory being pulled up was something of great meaning to the android. "It was a . . . unique situation. One of the few instances where an individual or individuals actually crossed over from one parallel universe to another—one being where Captain Kirk and several crewmen, as mentioned earlier, crossed into a parallel universe/time-line with a militaristic Federation. Tasha's experience was another. Unfortunately it . . . did not work out quite as positively as Captain Kirk's did."

Data lapsed into silence and Mary Mac understood immediately that he had said everything he felt needed to be said on the subject. But Data picked up on her expression.

"If you wish to question me further on the incident," Data said quietly, "you may feel free to do so. I won't feel imposed upon."

"Maybe not, but I'll feel like I'm imposing anyway. So I guess I won't." Then Mary Mac paused. "Actually, Commodore . . . I have something of interest to show you. Something along the lines of our discussion. A very intriguing turn of events that our monitoring of the Guardian's playbacks has revealed. And I think"—her green lips drew back into a broad smile—"I think you will find it very interesting."

Four

Riker sat in his guest quarters on the starship *Hood,* watching the stars hurtling by. It had been so long since he was in any sort of real motion that the view outside the port looked . . . *wrong* somehow. As insane as it sounded, he didn't feel as if stars were supposed to move.

"Do you miss it, Admiral?"

He hadn't even heard the door hiss open. He turned to face Capt. Wesley Crusher.

Crusher was standing in the doorway, his arms folded. He was half a head taller than Riker, which was disconcerting enough for the admiral. He sported a Vandyke beard, and his hair—graying ever so slightly at the temples—hung just over his ears. He stepped fully into the quarters upon Riker's silent gesture for him to enter, and Riker noticed with amusement that as he did so, he tugged slightly at the waistline of his black and green uniform jacket. Riker had not seen the gesture for quite a few years—the clothes straightening that had picked up the joking nickname of the Picard Maneuver, wryly named after the famous battle tactic that one Jean-Luc Picard had invented.

He saw Crusher standing and realized that it was in deference to himself. "Please, take a seat, Captain."

And Riker was even more amused when Crusher crossed to a chair and, without even thinking about it, reversed it and straddled it. "Pick up any other of my mannerisms, Captain?"

Crusher looked at him askance. "What do you mean, sir?" He looked down at the chair as if seeing it for the first time. "Did you used to sit like this?"

"Used to," said Riker. "Before some sore back muscles decided that they would say otherwise in the matter. In answer to your question of do I miss it, Captain . . . no."

"No?"

"You sound surprised, Captain Crusher."

Once upon a time, Wesley Crusher would have looked down nervously or stammered slightly or cleared his throat as he tried to compose himself. Just yesterday, it seemed to Riker. Now, though, the Starfleet captain merely shrugged slightly. "A little, I admit."

"You can take the man out of space, but you can't take the spacer out of the man, eh?" asked Riker.

"Something like that."

Riker slowly circled the quarters, never taking his gaze off Crusher. "You've carved quite a career for yourself, Mr. Crusher. Your father would have been proud."

"Thank you, sir."

"And what about you . . . Wes." It sounded odd to speak the name out loud. It was as if he were addressing someone who wasn't in the room. "Are you proud?"

"I've done my job. I've done it to the best of my abilities. And"—he paused only a moment—"I had the best teachers."

"The Academy has top people on their faculty."

"That's very true, but I wasn't talking about the Academy, sir . . . and I think you know that."

"We don't have to stand on formality, Wes. You can call me Will."

Crusher considered it for a moment, then said, "Actually . . . no. I'm not sure I can, sir. It would seem . . . presumptuous, somehow."

"Whatever you're comfortable with, then," said Riker easily. He caught a glance of himself in the mirror. Old. So damned old, and he felt older in the presence of the robust captain who sat before him. Robust, even in his fifties.

"What's your opinion of me, Wes?"

Crusher blinked in surprise. "Of you?" For a moment he seemed confused. "I . . . admire you tremendously. You're one of the greatest . . . probably, with all due respect, the second-greatest . . . Starfleet officer it was ever my honor to serve under."

Riker stared at him with a look that bordered on incredulity. "You can't *still* think that, can you?"

"Of course."

With a slow shake of his head, Riker sat down opposite Crusher. He did not, however, straddle the chair. "Wesley . . . everyone has people that they admire in their lives. People who they put on a . . . a heroic pedestal, as it were. But you can't possibly tell me I'm still up there on yours?"

Crusher shifted uncomfortably. "I wouldn't say 'pedestal,' Admiral. But I still admire you a great deal. In many ways . . . I still see you very much the way that I did when I first met you. Strong, decisive, heroic . . . everything a Starfleet officer was supposed to be. It's not unusual for first impressions to be lasting ones, Admiral . . . I mean, admit it"—now he smiled—"you find it just slightly difficult to seriously believe I'm an adult. Captain of a starship. Married twice, father of three. But you look at me and still think of the little kid on Farpoint who, once upon a time, only had two goals: to visit the bridge, and to have to shave more than once a week."

Riker laughed, the boisterousness of his amusement surprising even himself. "You're right, Wes. You're bang-on right. It's just that . . ."

"Just that what, sir?"

"Just that," Riker said soberly, "there comes a time in everyone's life where they start to see their heroes for what they really are: namely, people. Flawed . . . ordinary . . . people."

Crusher didn't say anything at first. Something very unpleasant seemed to be hanging in the cabin . . . an air of self-pity, maybe even a whiff of mortality. "Are you feeling particularly flawed and ordinary today, Admiral?"

"Wes, I haven't felt anything but that for years now. Look at me, Wes. Look at me and tell me that you don't see a broken-down, second-rate starbase commander. Someone who had potential he never fulfilled. Someone who was never everything he should have been. Tell me that you don't look at me and see someone in whom you're bitterly disappointed."

Someone else would have said such things in tones bordering on histrionic. Riker, however, did not. He spoke slowly, succinctly, and in a voice that indicated he had, quite simply, already decided these things about himself and come to terms with them.

Crusher's eyes narrowed, and when he spoke, quiet fire was in his voice. "If that is your opinion of yourself . . . Will . . . then you're certainly entitled to it. But if you're looking for someone to confirm it for you, I'm afraid you're just going to have to keep on looking."

Riker let out a slow sigh, tinged with faint amusement. "Is that your final word, Captain?"

"Yes, it is. And since we're on my ship, and it is my opinion . . . then we'll just have to make it so."

Crusher was about to say something else when suddenly he half-looked away, in that manner that had become so customary with the creation of the minicommunicators. "Excuse me, Admiral. . . . Crusher here." He listened to the voice that only he could hear and then nodded once. "Excellent. We'll be right there. Crusher out." He turned to Riker. "We're five minutes out of Betazed."

"Smooth and uneventful trip, Captain. You're to be commended."

"Thank you, sir."

Crusher rose from his chair and headed for the door. But there he stopped and turned back to Riker. "Do you want me there, Admiral?"

"Oh, I don't think that will be necessary, Captain."

"It's easily justifiable." Crusher took a step back into the cabin. "As a Starfleet captain, it would be eminently politic for me to be present. And as a . . . friend . . . I wouldn't mind being there to lend whatever support I could."

Riker was ready to dismiss the notion out of hand. But then he stopped and considered it—really considered it—and almost to his surprise, he found himself nodding. Feeling some words should accompany the nods, he said, "Very well, Captain. Perhaps it wouldn't be such a bad idea at that."

Crusher nodded. "Five minutes, then. Don't be late. Tardiness is mental slovenliness and is inappropriate for a Starfleet officer."

"Where'd you pick that up? The Academy?"

"No, sir. You told me that—the first time I was late for an astrophysics lesson with Geordi."

"Well, that being the case, I could hardly ignore such sound advice, could I."

"If it's good enough for the captain of the *Hood,"* Wesley Crusher said firmly, "it's good enough for you." He turned and walked out the door.

Through the viewport of his quarters, Riker could now see Betazed, coming up fast.

Help me, he said. *Help me get through this, Imzadi.*

There was, of course, no answer. Nor had there been for quite, quite some time.

Five

Betazed was nothing like he remembered it.

Then again, it had been many years since Riker had set foot on the planet. Not since the days when he had been first officer of the *Enterprise* 1701-D, under the command of Capt. Jean-Luc Picard.

Not since—

He wavered slightly, putting a hand to his head, and he felt Crusher's firm grip on his shoulder. "Are you all right, Admiral?"

All the anger, all the resentment and fury that he had thought he was long past, flashed through him once more with unexpected heat.

"I'm fine!" he practically snarled. "You don't have to sound so damned patronizing!"

Young Wesley Crusher would have taken a couple of steps back. He would have become dead pale, tried to stammer out some sort of a reply—and probably failed.

Capt. Wesley Crusher merely removed his hand from Riker's shoulder, then lanced him with a grim stare. "I was always raised to believe, Admiral, that being concerned over someone's welfare was considered, at the very least, good manners. Hardly patronizing."

Riker met Crusher's stare and said slowly, "Yes. Quite right, Captain. My . . . apologies."

Crusher nodded in a way that indicated that, as far as he was concerned, the minor incident was closed. Instead, he glanced toward the heavens. "Looks like the weather's turning nasty on us, sir."

At that, Riker nodded. It was something that he'd become accustomed to on Betazed. The majority of the time, the weather was calm, pleasant, bordering on the tropical. But when the atmospheric conditions shifted, they did so with startling and almost violent speed. One minute, cloudless and blue skies, and the next minute—bam.

Riker remembered that Lwaxana perpetually carried an umbrella with her when strolling about, particularly in the countryside. She had always prided herself on being ready for anything.

Anything.

"It's this way," said Riker.

They'd materialized on one of the more well-to-do avenues of the city. The homes were far apart and set back . . . but not too far. Betazoids walked a fine line between a desire for privacy and acceptance of its impossibility—for amidst an empathic society, privacy was at best a pretense and it was rude to pretend otherwise.

Crusher could have had them beamed right to their destination, but before he had specified anything, Riker had given specific coordinates that deposited them half a mile from where they wanted to be. It was as if Riker weren't all that anxious to arrive at his goal.

Riker set the pace, which was not especially fast, and Crusher fell into step next to him. The admiral did not seem particularly interested in talking, and they might indeed have gone the entire way in complete silence if an unexpected voice hadn't chimed in behind them.

"It *is* you."

Riker and Crusher stopped and turned, and Riker chuckled low in his throat. "Wendy Roper. I don't believe it."

The woman who stood behind them seemed a few years younger than Riker. She was small and slim, and her white hair, with a few remaining streaks of black in it, was twisted around in an elaborate braid. A sparkle in her eyes made it seem that a very amused young woman was hiding somewhere in the aged body.

"Will Riker, you old sleaze."

He walked to her and put his arms around her—tentatively, as if afraid that he might break her in half. They separated and he looked at her.

"Don't you dare," she said. "Don't you dare say I haven't aged at all."

"Why shouldn't I?"

"Because the thought that I looked like this half a century ago would be too much to cope with."

His smile widened. "Can I say you look great for a woman your age?"

"With my blessing." She ran fingers across his bearded cheeks. "When did you get so scruffy?"

"About forty years ago."

"Makes you look ancient."

"I feel ancient." He paused, then shook his head. "I can't believe you're still here. I mean, you can't *still* be assigned here with your father . . ."

Her expression saddened slightly. "Daddy died about ten years ago, Will."

"Oh." His face clouded. "I'm sorry. Oh . . . my manners." He stepped back and waved Crusher closer. "Capt. Wesley Crusher, this is Wendy Roper."

She shook Crusher's hand firmly but said, "Wendy Berq, actually."

Riker looked at her in surprise. "Married?"

"That's usually the way."

"When?"

"Actually, about two years after you left. My husband is Betazoid . . . a teacher. That's why I stayed."

"My God . . ."

She patted him on the arm. "Don't worry about it, Will. I know news travels slowly out in space."

He let out a slow breath. "I really am a sleaze. I've been back planetside a few times . . . but I never saw you. Never tried to contact you. Not even . . ."

"I was at the funeral."

Riker blinked in surprise. "You were? I didn't see you."

"As I recall, you weren't seeing much of anything that day."

To that, Riker said nothing. Then, slowly, he nodded. "That's about right." He paused. "I should have looked you up. I'm sorry."

"It's understandable. If there's one thing that living among Betazoids has taught me, it's to be respectful of people's feelings. If you ask me, the entire Betazoid credo boils down to one word: RaBeem."

Crusher looked momentarily puzzled. " 'RaBeem'?"

Riker glanced at him and said, "It means 'I understand.' "

"Very good, Will," said Wendy.

"I had a good teacher."

They stood there for a bit in uneasy silence, then Wendy cleared her throat. "I won't play games or pretend this was coincidence, Will. I knew you'd be coming. I knew she'd asked for you. And I thought—"

"You thought that I could use the moral support," he said, tossing a look at Crusher. "I've heard that quite a bit. Well . . . fine, Wendy. I suppose the more the . . ." Then he stopped. "I guess that's hardly appropriate to the situation, is it?"

"Hardly," agreed Wendy.

Riker stood there, feeling as if he'd been cut adrift. He felt that way a great deal these days—alone, floating. Unattached to anyone or anything in the galaxy around him. Clumsy with his speech, clumsy with his orders, just . . . clumsy. Unable to focus on anything or decide anything.

Make a decision, you idiot.

"Come on, then," he said. "Let's go."

The three of them walked up the small incline that led to the mansion that Riker knew so well. It had been years since he'd been there—a lifetime ago, it seemed—and yet every angle of the house, every aspect of it, had been forever etched into his memory. Tall and graceful, it was constructed on a reduced scale so that, although the upper stories were not abnormally high, they seemed to go on and on, almost touching the sky—the sky that was now darkening with the customary Betazed speed. And yet, somehow, it seemed as if it were holding back. Seemed as if it were waiting for something.

The door was opened before Riker even had the opportunity to knock. And filling the doorway was a figure that momentarily surprised Riker by its appearance . . . and then, he wondered why he had been at all startled. Of course *he* would be here. Where else would he be?

"Mr. Homn," said Riker, bending slightly and formally at the waist.

Wesley Crusher looked up in surprise. He had fleetingly seen Homn from time to time, back in his days on the *Enterprise.* His memory had been that Homn was incredibly tall . . . and yet, in later years, he had wondered how much of that recollection was shaped by the fact that young Ensign Crusher had been that much smaller. Now, as an adult, he found himself no less impressed by Homn's towering presence than he had ever been.

Wendy had never seen the towering manservant before. She just gaped.

And then, Homn did something totally unexpected . . . something that, to Riker's knowledge, he had only done once before.

His voice was low and surprisingly soft for so large a man—and there was even a faint hint of a lisp—as he uttered two simple words: "She's waiting."

The response echoed in Riker's mind—*Waiting for what? Waiting for me? Or waiting to die? Or are the two connected?*

Mr. Homn stepped aside, and Riker entered, Wendy and Crusher following him.

The house, in contrast to its elegant exterior, still smacked of being overdone to Riker, even after all this time. He knew why that was, of course. Lwaxana's late husband had designed the outside and left the actual furnishing to his wife. And furnish it she had . . . with a vengeance.

Every corner, every available bit of space, was crammed with . . . *stuff.* Everywhere Riker looked there was furniture or mementos: portraits, trophies, souvenirs, objects of art that ranged from the acceptable to the ghastly. The taste at casa Troi was, to put it mildly, eclectic.

Mr. Homn stood at the bottom of the central stairway and gestured. He remained immobile, like a monument. A living link to days gone by.

Riker started up the stairs. They seemed to stretch on forever. Once, once a very long time ago, he could have charged up these steps, taking them two, even three at a time. And a woman would have been waiting for him up there, her arms outstretched, her face mirthful and loving, her curly black hair cascading about her shoulders.

Back in the old days. Back when he was another person entirely, and the only thing he had in common with the old man who now trudged heavily up the stairs was the name.

He held on to the banister, pulling himself up as he went. He paused for a few moments on a landing to catch his breath before he continued upward. He knew that Crusher and Wendy were directly behind him, but they offered him no support or aid. Nor would he have wanted it.

The stairway opened up onto the second-floor corridor, which seemed to stretch almost to infinity. This effect was aided by the fact that the corridor was illuminated only by flickering lamplight, and also because full-size mirrors were at either end.

Appearances. Once again, appearances. They had always been so important to *her* . . . and now, it would seem that appearances were all she had left.

At first he didn't know which door she was behind . . . but then he realized. It was partly open, and from within he could hear slow, labored breathing. It sounded as if she was just barely hanging on. Hell, she might die any minute.

If he walked slowly enough, if he took enough time . . .

He saw the look in Wesley Crusher's eyes as the captain of the *Hood* stood next to him. He had a feeling that Crusher knew precisely what was going through Riker's mind.

Dammit, Riker, he scolded himself. *Be a man. For crying out loud, get it right!*

His hands curled into fists, and with a stride that indicated a confidence he did not feel, he walked toward the sound of the breathing.

When he was just outside the door . . . it stopped.

The cessation was abrupt; right in the middle of a breath, so it was very noticeable. Riker looked at Crusher as if for confirmation, and it was clear that Crusher had heard it, too. Wendy, feeling tired and labored, had just made it to the top of the stairs and so wasn't there yet.

For just the briefest of moments, relief flooded through Riker. And then it was immediately replaced by anger at his hesitation . . . cowardice, even. Quickly he entered the room.

He was stunned.

He had expected the most ornate of surroundings for this, the master bedroom. But such was not the case. In fact, it was quite the opposite.

Only a bed occupied the room. A canopied bed with black drapes hanging down. There wasn't a stick of furniture anywhere else.

It only took a moment for Riker to realize what had happened. All the furniture had been removed—the different sheen on various parts of the floor indicated that. He did not understand, though, *why* it had been done.

As if reading his mind, Wendy now said softly from behind him, "Betazed tradition. Some feel that you come into the world with virtually nothing. So when you leave, you try not to surround yourself with the things you've acquired. It's . . . excess baggage, for want of a better term."

"Oh."

He walked slowly toward the bed, but now there seemed to be no hurry. There was no doubt in his mind that she was gone. There was still that anger, bordering on contempt, that he felt for himself. *This is what you wanted. This is why you dragged your heels. So why aren't you happy about it?* The reason was, of course, that he also felt tremendously guilty.

Look at her. You owe her that much.

Slowly he parted the black drapery around the bed.

Lwaxana Troi lay there, unmoving. Her skin was taut, conforming uncomfortably closely to the outlines of her skull. Her lips and, incredibly, her hair, were the same parched color as her skin. Her arms and shoulders were bare—she was probably naked, just as was customary for a Betazed wedding, but a sheet was pulled up to just under her arms.

Her eyes were closed. Her chest was not moving.

Riker took a slow breath that seemed incredibly loud to him. The stink of death was heavy in the air, but it didn't stop him from sitting on the edge of the bed. Crusher and Wendy stood a respectful distance.

"I'm sorry," he whispered to her, and he meant it. He really, truly meant it. He knew now that she had really wanted finally to settle things with him. To bury the dead and put the ghosts to rest. And through his trepidation, through the fears and insecurities of an old man, he had allowed that moment to slip away forever.

He leaned over to kiss her on the forehead.

Her withered, clawlike hand shot upward and grabbed him by the throat.

Riker gasped, and the noise was partly cut off by the hand that was closing on his vocal cords with shocking strength. Lwaxana's eyes were open and blazing with pure, unbridled hatred.

"Admiral!" shouted Crusher, acting immediately and instinctively to protect the safety of the senior officer. He ran to Riker's side and was momentarily taken aback by the aura of undiluted fury that radiated from every pore of Lwaxana Troi.

From her ancient lips, as if ripped from the pits of her soul, Lwaxana Troi spat out a condemnation as if it were a curse: *"It's your fault!"* The voice was cracked and aged, not at all like the boisterous, sweeping tones that had once been the woman's staple. But there was still a vitality that would not be daunted by such trivialities as death.

"It's your fault!" she repeated, and the wrath of the woman shook her voice, shook her entire withered body. "You should have saved her! She asked you! She *begged* you! You were *Imzadi,* and you let her die!"

Riker tried to get out a reply, but the pressure was too much on his throat. Wesley tried to yank Lwaxana's hands away from Riker but they dug in. The long fingernails drew thin streams of blood.

"You let her die!" croaked Lwaxana. "It's not right! She was too young . . . too beautiful! And you let it *happen,* and I hope you *burn in hell* . . . it's your fault!"

Crusher tore her hands loose from Riker's throat and pulled the admiral away. Riker was gagging, but through the pain and mortification he still managed to gasp out, "It *wasn't!* I did everything I could! You have to understand!"

"Admiral—" began Wesley.

But Riker was shouting, "Please! It wasn't my fault! Lwaxana, I tried everything . . . it happened too fast! I—"

But Wendy laid a gentle hand on his. "It's too late, Will."

And she was right. Lwaxana's head had slumped back onto her pillow. Her eyes were still wide open, but there was no light in them. Her hand was still in its claw-like grip, frozen in its final gesture.

Wesley Crusher reached over, passing his hand over her eyes and closing them.

And Riker whispered to her, one final time, "It wasn't my fault."

But he didn't believe it any more than she had.

Six

The funeral had been surprisingly simple.

Surprisingly so because, considering the larger-than-life manner in which Lwaxana had lived her life, Riker had somehow expected a death that was . . . well . . . larger than death.

Instead, Lwaxana's instructions had been very, very specific. She had wanted only a handful of people there. Only the closest of friends, the one or two most highly placed politicians . . .

. . . and Riker.

Long after the others had left, Riker was left standing there, staring at Lwaxana's body in its clear, sealed entombment.

He kept trying to develop ways to ascribe to Lwaxana more pure motives than those of vengeance or hatred. After all, she hadn't been like that when he first met her. Strong willed, yes. Stubborn and meddlesome and—again—bigger than life. But anger? Vituperation? That hadn't been part of her makeup. Or so, at least, it had seemed.

Then again . . . the years have a way of changing people. Years, and unpleasant experiences that can harden the heart and blacken the soul.

Perhaps . . . perhaps she had wanted him there because she was genuinely trying to heal the rifts. Perhaps she had wanted him at her side in her final moments because she really did want to make amends—and it was only in the last, momentary panic, with icy death upon her, that hidden resentments had boiled over. Perhaps she had wanted him at her funeral not because she wanted to rub his nose in the notion of *See? See how your shortcomings have deprived me of happiness in life?* but rather because, ultimately, she wanted some sort of connection to her daughter to be present at her last rites. And he was, after all, Imzadi to her daughter.

Riker stood there in the chill air of the Troi mausoleum. They were somewhat rare items on Betazed—the more frequent modern method of disposal was cremation and then to be scattered on the winds; the northern cliffs in the Valley of Song were a popular point of such activity.

But the older families—and few were older than that of the Fifth House of Betazed—clung to the traditional method. The method was dictated by the notion that the best way to have a sense of who one's ancestors were was to have a perpetual reminder at hand.

Which was why Riker was now standing alone in the mausoleum, staring at Lwaxana's shrouded body, but being even more painfully aware of who was lying in the next room.

What, dammit. Not who. She hasn't been a who since . . .

. . . since you let her . . .

Riker tried to force away that line of thought. Blast it, he hadn't *let* it happen. It had just happened.

He couldn't go in and look at her.

He turned to head for the door, and that was when the uncommonly slow storm front chose finally to act. There had been a few passing drizzles earlier, and he had hoped that that would be the end of it. But now the full fury of the storm cut loose. Lightning ribboned across the sky, and rain began to fall in blinding cascades. Far in the distance, the Troi mansion was silhouetted against the stormy sky, something out of an ancient horror movie.

Riker stepped back into the mausoleum, turned and looked at Lwaxana.

"You arranged this, didn't you," he said with just the faintest hint of irony. "You're up there less than twelve hours, and already you're telling them how to run things."

Lwaxana made no reply. She didn't have to. The thunder did it for her.

Riker sighed. "All right."

He walked past Lwaxana and even rapped a quick knuckle on the clear encasement with just a flash of the old irreverence. He walked into the next room . . .

And there she was.

He approached her slowly, and for the millionth time in as many imaginings of this scene, he envisioned removing the clear covering over her body. Envisioned leaning over, kissing her, and her large, luminous eyes would flutter and open.

He placed his hands on the covering. He was amazed at his ability to remember things, for Deanna was even more beautiful than his recollection had been able to retain.

She was as her mother presently lay—nude but heavily swathed in pure, white shrouds. But unlike Lwaxana, the ravages of time had been spared her. Spared at a hideous price, but spared.

She was perfectly preserved. The black hair still thick and full, the perfect lips formed into a small, round O shape. Her chiseled features were immaculate—perfectly formed, perfectly preserved. Cut down in the prime of life, she had at least retained the look of that primacy.

He wanted to remove the spherical cover over her, to take her in his arms. But that would have been the worst move he could have made. The preservative atmosphere within the clear coffin would be compromised—her body would be subjected to the ravages of time. Besides, it wouldn't be holding *her* . . . no amount of preservation could put the warmth back into the soft skin, breathe the life back into her, open the eyes and put the soul back into place.

She could not be made whole. She could not open those eyes and drink in his presence. She could not open that lovely mouth and say—

"Will?"

Riker jumped at least three feet in the air, letting out a yell of shock. He twisted around and slammed his back into Deanna's coffin, turning to face an equally startled Capt. Wesley Crusher, who was holding his chest and seemed to have developed trouble breathing. When he found the air, he gasped out, "I'm sorry . . . did I startle you?"

Riker paused a moment to allow his heartbeat to approach somewhere near its normal rate. "Where in hell did you come from?"

Crusher was soaked to the skin. He pointed. "Out there. Beamed down. You said you hadn't wanted me at the funeral, and I respected that . . . but I thought now that it's over and all . . ."

"That I'd be ready to come back."

Crusher nodded, sending droplets of water spattering to the floor. Riker looked at him with mild amusement. "You look completely waterlogged. How long were you out in the rain?"

"About two seconds. It just seemed disrespectful somehow to beam directly into a—" He looked around. "Into here. Didn't think I'd get this drenched in such a short time, though."

"Typical Betazed storm," said Riker. "You're right, Captain. I'm ready to leave."

"Very well. Crusher to *Hood—*"

"However—"

"Cancel," said Wesley without missing a beat. He looked expectantly at Riker and waited.

"However," continued Riker, "it's not quite that simple. Lwaxana's will had an odd stipulation—she wants me to go through her memorabilia and catalogue it."

Crusher blinked. "I beg your pardon?"

"You heard me, Captain."

"But why in the world would she want you to do that?"

Riker lightly rested his hands on Deanna's coffin; Crusher wasn't even sure that Riker was aware that he was doing it. It was as if he were trying to draw strength from her. "Ostensibly because she feels I'm best qualified—which is nonsense. Mr. Homn is. The real reason, Wes, is because she wants me to relive it. Relive and remember all of it."

"But . . . but why?"

"Because," he said with a sigh, "I imagine that a day didn't pass where she didn't dwell on it. And perhaps she's under the impression that I was somehow able to put it past me. She credited me for more than she herself could accomplish—which is a compliment of sorts, I suppose. So she wanted one last opportunity to put me through what she's put herself through all these years."

"You don't have to do it, Admiral," said Crusher reasonably. "Tell them you simply can't take the additional time from your station. Tell them what you just said—that Mr. Homn is more qualified. Tell them—"

"Tell them whatever it takes to get me off the hook?"

Crusher shrugged. "That's one way to put it."

"Maybe. But it's not a way that I can subscribe to." He shook his head and stepped away from the coffin as he said, "I'm not going to deprive Lwaxana of her last shot at me. I was gutless enough to try and delay my coming to her until the last minute. I owe her this . . . I owe her something. I—"

He stopped as he realized that Crusher wasn't looking at him anymore. Instead Wesley's gaze was focused on Deanna's body, which Riker had partly been blocking from view. Riker said nothing for a moment, but instead simply watched the starship captain. Eventually Crusher rubbed the bridge of his nose, as if something stinging had lodged in his eyes.

"You had a crush on her, didn't you?" said Riker.

Wesley glanced at him. "Was it that obvious?"

Riker shrugged. "Teenage boys are very good at thinking they've got their feelings completely hidden. It helps to compensate for the fact that, more often than not, they're wearing them on their sleeves."

Crusher let out a slow breath as if a great weight had been lifted off him. "She was . . . the most exotic woman I'd ever seen. And you didn't have to pretend with her. No games, no posturing . . . she just accepted you as you were. All us guys had a thing for her, really. We'd sit around and—"

And then Crusher flushed slightly and cleared his throat.

Before he could continue, Riker said, "And wonder what it would be like to—"

"Yeah," admitted Crusher. Then, sounding slightly and amusingly defensive, considering his age and the years that had passed, he added, "We were just kids."

"We were all just kids. You, me, her . . . all of us. We just didn't know it at the time." Riker smiled. "Remember that blue-green outfit of hers?"

"Ohhh, yes. That was my favorite."

"Mine, too. Every so often, when I was feeling frivolous, I'd put it on and romp around the holodeck."

Crusher stared at Riker's deadpan expression. "You . . . ?"

"I'm kidding, Wesley."

"Oh." He laughed uncertainly. "Oh."

"Gave you a strange mental picture there for a sccond, though, didn't it?"

"Yes, sir. It did, sir."

Riker walked slowly across to the door, looking out at the thundering rain. "What else did you and the guys discuss?"

Crusher was looking at Deanna's coffin. "Truthfully?"

"That's usually the best way."

"We talked about how dumb you were to be just friends with her when you could have been so much more."

Riker looked at him askance. "Was the nature of my personal life such public knowledge on the *Enterprise?"*

Crusher shrugged. "A thousand people in an enclosed community for years on end . . . I'm sorry, Admiral, but there just weren't all that many secrets around."

"I see." Letting out a heavy breath, Riker said, "For what it's worth, Captain Crusher . . . we *were* 'so much more.' If we made any mistake . . . or if I made any mistake . . . it was allowing myself to take too much for granted. Like that she would always be there, like Old Reliable. Like that, if I wanted the nature of our relationship to change, I could do so anytime. That was probably my biggest presumption."

They were quiet for a time, listening to the rain falling on the structure. Every so often the thunder would crash, and they would involuntarily jump. Crusher could, of course, have beamed up to his ship anytime, but instead it was clear to Riker that Wesley had unilaterally placed himself at Riker's disposal for however long the admiral needed him . . . or however long Crusher believed he was needed.

Riker wondered obliquely how many strings Crusher had pulled, and how many noses he had put out of joint, to delay whatever missions the *Hood* might have in the hopper. Whatever it was that Crusher had done, Riker found himself extremely grateful.

"How did it happen, sir?"

"How did what happen, Mr. Crusher?"

For a moment, Wesley seemed reluctant to put it into words. "I read about it . . . about how she died. I read the formal reports. I know what my mom told me, but at the time she was so broken up about it that she really couldn't talk about it much. And somehow she never wanted to discuss it, even in later years. It hurt too much for her . . . for all of us, really. But now, I thought maybe—"

"You'd like to know what, precisely, was happening at the time."

"Well . . . I wasn't there," Crusher reminded him. "I was off at the Academy doing my extra year. And when I heard the news, I felt so removed, and I . . ."

"Wanted answers."

"Yes, sir. I remember, I just sat there in my quarters, shaking my head . . . I was too stunned even to cry . . . and I just kept saying, 'Why? Why?' "

"And now you're hoping I might have a few whys and wherefores."

"That's right, sir."

Riker shook his head. Then he walked toward the door and stepped just outside, allowing the rain to spatter on his face. The thunder cracked once more, and over its sound, Riker called out, "I have no answers for you, Wesley! None! But if you want to know what happened . . . I'll tell you. You're entitled to that. God knows we all are."

THE END OF THE BEGINNING

As if it were an old-fashioned campfire, or perhaps stories being traded in a haunted house, Adm. William Riker sat on the floor of the mausoleum and—holding nothing back—spoke to Wesley Crusher of those last days. . . .

Seven

"Come."

Comdr. William Riker, upon the command/invitation of his superior officer, entered the captain's ready room. Jean-Luc Picard, seated behind his desk, was studying his computer screen and gestured for Riker to sit in front of him. Riker did so, swinging the chair around and straddling it, then waiting patiently for Picard to conclude what he was doing.

He knew that Picard's first expression when he looked away from the computer screen would determine the thrust of the discussion. So Riker breathed an inward sigh of relief when Picard turned the computer display away and smiled up at Riker. Apparently there wasn't going to be any problem.

Still, it never hurt to be cautious. "You wanted to see me, Captain?"

"Merely to touch base, Number One. How are the delegates settling in?"

"Excellently, sir. I'd say the mood was even somewhat jovial. The Byfrexian, Luss, and Cordian ambassadors, and their aides, have absolutely no complaints with their accommodations . . . although the Byfrexians did request the atmosphere in their cabin be somewhat chilled. I've attended to that."

"How amazingly minor," said Picard, looking pleasantly surprised. "No problems at all?"

"Well . . . one small embarrassing moment, I suppose," admitted Riker. "One of the younger children stopped the Cordian ambassador in the hallway and said . . ."

Picard raised an eyebrow. "Said what?"

"He, um . . . well, the child seemed to be under the confused impression that the Cordian was, in fact, an accordion. He asked the ambassador to play 'Twinkle Twinkle, Little Star' on himself."

Picard moaned softly. "How did the ambassador react?"

"He took it in stride, actually. He said it's happened to him on several occasions in the past and suggested that it might be time, and I quote, 'to learn how to play the smegging thing.' "

"Good." Picard sat back in his chair in relief. "These sorts of missions are always delicate, Number One. Considering that ambassadors and delegates are supposed to promote interstellar harmony, it's amazing how often these things can degenerate into acrimony and emotional free-for-alls."

"True enough, but I don't think that's going to happen in this instance, sir. Everyone is just so relieved that the Sindareen are willing to put an end to decades of warfare."

"I'm not surprised. I was just updating myself on the conflict, Number One." Picard tapped the computer screen. "Truly amazing. The warlike attitude of the Sindareen is certainly on par with anything the Klingons or the Kreel ever had to offer. What is amazing is not only the aggressiveness with which they fought, and the zealousness with which they pursued every dispute, no matter how trivial . . . all of that, Number One, is secondary to the fact that they were able to keep it going for so long."

"From everything I read of them," said Riker, "they paid no attention to the fact that their economy was falling apart around their ears."

"Quite right. They kept telling themselves that whatever difficulties they had would disappear once they had conquered their enemies. Except even when they did achieve victories, the results were so devastating that there was nothing left to gain from the conquest—not riches, not any useful goods . . . nothing."

"A series of Pyrrhic victories."

"Precisely. Until the Sindareen reached a point in their war efforts at which they—to use the old-style vernacular—ran out of gas."

"Suing for peace was the first smart thing that the Sindareen have done in close to a century," said Riker. "They're just damned lucky that their closest enemies—the Cordians, the Byfrexians, and the Luss—were willing to listen. They could have put the screws to them."

"Yes. They could. Hopefully it's a lesson in tolerance and acceptance from which the Sindareen will learn. Nothing would better suit interstellar harmony than to have the Sindareen act in a civilized manner. At the same time, Will"—Picard leaned forward, steepling his fingers—"we have to make sure that whatever resentment the Sindareen might feel with the situation doesn't feed whatever fires of self-satisfaction the ambassadors might have burning in them. They are accomplished, intelligent individuals—but at the same time, in a situation like this, there can be a tendency towards smugness. We'll have to watch that.

"By the same token," Picard continued, "we'll have to keep a wary eye on the Sindareen. Yes, they've sued for peace. But we'll have to make sure they're sincere."

"That certainly sounds like it's right up the counselor's alley."

"I've already spoken with Counselor Troi," said Picard. "She had said that the Sindareen were not always easy to read; that their natural aggression could screen her empathic abilities to some degree."

"I know. But on the other hand, if she's with specific members of the Sindareen long enough, she can 'punch through' that resistance and get a very clear feeling for them."

Picard did not attempt to hide his surprise. "That's right. That's exactly what she said."

His captain's expression informed Riker that an explanation was anticipated. Riker simply shrugged. "Deanna had some experience with the Sindareen some time ago."

"And she told you about it?"

"Something like that."

"Is there something that's preventing you from volunteering more information about the counselor's Sindareen experience than you are currently doing?"

"Yes, sir."

"And that would be . . . ?"

Riker smiled. "My innate modesty, sir."

"I see," said Picard, and he harrumphed slightly. "Very well, Commander. Far be it from me to compromise your sense of modesty."

"Thank you, sir. Will there be anything else?"

Picard hesitated a moment and then said, "Let's watch ourselves on this one, Will. I agree that everything would appear to be going smoothly. On the other hand, we haven't reached Sindar yet. Once they get here, things could change very drastically. And we have to keep alert for anything vaguely out of the ordinary."

"If there's one thing I've learned, Captain, it's always to watch out for anything out of the ordinary."

"So have we both, Number One. And we've learned it through trial and error . . . sometimes costly error. And whenever possible—I'd like to avoid more costliness."

"Sometimes, sir, no matter how cautious we are . . . things happen."

Slowly Picard nodded. "That, Number One, is also something that we must both, reluctantly, agree upon."

Eight

After touching base with Worf to make sure that all security requirements were met, Riker headed down to Deanna Troi's quarters. It was, he felt, a reasonable thing to do—he had already spoken to her about her feelings vis-à-vis the state of mind of the various ambassadors, and because of her report, he had told the captain all was well. Still, it couldn't hurt to confer with her once more and see whether she had picked up on any second thoughts, hidden hostilities—anything that could conceivably interfere with the successful completion of the mission.

He walked up to the door of her quarters and rang the chime. "Deanna?"

At first there was no sound from within and Riker thought that he might have missed her. He tapped his communicator and said, "Computer, locate Counselor Troi."

"Counselor Troi is in her quarters," the computer calmly informed him.

This confused the hell out of Riker, and small alarms began to sound in his head. Was there a problem? Was she in danger? Why wasn't she answering?

More insistently now, he rang the door chime and said, "Deanna? Are you all right? It's Will."

The door slid open and Deanna was standing there, wrapped in a gold dressing gown that hung half off her bare shoulder. A naked leg was also visible through the folds, which she pulled shut as an afterthought. She appeared slightly out of breath, and her visible skin was slick and glistening, as if from perspiration—or perhaps some sort of skin moisturizing oil.

"I know it's you, Will."

"Is everything okay? I wanted to talk to you about—"

And then he saw him.

A man—a member of the Luss delegation, if Riker was remembering correctly—was seated on the bed. He was clearly naked and was self-consciously holding a pillow on his lap. Riker noted that the sheet was on the floor, out of reach.

The man's orange skin was likewise tinted with some sort of moisture, and his ears—normally elegantly pointed—were drooping somewhat, as if in disappointment or letdown.

Riker waited for the sixteen-ton weight that he was sure would momentarily show up to land squarely on his head.

"You're busy," he said lamely.

"I *was,"* was Troi's pointed reply.

Riker was trying to get himself to move, but his feet had apparently turned into large blocks of granite. Blowing air impatiently out between her lips, Deanna took him by the arm and yanked him into her cabin. The door hissed mercifully shut behind him.

Deanna brushed stray strands out of her face and said, with something remotely approaching civility, "Will Riker, this is Dann Lendann—aide to the ambassador of the Luss. Dann is an old . . . friend. Dann, this is Commander Riker."

"I know." Dann shifted his legs in a vain attempt to look casual. "He welcomed us when we came aboard."

"Yes, although . . . not as enthusiastically as you apparently did, Counselor," said Riker.

Deanna's dark eyes shot him a look that could have dented the deflector screens. And to Riker's surprise—since she did it so infrequently—her voice sounded in his head: *That was a cheap shot, Commander.*

"It was just a joke, Counselor," Riker said. "Just . . . to leaven the moment."

Dann looked from one to the other, sensing that something had just passed between them but unable to discern what it was.

"I think, Commander," said Deanna, readjusting the robe around herself as she held it shut, "that the moment would be sufficiently leavened if you left my cabin."

"Of course. Yes, I'll . . . I'll just be going." Riker backed up, feeling completely lost inside his own body. "Good seeing you, Dann . . . I mean, not that I expected to see this much of you—"

Deanna stared at him witheringly. Riker chucked a thumb in the direction of the door and she nodded. He turned, and mustering what few shreds of dignity he had left—which weren't much—he went back out into the hallway. The door closed with a very decisive hiss.

He leaned against a wall of the corridor. "Perfect."

Riker sat at his customary table in Ten-Forward, nursing his customary drink. A couple of times, crewmen started to wander in his direction. But when they got close enough to him to pick up on the unspoken body language that said *Leave me alone,* they would invariably back off.

Everyone, of course, except Guinan.

The Ten-Forward hostess glided up to the table and simply stood there until Riker looked up.

"The problem is the weather," she said succinctly.

He stared at her. "I beg your pardon?"

"A traditional entrée into conversation has always been to discuss something utterly inconsequential; something that no one can do anything about. The weather has always filled the bill. Saying things like 'I think it's clouding up' was always a good way to ease yourself into talking about something a bit more uncomfortable." Guinan inclined her head slightly toward the viewport. "But look at that. Not much to say, is there? 'Hmm . . . looks like a vacuum today. And they predict more of the same for tomorrow.' You see the difficulty."

"It's a formidable obstacle to casual chitchat," said Riker gravely.

She remained standing opposite him. "So is sending out waves of frustration."

"Have I been doing that?"

"Look around you, Riker. There were twice as many people in here when you came in. Half of them left to do something more fun than be near you—like shoot themselves out the photon torpedo tube."

"Bad as all that, am I?"

She waggled her head slightly. "Not *that* bad. People overreact sometimes. If you were an ensign on custodial detail, that would be one thing. But when the second-in-command looks like he lost his best friend, well . . . crewmen get a little unnerved by that."

"I'll try to be more sensitive to people's needs."

"Have you?"

"Been more sensitive?"

"No. Lost your best friend."

He stared into the contents of the glass. "I don't know. I acted like an idiot with her."

"I see. And were your actions unforgivable? Did you hit her?"

Riker looked shocked. "Of course not!"

"Rough her up a little?"

"No!"

"Call her obscene names?"

"Of course not, Guinan. I'd never do that, and she'd never tolerate it."

"How about beating up one of her friends? Would she tolerate that?"

"No. She wouldn't."

"Well, then," said Guinan, "how do you think she'd react to your beating up on yourself?"

Riker opened his mouth to reply and then closed it again without doing so.

"Uh-huh," said Guinan.

Then she looked behind her in that way she had, reacting to something before she'd even seen it. Riker craned his neck to see around her, already suspecting what would be there.

Sure enough, there was Deanna. She had entered Ten-Forward and was simply standing there, her arms folded across the top of her gray uniform with the purple V-neck. She was looking at Riker with an arched eyebrow. Her face was unreadable.

Guinan drifted over to her and Deanna glanced at her. "He's all yours," Guinan said. "If you want him, that is."

"I don't know," said Deanna with just the faintest hint of amused tolerance in her voice. "He looks pretty pathetic."

"Looks can be deceiving," said Guinan sagely. Then she looked to Riker, and back to Troi. "On the other hand, sometimes looks can be right on target."

"Thank you, Guinan."

"Don't mention it."

Deanna walked across the Ten-Forward with her usual purposeful stride. And then, in deliberate emulation of Riker, she spun the chair around on the opposite side of the table from him and straddled it.

"I am . . ." Riker tried to find the words, and nothing better than the obvious occurred to him. "So sorry."

He waited for Deanna to say something. All she did was stare at him before finally saying simply, "And . . . ?"

He looked at the drink again. "I handled it very badly. It was an embarrassing situation under any circumstances. Walking in on someone when they're . . . involved with someone . . . can be very disconcerting. And it's even more disconcerting when that person is someone you have . . . had . . ."

"Have and had?"

"Feelings for," he finished. "Feelings that you always think you've sorted out, but then every time you think you have a handle on them, something happens."

Again he paused, and again she simply said, "And . . . ?"

Now he was starting to get just a bit annoyed. "Well, I mean, Deanna—you're the counselor, after all . . . the one who's spent years getting in touch with her feelings. Can you say to me that you wouldn't feel the least little bit thrown off if you walked in on . . . I don't know . . ."

"Ensign Ro?" she said helpfully.

His face fell. "Bad example." But then he brightened slightly. "Actually . . . you know, I had this odd feeling of reverse déjà vu when I walked in on you, because if you remember, you didn't handle it particularly well on Betazed when—"

She waved it off quickly, saying, "Youth excuses a great deal," but Riker knew that he'd hit home with that reminder of times past. And she knew it, too. When she looked up at him again, it was with an expression that he'd come to know extremely well—understanding.

"Will," she said slowly, "we have a lot of history between us. A lot of reasons why our relationship is precisely where it is. Partly because we're serving on the same ship. Partly because . . . well, partly a lot of things. One thing that we both agree on, though, is that neither of us is interested in leading a celibate life."

"I know, Deanna. I don't deny that. I don't deny your right to be involved with whomever you want. In fact, I'm happy for you." He smiled sincerely, which wasn't difficult because he really was sincere. "You're entitled to every happiness that life has to offer you. And I understand that, since we've decided that our relationship is best served by remaining simply close friends—"

"There's nothing 'simple' about our relationship, Will," she said with her usual sparkle.

"Granted. What I'm saying is that I understand . . . hell, I *know* . . . that relationships of a more—physical—nature than we're pursuing with each other are natural. Expected."

Guinan appeared without saying a word, placed a drink at Deanna's right, and moved away as silent as a ghost. Deanna picked up the drink almost unconsciously, dropped in a small stirrer, and mixed it absently. "We've made no claims on each other otherwise," she pointed out.

"Right. And naturally we're going to be involved with other people."

"You keep saying that, Will. Do you repeat it because you want to emphasize it . . . or because you want to convince yourself of it?"

He smiled lopsidedly. "A little of both, I guess. What I'm saying is that I understand it intellectually. In the abstract. But being put face-to-face, unexpectedly, with the reality of it . . . it just caught me a little off guard, that's all. I felt surprise, and maybe . . . just maybe"—he brought his thumb and forefinger together to measure out a minuscule amount of space—"just a smidgen of jealousy."

"Just a smidgen."

"Nothing significant. I mean, after all, Deanna"—he spread his hands helplessly—"I'm only human."

"I've tried never to hold that against you," she said somberly.

And they clinked glasses.

Nine

In a time-honored tradition for getting attention, Captain Picard clinked his knife several times against his glass.

All around the banquet table, the delegates ceased their amiable chatter, putting down their utensils or drinks and giving their full attention to the captain.

Around the table were grouped the ambassadors from the Cordians, the Byfrexians, and the Luss. Also seated there were Data, Worf, Riker, and Troi.

Riker was not seated next to Deanna but instead several spaces down. That had not been the original seating arrangement, but when Deanna had arrived, she had been mildly surprised to find Dann next to her.

"Commander Riker insisted," said Dann, sounding just a bit puzzled. "I thought I was supposed to be sitting with my delegation, but . . ." And he shrugged.

Deanna had turned and looked at Riker, who was sitting next to the Lussian ambassador and speaking with him animatedly. The Luss was nodding his bald head thoughtfully, and giving that enigmatic half-smile that was so typical of the elders of his race.

As if sensing Deanna's gaze on him, Riker continued to talk to the ambassador but glanced in Deanna's direction. Her smile said it all—*The seating rearrangement wasn't necessary, but it's a sweet gesture. Thank you.* He cocked his head slightly in unspoken response and then turned his full attention back to the ambassador.

The evening had progressed quite smoothly as the *Enterprise* continued in its stately orbit around Sindar, the home planet of the Sindareen. Their arrival had been uneventful, which in and of itself was unusual. Once upon a time, anyone getting within a parsec of Sindareen space, much less the home world of Sindar, was met with challenges and hostilities . . . even if they were expected.

But the *Enterprise* had sailed through with nary a whisper from the Sindareen and had settled into orbit around Sindar while attracting nothing more than a muted greeting from the planetary government and an assurance that delegates would shortly be prepared to beam up to the *Enterprise* to begin the hammering out of a peace settlement between the Sindareen and their longtime opponents.

Those delegates were now seated at the head of the table and were paying polite attention to Picard as he rapped for silence.

When all was silent, Picard spoke. "The Federation is, at its heart, an organization dedicated to peace. So a mission such as this one is always particularly gratifying, since we are fulfilling the most fundamental function of the United Federation of Planets. I extend welcome once more to the delegates of the Cordians, the Luss, and the Byfrexians." As he mentioned each one, he raised his glass and moved it slightly in the direction of each in acknowledgment. "And now, it is my honor to welcome the delegates from the Sindareen . . . Ambassador Nici, and her retainer, Eza."

Nici slowly rose. She was tall, with her coal-black hair swept up and back, exposing her long, narrow throat. Her mouth barely moved when she spoke—instead, the sound issued predominantly from the nictating membranes that fluttered at the base of her neck.

"It is . . . *our* honor," she said carefully, "to meet with our . . . associates . . . in a place other than the battlefield. I have advocated the putting aside of hostilities for many years now. Our leaders have finally accepted the inevitability of . . ."

She paused, and immediately Picard knew why. She was waiting for one of the delegates to be classless enough to finish the sentence with the word *defeat.*

No one said anything, but simply waited expectantly and courteously.

". . . compromise," Nici concluded after a respectable pause.

Picard was pleased that the initial thrust from the Sindareen had worked out so smoothly, as they all raised their glasses and drank. He, along with the other delegates, knew perfectly well that the Sindareen used language as yet another weapon—to probe, prod, and generally to try to trip up potential opponents and reveal their true mind-sets. So no one at the table had any desire or intention of falling into one of the renowned Sindareen verbal traps.

Seated next to Nici, and just to Deanna's right, was Eza, Nici's aide. Eza was darker complexioned than Nici—perhaps a resident of another province, Riker figured. Eza had a dark scowl on his face and seemed even less enthused with the proceedings than Nici. But at least he properly kept his own counsel, and Riker hoped that Eza would not serve as any sort of impediment to the proceedings.

Also, Eza did seem capable of being swayed—the only times he smiled during the meal were when Deanna would engage him in conversation. He seemed grateful for the attention, and several times throughout the course of the meal he actually laughed rather boisterously, his nictating membranes flapping with furious speed. It seemed quite a positive sign. Clearly, Riker thought, the counselor's ability to charm people was not limited solely to Riker himself.

By the end of the dinner, everyone seemed in high spirits. It was as upbeat a beginning as anyone could have hoped.

Still, Riker and Picard managed to sidle up to Deanna during a leisurely time afterward, when the delegates had broken up into smaller groups and were chatting informally with each other. The full meetings were scheduled to begin the next day.

"Any feeling on the Sindareen?" Picard asked in a low voice. He kept his smile firmly fixed in place, though, and even nodded in the direction of Nici when she glanced at him from a corner of the room.

"On a surface level, Captain, their motives seem to be precisely what they say they are: they want peace."

"Any agenda beyond that?" Riker said.

Deanna paused, giving the question full weight. "I cannot say for sure. As I told you, Captain—and as Commander Riker knows—the Sindareen can be a challenge to read. Through continued exposure, however, as I gain a feeling for the individual's psyche, I might be able to tell you more."

"You'll do your best, I'm certain, Counselor," said Picard. "At least we're off on the right foot."

A hand rested on Deanna's shoulder and she turned to look into Dann's smiling face. "Are you about finished here, Deanna?" he asked, and then looked to Picard and Riker. "Sorry, gentlemen . . . I didn't mean to interrupt."

"That's all right, Dann," said Deanna. "We were finished." Then she looked to Picard for confirmation. "Weren't we, Captain?"

"By all means." But Picard's eyes narrowed slightly, and he watched as Dann led Deanna out of the room, an arm around her waist in a most familiar fashion. Deanna was laughing lightly at some comment he had just whispered to her.

Picard turned to Riker and noted that the muscles of his jaw were working under his cheeks. "Problem, Number One?"

"No problem, Captain," said Riker neutrally.

Picard took a step closer to his second-in-command and observed, "She seems rather friendly with him. That's not going to present a difficulty for you, is it, Number One?"

Riker regarded Picard with an arched eyebrow. "I already said there's no problem, Captain. I hope you don't think I'm lying to you."

"Number One, never in a million years would I believe that you would lie to me."

"Thank you, sir."

Picard paused only a moment before he added, "However . . . lying to yourself would be another matter entirely."

Riker had been turning away, but now he looked back at Picard with some surprise. "Deanna's happiness is my happiness," Riker said firmly, and then deciding that his tone sounded just a bit too aggressive for a statement directed to his commanding officer, quickly added a respectful, "Sir."

Picard nodded slightly. "A very commendable and adult attitude, Number One. If you are satisfied with the situation, then I certainly am—especially seeing as it isn't any of my business."

"As you say, sir."

One of the Byfrexians came up at that moment and engaged Picard in a discussion of Prime Directive ethics that had been a bone of contention in a seminar the ambassador had taught. Riker listened for a few moments before drifting over to Nici and striking up a polite and, he hoped, informative conversation with her.

But his gaze kept shifting over to the doors of the banquet room—the doors through which Counselor Troi had exited moments earlier with Dann. And Riker had taken note not only of the arm around her waist but also that Deanna had placed a hand over his as if she wanted to make sure he didn't remove that arm.

"I'm happy for you," he said to no one in particular.

Ten

Riker lay on his back, staring up into the darkness of his quarters.

His hands were interlaced behind his head, the pillow soft under him. He had been that way for over an hour as sleep refused to come.

Sorting out his feelings was rapidly becoming something of a royal pain. He still remembered that time a couple of years ago, in Deanna's quarters . . . Both he and Deanna had been in an extremely mellow mood, and he had also been allowing the more relaxing qualities of the Synthehol he'd consumed to have sway over his actions. A friendly good-night kiss had turned into something far more passionate, and for a moment they had been kissing each other eagerly, hungrily, and it had been just like the old days.

And then Deanna had whispered, pleaded, telling him that they shouldn't, reminding him of the difficulties of involvement while both served on the same ship. Yet even as she spoke, she would have let him . . .

But he pulled back. Her words had penetrated the Syntheholic haze on his brain and washed it away, bringing with it instant sobriety and a reminder of the line that they had drawn for themselves.

And nothing had happened.

Not that he hadn't wanted it . . . they had both wanted it . . .

But what had they wanted? Momentary gratification? Or something more . . . a rekindling of something that they had thought they'd left behind them?

Perhaps they'd been kidding themselves. Here he was someone accustomed to command situations, and here she was someone who was always in touch with feelings. So it was only natural that they would decide they could control their feelings, dictate their relationship. Turn their emotions on and off like an old-style light switch.

How realistic was that, though? Lying there in the darkness, imagining Deanna at that moment, wrapped in the arms of Dann, laughing or saying things softly . . .

Did she say the same things to Dann that she had to Riker?

For a moment there he had actually been drifting off, his feelings about Deanna lulling his brain and convincing him that everything would seem more clear in the morning. And then something, some impulse, made him sit bolt upright in bed, moving so swiftly that he had a momentary sense of disorientation.

Someone was there. He didn't know how, he didn't know why . . . but someone was there, hiding in a corner, lurking in the darkness.

He called out, "Lights!"

Obediently his quarters filled with light. And there he saw—

Nothing.

The doors had not opened. No one had entered. Except for himself, no one was there.

He had no way of describing the feeling that was cutting through him. What was the old saying? *Someone just stepped on my grave.*

"Hello?" said Riker tentatively, not having the faintest idea why he was saying it.

The ship's computer, aware that the room was unoccupied except for Riker, interpreted the salutation as an oddly variant, but no less legitimate, means of address to itself. "Working," replied the computer. It then waited patiently for further instructions.

He didn't know why he was asking, but he said, "Computer—who's in this room?"

"William Thelonius Riker."

"Anyone else?"

"No."

Slowly he nodded. "Lights off," he said after a moment.

He lay back down as the lights faded, wondering whether he wasn't making himself a little crazy over the situation.

At first he felt wide-awake, but then gradually the fatigue settled in, and slowly, gradually, he drifted off to sleep.

She filled his dreams. She was smiling at him, walking toward him, her arms outstretched, and somehow everything seemed to make so much more sense when she was there. Without her, there was no—

"IMZADI!"

The word screamed in his mind, throughout every part of his body, and he snapped to full wakefulness in a split instant. He didn't know how much time had passed since he had fallen back to sleep, and it didn't matter.

All that mattered was the voice, was the word, and it had been unmistakably no dream. Definitely, it was Deanna, and whatever was happening, it was utterly terrifying to her.

"Deanna!" shouted Riker.

The computer said helpfully, "William Thelonius Riker is the only occupant of—"

"Shut up! Lights!"

The lights immediately snapped on. He winced against it momentarily, but it didn't slow him as he ran to his closet and grabbed his robe. "Riker to Counselor Troi!" he called out in the more recognizable comm command that would, ordinarily, patch him through the ship's intercom to Deanna.

There was no response. She wasn't acknowledging—but he could still feel that cold, dark terror invading him. Whatever was happening, she was replying in a far more primal manner than via a ship's communication system.

Immediately switching gears as he yanked on his robe, he said, "Riker to Dr. Crusher!"

This time there was a response. Beverly sounded groggy—obviously he'd woken her up. But there was no hesitation to her voice because late-night interruptions were hardly unusual in her line of work. "Crusher here."

"Something's wrong with Deanna! Get a medunit to her quarters now!"

To her credit, Beverly Crusher wasted no time with confused questions such as "How do you know?" or "Why didn't you call sickbay directly?" To the latter question, she obviously, and correctly, reasoned that Riker had instinctively contacted the person he most trusted in a medical emergency. To the former question, when it came to matters of Riker and Troi, she was more than willing to accept a great deal on faith.

All she said was a stark "Acknowledged."

Riker didn't even hear her reply. He was already out the door.

He barreled down the corridor, attracting curious glances from passersby due to his state of extremely casual dress that contrasted with his air of barely controlled panic. Ensign Chafin had the poor luck to turn a corner without watching where he was going, which was directly into Riker's path, and Riker plowed into him like a linebacker. Chafin went flying and smacked into the far wall. Riker barely lost a step and kept on going, not even registering until sometime later that he had decked a crewman without so much as a word of apology.

Deanna's quarters were just ahead and he raced into them, heedless of his safety. After all, he had no idea what threat Deanna might be subjected to—for all he knew, berserk Sindareen were skinning her alive and were ready to turn on him next. Nothing mattered except helping her.

He entered her quarters and was horrified by the sight that greeted his eyes.

Deanna was lying on the floor, convulsions shaking her. She was nude except for a sheet that had been tossed over her, like a shroud. Dann was standing over her, having pulled on trousers, but otherwise looking confused and helpless.

"Deanna!" shouted Riker.

Dann looked at him, and his skin had gone a shade or two lighter. "I . . . I don't know what happened! She just—"

"Why the hell didn't you summon help!" shouted Riker.

"I don't know how!" said Dann. "I've never been on a starship before! Is there something I press or—"

Riker shoved him aside, unnecessarily hard, and called out desperately, "Riker to sickbay! Where the hell's that medunit!" He didn't even wait for a reply as he dropped down next to the trembling counselor.

Her skin was dead white. He took her hand in his and it was clammy. His hands moved helplessly over her, and he fought down his terror as he said, "Shh . . . everything's going to be okay. It's okay, Deanna."

Her eyes were clouding over. He didn't even think she could see him. He had no idea what was happening to her, and even more terrifying . . . neither did she.

"Imzadi," she whispered, voicing the word that had lanced through his mind and soul. "Please . . . help me . . . help."

He scooped her up into his arms urgently and was out the door, heading toward the sickbay. He was by nature a strong man, and now, driven by adrenaline and fear, he was so worked up that he hardly even felt her weight. He kept whispering to her, talking frantically, as if afraid that the only thing keeping her attached to the world was the sound of his voice.

He encountered the medunit partway. Beverly Crusher had not even bothered to toss on a robe—in her nightgown, she was guiding the techs with the antigrav crash cart. "Quickly! Quickly!"

Deanna's hand still gripped Riker's robe as he laid her down on the cart and ran alongside it. And again, she said, "Help me . . . please . . . so cold . . ." Her body was shaking faster.

"Stabilize her!" shouted Crusher, and Dr. Selar, who had been on duty when the call came in, jammed a hypo into her arm.

"I'll help you," Riker told Deanna, and the fear that ran through her leaped into him and clamped around his heart. He felt as if his world were disintegrating. "I promise, Imzadi. I'll do anything . . . everything. I . . ."

But she didn't hear him.

Her breath rattled once more in her chest . . . and by the time she was rolled into sickbay mere moments later . . .

. . . she was gone.

Thousands of light-years away, Lwaxana Troi woke up. And she began screaming.

She did not stop for two solid hours.

She was never the same after that.

EPILOGUE

Admiral Riker stared at Captain Crusher, who was stony faced. "Your mother blamed herself for quite some time afterwards," Riker said. "It was so unnecessary . . . she did everything she could. She worked on Deanna for . . . I don't know . . . it seemed forever, trying to bring her back. But nothing helped. Nothing . . . helped." And he added silently, *Not even me.*

"She blamed herself but she didn't have to, that's what you're saying?" asked Captain Crusher.

"That's right."

Wesley stared out at the rain, which had tapered off to a mere trickle. Within a minute or two, it would stop altogether. "And I guess another reason it wasn't necessary . . . was that you pretty much had a lock on the self-blame category."

Riker nodded slowly. "I guess the difference is that your mother did everything she could . . . and didn't succeed. And I kept feeling as if . . . as if I should have done something. Somehow, someway . . . I should have done *more.* And it was always a great frustration to me that I never figured out what that more should have been. All I knew is that I promised to help her . . . and I didn't do much except be by her side when she died."

"Maybe that was all she wanted."

Riker said nothing.

Crusher considered a moment and then said, "And Mom never found the cause?"

"Never," said Riker, shaking his head. "That's the most agonizing thing about a situation like that. You find yourself wanting answers, some sort of answers. And there were none to be had. Beverly couldn't find any cause for Deanna's . . . passing. It was just as if her body simply . . . stopped. Massive cardiovascular collapse, but there seemed no physiological reason for it. Beverly ran a full trace of all known foreign substances, for the purpose of ruling out foul play—which was pretty farfetched, but your mom covered all the bases—and there was nothing. Deanna just . . ." He struggled with the word and then exhaled it: "Died." He paused.

"And what happened then?"

Riker shrugged. "It all went downhill. The ship; my life . . . just . . ." And again he shrugged, this time a bit more fatalistically. "Sometimes you just don't really appreciate how key someone is to your world until they're gone. And then, of course, it's too late."

They sat there for a few moments longer, and then Wesley suddenly cocked his head slightly in that gesture that Riker had come to know so well. "Crusher here."

Riker didn't bother to stand by and watch Captain Crusher have a conversation with thin air. Instead he walked back into the other room where Deanna's body lay in a perfectly preserved state and rested a hand on the covering.

"I'm sorry, Imzadi," he said softly. "I tried."

He heard Wesley's soft footfall, and then the captain said, "I have to go. Sudden groundquake on Cygnia III. Code One disaster situation." He paused. "You're welcome to come along, Admiral. There's . . . well, I'm sorry, sir, but there's nothing here for you except fairly unpleasant memories."

"That may very well be, Captain, but as I mentioned to you, Lwaxana Troi's wishes in the disposition of her things were quite specific. And Lwaxana was always a tough woman to say no to."

"All right, Admiral. Whatever you say." Crusher paused. "It stopped raining. If you'd like, I'll walk you back to the house before I go."

Riker nodded.

They walked out of the mausoleum together, their feet squishing softly into the now spongelike ground. The clouds were passing and hints of sunlight were already streaming through. As they approached the house, the admiral turned to Crusher and took him by the shoulders.

"It's been a pleasure seeing you again, Wes."

Crusher grimaced. "I just wish it could have been under more pleasant circumstances."

"So do I. Maybe next time it will be."

Then, in a rather nonregulation but perfectly understandable move, Riker embraced Crusher firmly, patting him on the back. Then he took a few steps back, and both of them, without any intention of doing so, simultaneously tugged on their respective uniform jackets, straightening them. Each saw the other making the gesture, and they both laughed.

"Good sailing, Captain Crusher. The *Hood* is a good ship. I served on one of her predecessors. Fortunately she has a fine captain at the helm."

"Good luck in your future endeavors, Admiral Riker. I hope you find happiness . . . and some peace." Then Crusher tilted his head and said, "Crusher to *Hood.* One to beam up."

Wesley Crusher's body shimmered out, and Riker was alone.

He found the Holy Rings of Betazed. They were, for no reason Riker could determine, in Lwaxana's closet. He shrugged and put them with the pile of other materials, trinkets, and mementos that he was organizing in the living room.

Mr. Homn had vanished. There had been no word of explanation. No good-byes. When Riker had returned to the mansion, Homn simply wasn't there. It was as if he'd done his job to its conclusion and, once having reached that conclusion, had no reason to remain. And so he had left. Left Riker with a huge pile of material to go through.

Betazed had an excellent museum of antiquities, and Lwaxana Troi's collection was going to be a considerable and valuable addition. Riker had made the arrangements for it to be taken away, and they had only asked that he go through everything first to remove any possessions that might simply be considered personal and of no interest to the general Betazed public.

Lwaxana had left no family behind. The furniture had already been cleared out, donated to a local charity. All that were left were the keepsakes that Riker was now sorting through.

Having gone through all the other rooms in the house, he now approached the one he least looked forward to: Deanna's.

He opened the door, and sure enough, it was what he had anticipated. Lwaxana had left everything exactly as it was, like a shrine to her daughter. The room was decorated in large splashes of purple, with various small statues—the type that Deanna had liked to stare at for hours on end.

And in Deanna's closet, he found a box.

It had a lock on it, but the lock wasn't closed. Riker opened the lid, curious as to what he would find.

He recognized everything that was in the box.

Everything had been perfectly preserved, no matter how arcane or trivial. There was a piece of vine from the Jalara Jungle. There was the headband that she had been wearing at Chandra's wedding. There was her study disk on "Human Dysfunctions." There was . . .

"Good lord." He reached down and picked up a small but sharp rock. It had a discoloration on it that was quite clearly blood. "She even kept this."

He looked further and found the poem.

He read it over, separated by decades from the youthful exuberance with which he'd penned it. Phrases that he could remember sounding so clever to himself when he'd come up with them now sounded trite, facile. A kid who knew nothing, trying to sum up in a few lines of poetry feelings that even now, as an old man, he couldn't completely frame for himself.

"This is terrible. I can't believe I wrote this." And then he picked up the headband, fingering it. "And I can't believe you liked it. I can't believe you—"

He was surprised to find that his face was wet. He wiped the tears with the headband and felt the softness of it against his face and started to cry harder.

He had thought he'd finished with the grief. He'd thought he'd been able to move on. But there, sitting on the floor of a room once belonging to a young, vital woman, he realized that he had never moved on. Never put it behind him. His entire life reeked of unfinished business. And he would never be able to finish it. There had been so much he had wanted to say—and would never be able to because time had outsped him before he'd even fully grasped the notion that he was in a race.

It was never going to get better. Despite all his accomplishments, his great failure—the failure that everyone had told him he'd had no reason for shouldering—would always be with him. Always.

He clutched the headband even tighter and tried to remember a time when he felt no pain.

THE BEGINNING

Eleven

Lieutenant William T. Riker punched the bulkhead and managed to bruise his hand rather badly. The bulkhead, for its part, didn't seem to care all that much.

He stared once more, with utter hatred, at the packed suitcase that sat in the middle of his bed, as if angry the thing even existed. "This really stinks," he informed the case, and went on to add, "I can't believe you're doing this." The suitcase showed as much interest in Riker's anger as had the bulkhead.

"Lieutenant Riker to the bridge," came his captain's voice through his communicator.

He tapped it with his hand, which made it feel sore all over again: "On my way." He cast one last angry glance at the suitcase and the bulkhead, which had obviously conspired to make his life just that much more miserable, before heading out the door and up to the bridge.

He drummed impatiently on the railing grip of the turbolift. Everything about the ship seemed slow and frustrating. For that matter, everything about his *life* seemed slow and frustrating. He had places to go, a career to forge . . . and the fates had conspired to slow that career to an agonizing, frustrating crawl.

The 'lift door opened out onto the cramped bridge of the *Fortuna,* and Riker stepped out. He nodded a brisk acknowledgment to Captain Lansing and took his place at the survey station.

Lansing, middle-aged and content with the relatively low point in the pecking order that he had reached in his career, swiveled in his chair to face Riker. "I thought you might want to know, Lieutenant, that we'll be arriving at Betazed in . . ." Lansing paused and glanced at the helmsman.

"Twenty-seven minutes," said the helmsman.

Riker noticed that everyone on the bridge seemed to be staring at him.

"And we thought that you might want to spend your last half hour aboard our vessel with our small but sturdy bridge crew," continued Lansing.

Riker frowned. "That's very kind of you, sir."

Lansing rose, drawing his portly frame out of the command chair. "You did make it quite clear that you did not want any sort of going-away function."

"Yes, sir. And I appreciate your honoring my request."

"You know the wonderful thing about being in command, Mr. Riker?" Without waiting for Riker to respond, Lansing continued, "You get to ignore the wishes of your junior officers whenever it suits you. Mr. Li, if you don't mind."

Navigator Kathy Li rose from her chair and brought her hands around. Riker saw that she was holding something, and he fought down a grin when he saw what it was: a large cupcake with a sparking candle lodged serenely in the top. And the words *So Long, Cupcake*—Li's nickname for him—were scrawled across the top of it in pink icing.

Captain Lansing said, "Computer. Run 'Riker Farewell Program One-A.' "

The bridge was promptly filled with the sound of Dixieland music, and now Riker laughed out loud in spite of himself.

Over the music, Lansing called out, "We decided to compromise, Mr. Riker—a send-off, but with a very proscribed time limit, namely twenty-seven—excuse me, twenty-six now—minutes."

Riker made the round of the bridge crew, shaking hands and laughing and nodding, accepting with good grace their best wishes for his new assignment. Kathy Li kissed him rather passionately—they had made some minor effort to be discreet over their relationship while serving together. They had, of course, fooled absolutely no one, and with his imminent departure she saw no need to pussyfoot around. They broke for air and she patted him on the face. "It's been a lot of laughs, cupcake."

"No more than that?" he said mischievously.

She looked at him, feigning total astonishment. *"More* than that? With Will-the-Thrill, I-Never-Met-a-Woman-I-Didn't-Like Riker? Oh, come on, Lieutenant. You wouldn't *want* more than that. Doesn't fit in with your game plan."

"Are you saying the good lieutenant isn't the type to commit to one woman?" said Lansing in mock horror.

"I'm really enjoying discussing my psychological profile in a public forum," Riker said.

As if Riker hadn't even spoken, Li said cheerfully, "Remember the old days of space travel, Captain? Where every single article had to be carefully measured and accounted for because of fuel consumption? If you had weight that you didn't allow for, it could cost the early astronauts their lives. Well"—she squeezed Riker's shoulder—"the lieutenant operates on the same principle. A real, solid romance—true love and everything—would amount to additional weight in his travels through space. Our Mr. Riker doesn't like to deal with excess baggage."

Riker looked at her. "Kathy, are you mad at me?"

She blinked in surprise. "No. Not at all. I just know how you are. Or am I wrong?"

He thought about it and said, "No, you're probably right."

"See there?" said Lansing. "Mr. Li is probably right. And that is good enough for me. Mr. Riker, do you have any final things you'd like to say before you embark on your new and exciting assignment?"

Science Officer Sara Paul was going around from person to person, holding a bottle of champagne. Glasses had been produced and she was filling each of them up about halfway.

"Anything I'd like to say? Truthfully?"

"The truth is preferred aboard the science exploration vessel *Fortuna,"* said Lansing.

Riker stared at his cupcake. "Well . . . to be honest . . . I wish I weren't leaving."

This caused a fairly surprised reaction from the others. "But Lieutenant," said Lansing, "being promoted to first officer on the *Hood* . . . it's a sizable step up. And—"

"If I were going to the *Hood,* sir, I'd be ecstatic. But I'm not. I'm going to be cooling my heels planetside for the next few months. I could be far more use remaining on the *Fortuna."*

"Lieutenant," said Lansing understandingly, "it's an unfortunate piece of luck, I'll admit. But let's try being unselfish, shall we? We can just thank the stars that the *Hood* is still in one piece. From what I've heard, those Sindareen raiders gave her quite a shellacking. It's a testament to the *Hood,* her capabilities and her crew, that she not only survived the sneak attack but destroyed the raiders. Still, she's going to be in dry dock for the next two to three months, undergoing repairs and overhauls which were past due anyway. Look at it this way—you'll be getting a ship that's better than new."

"But to be planetside . . ." Riker shook his head ruefully. "I feel like I'll lose my space legs. The timing is so lousy."

"True enough," admitted Lansing. "But what are we supposed to do? Your transfer to the *Hood* was arranged a month ago. Who expected a Sindareen attack on her? And the same time your transfer was arranged, so was the transfer of your replacement. We rendezvous with him in eighteen hours. We don't need the both of you here, and when the vacancy in the Betazed embassy opened up—"

"So why not let *him* stew on Betazed for a few months?" said Riker, hoping he wasn't sounding too whiny.

"Because Starfleet wanted the more experienced officer there, Lieutenant, and that's you. Face it, Mr. Riker . . . you're just too popular. Everyone wants you."

Riker shook his head. "It's been years since I've been planetside for more than seventy-two hours."

"You'll get the hang of it," said Lansing consolingly. Then he raised his glass. "Lt. William T. Riker: Here's wishing you all the success in the galaxy, and hoping for a great and glorious future. To your future."

"To your future," chorused the crew of the *Fortuna.*

Riker nodded and smiled. "To the future," he said, and drank the champagne.

Twelve

Riker's first view of Mark Roper, the man who headed the Federation embassy of Betazed, was what would become a fairly typical view of him—behind his desk, looking utterly besieged. Roper, for his part, didn't seem to notice Riker at all.

Roper was heavyset, with graying hair and a thick, red nose that God seemed to have slapped on one day while He was in one of His more puckish moods. Roper had two computer screens on his desk and was going from one to the other, tapping notes into a small padd in front of him and muttering to himself much of the time.

Riker cleared his throat. Roper glanced up at him, nodded briskly in acknowledgment, and then promptly, and rather obviously, forgot Riker was standing there. Instead Roper continued with his work, saying things like, "Unbelievable. Can't expect me to be everywhere. They want me to . . . ? That's two conflicting appointments. *Now* the Rigelian ambassador wants to come through? *And* he expects me to set up a reception. Lord . . . Grace!"

The last word was shouted, and for a moment Riker thought that Roper was loudly calling for divine intervention. But then the harried but determined young woman who had greeted Riker when he first arrived outside Roper's office barreled in in response. She sidled past Riker, who had the distinct feeling that he had been thrown into the middle of carefully, but barely, controlled chaos.

"Grace," Roper said, "get me Harras at the catering facility. I have to meet with him as soon as possible. Also with Counsel Head Timbor—"

"You just met with him yesterday," Grace reminded him, sounding slightly confused.

"Yes, but I didn't know about the Rigelian ambassador yesterday," replied Roper in exasperation. "Utterly paranoid people. Never like to give anyone more than forty-eight hours' notice. And he probably won't even show up! Cancel at the last minute. Typical. Typical."

Riker wasn't sure precisely whom Roper was talking to—Grace, Riker, or himself . . . or some combination of the three.

"When's the earliest I can see Harras? Tonight," he said, answering his own question. "It has to be tonight."

"You have the Xerx wedding tonight."

Roper held his face in his hands. "Perfect. Just perfect."

He was silent for a long moment, and Riker seized the break in the steady flow of conversation. "Mr. Roper? I'm Lieutenant Riker. I presume you were told about me?"

Roper stared at him through his fingers. "When was our appointment?"

"Appoint—?" Riker looked from Roper to the woman who'd been addressed as Grace. "Is *anyone* here expecting me?"

Grace said to her boss with a gentle, prodding tone, "Starfleet? Remember, Mark?"

Roper still looked blank for a moment, and then understanding flooded through his face. "Riker! William Riker!"

"Yes, sir," said Riker with a sigh of relief.

"The new Starfleet liaison! My boy, please accept my apologies." Roper circled around his desk and took Riker's hand, pumping it furiously.

"I'm sorry if I came at a bad time."

"Daytime is generally a bad time," said Roper. "The second worst time is nighttime. Nevertheless, it's good to have you aboard. As you can see by my perpetually discombobulated state, the more help we have here, the better."

"Whatever I can do to help, sir."

"Yes, well, the first thing you can do is take a load off." Roper gestured to the chair opposite him. "And have patience with my natterings and ramblings. Would you like some coffee?"

"That would be great, thanks."

Roper started to head for the door, but Grace stopped him. "It's okay, Mark. I'll get it." She looked to Riker and said, "Cream?"

"Black."

"Coming up." She smiled and flashed two rows of clean white teeth at him before walking out.

Roper looked at Riker with what appeared to be newfound respect. "I admit, I'm impressed, Captain."

Riker looked at him with mild confusion. "It's 'lieutenant.' And why are you impressed, sir?"

"Because Grace has been my assistant for three years and she rarely sees fit to bring me coffee . . . and she never volunteers. But you—" Roper paused. "Have a way with the females, do you, Captain?"

A slow smile spread across Riker's face. "Women seem to . . . appreciate me. Why do you keep calling me captain?"

"Starfleet forwarded me your file. Very impressive body of work. The word on you is that you're an aggressive, hotshot, up-and-coming young officer, with a flair and aptitude for some of the finer points of diplomacy. The general poop—do you Starfleet types still use nautical terms like *poop?"*

"On occasion." At first put off by Roper's style—if such a term could be applied to it—Riker was slowly finding himself amused by, and even liking, this somewhat harried diplomat.

"Okay. The general poop is that you're on a fast track, my young friend. Some even believe you might beat out Jim Kirk's record for youngest captain . . . and that's stood firm for close to a century."

"That's the poop, is it?"

"And nothing but the poop. So I figure I'll start calling you captain now and beat the rush." Roper leaned forward. "Unless you'd like me to just skip straight to 'admiral'?"

"That's quite all right, sir, you run the embassy. You can address me however you want . . . although I would appreciate it if, in the presence of other Starfleet personnel, you addressed me by my proper rank. Genuine captains might not consider it amusing."

"Whatever," said Roper with a casual air.

Grace came back in with a cup of black coffee, which Riker took carefully from her. She stood over him and said, "Anything else I can get for you?"

"This will be fine."

"Grace, see that we're not disturbed."

"All right, Mark," she said, but her smile and gaze were directed to Riker. Then she turned and walked out.

Roper shook his head. "Oh, yes. *Very* impressive. So . . ." His tone changed to a more businesslike timbre. "What have they told you?"

"About this assignment? Well . . . Betazed is supposed to be environmentally quite lovely." Riker turned his attention to a large window that opened out onto a dazzling vista. The sky was dazzling blue with pink clouds hanging against it as if they'd been painted there. They were on the twentieth floor of the building, and Riker had an overview of the city. Rather than being a combination of a variety of styles, as in so many cities, the buildings seemed to flow seamlessly one into the other. Either the city had been meticulously planned from the beginning or else the growth of it had been consistently smooth and organic. Far, far in the distance, Riker could see the barest hints of a mountain range. "In that," he continued, "I would have to say the word *understatement* comes to mind."

"It is a lovely world. A lovely people," confirmed Roper. "Sensitive to a great degree. Thoughtful and caring, and utterly cooperative. A people steeped in tradition, and a world filled with great thinkers. I am not—it pains me to admit—a great thinker, Captain. How about you?"

"For the moment, I'm happy to be a quick thinker. I presume the rest will take care of itself."

"A very mature attitude. What else do you know?"

"Betazed is a long-standing Federation ally, and quite valued." Then Riker's face darkened. "I also understand there have been some recent difficulties with the Sindareen."

"Quite correct," said Roper gravely. "The Sindareen have a history of belligerence. They also seem to operate in shifts."

"Shifts?" Riker didn't quite understand.

"They have a number of planets and peoples with whom they have disputes, or just perceive as being ripe pickings. But they don't attack them steadily. They go after them for periods of time until they've reached the point where they're almost crossing the line from nuisance and threat to genuine menace . . . and then they pull back. They won't be heard from for months, even years at a time . . . until they've been pretty much forgotten about. At which point they start their assaults and raids all over again."

"And right now they're picking on Betazed."

"That's right. There have been three attacks in as many months at various points throughout the city."

"What about the outlying cities?"

"Small. Primarily agricultural. A lot of farmland on Betazed, or cities that are devoted primarily to philosophical studies. Here is where the real economic action of Betazed occurs—almost all of the trading, the commerce, funnels through here."

"Not the smartest way to arrange things," said Riker grimly. "Apparently they've never heard about putting all the eggs in one basket."

Roper shrugged. "It's their planet, Captain. We can't tell them how to run things. We can, however, take steps. A squad of Starfleet security has been stationed here. As the ranking Starfleet officer, you'll be in charge of them."

Riker nodded. He was familiar with ground-based Starfleet security men—essentially, they were security guards without a ship. They would be dispatched by the UFP to situations where a Federation presence was going to be required for an extended period of time. You couldn't leave a starship in orbit around a planet for weeks, even months—but you could send in a squad of Starfleet security men and leave them there for however long it took to solve the problem.

Riker had encountered ground security teams on a couple of occasions. They were generally tough, strong headed, sometimes contemptuous and even distrustful of officers who spent their careers in "fancified starships," as one ground security man had put it. They were also, Riker knew, extremely formidable.

"Anything else I should know, Mr. Roper?"

Roper nodded and leaned forward. "Don't try to con these people, Riker. Their sensitivity to thought processes is second to none."

"I wouldn't try to 'con' anyone, sir," said Riker, feeling a bit indignant.

"Oh, come on, Captain, we all do it. For example—you run into a woman at a party and she's wearing a dress so ugly it looks like a Klingon Targ vomited on it. Do you say to her, 'Hello, how are you—why are you wearing such a god-awful dress?' Or do you say, 'Hello, my dear, you look lovely tonight.' "

"Well . . . the second, I suppose. I mean, just to be sociable."

"Save it. On Betazed they know precisely what you're thinking. The fortunate thing is that, because of that, these people are hard to offend just on the basis of pure unspoken opinions. They've had to develop a high tolerance for unexpurgated thought . . . it was either that or kill each other. The only thing they have little tolerance for is prevarication. They'd consider that to be insulting. Be straightforward and honest with the Betazoids and they'll appreciate and respect you for it."

The door to the office hissed open and Roper looked up in irritation. "Grace, I thought I said I didn't want to be disturbed."

A young, cheery-eyed woman with straight black hair and a bit of the devil in her eye flounced into the office. "Hello, Daddy."

"Oh! Wendy!" He gestured to Riker, who got to his feet. "Lieutenant Riker, this is my daughter, Wendy. Wendy, this is William Riker."

"Nice to meet you," said Riker, taking mental note of the fact that Roper had introduced him using his correct rank. For that he was most appreciative.

Wendy pumped his hand in much the same manner that Roper had. "We have the same initials," she observed. "W.R." She was looking at him with a frank, appraising attitude.

"So we have," agreed Riker.

"Good." She grinned impishly. "When we get married, we can have identical monograms on our towels."

Riker blinked in surprise and looked at Roper, who shrugged. "Wendy's been here with me the past three years. She's gotten into the habit of stating her mind . . . even with those people who can't read it."

"Saves time," she said. She released Riker's hand but continued to smile. "If you could read my mind, though, Lieutenant, you'd know I was just joking."

"Oh." Riker felt a little foolish. "Of course you were."

"You're cute, though. I like your eyes. They look like they've seen a lot . . . a lot of amazing things, and a lot of nasty stuff."

Riker was beginning to find her forthrightness somewhat refreshing. The idea of an entire planet where people said what was on their minds began to seem a little less daunting. Since when was the notion of honesty something to be concerned over?

"You're right," he said. "I'll be happy to fill you in on some of it."

"I'll be happy to listen."

"And I'm happy everyone's happy. Oh, happy happiness," Roper put in, sounding a bit curmudgeonly. "Wendy, was there something in particular you wanted to discuss?"

"Yes." She turned to her father. "I just wanted to know, which do you think would be better to wear to the Xerx wedding tonight? The blue dress with the ruffles, or the green dress that's cut low?"

"What difference does it make?" asked Roper. He looked at Riker. "Yet another one of the social engagements that this office is expected to participate in. Chandra Xerx, a daughter of the third house of Betazed, is getting married tonight. The Federation is to send a representative. Guess who."

"Well, *I'm* looking forward to it," said Wendy.

"What third house?" asked Riker.

"Oh, that. Well, Betazed society has a number of families that are considered founding families, tracing ancestry back all the way to the earliest writings of Betazed history and culture. There are twenty of these senior 'houses,' as they're called. The house of Xerx is the third oldest, hence the designation 'third house.' Chandra is the eldest daughter of Gart Xerx, and as Wendy mentioned, the wedding is tonight. I hate Betazoid weddings," he added darkly. "And the timing of this one in particular . . . when in hell am I going to meet with Harras to discuss this sudden reception I have to pull together?"

"Look, sir, if it's too much of an inconvenience for you, I have a simple solution," said Riker. "I'll go."

Roper looked up. "You?"

"If," said Riker, and he turned smilingly to Wendy, "it wouldn't bother you to have me as your escort instead of your father."

She looked him up and down in an even more appraising manner than before, and Riker couldn't understand why she was grinning so widely. "That sounds great."

"You really wouldn't mind, Lieutenant Riker?" said Roper. "You'd be doing me a tremendous service—clearing up some free time for me to attend to other matters, and sparing me yet another one of those ceremonies."

"I don't see what the problem would be," said Riker. "I'm glad to pitch in and help wherever I can."

"That's settled, then," said Wendy cheerfully.

"Good," said Roper, slapping his ample belly. "I must admit, I think that you'll present a much more dignified presence for the Federation than I usually do."

Riker smiled politely, not completely understanding what Roper meant.

But later, he would.

Thirteen

The wedding chapel was small and sedate, a one-story building shaped like a trapezoid.

It was a crisp, cool evening, and Riker in full dress uniform had called on Wendy at her home to pick her up. He saw that she had indeed decided on the low-cut green dress, and he felt somewhat appreciative of that. The cleavage it revealed was most attractive, and she had a long and slender neck that was nicely accentuated as well.

She smiled at him and said, "Very chic, Lieutenant."

"I wanted to make a good first impression on all concerned. And please, call me Will."

"Try and stop me." She inclined her head slightly. "The chapel's less than a kilometer away, and it's a lovely night. Feel like walking?"

"That sounds charming." He proffered his elbow and she took it.

They headed down the street, keeping up a pleasant and enjoyable string of chitchat between them. Riker found out that Wendy was a sociologist; that her mother had passed away some years previously; and that she preferred new age music.

Riker feigned being wounded. "I *must* introduce you to the joys of real music. This new age stuff is just noise."

"So what's real music, then?"

He grinned. "Dixieland. Swing. The big-band era."

"Big band?" she said, sounding puzzled. "You mean they're excessively tall?"

"I'll explain it later," he said, for he had spotted the chapel just up ahead.

He saw a number of Betazoids filing in through the doors, smiling and greeting one another. It was his first opportunity to see a large number of them together, and he was struck by the feeling that something seemed a bit wrong. Then he immediately realized what it was.

There was hardly any talking.

People would nod, smile to each other, tilt their heads as if they were listening intently to one another. But except for the occasional stray word of exclamation, or some random laughter here and there, not a word was spoken.

"They're communicating telepathically, aren't they?" said Riker in realization as they approached.

"Of course."

"Then this is liable to be a fairly dull ceremony. Everyone standing around thinking things at each other and we can't hear them."

"Oh"—Wendy waved off the concern and laughed—"that won't happen. Weddings are always done out loud, in consideration of any offworlders who might be in the audience."

"That's a relief." He thought about it a moment. "Will I be able to communicate with any of them? Mentally, I mean? I've never met a Betazoid . . . I'm not sure what's involved."

"You won't be able to, no. Oh, they'll be able to pick up on what's going through your mind easily enough. But for you to send and receive projections, well . . . it's a technique. It's something that you have to learn, involving mental discipline and learning how to clear your mind. Unless, of course, you're dealing with a really strong telepath."

He looked surprised. "You mean they're not all equally adept?"

"Of course not. Are all humans equally intelligent? Equally athletic? Equally eloquent? No. All Betazoids are telepathic to some degree. Most can read minds without too much difficulty. But only a small percentage are really so powerful, so . . . formidable," she said, for want of a better word, "and they're the ones you have to watch out for. They're the toughest."

"Toughest?"

"To know how to act around. They're so casual about their abilities, it's hard to feel like anyplace inside you is . . . I don't know . . . safe."

"I'll watch out for that."

They entered the chapel. The air inside was cool and fresh. They entered a large room where everyone seemed to be milling about, just conversing . . . or whatever one would call it . . . with each other.

Riker looked slowly around the room. It was fairly plain, although inscriptions written in Betazed lined parts of the wall. What was also odd were the recesses all along the side, and dangling from the recesses were what appeared to be clothes hangers of some sort. On the floor was a series of small boxes. Riker idly tapped one with his toe and the hollow sound confirmed that it was empty.

Hangers and empty boxes. Probably for days when the weather was inclement and people brought coats and such.

At the far end of the room was a set of ornate doors, closed. Riker presumed that the actual ceremony would be through there, but they probably weren't ready yet.

Several of the Betazoids seemed to pick up on Riker's presence. They looked in his direction, smiled and nodded. It was as if to say, *We know you're here. Welcome.* And then they went back to their own communications.

Riker had once been to a world where none of the occupants had standard auditory or verbal equipment. They communicated entirely through hand movements. Riker had been to a party there, and the silence was positively eerie. The only sound that had broken the quiet was the slap of skin on skin as their hands would come together to form certain words.

This wasn't quite as bad as that . . . but still, it was rather disconcerting.

"A little difficult to deal with, isn't it," said a voice from behind him.

Riker turned and saw a thin but pleasant-looking Betazoid smiling at him. "Pardon?" asked Riker.

The Betazoid gestured. "All this. The quiet communion. You are from Earth, are you not?"

Riker realized the man knew the answer to the question already, but was doing Riker the courtesy of allowing him to answer it. "That's right. Lt. William Riker."

"Gart Xerx, your host."

"Ah. Congratulations, Mr. Xerx."

" 'Gart' will do." Xerx nodded at Riker's companion. "Good to see you again, Wendy."

"You too, Gart. I'm very happy for you and Chandra."

"Thank you, Wendy." Xerx indicated the closed doors with a nod of his head and said, "They should be ready to start in just a moment or two. Chandra's quite nervous, of course. She wants everything about her appearance to be perfect."

"I know how it is," said Riker. "The bride wants to make sure the dress looks just right."

Gart Xerx smiled politely. "Well . . . that might be true in *your* culture, Lieutenant. We don't have that problem, actually."

"Then you're very fortunate," said Riker.

The edges of Xerx's mouth turned upward slightly. "You don't know, do you." It wasn't a question.

"Know what?"

At that moment, the doors at the far end opened. They moved very slowly and ponderously, and Riker watched them, interested to catch a glimpse of the wedding sanctuary within.

It was dazzling, filled from ceiling to floor with flowers, all exotic and tropical. It seemed as if a small jungle had been grown inside the sanctuary specifically for the purpose of the marriage. Riker caught a whiff of moist air—obviously the climate was carefully maintained in order to preserve the flowers to their maximum advantage.

He turned back to Gart Xerx to compliment him on the arrangement and was astounded to see that Xerx had removed his shirt, revealing a bare chest that was amazingly smooth.

"Excuse me . . . what are you doing?" asked Riker, trying to keep the astonishment out of his voice. He turned to Wendy to see her reaction.

What he saw was Wendy's low-cut green dress even lower than it was before . . . namely on the floor. She was stepping out of it, and Riker was seeing a lot more of her cleavage than had been displayed previously . . . to be specific, all of it that there was to see.

His now-nude escort looked up at him with innocent doe eyes. "What are you waiting for, Will? Musical accompaniment?"

She laughed lightly, turned, and headed toward the hangers, her dimpled backside swaying cheerfully back and forth. And now Riker saw, to his utter shock, that all of the guests were stripping off their clothes and placing them on the hangers provided.

Gart, who was naked and holding his clothes draped over one arm, looked at Riker sympathetically. "I'm very sorry, Lieutenant. They should have told you. Perhaps Mark Roper was concerned that, if you knew, you wouldn't be interested in attending."

Riker's mouth was working, but at first he couldn't get any words to come out. Finally he managed to stammer, "Is this . . . *standard?"*

"Oh, yes," said Gart calmly. "At a Betazed wedding, the bride, groom, wedding party, and guests all attend nude."

"Why?"

"To symbolize that, physically and spiritually, there is nothing to hide. That all are sharing in complete cooperation in the spirit of harmony and unity."

Riker had a feeling that all the blood had drained from his face. "Well . . ." He cleared his throat, unsure of what he should do. Starfleet protocol required cooperation with local mores and customs wherever possible, so long as no violation of the Prime Directive was involved. There was nothing in the Prime Directive about getting naked in front of over one hundred strangers, so he was clear on that score. But even so . . .

"Lieutenant," said Gart, trying not to show as much amusement as he was clearly experiencing. "If you don't go naked, I assure you, no one will think the less of you. We believe in not asking more of an individual than he is capable of giving. This is a time of celebration, not embarrassment. Attend the wedding in whatever manner you will feel the most comfortable."

"I don't want to insult anyone . . . " said Riker uncertainly.

"Nor will anyone take offense. Now, if you'll excuse me . . . I have guests to attend to." Gart walked to the hangers, leaving Riker alone in the middle of a room of stripping people.

Wendy walked back up to Riker and looked at him reprovingly. She placed her hands on her hips in a fashion that was probably chosen to look especially provocative. "What's this, Will? Having trouble? Here . . . I'll help." She reached up to the fastenings on his uniform.

He grabbed her wrists, though not particularly hard. Through a tight smile he said, "You could have told me beforehand, you know."

"What?" She looked shocked. "And miss the opportunity to see your expression?"

"You've seen it. How did it rate?"

"I think you'd look at a firing squad of Klingons with less trepidation than you're looking at a bunch of naked people."

"At least with the firing squad, I'd have a bit of warning."

"Oh, Will." Now she was grinning widely. "Come on. You have nothing to be ashamed of." Then she paused and raised an eyebrow thoughtfully. "Do you?"

"No!" said Riker a bit too loudly, so he repeated, "No," but more softly this time.

"Well then . . . ?"

"Well, to be honest . . ." He put his fingers to his forehead, trying to figure the best way to put it. "I've never been in a position where I'm trying to maintain my dignity and status as a Starfleet officer without benefit of the uniform . . . or anything else."

"Then don't worry about your position. Worry about joining in the celebration. Look . . . if you don't want to strip, then don't. Come in anyway."

"Okay. Fine. Thanks for understanding."

He went in with her to the chapel, and the full fragrance of the flowers wafted through the air. It was as if he'd stepped out from the city and straight into the jungle.

Wendy guided him to an aisle seat about halfway down. He looked around.

Naked people to the right of him, and to the left. In front and behind.

Everyone seemed utterly casual, even oblivious of their nudity. No one was tense or embarrassed. In fact, they seemed even more relaxed than they had been outside. Even men and women who, by the standards of the human ideal, would have been far better served wearing clothes (if not pup tents) weren't the least bit bothered by their nudity.

He felt as if everyone were staring at him. Riker knew they weren't, of course . . . but he felt that way.

Turning to Wendy, he said, "Excuse me . . . be right back," and he got up and walked out before she could ask him where he was going.

She sat there, staring at his empty chair, nodding and smiling to the other people, and wondering where in hell Riker had gone off to. Then she heard him say, "Thanks for saving my seat."

She looked up and grinned. "So you decided to join the party after all."

He sat down next to her, not precisely sure how to place his bare legs. He wound up just sitting with them flat, his hands on his thighs. He noted for the first time that the seats were nicely cushioned, for which he was grateful. Cold metal would not have been especially appreciated right about then.

Wendy leaned over and said softly into his ear, "You were right, by the way . . . you have nothing to be ashamed of."

He liked the tone of her voice as she said it . . . it had a certain degree of promise to it. "Thank you. You're very kind."

She sat back and said, "I'm not sure why you were so nervous. I mean, what did you think was going to happen? Women were going to point and laugh?"

"I don't know. It's just a different situation for me, that's all. I thought people might say things that made me feel self-conscious."

"Oh, don't be silly. Like what?"

An older Betazoid woman was being guided toward the front by Gart Xerx. Riker assumed that it was probably his mother, or perhaps a great-aunt. She stopped, looked at Riker, and frowned. "You human men are very hairy. Why is that?"

Xerx rolled his eyes in mild mortification. Wendy put her hand over her mouth to cover her grin.

But Riker, nonplussed, merely said, "Traction."

Wendy emitted a quick burst of laughter, which she just as quickly stifled. Xerx was grinning openly. The old woman looked at Riker through narrowed eyes and then allowed herself to be led away.

"Traction?" whispered Wendy.

"I had to say something."

"Well, what you said was wonderful. You see? And you were worried that you wouldn't be able to maintain your dignity while naked. You handled that in a very dignified manner."

"Thank you."

Wendy appeared to be sizing him up for a moment, and then she coyly fingered a strand of his chest hair.

Riker crossed his legs.

At that moment, the ceremony started . . . a moment marked by the sound of a very loud gong.

The lieutenant focused his attention toward the front of the wedding sanctuary. The wedding party was entering, and yes, they were naked as well. From one side of the sanctuary entered the groom, in the lead, followed by his mother.

To Riker's surprise, the mother was pulling on his arm, trying to stop him. He ignored her, taking one implacable step after the other, toward the middle of the room. Into his path stepped a man whom Riker assumed to be his father. The father raised a hand, putting his palm up, signaling the groom to stop. The groom took his father by the forearm and shoved him aside . . . not roughly, and in fact, Riker saw that the groom was taking care not to make the action too violent, for fear of actually causing the older man to stumble.

"Symbolic, I take it," Riker said in a low voice to Wendy. She nodded confirmation.

The groom stopped in front of a clergyman (presumably), who stood dead center of the room with a long scroll between his hands. They looked off to the right, and now the parents of the bride entered—the bride's mother sobbing loudly onto the shoulder of Gart Xerx. Too loudly—clearly more symbolism, but Riker thought the mother might be playing it up just a bit too much even for something that was supposed to be representational.

And then the bride walked in. The bride . . .

Walked . . .

Riker blinked in that way people do when they're not entirely sure they're seeing what their eyes are telling them they're seeing.

She was gorgeous.

Her eyes were the most luminous that Riker had ever seen. She held her pointed chin in an almost aristocratic manner, and her dark hair hung in thick ringlets around her head. Her neck was slender, and her figure . . . well, as they said in old detective novels, her body had the kind of curves that, if you were a car, made you want to hug the road.

Thoughts of what he would like to do with that body ran rampant through his imaginings, but he had to tell himself that, for crying out loud, she was taken. She was the bride. She was about to get married. She—

She stepped aside and gestured to a young woman who was seated in the front row.

"I summon you to the place of marriage," she said. Her voice was low and musical and had an exotic accent that Riker had never heard before. It sound vaguely like a combination of three Middle European intonations, and yet a bit different.

The young woman rose. She had blond hair, tied back in a white band. She took the hand of the woman who had "summoned" her and stepped up to the side of the groom. They took each other's hands and turned to face the clergyman . . .

And that was when, belatedly, it hit Riker. The brunette wasn't the bride. She was some sort of equivalent of the maid of honor.

Unbidden, uncensored, thoughts about getting to know the maid of honor on a variety of levels stampeded back through his mind. His eyes drank her in hungrily as she stood with her back to him. The sumptuous lines of her hips, the elegant arch of her spine, and the way her shoulder blades played against the skin . . . and the way the light shined off that skin . . . the richness of her smile . . .

Her smile.

Her back was to him but he could see her smile . . .

Because she'd turned her head.

And she was looking at him.

Right at him.

At him. And smiling.

Oh, my God, he thought, *she knows what I'm thinking. She knows what I'd . . .*

Wendy looked at him and saw that his face had gone several shades of red. "Will . . . are you okay?"

"I'm fine." His voice was thick and hoarse. It didn't even sound remotely like his. "Just fine."

"You sure? You're sweating."

"It's hot in here. That's all. Just hot."

She was still smiling at him, for what seemed to Riker to be an eternity. Her bosom *(God, her bosom)* shook slightly in what he took to be (correctly) silent laughter. And then, mercifully, she turned away from him and put her attention back on the ceremony.

Riker didn't hear a word of the rest of the proceedings. He had his own proceedings in mind. The only question was how best to proceed with the proceedings.

A reception had been arranged out in a garden behind the chapel. Large lights had been set up that flooded the evening with illumination.

Riker paid absolutely no attention to the types of food he was eating or how much . . . indeed, he would pay for it later that night with a major bellyache. For now, though, he popped various hors d'oeuvres into his mouth, one after the other, but his mind was elsewhere.

The guests were now all clothed, and the fact that Riker had his uniform back on was something of a blessing. It enabled him to—to a degree—put his mind on autopilot, speaking pleasantly and adroitly to all those who approached him in his capacity as representative of the UFP. He wondered if they were aware that his thoughts were only partly on his surroundings.

His eyes kept scanning the crowd for some sign of the maid of honor. The bride and groom hadn't materialized either—apparently there was ceremony and delay involved in this, too.

He couldn't get her out of his mind. He had encountered so many women in his lifetime, and yet when he had seen her, there had been something . . . something he couldn't put his finger on. It was almost as if he *knew* her somehow, from somewhere.

But he had never seen her before. He was sure that he hadn't. Hell, she wasn't even the kind of female that he usually considered his "type." But there was *something* about her that—

A burst of applause brought his attention back to focus, and there she was. She had emerged from the chapel with the bride and groom, and several other friends of the newlywed couple were crowding around them, congratulating them, laughing and smiling.

He waited for the maid of honor to look his way, to catch his gaze. But she didn't. In fact, she seemed to look everywhere except in his direction. He wasn't sure if this was intentional or not. Whatever it was, it was damned frustrating.

There was a tap on his shoulder. He turned and Wendy was looking up at him with those large doe eyes of hers. "Is there some problem, Will? You seem to have time for everyone except me, and I'm supposed to be your date."

"No problem. No problem at all." He draped an arm around her and kept her close to him the remainder of the time. Almost as if she were a shield; a reminder that there were plenty of other women in the galaxy.

Almost as if he were a little afraid of the way that the young Betazoid maid of honor had gotten to him.

It was crazy. He didn't know her . . . not at all. Oh, sure, he knew she looked good naked—okay, great naked—okay, spectacular beyond belief naked—but even so, nothing about her could account for this feeling of urgency he had whenever he looked at her. This feeling that he had to get to know her better.

"Do you believe in love at first sight?" he asked Wendy.

"Nope. I think you can look at someone and be attracted on a physical level. That's easy. But true, genuine love? No. You can even be attracted to someone and fall in love with them subsequently. That doesn't make it love at first sight though. That just makes it . . . I don't know . . . fortuitous infatuation."

"Absolutely right." He even felt a measure of relief. Here was someone to throw a bucket of cold reality into an unreal situation. "I feel the same way. You find something, you study it, you draw conclusions, and you proceed. You don't just leap into something on blind faith."

"Will," Wendy said, smiling coyly, "is this your way of telling me that you find me attractive? I mean . . . what are you saying? That you think you might be falling in love with me at first sight?"

"Of course not. I thought we agreed . . . there's no such thing. Don't you remember?"

"Ooooh, yes. So we did."

All the young women were clustering together now, including the maid of honor. Riker watched with curiosity and Wendy said, "You know the old Earth custom of the bride throwing the bouquet?"

"Yes."

"Well, there's something similar here. Except it's not a bouquet. The bride wears a white band in her hair, and she tosses that."

"Oh."

Chandra, the bride, stood with her back to the young women and after a moment of hesitation tossed the headband over her right shoulder. It fluttered through the air toward the throng of grasping hands, and one pair of hands snatched it from its flight. There was a burst of applause as the maid of honor came up with it triumphantly.

"Oh, how nice! Deanna caught it," said Wendy. "She and Chandra have been friends for years."

"Deanna?"

"Deanna Troi. She was the maid of honor."

"Was she?" said Riker with very carefully cultivated neutrality in his voice.

So carefully, in fact, that it drew a strange look from Wendy. "Yes, that's right. I'm surprised you don't remember."

"Well, you know how it is . . . all naked bodies tend to blend in with each other. So what does catching the white cloth signify? That she's the next to get married?"

"No. What it means is that the great love of her life is at this gathering."

"How romantic." Riker found himself turning the full force of his gaze, of his every thought, directly at the young woman who he now knew was called Deanna Troi.

She did not so much as glance his way the rest of the evening.

Fourteen

"You could have told me, you know."

Mark Roper looked up at Lieutenant Riker and grinned. "Good morning, Captain."

"Don't call me that." Riker's stomach felt achy, which matched the condition of his head. "Why didn't you tell me that no one wore clothes at the wedding?"

Roper sat back in his chair and looked with mild scorn in Riker's direction. "Oh, come now, Captain. All throughout Starfleet they teach you how to adapt and deal with the unexpected. I'd have thought that you wouldn't be fazed for a moment by the situation."

"They didn't cover stripping in Starfleet Academy." Riker sagged into the chair opposite Roper.

"Maybe you should suggest it be added to the curriculum," Roper said helpfully.

"I'll do that," lied Riker.

"Wendy was, I take it, an excellent companion?"

"Very socially adept."

"Did you take her to bed with you?"

Riker's jaw dropped as he stared at Roper's mirthful expression.

"What *is* it with this planet?" said Riker incredulously. "Casual nudity. Fathers inquiring about the sexual activities of their daughters first thing in the morning . . ."

"Would you prefer I wait until midafternoon?"

"Mr. Roper," Riker said after a moment, "I really don't think it's any of your business."

"Riker, Riker, Riker. You don't understand. I'll find out anyway. My daughter and I have a very open relationship. We've learned that technique from our stay here on Betazed. Honesty—that's the key whenever possible. And if you and my daughter enjoyed each other, then I'll take pleasure in that enjoyment."

Riker stared at him. "You know . . . I never thought of myself as a prude, by any stretch of the imagination. But in comparison to what goes on with you people here . . . I feel positively archaic."

"You'll get used to freedom. Everyone does after a while. Sometimes it just takes a bit of adjusting, is all."

"All right, then. For the record . . . no, I did not take your daughter to bed. Nor did she take me. It was late, we were tired . . ."

And I couldn't get Deanna Troi out of my mind. But he didn't say that part, though.

"Whatever," said Roper casually. "My daughter is a perfectly capable young woman. I trust her decisions whenever she makes them, and whomever she makes them with." He paused. "That Chandra Xerx was quite a lovely bride, I'll wager."

"Yes. Yes, she was." This was the perfect opportunity to bring up what he was really thinking about. "So was her maid of honor . . . what was her name? Donna? Dena?"

"Deanna? Deanna Troi?"

"That's right," said Riker, hoping that his affected casual air was remotely convincing. "That was the name I heard mentioned. Deanna Troi."

"Lovely girl. Just lovely. Now what is she up to these days?" Roper glanced outside for a long moment, as if the answers he sought were in the clouds. Perhaps they in fact were, because he turned back to Riker and said, "Psychology student. That's it. Over at the university. Near the top of her class . . . I should remember that since Lwaxana's always boasting about her."

"Lwaxana is her mother?"

"Ohhhh, yes. Quite a character, that one. You know the old axiom about how, if you want to get a feeling for what the daughter will be like twenty, thirty years down the road . . . all you have to do is look at the mother?"

"Yes."

"Case in point."

Riker looked surprised. "What, is she that ugly?"

"Lwaxana? Oh, not by any means. In fact, she's a very striking woman. Quite attractive, and she knows how to use her appearance to her advantage. But she can be very . . . overpowering."

"Overpowering in what sense?" But before Roper could respond, Riker added, "Wait . . . Wendy was talking about a small percentage of Betazoids who are, telepathically, pretty formidable."

"She may have been speaking specifically about Lwaxana," Roper affirmed. "I think 'formidable' is a perfectly apt description. For that matter, according to what Wendy's told me . . . and believe me, that girl is up on all the latest scuttlebutt . . . if you happen to be a suitor, then Lwaxana can be downright intimidating. Poor Deanna doesn't see much in the way of a social life."

"What a waste."

His tone of voice had slipped more than he'd have liked. Roper looked at him with a cunning expression. "You're interested in her, aren't you."

"Mark, I don't even know her."

"You're dodging the question."

"No, I'm not. How can I possibly decide if I'm interested in someone if I haven't even exchanged ten words with her."

Roper looked wistful. "Other than my marriage, the most memorable relationship I had in my life involved a young woman and an exchange of less than five words." He regarded Riker. "That, of course, was when I was a very young man. Vital, alive, and feeling my oats. Much as you are now."

"My oats are reined in, thank you, Mark," Riker told him firmly. He stood and said, "If you'll excuse me, I have a meeting with the commanding officer of the security team."

"Sergeant Tang? Good man. He knows his stuff." Roper swiveled the computer screen around to check his itinerary for the day. "Give him my regards."

"I will."

"And I hope I didn't offend you with my observations about young Troi."

"Not at all," said Riker, heading for the door. "But to be perfectly honest, I have far more on my mind right now than Deanna Troi."

"I'm sure you do. You know where the university is?"

"No, but it shouldn't be hard to find . . ." And then Riker's voice trailed off as he realized what he was saying. He turned back to Roper and said, "That is, of course, if I were interested in finding it."

"Of course," said Roper calmly. "If you were interested. Which you're not."

"Not at all."

"Glad to hear it."

Fifteen

Deanna Troi walked across the campus, her thoughts still on the topics they'd been discussing so forcefully in her psychological ethics class. So she paid no attention whatsoever to the young, dashing Starfleet officer who ever so casually, ever so coincidentally, strolled past her.

But then a voice called out, "*I* remember you."

She stopped in her tracks. She couldn't place the voice at all, but the *sense* of the person behind her was damned familiar. Then she smiled . . . inwardly. *I should have expected this,* she thought, and turned slowly.

He walked toward her, making a great show of trying to place precisely where he recollected her from. "The wedding yesterday. You were at the wedding, weren't you."

Slowly she nodded, making sure to maintain a very carefully constructed air of disinterest.

He stuck out a hand. "Lt. William T. Riker, at your service."

She looked at his proffered hand for a moment. Then extremely carefully, as if handling a specimen, she took the tips of his fingers in hers and shook his hand very lightly. "What does the *T* stand for?"

"Terrific." He waggled his eyebrows slightly to put across, just in case she didn't get it, that he was making a joke.

She got it. But her expression made it quite clear that she didn't care for it.

Or him.

"I'm new here . . . to the planet, I mean . . . and I'm just trying to get to know as many of the residents here as I can."

"I see." She had been holding a computer padd under her arm. Now she crossed her arms over her breasts, holding the padd over them as if it were a shield. She was dressed in flowing blue, a loose-sleeved tunic and a long blue skirt that the wind was swishing about her legs. "So you're going around and introducing yourself, one person at a time. That could take quite a while."

"It'll take even longer when the people I'm introducing myself to don't even tell me their names."

She angled her head slightly, regarding him with that outthrust jaw of hers. "Why should I bother? You know my name."

Now he folded his arms. "You know . . . it's going to be very difficult being at ease with a population that considers my mind an open book."

"I didn't read your mind. I hazarded a guess. All you did was confirm it."

"Oh. I . . . just assumed . . ."

"Assumptions can lead to great embarrassments, Lieutenant. As I'm sure you can attest."

She turned and walked away from him.

He stood there for a moment and watched her go.

Don't give up.

The thought entered his head, and he wasn't entirely sure where it came from. Was it his own mind . . . or was the source elsewhere? Was there a remote chance that the encouragement had come from her . . . either consciously or unconsciously?

A remote chance, yes. Remote. Very, very slim. Pathetically thin, as a matter of fact. So thin as to be virtually nonexistent.

But still worth a shot.

He kicked into high gear and trotted after her. It was surprising how quickly she moved, with brisk, rapid steps. His quick pace brought him alongside her and he said, "You used to do some geology, didn't you."

That brought her up short and she stared at him.

"A lot of fieldwork," he continued.

"When I was a teenager, yes."

"Why did you give it up?"

"My true talents lay elsewhere. How in the world did you know?"

"The way you walk. I had a friend, she was also a geologist, except she made her life's work out of it. She walked the same way . . . a very precise, measured stride. And she knew exactly how much space each of her strides covered. That way she could always measure off distances even if she didn't have an instrument handy to measure them."

Slowly she nodded her head. "Very good, Lieutenant. I'm impressed."

"And I'm impressed that I impressed you." Once more he stuck out a hand. "I'm Lt. William T. Riker. And you are . . . ?"

She sighed. "We've been through this, haven't we?"

"I have. You haven't."

This time she took his hand and shook it firmly. "Deanna Troi. The answer is no."

He wished he could get more than a handful of sentences out of her at a time. He loved listening to her voice. "The answer to what?"

"The answer, I would presume, to just about any question you'd care to pose." She folded her arms once more. "Look, Lieutenant . . . I really don't mean to be rude here . . . but I don't have the slightest intention of leading you on. I know you saw me at the wedding last night. In fact, we both know you saw me, and we both know what was going through your mind."

He took a step closer to her, sounding as suave as he possibly could. "Then we're not exactly on even footing. I don't know what was going through your mind."

"Then I'll tell you now. I'm very flattered by your intentions, Lieutenant. I'm vain enough to be pleased that I could provoke such . . . strong feelings from you . . . merely by the display of my body. Your reaction, however, would indicate an obsession for surface attributes only."

"That's hardly my sole interest," he said defensively.

"No, but it's a driving one."

He drew yet another step closer, trying to discern whether his growing nearer was having any sort of effect on her. She wasn't stepping back, which either meant that she wanted him near her, or else she just figured it wasn't worth the trouble to back away from him. "Even if it is . . . it doesn't mean that I wouldn't want to get to know you better on a variety of levels."

"That might be. But it's the order of the levels that I have difficulty with. I also have difficulty with the transient nature of your personality."

That stopped him. "Transient?"

She looked down and seemed almost reluctant to speak. "I don't wish to say things that will upset you."

His voice took on a deeper, somewhat annoyed air. "You won't upset me, I assure you."

"Very well." She looked him in the eyes. Other students passing by afforded them quick glances before going on about their business. Her voice took on a clinical air as she said, "I sense that you're someone who thrives on quick encounters. Who enjoys the physicality of relationships without the deeper emotional attachments those relationships can and should bring with them. And that natural tendency of yours is heightened by the fact that you're only going to be on Betazed a few months. That's much more incentive, then, to engage in passing romantic assignations without any concern of long-term relations since, by definition, you won't be here long enough. Well? Am I close?"

His lips thinned almost to nonexistence. "I suppose you feel you have me pegged pretty well."

"Well enough for my purposes. Good day, Lieutenant."

She turned and walked away, and this time there was no additional beckoning in Riker's mind, leaving him totally in the dark about where his mind was at, where her mind was at, and what precisely he should do next . . .

. . . if anything.

I'm home.

Deanna nodded to Mr. Homn, who stepped back away from the front door of the mansion as she entered.

In her head, her mother's voice replied, *I'm up here, Little One.*

Deanna looked in the direction of the upstairs bedroom. *What's wrong, Mother?* It was very unusual for Lwaxana Troi to be upstairs at this time of day . . . usually she was bustling around, tending to this, that, and the other, or perhaps entertaining some head of state. Her absence was reason for curiosity.

Deanna trotted upstairs and into her mother's bedroom. Lwaxana lay in her bed, looking utterly spent. She blew her nose loudly into a cloth.

"Oh, Mother, what happened?"

It snuck up on me, replied her mother, responding to Deanna's verbal expression of concern. *One minute I was fine, and the next minute my head felt ready to explode. Treasure your health, Little One. You never appreciate it until it's gone.*

Is there anything I can do, Mother?

Lwaxana sneezed loudly, then thought, *Yes, there is. Substitute for me.*

Where?

The Federation embassy is hosting a reception for the Rigelian ambassador tonight. As a daughter of the fifth house, it's my responsibility to be there. Obviously I can't go when I'm in this shape.

Deanna sat on the edge of the bed and fidgeted with her hands. Out loud she said, "I'd really rather not, Mother. I was out late yesterday with Chandra's wedding. I've been working late hours on my studies. I—"

Lwaxana sat up, but her expression had changed from self-directed misery to a puzzled frown. "Who's Lieutenant Riker?"

With a loud sigh of annoyance, Deanna said, "He's no one, Mother. And you know, after all this time, I still hate it when you do that. If I wanted to discuss him with you, I'd discuss him."

"You would have sooner or later." But then the draining of Lwaxana's sinuses prompted her to lie back down, and as she blew her nose again, she thought, *So who is he?*

I told you, he's no one. Just some Starfleet officer who can't keep his . . . more base thoughts . . . under control. He's of no consequence to me.

He's of enough consequence, Little One, to be the primary factor in why you don't want to go to the embassy tonight.

Deanna made an irritated noise. *I'll go, Mother. All right? I'll go. I'll be charming and wonderful and I assure you I'll have absolutely no trouble with Lieutenant Riker. All right?*

Her mother reached up and patted her affectionately on the cheek. *That's my girl.*

And deep enough down in her psyche that she hoped even her mother wouldn't be able to discern it, Deanna thought, *Great. Just great.*

Sixteen

The Federation embassy was fully lit up that evening and was alive with the boisterousness and frivolity of the gathering.

Unlike the wedding ceremony, which was almost entirely attended by Betazoids and hence was rather quiet, protocol required that conversation at embassy gatherings be primarily verbal, in order to accommodate offworlders. So it was that Riker found himself eminently more relaxed this time out.

He watched Mark Roper working the crowd, overseeing the catering functions, and doing everything he could to make the Rigelian ambassador feel at home. Considering that up until that point Riker's sole exposure to Roper had been watching him fuss and bother over the details of his job, it was somewhat comforting to observe that Roper was indeed a perfectly talented diplomat when in the proper circumstances.

Riker was no slouch at such activities himself. He had his charm cranked up to all burners and continually made all the right moves and said all the correct things. At one point Roper drifted over to him and said, "You ask me, Captain, I think you've missed your calling. You have a real flair for this line of work."

"I'm just a gifted amateur, sir."

"Oh, now don't be modest."

But Riker hadn't heard the last thing Roper had said because his attention had been distracted when Deanna Troi came through the door. He watched as she looked around, trying to spot someone she might know. She attracted the attention of one of the older counsels and immediately went off with him.

Roper watched the entire thing and his mouth twitched in amusement. "Your mind seems to be elsewhere, Captain."

"Hmm? Oh." Riker looked down, slightly abashed that he'd allowed his attention to be so easily diverted. What the hell kind of training was that? "Sorry, sir."

"Once again your famed noninterest in Deanna Troi appears to rear its head."

"Frankly, Mark . . . she's not a particularly friendly person."

"Really?" Roper seemed genuinely shocked. "She's been nothing but friendly to me, and everyone who's gotten to know her. Are you quite sure?"

"Well, she was extremely standoffish with me."

"When was this?"

"I . . . happened to run into her. In the city."

"I see. And how do you think you behaved?"

Riker stared at him. "I was fine. Polite." Then he paused and admitted, "Frankly, I was damned uncomfortable."

"Why, in heaven's name?"

"Well . . . I had a hard time becoming totally at ease with a woman who can read my every thought."

Roper looked from the young lieutenant to Deanna, who was across the room, and back to Riker once more. "Who? Deanna? She can't read your every thought."

"What? But—" Now Riker was clearly confused. "I thought that . . . I mean, I just figured . . . and you said her mother was so—"

"That's her mother. But Deanna isn't anywhere near the telepath that her mother is. To be specific, she's half the telepath her mother is. Deanna's father was human."

"Human?" Riker was astounded. Here he couldn't figure out how to come to terms with even *talking* to a Betazoid, and some man had actually found a way to marry one. And a powerful one, at that.

"That's right. Deanna's no mind reader. She's an empath. She senses moods, emotions, feelings. She can sense honesty, duplicity, sexual desire . . ." Roper paused after saying that, waited for Riker's expression of surprise, and when he got it, continued, "She's very, very adept at that . . . but only in a general sense."

"I see." Then Riker nodded and grinned. "Well . . . perhaps I'd better try and rectify the situation."

He took a step forward and suddenly Wendy was in the way. She was holding a drink and looked extremely mellow.

"Will, have you been avoiding me?" She placed a hand on his shoulder and assumed a distinctly pouty air. "I'd be very hurt if you were."

Riker tried to come up with a smooth response that would ease him through the situation, but now Roper stepped in and said, "Wendy . . . there's someone I'd like you to meet. The Rigelian ambassador."

"Really?" she chirped. It was becoming rapidly clear that the drink she was holding was hardly her first of the evening.

"Yes, really. He's right over this way." Roper took his daughter by the arm and guided her away into the crowd, leaving Riker alone. Roper slowed only long enough to toss a wink in Riker's direction.

Riker immediately seized the opportunity and cut his way through the crowd like a shark. Within moments he had drawn up behind Deanna and simply stood there, waiting for her to turn around.

He knew that she was aware of him almost immediately, but for what seemed an eternity she only presented her back. The diplomat she was talking to was suddenly distracted by someone else clamoring for his attention, and he allowed himself to be pulled away with an apologetic nod to Deanna. Then she sighed and her shoulders slumped just a bit.

"Why are you just hovering, Lieutenant?"

"How did you know?"

"I could feel you breathing down my neck."

"No, not that. I mean how did you know that I was only going to be assigned to Betazed for a few months?"

Slowly she turned to face him, an amused expression on her face.

"I mean," continued Riker, "I had assumed you'd just picked it out of my thoughts. But someone who's an empath wouldn't be able to focus that tightly, would she?"

"No. She wouldn't."

"Well? I'm waiting." He even made a show of tapping the toe of his boot with impatience.

She studied her fingernails as she said, "I asked around. All right?"

"Now why did you do that?"

"I was curious. Are you satisfied, Lieutenant?"

"Call me Will."

"For the moment, I believe I prefer 'Lieutenant.' "

"For the moment?" He smiled ingratiatingly. "Does that mean you anticipate that there will be opportunities in the future to address me?"

"Right now, Lieutenant, I'd like to address you to Vulcan and send you out with the next batch of communiqués."

He mimed being stabbed to the heart. "Oh! How you sting, Miss Troi! To be at the receiving end of your rapier wit . . ."

"Lieutenant," she said with a heavy sigh, "what do you want from me? No . . ." She put her hands palm up in a don't-move gesture. "No, strike that. I know what you want. The question is, what will it take to get through to you that I'm not interested?"

He set his jaw determinedly. "Go out with me."

"Go out with you?" She laughed. "You feel the best way to *dis*courage you is to *en*courage you? Now that is truly a unique piece of logic."

"I didn't say it was logical."

"That's a relief."

"What I do say is that it gives you a chance to make a decision based on something other than first impressions. If we spend some time together and you decide that you're not interested . . . then fine. I'll accept that. Believe me . . . I don't go where I'm not wanted."

She couldn't resist. "You must not get around much, then."

His eyes narrowed, then slowly he nodded. "Fine." He put up his hands. "Fine. Have it your way."

He started to turn away from her; then to his surprise she placed a hand lightly on his arm. He turned and looked back at her.

"Tomorrow's terrible for me," she said. "The day after. Pick me up around midday, at my home. We'll go on a picnic. I'll pack it."

"I don't want you to feel like you have to do me any favors, Miss Troi. I mean, don't go to any trouble, or—"

"Lieutenant, don't push your luck."

"Midday it is."

"Good." Then she paused. "Tell me, Lieutenant. There are any number of women around . . . and quite a few might be much more inclined to be impressed by your—peculiar—brand of charm than I would. Why so interested in me?"

"Because, I like a challenge."

"Well, that's splendid. In that case, when you come by to pick me up, the two of you will probably hit it right off."

"The two of us?"

"You and my mother. You see, she likes challenges, too." Deanna smirked in a way that made Riker extremely uncomfortable. "And I have a feeling she's just going to *adore* you."

Seventeen

Sergeant Roger Tang, grizzled veteran and squad commander of the security unit assigned to Betazed, caught a glimpse of Riker as he headed for the door. "Lieutenant," he said, and snapped to a salute.

Inwardly, Riker shook his head. Salutes hadn't been in style for two centuries now, but Tang was retro enough to harken back to those days of extreme discipline. Riker waved his hand in close approximation of a salute and said, "At ease, Sergeant."

Tang stroked his round, stubbled chin. The large phaser he always wore was clipped to his waist and slapped against his thick leg. Riker was willing to bet he wore it to sleep. "Lovely day today, Lieutenant. Where you off to . . . if you don't mind my asking," he added quickly.

"Out."

"Yes, sir, I can see that. The general direction of your path would seem to be leading you out the door. I was just curious as to where, sir. Security reasons. Can't be too careful, you know."

Riker sauntered over to Tang and draped his hands behind his back. "If you *must* know, Sergeant, I have a date."

Tang appeared to consider that for a moment. "Local girl, sir?"

"That's right. A local girl. I tried to bring a girl with me from the *Fortuna,* but she didn't fit in my suitcase."

"Damn shame," commiserated Tang. He lowered his voice to confidential tones. "You don't mind a piece of advice, sir?"

Riker shook his head.

"These people can ruin you."

At that, Riker blinked. "Pardon?"

"They're soft. They're pleasant." He tapped the side of his head. "They're always philosophizing about things, dwelling on things, pondering things. They think too damned much, if you ask me."

"Thinking about things is a good habit, Sergeant."

"Oh, of course. But not to the point where it's *all* you do. Not to the point of overintellectualizing. They don't fight . . . they'd rather talk about the reasons for disputes. I told one of them that the only thing the Sindareen understand is force, and the guy looked at me like I'd just dropped down from outer space."

"Well . . . in all fairness . . . you did."

Tang emitted a short laugh that sounded like a bark. "Yeah, I suppose I did at that. Look, Lieutenant . . . all I'm saying is, remember who you are. And who they are. Getting to know different cultures is fine and all that . . . but just remember that the galaxy is divided into two types."

"Those being?"

"Starfleet . . . and everyone else." Tang put a finger to his lips and then added, "Enough said."

"Thank you, Sergeant."

Tang tossed off one more salute and said, "All part of the service." Then he turned and walked off, the phaser continuing to slap comfortingly against his thigh.

Riker stood outside the mansion that was the home of Deanna Troi. Impressed by the structure, he hesitated a moment before rapping on the door.

He heard no footsteps, but then slowly the door opened.

Riker looked up.

And up.

A towering man loomed over him. He didn't look precisely Betazoid. He didn't look precisely anything. He stared down at Riker impassively.

"I'm Lieutenant Riker. I'm here to pick up Deanna Troi." Then Riker hesitated. "This is the Troi residence, isn't it?"

The man nodded slowly and stepped back, providing space for Riker to enter. He did so, looking around the opulent setting in curiosity.

"Where should I wait?"

The giant closed the front door, but did not answer Riker's question. He studied the looming figure, utterly perplexed, and then a voice behind him said, "So I see you've met Mr. Homn."

Riker turned and saw an attractive woman with long dark brown hair, and a very aristocratic bearing. She came sweeping toward him in a pink and gray gown that set off her dark eyes and rosy-complexioned face. "And you're Mrs. Homn?" he asked.

She laughed lightly. "No, no. I'm Deanna's mother."

He took her extended hand and bowed slightly at the waist. "Lt. William Riker. But please, feel free to call me Will. Or William, whichever you prefer. And I should call you . . . ?"

"Mrs. Troi."

"Oh." He smiled gamely. "All right, Mrs. Troi. Um . . . Deanna and I have an appointment."

"Yes, I know." She took him by the arm and led him into the spacious living room. "She'll be with you in a moment. She's just getting ready . . . and I thought it would be nice if we had a few moments to chat."

"That sounds very nice."

He sat down on a couch, sinking unexpectedly deeply into the cushions. Lwaxana took a seat nearby that bore a striking resemblance to a throne. "Now . . . tell me all about yourself."

He stroked his chin and said, "Why don't you tell me about myself?"

She chuckled at that. "Oh, that's very good, Lieutenant. Instead of voicing statements that you know I can puncture, you instead ask me to take the first step so that you know what you're in for. All right." Suddenly the sound of her voice changed just a bit. "You're aggressive, hardworking, dedicated, cautious. You're someone who's guarded, and so finds himself ill at ease in an environment where your only option is forthrightness. Oh, and you are extremely attracted to my daughter and have had a variety of sexual fantasies about her. In fact, you are hoping that this outing will be in a romantic enough setting that you can employ your considerable charm to break through Deanna's defenses and introduce her to the full joys of your masculinity. Your preferred position for intercourse is—"

"Mrs. Troi!" said Riker, more sharply than he would have liked.

"And what's this about lime-flavored oil rubs?"

He got to his feet. "Mrs. Troi, I must admit, I'm shocked."

"You're shocked?" She looked up at him with overwhelming innocence. "Lieutenant, they're *your* thoughts."

"That may very well be, but it was my understanding that Betazoids prided themselves on courtesy. By my definition, your treatment of me here is not particularly courteous."

Her expression was stricken. "You're right. Where in the world are my manners? I haven't offered you anything to drink. Mr. Homn!" She clapped her hands together briskly. "A drink for our guest."

"That's not what I'm referring to. You're speaking . . . like I'm the enemy."

"That's your interpretation, Lieutenant. I don't think of you as an enemy. No, not at all. At most, I think of you as . . ." She paused, considering. "As an experience. A transient, passing experience that Deanna will encounter, learn from, and grow from. That's all. *Enemy* is much too strong a word. As for the things I'm saying, Lieutenant—my assessment of your nature and thoughts—you invited me to comment. You can hardly take me to task just because I took you up on your offer."

Mr. Homn appeared at Riker's side with a drink, balanced perfectly on a gleaming silver tray. Riker took it without even really noticing.

"You have to understand, Lieutenant. There are certain responsibilities that come with being who I am. I am a daughter of the Fifth House. Holder of the Sacred Chalice of Riix. Heir to the Holy Rings of Betazed. I am accustomed to speaking my mind, and I am also accustomed to watching out for the best interests of my daughter. She is an attentive, intelligent young lady. She will inherit from me the tremendous responsibilities that are presently all on my shoulders. Unlike you, whose life in Starfleet means that endless vistas are open to you . . . Deanna does not have that luxury. There are certain dictates upon her that come with who she is. She accepts that. She welcomes that. I want you to be considerate of those dictates. And I want you to do nothing that will interfere with her destiny or sense of purpose."

"Nothing meaning . . . ?"

"Nothing," said Lwaxana firmly, "meaning *nothing."*

"Mrs. Troi," Riker said slowly and deliberately, "I understand what you're saying. I appreciate your position. But with all due respect . . . you can't give me orders."

"Quite true," she replied with utter calm. "But Starfleet can. And believe me, Lieutenant . . . if a daughter of the Fifth House complains to Starfleet, there will certainly be those who listen. Do we understand each other?"

She gestured that he should take a drink. He stared at the contents of the glass and for just a moment tried to see any telltale residue that indicated poison.

"It's perfectly safe, Lieutenant."

He looked up and once again realized that his thoughts were completely open to her.

"I never seriously thought it wasn't."

She smiled sweetly.

Deanna chose that moment to make her entrance. Riker felt a flash of disappointment—her long, thick hair was tied up in a small, tight knot. The lines of her shapely figure were hidden under a loose-fitting, caftanlike outfit. In front of her she held a small basket. "Hello, Will," she said genially.

He got to his feet. "Deanna, you look lovely."

"Aside from the fact that he hates the dress and the way you're wearing your hair," said Lwaxana.

Riker fired her a poisonous glance, and Deanna said, sounding a bit confused, "Mother . . . you suggested the hairstyle and dress."

"Did I?" She smiled disingenuously. "So I did. Not too fond of my taste, Lieutenant?"

Gamely, he replied, "It wouldn't matter if she shaved her head and wore sackcloth and ashes. Deanna would still look lovely."

Mother and daughter exchanged a glance, and Lwaxana looked back to Riker. "Very smooth, Lieutenant," she said.

"Thank you."

He went to Deanna and gestured toward the front door. She continued to clutch the picnic basket in both hands, but smiled at her mother as they went out.

Lwaxana did not smile back.

"I hope she wasn't too hard on you."

Deanna and Riker were seated up on a grassy knoll overlooking a particularly lovely stretch of Betazed countryside. The picnic basket sat open next to them, the contents scattered about the ground around them.

Much of the time they had eaten in silence. Every so often Deanna would look up at Riker and either frown or smile. He had the distinct feeling that they were having a conversation without a word being spoken, or for that matter, without him even being fully aware of what was being said.

The statement she had now uttered was just about the longest of the afternoon.

"Nothing I couldn't handle," he said easily. When he said that, she laughed in a manner that he found very peculiar. "Why did you laugh that way?"

"Well, it's the way you responded. I asked you a question about how something made you feel. And your basic response was to make it clear that the situation was something within your control."

He stared at her uncomprehendingly. "So?"

"So, not everything has to be defined in terms of whether you can handle it or not. Sometimes it's enough to acknowledge that a situation has occurred and that you're aware of it."

"That doesn't seem like it would accomplish all that much."

"Why not?"

He lowered himself onto the grass, propping up his head with one hand. "Just acknowledging that a situation exists is rarely enough in my line of work. You have to deal with it."

"That's not true. What about your Prime Directive? Doesn't that tell you that you're not to get involved?"

"What it tells us is the preferred way of handling a particular type of situation . . . namely one involving interference with cultural development. But it still boils down to the idea that every situation must be dealt with in some way . . . even if occasionally the method of dealing with the situation is to keep your hands off."

"I see." She lifted the napkin off her lap and folded it carefully, replacing it in the picnic basket. "Is control very important for you, Lieutenant?"

"Not letting things get out of control is very important. There's a difference."

"And what might that be?"

"The difference is that you can have a specific situation with specific parameters . . . and as long as the elements within that situation don't go beyond those parameters, then everything is fine. You don't have to do much beyond sitting back and letting things run their course. This is as opposed to having to be in control, where you are handling every element personally every step of the way. It's a bad way to command. Shows a lack of ability to delegate."

She cocked her head slightly. "Do you think of everything in terms of Starfleet?"

"Not everything."

They looked at each other for a long moment, and Riker saw something in her eyes . . . something that beckoned to him.

He reached across, grabbed her by the arm, and pulled her to him. She fell to the ground with a startled cry of exclamation. For a moment he felt her body go limp against him, and he brought her face to his, pressed his mouth against hers. He felt something electric pass between them. . . .

And then he felt her knee in the pit of his stomach.

Riker gasped and rolled away, clutching his belly and moaning softly. He came up, gasping, and saw Deanna smoothing out her dress and looking utterly composed.

He sucked in air gratefully and tried to force the pain to go away. Deanna, for her part, reached into the basket and pulled out a brown pastry. "Dessert?" she asked innocently.

"Wh . . . why did you do that?" he managed to get out.

"Will, why are you asking obvious questions?" She held out the pastry to him. "I mean, I'm not asking you why you mauled me just now. I think it's fairly self-evident. I think my reason for stopping you is equally self-evident. So tell me . . . do you still feel in control?"

"Not . . . particularly." The soreness was just starting to recede.

"Now you see . . . that's just how I felt a moment ago. Lovemaking, Will, is when two people voluntarily decide to give control over to the partner. I wasn't voluntarily relinquishing anything. So I needed to reclaim it, quickly."

"You . . . could simply have said no."

She frowned at him. "I did."

"No, you didn't."

"I distinctly remember—"

"You didn't. If you'd have said no, I'd have stopped." Slowly he sat up, still rubbing his sore middle. "That I can assure you."

Her eyebrows knitted together, a puzzled expression on her face. "I was quite sure that I—"

"You know what?" said Riker, pointing at her. "You may have thought you said it . . . but you didn't. And maybe that's because you didn't really want to. For a moment there, you weren't resisting. As a matter of fact, you were pretty damned encouraging. I'll tell you something—you're so certain that you know my mind. Well, I don't even think you know your own."

"Is that a fact?"

"Yes."

"Well, then, just answer me this. . . ."

He waited for the question. "Yeah?"

"Do you want the dessert or not?"

He shook his head in confusion. "That's the question?"

Even she looked puzzled by it. "Yes."

"No. No dessert, thanks. Between the filling meal and your knee, my stomach's pretty much finished for the afternoon."

"Okay. Fine, then." Never taking her eyes off Riker, and regarding him with a very suspicious air . . . probably because she wasn't sure herself how he was making her feel . . . Deanna Troi ate Riker's dessert along with her own. Riker said nothing as he watched her do it.

Finally he asked, "Have you met a lot of humans?"

"A few. Mostly friends of my father."

"Formed an opinion?"

"Not especially. They're people, just like anyone else. Sweeping generalizations are rarely much use. I prefer a case-by-case diagnosis."

"Spoken like a true student of psychology. So . . . what are you going to do with your degree once you've gotten it?"

"Do with it?" She shrugged. "I don't know. Probably nothing."

He stared at her. *"Nothing?"*

"Well . . . knowing how the mind operates, and being able to talk to people . . . these skills will certainly be helpful to me in my societal responsibilities. Far more so than geology would have been."

"But . . . but don't you want to forge a career?"

"My life is my career. My responsibilities that are part and parcel of Betazed tradition. I'm not like you, Will. Many aspects of my life are already set."

"You know, I've had this conversation before," said Riker grimly. "With your mother. It's a shame you haven't got a mind of your own."

"I have a mind of my own," shot back Deanna hotly. "It's hardly my fault if my opinion concurs with that of my mother, now, is it?"

"You're right, you're right. I'm the poor dumb human who barely understands what's going through his own head, and you're the all-wise Betazoid who knows everything. Does that pretty much cover it?"

Making a sound of great frustration, Deanna began shoving all the picnic materials back into the basket. "This was stupid," she muttered partly to herself. "I don't know why I let myself be talked into this."

"Because you wanted to be talked into it."

"Oh, nonsense."

"You know what your problem is, Deanna?"

"Yes. My problem is you."

"No." He drew himself closer to her and hunkered down in front of her. When she wouldn't look at him, he took her pointed chin in his hands and brought her around to face him. "Your problem is that you overanalyze everything. You are so damned used to studying feelings, and thinking about feelings, and contemplating feelings, that you have no idea of how to just *go* with feelings."

"And you," she shot back, pushing his hand away, "can *only* go with feelings. You're going to make *some* Starfleet officer, Lieutenant. Someone who's incapable of studying a situation and deciding what to do about it calmly and rationally. I bet you'll never ask anyone for their opinions. I bet you'll never look for suggestions. You'll just do what you want, when you want, on impulse, because your feelings tell you to do so, and you'll just drag the rest of the crew along with you. And heaven help them if you're wrong."

He sat back on his heels. And looking somewhat stupid, he grinned. "You must really like me if you get that worked up over me."

"Oh, you're intolerable."

She picked up the picnic basket and started to walk, her large caftan swishing around her. Riker got to his feet and walked along next to her.

"And I bet you don't believe in love at first sight," he said challengingly.

She didn't even glance at him. "Now you're saying you love me?"

"No, I'm not saying that. I'm asking about the idea in principle. Do you believe in love at first sight?"

He fully expected that she would say no, just as Wendy had. So he was surprised when she slowly came to a halt and turned to look at him full in the face, her eyes large and thoughtful.

Then she turned and walked off in another direction. Puzzled, he followed her.

The terrain got more steep and hilly, and she put down the picnic basket and used her hands to help pull herself up. He followed her, unsure of what was happening, but reluctant to say or do anything that would possibly stop her. He wanted to see what she was up to.

Eventually Deanna reached what appeared to be a peak, and she sat down carefully, meticulously arranging her caftan. Riker climbed up next to her, and his breath caught in his throat.

It was a stunning vista. The view earlier paled in comparison. The sky was now pale orange, and hundreds of feet below a river ribboned between two high banks. Long, untamed blades of grass sprouted here and there, on the one hand appearing random, but on the other, adding to the overall look and feel of the place as if it had been carefully planned.

"I like to come here to think. It's one of my favorite places."

"What do you think about?"

"Love at first sight." She paused. "Yes. I do believe in it."

"Well, now, I must admit, I'm surprised. That's hardly the sign of a rational, nonimpulsive mind. Love at first sight is the ultimate leap of faith."

"Nothing about it is particularly rational," she admitted. "I'd suppose you'd say my rationale is more romantic than anything else."

"And what's your rationale, may I ask?"

At first she said nothing, as if trying to figure out the best way to put her thoughts. "I think that, to some degree, all of us are fractured souls. Cut in half. And we wander through life looking for the rest of ourselves. And sometimes we're fortunate enough to meet someone who possesses, in themselves, the part of ourselves that we've been missing. We may not realize it on a conscious level, but definitely on a subconscious level. We see in someone else . . . something of ourselves."

She held her hands up in front of her, palms facing each other. "That's why sometimes you meet someone and you just immediately feel comfortable with them. You feel like you've known them all your life. The reason is that they're a part of you, and you're a part of them. You're soul mates. You . . . fit." She interlaced her fingers. "And once you've fit together, nothing can pull you apart unless you let go." She released her grip, drawing her hands apart.

"And how did you develop this . . ." He coughed politely. "This theory?"

She smiled gamely. "It seemed the most reasonable explanation for why my parents came together. I mean, no rational being would have seen them as any sort of workable couple. Yet my mother claimed that the moment they met they just . . . just knew." She shrugged. "So who knows?"

"But that's kind of sad, really."

"Why?" she asked, puzzled.

"Because, since you're such a rational type, if you ever met your 'soul mate,' you'd probably intellectualize it to death. How could any sort of pure romantic notion stand up to being rationally disemboweled? You'd never follow your impulse."

"Love at first sight is hardly the sort of thing that happens all the time. My attitude is different from yours. You always follow your impulse. And you have good impulses, I'm sure, by and large. You're very confident, and that's a requirement in your career. But it's not the kind of mind-set I'm used to. I doubt there's any sort of future for us."

He slid closer to her and then said, "Change me."

She stared at him. "What?"

"You're studying to be a psychologist. The entire point of that is to help people. If you think I have some sort of emotional shortcomings, then you can try and do something about it."

"I'm hardly a fully trained therapist, Will. I'm not qualified. You'd be . . . you'd be little more than a guinea pig. It wouldn't be ethical."

"Why not? It's only unethical if you pass yourself off as something you're not. And I'm perfectly willing to be a guinea pig. Believe me, I doubt if anything you'd say or do could be any more grueling than officer training at Starfleet."

He stuck out a hand. "What do you say? Deal?"

She stared at him for a moment. "You're just hoping that this will afford you an opportunity down the road to make love to me."

"That's right," he said without hesitation. "And you're hoping it will, too. Secretly, you're grateful for the chance to bring me 'up' to your level so that you can then feel better about allowing yourself to come 'down' to the more basic altitude of *my* level."

He spoke with such conviction and such certainty that Deanna actually felt an unusual sensation . . . her cheeks were burning.

Riker noticed the flush in an instant and then said, using precisely the tone she had the other day, "I didn't read your mind. I hazarded a guess. All you did was confirm it."

And he looked at her with such challenge in his eyes that she took his hand and squeezed it firmly . . . so firmly that it left him numb for a few minutes as she said, "It's a deal. Prepare to be a guinea pig, Lieutenant Riker."

"Miss Troi, point me to the maze."

Eighteen

In a café just outside the Federation embassy, Mark Roper sat down for breakfast. He studied the menu, then thought about what he'd like to have. Moments later, it arrived, courtesy of a smiling waitress, who knew that he would want nothing else, knew the name on his credit account, and went off to deduct from it not only the cost of his breakfast but how much he would want to tip her.

To Mark Roper, it eliminated a lot of the fuss and bother of meals.

A rap on the window of the café next to Roper made him look up. Outside was Lieutenant Riker, looking pleasant and refreshed. Roper gestured for Riker to join him, and the youthful officer entered the café and sat down across from him.

"So how did it go with young Deanna yesterday?" asked Roper.

"Very nicely. Very nicely."

"Lwaxana was something else, I'll bet."

"Oh, yes."

"So tell me . . . did you do it with Deanna?"

Riker's whole body sagged in disbelief. "Mark . . . what is this obsession with my sex life?"

"I have none of my own," replied Roper a bit sadly. "I have to get my enjoyment vicariously."

"May I suggest you find someone, and quickly. This is becoming a bit obsessive. Besides, aren't you concerned about how your daughter will react if I take up with Deanna?" And then Riker's eyes narrowed. "Wait a minute. That's it, isn't it."

"That's what?"

"You'd *prefer* if I became involved with Deanna because then you figure I'd stay away from your daughter."

At that, Roper laughed loudly, so loudly that he started to cough. Finally, upon composing himself, he said, "Captain . . . you're giving me motives that are far too Machiavellian. Whatever my daughter and you do is fine by me. Whatever you do with Deanna is fine by me. To be honest, whatever my daughter and Deanna did with each other would be fine by me. Although, I must admit, it'd be surprising as hell. I'm just curious, that's all."

"Well, to satisfy your curiosity . . ."

"Nothing happened."

"Right."

"As a matter of fact," said Roper, leaning forward and pointing at Riker, "I'll bet that you put some moves on her, and you were shot down cold."

"Well . . ." Riker coughed politely. "As a matter of fact, yes."

"Thought so."

Riker looked puzzled at that. "Why did you think so?"

"You're not Deanna's type. I know her, I know the kind of background she comes from. Her taste would run towards someone more intellectual—no offense."

"None taken," said Riker, although he wasn't entirely sure how to react. "But I'm hardly a mental midget."

"Oh, I didn't say that you were. Far from it. You're an extremely bright fellow. But you just don't think along the same lines she does. She's a gentle rainstorm, and you're lightning in a bottle. I doubt either of you would have the patience with the other to get anything going."

"Actually, we're going to be seeing each other again. Tomorrow, in fact."

"No!"

"That's right."

"Up to you, Captain. I just hope that you're not counting on Deanna to be the one who breaks your streak of celibacy while on this fair planet."

"I have no intention of being celibate, Mark," said Riker, leaning forward and dropping his voice. "And if you absolutely *must* know . . . she definitely wants me."

"Nonsense."

"It's true. She just hasn't admitted it yet. But she'll come around."

"When? On her deathbed?"

"A lot sooner than that."

"Never happen."

"It will, Mark. Bet on it."

Roper looked at him with mischief in his eyes. "All right. One hundred credits says you never 'become intimate' with her."

Riker laughed in disbelief. "Mark! I'd never bet on anything like that! It's . . . it's crass, it's tasteless, it's . . ."

"Two hundred credits."

"It's a bet."

Roper raised a warning finger. "And no funny stuff. No getting her drunk. Has to be utterly mutual. You can't force her."

"Force her! Mark, I've never 'forced' a woman in my life. Honestly, now. What do you take me for?"

Roper patted the top of Riker's hand. "Captain . . . I believe I've taken you for two hundred credits."

Nineteen

The Betazed museum of art was a tall, impressive building, and extremely ornate. Deanna and Will stood outside as she explained to him the history of the structure, the design work and theory that had gone into it. She spoke at length for some minutes.

Riker, for his part, was happy that she was once again wearing her hair down, and that the outfit she was wearing was more flattering to her figure. Much of what she said barely registered until finally she turned to him and said, "Why am I bothering?"

"What?"

"You don't seem at all interested in what I'm saying, Will. I'm trying to explain to you why this building is, in and of itself, a work of art."

"And I'm trying to explain to *you,* Deanna, that I can only appreciate one work of art at a time."

"And right now you're still appreciating me."

"I guess so, yes."

She sighed, took him by the hand, and said, "Come on." She pulled him toward the building and through the large columned doors.

Inside there was music playing, loud and sonorous, and it sounded somewhat like organ music.

It was coming from a large, multiple-piped instrument in the middle of a great rotunda. Seated in circles around the musician were various Betazoids, who were listening to the music, their eyes closed, their faces blissful. Riker looked around and tried to get a feeling for what was going on. The music sounded okay to him, but nothing particularly special. He couldn't understand why it seemed to be affecting the listeners so deeply.

He looked at Deanna, and she, too, appeared to be totally taken by it. Her eyes were half-lidded, and she was swaying slightly to the tones. Riker whispered, "Are you all right?"

She opened her eyes and looked at him. Her stare was almost incredulous, as if she couldn't believe that he was still capable of speech. "This is soul music," she whispered. "Listen to it. Let it pervade you. What does it say to you?"

He listened. He let it pervade him.

"What is it supposed to say?" he asked.

With an irritated noise, she pulled at him and dragged him off down a large corridor.

The air in the cavernous building was cool. Riker looked around, trying to take things in. His eyes adjusted to the dimness, and he kept trying to find something that would be startling and revolutionary to him. Something that would give his innermost thoughts a voice and fill him with understanding. Nothing in particular seemed to leap out at him, however.

Deanna led him into a room and made a sweeping gesture.

Paintings hung on the walls. All of them appeared to be what Riker would term "abstract" . . . that is, they didn't seem to be pictures of anything in particular. In front of every single painting was a small bench, and in a number of instances, Betazoids were seated on the benches staring intently at the works.

"I come here once a week," whispered Deanna. Her voice, although it was as low as she could possibly make it, still attracted glances from the occupants of the room. Silent communion was the norm here. People looked from her to Riker and then back to her, and their expressions changed from mild irritation to understanding tolerance . . . and even, in a couple of cases, a degree of pity—much to Riker's annoyance.

"Once a week? Why?"

She led him over to one work in particular, which was concentric splashes of red, blue, green, white, black, and a couple of colors that Riker didn't recognize. Here, in one of the more far-off sections of the room, no one else was sitting nearby at the moment.

"Because, Will," she said quietly, "it's one of the methods I use to stay in touch with myself." At his blank expression, she continued gamely, "In order to fully understand others, you must learn to understand yourself. Only by being in touch with what motivates you can you then grasp what motivates others."

"I studied this in the Academy. The course was called Dynamics of Command."

"Commanding who?"

"Other officers. Crewmen."

"Yes, well, you see . . . here the only person you're trying to command is yourself. Now . . . I want you to look at the painting and tell me what it says to you."

"This is supposed to talk to me, too? Can't anything on this planet keep its mouth shut?"

His comment came out sounding a bit more sarcastic than he would have liked, but Troi appeared undeterred. "On Betazed, we believe in full communion. Communion with each other. Communion with our world. But before any of that can occur, we must have communion with ourselves."

"What's the painting called?"

She stared at him in confusion. "What?"

"What's it called? What's the name of the painting? At least I'll have *some* clue to what the artist was trying to put across if I know what he called the damned thing."

"The 'damned thing' doesn't have a name. That would be presumptuous . . . it would be as if the artist were trying to impose his own worldview upon the viewer."

"Terrific. Look, maybe we can start with another painting? Something that *looks* like something?"

He started to rise and she pulled him back down again. "Will, you're not even trying. You said you were going to cooperate."

"I'm sorry," he sighed. "I'll try, all right?"

The problem was, every time he looked at her, he kept thinking about trying to get her clothes off. But he knew that such unguarded thoughts were only going to get him into trouble again. So, gamely, he focused on the picture again.

It was swirls. Splashes of color. No matter how long or how intently he looked at it, it still looked like jumbled paints and nothing more.

"You're trying too hard."

He blew air through his lips in exasperation. "First you tell me I'm not trying at all, and now you tell me I'm trying too hard. Now which is it?" He looked at the painting. "Would you mind telling me what it is you want of me?"

Then he felt two strong fingers at the base of his skull, squeezing together and massaging him. Deanna's arm moved in a steady, circular motion.

He started to feel tension that he didn't even know he had ebb from him. He was glad that he couldn't see his face because he had the distinct, detached feeling that he had a rather goofy expression at the moment.

"Now," she said softly, "while you're relaxing . . . look at the painting and tell me what you see. Learn to look below the surface, beyond the superficial. What is there to learn from the painting . . . and what can we learn from ourselves?"

His head swayed back and forth in gentle rocking motions. He stared at the painting for what seemed an eternity.

"I see . . ."

"Yes?"

He was silent for a moment and then said, "I see . . . paint swirls."

She stopped the rubbing. "That's it?" she said with flat disgust.

"That's it. I'm sorry." He turned to her, not sure whether to be more irritated with himself or with her. "You wouldn't want me to lie to you . . . and I doubt I could, even if I wanted to. I see paint swirls. Big, goopy paint swirls."

"Goopy? This is a word? *Goopy?*"

"I don't have much taste for abstract art. When I look at something, I like it to look *like* something."

She paused, her hands carefully arranged on her lap. "Tell me, Lieutenant. As you further explore the galaxy, you will inevitably run into things that don't look like anything you've ever imagined that anything could look. What are you going to do in those instances? Are you going to decide that they're inferior somehow? Or that there's something wrong with them? How are you going to judge? By their degree of goopiness?"

"In those instances, when encountering new life-forms beyond my experience, I'll have instrumentation to help me. Sensor arrays. Medical scans. Instantaneous translators and communications devices. I won't have to—"

"You won't have to depend on yourself."

"Now I didn't say that."

"No, you didn't. But that's what it boils down to, Lieutenant. And believe me, you're going to find yourself in situations where all the instrumentation in the world isn't going to do you a bit of good. They can guide you, but you're going to have to rely on something beyond that. As a matter of fact, I'll wager that there will be times when you have to act in ways that are contrary to what instrumentation is telling you . . . that are contrary to what *people* are telling you, for that matter. And you have to be fully conversant in *why* you think what you think, because otherwise you're going to find yourself heading down the wrong road."

"Thank you for your opinions, Miss Troi . . . drawn, no doubt, from your many years of experience with Starfleet."

"I don't have to be experienced with Starfleet, Lieutenant, in order to be aware of the importance of knowing your own mind."

"Really?" He took her hand in his and squeezed it firmly. "And what does your mind tell you about your feelings for me? Hmmm?"

She met his gaze levelly. "It tells me that perhaps we have to begin with something a bit more fundamental than this." She stood. "Come on. We're getting out of here."

"Where are we going?"

"Back to basics."

The tree towered over them, its trunk brown and gnarled. There were no leaves on it, and its branches seemed to stretch up forever.

The trunk was so twisted that climbing up it was easy. Deanna did so and gestured for Riker to follow. He climbed, relieved that this was at least something that was mildly entertaining . . . particularly because he liked watching the play of Deanna's muscles under her tight clothes.

She stopped at a point about ten feet above the ground. Large branches stuck out in either direction. She sidled out onto one, and when Riker started to follow her, she shook her head and indicated that he should go in the other direction. With a shrug he did as instructed.

"Your problem, Lieutenant, is that the demands of your body have too much sway on your mind," she said once they were both perched on their opposite branches.

"What do you mean?"

"Your attraction to me, for example. Indeed, your attraction to most women, I would think. It's purely hormonal. It's being fueled entirely by your sex drive, which is biological, not intellectual. But you are more than willing to turn your intellect over to the requirements of your biology."

"What about what you were saying before? About love at first sight being something you believe in? Where does biology figure into that?"

"It doesn't. Love at first sight is spiritual. You're too primal for that."

"You're saying"—he smirked slightly as he spoke—"that I'm incapable of falling in love with someone at first sight because I think with my glands and that automatically pushes out all higher emotions?"

"That's correct."

"Well, thanks a lot, Miss Troi."

"It wasn't a compliment," she said primly. "Higher emotions are what separate us from the lower orders of life."

"Is that all?"

"Higher emotions, and table manners."

"Tell me, Deanna, have you ever had really good sex? Or is that just a theory to you?"

She actually laughed at that. "You really can't figure me out, can you, Lieutenant. You think that all you have to do is smile at me, wink devilishly, overpower me with your charm and strength, and I will willingly succumb to your overwhelming manliness."

"Something like that."

"Commander, welcome to the twenty-fourth century. I don't know what goes on on Earth, or even aboard starships . . . but on Betazed, a woman wants more from a man than for him to simply be a strong hero figure. Someone who is going to carry the helpless damsel off in his big, muscular arms, causing her to swoon and give herself over to him in hot and sweaty throes of passion. Women aren't like that here. *I'm* not like that."

"No, of course not. You're much too busy doing precisely what Mommy tells you, and being precisely what she wants you to be, to let yourself be influenced by anyone as down-and-dirty as me."

Her expression was not a particularly pleasant one. "Listen, do you want to do this or not?"

"Sure. Sure. You were going to show me how to separate the needs of my mind from the needs of my body."

"All right. It's very simple, really. I want you to get a solid grip on the branch, just like I'm doing." He followed her demonstration and she continued, "Then we're going to just drop off from the branch and hang on for as long as possible."

"This is a test of muscular strength . . . which seems kind of silly, since obviously I'm stronger than you. So if this is some sort of competition . . ."

"The only one you're going to compete with, Lieutenant, is yourself. And furthermore, it has nothing to do with muscular strength because muscles, and the body, invariably have limits, no matter how well trained they are. You reach a point that can't be surpassed. But the properly trained mind, on the other hand, has no limits. Ready? And . . . go."

Deanna dropped down off the branch and hung there, her feet suspended more than a meter above the ground. Riker did likewise.

He stared at her, noticing that her toes were not pointed downward, but rather were straight out. Her eyes were fluttering closed as she said in a low, melodious tone, "Now . . . sooner or later, your fingers will want to release. Your instinct will be to fight this impulse. Do not fight it. Instead . . . simply ignore it. Banish it to the inner core of your being, and instead focus on something else."

"Like what?"

"Like anything. Anything that will take your mind away from your body—the sky. The clouds. Birds in flight. The creation of a star. Anything to disassociate yourself from the demands of the physical. Now do what I'm doing—bring an image to mind, a focal image. Close your eyes. Breathe slowly and steadily, in through your nose, out through your mouth, like this," and she demonstrated. "Slowly, steadily, gradually . . . that's it."

Riker had closed his eyes, but now he turned and peered again through narrowed lids at Deanna.

She seemed perfectly at ease. Her breasts were rising and falling so slowly that the motion was almost imperceptible.

Clear his mind. Think about something else other than the fact that his fingers were starting to ache a bit, and his upper arms were feeling a tad numb.

He thought about Deanna.

He pictured her as he had first seen her at the wedding—naked and smiling.

She stood on a beach, having just come out of the water, her body covered with thin rivulets of moisture. She shook her head in slow motion, water spraying out in all directions from her thick hair. Then she came toward him slowly, smiling, her arms outstretched toward him, her fingers gesturing for him to approach her . . .

Her fingers waving . . . her arms outstretched . . .

He felt an ache growing beyond his ability to ignore it. He opened his eyes and found that his fingers were covered with perspiration and were slipping, losing their grip. He tried desperately to readjust, but now his fingers felt nerveless. He had no idea how long he had been hanging there, for he had lost track of time . . . but however long it was, it was enough for him to have lost all feeling above the elbows.

With a low, muttered curse, he dropped from the branch and landed with a hard thud.

He sat there, dusting himself off, and looked up.

Deanna was still hanging there. Serenely. Calmly. Looking as if she had all the time in the world. Her eyes were still closed, her breasts still rising and falling at the exact same pace as before . . . no. As a matter of fact, they were moving even more slowly.

He sat there and watched her, shaking his arms to try to restore circulation.

Deanna hung there.

As blood began to return to Riker's upper arms, he felt a fierce pain, and he winced as he touched the abraded skin on his palms. He looked back to his teacher.

Deanna hung there.

And hung there.

He had no idea how long it was . . . ten, maybe fifteen minutes. Maybe longer. Her slim body continued to display no ill effects whatsoever.

After what seemed an interminable length of time, Deanna began to rock back and forth, slowly and gently. Her eyes remained closed. She gained enough momentum to swing upward like a gymnast, wrapping her legs up and around the branch and bringing herself back to sitting.

"What are you doing down there?"

"What are you doing up there?" he countered. "Finally get tired?"

"No. I could have continued that way for quite some time. A shame that you couldn't. Maybe the weight of all those muscles dragged you down. What an inconvenience, being so much stronger than little me."

He stood, brushing himself off, and walked toward the base of the trunk. As he did so, Deanna clambered upward, standing on the branch as if she were a tightrope walker. She looked completely at ease.

"All right, you've proven your point," he said, trying to keep the disgust out of his voice. "You can climb down now."

Deanna took a step toward the trunk so that she could get a grip and descend . . .

And her foot slipped.

Her arms pinwheeling, and with a startled shriek, Deanna lost her balance and tumbled off.

Riker, still a short distance away, moved like lightning. His arms outstretched, he skidded in and caught Deanna before she hit. But he hadn't had time to brace himself, and the weight of her carried him down. He dropped to his knees, the shock rattling his teeth, but he still held on to her.

Reflexively her arms had gone around his neck. She tried to compose herself, automatically doing the breathing exercise to regain her equilibrium. Riker, meantime, shook his head briskly. Then he looked at her . . . and grinned ear to ear.

He got to his feet, still holding her in his arms. "You okay?"

"I'm fine. You can put me down—"

Their faces had been mere inches from each other, and Riker now seized the initiative. He kissed her full on the lips.

They held like that for a long time, and he felt her body go limp. And then she just seemed to melt against him, and reflexively her hands squeezed his shoulder blades, as if afraid he might vanish, or the moment might end.

But ultimately it was she who ended it, breaking off with an audible popping sound. "Put me down," she whispered.

He grinned and said, "But we were just getting—"

Put me down NOW!

He dropped her.

He hadn't intended to do it. But the imperative was so startling and so overwhelming that it caught him completely unawares. She fell at his feet and, quickly scrambling to hers, backed away from him.

"I heard you," he said, "in my head. That must mean I'm getting better at this. Right?"

"You couldn't have heard me in your head."

"I know I—"

"You *couldn't* have!" she said with an infuriated stomp of her foot.

She turned away from him in an obvious attempt to compose herself. He made no move toward her, stayed as far from her as he could.

She was in pain. My God, she was in pain over him.

At that moment, he cleared his mind because instinctively, he didn't want to think or even feel anything that she might pick up on and cause her more distress. Just like that, he was suddenly thinking about nothing at all. And he felt totally relaxed.

"Deanna—"

She said nothing. Her hands were pressed against each other, palm to palm, and she had slowed her breathing down. When she did turn back to face him, all the confusion was gone. Instead she was lit with inner calm.

"Your problem earlier," she said, sounding very clinical, "was that you were once again entertaining erotic thoughts about me. All that did was focus you on the needs of your body. You can't put yourself beyond those needs if you use that as your focal point. You should watch out for that, Lieutenant."

"Really." He took a step toward her. "Well, you know what I think, Miss Troi. I think your body and mind aren't quite as synchronized as you like to think. I think your body wanted to fall into my arms, contrary to what your mind might think of me. And so your ever-so-sure feet deliberately betrayed you."

"I subconsciously threw myself at you, is what you're saying?" She laughed lightly.

"It's possible, yes."

Again she laughed. "No, Lieutenant. It's not possible. For your information, a piece of bark broke off, and that's what caused me to slip. That's all. If you look around on the ground, I'm sure you'll find where it fell. Now, if you'll excuse me . . ."

She turned and walked off. He called after her, "When is our next lesson?" But she didn't respond.

He spent the next twenty minutes searching every inch of the ground, trying to find the stray piece of bark.

But he never did.

Twenty

Dinner that night in the Troi household was subdued. The only sound was a persistent and gentle chiming as Mr. Homn stood at the middle of the table repeatedly striking the small instrument that gave thanks to the gods of Betazed for the food being eaten.

Lwaxana kept glancing up at Deanna. Her daughter seemed preoccupied this evening, her gaze and thoughts focused entirely toward herself. When, out of habit, Lwaxana sent a gentle and subtle probe into her daughter's mind to find out what was troubling her, she was astounded to find that her mental inquiry was turned aside. She could have, of course, immediately pushed more deeply and with more force, but that would have been utterly out of line. Casual mind brushing was one thing; shoving one's way in after meeting initial resistance was quite another thing entirely.

Deanna . . . ?

There was no response, and with an annoyed air, Lwaxana resorted to the far more inconvenient, since it meant she had to disrupt her eating, verbal "Deanna."

Deanna looked up. "Yes, Mother?"

"What is troubling you, Little One?"

Her daughter smiled gamely. "Nothing, Mother."

"Casual lies?" Lwaxana looked disapproving. "First you thwart a mind brush, and then you resort to telling me that nothing is bothering you when something clearly is. I thought we were more open with each other than that, Deanna. Frankly . . . I'm a little hurt."

"There's no reason to be hurt, Mother, just because I don't want to share every intimate detail of my life every moment."

Lwaxana raised an eyebrow. "Intimate?"

"Mother, I don't want to get into it."

Lwaxana let a rather crude response float from her mind into Deanna's, and it got the expected reaction. Deanna flushed slightly and said, "Mother, that was uncalled for."

"Perhaps. But how accurate was it?"

"Mo-ther . . ."

"It's him, isn't it. That Starfleet officer, Striker."

"Riker."

"Him." Lwaxana carefully arranged her napkin in front of her and turned to her manservant. "Mr. Homn, I'll want to send a communiqué to Starfleet."

Deanna slapped the table impatiently and said, "Don't you dare!"

She might just as easily have spit into Lwaxana's food and gotten the same response as she received. Slowly, with an air of complete and utter shock, Lwaxana turned and openly gaped at her child. " 'Don't you *dare'?"* she repeated incredulously. Deanna looked down, her mouth moving but no sound coming. "You're telling *me,"* continued Lwaxana, "what *I,* the keeper of the Sacred Chalice of Riix, should and should not *dare?* May I ask you, young lady, who in the Great Fire you think you're talking to?"

"Mother, please, I'm sorry—"

"I will *not* be addressed in that . . . that cavalier, offhand manner. I am *not* one of your 'pals,' Deanna. I am not one of your casual acquaintances. I am certainly not one of your Starfleet friends."

"He's not a friend! He's not even . . . Mother, I don't even *like* him!"

"Then what is he?" demanded Lwaxana. "What is he to you?"

"A frustration. A big frustration, that's all. He's a . . . a case study in surface arrogance. He's . . . he's nothing. *Nothing.* Not on a personal level."

"Need I remind you," said Lwaxana stiffly, "of your commitment to Wyatt?"

"I know about that, Mother. But frankly, I can't believe that you're really going to hold me to that . . . that agreement."

"Little One, *I'm* not holding you to anything! This is tradition and custom we're talking about. I don't just fabricate things to inconvenience you and make your life more difficult. I simply teach you what they are and expect you to abide by them. And you, knowing your place in society and the responsibilities that place entails, are going to abide by them. Aren't you." The last was not a question.

Deanna looked down.

"Aren't you." This time there was even a bit more of an edge than before.

"Yes, Mother," said Deanna automatically, a phrase she had repeated any number of times before on a variety of occasions.

"Good, because frankly . . . and I'm only giving you my surface interpretation here, since you seem uncomfortable with allowing me to probe more deeply on this . . . you're making it quite clear that you can't exactly control yourself when it comes to this lieutenant."

Now Deanna looked up, her jaw set. "I can control myself just fine, Mother. I'm not some . . . some animal in heat."

"I never said you were."

"No, but you implied it."

"I didn't—"

"You *did."*

"All right, maybe I did," said Lwaxana, putting her hands up. "But it's understandable. You don't seem yourself when it comes to thoughts of him. Perhaps I should have a talk with the people at the university. If this lieutenant is merely a case study for you, then I think that the university is doing a pretty shabby job of teaching you something as simple as clinical detachment."

"They're doing a fine job, Mother. Please . . . stay out of it. I can handle Lieutenant Riker just fine."

Lwaxana stared at her piercingly. "And how do you define 'just fine'?"

"I define it as being capable of rising to a situation without your help."

Lwaxana appeared to consider this a moment, then speared another piece of fish with her prong. And then she said simply, "See that you do."

Mr. Homn hit his chime and Deanna winced slightly. Funny how, after all these years, she'd never realized just how damned annoying that persistent chiming was.

* * *

Riker lay in his quarters at the embassy, reading a primer on Betazed philosophy that Deanna had recommended.

It was puzzling to him. In example after example, situations were presented and the reader was asked, basically, "What would you do or say in such a situation?" And Riker was consistently getting it wrong.

He went on to the next example and read it out loud to see if it would make more sense: "A friend tells you that she is very upset. Her immediate supervisor has said several overly critical things in regards to her work, and she feels frustrated and hurt over the situation. How do you respond?"

Riker thought about it and then said out loud, "All right. I tell her one of two things: either she can analyze her work habits, see where she's being remiss, and improve her performance, or, if she firmly believes that the criticism by her supervisor is unwarranted, she can tell her supervisor that and demonstrate why. If he continues to be overly critical, she can inform him that if he does not cease and desist in his unreasonable demands, then she will go to the next level in the chain of command and file a grievance."

He pondered that for a moment, decided that it was a good, solid, reasonable response, and moved on to what the text claimed was the proper way to handle it.

He read it out loud without understanding it.

" 'Tell your friend' "—and there was incredulity in Riker's voice—" 'that you understand her frustration. That you know she's in a difficult situation, but have confidence she'll work it through. Cite an instance in your own life where you experienced similar feelings of anxiety. Let her know that she's not alone and that she can count on you as a source of emotional support.' "

He stared at the words floating there on the screen and shook his head. "But what's that going to solve?" he asked in frustration. "Sitting there and commiserating about how difficult life is? That's not going to do anything to address the problem! It's not going to make things better. I mean, why would she come to me with this problem if she didn't want me to try and come up with ways to solve it?"

He pushed the screen away in annoyance, shutting it off. This was ridiculous. Tang had been absolutely right about these people. They seemed to dwell endlessly on how everyone felt.

He resolved to ask Deanna about it the next time he saw her.

Which was not the next day.

Or the day after that.

Or the day after that.

By the end of the week, the silence on the part of his "tutor" had become somewhat puzzling, if not downright irritating. He made several calls over to the mansion and was repeatedly told that Deanna wasn't there or wasn't available. He asked that she return his calls, but she never did.

He was starting to become irritated, and his irritability showed through when Sergeant Tang happened to stop by to chat about a new piece of ordnance. Riker was short-tempered with him and then immediately regretted his tone.

"Sorry, Sergeant. That was uncalled for."

Tang stared at him and rubbed his beard stubble thoughtfully. Riker wondered for a moment how in hell Tang perpetually managed to look as if he needed a shave. Did he just scrape along the edges of the stubble, cutting it to a particular disheveled length?

In a manner that was a bit too overfamiliar for a sergeant to deal with a lieutenant—but nevertheless seemed utterly in keeping with Tang's personality—the veteran spacer slapped Riker on the forearm and said, "C'mon with me, Lieutenant. I got something set up downstairs that you look like you could use."

Riker followed Tang to the lower sections of the embassy, to rarely used storage facilities. At the moment, the facilities were relatively empty, particularly because the reception for the Rigelian ambassador had depleted much of the stock. Riker knew there would not be a ship along to restock for several weeks.

Riker was surprised—but not *too* surprised—to see that Tang and his men had converted the large facilities into a makeshift armory. "We're good at making do with what we have," said Tang. "Every so often, though, we fall into a bit of luck."

"Good lord." Riker was looking at one of the most massive pieces of armament he'd ever seen. It hung on the wall and was almost as large as Riker himself. He looked around to Tang and said, "May I?"

Tang waved toward it. "You're the CO. Be my guest."

Riker lifted the long, cylindrical weapon down and staggered under the weight of it. He had trouble placing his hands correctly and felt it slipping off his shoulder. But then Tang was there, steadying him, although actually he seemed a bit more concerned about the weapon's safety than Riker's.

"Here, you take it," said Riker, handing it off to Tang. Although Tang was a head shorter than Riker, he hefted the weapon as if it weighed a fraction of what it actually did. Riker tried to suppress his astonishment at the display of strength and was only partially successful. "What *is* that?"

"This," said Tang, patting it proudly with his free hand, "is the latest in mobile ground-to-air defense. The portable Level 10, shoulder-mounted phaser cannon, Model II."

"Makes you wonder what Model I was like."

"Model I blew up during field testing and destroyed half of Pluto. No one cared—it was a boring planet, anyway." Then, when he saw Riker's expression, he grinned, showing slightly irregular teeth. "I'm kidding, Lieutenant."

"I knew you were," Riker lied. "How powerful is that thing?"

"On full strength, I'd probably have a shot at knocking one of Betazed's moons out of orbit."

"You're kidding again."

Tang looked at him, his face inscrutable. "I didn't say I'd have a *good* shot at it."

He placed the gun back on the wall and took a couple of small target-practice phasers out of their mountings. "Come on. I'll show you what we got set up."

He led Riker over to another area, which was somewhat darkened, and handed him one of the phasers. Then from his belt he unclipped a couple of small, diamond-shaped devices. "Standard issue for ground security," he said. "Keeps us from getting stale no matter where we are."

He tossed them into the air, and on their own, they started hurtling around the chamber. "Pick your shot and start firing, Lieutenant."

Back to back, Riker and Tang began firing at the diamonds, trying to nail them in midflight. They glistened as they darted about the room, bobbing and weaving in no particular pattern. Riker managed to land a couple of shots; Tang landed far more.

And as if the tricky piece of firing only required part of his attention, Tang said, "It's a woman, isn't it."

"Pardon?"

"One of the local girls, like you said you were going to be going out with. She's got you hooked . . . no disrespect intended."

"I'm not *hooked,* Sergeant. They have interesting philosophies. I'm trying to understand them."

"How much philosophy do you need to get through life? If something attacks you, shoot it. If it doesn't attack you, leave it alone. Everything else is just window dressing."

"That's a very narrow mind-set, Sergeant."

"That mind-set is what keeps you alive, Lieutenant Riker. I'm still here. My men share my mind-set. They're still here. That's all that matters."

"Hello, Will."

The two men stopped and turned, and there stood Wendy Roper. She was wearing a white jumpsuit that clung to her like a second skin. "Hi, Sergeant."

"Ma'am," acknowledged Tang.

She turned back to Riker and wasn't able to hide the disappointment in her face. "Will. . . . I haven't seen you around much."

"I, um . . . I've been very busy lately, Wendy."

"Really?" she said with a pert angle of her head. "Doing what?"

"I've . . ."

"The lieutenant has mostly been preoccupied with perimeter inspections, ma'am," Tang said stiffly. "Word on the line is that we're ripe for an attack at any time."

"Yes, any time," echoed Riker.

"A great deal of time being spent in security procedures. All out of concern for your safety, ma'am."

"I see. Well . . . when you do have some free moments, Lieutenant . . . it'd be nice to get together. I thought we were hitting it off rather well." She nodded to Tang. "Good seeing you, Sergeant." And she walked off. Riker could hear her light footsteps receding up the stairs.

"She's a nice girl," Tang observed. "Very pleasant companion, I'd think. And best of all—no offense intended—not overly intellectual, if you catch my drift."

"I'd have to agree."

"But I take it she's not the young lady . . . ?"

"No. She's not."

"Never burned the candle at both ends, Lieutenant?"

Riker looked at him askance. "You mean juggled more than one relationship at a time?"

"If you want to put it that way, sir, yes."

"To be honest . . . yes. But somehow, until I get things sorted out with Deanna—"

"Deanna's the local girl?"

"Yes. I don't know how to put it, Sergeant, but it wouldn't seem . . . I don't know . . . *right* somehow."

Tang made a disapproving clucking noise. "Bad sign, Lieutenant. Very bad sign. Shields up, proceed with caution."

"Noted and logged, Sergeant. Oh, by the way." Riker started targeting the flying diamonds again. "You didn't have to lie for me to Wendy."

"I know, sir. On the other hand, I'm rather experienced with laying down covering fire. Just consider it all part of the service."

"Well . . . it's appreciated. I didn't exactly know how to tell her about Deanna . . . especially when I'm not even sure if there's anything to tell."

"No problem, Lieutenant."

"I haven't even seen her in close to a week. Maybe I should head over to the university where she's got classes . . ."

Tang shook his head violently, although it did nothing to spoil his shot. "Big mistake, sir. Very big mistake. Keep in mind that she hasn't heard from you either. Now either that's weighing on her mind, in which case you should just let it simmer until she can't stand it anymore, or else she's not thinking about you at all, in which case you certainly don't need her. But you go pursuing her, you're giving her the strategic advantage. Not a good maneuver at all."

"You make it sound like a military campaign."

Tang looked at him. "Well, sir . . . they *do* call it the war of the sexes. Wars are wars. Strategies are strategies. And winning"—Tang fired again, in rapid succession, and this time nailed both floating diamonds dead center, disengaging them. They clattered to the floor—"is what counts."

"Winning isn't everything, Sergeant."

"Winning isn't everything, sir . . . but losing isn't anything."

Riker tried to come up with a response to that, but couldn't. "That's true, I suppose."

"Can't claim credit for it, sir. I was told a twentieth-century philosopher came up with that. They sure knew their stuff back then."

"What philosopher?"

Tang paused and frowned. "Can't say I rec—wait. I do remember. His name was Charlie Brown."

Riker considered it and nodded. "This Charlie Brown must have been a very wise man."

"I expect he was, sir. I expect he was."

Twenty-one

Mark Roper was chuckling. "So when do I get my two hundred credits?"

They were seated across from each other at the café, where meeting for breakfast had evolved into a morning ritual. Riker looked up at Roper innocently while buttering a piece of rye toast. "What do you mean?"

"The two hundred credits you owe me over the bet about Deanna."

"I've got considerably more time on that, don't you think, Mark?" said Riker evenly.

"Time?" Roper laughed. "Captain, time doesn't make any difference. She's cut ties with you. Now or doomsday won't make any difference. It's not going to happen. Lwaxana told me—"

"She told you what?" demanded Riker, his eyes turning keen and a bit angry. "When did you speak to her?"

"Casual conversation a week or so ago."

"Why didn't you tell me?" He crunched down on the toast.

"I *am* telling you. Frankly, you weren't even the topic of conversation. We were comparing notes about the difficulties of raising daughters. And Lwaxana was boasting about how Deanna listens to, and does, everything Lwaxana tells her to do because she has Deanna so well trained in her responsibilities as a daughter of the Fifth House. And an example she gave was how she shut down the relationship between Deanna and 'that Starfleet fellow' because it wasn't appropriate."

"Oh, she did," said Riker icily. "Odd. That's not how I see it."

"I don't imagine you would see it that way," was Roper's calm response. He speared a piece of egg and said, "But then again . . . I suppose how *you* see it doesn't matter all that much, does it, Captain?"

Riker looked daggers at Roper, but the older man was the picture of tranquillity. And why shouldn't he be? As far as he was concerned, he'd won a two-hundred-credit bet.

But Riker saw it a bit differently.

The problem was, Sergeant Tang had made a valid point. Running in pursuit of Deanna, making calls to the mansion, trying to start things up when she was clearly so intimidated by her mother . . . it didn't sound like a pleasant experience. The question was, which was the potentially more humiliating? Throwing himself at Deanna? Or losing the bet?

He kept hearing Tang's voice in his head, warning him about strategy. Warning him . . .

. . . his voice in his head.

That's when it hit him.

The next day, after an early-morning meeting with Tang to review the latest Starfleet reports about raider activity, Riker headed over to the university. He staked out a place for himself, seated on the edge of a large, ornate sculpture in the middle of the campus. And he simply waited. Sooner or later, Deanna was going to have to pass by.

He spent half a day there, watching the sun pass over in the sky, watching the shadows shift position. They were simple, meaningless things. But he stared at them, focused on them, practicing. And as he did so, he slowed down his breathing, drawing out each breath. In through the nose, out through the mouth.

He did so with more than just an interest in finding his calm, inner self. He had a purpose, a drive to his actions. He used the urgency and determination to focus his thoughts, focus everything he did.

He had completely lost track of time, but something made him look up.

There she was.

She was walking across the campus, chatting with a couple of friends. She was laughing at something, and for a flash of an unreasonable instant, Riker felt tremendous resentment. Why should she be cheerful when he was feeling so much mental clutter?

But that wasn't what this was about. He couldn't submit to that clutter; he had to brush away the confusion, concentrate fully on the matter at hand.

He didn't look at her. Instead he was staring at the lengthening shadows, once again performing the steady in-and-out breathing. He reached down into himself, down into that determination that fueled the drive of his career. Except now that core of energy was going to fuel something else.

He felt it welling up inside him, felt—or at least hoped he felt—the ability, the potential, there for him to tap. And now he sought out Deanna.

There she was, her measured strides having taken her only a couple of meters beyond where she had been before. And she was looking his way. Apparently she had just noticed him, and she gently elbowed one of her girlfriends and nodded in Riker's direction. The other girl looked, too, and all three of them seemed to be sizing him up for a moment before putting their heads together and giggling.

And Riker took Deanna's image, took a mental snapshot, and imprinted it onto his mind. And then he cut loose in an undisciplined, inelegant burst.

You're afraid of me, he informed her.

The reward to his herculean effort was immediate. Deanna was thrown off-step, and her head snapped around in astonishment. She looked right at him, and on her face was utter shock.

To her credit, she recovered immediately. She fell back into step and made every effort to act as if nothing unusual had happened.

But Riker knew, dammit, *he knew.*

He tried to send again, but now his thoughts were cluttered, whirling and flushed with the excitement of his success. He couldn't pull himself together again fast enough—he hadn't developed nearly enough discipline.

He realized that he'd had the equivalent of beginner's luck. That didn't change the fact, though, that he had let Deanna know precisely what he was thinking. He had, in essence, thrown down the gauntlet right on her own turf of the mind.

She studiously looked away from him as she and her friends made their way across the campus. Deanna had, in fact, picked up the pace. It was clear to Riker why: she was concerned that he was going to come running after her.

However, he had no intention of doing that. In fact, when Deanna was almost out of sight, she risked a quick glance behind her. All she saw was Riker sitting precisely where he had been before, his legs crossed, looking like a smug Buddha.

Riker was sound asleep when an insistent rapping came at his door. He sat up in confusion, checking his chronometer. It was the middle of the night.

The first thought he had was that there was some sort of attack. He tossed the blanket around himself and ran to the door.

Deanna was standing there, her arms folded, her eyes bright.

"I am *not* afraid of you."

It took a moment for Riker to shift gears and realize that there was no danger from imminent alien assaults. Still, he composed himself quickly. "You could have fooled me."

"Obviously you're not all that difficult to fool. On what grounds do you say that I'm afraid of you?"

"On the grounds that you cut off all communication with me. On the grounds that you're steering clear of me."

"I cut off communication with you because, as far as I was concerned, I had better things to do with my time than devote it to someone who couldn't possibly understand the subtleties of our philosophies."

"Well, obviously I'm understanding something," he said, leaning against the doorframe, "because I projected thoughts to you."

"A fluke. Pure happenstance. Besides, you didn't do it for the satisfaction of opening up your mind. You did it so that you could get my attention; maybe even get back at me, in some crude way. As for steering clear of you, my presence here should be enough to show how ridiculous that is. On what grounds can you—?"

"On the grounds," Riker interrupted remorselessly, "that every time you're close to me you start to lose control. Your body starts sending you signals that your brain doesn't want to accept. Face it, Deanna . . . I'm upsetting your nice little intellectual applecart."

Her gaze was steady and unrelenting. "Get dressed."

"Where are we going?"

"Out."

"Where? Why should I go with you if you won't tell me where it is we're going."

She looked at him defiantly. "What's the matter, Lieutenant, afraid of me?"

"All right," he said after a moment. "Give me a couple of minutes."

"Take all the time you want."

It was a fairly warm night. Where Deanna stood, she was framed in the moonlight reflecting off a large lake, providing some degree of illumination. Her arms were crossed as if she were cold.

Riker stood behind her, waiting patiently. "Lovely area," he said tentatively. "You come here often?"

"Yes." She sounded distracted. "From time to time."

"It's pretty remote."

"That's deliberate."

They were at the edge of a forest. Riker glanced up at the trees with their outstretched branches, like fingers that wanted to drag him into the darkness of the woods. "So now what? We hang from branches some more?"

She turned to face him. "Take your clothes off."

He stared at her. "I beg your pardon?"

"It's a therapy technique I learned in class a couple of days ago. Take your clothes off. All of them."

He grinned lopsidedly. "Okay. What's the joke? One of your girlfriends hiding in the woods here? I get naked, you guys grab my clothes and run off. I have to make my way back to town, show up at the door of the embassy, and explain why I'm seriously out of uniform. Big laugh on the human. Right?"

Deanna gave a loud sigh and reached back around to the back of her tunic, undoing some fastenings. Within seconds she stood naked in front of Riker and tossed her outfit to him. It landed in a small bundle at his feet.

"Take your clothes off."

Riker did so.

They stood nude in the moonlight, facing each other, and then Deanna walked toward him. Riker's body was trembling inwardly, but he tried not to show it.

"Lie down." Her voice was firm, but Riker wondered if she was just as nervous inside as he was.

Now why in hell was he nervous? It certainly wasn't as if she were his first.

Deanna saw him standing there, unmoving. "If you want, and if you still think this is some sort of prank, you can keep your hands on your uniform so no 'accomplice' can grab it."

Slowly Riker lay down on the ground.

"On your side. Your back towards me."

Completely puzzled, Riker did as she asked. He tucked his legs up slightly, looking slightly fetal and feeling slightly foolish.

He heard motion behind him and then Deanna was lying next to him. She curled up against him in the manner that humans still called spoons, for the way that spoons fit together when stacked. She slid one arm under him and brought the other over, wrapping herself around him.

He felt her chin against his shoulder, and that particular connection was easily the least incendiary that occurred to him. The rest of her front was pressed against his back, and his pulse and mind were racing. She felt incredibly warm against him. Every muscle was aching; he felt as if his entire body had too much blood in it . . . that it didn't know where to go, and any moment he was going to explode out every pore.

"Now," she said softly, "we're going to talk."

His voice was strangled. "T-talk?"

"Yes. You see . . . you still have to develop mental discipline. You still have to learn control. You have to be able to deal with me without thinking about me on a physical level."

"And *this* is supposed to make me stop thinking about you physically!" He wanted to flip over and face her, to grab her, to turn her over and—

"That's right." She sounded inhumanly calm. "We are going to chat about whatever you want and just stay like this. You are going to become comfortable with the notion of my sexuality and yours, and that way you'll be able to move beyond it to more spiritual matters."

"I can—" But his voice had gone up an octave. He cleared his throat, trying to ignore the horses galloping through his brain, and started over. "I can think of a far better way to get comfortable with sexuality—and it'll be a lot more fun than the way I'm feeling right now."

"How are you feeling right now?"

"My body hurts, and I want to bay at the moons."

To his surprise, this actually prompted a soft laugh. But then she said, "To give in to those impulses, Will, only undercuts everything I've said. The desires of the body must be secondary to the desires of the mind."

Riker was ready to kill her. "Why in hell are you doing this?" he grated. "Why are you making me feel like I want to jump out of my skin? I mean, obviously it has no effect on you, but it's making me crazy!"

She said something so softly that he didn't hear it at all. "What?"

"I said," she repeated, not without effort, "that it is definitely having an effect on me."

"It is? What . . . um . . . what sort?"

One of her hands moved across his chest, and she said, sounding somewhat frustrated, "Well, now, what do *you* think?"

Doing the best he could to control his voice and keep the tremble out of it, he said, "Deanna . . . if both of us are feeling this way . . . then maybe it would make sense if we . . . ?"

"Will." For the first time she actually sounded pleading. "Will, I can't. Don't you see? First and foremost, two people have to connect on an intellectual and spiritual level. If they make love purely because of the physical attraction, then it's just . . . just a sex act. It would be a mistake."

"Deanna . . . how could giving in to what we both want be a mistake?"

"I don't want to, Will."

"But you said . . . ?"

"I don't want to give in to the impulses that I'm feeling. How can you not understand? It would undercut everything that I believe in. I don't feel a connection to you on a spiritual level. I don't feel *comfortable* with you. I can't just give myself over, I . . ."

"You're afraid of me." This time when he said it, there was no challenge in his voice, no mockery. This time he said it and there was . . . sympathy? Understanding? He wasn't sure what it was, but all he knew was that he wanted to comfort her. He wanted her to feel better.

He held her arms tightly against himself, and there was nothing sexual about it. It was as if he were trying to send some of his strength into her.

"A little," she said in a voice so small he had to strain to hear it. "I feel a little afraid. When you live by a certain philosophy, and then you meet someone who disrupts that philosophy . . ." She paused a moment. "It goes back to what we were talking about . . . about love at first sight. I can accept love at first sight. I can accept lust at first sight. But the latter is something I don't feel I want to be a part of."

"There's something to be said for just giving yourself over to the pleasure of the moment."

"I'm sure you'd be the expert on that, Will."

They were silent for a long time after that. He still felt the heat from her, and the slow in and out of her breathing. But it wasn't affecting him quite the same way.

"So . . . so what do we do now?" he asked.

"We talk."

"About what?"

"About anything you want . . . anything except sex. The whole point of this is—"

"To rise above the impulses of our bodies. Yeah, I know." He thought about it a moment. "Okay. Okay, I've got something to talk about."

"What?" She sounded almost eager.

He tried to ignore the musical way her voice seemed to float, and the soft feel of her breath against the back of his ear. "This stuff I was reading about Betazed philosophy . . . the one you recommended to me."

"Yes?"

"I don't get it."

"What don't you get?"

"Well, for instance . . . there was this example about a woman being criticized unduly by her supervisor. And she comes and tells me about it."

"Yes, I know the scenario. And let me guess: you came up with ways to solve her problem."

"Right."

"And the text informed you this was the wrong approach."

"Right."

"And you don't know why."

"Right. So what can possibly be wrong about wanting to solve her problem, instead of just moaning and wailing about it."

"There's nothing wrong with it, if that's what she wanted. But that's not what she wanted. The problem is that you're insensitive to her desires."

"Insensitive?" Riker propped himself up on his elbow. "How was I being insensitive? I listened to her difficulties and tried to make her life better for her."

"She wasn't asking you to do that."

"But if she—look, let's make up a name for her . . . 'Jane' . . ."

"Catchy name," said Deanna dryly.

"If Jane came to me with her problem, obviously she was coming for help in solving it. That's a given."

"No, it's not."

"Yes it is," he insisted. "Look . . . if a technician goes to the chief engineer and says there's trouble with the warp core, the chief engineer isn't going to say, 'Oh, what a shame, that's too bad, I know how difficult this must be for you.' He's going to say, 'We've got to get that fixed!' A busted engine, an abusive boss . . . it all boils down to the same thing. Namely, a bad situation that needs to be repaired."

"You're missing the point, Will."

"No, I'm not missing the point." He turned over to face her. Their bodies were now pressed up against each other, flesh to flesh. And incredibly, Riker wasn't paying attention. "You're just being obstinate."

"And you're in command mode, Will. The universe isn't Starfleet. Emotions aren't regulated. And Jane, as you call her, wasn't looking for you to solve the problem."

"Then why in hell did she come to me!" demanded Riker.

"She came to you because she was looking for emotional support," said Deanna patiently. "She knew she had a problem. She knew it had to be solved; or perhaps she wasn't going to solve it but simply live with it. Either way, though, she had to deal with it in her own way because *it was her problem.* What Jane was looking for from you was an augmentation of her emotional strength. She needed you to say that you were sympathetic to her difficulties and were supportive of her. This is the philosophy of RaBeem, which, simply translated, means 'I understand.' An even better way to handle it is to tell her of a time when you faced a similar situation—"

"And describe how I solved it?"

"And describe how it *made you feel.* So she knows that whatever frustration and embarrassment she might be encountering is not unique to her. When you're unhappy or discouraged, it's very easy to believe that you're the only person in the world who has ever felt this way. Teenagers experience that feeling most sharply, but adults do also. And what Jane was simply looking for was a sense that she was not alone."

"But . . . but then how does the problem get solved?"

"It gets solved by her, in whatever manner she chooses. And she's also looking to you to say that whatever she does, you will support her because it's the action that she has decided to take."

"I'm still not sure I get it."

"Oh, you're starting to." Deanna smiled. "You just haven't admitted it."

"What you're saying is that I'm faced with a problem and I shouldn't make the slightest effort to solve it."

"That's not such a bizarre notion for you to have to deal with, Will. Isn't that what the Prime Directive is all about?"

"Not at all. We talked about that, it's completely different."

"Only in scope, not in practice. Just because the problem involves a close friend rather than a civilization of strangers, it doesn't make the theory any less valid."

He was about to reply but realized that he couldn't think of anything to say.

Smiling sympathetically, she ran the back of her fingers across his face. "I know it's difficult for you, Will. Your impulse is to take command. It's what you were trained for. It's what you long to do. But command isn't the be-all and end-all of life."

"It is to me. I hope that doesn't sound egotistical, but . . . it's all I want to do. It's what I'm aiming for. I want to beat Kirk's record."

She frowned politely. "Pardon?"

"Youngest starship commander in Starfleet history. That's my goal. I want my own command . . . and I guess my mind-set sometimes shapes all of that, and makes me . . ."

"Want to command every situation? Every person you meet?"

He saw the slightly mocking way she raised her eyebrow. "Not exactly . . . but maybe a little," he admitted.

"Well, who knows? Someday you might find yourself in a situation where you find that you enjoy following someone more than you would commanding."

"Never happen. Every person I serve under is just a means of learning more and more so I can have my own command."

"You can't see yourself serving with someone simply for the sheer joy of serving with them? Or with the others on board the ship?"

"Never happen. No matter how much I liked the ship or crew, if I was then offered my own command, I'd be out of there in a heartbeat. Trust me on this." Then he paused. "You probably don't understand."

"You're wrong, Will. I do understand. I may not agree. But I understand. So," she said after a moment's thought, "tell me what other things about Betazoid philosophy puzzle you."

And they remained that way, naked, wrapped around each other, talking. Just talking, until the early-morning hours, when the first rays of the sun stole across the treetops. They dressed, Riker feeling extremely self-conscious, Troi feeling . . . he didn't know how she felt.

"Thank you for an . . . interesting evening," he said.

"I think we've made some progress."

"When can we get together again?"

"Why do you want to get together again?"

"I . . . well . . ." He smiled. "A lot of reasons."

"In that case, I think we've made even more progress than I thought," said Deanna teasingly. "I'll be in touch with you, Will." And she turned and walked off.

When she snuck into the mansion, Lwaxana was waiting for her.

Her mother was standing there, hands on hips, lips thinned virtually to nonexistence. "Would you mind telling me where you were?"

Deanna looked downward. "Yes, I would."

"Deanna, we've never kept things from each other."

"Not quite, Mother. I've never kept anything from you. I've never had much choice."

Lwaxana pointed to the stairs. "Go up to your room, Little One. We'll speak of this later . . . maybe."

"Mother, I'd rather—"

"I don't care!" Lwaxana's voice was filled with more fury than Deanna had

ever heard, and it occurred to the young Betazoid that now would probably not be the best time to discuss matters in more detail . . . particularly considering the details.

Nevertheless, though, she felt she had to say something.

"Mother," she said very quietly, "don't you trust me?"

The muscles under Lwaxana's face worked for a moment, flexing and unflexing. And then, softly, she said, "Of course I trust you, Little One."

"Well, then . . . ?"

"It's others that I don't trust. Deanna"—she took her daughter's face in her hands—"you have a purpose in life. A higher purpose. And I distrust anyone and anything that seems as if it will dissuade you from that purpose."

"But don't I owe an obligation to myself to—"

"Your obligations," said Lwaxana sadly, "are far greater than those to yourself. You have history to protect. You have tradition to uphold. People who died years, even centuries ago did so with a sense of comfort. Even completion. Because they knew that they were part of a larger tapestry; that they were part of something greater than themselves. It is not easy, Deanna, to sublimate your interests and desires to those long gone and those to come. But the happenstance of your birth and lineage means that you owe it, not only to those who preceded you, but to those who will follow. Please, Deanna . . . tell me that you won't let me down."

In her face was more of a pleading expression than Deanna had ever seen. At that moment, as they had so often before, her own interests and willpower wilted before the needs and demands of the woman who had so shaped her life.

"Of course, Mother. I won't let you down."

"Are you certain?"

"Yes."

Lwaxana drew herself up, almost looking embarrassed about her heartfelt plea. "Well . . . that's . . . that's good to hear. Um . . . it's early, but . . . how would some hot chocolate sound to you about now?"

Deanna had to smile at that. Chocolate was one of the few tangible reminders—aside from Deanna's presence, of course—of her father. He had absolutely adored chocolate, and it was a craving that he had imprinted on his wife and, apparently, passed on to his daughter. She licked her lips at the thought and said, "That would be wonderful . . . but I wouldn't want you to go to any trouble."

"Oh!" Lwaxana waved dismissively. "It won't be any trouble at all." She turned, cupped her mouth, and bellowed in a voice that shook the rafters, *"Homn! Wake up! Deanna wants some hot chocolate!"*

"Mother! I thought you were—" And then she saw Lwaxana's stunned expression and amended, *"I* could have made it."

"Oh, nonsense. A daughter of the Fifth House? What an absurd notion."

"But why did you have to yell?"

"Because Mr. Homn has an annoying habit of sleeping through my thought-castings. Amazing. The only other person I ever met who could do that was your father."

Mr. Homn appeared moments later. To Deanna's surprise, the towering manservant was fully dressed. She wondered if he was simply a fast dresser, or whether he just slept that way in the event that Lwaxana needed him for something. Actually, for all she knew, he never slept. Certainly life with Lwaxana would seem to preclude the opportunities for such mundane activities.

"Deanna wants some hot chocolate," Lwaxana informed him.

Mr. Homn looked at Deanna impassively, and Deanna gestured in a manner that silently said, *I'm sorry about all this.* Homn merely inclined his head slightly and headed off toward the kitchen.

"Now you see, Little One?" said Lwaxana, looping her arm through Deanna's. "There are still some people who know how to give proper respect to those who are entitled to it. I suggest that you keep that in mind . . . particularly in the way that it applies to Lieutenant Riker."

Deanna looked at her nervously. "You're not going to contact Starfleet, are you? We're just friends, Mother."

"Just friends because of your actions, my dear, not his. But no . . . I doubt I'll really speak to Starfleet about him. After all, Little One"—Lwaxana patted Deanna's cheek—"you do want me to trust you, don't you?"

Twenty-two

Breakfasting at their customary café, Riker and Roper looked up in surprise when Gart Xerx appeared next to them. "So here's where you're hiding, Roper," he said in mock annoyance to the Federation ambassador.

Roper shrugged. "This is where I am every morning. Ask Mr. Riker here."

"He is," said Riker solemnly. "I can vouch for him."

"Although actually," said Roper, putting his napkin down, "I hate to say this, but I have to cut our usual morning ritual short. I have an early meeting this morning."

He started to rise, and Riker automatically started to put his own food aside, even though he hadn't finished it. But Roper quickly stopped him. "Just because I have to abort breakfast, Captain, doesn't mean you do. Stay. Chat with our great friend Xerx."

"Great friend," said Xerx with an exaggerated *harrumph.* "Didn't come to my daughter's wedding weeks ago."

Roper shrugged. "My daughter and the captain here attended on my behalf. And I did send a lovely gift, didn't I?"

"Quite true," said Xerx diplomatically.

"So there you are then," said Roper with satisfaction. He gestured to the now empty chair. "Sit. Order something and charge it to me."

"As you wish, Mark." Xerx sat and then waited patiently until Roper departed. "He'll regret that," Xerx told Riker.

"Why?"

A moment later, the waitress walked up with a steaming plate of food and placed it in front of Xerx. Riker stared at it and said, "That's the most expensive thing on the menu."

"Yes, I know," said Xerx cheerily. "Want some?"

"No thanks."

Xerx looked at him quizzically. "By the way . . . 'captain'? I thought you were a lieutenant?"

"That's right. It's a . . . well, a sort of running joke between myself and Mark."

"Yes. He does have a peculiar sense of humor."

"So," said Riker, taking a sip of coffee before continuing, "how is your daughter doing?"

"You know how it is with young marrieds," said Xerx with a small laugh. "They live in a world of their own making. At the moment they're still doting on virtually everything that the other one does. The way each of them walks, talks, breathes. We had them over the other night, and it was amusing to see how Chandra simply sat and adored the way her new husband chewed his food."

"Chewed his food?"

"Newlyweds. What can I say?" Xerx shrugged, and then his eyes narrowed slightly. "And how goes it with you and young Miss Troi?"

Riker raised an eyebrow. "Reading my mind, Gart?"

"Merely enough to confirm what I already knew. I noticed the way you were staring at her at the wedding and reception. And I also know that you've been seeing her socially. I've overheard Deanna and her friends discussing it at the university."

"What were you doing at the university, if you don't mind my asking?"

Xerx took another forkful of food. "I'm a professor of psychology. Where else would I be?"

"Oh. I didn't know that."

"Somehow it never came up. I even have Deanna in one of my classes."

"Is it the class where they teach about nude therapy?"

Xerx stared at him. Gart had been about to eat another forkful, but now it remained suspended several inches from his mouth. "I beg your pardon?"

"I'd heard there was this . . . technique . . . where a patient and his or her therapist take off their clothes and lie next to each other . . . even . . ." He cleared his throat. "Even pressing up against each other."

"I'd think that would probably lead to sex," said Xerx, looking amused.

"Well, no. It's done in order to move past physical considerations and deal with each other in a purely intellectual manner. But . . . why am I explaining this to you? I mean, certainly you know about . . . ?"

Xerx was trying not to laugh. "Lieutenant . . . I've been teaching, and practicing, psychology for going on thirty years now. And I can assure you I've *never* heard of any 'technique' that has therapist and patient removing their clothes and lying against each other . . . except in those cases specifically involving sexual dysfunctions and therapy for those dysfunctions. Was this a case involving dysfunctions?"

"N-no," stammered Riker, looking utterly befuddled.

"In that case," said Xerx, spreading his hands, "I would see little purpose for that sort of contact beyond the obvious gratification." Then he leaned forward. "Who told you about this 'technique'?"

"No one," said Riker quickly. "I just . . . just heard it around."

"Well, it sounds to me as if such actions would be extremely pleasurable, but other than that, I wouldn't attach much psychological value to them."

Riker sat back in his chair, and then a slow grin spread across his face.

"Lieutenant, is there something you'd care to discuss with me?"

"No," replied Riker, unable to wipe the smile off his face. "No, nothing at all. I just find the entire thing . . . funny."

"I see."

At that moment, Riker's communicator beeped. He was mildly startled. Whereas the page was certainly common enough on board a ship, here in the more leisurely surroundings of Betazed, it was extremely unusual. So much so, in fact, that Riker had a dim sense of worry even as he reached up to tap it. "Riker here."

"Lieutenant, this is Tang," came the sergeant's voice.

"What is it, T—"

Tang didn't even give Riker a chance to get out the entire question. "Planetary sensors detect incoming ship moving extremely quickly, ignoring all attempts at hailing it. General shape would indicate Sindareen origins."

Immediately Riker was on his feet. "Planetary defense systems—"

"Too late, Lieutenant. These Betazoids are so damn peaceful, they hardly have anything anyway. And what they do have is too little, too late."

Xerx was looking up at Riker with tremendous worry reflected in his eyes, but Riker had no time to try to quell fears. "Scramble the squad."

"Already done."

"And track the vessel's likely destination, based on trajectory."

"Already done, sir. Our calculations have them making planetfall right in the heart of this city."

Riker was ecstatic. "Right where we'll be waiting for them. Their overconfidence is their first and last mistake. I'll be right there. Riker out."

All in the café were now looking at Riker with tremendous worry on their faces. Even though no one was saying anything, he could almost sense the anxiety level skyrocketing. He started to head for the door, but for a moment, Xerx stopped him.

"An open area makes them easy targets," said Xerx. "But densely populated as we are here, means that you have to worry about innocents. Don't let your determination to capture your targets be *your* first and last mistake."

Riker regarded him for a moment, then nodded briefly.

"Understood," he said, and then ran out of the café.

Twenty-three

Deanna and Chandra stared at the painting. They had stared at this particular painting once a week, every week, for the last ten years. Every time they did, they saw something new . . . although whether it was something new in the painting or in themselves, neither of them could have said for sure.

Deanna crisscrossed her arms and ran her hands up and down as if to shake off a chill. Chandra noticed the gesture and said, "Are you okay?"

"I'm fine. I just . . ."

Her voice trailed off, and gently Chandra said, "It's that Riker, isn't it? The one from the wedding."

Deanna nodded hesitantly.

Chandra turned away from the painting. "What is it about him, anyway?"

"I don't know. He's not at all like any of the men I . . . I mean, he's so *un*intellectual."

"You mean he's stupid?"

"No! No, not at all. He's very bright. Very quick. Very intelligent, really. He's just so . . ." She tried to think of the best way to put it. "So primal. His actions seem governed as much by instinct as any sort of rational thought."

"What's wrong with that? There are few things in the world more natural than instinct. When I met Teb," Chandra continued, referring to her new husband, "there was a sort of instinctive attraction."

"But at least you two were compatible. Riker and I, we're . . ."

"You're what?"

Deanna shivered slightly again. "Every single bit of rational thought tells me that Will Riker is completely wrong for me."

"And your irrational thought?"

"My irrational thought," she admitted, "makes my skin tingle."

"Well!" Chandra smirked. "And what does your mother say to that?"

"Ohhhh, don't ask. You think *I* have trepidation about him? He's not at *all* the type of man my mother wants me with. No social standing. No ties to Betazed or Betazoid society. No . . ."

And suddenly her voice trailed off, and her dark eyes went wide. Her face took on the color of paste.

"Deanna," said Chandra in alarm. "What's the matter with . . . ?"

Then she sensed it, too. "Oh, Gods," she muttered.

Deanna grabbed her arm and grated, *"Come on!* Let's get *out* of here! Before we—"

Other Betazoids were reacting as well. They were already in motion in response to the strong and frightened thoughts that were affecting the crowd to various degrees.

But their actions weren't fast enough.

All over the gallery, doors burst inward. At one end, a powerful ray blast blew in a chunk of the wall. The hurtling fragments flattened a man, pinning him writhing on the ground.

Sindareen warriors entered, dressed in glittering armor, cradling pulse blasters under their arms. One of them fired in the air, and the deafening noise froze a number of people in their tracks.

Deanna and Chandra spun and dashed toward one exit that remained clear. They were several steps short of it when it slid open, and the open space seemed to be completely filled with a massive and extremely formidable-looking Sindareen.

His lips pulled back, and his entire face was cast in a death's-head glow. He leveled his weapon at the two women and said, in a deceptively pleasant voice, "Step back."

Chandra whimpered slightly as Deanna guided her back. In a low voice Deanna advised, "Don't show them you're afraid." She was no less frightened, but she found it easier to ignore her fear by focusing on calming her friend.

She sensed the terror running rampant through the mind of her friend. Newly married, her main concern was that she was never going to see her husband again. Deanna, for her part, hadn't taken it quite that far; she hadn't really accepted the notion that she might die here, pointlessly and unexpectedly. Her main concern was survival.

As the Sindareen prodded and herded the thirty-plus Betazoids together into a small circle in the middle of the room, Deanna's mind was racing with thoughts of rescue. She was certain that the Sindareen's presence here could not possibly have gone undetected. She knew that, even now, steps were certainly being taken to rescue them.

And somehow, beyond any shadow of doubt, she knew that it would be Lt. William T. Riker who would be spearheading that rescue operation. For no rational reason, she derived great comfort from that, and a certainty that everything would work out.

She felt that way up to the point where the barrel of one of the Sindareen blasters was shoved into her mouth.

"What have we got?"

Riker was standing next to Tang, about a hundred yards away from the art building. Betazoids were trying to get near, sensing as one the terror emanating from the building and instinctively wanting to help and soothe those who were trapped within. But Tang had ordered his people to keep everyone back, and they were busy shooing the concerned citizens away from the immediate area. Tang was stroking his perpetually grizzled chin.

"There's the ship they came in." Tang pointed. Sure enough, situated on top of the building was a small Sindareen vessel, of the style commonly called a Spider, so nicknamed for its odd sectional style and eight leglike extensions.

"Can you pick it off from here? Disable it?"

Tang studied Riker for a moment and said, "Yes. Do you want us to?"

Riker pondered that. "No. It wouldn't be a good idea. Then they'll be trapped, and desperate. The first thing we have to do is secure the safety of whoever's inside."

Tang nodded briskly and Riker realized that the veteran spacer had already come to the same conclusion. For some reason, Riker felt a brief flash of pride. But his mind was already racing ahead. "Who's your communications expert?"

"Hirsch," said Tang, and before Riker could say anything further, Tang tapped his communicator and said, "Hirsch—haul your butt over here."

Riker studied the building as they waited for Hirsch to show up. "Do we know how many people are in there?"

"Not for certain, sir. Some people on the lower floors managed to get out. One of the more sensitive mind-types said she detected about thirty or so locals, and about nine Sindareen—which would be consistent with the known crew complement of ten for a Spider."

Hirsch, a stocky brunette woman, ran up to them. She was cradling a small phaser rifle, but also had with her a portable comm unit. Of greater power and range than the standard portable communicators, it was also capable of more functions.

"Yes, Sergeant?"

Tang merely pointed to Riker, and she turned to face him, waiting.

"I want to talk to the Sindareen," said Riker. "The odds are that they left someone behind in the ship with whom they're in communication, to be their eyes and ears outside."

"You want me to find the frequency they're talking on and break in so you can come on?"

"That's right. Keep in mind their communications might be scrambled."

Hirsch's contemptuous expression showed precisely what she thought of Sindareen scrambling capabilities. "No disrespect, Lieutenant, but I thought you were going to give me something hard to do." She dropped down to one knee, removing the large comm unit from her equipment pack and studying the frequencies registering over it. Her fingers flew over the touch padds.

"Got it, Lieutenant," she announced after less than thirty seconds. "Just need a few more moments to unscramble." She smirked. "Apparently they think we can't do it."

"Enlighten them, Hirsch," said Riker, "as to the error of their ways."

The Sindareen who had cut off Deanna and Chandra's escape was apparently the leader of the group. As was mostly the case with the Sindareen, his hair was tightly swept back and coal black. His skin was pale, virtually to the point of the chalk white shade of an albino. Although he possessed a mouth, it existed exclusively for eating. Speech issued from the nictating membranes on his long throat.

"Baytzah!" he snapped to others of his group. "Zroah! What are you standing around for? Charoset, you and Chazeret get to the other room and clear that out. And you others—move! We don't have all day!"

The Sindareen were moving through the great museum, carrying with them large cases. They hurriedly pulled paintings off the wall, shoved glittering sculptures into the cases. Each action was greeted by gasps and audible protestations by the Betazoids—which were quickly silenced by the leader's subtle movement of his weapon in the direction of the prisoners.

"My dear Betazoids," he said, sounding unexpectedly reasonable. "I am called Maror. If you would be so kind as to cooperate, we can do this briskly and without serious difficulty for any of you."

"But why!"

The uncontrolled outburst had originated from Deanna, who had said it without thinking. Chandra tried to pull her back into the relative obscurity of the crowd, but it was too late. She had attracted Maror's attention. Somehow, though, surviving the emotional trauma of being shoved, courtesy of a blaster in her mouth, had emboldened her.

Maror's gaze wandered along the lines of her body in a manner that made Deanna suddenly feel dirty. She derived the feeling purely from the surface, however. She found that she couldn't get an empathic lock on any of them, which was unusual and frustrating for her. The uncontrolled, and unwise, question had been a manifestation of that small but aggravating defeat.

"But why what?" asked Maror. Behind him the rest of his men continued with their task. "Why should you not interfere with our little procedure?"

Deanna, keep quiet! Chandra's voice rang in Deanna's head. But she knew that wasn't possible. Her outburst had already attracted the Sindareen's attention. Besides . . . some part of her genuinely wanted to understand what in the world could be motivating these beings into these destructive acts.

She called on the image of her mother, who had never seemed intimidated by any situation. She squared her shoulders and firming up her voice, demanded, "Why are you stealing our art treasures? They can't hold any meaning for you. They're works that spring from the hearts and minds of Betazoid artists."

Maror made a noise that must have been the Sindareen equivalent of laughter—it was a more rapid fluttering of the membranes, unaccompanied by any noise other than the flapping sound. "Are you really under the impression," he asked when he had recovered himself, "that we are going to sit around and look at the pretty pictures? Don't be ridiculous. What we have is a client who is a very avid collector, with a taste for one-of-a-kind pieces. And he is very wealthy, and very willing to pay whatever it takes to obtain those things that have struck his fancy.

You should be flattered that your work has attracted his attention—he's very discriminating."

And now whatever fears Deanna might have had were overwhelmed by a fundamental sense of indignation. "You would deprive a people of their cultural heritage just to satisfy the greed of an individual? What sort of beings *are* you?"

His mouth turned up slightly as he replied, "Entrepreneurs." Then he stepped back, clearly ending the discussion, or at least his interest in it. He tapped his wrist comm unit and said, "Karpas. Report."

Over the comm unit came back a voice, saying, "There's a fairly large assemblage on the street. Typical bunch of Betazoids—everyone standing around, trying to understand how everyone else feels about the situation, and nobody doing anything about it."

"Yes, that *is* typical," grunted Maror. "Anything else?"

"Yeah. What appears to be a squad of Starfleet security men. Apparently they're taking charge of the situation."

"Let them. I know their regs. As long as we've got the hostages in here, they won't dare make a move against us. Keep the engines primed. I estimate we have another three to four—"

But before Maror could complete the instruction, another voice broke in on the comm unit. "Attention, Sindareen raiders. You are completely surrounded and cannot escape. Surrender is your only alternative."

Deanna's dark eyes widened and she looked at Chandra, who immediately knew what was going through Deanna's mind. For the briefest of moments, Deanna wanted to shout out, "Will! I'm trapped in here with them! Do something!" But fortunately, and wisely, she held her tongue. Riker certainly did not need personal involvement dragged into the middle of all this.

Maror, for his part, bubbled in fury. "Who is this!" he demanded.

"Lieutenant Riker, of Starfleet," came the stern reply. "Who is this?"

"Maror of the Sindareen. So tell me, Starfleet man . . . where's your ship? We didn't see it coming in, and there's none within light-years of here. We checked."

"A ship isn't necessary to deal with this situation."

"You flatter me," said Maror sarcastically.

"No. I warn you. I have an entire squad of men, with more on the way. The entire area has been sealed off. You cannot escape. If you surrender now, your cooperation will be noted."

" 'Noted.' How nice. That will make a lovely tombstone: 'Here lies Maror. He cooperated.' I think I'll take my chances, Lieutenant, thank you. Now if *you're* interested in taking chances, then I invite you to try and impede our departure." Then Maror's voice grew cold and harsh. "And you can explain the three dozen Betazoid corpses to your superiors! Do we understand each other, Lieutenant?"

Riker's reply was firm and unyielding. "You will not escape."

"You will not stop me," shot back Maror. "Now get off my comm unit."

"We are scrambling your transmissions. You will not be able to communicate with your ship for as long as you refuse to cooperate."

"Oh, really." Without hesitation, Maror swung his weapon around and squeezed off a shot.

The blast struck Chandra in the upper thigh. She went down with a shriek that echoed throughout the museum and certainly was audible over the comm unit.

Deanna dropped to the floor with her, Chandra clutching her leg and whimpering. An ugly carbon-scored gash was across her thigh.

"Did you hear that?" demanded Maror. "I could have killed her just then! That is the extent of the cooperation you'll have from me, Lieutenant! The next time I fire it's going to be at somebody's heart, and I assure you, Riker, I hit what I aim at! Now unclutter my transmission or somebody dies in the next ten seconds—and that's on your head, Lieutenant Riker. *Yours!*"

There was only the briefest of pauses before Riker's voice came back. "In the interest of cooperation, I'll put you back in touch with your ship. I anticipate you'll extend further good-faith courtesies in the future."

A moment later, Karpas's concerned voice was back on the air. "They're going to give us trouble, Maror! Did you hear what they—"

"Of course I heard, you idiot," snapped Maror. "And what's more, they're going to hear. Namely, they'll hear everything that's being said over this frequency. I don't need them eavesdropping! Maintain radio silence except in case of extreme emergency! Maror out!"

He lowered his comm unit and turned to the Betazoids. Deanna had ripped a length of cloth from her sleeve and wrapped it around the burn that was blistering the skin on Chandra's leg. She looked up at Maror with anger and defiance flashing in her eyes. Maror, for his part, looked utterly calm, and again Deanna met frustration in being unable to get any sort of feeling for what was going through his mind. Something in his psychological makeup—in the makeup of all of them, in fact—rendered them impervious to Deanna's empathy. Or at least, for the moment it did.

"Your rescuers," said Maror, "are only going to make matters worse for you. I suggest you pray to whatever gods you believe in that the Starfleet security and their noble lieutenant are less effective than they think they are. Because their effectiveness will be measured entirely in the number of deaths that arise because of them."

Twenty-four

Riker turned away from Hirsch and looked at Tang with frustration. "That could have gone better," Riker said.

"It could have gone worse," replied Tang. "At least nobody's dead."

"We have to determine what they want. What their demands are."

"No, we don't. We know what they want," said Tang reasonably. "It's whatever is in this building. We know what their demands are—they demand we let them get away with it. The only question becomes, do we let them?"

Riker's face was set. "No. We don't."

"Even if people die?"

"We try to avoid that at all costs," Riker said slowly. "But the bottom line is that if we let them get away, we simply invite them to continue their activities at the expense and lives of other innocent people. It has to stop here and now."

At that moment, Gart Xerx appeared at Riker's side, his huffing and puffing indicating that he had been running the entire way. "Sindareen raiders!" he gasped out.

Riker glanced at him and said, "Yes, sir, we know. We're handling this. Now if you'll just—"

"Chandra's in there!"

"What?" Riker turned back to him. "How do you . . ." And then he caught himself, remembering with whom he was dealing. "Yes, of course you'd know, wouldn't you. Is she all right?"

"She's been hurt. The bastard shot her in the leg."

Riker's face darkened, thinking of the sweet, eager bride he'd seen all those weeks back. "Is she all right?"

"As all right as can be expected, considering she's been shot," said Xerx evenly. Clearly he was trying to fight down the panic that threatened to overwhelm him. He was obviously searching for that place of central calm that Deanna had told Riker about. And then, almost as an afterthought, Xerx added, "Deanna's with her. She's bandaging the wound as best she can."

Riker tried not to show his reaction to this latest bit of information. In fact, instead of acknowledging the news, he merely said, "Good." But the way Xerx looked up at him spoke volumes to Riker; Xerx must have immediately intuited precisely what was going through Riker's mind, and what his true feelings about learning of Deanna's presence were.

Riker was determined to remain all business. "Can you communicate with her? Find out information?"

"What do you want to know?"

"Everything."

Deanna dabbed at the wound with the cloth, the bleeding having slowed down significantly. She looked up at Chandra, ready to offer some words of comfort, but she saw from Chandra's expression that her friend's mind was not on the trouble at hand. At first she assumed that Chandra had merely separated herself in order to spare herself the pain. But then she realized precisely what was going on: Chandra was communicating with someone outside. Chandra took a moment to glance at Deanna and nod slowly in confirmation.

Maror came up behind them and looked at them once before nodding brisk approval. "Good. No whimpering. Keeping things to yourself. That's what we like to see. You're making this much easier on all of us." Then he raised his comm unit to get a very brief assessment from Karpas as to the movements of the Federation personnel . . . brief since he was perfectly aware that Riker was doubtlessly monitoring every word.

"Precisely thirty-two of our people in there," said Xerx to Riker. He wasn't looking at Riker, but instead seemed to be staring off into thin air. "There are nine of the Sindareen. This Maror you spoke to is definitely the leader. They aren't threatening the hostages beyond telling them to keep out of trouble. They seem intent on stripping the museum of its works for the purpose of selling them to some private collector." Xerx shuddered slightly. "What a barbaric idea."

"Compared to some of the things I've heard about the Sindareen doing, that's positively civilized," replied Riker. "They're probably the only race in the galaxy that the Ferengii actually enjoy dealing with. All right, Gart . . . tell her that she should let us know the moment that the Sindareen start moving for their ship. Tang, I want your people deployed—"

"Already done, sir." Tang pointed to several different locations.

Riker looked around and smiled grimly. The security personnel gathered in the street served as a distraction. In the meantime, more of them had been deployed to strategic points in surrounding buildings, crouched on rooftops or poised in windows. They had phasers armed and targeted on the rooftop where the Spider perched like an oversize predator.

"Problem is," continued Tang, "the Sindareen may not look it, but they're pretty tough. Phaser blasts can stop them, but not on lower settings. Ranges that stun the Sindareen can severely injure, even kill other humanoids."

"Humanoids such as Betazoids," said Riker slowly.

"Right. Which means if they bring any of the hostages along as potential shields . . ."

"You'll have to work around it, Sergeant. Alert your marksmen to take extreme care. We're not going to lose these raiders, under any circumstances."

"Yes, sir. And just in case they do make it to their ship . . ." Tang gestured to one of his security team. He was lugging a large case, and he staggered over with it to Tang and placed it at his feet. Tang snapped it open and Riker saw within the case the formidable Level 10, shoulder-mounted phaser cannon, Model II. Tang hefted it out of the case, and Riker was impressed again by the display of strength on the part of the smaller man. As he had before, he patted it affectionately and said, "Believe me, Lieutenant . . . they're not going to get away."

"That's good to hear. All right, Sergeant. Apprise your people that we definitely have nine Sindareen in there. I don't want any, repeat, *any* shots fired until we've counted nine of them emerging and approaching the ship. As soon as the last one is out, which means the hostages are unguarded—start firing. If they manage to get airborne, I'll be counting on you to bring them down. I do *not,"* he reiterated, "want to see them get away. We're going to be sending a message to them and all of their kind, and we're sending it now."

"Understood, Lieutenant."

"Good. Oh . . . and watch your aim, Sergeant," Riker cautioned. "You miss them and hit the Betazed moon, and we'd have a problem on our hands."

"I won't miss, Lieutenant. Count on it."

The cases were loaded and the other Sindareen were bringing them up toward the roof. Maror stood in front of the Betazoids, studying them apprisingly for a moment.

"As charming as this has been," he said, "we really have to take leave of you now. However . . . it's my concern that the Federation men might decide to give us problems upon our departure. And so, just for some added protection, I'd like one of you to accompany me. Ideally, I'd bring all of you . . . but our ship is small, and we're heavily loaded already. So it's going to have to be one. Now, let's see . . ." He scanned them briefly, and then, tucking his weapon under one arm, he said firmly, "You. You're wounded anyway, so you won't give any trouble." And he reached for Chandra.

"No! Leave her *alone!"* shouted Deanna as Maror grabbed the frantic Chandra by the arm. Deanna leaped forward, her fingernails raking across Maror's face, and Maror howled in fury as lines of blood welled up on his pale cheek. His face contorted with rage, he hurled Chandra to the parquet floor, and her head cracked with explosive force against it.

Deanna instinctively turned toward her friend, but Maror grabbed her and swung her around. He yanked her forward and snarled in her face, "You know, I thought you had nerve. And intelligence. Out of respect for that, I was going to leave you be. But you weren't intelligent enough to know when you were getting off lucky. So now, foolish little Betazoid . . . it's going to be you."

Xerx actually gasped in fright and staggered slightly. Riker put a hand behind him to steady him and was almost afraid to ask what had happened.

He didn't have to ask as Xerx said, "I've lost contact. Chandra's unconscious." Riker waited for Xerx to pull himself together sufficiently to provide more information, and Xerx did so. "There was something . . . they—the Sindareen—were going to take one of the hostages with them. For a shield. And they were taking Chandra. And she struggled and fell . . . and now I have no sense of her. Lieutenant . . ." And there was pure terror in his voice.

Tang's comm unit crackled to life. "This is Sommers at Gamma Point," snapped a voice. "I have a visual. They're coming out, sir!"

"All units are to wait for my signal!" barked Tang. "Repeat, not a shot is to be fired until you have the clearance from central command!" He looked to Riker. "You're the CO, Lieutenant. Gonna be your call."

"We stick with the plan. When all nine are exposed, we open fire," said Riker firmly.

"My daughter! Gods, Lieutenant . . . you can't shoot my child!"

"They'll shoot clear of her, Gart," Riker said, looking to Tang for confirmation.

Tang nodded his head in agreement. Then from his supplies belt, he removed a small pair of electronic sensor binos and, putting them to his eyes, studied the rooftop.

"Get me one of those," ordered Riker.

"Binos for the lieutenant!" snapped Tang, not removing his gaze from the rooftop. Moments later, Hirsch reappeared and handed a pair of the instruments to Riker. Now he had the roof under close scrutiny as well.

At first there was no movement at all, and for a moment Riker toyed with the notion that this was all some sort of scam—that, in fact, another means of escape was all set up, and the ship was simply there as a distraction. But then he saw the door to the roof slide open and the first of the Sindareen appeared—two of them, lugging a large crate between them.

"Hold fire," said Riker softly, and the order was repeated by Tang. It wasn't necessary, really. Everyone knew what their orders were and what they were supposed to do.

There was an eerie silence over the area. When Tang had been in similar situations, the buzz of the crowd was positively deafening, and sometimes came close to interfering with the job. Whatever was going through the minds and hearts of the Betazoids, they were having the exquisite courtesy to do it quietly.

More of the Sindareen appeared, lugging more crates. Riker counted them off softly to himself . . . five . . . six . . . and then he said, "Have we got them targeted, Tang?"

"Target report," said Tang into his comm unit.

"Alpha Point, target acquired," came the first reply. The snipers had chosen their targets in order of appearance based on their designation: Alpha took the first target to appear, Beta took the second, and so on.

One by one the rest of the snipers reported in. All of them had targets in their sights.

Eight of the Sindareen had made themselves visible. Riker muttered a low curse. The lead two were approaching the confines of the ship. Sure enough, a second later one of the snipers reported, "This is Alpha Point. About to lose target acquisition. Awaiting instructions."

Riker could envision the finger of the sniper, poised over the trigger. He wanted to give the order to cut loose, and he could feel Tang's gaze upon him. But there was no way that he could give the clearance . . . not when the ninth raider was still unaccounted for.

Then there was more movement, and the final member of the Sindareen raiding party made his appearance.

In his right hand, he was cradling a blaster. His head was turning slowly, clearly trying to spot whatever Federation people might be trying to target him. His left arm was curled around the throat of a woman.

"Deanna," breathed Riker.

He zoomed in on her face. Her jaw was set, her eyes unblinking. If she was afraid, she was making a great show of keeping her feelings to herself.

"That's nine," said Tang. "Lieutenant—?"

"They have a hostage," Riker said tonelessly.

"I know that, sir."

Riker was silent. "Who's your best marksman?"

Tang anticipated the request and tapped his comm unit. "Sommers. Shift target to the Sindareen in the rear. Lorie, pick up Gamma's target."

"Acquired," came Lorie's voice from Alpha Point.

This was immediately followed by Sommers saying, "Got him in my sights."

"Clear shot?"

"Negative," replied Sommers, "repeat, that's a negative. Target's moving too much."

Riker saw immediately that Sommers was correct. Maror was too experienced at this. He kept shifting his position, swinging Deanna around so that she was constantly in the way.

Riker pressed the binos so hard against his eyes that he thought they were going to come out the back of his head. He knew what he should do. The vast majority of the hostages were already in the clear. Only one was left . . . one who might still survive if everything fell right. But if they made no move, then the raiders would escape, and more people would pay down the line.

Deanna, he thought bleakly.

At that moment, Deanna was swung directly into Riker's sight line . . .

And she looked straight at him. Straight and proud and unafraid.

Two words rang in his head.

I understand.

"Take them," said Riker.

"Take 'em," Tang ordered. "Take 'em."

Deanna flinched.

From all around, phasers blasted outward, enveloping the surprised Sindareen in coronas of energy. Several staggered and went down. One of them managed to survive the blasts and tumbled into the ship.

Sommers missed Maror. Deanna's instinctive, uncontrollable shiver, anticipating the barrage that was about to occur, had been enough to warn the

Sindareen leader that something was about to happen. As a result he'd dropped to a crouch, dragging Deanna down with him. Sommers had been aiming high anyway, banking on Maror's exposing his head for the brief moment that Sommers would need. But it didn't happen, and now Maror dashed for the ship, dragging Deanna with him. The marksmen shot around him, steering clear of the trapped Betazoid.

For a split instant, Maror's back was exposed, and Sommers fired. The high-power phaser beam, which would have severely burned and possibly even crushed Deanna Troi, staggered Maror. It caused him to stumble forward, almost falling atop his prisoner, but then he recovered and reached the inside of the ship, shoving Deanna inside ahead of him. The hatch rampway closed, with several crates of Betazoid art treasures—along with five of the Sindareen—left lying on the rooftop.

"Dammit!" shouted Riker. "Dammit!" It was a totally un-Starfleet response. It was also understandable.

With a roar of impulse engines, the Spider swayed into the air. Obviously whoever was piloting the ship was doing so in a god-awful hurry, not taking time to engage in proper navigational procedures, but instead concentrating only on getting the hell out of there.

Riker didn't even have to look behind him to know what Tang was doing. The hard-bitten sergeant had swung the phaser cannon onto his shoulder and activated it. "Can you bring them down?" said Riker without turning.

"I can blow them out of the sky. Quick and fast."

"Can you cripple them?"

"Trickier. Not as sure. And," Tang added quietly, "there's no guarantee she'll survive the crash. You may not be doing her any favors."

"I know."

The Spider had now gained the skies and was heading west, angling upward. In a moment it would pick up even greater speed and hurl itself far, far away from Betazed.

"Cripple them," said Riker.

Tang made an adjustment on the power and fired.

The intensity of the phaser blast was beyond anything Riker had ever experienced directly. The air crackled around him, and he thought he was going to choke.

The blast took out the starboard engine and the navigational instrumentation of the Spider. The ship lurched wildly, tried to regain control, and failed. It spiraled downward, leaving a trail of thick black smoke behind it miles long.

"Where's it going to come down?" said Riker tonelessly.

"Judging from the speed and trajectory," Tang replied, "somewhere in the region known as the Jalara Jungle."

There was silence for a moment, and then Gart Xerx said, "If she makes it through the crash, she has a good chance. The jungle has its dangers . . . mud pits and such . . . but there are few really dangerous animals to contend with."

Riker turned and stared at him. "You're forgetting the most dangerous animals. They're the ones steering the ship."

Twenty-five

Maror didn't know what he was running from, or what he was running to.

No. That wasn't precisely right. He knew what he was running to. He was running straight to hell. But if there was one thing of which he was resolved, it was that he was going to take the damned Betazoid woman with him.

She sat on a rock nearby, and to his frustration she looked exactly as she had the day before, and the day before that. Even though her clothes were ripped and dirty, her face filthy, her hair hanging in stringy ringlets that had lost all their bounce in the moisture of the jungle. Even with her shoes gone, her prospects slim.

Still, she had composure.

He couldn't take it anymore. He wanted her to be like other women he had captured. He wanted her to beg or plead. He wanted her to whimper or moan. He wanted her to . . . to *something.*

He swung his gun up and aimed at her. "Ask for your life."

With a small shrug of her slim shoulders, she said evenly, "Please do not kill me."

He stared at her in disbelief. "You call that begging?"

"No. I call that asking. To be honest, it's pointless. You'll kill me or not. I can't stop you. Begging will demean me and accomplish nothing. I see no advantage to it, and I won't do it."

With a roar of unbridled fury, he stalked over to her and grabbed her by the back of her head. He yanked down hard, and the angle in which he pulled her skull made her mouth open involuntarily. He shoved the barrel of the gun into her mouth, angling it so that the ray blast would be certain to blow her brain up through the top of her skull.

"I said beg," he repeated.

Her eyes rolled up to regard him for the briefest of moments, and then up into the top of her head. Her breathing slowed, and her entire body went limp.

For an instant he thought she'd passed out, but then he realized what she had done. She'd put herself into a trance, or into some sort of deep meditative state. When she was like that, nothing he could say or do would bring her out of it until she was ready to be brought out. He could blow her brains out and she would never know or feel it.

So there he was, feeling like something of a fool. You couldn't threaten someone who wasn't aware of you. Which meant either he should kill her or not. If he killed her, he had a corpse and nothing to hold over any of the Fed men should they catch up with him. There was no point to it. Hell, there was no point to any of it.

With a curse he released her and took some small measure of satisfaction in watching her thud to the ground like a bag of stones. Then he perched himself on the rock that she had occupied moments before and stared down at her, waiting for her to come out of it.

Slowly, after some minutes, she did. She lay there, staring up at him.

"You wonder why I haven't killed you yet?"

She tilted her head slightly and said, "You hope that I will serve some purpose in the near future."

The membranes on his neck fluttered a bit faster as he asked, "And have you wondered why I haven't raped you?"

"You're not a rapist. A thief, yes. A killer as needed. But not a rapist."

Maror studied her. "You're that certain?"

"I wasn't at first." She drew her knees up under her chin. "At first I was terrified that you might do that. When the two of us were the only survivors of the crash, I was certain you might take that course. But as time has passed, I have begun to have a sense of you. Prolonged exposure to you has enabled me to get an empathic feel for you that I didn't have before."

"Keep your empathic feelings to yourself." He walked toward her and yanked her rudely to her feet, as if to try to make up for the fact that he wasn't the type to assault a woman sexually. "I still can't believe," he grumbled, "that you survived the crash when others of my men didn't."

"I was not tense," she said simply. "I had relaxed myself. Your men were tense. The stiffness resulted in the internal injuries that killed them."

"Thank you for that diagnosis," he snarled.

He led her through the jungle, watching carefully all about him for any sign of pursuit.

Deanna, for her part, took the opportunity to expand her senses and get a feel for the life that throbbed all about her in the jungle. It was rare that anyone really ventured any real distance into the Jalara, and rarer still for anyone to be out this far. In a way she found it exciting. She just wished that that excitement wasn't coming at the expense of those who loved her.

She was certain that her mother must be frantic by now, and not for the first time she silently cursed the fate that had made her half-human. Had she been full Betazoid, there was a great likelihood that she would be able to send free-ranging thought broadcasts as far back as the city. Summon help right to the spot where she presently was. It wouldn't matter that geographically she didn't have a clue as to her whereabouts. They would simply be able to sense her.

But her ability to send and receive was diluted by her human heritage. She needed greater proximity to be at all reliable. And out here, in the middle of nowhere, proximity was not exactly easy to come by.

Birds fluttered past her, and she had to step carefully to avoid treading on a small serpent that slid past her. It was not poisonous, but she had no desire to injure something innocent. The thing she found most heartening was that she had sensed the creature's presence rather than seen it.

The vegetation around them was thinning out, and ahead of them was a cleared area that prompted Maror to let out a sigh of relief. It was a watering hole.

He turned to Troi. "Even you have to be thirsty. You're made of ice, but ice requires water."

"I'm hardly made of ice," she said, brushing strands out of her face and trying not to let the fatigue she felt be betrayed in her voice. "That water will taste as good to me as it does to you."

"That's very comforting." He gestured with the gun. "You first."

"Thank you."

She went to the water and knelt down before it. The rips in her dress exposed more skin than she would have liked, but at this point there was no use getting overly concerned about such things. She cupped her hands, scooped up water and brought it to her lips, sipping gingerly and being careful not to take the big gulps that her impulses urged.

He frowned as he watched her. "You drink like a bird."

"There's no point in overdoing it," she replied evenly. "If I overindulge, the result will simply be stomach cramps. I see no advantage to that."

"Fine. Fine. Do what you want."

She looked at her reflection in the water and moaned softly. Then she shoved her hands in once more, wetting them thoroughly, and brought them up to her face, making an effort to wash away as much of the dirt as possible. After a few moments she studied the result and decided that, while it wasn't perfect, at least it was an improvement.

"You realize," she said, "that you're not heading anywhere in particular. You're just marking time. You have no one waiting to pick you up. No rendezvous. No secret hideout."

"I've never been caught. I take tremendous pride in that. I'm not about to get caught now, no matter what. Besides, I'm betting that they stop looking for us. They've probably found the ship by now. They found the bodies of the others. Maybe they'll even continue the search for a couple of days. But sooner or later, they'll conclude that we couldn't have survived—that we probably fell into a . . . what did you call it?"

"Mud pit," she said evenly.

"Right. Mud pit. Or maybe a ravine. Or maybe even got eaten by some huge animal they didn't even know hung about in these woods. They won't search for us forever."

"Oh, yes, they will," she replied with quiet confidence. "I don't believe they'll ever stop. And neither, in all honesty, do you."

"Really? Then why am I going to all this trouble if it's so certain that I'll be caught?"

She turned and looked at him with her ebony eyes. "You are afraid. You are afraid of whatever actions might be taken against you by Starfleet. Afraid of giving up some measure of your freedom. So afraid, in fact, that you would much rather live a handful of days fighting for survival, but free . . . than you would live many days, or months or even years, in captivity or under the supervision of the Federation."

His eyes narrowed, but he said nothing.

After one more brief pass of the water over her face, she rose and pointed to the water. "All yours."

He nodded and gestured for her to step away from the water. "You know, I was just tired of you before. But now I'm really, really sick of you. All you're doing is slowing me down." He crouched in front of the water and scooped some up. He was able to bring it to his mouth and continue to converse at the same time. "You yammer at me. You analyze me. You try to make me feel like some sort of coward. I'm starting to think that whatever minimal use you might have had as a hostage would pale next to the sheer, selfish pleasure I'd feel at blasting the top right off of your pretty little—"

She kicked him in the small of the back.

With a yell, Maror stumbled forward, wet soil slipping beneath him, and he fell headfirst into the water. He floundered around and was about to pull his upper body out when some inquisitive water snakes, which Deanna had sensed were in the area, came to investigate and did so by wrapping themselves around Maror's throat.

Deanna, for her part, bolted.

For a moment she had considered the idea of making a grab for the gun, but a tentative step she had taken toward it quickly dissuaded her of that notion. Maror's hand was firmly on the grip, and she had a feeling that if she'd pulled at the gun, it would simply have told him, without any shadow of doubt, precisely where his target was located.

And right now she did not want to be a target. That was why she had chosen that moment to make a bid for freedom. For she had sensed, beyond any doubt, that Maror really had had enough. That he was beginning to realize that his flight was hopeless and was becoming angry enough and frustrated enough to take that realization out on anyone who happened to be near.

In other words, he was genuinely ready to kill her as the likelihood for her serving any purpose faded.

So she ran.

Maror sputtered in indignation as he lurched to his feet, pulling at the snakes. The snakes, for their part, were uniformly startled to be removed so unceremoniously from their natural watery habitat. The shock caused them to lose their grip on Maror, and he was able to yank them free. He threw them back down into the water with loud splashes, spun, and roared Deanna's name in a frenzy. He even fired blindly into the jungle with his weapon and by blind luck came within two feet of blasting Deanna's head off.

There was no rational reason for him to pursue her at that point. Dashing pell-mell through the jungle the way she was, the odds were that she was just going to get even more lost and maybe even run headlong into something that was lethal. Whatever pleasure that knowledge might have brought him, however, was diluted by the fact that she had royally embarrassed him. And that was something that he was simply not going to tolerate.

With a howl of vexation he lashed his weapon around himself and took off after her.

It wasn't difficult to track her. Her rush through the jungle left a series of broken branches and crushed shrubbery in her wake. He could have followed the trail if he were blindfolded.

Deanna hadn't been sure if he would try to chase her, or whether he would be happy just to be rid of her. She was banking to some degree on the latter. When she heard the crashing of the jungle underbrush behind her, her heart sank.

She looked around desperately, trying to find some sort of weapon, or perhaps some place to hide so that he would run past her. But no place seemed to be sufficient shelter.

She dodged to the right and stumbled on an outstretched root. She fell forward, catching herself by hitting her palms against the ground, and she felt pain stab through her forearms. She lifted her right hand and found a small, pointed rock, which she wrapped her fingers around for reasons she didn't even fully understand. Then she scrambled to her feet and kept going.

She heard his pursuit getting closer and closer. Between the noise of shoving shrubbery aside, and his loud and constant string of profanity, it was hard to miss him.

His blaster roared behind her and she could feel the heat. He must have used it, she realized, to clear away some underbrush so that he could make better time. She would have given anything to have some sort of weapon or tool like that.

For one insane moment, she envisioned Will Riker coming to her rescue. Striding forward like some great hero, showing up out of nowhere at the penultimate moment, drawn there by fate, happenstance, and that incredible timing that always seemed to accompany such last-minute saves. She wanted it more than anything, to believe that such things could occur in real life. Because it would mean that in real life people really could be drawn together not because it was the intelligent or smart thing to do, but simply because *not* to be together would be completely wrong. It would mean that in real life there were greater things than that which her mind could grasp, analyze, and study.

She wanted him. Gods, she knew that, had known that all along, and she had been such an idiot to fight it for all sorts of reasons that had made sense then but now seemed pointless. If only she had that time back. If only she could see him again.

But she knew, in her heart, that that wasn't going to happen. It was up to her; live or die, it was up to her, and there would be no rescue, and the chances were extremely good that in a few minutes, there would be no Deanna Troi either.

Abruptly the ground in front of her angled upward sharply. She'd come to the base of some sort of small slope. It would take her more time to make her way up it, but backtracking wasn't possible. She took a deep breath and started upward. Roots and small outcroppings of rock provided her with handholds that sped her on her way.

But they did not speed her nearly enough, and suddenly she heard a triumphant yell from behind her. She tried to climb higher, but a hand wrapped around her foot.

"Got you, you Betazoid bitch!" growled Maror.

She screamed, her fingers clawing for purchase, but he dragged her down toward him and spun her around so that his face was mere inches from hers. "You have been far more trouble than you could possibly be worth," he snarled, "and I'm going to . . ."

In her palm she felt the hardness and sharpness of the rock she'd grabbed mere moments before. She didn't hesitate as she brought the pointed end around and slammed it squarely into Maror's forehead.

The Sindareen raider shrieked, a high-pitched sound emanating from the sides of his throat, as blood trickled down his face. Deanna, animalistic, fighting for her life, twisted the rock around and tried to drive it farther into his forehead. But the Sindareen was far too strong. With a roar he shoved Deanna back, but she maintained her grip on the rock as she fell and it tore loose from his forehead. More blood poured freely down his face.

He shoved one hand against it to staunch the wound as he approached her, his gun trembling because of the sheer fury filling him. "You—!" And his rage was beyond his ability to articulate, so he stammered out again, "You—!"

He dropped down on top of her, pressing his full body weight against her. She squirmed under him but couldn't dislodge him as he pressed the gun squarely against her stomach and snarled, "Belly wound. Very slow, very painful, and you'll die anyway. It's what you deserve. You've ruined everything—"

"I didn't—"

"Shut up! You never *shut up!* But I'm going to shut you up! I'm going to blow a hole in your—"

And from above them, a voice spoke in a tone that was deliberately cool and controlled. "Back away from her."

Maror looked up and his already pale face went one shade lighter. Deanna twisted her head around, her eyes wanting to confirm what her ears and her mind had already told her but she still couldn't quite believe.

Riker was standing about ten feet higher up on the slope. He held a phaser, aimed squarely at Maror. He was dressed in survival gear, with a utility jacket, and a supply belt strapped around his middle containing food rations, a patch holster for the phaser, and other miscellanea in small pouches.

His emotions flooded over Deanna, he being open to her in a way that no one outside of her closest friends or her mother ever was. Relief mixed with fear, all carefully bottled up so that he could present an image of utter composure to the frazzled and desperate Sindareen.

"I said back away from her." Riker's phaser wasn't wavering. "Put your hands over your head."

"No, Federation man!" snapped Maror. He twisted his body around, his legs wrapped around Deanna's middle and exposing no part of himself to a clear shot. "No, you're going to put your phaser down! You're going to put your hands over your head! You got that? Just do it! Or I swear I'll kill her. I swear!"

Don't listen to him, Will, he heard in his head. *Don't do what he wants. He'll kill you.*

"Kill her," said Riker evenly, "and you'll have nothing to bargain with."

"I don't *care* whether she lives or dies!" shot back Maror. "If you don't care either, then that's that. So I kill her, put my hands over my head, and surrender. You won't be able to do a damned thing except turn me over to the authorities. And she'll be dead. Now if that little scenario doesn't bother you, then fine! Or maybe you just want to take a whack at shooting the both of us. But I don't stun easy, Lieutenant! You'll probably fry her while you're trying to knock me out. And if you fail to stun me, then I'll kill her anyway. From where I sit, you don't have a hell of a lot of choices!"

"I have plenty of choices."

"No, you don't! I know that and you know that!" His voice went up in register, his barely restrained panic starting to overwhelm him. "Now throw down the weapon! Come on! Do it! Throw it down or I'll kill her, I swear I will, now do it, throw it down, *throw it down now or she's dead right now!"*

"All right!" And Riker tossed the phaser to one side. It clattered away, out of sight.

Deanna sagged against Maror, her thoughts black.

"The jacket, too! You might have some weapons hidden. And the belt! Slowly! Keep your hands in sight! So much as one twitch and she's dead. Her life's in your hands now, Lieutenant. Yours!"

Carefully, making no sudden moves, Riker slid the jacket off. Then he reached around and undid the fastening on the belt. He ran it slowly through his hands, saying, "See? Nothing on it. I don't have any other weapons." Then he dropped the belt to the ground.

Grinning, Maror raised his weapon and took dead aim at Riker. But to Maror's surprise, Riker remained as calm as if he had the upper hand and said, "Now lay down your weapon and no one will hurt you."

"You've got to be kidding me."

"No, I'm not kidding you. You see . . . you're surrounded."

For the briefest of moments, Maror seemed confused. Then, firming up his convictions, he said defiantly, "You're lying! This is just some . . . some pathetic bluff!"

"No bluff. There are Starfleet people on either side of you. And although they're trained to give innocents priorities, they're also trained to protect ranking officers. Put down your weapon now, and you won't be injured. But if you take any offensive action against me, my men will shoot. Even if it means injuring or killing your hostage. They will endeavor to save my life over hers."

"You can't fool me. That's against Starfleet policy," Maror snarled.

"True. But security men sometimes follow their own dictates. And frankly, you're not in a position right now to question their priorities."

Maror was silent for a long moment. Then he stood and hauled Deanna to her feet, shoving the blaster against her.

"I think," he said slowly, "that you are bluffing. I think that all of you split up in order to cover more ground. This is a very, very big jungle. Oh, you may be in communication with them, but there's no way that they can possibly be close enough to make any sort of difference. In fact, it'd probably take you a couple of days to rendezvous with them, seeing how much time has gone by. And so I'm calling your bluff, Lieutenant. Tell them to shoot. Go ahead."

"This is your last warning," said Riker sternly.

"I know. I'll chance it."

Riker looked bleakly at Deanna and said, "I'm sorry." And then, suddenly, he spread his hands wide and shouted, "All right, men! Fire!"

For a second there was nothing, and then, to his shock, Maror caught movement out of the corner of his eye, to his right. He snapped his weapon around and fired, and then he saw something over to his left. He spun, not sure where to look first. He had been so certain that Riker was alone, and now there was movement behind—

The distraction was all that Riker had wanted, all that he had time for. Without hesitation he took two quick steps and leaped off the slope, arms outstretched, directly toward Maror.

Maror looked up in alarm, realized his error, swung his blaster around, and fired. Deanna chose that moment to shove upward and back, and the sudden movement sent Maror's shot wide, just missing the fast-moving Riker.

Riker plowed into Maror, pushing Deanna clear with one hand while grabbing at Maror with his other. The two of them went down, rolling and shoving, struggling desperately, each of them trying to get leverage.

"Will!" shouted Deanna, for Maror had temporarily gotten the upper hand and was now trying to bring his weapon to bear on the Starfleet officer.

She ran toward them and grabbed at Maror, trying to yank him off Riker. Maror rammed the stock of his blaster back, slamming Deanna in the stomach. She went down, gasping and retching, the agony threatening to overwhelm her.

It was all the delay Riker needed. He swung his hands up and boxed Maror on either side of the throat, at the base of the nictating membranes that served as his vocal apparatus. It was the equivalent of slamming a punch to the Adam's apple in a humanoid.

Maror gagged, his breath momentarily cut off, but his strength was still far superior to Riker's. So when Riker got his hands on the blaster, Maror was still able to hold on to it as his injured membranes fought to regain their equilibrium.

The combatants shoved against one another, pitting their full weight and strength, grunting and growling low and incomprehensible noises. A twist, a turn, jockeying for position, and Riker managed to get his feet planted. With a quick twist of his hip he slammed Maror up against a tree with a bone-jarring jolt.

Maror lost his grip on his blaster, and it clattered to the ground at his feet. Riker had a split instant to make a decision. He released his grip on Maror, gambling on his speed and the damage he'd inflicted on the Sindareen thus far, and lunged for the blaster.

It was the wrong move. Maror's foot lashed out, kicking the blaster away into the underbrush. Riker was off-balance, and Maror drove his foot up into Riker's face.

Riker went down, rolling, tasting his blood welling up in his mouth. Maror came after him, kicking furiously, Riker just barely staying ahead of him.

Riker managed to scramble to his feet, and Maror came in fast. Riker braced to meet the charge, his back against a tree, and only at the last moment did he see the knife flashing in Maror's hand. Where he'd pulled it from, Riker hadn't a clue . . . probably he'd kept it secreted up his sleeve.

Riker immediately switched tactics, twisting and just barely avoiding the slashing attack. The blade sank into the tree trunk. Riker's hands swept up and he slammed his head forward, his forehead cracking against Maror's face.

Maror fell back toward some brush . . .

And his questing hand came up with the blaster that had been knocked over there.

Riker dove for cover as the blaster bolt sizzled over his head. Maror pivoted, dodging to the right to try to get a clear shot at Riker.

And Riker saw where Maror was heading.

"Wait!" shouted Riker. "Stop! Don't go there! Don't move!"

Maror, his voice returning, cackled, "Why not, Federation man? Because this will give me the best angle to turn you into a sack of boneless skin? Or maybe security men lie in wait for me? I'm tired of your bluffs, Lieutenant! I'm tired of you!"

Maror leaped to his right, landing with an odd squishing noise, and aimed his blaster at Riker, whose hiding place was now fully exposed.

Incredibly, Riker had not given up the apparent pretense that he somehow had the upper hand. In what seemed a masterpiece of acting, Riker shouted, "Move! Before it's too late!" and he waved his hands wildly.

"The one who it's too late for is—"

And that was when Maror realized that he was getting shorter.

He looked down.

He was standing squarely in one of the infamous Jalara Jungle mud pits.

He knew what they looked like. Yesterday a small animal he'd been chasing for food ran headlong into one and had sunk from sight in a little under two seconds.

From the speed with which Maror was vanishing into the dark, pasty nonsoil, it appeared that larger creatures, such as humanoids, took a bit longer. Like, five seconds.

He looked back up and finished the sentence with slow realization. "Is me," he said as the mud crept up to his shoulders.

Riker scurried forward, arm outstretched, watching for the edges of the mud pit so that he didn't slip in. "Hold on!" he shouted.

Maror actually seemed amused. "To what?"

That was the last thing he was able to say as the mud covered his throat. Riker got to the edge of the pit, which he could discern by the dark rim, and reached out, trying to grab at Maror's hair. But Maror was just beyond Riker's grasp, and then five seconds were gone . . . and so was Maror. He vanished beneath the surface of the mud pit without a trace.

And insanely, Maror's final expression had been one of quiet triumph.

Twenty-six

Riker went to Deanna and saw how she was staring at the center of the mud pit. In a low whisper, she said, "He won. He was never caught."

"Are you all right?" asked Riker, taking her by the shoulders. "Did he hurt you?"

"I'm fine." She got to her feet, pausing only to nurse the dull ache in her stomach. "I'm fine. I want to get out of here."

"All right. Let's just wait a few minutes until—"

"No. Now." There was an urgency in her voice, a desperation to try to distance herself as much as possible from the site of these events.

"Okay. Let me just get my equipment together."

She nodded, her gaze never wavering from the mud pit.

Riker quickly got his jacket and belt and retrieved his phaser from where he'd tossed it. Then he tapped a small button on one of the belt compartments, and Deanna blinked in surprise as two small diamond-shaped objects shot past her. "What are those?"

"Target-practice devices. Standard issue for ground-based security personnel. They're what I used to distract Maror."

"Oh." She nodded, and her voice sounded very distant. "That was quite clever, Will. Quite clever."

He stared at her. "Are you sure you're all right?"

"Positive. Let's go."

Riker didn't say anything further, but simply guided her gently away from the mud pit site. He studied her bedraggled condition and, insanely, still couldn't help but think how good she looked despite her ordeal. She seemed to have an endless reserve of inner strength.

Once they began walking, Riker contacted Tang. Maror had indeed been correct in his guess. Riker and the various members of the security crew had split up, the better to cover the vast distances of the jungle. It had been Riker who was fortunate enough, after several days of searching, to detect the life readings of Deanna and Maror using his tricorder.

He informed Tang that Deanna had indeed been recovered (he avoided using the word *rescued* . . . it sounded melodramatic somehow) and that they would now be heading toward the rendezvous point. It would take a few days to get there, but Riker was still well stocked with provisions, and no abnormal delays were anticipated.

Riker had been preoccupied with his mission throughout the past few days and had not paid all that much attention to the jungle, other than to avoid its pitfalls or obstructions. His judicious use of a phaser to carve himself a path now served him in good stead, making it that much easier for him to make his way back . . . even if the tricorder weren't capable of enabling him to retrace his steps.

With the pressure off, he was really able to take notice of the true beauty of the Jalara Jungle. He realized now that the flowers and vines that had decorated the interior of the wedding chapel must have been taken from the jungle. The flowers and growths were exotic combinations of colors. The air was warm, even steamy, without being irritatingly humid. It was filled with a scented mist that was invigorating, or perhaps simply smelled all the sweeter with Deanna's freedom now a reality.

He turned and looked to Deanna, who had been extremely silent for the past half hour.

She was shivering. Her arms were wrapped around herself, and there, in the midst of a warm jungle, she was shivering. Her teeth were chattering.

Immediately he knew what was happening. All during the time when she was in danger, she had managed to keep everything bottled up. She had detached herself from the fear and uncertainty, from the terror that must have accompanied every moment. Such feelings could be repressed or ignored for the duration of a crisis. But sooner or later they would come roaring back and would have to be dealt with.

He went to her and put his arms around her, settling her into a seated position. "Shh. It's okay. Let it out, Deanna. That's all right."

She trembled more violently, staring not at Riker but straight ahead, as if she expected someone or something to come at her from the underbrush. Her hand clamped onto his upper arm, her fingernails digging into the skin with such fierceness that Riker had to stifle the impulse to push her hand away. As it was, he kept his mouth shut, not letting on that it hurt like hell.

He stroked her face, continuing to make soft, comforting noises. Letting her know that it was okay to be frightened. Reminding her that she wasn't alone. Telling her that everything was going to be all right, that she was out of danger and soon all of this would just be a distant, bad dream.

As he spoke, she drew herself closer to him, pressing against him and readjusting his arms so that he completely enveloped her. The quaking still convulsed her body, and her lower lip trembled. Tears rolled down her face, but she did not cry out loud. Her complete silence was almost eerie.

He didn't say anything further. He merely rocked with her, back and forth, gently, letting his mere presence be something from which she could draw reassurance. And slowly, ever so slowly, the trembling diminished and eventually stopped. The tears ceased, and then she brought her hand up and wiped away the remainder of the moisture.

Then she looked up at Riker. He smiled down at her and, wondering if she was prepared to move on, said, "Ready?"

She nodded. "Yes. Yes, I am." She reached up, wrapped her hand around the back of his head, and drew his face to hers.

The kiss was very long and very sweet and filled with promise. Their lips parted and he looked at her, the jungle air making him feel giddy. There was an unreality to it all. *Going native* was the old phrase.

"Deanna," he said, his voice low. "This . . . this isn't right. This isn't the time. You aren't thinking straight, you've been through a lot, you—"

"Let me"—she held his face in her hands—"let me put this to you in a way that I know you'll understand."

He waited. With her eyes wide, her lips mere inches from his, she whispered, "Shut up and kiss me, Riker."

He did.

Moments later, all the perfectly logical reasons why this was wrong, inappropriate, completely incorrect behavior for a Starfleet officer . . . all those blessed reasons flew completely out of Riker's mind. Instead all there was was *her,* was the moistness of the jungle combined with the sweat of her. The rustling of trees mixed with the rustling of clothes, and this time when their nude bodies pressed against each other, there was no intellectualizing, no deep discussions that required anything beyond soft, whispered words, punctuated by faint, occasional gasps.

In that moment they knew all there was to know of each other . . . body and soul, flesh and spirit, all combined and permeating every inch of both of them. Instead of moving away from each other, instead of resisting the pull, they gave in to it completely. They complemented each other, became each other, filling out each other's needs and rejoicing as pressures built in them. Throughout the Jalara Jungle it seemed that all noise had ceased. That there was nothing in the jungle, nothing in the planet, nothing in the universe except the two of them and their discovery, their admission, of their mutual need and hunger.

The pressure built beyond their ability to contain and they released, clutching each other, as if hoping they could meld their bodies into one as seamlessly as they had with their souls. And somewhere, somewhere deep within Riker's mind, merged with his spirit, a word echoed. A word that he had never heard before. A word filled with mystery and promise and a future . . .

And the word was *Imzadi.*

They lay next to each other, Deanna's head against his shoulder. She ran her fingers idly across his chest hair.

"I hear that's for traction." It was the longest sentence she had uttered in half an hour . . . the first sentence since their lovemaking. Their most recent lovemaking, to be precise, although how many times they had engaged in their mutual sexual calisthenics was a bit of a mystery to both of them. Things had blurred one into the other; had just finished and begun again with hardly a word passing between them. It was as if, having decided upon a course of action, they were both afraid to speak after that for fear of botching it up somehow.

They had not moved from the spot where it had all first begun untold hours ago, and Riker had a feeling that impressions had been dug into the ground that would probably mystify future geologists.

"You heard about that, did you?" he asked.

She nodded. "Chandra's father told her. She told me."

"Oh. Well . . . yes. Traction." Riker paused, trying to find something to say.

She said it for him. "So where do we go from here?"

"To the rendezvous point. But I have a feeling we're going to be pretty late."

"That's not what I meant."

"I know." He turned over, propping himself up on his elbow, and ran his fingers through her hair. He picked out a length of vine that had become tangled up in it and was about to toss it aside. But she took it from him.

"No. I want to keep that. As a souvenir."

"A piece of vine?" he asked incredulously.

She shrugged.

"In answer to your question . . . I don't know. I know how you make me feel. I think I know how I make you feel. But I . . . I don't have any answers. I'm still getting this all sorted out. I mean . . . you're the expert on feelings. What do *you* think?"

She sighed. She felt slightly chilled, even in the warm jungle air, and she drew her naked body tightly against his. "I don't know. That's . . . that's what I find appealing about you, Will. When I'm with you . . . I don't think."

He raised an amused eyebrow. "I'm not sure how to take that."

"When I'm with you . . . when I think about you . . . all my training, all my . . . my overintellectualizing, as you put it . . . just vanishes. I've never felt this way about anyone and I . . . I finally decided I wanted to give in to it. To fully experience it. How can I be any sort of complete person if I'm not willing to go where my . . . where my spirit wants to take me."

He brushed back a lock of her hair. "I think you have a very beautiful spirit."

"Why thank you, Lieutenant. It's nice of you to notice it. And so do you."

He paused. "This is going to sound so . . . so trite, but believe me when I say . . . I've never felt like this with anyone. More than just the physical part . . . which was great, don't get me wrong," he added hurriedly. "But there was . . ." He felt tongue-tied. "I really don't have words to express it."

"There are none. There don't have to be."

"There was . . . when we were . . ." He cleared his throat. "There was a word. You thought it at me . . . at least, I presume it was you. I don't think there was anyone else rattling around in there. 'Imzi' or something?"

Now she propped herself up as well and faced him fully.

"Imzadi," she said softly. When she said it, there was a musical, loving tone to her voice such as he had never heard.

"That's it. Imzadi. What does that mean?"

"Well . . . it has several meanings. The surface level is simply 'beloved' or 'dear one.' But when used with certain people, under certain circumstances . . . well, you need to know the further nuance to it to understand its full meaning."

"So what is its full meaning?"

She smiled shyly, which was a direct contrast to the casualness of her nudity. "It means . . . the first."

"The . . . the first?" He wasn't sure he had heard correctly, or perhaps didn't want to.

"Yes. No matter what happens from here on . . . we will always be true Imzadi. We will forever be each other's 'first.' "

She looked up at him with those large, dark eyes, and he felt like a total cretin.

"You mean . . . you mean I'm the first man that you . . . that you ever . . ."

She nodded.

"Had sex with?" he managed to finish.

She nodded again.

"Oh, my God."

"You seem surprised," she said, looking quite amused. "Is it so difficult to believe?"

"Well, I mean . . ." He couldn't remember when he'd felt quite this embarrassed. "I mean, you're such an open society and all . . . and you're so gorgeous . . ."

"Thank you," she said demurely.

"That I'm . . . I mean, it never occurred to me that no man had ever . . ."

"Bagged me?" she asked, her eyes twinkling slightly.

He winced. "That's one term that's occasionally used . . . although not by me."

"Oh, of course not. Never by you."

"And . . . um . . . look. Deanna. I . . . I don't know if I said or did anything to give you the impression otherwise, but . . . but you're not my first. I mean . . . I've been with other women."

"No, you haven't," she said serenely.

"Yes, I have. I mean, I was there. I think I'd know."

"Oh, *I* understand. You mean you've had sex before."

"Well . . . well, yes. I thought that's what we were talking about."

"You still don't understand, Will. The physical part, as pleasurable as it was . . . and as exciting as it was for me, I must admit . . ." She hesitated and suddenly looked vulnerable. "Did I do all right?"

"Oh, yes! Yes. You did . . . you did great. I'd never have known if you hadn't told me that . . ." He gestured, trying to sum up his conflicting feelings.

"All right, then. But you see . . . the concept of Imzadi goes beyond the physical. You've had other women physically. I know that. And even though I haven't had other men before you, that's almost incidental. To be Imzadi is to go far deeper than that. Don't you understand, Will? Other women may have had your body"—she smiled—"but I'm the first who's ever touched your soul."

And he realized, with a dim astonishment, that she was right. Sex for him had always been directed toward the pleasurable aspects. Even when he had thought he was in love, it had turned out to be purely superficial . . . an excuse to add some additional excitement to the physical gratification.

Was he in love now? Thoughts were tumbling around far too fiercely for him to assimilate fully. It was the kind of sensation that he had always wanted to avoid. He liked knowing precisely what he was doing at all times. He liked being in control. But to be in love was to surrender some degree of that control, and he had never been willing or able to do that.

And now, here with Deanna Troi, he still wasn't sure if he was able. But for the first time in his life, he realized that he was genuinely willing.

"Imzadi," he said, and smiled.

She returned the smile and nodded. "I understand."

He sat up and saw that the sun was setting. It hung low, streaks of pink and orange dancing like liquid fingers across the Betazed sky.

"You know," he said slowly, "I've been looking at stars in space for so long . . . that I completely forgot how utterly beautiful a star can be when it's setting. And you know what else? Those clouds right there"—he pointed—"the way they're coming together . . . they look like two dragons battling."

"You see conflict in the sky. That's understandable. When you launch yourself into space, then to a very large degree, it's you against the vacuum."

"It's like the painting, isn't it."

"To some degree," she acknowledged. "When you look at any sort of tableaux, be it hanging on a wall or hanging in the sky . . . you see in it a reflection of your innermost wants and desires. That is, if you look at it in the right frame of mind."

"You want to watch the sunset and wax philosophical?"

"By all means."

She drew her body next to his and they sat there, staring up at the setting sun and seeing in it all sorts of aspects of their souls that they had never before examined.

Riker was thoroughly enraptured.

But after about thirty seconds, Deanna turned to him and said, "Right, then. That's enough of that. Come here, Imzadi." She pressed against him and bore him tenderly to the ground.

The sun set the rest of the way without them.

Twenty-seven

Riker stared at the paper, shaking his head. What could he possibly have been thinking?

He started to shove it back into the supplies belt when he heard Deanna's soft footfall behind him. Her unexpectedly fast return from her morning ablutions had caught him by surprise. As a result he fumbled slightly, and the sheet fluttered to the ground.

Deanna picked it up, staring at it in surprise. "Paper. Now here's something you don't see every day."

"Federation security men believe in being prepared for any eventuality—even leaving a message stuck to a tree. Give it here."

She looked at him, her head slightly tilted. "Will, we've been traveling together through this jungle for five days now . . . covering distance that we could have covered in three days, if we weren't always . . . interrupting ourselves."

At that he had to laugh. Deanna's enthusiasm and positive lustiness for the newly developed physical part of their relationship was almost overwhelming. Apparently Deanna Troi didn't do things in half measures. When she was being cerebral, she was totally cerebral. But now that her attention had been drawn to the pleasures of the flesh, all of her enthusiasm was directed toward exploring all the various possibilities and extremes to which such pleasure seeking could be taken.

"We have to watch out for those interruptions," Riker said dryly. Then he reached for the paper again and she snatched it away.

"The point is," she continued, "that even if we hadn't been drawn so close through our physical activities . . . and even if my empathic feelings for you weren't so strong . . . it would still be obvious to me that you've written something on here that you're embarrassed about."

"All right, I agree with that," said Riker evenly. "And don't you think that's something that you should respect?"

"You're right. I *should.*" Grinning mischievously, she unfolded the paper and started to read it.

Riker moaned softly. "I really wish you wouldn't. I wasn't going to show it to you until it was finished. Hell, it'll probably never be finished. I'm terrible at things like that. I never even tried before. It's lousy. I—"

"Shhh!" She looked up at him with genuine irritation on her face. Then she returned to reading the paper, her lips moving silently to the words.

Riker made no further attempt to interrupt. Instead he made a great show of nonchalantly checking his chronometer and tricorder, and then nodding in satisfaction. He was, in fact, satisfied. They were late, that much was true . . . but within an hour they'd be at the rendezvous point, and from there it was only a short ride back to the city.

He worked up the nerve to look at her. She was studying him frankly, her lustrous eyes seeming to take in the whole of him. Just as she had taught him—and just as he had perfected over the past several days—he took in and let out a slow breath, clearing his mind with facility.

This is beautiful, Imzadi, she told him.

He smiled, inwardly and outwardly. *Do you really like it?*

You'd know if I were lying.

She studied the paper and read out loud:

> "I hold you close to me.
> Feel the breath of you, and the wonder of you
> And remember a time
> Without you
> But only as one would remember
> A bleak and distant nightmare
> And you shudder against me in your sleep
> Do you share the memory with me of dark times past?
> And you smile
> Do you share the memory of times to come?
> The future holds such promise
> And just as I cannot imagine how I survived the past
> Without you
> I cannot imagine a future
> Without you."

"I don't know," Riker said, trying to keep the pride of authorship out of his voice. "I thought maybe it was a little syrupy."

"Oh, you thought no such thing," admonished Deanna. "You thought it was a perfect statement of how you felt. You were proud of it. In fact, you still are."

He grinned. "I should have known better than to try false modesty with an empath."

"Absolutely right. That will get you nothing except embarrassment."

"Speaking of embarrassment, we better get moving. We're already so late that that, in itself, is pretty damned embarrassing. Sergeant Tang's been in touch with me four times in the past two days, just to make sure that I'm still alive."

"It's nice that he's so concerned about you." She folded up the paper and tucked it in her bodice, and Riker looked at her in surprise.

"Aren't you giving it back to me?"

"Please don't make me. I'd like to keep it."

He sighed. "Only if you promise not to show it to anyone."

"Deal."

Forcing themselves not to yield to temptation, they went the rest of the way without any more impromptu interruptions. They held each other's hand tightly, their fingers intertwined, and it was only when they were within sight of the encampment that they released their hold on each other, mutually deciding that it would probably look better if they didn't arrive at the rendezvous with the flush of new love upon them.

Tang and several other security people were waiting for them. The recovered art treasures of Betazed had already been sent on ahead back to the city and were safely ensconced back in the museum. Tang had also arranged for the bodies of the Sindareen raiders to be shipped back—without comment—to the Sindareen homeworld.

"Good work, Sergeant," said Riker approvingly. He turned and extended a hand to Deanna, who took it while maintaining as neutral an expression as she could. "This is Deanna Troi."

"Ma'am," Tang greeted her with a slight inclination of his head. Then he exchanged looks with Riker. If Tang had any inkling as to what had gone on in the Jalara Jungle, he gave no indication whatsoever. He was far too much of a veteran, in every sense of the word, to be that open with whatever was going through his mind. "You're certain that the leader of the raiders was attended to?"

"Oh, yes," said Riker. "It's not the most pleasant thing I've ever witnessed . . . but he's definitely attended to."

"Very well then, sir. Shall we go?"

"By all means, Sergeant."

The journey back to the city took relatively little time. All the way back, Deanna and Will exchanged only the most minimal of conversation, most of it carefully polite inquiries into the health and well-being of the other. But then, as they approached the outskirts of the city, Riker heard in his mind . . .

Why don't you come over to the house tonight.

Are you sure your mother wouldn't mind?

Mind? Deanna's voice sounded almost scoffing. *How could she mind? I imagine that she'll want to thank you for saving me. I'd like to have her more kindly disposed towards you.*

That would be nice. The thought of her being less *kindly disposed towards me is a really chilling one.*

"I want details."

Riker stared across Roper's desk at the senior Federation representative. "Details on what?" asked Riker politely.

"On what?" Roper looked incredulous. "The entire thing! What do you think?" He gestured toward the chair for Riker to sit down. "And don't hold anything back!"

With a shrug, Riker started to sit . . . and then, just on impulse, he swung the chair around and straddled it. "It was a fairly straightforward operation. We searched the jungle. I was fortunate enough to come upon the Sindareen raider before he had the chance to injure Deanna. He resisted my attempts to capture him and died in a mud pit. I brought Deanna to the rendezvous and she is, at this moment, safe and sound at home. End of story."

"No," said Roper, waggling a finger. "No, not end of story. You and her, out in the jungle. The steamy, romantic Jalara Jungle. You having just saved her life, her incredibly grateful. The atmosphere, the mood. Our bet. Our *bet,* dammit. You're not going to tell me that with all that falling your way, you didn't take the opportunity to . . . ?"

Riker sighed and said, "All right, Mark. I have to admit it."

Eagerly Roper clapped his hands together. "Tell me. Go on. Give an old man his vicarious thrills."

"I'm afraid I can't do that," said Riker slowly. "What I can give you is your two hundred credits."

Roper's face fell. "You're telling me that—"

"Pure as driven snow, Mark. And I grew up in Alaska, so believe me, I know what I'm talking about."

Roper sat back, his expression that of a child having just been informed that Santa's existence was, at best, a dubious proposition. "I can't believe it."

"Believe it, Mark. To use the old baseball parlance, no one bats a thousand. I gave it my best moves, but I'm afraid that it just didn't happen. And I'm tired of bruising my ego trying."

"I must admit," said Roper, shaking his head, "I'm just a bit disappointed. I generally can get a feeling about people, Captain. And despite my posturing to the contrary, I just had this gut instinct that you and Deanna would make a good couple. I've generally learned to trust that instinct. I hate to find out that I was that much off target."

"It happens to the best of us, Mark. As far as Deanna and I go, I'm afraid I just wasn't in her league. But look at the bright side. Sure, we both feel frustrated. But at least you're frustrated and got two hundred credits out of the deal."

"Is that supposed to make me feel better?"

"It's supposed to make one of us feel better."

Roper studied him for a moment, with Riker maintaining a carefully neutral expression. "You know what I think?" said Roper after a time.

"No, Mark. What?"

"I think that you are the most self-satisfied-looking 'loser' I've ever seen."

Riker smiled enigmatically.

Twenty-eight

Riker stood at the entrance of the Troi mansion, waiting patiently for the door to open. But he waited for what seemed an extraordinarily long time before it finally did.

Mr. Homn wasn't standing there. Lwaxana was.

Riker smiled graciously. "Mrs. Troi," he said by way of greeting.

She forced a smile, but did not step aside to allow him admission.

"Lieutenant," she said slowly, "I want you to believe me when I tell you this is not easy for me."

"What isn't easy, Mrs. Troi?"

"First, I have a moral obligation to thank you. You rescued my daughter from a very dangerous situation. You have, for that, my eternal gratitude and sense of obligation. I will always keep your heroism in mind whenever I think of you in the future."

"Thank you."

But she had clearly not finished. "Because of that, I am not using my considerable influence with Starfleet to see that you're severely reprimanded."

"I . . . I beg your pardon?" But even as he said it, the thought flashed through his mind in bleakest fashion: *She knows.*

Of that, Lwaxana promptly left no doubt. "Your subsequent actions with my daughter were completely out of line. You took advantage of a very incendiary situation."

"What happened between Deanna and myself, Mrs. Troi," said Riker hotly, doing everything he could not to lose his temper, "was entirely mutual and entirely our business. I want to see Deanna." He started to step past Lwaxana.

She put her arms out rigidly and her voice was iron. "So help me, Lieutenant, no matter what obligation I have to you, if you set foot in here without my permission I will have you up on charges for criminal trespass. *Is that clear?*"

He halted in his tracks.

"I want to see Deanna," he repeated in a low but forceful tone.

"And do what? And say what? What do you have to offer her, Lieutenant? What, except a further dilution of her purpose."

"Further . . . ?"

She stamped her foot in anger. "Don't you understand anything? *Anything?* Do you have *any* comprehension of what you've shoved your way into the middle of? A line of obligation that stretches back centuries! Tradition that was already old at a time when your ancestors were still discovering the mysteries of footwear! Blast it, Lieutenant! Deanna isn't like the others! She isn't like the other women you've known! She isn't even like other Betazoids!" Lwaxana slapped one hand against her palm for emphasis. "Every step of her life has been mapped out for her! Her education, her career, her place in Betazoid society—all of it!"

"By you," he said tonelessly.

"Yes, by me. Of course by me. You think I'm eager to shoulder that responsibility? No, Lieutenant. No, I'm not. But I do it because it's my obligation and I accept it. And Deanna has accepted hers, and her obligation and her future. And I'm telling you, Lieutenant, right here, right now, that it's a future in which you don't figure."

His gaze ice, he said, "That's for Deanna and me to decide."

"Oh, really," Lwaxana said, making no effort to keep the sarcasm out of her voice. "And where's that decision going to lead? Are you going to give up your career exploring the galaxy? Pass it up for a permanent position here on Betazed? Clip your star-faring wings? Trade in your space legs for walking shoes?"

"I want to see Deanna—"

"And where's that going to lead, Lieutenant?" Lwaxana continued relentlessly. "Are you really prepared to give all that up for Deanna? And if you do, then how long, Lieutenant? How long before the prospect of one planet wears thin on you? How long before the sight of the same old sun, rising and setting, day after day after day, weighs on you, chokes and suffocates you? How long before you blame Deanna for making you give it all up? A year? Two? Five? When the first rush of unbridled romance is faded, Lieutenant, and the fires don't burn anywhere near as hot as the stars that were once your home . . . what's going to happen then? Answer me."

Cold fury choked him and at first he couldn't reply. But then, in the hallway behind Lwaxana, he spotted her. She was standing there, near the bottom of the stairway, a haunted look on her face.

"Deanna!" he shouted to her.

Her hands moved in small, vague circles.

Lwaxana looked from one to the other, and then she said firmly, "Tell him, Deanna."

Deanna looked down, unable to put words together.

"Deanna," said Riker, and then he said, "Imzadi."

Lwaxana fired him a look that could have extinguished one of those blazing stars to which she'd referred moments before.

And Deanna now looked him square in the face. She stood mere yards away, but her tone and words made her seem much, much farther.

"She's right, Will," said Deanna tonelessly.

"She's not right! She—"

"Sooner or later," continued Deanna, as if Riker hadn't even spoken, "you're going to want to leave. Your place is out there. Mine's here." She hesitated, then said, "I have to be adult about this. We both do. It's never going to get any better for us than it was in the jungle, Will. That was it. That was the high point. I . . . I want to remember it that way. Before your nature leads you to other places, other women . . ."

"Deanna," he said hopelessly, feeling as if she were fading from sight even as she stood there.

"Let it end on a high note, Will. Not in the downward spiral of a relationship gone wrong. Think about what we had. That's what's important. Because there's really nothing for us in the future. Nothing."

She turned on her heel without another word.

Imzadi, he hurled at her bleakly.

She didn't even slow down as she walked . . . no, ran from him . . . up the stairs and out of sight.

Lwaxana regarded him steadily. There seemed no triumph in her eyes, he thought, which was odd.

"No, it's not odd, Lieutenant," she replied to his unspoken thoughts. "I'm not some ogress. Believe it or not . . . all I want is what's best for Deanna. Perhaps if you have children someday, you will realize that watching out for what's best is not something that brings a great deal of pleasure. Sometimes—at times such as this one—it's a responsibility filled with much pain. As a Starfleet officer . . . William . . . this should not be a particularly alien concept to you. You've promised to assume responsibilities that are not always going to be gratifying: obeying the orders of a superior, even when you disagree. Or staying your hand in the name of the Prime Directive, even when your sense of morals would have you do otherwise. Well, you don't have to be in Starfleet to face such difficult moments. Deanna's facing one such now . . . and so am I. And believe it or not, I take no joy in it. Because it's causing my daughter sorrow, and I hate having to do that. But we all face our responsibilities, Lieutenant. We do what we have to do. I know and accept that, as does Deanna. And now I think it's time that you faced up to that as well. Good day, Lieutenant."

The door closed in his face.

Twenty-nine

The Scotch burned as it went down Riker's throat.

He had gotten it from Tang. The sergeant had seen Riker's bleak mood when the young Starfleet officer had returned from the Troi homestead and without a word had extracted the bottle from his private stock, offering it to Riker with the contention that it could make everything go down more smoothly . . . frustration, pain, hurt, whatever.

Riker stared at the bottle, then gripped it firmly by the neck. He had looked at Tang and asked, "Are you interested in joining me?"

Tang had placed his hands behind his back and rocked on his heels thoughtfully. "Frankly, sir," he had said after a moment's thought, "I don't think you'd want me there. There are times when a man just wants to get stinking drunk on his own."

Riker had nodded. "Sergeant, you're wise beyond your rank."

"Thank you, sir. All part—"

"—of the service," Riker had finished along with him.

Now Riker, alone in his quarters, poured himself another glass. He resisted the impulse to just swig it directly from the bottle. Somehow such action didn't seem remotely in keeping with Starfleet decorum. He was sure that somewhere, in some regulations book, he had read that rule one of being an officer was that an officer always drank from a glass.

He tossed back another shot and tried to remember what in hell had gotten him so upset in the first place.

"Deanna," he said out loud, and consequently reminded himself.

What in hell had he been thinking of, anyway? Getting involved with a local that way. That kind of thing never led to anything but trouble. And not just involved, no. He'd actually had to go and get . . . *feelings* for her.

"Not feelings," he muttered to himself, and tried to take consolation in that. Yes, that had to be it. He hadn't *really* felt anything for her. Not really. It had all been . . . been self-delusion. An attempt to convince himself that there was some sort of genuine love for her rattling around in that brain of his, because that was the only emotion that *her* type would accept before they would get to the really *worthwhile* part of a relationship. Yes, the worthwhile part, which was . . . which was . . .

He frowned. "What was the worthwhile part again?" he said.

The door chimed.

Riker tapped his communicator. "Riker here." He waited for a response.

The door chimed again.

Again Riker tapped his comm unit. "Riker here," he said with growing irritation.

"Will?" came the voice of Wendy Roper through the door.

"Speak up, Wendy," he told the communicator. "We have a lousy connection."

"Will, I want to see you."

He shrugged. "Sure. Come on over."

The door slid open and Wendy entered. Riker blinked in surprise. "That was fast."

Wendy didn't quite understand what he was talking about, but didn't pretend to. "I heard you were upset about something, Will."

"Nonsense!" he declared, rising slowly to his feet. "Do I sound upset?"

"No. Actually, you sound drunk."

"Drunk!" said Riker indignantly. "That, young woman, is an ugly rumor, spread by people I've tripped over."

She giggled slightly at that. "Well, if you are drunk, at least you're funny about it. Daddy sticks mostly to Synthehol when he drinks."

"Synthehol!" sniffed Riker. "That stuff's for infants! You'll never catch me drinking that Ferengii garbage."

He circled his room, taking slow and steady steps that were a bit exaggerated. Without any preamble, he turned to Wendy and said, "She wasn't even that good-looking!"

"Who?"

"Her! Her . . . her nose was too long. And her mouth was too wide. And . . . and her cheekbones were too high. Frankly . . . she was ugly."

"Her who?"

"Someone I knew. Or thought I knew." He dropped down onto the edge of the bed and stared off into space for a moment. Wendy sat next to him, waiting for him to say something else.

"You know," he said after a time, "you get in your head this . . . this picture of the way you think things are going to go. And they never match up. Nothing ever turns out the way you think it's going to."

"I know how that is."

He looked at her. "You do?"

"Of course I do. Fate's always kicking you in the teeth."

"But why me?"

"Not just you." She almost laughed at the persecuted look on his face. "Everyone. I've had my share of busted romances. And my dad—well, how do you think he took it when my mom died?"

"Not well?"

"Not well at all. He was wrecked up about it. But just because fate kicks you in the teeth doesn't mean you have to grin and give him more targets. You fight back, that's all. You just let him know that you're not going to take it. You're just not."

"She didn't understand," said Riker bleakly. "I thought she did, but she didn't. She can't see anything beyond this . . . this lousy little planet. A whole galaxy of opportunity, and she's got her head buried in the sands of Betazed. . . ."

"Not me," said Wendy firmly. "I'm not living out my life here, you can bet on that. Not on this overphilosophized ball of rock. Uh-uh."

"No?"

"No. No attachments for me. No strings. I want my freedom," Wendy said with fire in her voice. "Another year or two here, tops. Then I'm gone. Diplomatic corps, maybe. An attaché or something. Or who knows? Maybe I'll just hitch. See the galaxy. Grab rides on star freighters, doing odd jobs for passage."

"No attachments."

"No strings."

He stared at her. "Has anyone told you," he said, feeling an extremely pleasant buzz in his head, "how terrific you look?"

She grinned. "Not for a long time."

"And"—he paused—"has anyone *done* anything about how terrific you look?"

"Not for an even longer time."

He kissed her, feeling giddy. She was warm and supple against him. Undemanding. Yielding. Wanting nothing more from him than he was capable of giving.

He broke from her for a moment. "What do you think of art?"

"Boring."

"Thank God," he said, and they sank down onto the bed.

Lwaxana sat in her favorite chair in the study, reading and feeling totally relaxed. Deanna sat at a desk nearby, surrounded by texts for various psychology courses.

"What are you studying, Little One?" Lwaxana called to her.

Deanna did not respond.

Lwaxana turned to look at her and saw that Deanna was staring off into space. *Deanna,* she tossed into her daughter's head. Deanna looked up, and Lwaxana continued, *What are you studying?*

"Oh." Deanna looked blankly at the texts in front of her. She held one up. "Human dysfunctions."

"Well," Lwaxana said with a faint smile, "we've certainly had our up-close-and-personal study of that for today, haven't we."

"Mother, that's not nice," said Deanna tightly.

"You know," Lwaxana said with a thought, "you might be able to get some genuine use out of your extended contact with him—purely on a clinical basis. He's a fascinating study in obsessive behavior, don't you th—"

Deanna rose from her chair and started across the study. "I'm going out."

Immediately Lwaxana frowned, getting up from her chair. She didn't precisely block Deanna's way, but Deanna was definitely going to have to go around her. "It's late," Lwaxana said.

"I think I'm a little old for a curfew, Mother."

"Maybe. But not too old to exercise common sense. You're going to see him, and don't bother trying to lie to me."

"It was too abrupt, Mother. It—"

Lwaxana raised a stern finger. "It was exactly as abrupt as it needed to be. It's what you both needed. Simply dragging things out would have done neither of you any good. It's over. It's finished. That's it. Now go back and study."

"Mother, I don't want to. I can't. I—"

I don't care what you want, Lwaxana's voice echoed sharply in Deanna's head for emphasis. *Do as I tell you!*

Deanna took a step back, a physical reaction to the mental rebuffing. Then her eyes narrowed, her fingers rolled up into tightly clenched fists.

"You don't, do you," said Deanna carefully. "You don't care what I want."

"I care about what's best for you—"

And with such force that it seemed as if the air molecules crackled, Deanna hurtled a blistering, *NO YOU DON'T, MOTHER!* right at Lwaxana.

Lwaxana staggered, paling under her makeup. "How dare you think at me that way! To imply that I—"

"I'm not implying it, Mother! I'm saying it outright!" For a moment Deanna felt as if her courage were going to falter, and then she realized that if she'd been able to face up to the fear that had pervaded her in the jungle, then this should be easy in comparison.

It all burst from her at once. "For years, Mother—*for years*—while you've done whatever you wanted, wherever and whenever you wanted, you've told me what I'm *supposed* to do, what I *have* to do. And you keep telling me it's for me, all me. But it's not for me, Mother! It's for you! It's to satisfy *your* needs and *your* desires and *your* decisions. You've never asked me whether I care about any of these so-called responsibilities! You've never cared! You just . . . just assumed that I would embrace them because they were important to you. Well, they're not important to me, Mother! I'm sorry! I don't want to hold the sacred chalice! It's all yours! Make wind chimes of the Holy Rings for all I care!"

"Deanna—!" Words could not begin to express the shock flooding through Lwaxana. "I'd have sooner died than talk to *my* mother this way!"

Deanna didn't stop. She was afraid that if she did stop, she'd never have the nerve to start again. "I want my own priorities, Mother!" She thudded her fists against her own bosom for emphasis. "I want to make my decisions! My choices! Not yours. Not hundreds of years worth of tradition. Mine! I'm entitled to that! Every single thing I've done, I've done because you've made that decision for me! So when do I get a chance, Mother? When do *I* get to make decisions about careers and opportunities and marriages? *When?"*

"When you have a daughter! Just the same way that I did!"

Deanna gaped at her mother, appalled. "I can't believe you said that."

Lwaxana was silent.

"I cannot believe that you said that," repeated Deanna. "Generation after generation, women not being allowed to think for themselves . . . perpetuating that pattern, child after child . . ." Deanna drew herself up. "It stops here, Mother."

"It's that Riker," Lwaxana said angrily. "He put these thoughts in your mind."

"No, Mother. The thoughts were always there. I just never had the nerve to say them. And what's worst of all is, you knew they were there. You must have known. You knew that I was unhappy, and that didn't stop you from doing whatever you pleased with my life, counting on my obedience and 'dutiful daughter' mind-set."

"I knew that when you were older, you'd understand—"

"Well, you were wrong, Mother."

Deanna walked around Lwaxana and headed for the door. Her mother turned and called out, "You'd take him over me!"

Deanna spun and shouted back defiantly, *"Yes!"*

"You can't do this! You have studies . . . duties . . . a destiny!"

"I want to be with him, Mother! I was wrong to let you intimidate me into submission again. I was wrong to let him just walk away. We can't go back to the way it used to be, Mother. It's not going to happen. It would be a lie, and I won't live a lie!"

Lwaxana placed her hands on her hips and said sarcastically, "And what are you going to do? Quit your studies?"

"Probably."

"Marry him?"

"Maybe. Maybe not. Maybe I'll just go with him, be happy to be near him. When he ships out for his next assignment, I'll try to sign on. Some sort of job, I don't care what. Chief cook and bottle washer—it doesn't matter as long as we're together."

"You on a starship?" Lwaxana said, appalled. "A beautiful, free creature like you, cooped up in a ship for years? Millions of light-years away from home? It's insanity!"

"I've thought about Starfleet for years. A life of adventure, of experiencing minds and philosophies beyond what I have here. But I never really considered it as an option. Now, though, I understand. There's a galaxy of possibilities out there—even for a daughter of the Fifth House, if she simply has the nerve to take them. And who knows? Maybe I won't join Starfleet. Maybe I'll go back to geology. Maybe I'll paint myself blue and become a naked dancing girl in the Zetli system. But whatever I do, it will be *my* choice, not yours."

Deanna headed for the door, and in her head she heard, *If you go out that door, don't come back.*

Deanna went out the door.

Thirty

Deanna entered the embassy, which was quiet since it was after hours. But she stumbled upon several security men, whom she remembered from having met them in the jungle at the rendezvous point.

"Evening, miss," said Sommers, nodding slightly.

"Hello. I'm . . . I'm here to see Lieutenant Riker."

"Yes, miss. I'm sure you are," Sommers said. "You know the way?"

"Oh, yes."

He waved her past and Deanna disappeared down the hall. Sommers whistled softly to himself. "The officers get all the women."

Deanna went straight to Riker's quarters, her heart pounding. She had envisioned what he would say, what he would do. He was going to be so proud of her. The way that she had stood up to her mother, the way that she had taken control of her life. He would congratulate her, he would be thrilled at her love for him, he would take her in his arms . . .

She walked into his quarters and stopped dead in her tracks.

The room was only partly lit, but she could see Riker was lying in bed, naked. His uniform was tossed in several places around the room. He was asleep . . . and curled around the naked form of a woman whom Deanna immediately recognized as Wendy Roper.

Deanna made no sound, but her mind screamed in embarrassment and mortification.

It was more than enough to awaken Riker.

He sat up, confused and disoriented. He also sat up much too quickly because he was solidly hung over, and for a moment he thought his head was going to ricochet across the room. He sputtered uncomprehendingly . . . and then he saw Deanna, standing in the doorway, backlit by the hall light.

It took him a moment to reach the full realization that this wasn't a dream, or for that matter, a nightmare. "Deanna?" he said in a voice that sounded distant and ill.

She wanted to run shrieking down the hallway, but there was no way that she was going to retreat in that manner. "My apologies, Lieutenant. I seem to have come at a bad time. Perhaps if I'd called ahead, you might have been able to fit me into your schedule."

Her tone made Riker's hair hurt. "Deanna," he said again, and started forward. But his coordination was way off and instead he crashed to the floor.

The noise awakened the stone-cold-sober Wendy, who sat up in confusion and looked around. She saw Deanna, blinked in mild chagrin, and pulled the blanket around herself.

"Deanna," Riker began again. He grabbed at his uniform and started to pull it on.

"How nice. You have a thorough command of my name," she said, her arms folded.

"This isn't what it seems." Then Riker looked at Wendy, and the rumpled bed, and back to Deanna. "All right, it is what it seems. But I . . . you said you didn't want to see me anymore. You said we were finished and—"

"And it had been less than twenty-four hours since you'd had female companionship, so naturally you got over me. In fact, not only did you *get* over me, you practically *vaulted* over me," Deanna said, her voice getting louder.

Riker made shushing noises, which only prompted her to raise her voice more. "Are you afraid someone will hear?" she demanded.

"No," he whispered. "It's just . . . my head hurts."

"I'm sorry about your head," she said, not sounding remotely sorry. "I won't burden it further."

She spun on her heel and walked away. Riker, his uniform disheveled, nevertheless ran after her. He caught up with her halfway down the hallway and spun her around.

"You said—" he began.

"I know what I said. And would you like to know what I said to my mother? I told her I'd been wrong to toss you away. That it was time for me to find my own path. And that I wanted that path to be with you." Hot tears welled in her eyes and she fought them down. "But I foolishly assumed that you wanted that as well."

"I do—"

"No, you don't. I crawled out on a limb for you, and you chopped it off behind me."

"It wasn't like that. I wasn't thinking straight, and Wendy showed up, and—"

"And it was an opportunity."

"Yes."

"And it didn't really mean anything."

"That's right."

"And how do I know," she said icily, "that our time together didn't fall into the same categories?"

He took her by the shoulders. "You know that it didn't."

"I thought I knew that. But now I'm not sure. And what's worse, you're not sure either. Will . . . I thought we had something special. The physical and the spiritual. But for me, one hinges on the other. For you, it doesn't. And I don't think that's ever going to change for you."

Riker felt something slipping away from him, something very important—more important than he could have guessed—and suddenly, desperately, he wanted to save it. "I can change," he said. "I can—"

"Not overnight. Maybe someday, but maybe not ever. It may be, for you, something that can only come with maturity. I can't hinge my life on maybes. Because you're going to go away and I have to make decisions, and I can't base those decisions on uncertainties."

For a moment he bristled. "You sound so damned holier-than-thou. How do you know how it's going to be for you? Maybe as you mature, *you'll* change. Maybe you'll decide that you don't have to be heels over head in love in order to be intimate with someone. Maybe you'll discover that the physical side can have its own rewards, now that you've allowed yourself to experience it."

"Perhaps," she said evenly. "But there's one thing of which I'm reasonably sure at this point."

"Oh, really? What?"

"That you're not going to be there to find out."

He tried to think of a response to that, but before he could, she put a hand to his cheek and said, sounding not angry, but simply sad, "I'm sorry, Will. I just don't think there's a future for us."

And she turned and walked away.

Riker stood there, unmoving, watching her go. Wanting to say something, but unable to. Perhaps it was the drink still buzzing in his head, or perhaps there simply were no words . . . or even thoughts.

He turned and there was Sergeant Tang, leaning against a wall and regarding him thoughtfully.

"You were right to let her go, sir," said Tang. "Mark me, there's a twinkling star for every broken heart that a Starfleet man leaves—"

"Shut up, Tang," said Riker, and walked past him, heading back to his quarters.

Tang, unruffled, merely nodded. "Shutting up, sir. All part of the service."

* * *

Deanna Troi peeked into the study, sensing that her mother was still there.

Lwaxana was staring at a small holograph. She said nothing to Deanna, but Deanna sensed that her mother was not mentally wishing her to stay away. Tentatively, she entered the study and peered over her mother's shoulder.

"That's Grandmother, isn't it," said Deanna.

Lwaxana merely nodded.

There was a long silence, and then Deanna said, "I just came to get some of my things."

Her mother stared at the holograph for a time longer and then said, "You know . . . when I said that if you went out the door, you couldn't return . . . the words sounded familiar somehow. I racked my brain trying to remember where I'd heard them."

"And did you?"

"Mm-hmm. My mother"—Lwaxana waved the holograph slightly—"said it to me. When I told her I wanted to marry your father."

"She had her own plans for you?"

"Of course. Just as you are promised to Wyatt, I was promised to . . . what was his name?" She paused, and then remembered. "Stahly. That was it. But when we were of the proper age, we met for the first time, and . . . well, things just didn't . . . work out."

Deanna hunkered down next to her mother, fascinated. Lwaxana had never spoken of this before. "Why not? Didn't you like each other?"

"Oh, we got on quite well. I liked him, he liked me. But . . . I knew moments after we were introduced that it was hopeless. For one thing . . . he was in love with someone else."

"Another woman?"

Lwaxana looked at her bleakly. "Another man."

All Deanna could say was, "Oh."

"The hell of it was," admitted Lwaxana, "they made a cuter couple than we did."

Deanna tried not to smile. "It must have been very difficult for you."

"Well, fortunately it was shortly after that that I met your father. But my mother was stung by the lack of success for her match, and so she rejected out of hand whomever I brought home. We had an explosive argument about it. She disliked everything about your father."

"As much as you dislike Will Riker?"

"Oh, no . . . my dear, you thought I was difficult?" Lwaxana laughed mirthlessly. "She was much worse. Much much worse. Because to her, it was a matter of wounded pride. The notion that I could find a mate for myself where she had failed. And when I stormed out, through that very door, in fact"—she pointed to the front door—"she told me that I shouldn't bother coming back. Oh, she didn't mean it, of course. Well . . . maybe at the time, she did."

"And did you mean it when you said it to me?"

Lwaxana regarded her thoughtfully. "At the time." Then she spread her arms. "Oh, Deanna . . . I'm so sorry."

Deanna leaned forward and her mother embraced her. "Sorry for what, Mother?"

"Sorry because I know what happened when you went to see Lieutenant Riker. I mean . . . a mother knows these things."

"Especially when a mother can read minds."

"That's true. And also . . . I'm sorry because you were right about something.

About how . . . things between us have changed. And we can't go back to the way they were."

"Why are you sorry about that, Mother?"

"Because I *liked* the way things were," said Lwaxana plaintively. "It was nice, simple, uncomplicated." But then she sighed and patted Deanna's hand. "But it wasn't what you wanted. I understand that. And I really am *not* an ogress, Deanna."

"I know, Mother."

"I just ask one thing. Please . . . please don't become a naked blue dancer on Zetli. It's so chilly there, I can guarantee you, you'll catch your death."

"All right, Mother." Deanna smiled. "Tell you what. Not only do I promise not to become a naked dancer of any color, but I'll stay with my psychology studies. Although . . . I don't rule out Starfleet as an eventual outlet for my career."

Lwaxana appeared about to object, but instead she simply nodded her head. "Whatever will make you happy, dear."

"Thank you, Mother."

"You know, it's so late at night, and you ran out without having dinner. You must be starving."

"I . . . am a little hungry," admitted Deanna.

"Would you like something to eat?"

"That'd be nice."

As soon as Deanna said it, she realized she'd misspoken, and she thrust her hand forward and put it gently over Lwaxana's mouth before her mother could bellow for Mr. Homn.

"Mother," she said softly, "I'll make my own dinner. In fact, if you'd like, I'll even make something for you."

Lwaxana looked thunderstruck. "Yourself?"

"Yes, Mother."

Lwaxana let out an amazed breath. "You *are* full of radical ideas today, aren't you. All right . . . let's go." She stood and looked around, momentarily confused. "Now . . . which way is the kitchen?"

Deanna took her by the elbow. "I'll show you, Mother," she said with a smile.

Lwaxana shook her head as Deanna led her off. "Children nowadays and their crazy notions. Starfleet. Cooking. I don't know what the world is coming to. . . ."

Thirty-one

Roper looked up as Riker walked slowly into the café. "You're late, Captain," he admonished him.

Riker just nodded . . . very slowly. He sat down and the waitress brought some black coffee over to him unasked. He was silently grateful.

"I hear," said Roper casually, "that there was something of a brouhaha last night."

"Something like that." Riker didn't even want to ask him where he'd heard it. Either it was from one of the security men describing the idiot behavior of a senior officer, or else it was from Roper's own daughter describing the aftermath of an assignation. Either way it wasn't something he wanted to dwell on.

"Planetside relationships can get somewhat tangled, eh?" said Roper. "That's the advantage of being in a ship. Hit and run, as it were."

Riker just nodded and let the coffee flow into his veins, reestablishing some measure of coherency.

"You must be happy about getting out of here."

Something about the phrasing caught Riker's attention, burrowing through the alcoholic haze. "I've . . . I've got at least another month here."

But Roper shook his head. "I thought you'd heard. *Hood* repairs finished faster than anticipated. You're out of here in twenty-four hours, Captain."

Riker felt a charge in his head as if a life-support system had come on line. "You mean . . . you mean I'm shipping out?"

"That's right. So you'd better get yourself shaped up. There's paperwork for you to finish up. Forms to be filled out, reports on the Sindareen business. Got to have everything tied off nice and neat before we kick you loose."

Riker stood quickly, tossing the coffee down his throat and trying to ignore the fact that, in so doing, he'd just burned himself. "Mark—Mark, thank you. This is great news. This is . . ."

Mark pumped his hand and said, smiling, "When you're out carving yourself a career, just think about us poor planet-crawlers every now and then, okay?"

"I will, Mark. You can bet on that."

"Then get a move on, Captain."

Riker released Roper's hand and bolted out of the café. Mark watched him go and then sighed. "Kids."

Everything had been attended to.

Almost.

Riker told himself that he was making a final stop at the art museum to verify for himself that everything was back in place and restored to order. After all, Starfleet would want nothing to be overlooked.

But he found himself standing for an overlong time in front of one particular painting: the one Deanna had showed him, the one with all the large concentric "goopy" swirls.

He stared at it.

Then he heard the music floating from nearby. And somehow, in a way that he couldn't quite explain, the music seemed to enhance what he was looking at.

As if dancing to the notes, the colors began slowly to swirl. It bore a striking resemblance, Riker realized, to stars swimming about in a sort of galactic whirlpool. No, not just stars . . . stars and planets, and perhaps . . . perhaps that was something like what the universe had looked like in the throes of creation. Void and miasmic and filled with promise and possibilities . . .

He sensed her standing next to him. But he couldn't turn to face her.

"You're leaving," said Deanna.

"Yes."

"I wish you safe voyage."

"I wish you . . ." He stopped and found the strength to look at her. He had turned quickly, and for a moment his mind's eye superimposed the flow of the painting over her. For one insane second, she was, literally, the center of his universe. "I wish you could come with me," he said at last.

She shook her head. "You know, Imzadi . . . for a time there, I was ready to change my universe for you. But now . . . now I don't think either of us is ready for that."

He tried to say that she was wrong, but he couldn't. So instead he tried to find some way to say good-bye. But he couldn't do that either.

He turned and looked back at the painting. Such vastness that encompassed everything there was . . . and yet somehow, now, it seemed completely empty.

"Deanna." He turned back to her. "Maybe . . ."

But she was gone.

He hadn't even said good-bye. Dammit, he'd said nothing to her . . . because he hadn't been able to find the words. And so he'd blanked his mind, and now she probably thought that he didn't care all that much. If he were able to part from her with such apparent ease, without even a word . . .

He took a step in the direction he was sure she had gone . . . but then stopped. Because he knew, beyond any question, that this was the way she wanted it. And somehow, somewhere along the way, what she wanted had become more important to him than what he wanted.

Thirty-two

Captain's Log, Stardate 42372.5:

Of the twenty-four hours Q allotted us to prove ourselves, eleven have now passed without incident. And yet I cannot forget Q's prediction that we will face here some critical test of human worth.

As the *Enterprise* continued to orbit around Cygnus IV, Commander Riker sat across from his new captain in the ready room. Both of them were equally concerned about what they perceived as oddities on Farpoint Station, but neither was certain precisely how to proceed.

The thing that Riker was pleased about, however, was that Picard had so clearly accepted him without reservation. Once Picard had welcomed him aboard and set out the ground rules, it was as if the captain had left any sort of doubt behind him. Unlike other commanders under whom he'd served, Riker felt no pressure that he had to impress Picard. Instead Picard was clearly going to deal with him in a straightforward, no-nonsense manner. It was an attitude that Riker welcomed.

Studying his notes on Cygnus IV, Riker said, "This planet's interior heat results in abundant geothermal energy, sir. But it's about all this world *does* offer."

Picard looked thoughtful. "And it's your belief that this is what made it possible for them to construct this base to Starfleet standards?"

"Yes, sir." Riker leaned forward. "We have to assume that they've been trading their surplus energy for the construction materials used here. According to our ship's scans, many of the materials used are not found on this world."

Picard smiled slightly. "Perhaps it's like those incidents you describe in your report as 'almost magical' attempts to please us."

From any other captain, that might have sounded patronizing. But Picard was merely stating the facts. Accordingly, Riker nodded. "Those events *did* happen, sir."

"And in time we'll discover the explanation. Meanwhile, none of it suggests anything threatening. If only *every* life-form had as much desire to please Starfleet."

Riker knew what Picard meant. With the Ferengii to contend with, not to mention the Orions, the Sindareen . . . plus the ever-present notion that the Romulans might be heard from again . . . there were certainly enough hazards for the Federation to deal with. And then this Q had shown up, whose actions Riker had reviewed earlier, just to make things even more difficult.

Picard rose. "Ready to beam down? I'm looking forward to meeting this Groppler Zorn."

Riker waited for Picard to come around the desk. After Riker's big speech earlier about being protective of the captain, he wasn't thrilled that Picard was immediately going to beam down and meet with the head of Farpoint Station. If there was some unknown danger, it would be extremely bad if that danger suddenly became known in the course of Picard's visit planetside. Still, there appeared to be no jeopardy at the moment, and so Riker kept his counsel. As Picard preceded him to the door, Riker said, "I'm convinced there's more to it than just 'pleasing us,' sir."

Picard looked thoughtful. "Like something Q is doing to trick us?"

As they stepped out toward the turbolift, Riker noticed the turbolift door opening. His view of the occupant was momentarily blocked by Picard's raised arm as the captain gestured and said, "Over here, Counselor!" He turned to Riker and said, "I've asked her to join us in this meeting."

A ship's counselor. Riker had never served on a ship large enough, or on a long enough mission, that a counselor was required. Besides, the position was a relatively new one to Starfleet, only having been developed over the last few years. Since Riker had unbounded confidence in his own mental balance, he doubted that he'd have much need for a counselor's services, but thought a lot of people on the *Enterprise* could probably make good use of one. He just hoped that he or she wasn't going to be one of these excessively cerebral types who tried to read something into everything that was said, no matter how casual.

Now Riker had a clear view of her . . . and he felt all the blood drain from his face. Picard had turned to the woman and was saying, "May I introduce our new first officer, Comdr. William Riker. Mr. Riker, our ship's counselor, Deanna Troi."

Picard was now looking back at Riker, and his tone changed slightly as he saw the expression on his first officer's face.

Ten years it had been, but the old feelings flooded over him with the same sting as if the wound were still fresh.

She had her hair back up in that tight knot—the one that was so unflattering—that she'd worn when she wanted to discourage any advances from him. She'd known . . . *she'd known* . . . he was going to be here. Of course she would have. As a counselor, she would have reviewed the files of all the senior officers.

His mind was running riot. He was out of practice, *years* out of practice. He'd been caught completely flat-footed.

Deanna, for her part, looked utterly serene. And then there was that sensation, the one that he'd thought he'd never experience again. Her voice in his head, in his soul, as she asked, *Do you remember what I taught you, Imzadi? Can you still sense my thoughts?*

She was so smooth, so collected, that even as she thought-cast to him, she extended her hand formally. "A pleasure, Commander," she said, placing a slight emphasis on the rank.

Riker took her hand and said, "I, uh . . . likewise, Counselor."

From Riker's flustered expression, Picard now knew that something was definitely up. "Have the two of you met before?" he asked Riker.

Met? Oh, nooo . . . just had one of the most involving, intense, frustrating, and torrid relationships I've ever had with anyone. That's all. Out loud, he simply said, "We . . . we have, sir."

Riker wasn't sure whether Picard had picked up on the subtext of the statement and tumbled onto just how well Riker and Troi knew each other, or if he was simply assuming that they'd become acquainted on some previous occasion. All he said was, "Excellent. I consider it important that my key officers know each other's abilities."

Riker wasn't sure, but he thought he could hear Troi's silent laughter echoing in his brain.

"We do, sir," Troi assured him. "We do."

Picard stepped into the turbolift, and Riker and Troi followed him silently.

There was so much he wanted to say . . . so much he wanted to tell her. But his mind awhirl, and out of practice as he was, he couldn't find any way to project the thoughts to her. And now they would not have the time to speak privately before being thrust into a new and hazardous situation. A situation in which they would have to interact smoothly and professionally. But would that be possible, considering all that they had been through together? And considering the way they had parted, with so much left unsaid? Did she know he cared? Did she know the things he had wanted to say? Or had she been nursing a grudge all these years, not understanding how . . . ?

And then, there was her voice again, in his mind, carrying her thoughts to him like a dove finding its home. *I, too, would never say good-bye, Imzadi.*

Relief washed over him. He should have known better. He should have known that she would understand, and that there was indeed going to be a basis on which to build a relationship.

He wasn't sure where that relationship would go, or what its ultimate fate would be . . . but at least whatever happened in the future, they would be facing it together.

It had taken them some time to work it out. At first the impulse was to pick up where they had left off . . . but they found quickly that they couldn't. Too much time had passed, and neither of them could find some way to bridge that gap and reconcile the young people they had been with the Starfleet officers they were now.

Nor were they sure what would happen should they rekindle the passion that had burned so brightly. If things didn't work out, then it would be extremely difficult for them to work with one another without a great deal of tension. And there was a very distinct possibility it might not work out, for their predictions about each other had been remarkably on target. Riker still tended to have a roving eye. And Troi had indeed come to appreciate the pleasure of experimentation . . . so it wasn't as if she had lived like a monk in the intervening years.

With all the complications that came with becoming lovers again, they had decided simply not to rush things. Neither of them was willing to risk everything to stoke the embers of their relationship.

"Time has a way of working things out," Deanna had said to him. So they gave the relationship that time.

They did not, however, give the relationship much of anything else. And the laws of inertia tended to govern human interaction along with most other things. As their years together on the Enterprise *rolled past, their relationship, since it was at rest, tended to stay at rest.*

The only force that could have acted upon them to change it would have been the idea that they might not be able to alter the course of things any time they felt like it. Then again . . . why should they have considered that possibility?

After all . . . they thought they had all the time in the universe.

And then came the peace conference with the Sindareen . . .

Thirty-three

Riker lay on his back, staring up into the darkness of his quarters.

His hands were interlaced behind his head, the pillow soft under him. He had been that way for over an hour, as sleep refused to come.

Sorting out his feelings was rapidly becoming something of a royal pain. He still remembered that time a couple of years ago, in Deanna's quarters . . . Both he and Deanna had been in an extremely mellow mood, and he had also been allowing the more relaxing qualities of the Synthehol he'd consumed to have sway over his actions. A friendly good-night kiss had turned into something far more passionate, and for a moment they had been kissing each other eagerly, hungrily, and it had been just like the old days.

And then Deanna had whispered, pleaded, telling him that they shouldn't, reminding him of the difficulties of involvement while both served on the same ship. Yet even as she spoke, she would have let him . . .

But he pulled back. Her words had penetrated the Syntheholic haze on his brain and washed it away, bringing with it instant sobriety and a reminder of the line that they had drawn for themselves.

And nothing had happened.

Not that he hadn't wanted it . . . they had both wanted it . . .

But what had they wanted? Momentary gratification? Or something more . . . a rekindling of something that they had thought they'd left behind them?

Perhaps they'd been kidding themselves. Here he was someone accustomed to command situations, and here she was someone who was always in touch with feelings. So it was only natural that they would decide that they could control their feelings, dictate their relationship. Turn their emotions on and off like an old-style light switch.

How realistic was that, though? Lying there in the darkness, imagining Deanna at that moment, wrapped in the arms of Dann, laughing or saying things softly . . .

Did she say the same things to Dann that she had to Riker?

For a moment there he had actually been drifting off, his feelings about Deanna lulling his brain and convincing him that everything would seem more clear in the morning. And then something, some impulse, made him sit bolt upright in bed, moving so swiftly that he had a momentary sense of disorientation.

Someone was there. He didn't know how, he didn't know why . . . but someone was there, hiding in a corner, lurking in the darkness.

He called out, "Li—"

But he didn't get the word out.

A hand clamped over his mouth and shoved him back down onto the bed.

Riker struggled fiercely, shoving at the arm that held him down. He reached upward, grabbing at his assailant's face, feeling skin that was like parchment and a bristling beard.

And then a voice said, "Lights!"

Riker froze. Because the voice sounded insanely familiar.

The lights came up on command. He blinked against the sudden brightness and the voice amended, "Half lights." They dimmed 50 percent, and now Riker could make out the features of the intruder.

The hair and beard were thick and gray. The skin was wrinkled and timeworn. But the eyes burned fiercely with determination, and the face . . . the face was unmistakable. He was looking up at himself . . . except he was decades older.

"Shut up!" hissed the elder Riker. "We haven't much time."

Riker's eyes were wide with stupefaction. For one moment he thought he might still be sleeping, and he started to struggle again, tried to shout over the hand that was clamped on his mouth.

"Didn't you hear what I said?" snarled the old man. "Shut up, you idiot! They may be here to try and stop me at any moment! So lie still! Listen to me, and be prepared to do exactly what I tell you. Deanna's life hangs on what you do next."

THE MIDDLE

Thirty-four

The curator of the Betazed national archives shook hands with Admiral Riker and bowed slightly in acknowledgment. "Your donation of Lwaxana Troi's effects will be quite a boon to our collection, Admiral."

Riker smiled indifferently. "I'm glad I could be of service, sir. And now . . . if you'll excuse me, I believe that my transport back home is here."

"Ah, yes," said the curator. "I understand the *Enterprise* herself has come to get you."

"Just happenstance." Riker smiled evenly. "It was the closest ship. It's not as if I'm anyone particularly important."

"Oh, now, Admiral, let's not sell ourselves short. Some of us still remember your handling of the Sindareen raiders all those years ago. They stayed well clear of Betazed after that." The curator frowned. "Although it's a pity . . . they've become much more aggressive in the last decade or so. My understanding is that they've resumed many of their warlike ways. Truly a shame."

"Yes," agreed Riker, at this point anxious to just get out of there. He felt as if he would say just about anything to escape.

At that moment the air hummed a few feet away with a familiar sound, and Riker grinned openly. It was rare that he smiled these days, but when he did, it was genuine.

"Commodore Data," he said evenly. "It's a pleasure to see you again. You haven't aged a day."

Data cocked his head slightly. "Why would I, Admiral?"

Riker chuckled silently. "You may have gotten the hang of a lot of things since I first met you, Data, but humor still eludes you. Comforting to know some things don't change."

"I'm sure it is." Data turned and indicated his second officer. "You remember my science officer, Lieutenant Blair."

"Yes, of course," said Riker, and shook Blair's large, furred hand. "Well, gentlemen . . . shall we get going?"

"Whatever you say, Admiral . . . if you're done here, that is."

Riker looked at the curator questioningly.

"As far as I'm concerned, Admiral, we're finished. Oh," the curator added as an afterthought, "a woman stopped by . . . Wendy, I believe she said her name was . . . and said that you should stop by and say good-bye before you leave."

"We can wait if you wish, Admiral," offered Data.

But Riker just shook his head. "No," he said softly, and the general melancholy that routinely hovered over him these days enveloped him once more. "No, I've never been particularly good at saying good-bye on this planet."

Data didn't pretend to understand. He merely tilted his head and said,

"Enterprise. Three to beam up." And a moment later, with a crackle of blue energy, they were gone.

When Riker first set foot on the ship that bore the name of that vessel he'd once served aboard, he felt a rush of pleasure. But it was quickly borne away by the realization that this wasn't really that *Enterprise* . . . that there would never be another one like it. It had been a unique, special time in his life, and . . . he realized bleakly . . . probably the high point. Certainly nothing since then had come close to approaching the pure joy and wonder that that particular assignment had given him.

He was more than happy to inspect the ship, examine all the various new and exciting wrinkles that had been added. Ultimately, though, once all that had been done, he was more than content to sit in his cabin, alone and comfortable with the loneliness to which he'd grown so accustomed.

It was in this state that Data found him when he came to inform Riker that they would be arriving shortly at Starbase 86.

"Thank you, Data," Riker said simply upon being given the news. He went back to staring out the viewport.

"You seem to be preoccupied, Admiral," observed Data.

"I'm watching the stars." Riker smiled thinly. "Did you know, some people believe that whatever happens to us is decided by the stars. That we have no control over our fates. I think Shakespeare even wrote that 'the fault is in the stars.' "

"Actually, Admiral, that is incorrect."

"You're going to tell me that it's ridiculous to believe that interstellar phenomenon could possibly have any sort of effect on the affairs of men?"

"No, sir. That's so self-evident it's not even worth pointing out. No, I was simply going to tell you that your endeavor to quote Shakespeare was not only imprecise, but in fact wildly wrong."

"How wildly?"

"If you're quoting the passage I believe—namely *Julius Caesar,* act one, scene two—then you have reversed it. The proper line is, 'Men at some time are masters of their fates: The fault, dear Brutus, is not in our stars, but in ourselves, that we are underlings.' "

"Really? Huh." Riker thought about that a moment. "Hell of a thing to screw up. Who said it?"

"Shakespeare, sir. You were correct about that."

"No, I mean, who in the play?"

"Cassius, in conversation with Brutus. Two of the conspirators who assassinate Julius Caesar."

"Hmm. Ironic, isn't it, Data? Men who try to decide they're going to take their fate into their own hands . . . and the only way to do that is to try and kill a man whom they admire."

"It has always been a great puzzle to me how people can do utterly immoral things in the name of morality. Certainly the philosophy of guiding your own fate is a laudable one. But how can anyone applaud the notion of murder?"

"Sometimes, Data . . . you do what you have to do. You just make a decision that something has to be done and damn the consequences."

Riker said nothing further, and even though Data simply stood there, watching him, Riker didn't feel any need to comment. "My standing immobile in this manner once bothered Captain Picard greatly," Data said after a time.

"Did it?" Riker shrugged. "Data, you'll find that nowadays, there's very little that bothers me."

"Is it because of Deanna Troi?"

Riker turned and looked up at him. "Ancient history, Data," he said in a hollow voice. "Very ancient."

Data seemed pensive, which was most unusual for him. "I am aware of something, Admiral, that—if you take it in the proper frame of mind—might serve to put much of your long-standing frustration to rest."

"Really?" Riker was more amused than anything else. "And what precisely do you know, Data?"

Data paused, and his next words were the last that Riker could possibly have expected.

"What would you say, Admiral, if I informed you that . . . somewhere . . . Deanna Troi is still alive."

The statement hung there for a moment, untouched. And then, to Data's surprise, Riker actually smiled again. "Data, you're turning philosopher on me."

"I am, sir?"

"You're about to tell me that Deanna lives on in our hearts and minds and memories, right?"

"No, sir. She lives on in an alternative time line."

Riker's smile was frozen, but the rest of his expression was an utter blank. Finally he said, "Data, what in hell are you talking about?"

Data sat down across from Riker, endeavoring to select the method of explanation that would be simplest for Riker to follow.

"Our stop right before Betazed," began Data, "was at the world of the Guardian of Forever. You're familiar with it?"

"Of course," said Riker impatiently.

"In the course of my visit there, the scientists showed me a temporal irregularity they have discovered. These irregularities are known, interchangeably, as alternative time lines or even parallel universes. There have been several encountered in Federation history. For example, the alternative universe and/or time line wherein the Klingons and Federation remained at war, from which Tasha Yar crossed over and eventually became the mother of Sela. Then there was the alternative universe and/or time line which James Kirk and several of his command crew encountered that was a 'mirror' representation of our—"

"I know all that! Dammit, Data, what does any of this have to do with Deanna?"

"It has to do, sir, with how these alternative universes and/or time lines—"

"Stop saying it that way! It's getting on my nerves! Pick a term and stick with it!"

Data blinked. Riker was showing more fire and anger in the past five minutes than he conceivably had all during the past five years. "It has to do," Data began again, "with how these time streams . . . ?" He paused on the last word, adding a slight interrogative to his intonation to see whether or not Riker approved of the terminology. The admiral nodded and gestured for him to continue. "It has to do with how these time streams are begun. No one knows how many there are; perhaps an infinite number. But apparently they key off of significant moments in time. *Focal points* was the term that then–science officer Spock coined, I believe.

James Kirk's Edith Keeler, who inadvertently lived when she was supposed to have died, represented one such focal point. The constant surveying of the events that the Guardian displays will sometimes reveal one of these offshoots."

Riker swallowed hard. "And they've . . . they've found one involving Deanna?"

"That's correct, sir. Curiously, it revolves around the moment of Deanna Troi's death at the Sindareen peace conference. In the alternative time stream, Counselor Troi in fact did not die."

"How did she survive?" Riker's voice was barely above a whisper.

"They have been unable to make that determination. What they have discovered, however, is that the counselor was present at the peace conference . . . and her empathic abilities were able to discern that the Sindareen were lying about their peaceful intentions. Once she uncovered their duplicity, it was quickly learned that the entire peace conference was a scheme to use Federation resources to rebuild so that they could, years down the line, launch new and devastating forays against the Federation."

"Which they wound up doing."

"Yes, sir, in our time stream—the 'correct' one, for want of a better term. In our time stream, the Sindareen are a powerful and formidable people. In the alternative time stream, however, the Federation refused the peace initiative, pulled out, and the Sindareen economy eventually fell apart completely. At that point, the Federation then stepped in with restoration efforts, but under far more controlled and less trusting circumstances. The Sindareen were able to rebuild, but were a far more docile and chastened race."

"And Deanna lived." Riker looked to Data, his eyes sparking like flint struck together. "She lived."

"Yes, sir. So you see, Admiral . . . you can take heart. Although the counselor's death was an unfortunate and tragic thing, there is a 'cosmic justice' of sorts . . . a sense of balance. For in an alternative time stream, Deanna Troi lived and accomplished great things."

Riker was silent for a long moment . . . and then he seemed to be muttering to himself. Whispering. His voice was a low and gentle singsong, and it sounded as if he were trying to reason something out.

"Admiral?"

Riker started to get to his feet and put a hand out to Data. The android assumed that Riker needed his help getting up and so lent him support. But then Riker's hand closed on Data's shoulder with a fierceness that might have been appropriate to a man less than half his age, and he whirled Data around, galvanized by inner fires.

"Turn the ship around," Riker said hoarsely.

"Admiral?"

"You heard me. Bring us back to Betazed. Fastest possible speed."

"Sir, I'd like to be as accommodating as possible, but I don't understand why—"

With a red-hot fury, and a voice like iron pounded on a forge, Riker shouted, *"Turn the goddamn ship around, Data! That's a* direct *order from a superior officer. Do it* now, *or so help me, I'll have you* relieved *of command and I'll steer us back there* myself!"

Thirty-five

It took a day to get all the clearances from the Betazed government. But Data did it as quickly as he could because he was of the firm conviction that if he didn't get an official release for the body of Deanna Troi, then Admiral Riker might very likely go down and bring the body back himself. In the current state that he was in, he was probably single-minded enough to haul the corpse onto his back and find a way to carry it piggyback to the *Enterprise.*

Riker had lapsed into silence, but that silence was hardly benign. He fairly radiated urgency, bordering on controlled desperation. He stood there and watched as Deanna's body, still in its encasement, materialized on the cargo transporter. It floated on small, controlled waves of antigravity emanating from floater units that had been attached.

Data, Blair, and Chief Medical Officer Hauman, along with two medtechs, were all waiting there for it when it arrived. Hauman, tall and gangly with thick brown hair, looked at his commanding officer questioningly. "Sir, am I understanding this correctly? You want me to run an autopsy on a four-decade-old body?"

"That is the plan," Data said with as close to a sigh as he was capable of producing.

Riker put up a hand. "Hold it," he said as the medtechs came around to move the encasement. "Hauman . . . run a tricorder scan. Look for life signs."

Hauman stared at Riker, then at Data, and then back at Riker. "Are you expecting me to find any, sir?"

Riker looked at him coldly. "I'm expecting you to follow my order."

Hauman did as he was told, passing the small unit over Deanna's body. "Nothing. Not so much as a blip. I'm sorry, Admiral, but this is a forty-year-old corpse. Nothing more."

"It's something more than that, Doctor," said Riker. "It's a hope in hell. Now get her . . . get it . . . down to sickbay."

"What am I looking for, if I might ask."

"Cause of death."

"Sir, wouldn't that be in the autopsy performed at the time of the death?"

"Yes, it would," said Riker, sounding amazingly reasonable. "So what I want you to do is pull that autopsy from the records."

"And then?"

"And then," said Riker, "look for something that isn't there."

While the autopsy was performed, Riker stayed in his quarters. He had an inkling of what autopsies used to be like, back in the primitive days of surgical knives and catguts. Cutting up the body, studying each of the organs, searching through and running tests while a nauseating stench filled the air.

Deanna's body would not be cut or harmed. A battery of tests would be run without mussing a hair on her head. Nevertheless, Riker couldn't find it within himself to stand there while Deanna's body was treated like a large slab of meat . . . no matter how comparatively delicate that treatment might be. He'd gone through it once. Twice would be unendurable.

He stared down at Betazed, which turned under them in leisurely fashion.

Imzadi, he whispered to someone who had not been able to respond for nearly two generations. *Imzadi . . . tell me I'm not losing my mind.*

There was a buzz at his door and he said urgently, "Come in."

Data entered with Dr. Hauman at his side. Data's face was, as always, unreadable. But Riker could immediately tell from Hauman's expression that something had happened. Something had occurred that had surprised the good doctor. That alone was enough to give Riker hope. "Well?" he demanded, waggling his fingers impatiently. "Tell me."

"It's, um . . ." Hauman looked uncomfortable. "It's . . . extremely puzzling."

"What is?"

"It would appear, Admiral," Data said, "that we have something of a paradox on our hands."

"Oh, really. Explain it to me, if you'd be so kind. No . . . better still . . . I'll explain it to you."

Riker rose from his chair and faced Hauman. "You found," he said slowly, "traces of something that didn't exist at the time of Deanna's death."

"That's . . . that's correct, sir," said Hauman. Not only did he feel foolish that his previously expressed doubts over the point of this exercise were now without foundation, but he felt even dumber over the fact that Riker was apparently one step ahead of him. "We found minute traces of Raxatocin . . . so minute that the medical equipment of the time would not have been able to detect it. It wouldn't have even shown up as an unknown substance."

"Raxatocin," said Riker slowly. "That's a poison, isn't it?"

"Yes, sir. It . . . well, it causes precisely the types of symptoms that killed Counselor Troi. Massive circulatory collapse. It was developed thirteen years ago, and as recently as five years ago it was still undetectable."

"How is the poison transmitted?"

"Any number of ways. Injection. It can be ingested. In sufficient concentration, it can even be inhaled."

"All right." Riker took a deep breath. "Has Deanna's body been returned to the proper authorities?"

"Yes, sir," said Data.

"Good. Okay, Mr. Data." Riker clapped his hands together and then rubbed them briskly. "Take us to the Guardian of Forever."

There was a dead silence in the room, and then Data turned to Hauman. "Doctor, I thank you for your time. That will be all. And make certain the file on Deanna Troi is sealed."

Hauman nodded. Riker stared at Data and said, "What?"

Data raised a finger, indicating that they should not say anything until Hauman left. Riker waited impatiently until the doctor was out the door, and then he said, "What's the problem here, Data?"

"Admiral . . . I didn't want Dr. Hauman here because, frankly . . . I was afraid that you would say things that would be incriminating and I didn't want there to be a witness who had less loyalty to you than I do."

"Incriminating? Data," Riker said, trying to keep his anger down, "what do you mean? Isn't it obvious what's happened?"

"I blame myself, sir. I tried to tell you something I hoped would give you some measure of peace. But instead it is moving you toward thinking the unthinkable.

It's obvious to me, sir, what's going to happen. You intend to try and step through the Guardian of Forever. To go back in time and save the life of Counselor Troi, and by doing so, change history."

"No, Data. Fix history. Don't you get it?" Riker started to pace the room, unable to contain his excitement. "She wasn't supposed to die! Someone went back, from right now, or maybe even years in the future. And they poisoned her!"

"We don't know that."

"We *do* know that! The poison came from the future! Maybe our future, or perhaps her future which is our past, which is . . ." His voice trailed off. "Give me a minute. I get confused sometimes when I discuss time travel."

"I understand what you're saying, sir. But I must point out that Raxatocin has been known to occur in nature, even before it was developed as a poison. It's possible that somehow she acquired it through some unique and bizarre combination of circumstances."

"Remotely possible, but not likely. I'm telling you, Data, you were absolutely right about her being a focal point in time. But it's the reverse of Edith Keeler. Deanna wasn't supposed to die. She was supposed to live. Our world, this world—it's not the 'correct' time line. It's the wrong one!"

"And your hope is that, if you're allowed to go through the Guardian of Forever, you'll have the opportunity to set things right."

"That's correct."

Although Data's expression didn't change, it was clear that a great deal was running through his mind. And all of it involved trying to determine some way to deal with this new and bizarre situation.

"Admiral . . . you cannot be allowed to do it."

"I'm giving you a direct order to—"

But Data shook his head. "No, sir. Not this time. It's not going to work, and pulling rank is going to be of no use whatsoever. Starfleet regulations in this matter are very, very specific. Ever since the first *Enterprise* slingshot back through time and proved that it could be done, a set of specific guidelines were developed regarding time travel. And the foremost of those guidelines is, no tampering."

"Dammit, Data, someone *already* tampered!"

"We can't be certain of that. What we can be certain of is Starfleet regulations—"

"The hell with regulations!" Riker stood barely two feet from Data, his fists clenched, his temper flaring beyond control. "Deanna's life is at stake!"

"Deanna has no life, Admiral. Deanna is dead." Data's calm was a striking contrast to Riker's fury. "She has been dead for four decades. Her death helped determine the universe in which we've lived all these years."

"Then I don't want to live in this universe. I want to cross over, like Tasha did."

"That's not possible, Admiral. And if you enter the Guardian, you put at risk the lives and reality of uncounted innocent people. Many things have happened since Counselor Troi died. I've evolved, both in terms of self-expression and in command ability. You have your Starbase to command."

Riker laughed bitterly.

"Wesley has his own command," Data continued. "Geordi, Worf, Alexander . . . all of them have lived their lives as the fates have determined. People have been born and died for forty years since the death of Deanna. Things have happened as they were meant to happen. You cannot now suddenly flip open the books of history, erase what's been written, and reinscribe it with a story more to your liking."

"I could go before Starfleet—"

"That's certainly your prerogative," agreed Data. "But I do not foresee any instance where Starfleet will be willing to risk sacrificing all reality for the sake of one woman."

Riker was hushed. Sensing that perhaps he was getting through to him, Data pressed on. "Have you considered something, Admiral? You say that all you wish to do is save Deanna. But have you considered the possibility that—even if you accomplish your task—you might, in the midst of doing it, make matters worse? With knowledge of forty years' worth of events, you could easily say something, do something, that has either an immediate impact or an influence further down the time stream. If knowledge is power, then knowledge of the future is the ultimate power. No one, Admiral . . . not you, nor I . . . no one has the wisdom to wield that power. The nontampering rule of time travel is in place for just as solid a reason as the Prime Directive. And as in the case of the Prime Directive, it may be something that's difficult for us to live with . . . but it is, nonetheless, necessary."

Riker stood with his back to Data. And Data could see, slowly but surely, a lot of the fire and spark slowly draining from him. His shoulders slumped, his posture drooped. His hands, which had been tightly curled around the edges of the table, slackened.

When he spoke, it was with the air of defeat that he had carried with him all these years. "She is just one woman, isn't she."

"Yes, sir. And you, sir . . . are a conscientious and ethical man. You would not put at risk an entire reality . . . for the sake of one woman."

"All right, Data," Riker said tiredly. "You've convinced me. Maybe it's . . . maybe it's time I just realized that I have to let go."

"I think, sir, it would be for the best."

Riker turned to face him, and there was the same despondency that Data had seen when he picked up Riker on Betazed.

"Take me home, Data," he said quietly. "And we'll let Deanna rest in peace."

The second return trip to Starbase 86 was uneventful. There were no more sudden outbursts from Admiral Riker, no more abrupt flurries of activity. He stayed in his cabin the entire time. Several times Data went to him, tried to engage him in casual conversation about routine matters of policy, or sought his advice on various topics that had come up in the normal course of activity.

In each instance, Riker's replies were terse and to the point. He did not try to drive away companionship, but he did not welcome it. He simply . . . existed. Data noted that Riker didn't seem interested in meeting the world on any sort of terms.

For a time, Data was concerned that Riker was making some sort of plan to head for the Guardian of Forever the moment he was dropped off at 86. Although Data hated resorting to subterfuge, he nevertheless sent his ship's counselor to try to draw out Riker on what was bothering him. The admiral was not particularly responsive, but that didn't matter. He didn't know that the counselor was a full Betazoid who, upon being told that urgent matters were at stake, forced himself to probe more deeply—albeit very gently—than he would normally have.

He reported back to Data and the account was precisely what Data had hoped to hear. "He is rather despondent, Commodore," said the counselor. "But if I had to select any single word that would most describe him at this moment, I would have to say . . . resigned."

"Resigned to what?"

"Resigned to whatever years he has left. Resigned to his life. For all intents and purposes . . . he's given up."

To a large measure, this was good news. And yet, Data could not help but feel a great sense of loss upon hearing this. As if he had somehow passed a sentence of living death upon his friend.

When he informed Riker that they had arrived at Starbase 86, the information received the merest nod of acknowledgment from him. He packed his bags quietly, and Data accompanied him to the transporter room.

"If it's all the same to you, Admiral," Data said, "I'd like to beam down with you."

Riker shrugged. "The space station is open to everyone. Why should the commander of the *Enterprise* be excluded?" It was the longest single sentence he had uttered in twenty-four hours.

Lieutenant Dexter was waiting for them at the transporter platform of the starbase and gave that customary, slightly puckered smile that he specialized in. "It's good to have you back, Admiral. I trust everything went smoothly on Betazed?"

"Fine." Riker nodded his head in Data's direction. "You know Commodore Data?"

"Actually I don't believe we've had the pleasure," said Dexter, shaking Data's hand.

Riker stepped around them and headed for his office. Dexter started to follow at his heels, but Data held him slightly back and spoke in a low undertone. "The admiral went through something of an ordeal on Betazed. I would be most appreciative if you could keep a close eye on him for the next few days."

"What?" said Dexter nervously, casting a surreptitious glance at Riker. "He's not sick or anything, is he?"

"I don't believe so. But he is quite dispirited. I would strongly suggest that you make every endeavor to proceed with business as usual. And if he should do anything out of the ordinary . . . please contact me via subspace radio."

"All right. Consider it done, Commodore."

"Thank you." In a slightly raised voice, Data now called out, "Admiral—I must return to the *Enterprise.* If I can be of further use . . ."

Riker stopped and turned, looking at Data sadly. "No, Commodore. I believe you've done more than enough." And he entered his office, the doors hissing shut behind him.

Dexter shivered slightly. "Now that is someone who is in a very bad mood."

"Yes," confirmed Data. "Unfortunately, the mood has persisted for forty years."

"And the *Chance* will be arriving by this time tomorrow,"said Dexter. "We're prepared for restocking. Oh . . . and Starfleet sent another reminder about processing paperwork on time."

Riker regarded Dexter with a steady gaze. "Tell Starfleet," he said thoughtfully, "that we'll speed up the paperwork as soon as they send us paper."

Dexter blinked owlishly. "Sir . . . no one really uses paper anymore, to any great degree. It's . . . it's just a phrase, sir. Relatively speaking."

"Fine. Then tell Starfleet that we'll be processing our figurative paperwork on time . . . relatively speaking. Time, after all, is relative."

"Yes, sir," said Dexter tiredly.

"Is there anything else?"

"No, sir," said Dexter, tapping his computer padd.

"I didn't think so," said Riker slowly. "There wouldn't be, would there. Same old thing. Day in, day out. And time passes."

"Yes, sir." Now Dexter was starting to sound nervous. "Admiral, are you all right?"

"I'm fine." Riker sighed loudly. "Just fine."

Dexter nodded and then backed out of the office, taking as much time as he could to watch Riker. Riker, for his part, had his chin propped up on his hand, but spared a moment to toss off a cheery wave at Dexter before the door closed.

And then he was alone.

He swiveled in his chair and looked out at the stars. The *Enterprise* had departed orbit around the space station, off to whatever their new great adventure was. For there was still adventure out there, that much was certain. Still a big galaxy with a lot going on. Just not a lot that interested him.

He heard it behind him.

Tick.

Tick.

Tick.

The grandfather clock. His pride and joy.

His symbol of the passing hours.

He watched the pendulum slowly, ponderously, swing back and forth. Back and forth.

Like a large, heavy scythe. Slicing through the air, cutting through time, minute by minute, cleaving it neatly. Each second unaffected by the previous second, and uncaring of the next. Every second was the same to the pendulum.

Nothing mattered.

It just marked time.

Tick.

Tick.

Tick.

The sound grew louder in his head, louder throughout his entire being. The sound that reminded him that this was it, that time was unyielding and pointless and there was nothing to be done about it, it was just there, that's all.

The cogs of the clock irrevocably moved against each other, each tooth engaging smoothly and flawlessly, unheeding of anything except its relentless clockworks.

And he saw her.

In his mind's eye, he saw Deanna, lying there on one of the cogs. The teeth of the cogs calmly integrated, and without uttering a whimper she was mashed in between. The cogs moved on and spit her out, her remains littering the clockworks, and nothing mattered because she was just another piece of garbage to be crunched and tossed aside.

Tick.

Tick.

Tick.

With a barely controlled scream of rage, Riker grabbed the grandfather clock from behind and, with all his strength, shoved. The heavy clock toppled forward and crashed to the ground like a giant redwood, the crash virtually exploding throughout the space station. Glass shattered, wood cracked and splintered, and there was the eminently satisfying sound of clockworks screeching to a halt, cogs and wheels skittering out and across the floor and rolling in small circles before clattering to a halt.

Dexter ran in, alarmed at the racket, and saw Riker standing over the mess, his fists clenched and a crooked smile on his face. Riker looked up at him and all he said was, "Whoops."

When the surveying ship *Chance* arrived barely twelve hours later, Riker was ready.

Thirty-six

The *Enterprise* 1701-F was halfway to its next port of call when a subspace communication came in that immediately got Commodore Data's full attention.

"This is *Enterprise,"* he said when the computer's automatic hailing program informed him of the incoming message and the point of origin. "Go ahead."

"Commodore Data?"

It was precisely the voice Data would have preferred *not* to have heard. "Yes, Lieutenant Dexter. Computer, on vid."

A three-dimensional image appeared directly in front of Data, projected there by a free-floating chip. It was Dexter, and he wiped his brow with considerable discomfort. "Commodore, we have a problem."

"Specify."

"It's the admiral."

Blair and Data exchanged glances. "Is he ill?" asked Data.

"No. He's gone."

"Do you have any idea as to where?"

"Not in the slightest," said Dexter, sounding uncharacteristically put out. "He beamed up to the *Chance,* supposedly for some sort of routine business. The next thing I knew, the *Chance* had blown out of here at warp three . . . with the admiral."

"Have you endeavored to contact them via subspace?"

"Oh, I've endeavored, all right. They don't answer. They're maintaining total radio silence."

"Yes," said Data, sounding extremely practical. "They would. The admiral would make certain of that."

"But why?" demanded Dexter. "Why? What in hell is he doing? Commodore, do you have any idea?"

"I have an excellent idea, Lieutenant. However, it is only an idea . . . one that I would prefer not to bandy about unless I have confirmation. Thank you for alerting me to the situation. I will attend to it. *Enterprise* out."

Dexter's image blinked out of existence before he could get out another word.

Data swiveled in his chair to face Blair, who said worriedly, "You know where he's going, don't you, Commodore. It's connected with what happened on Betazed, isn't it?"

Data felt the worried eyes of all his bridge crew upon him. He wished that somehow he had been able to impress on the admiral that all these people, these people right here, had something at stake in the way that things were. But Data had not been able to do so, and now the best he could do was to perform damage control.

And he would have to perform it no matter what the cost.

"The top speed of the *Chance* is warp six," Data said, accessing his thorough memory of all ships in the registry. "There is little doubt that they are heading for the Forever World. Helm, set course for the Forever World, warp eight."

"Course plotted and laid in, sir."

"Engage," said Data calmly.

The *Enterprise* leaped into warp space, and Data rose from the command chair. "Mr. Blair, come with me to the briefing room, please. We need to discuss worst-case strategy."

Blair followed his commanding officer into the ready room, and Lamont at conn looked over to Tucker at Ops. "You know," she said, "I don't know which is preferable. Not knowing what's going on . . . or finding out."

"Approaching the Forever World, Commodore."

Data had sat rigid and unmoving, staring intently at the screen, all of his considerable brainpower focused on the problem that awaited them. In an even more sedate tone than he usually used, he said, "Sensors. Is there another ship in orbit around the planet?"

"Negative," said Margolin at tactical, but then he paused and said, "No . . . wait. There's—"

The *Enterprise* was jolted slightly as they came within range of the time distortion ripples that were standard for the vicinity of the Forever World.

"—a ship in standard orbit," continued Margolin. "Markings and registry indicate that it's the *Chance.* Sorry about the confusion, sir. The time distortion ripples are especially—"

Once again the ship was knocked around, this time to a sufficient degree that automatic restraints snapped into place on the chairs of the bridge, holding the personnel firmly in their seats.

"—fierce," Margolin persevered, as if the severe buffeting were only a minor inconvenience designed to slow down the dissemination of information. "It's interfering with our sensors."

"Compensate, Mr. Margolin. Give me a hailing frequency to the *Chance."*

"You're on, Commodore."

"Chance, this is the USS *Enterprise,* please acknowledge."

There was no response from the smaller ship. There was, however, continued pounding from the waves of time distortion, and Data could practically sense time slipping away from him—in more than one sense of the word.

A second hail brought continued radio silence, and now Data gave an order that even he didn't quite believe. "Mr. Margolin," he said quietly, "arm phasers."

"Sir?" Margolin was thunderstruck.

They were all looking at Data with shock on their faces. Nevertheless, the commodore knew he had no choice. "Carry out my order, Mr. Margolin," he said quietly.

"Yes, sir," said Margolin hollowly. "Phasers armed and locked on target."

"Mr. Blair, inform the transporter room that you and I will be beaming down to planet surface within two minutes. Attention *Chance,"* Data continued, raising his voice and thereby activating the comm link. "Our phasers are armed and locked on you. Unless you respond immediately, we will be forced, in this state of emergency, to fire on you. Acknowledge or suffer attack. Acknowledge."

The intership radio crackled to life immediately. *"Enterprise,"* came an irritated gravelly voice, "this is Captain Tennant of the *Chance.* What in hell do you think you're playing at?"

"I believe," responded Data, "that the same could be asked of you, Captain."

"We're simply obeying orders," shot back Tennant, "as part of a confidential mission, the contents of which I am not at liberty to disclose. Not even to one of the flagship vessels of the fleet."

"Disclosing them would be pointless," Data said. "I have no doubt that they are utter fabrication. I would assume radio silence is one of those orders. One moment, please." Data turned to Margolin. "Are we within range of the Forever World yet?"

"Yes, sir."

"Raise them . . . Captain Tennant," Data continued the first conversation, "am I correct about the assumption of radio silence?"

"Yes, you are. And to be blunt, I'm jeopardizing the safety of that mission by conversing with you. But with the safety of my crew on the line, I decided to acknowledge your hail, in direct contradiction of my orders."

"Excellent judgment, Captain," said Data calmly. "Am I also correct in assuming that Admiral Riker is not there?"

"That is correct. He beamed down to the surface fifteen minutes ago. He told us to maintain orbit and radio silence."

"That does not surprise me."

"Sir," said Margolin, "we're unable to raise anyone on the surface."

"That also does not surprise me. Transporter room, can you lock on any life-forms on the surface? If so, I want them all beamed up immediately."

There was a pause as the transporter chief ran a quick scan. Then her voice came over the comm: "Negative, bridge. Readings are too sketchy. If someone is down there and gives us coordinates, that's not a problem. But as it is, I'd be afraid to try and lock on and bring something up. I might get nothing at all, or maybe a puddle of protoplasm. There's no predicting without solid confirmation."

"Very well. Mr. Blair," said Data, "with me."

Data crossed quickly to the turbolift, Blair right behind him. Almost as an afterthought, Data called out, *"Chance* . . . maintain position. We will inform you if there is anything you can do."

"Enterprise, would you mind telling us what's going on?" came the voice of Captain Tennant. "Admiral Riker said that we were being commandeered as part of a top-secret mission for Starfleet. He even had orders—"

"I'm sure he did," said Data. "I assure you, however, they were forged. You are on a mission, *Chance* . . . but it's not on behalf of Starfleet. It's on behalf of Admiral Riker."

"What? What in hell is this about, *Enterprise?"*

"Don't concern yourself about it, Captain Tennant. Whether the admiral's mission succeeds or not . . . either way, you'll never know. *Enterprise* out." And then he cut the transmission rather than waste more time.

After all, the entire conversation might end up being moot.

* * *

When Data and Blair arrived on the planet's surface, they discovered precisely what they thought they would find.

The bodies of the scientists were scattered about. A quick inspection revealed that they were alive, but clearly phaser-stunned. Riker must have secreted a small hand unit . . . perhaps several . . . on his person. He'd done it in such a way that Tennant hadn't known . . . otherwise he'd certainly have let *Enterprise* know about it.

What tissue of lies had Riker constructed? Data wondered as he and Blair quickly made their way across the compound. Sindareen scheme? Romulan incursion? Or perhaps the Ferengii were up to their old tricks? There was no end to the possibilities that an inventive mind could conjure, and Riker's mind was as inventive as anyone's.

Data scanned the entire area and came to an immediate realization. "Mary Mac is not here."

"Which means—"

"She's with him," concluded Data. "Odds are it's an unwilling accompaniment."

Above them the air swirled and crackled, and more than once lightning lanced across the sky. Data felt forces gathering around him, as if some massive, insane celestial experiment were in the works.

Quickly they ran through the compound, small bits of dirt and rock swirling around in whirlpools that moved, Data noticed, in opposite directions from one another. Somehow that seemed perfectly in keeping with the rest of the environment.

"He's crazy," Blair was muttering. "He's completely crazy."

"No, Mr. Blair," Data replied, speeding up slightly. "He's not crazy at all. He's merely determined, and certain he is doing the right thing."

The wind grew louder, and Blair raised his voice. "And what if he is? How do we know for sure?"

"We don't. But we cannot take the chance."

They raced to the top of an outcropping. Far, far in the distance, the ruins of the city were still there, as silent and unproviding of information as they had ever been. There below them was the Guardian of Forever.

The protective force field surrounding it was intact.

Riker, however, was on the inside.

So was Mary Mac. He had a firm grip on her wrist, but now she was struggling with the fierceness of her Orion heritage. Her teeth were bared, her fingernails flashing. Riker had been holding a tricorder, but it had clattered to the ground. Data saw that Riker needed both hands to keep off her savage onslaught.

She was shouting something that even Data, with his supersensitive hearing, couldn't make out over the howling of the winds. And then Data also saw, on the large screen that had been erected nearby the Guardian, events being played out that were horribly familiar. There was Deanna Troi, on the floor of her quarters, writhing and gasping, and a terrified and confused Commander Riker leaning over her, looking more helpless than he ever had in his life. On the ground nearby, the fallen tricorder continued to record the information with precision.

Data gestured for Blair to follow and the two Starfleet officers made their way quickly down toward the Guardian.

Mary Mac swung Riker's arm around and clamped down with her teeth. Riker howled in pain and slammed her in the face with as hard a punch as he could remember ever using. Mary Mac released her grip and staggered, wiping at the blood trickling down her mouth.

"You'll destroy *everything!"* she shouted.

"This 'everything' has no right to be!"

"You're not the one to make that decision!"

"Wrong! I'm the only one!"

She leaped at him again, a feral snarl ripping from her throat. Riker ducked and she sailed over him, and he stood quickly, catching her in midlunge. Before she could make a countermove, he deliberately threw himself backward and body-slammed her to the ground. He twisted quickly around while she was stunned and, giving it everything he had, slugged her on the side of the head. The green-skinned woman's eyes rolled up into the back of her head, and she went limp.

Quickly Riker felt under her chin and checked her pulse. He wasn't entirely sure what was normal for an Orion, but this felt strong and firm. Good enough.

He grabbed his fallen tricorder and forced himself to be dispassionate as he programmed it. Carefully, he began to calibrate the tricorder to the enlarged screen designed specifically to display the Guardian's readouts. The tricorder would be able to measure the speed of the Guardian's actual display against the time-delayed playback of specific moments as depicted on the screen. Once it was all fed in and cross-programmed, the tricorder would be able to tell him exactly when to jump through the portal.

There would still be no guarantee of 100 percent accuracy. But it was the only shot that Riker had. His determination was to try to leap through as close to the actual event as possible. He knew that the longer he was back in the *Enterprise* 1701-D, the more chance he had of affecting things he wanted to leave alone. So he had to bring himself as near to Deanna's death as he could without missing it . . . while leaving himself enough time to do something about it.

His fingers flew over the tricorder's controls, cross-referencing the two displays. He programmed in, basically, a countdown. When the correct moment was approaching, a small green light on the tricorder would snap on. The moment that happened, Riker had to leap through precisely five seconds later . . . a built-in delay factor, as he had calculated how long the actual, physical act of taking two steps forward and jumping through would require.

"Guardian!" he shouted. "The display I just witnessed—on my mark, begin again. Three . . . two . . . one . . . now!"

Images began to coruscate across the face of the Guardian of Forever. The same dizzying blur that Riker had seen before. The primary command had been simple: Riker had asked to see the history of the *Enterprise.* The Guardian had proceeded to show it—except that the display had begun with the first event that the Guardian had considered to be instrumental to the creation of the mighty starship. Unfortunately for Riker, that event had been the invention of fire. Images of beings that were barely recognizable as ancestors of humanity, clustered around a small pile of sparking wood, was hardly what Riker needed.

Fortunately enough, the Guardian was renowned for its speed. In an eyeblink Riker witnessed the creation of the wheel, the development of tools. They were wonders that, under other circumstances, Riker would have been spellbound to witness. As it was, he was merely impatient to get past them.

The tricorder's programming had brought it on line as soon as the Guardian began the playback. It hummed along silently, matching and timing the display. Inside its circuitry, the countdown had begun.

Riker patted the vial that he had hidden in his jacket.

"Admiral!" came the shout from behind him.

Riker spun, and he saw Blair and Data approaching. For a moment he was startled and even frightened that they would stop him when he was so near to his goal . . . and that he would never get another opportunity. But then he remembered the force screen that was serenely in place. "It won't do any good, Data!" Riker called. "My mind's made up!"

Data and Blair came to a halt just on the other side of the force field. Blair's thick fur was blown this way and that in the fierce windstorm that surrounded them. Data called out, "Is Mary Mac all right?"

Riker checked the Guardian. Leonardo da Vinci was stroking his chin thoughtfully, studying his designs for a primitive flying machine.

"She's fine, Data! She was less than cooperative when I forced her, at phaser point, to open up the forcefield. I told her I'd just stun her and used her handprint and retina pattern even if she was semiconscious. She chose to remain conscious, hoping that she could talk me out of this. And when she realized she couldn't, she seized a moment when I was distracted and tried to take me out. Damn near did, too," he said, rubbing the back of his neck ruefully.

"Admiral, you must turn away from this destructive course."

Riker glanced back at the Guardian. Alexander Graham Bell was just informing Watson that he needed him, and in an overlapping image, Thomas Edison was staring in wonderment at the glowing light in front of him.

"I'm going to save her, Data! For forty years, I've been eaten up by the thought that I should have done something! She begged me to . . . I promised that I would, and then all I did was stand there and watch her die!"

"She wouldn't have wanted this, Admiral! You're risking everything!"

"Don't you remember, Data?" called back Riker. "The name of James Kirk's autobiography?"

Data needed only a moment to recall it. "It was entitled *Risk Is Our Business.*"

"Damn right! I owe Deanna nothing less than to try everything! You hear me, Data? Nothing less!"

"Admiral, if you do not come out of there immediately, I shall order the *Enterprise* to open fire and use ship's phasers to penetrate the force field! You may very well be destroyed if that happens!"

"And the Guardian might be as well!" shouted back Riker. He took a step toward the time gate. Seconds before, a Saturn V rocket had been lifting off. Now Zephram Cochrane was about to activate the first warp drive unit. "Would you do that, Data? Would you risk destroying the Guardian? Don't you see, Data? You've longed to understand humanity! You've longed for a soul! Well, Mr. Data—the Guardian is the resting place of all the souls, throughout all time! It's God's window on eternity! Who are you to destroy it?"

And with icy calm, Data replied, "I have already contacted Starfleet, Admiral. Their orders were very specific. Protect the time stream, no matter what. Deanna Troi must die . . . and if it takes the destruction of God's window, then who better, Admiral, to assume that responsibility? After all . . . I am not one of God's creatures." And Data angled his head upward and said, *"Enterprise* . . . target the shielding directly in front of me. On my command . . . fire."

"Don't do it, Mr. Data!" called Riker with genuine pleading in his voice. "Don't kill Deanna!"

"I did not kill her, Admiral. But if maintaining the integrity of the space-time continuum were at stake, I would take her life with my own hands. I would derive no satisfaction from it. Indeed, the counselor was as dear to me in my own way as she is to you in yours. But I am prepared to accept that her death is a requirement in the natural order of things, and to preserve that order, I will do whatever I have to do."

Data had spoken with certainty and a sense of implacable decision. And Riker knew that lines had been drawn. "So will I, Mr. Data."

"Enterprise," said Data tonelessly. "Fire."

From orbit, the mighty phasers of the *Enterprise* cut loose. They struck the force field directly above Riker's head. The force field sparked and shimmered under the barrage, resisting the power of the weapons.

It was the strongest force field that Federation technology had to offer . . . on par with the deflector shields of the *Enterprise* herself. Furthermore, the Forever World had been equipped with its own heavy-duty defense array, protected by similar shields. If a hostile vessel had shown up, the scientists below could very easily have given a very formidable accounting of themselves—in all likelihood, blowing the attacking ship out of orbit.

But the *Chance* had not been a hostile vessel, and the renowned and esteemed Adm. William T. Riker was hardly considered to be a malevolent presence. It had been the scientists' error to take Riker's word that there was urgent Starfleet business to discuss.

By the time they had realized their mistake, it had been too late.

Data was trying to make up for that mistake now. He watched, stone faced, as the *Enterprise* pitted her phasers against the force field. That they would eventually penetrate, he had no doubt whatsoever. The question was whether they would break through in time.

Riker took a step back, watching the phasers with a sense of grim desperation. There was nothing he could do. He was trapped inside, and besides, getting out would simply put him farther from the Guardian. He heard a low moan behind him—Mary Mac was coming around. Perfect—that was all he needed.

The field began to buckle. He could see the power reserves straining, the field integrity collapsing. How incredibly ironic that here he was at the gateway to all time, and time was the one thing he did not have.

He glanced down at the tricorder.

The green light was glowing.

He emitted a horrified yell. He should have been standing in front of the Guardian the whole time, watching, monitoring, waiting for the signal to flash to life. Had it just come on? Had it been on for a few seconds?

Too far! his mind screamed. *Too far from the Guardian!*

He spun and charged at the gateway. The sand crunched beneath his boots. On the display face of the Guardian, he saw a brief image of Q dancing with Lwaxana Troi, and then Locutus threatening the ship, and it was all merging and blending together . . .

"Admiral, we will stop you!" came Data's voice, rising above the wind and the screaming of the *Enterprise* phasers, and he heard Blair's voice shouting something as well.

No time! No time!

Help me, Imzadi . . . the voice seemed to reach back through the years.

Riker leaped.

And then he was out of time.

Literally.

Thirty-seven

Lieutenant Barclay stood in the holodeck of the USS *Enterprise* 1701-D and cracked his knuckles.

He knew that he shouldn't. He knew he might get caught. But the odds were slim. Captain Picard, Commander Riker, all the senior officers had been involved with a major diplomatic bash that evening. So the chances were that they wouldn't be anywhere near the holodeck that night.

Besides, he was off duty now. And he had pared down his holodeck activity to once a week. It wasn't interfering with anything important. And if he had his own ways of entertaining himself, well—as long as he didn't hurt anyone, and as long as he wasn't overdependent on it . . . well, where was the harm in that?

He had already informed the computer precisely what he wanted. Now he said simply, "Run program."

A moment later he was standing on a vast, grassy plain. Far in the distance, ancient Rome stood in all its glory. But right in front of him was a small temple, circular with tall pillars.

Standing in the middle of the temple was Deanna Troi. She was scantily clad in gauze, flowing robes. She extended her arms to him and in a musical lilt said, "I am the goddess of the mind."

Barclay started toward her, his voice robust and deep. "And I am the one who worships you . . . and whom you will worship in return."

And at that precise moment, something else appeared on the holodeck—seemed to just step right out of nowhere.

Barclay stopped, utterly confused. It was a man in what appeared to be some sort of uniform. It even looked vaguely like a Starfleet uniform, but the coloring was different and—

Then Barclay took a close look at the face.

"What the hell . . . ?" he breathed.

The new holodeck image, which appeared for all the world to be an older version of Riker, looked around in what seemed to be momentary disorientation. Then "Riker" turned, looked at Barclay, then to the image of Deanna, and back to Barclay. Riker put his hands on his hips and addressed Barclay with a voice of utter authority. "So . . . I should have known. Still at it, Lieutenant?"

In total confusion, Barclay called out, "Computer. Remove image of . . ." He wasn't sure what to call it. "Remove new image and run a systems check."

Riker merely stood there, showing no signs of disappearing. "I," he said, "am a holodeck failsafe, built in to monitor the types of programs you're engaging in, Mr. Barclay. I am *very* disappointed to see you still perpetrating such . . . bizarre . . . scenarios. I want it halted immediately." He pointed at Barclay sternly. "Is that clear?"

"Y-yes sir!" stammered Barclay uncomprehendingly. "Computer! Cancel this program! In fact . . . in fact, cancel all programs that I've created. As a matter of fact—cancel all my future participation in holodeck activities!"

Rome, its environs, and the image of Deanna Troi, all vanished back into the nothingness they had come from. The only things remaining in the room were the glowing yellow grids, Barclay, and Riker.

"Very good, Lieutenant," said Riker approvingly.

"Are . . . are you going to go now, too?" asked Barclay hopefully. He had no idea why, of all images, an older Riker had been chosen. But whatever the reason, it was a damned effective selection. He was totally unnerved by it.

"Yes, I'm going to go, too," said Riker. "And I'll tell you what. If you don't mention this incident to anyone, then I won't, either. We'll keep it just between us."

"Th-thank you, sir," Barclay said.

The image of Riker headed for the door. Barclay waited for it to vanish, as all holodeck creations did if they tried to leave the holodeck. Instead the doors hissed open obediently, and the elder Riker walked out, turned left, and headed down a corridor. The doors hissed shut behind him.

Barclay stood there for a long time. And then he went out, turned right, and returned to his cabin.

He didn't go near the holodeck for the rest of his stay on the *Enterprise.*

Admiral Riker walked quickly down the corridor, looking neither right nor left. He passed a couple of crewmen, some of whom did double takes upon spotting him. Perhaps they would assume that some uncle of Riker's had come to visit the ship, or maybe the commander was coming from some sort of costume function. He didn't slow down enough for anyone to get a really clear look at him, and he certainly didn't stop to answer any questions.

He had to get his bearings. Figure out precisely when he was. He could have asked Barclay, but he hadn't wanted the lieutenant to question his existence as anything other than some sort of confusing holodeck manifestation. It had saved him time—and he didn't know how much time he had.

He ducked into a room to his left that he knew was going to be vacant because it was one of the guest quarters. Once inside, he called out, "Computer! Tell me the stardate and time."

There were few moments in Riker's life that he could precisely remember down to the second of their occurrence. But the day and time of Deanna Troi's death was certainly one of those. He was able to recall the exact sound of Beverly Crusher's voice as she had labored to bring Deanna back to life. And when she had failed . . . when she had finally realized that nothing was going to help, and her best friend on the ship was forever gone . . . she had said, in a voice that sounded choked with dirt from a grave, "Record the time and date of death." The computer had obediently, and uncaringly, said it out loud for the record.

Riker had been standing there and had heard it—heard it punctuated by a choked sob from Beverly Crusher. There had been no noise from Riker himself—already the cloud was settling over him. The cloud that would cloak him for forty years.

Now, in the vacant guest quarters, the computer informed him of the day and time. He felt his breath catch in his throat, the blood pounding in his temple.

He had hoped to arrive a day or two beforehand. Somehow, cautiously, make contact with Deanna. Inform her of what was to happen. Convince her, put her on guard. And even more importantly—give her the antidote for the poison that he had brought back with him, securely stored in his jacket.

He had known that it would be dangerous. Somewhere, somehow, Data might have sent people back, anticipating his moves. Trying to block his plans. But Data would have to be judicious—he didn't want to upset the applecart of time, and he would be very, very careful as to what he did and how he did it. Riker had anticipated that there would be something of a chess match of strategy, played out through the corridors of the *Enterprise* 1701-D.

But he had been wrong.

He didn't have time for subtlety. He didn't have time for finesse.

What he had was twenty-three minutes.

Twenty-three minutes from right now, until the point where Deanna Troi would be lying on Beverly Crusher's medtable, a lifeless bundle of flesh.

"Damn!" he snarled.

He charged out into the hallway, resetting his chronometer, and bolted down the corridor, running full-tilt toward Deanna's quarters.

His arms pumped furiously, and as he turned a corner, his pounding footsteps alerted a security guard. The guard turned, and Riker didn't recognize him. That, in and of itself, didn't mean anything. Even when he was the second-in-command, he didn't necessarily know every single crewman on sight—particularly if it was a relatively new arrival. And he wasn't even the contemporary Riker—forty years had passed, and faces blurred with the years.

Then again—it might be someone sent back by Data.

The security guard frowned and started to reach for his phaser. "Hold it!" he called out.

Again, Riker had no way of knowing for sure. Certainly, with so many dignitaries presently on board the *Enterprise,* it would be standard operating procedure for guards to be on alert to anyone who didn't seem to belong there. And Riker certainly seemed out of place.

Then again—the "guard" might know precisely who the gray-haired man was, and what his mission was.

Riker raised an arm in front of his face to block the guard's view and slammed into him, knocking the younger man back before he could bring his phaser up. "Security alert, deck fourteen!" shouted the guard, and then Riker grabbed him up, pivoted, and slammed him headfirst into the wall. The guard went down, unconscious, and Riker scooped up his phaser.

Riker knew security would be all over the place within a minute. If Riker were to be captured, dragged down to the brig, interrogated . . . by the time he got everything straightened out, it would be too late.

There was only one person he could think to trust.

More to the point—there was only one person he could trust whose cabin was close enough.

The thoughts had gone through his mind so quickly that he was already dashing down a side corridor before the guard had even completely slumped to the ground.

A right, then another left, and he was standing in front of the cabin. He took a deep breath. The door was locked, which was not unusual when someone had retired for the evening. But his voice was still his voice, and he said briskly, "Computer, override lock and open for William Riker."

The computer checked that this was indeed the voice of William T. Riker, authorized occupant of the cabin, and consequently, the doors hissed open. The admiral stepped inside.

He heard soft breathing in the bed. He squinted, his eyes adjusting quickly to the darkness as the doors slid shut behind him.

He hadn't been quite sure how he would react upon seeing his younger self. He was pleased to discover that, for the most part, he didn't really care. His younger version was simply a means to an end.

Perhaps, when all this was over, he would get a massive case of the shakes. Just as Deanna had those many, many years ago.

For the briefest of moments he was distracted by the mental image of Deanna from their steamy encounter in the jungle, and then he was immediately snapped back to business when his younger self suddenly sat up in bed.

Commander Riker squinted into the darkness, looking straight at his older self, but wasn't able to make out anything clearly. He started to say, "Lights."

But the admiral moved quickly, moving with assurance in the darkness since, after all, it was his old quarters and he remembered where everything was. He dropped onto the bed next to his younger self and clamped his hand over Will Riker's mouth.

The commander struggled fiercely, shoving at the arm that held him down, grabbing upward at his face. The elder Riker, for his part, felt nothing but impatience and quickly called out, "Lights!"

He felt the younger man freeze in momentary confusion at the no-doubt familiarity of the voice. The lights came up, too bright for Will, and the admiral snapped, "Half lights," bringing the illumination to a more bearable level.

Commander Riker stared up in shock at his future self. The latter hissed, "Shut up! We haven't much time!"

Momentarily startled, Will began to struggle again, trying to make some sort of noise. The admiral, losing what little patience he had, and aware of the rapidly passing time, snapped, "Didn't you hear what I said? Shut up, you idiot! They may be here to try and stop me at any moment! So lie still! Listen to me, and be prepared to do exactly what I tell you. Deanna's life hangs on what you do next."

That was more than enough to get Will's attention. He stopped struggling, slowly realizing that he was not under direct attack; that he was not dreaming; and that there was more to this than he was going to be able to discern upon first exposure.

"I'm going to let go of your mouth now," said the admiral. "So help me, if you shout or try to get attention, I'll knock you cold and take care of this myself. And if I have to do that and get nailed because I'm easily spotted, then you will quite literally have no one but yourself to blame for the rest of your life."

Will nodded, indicating he understood, and the admiral slowly released his hand. He stepped back off the bed as Will sat up. There was still confusion in his eyes, but also amazement. "Who . . . *are* you?"

"The Easter bunny," snapped the admiral. "Who in hell do you *think* I am. We're wasting time . . . time we haven't got. Get dressed. Move. *Move!*"

Will rolled off the bed, never taking his eyes off the senior Riker, even as he started to pull on his uniform. "You're from the future, aren't you?"

"That's right. You don't sound surprised."

"After the time that Captain Picard ran into himself, I swore that nothing would surprise me."

"Oh, yes," said the admiral. "I did swear that, didn't I." Then he turned deadly serious. "Listen to me and don't interrupt. Deanna's life is in mortal danger."

"Then why in hell am I taking the time to get dressed?"

"Because they may be watching for anything unusual—and you running down the corridor in your nightclothes would qualify."

"Who is 'they'?"

"I said don't interrupt. Just listen: Deanna is going to be poisoned." He pushed on despite Will's expression of astonishment and held up the vial from his jacket. "This will counteract it. You've got to get to her quarters and get her to drink it. And you've got"—he glanced at his chronometer—"just over fifteen minutes to do it."

At that moment, Will's communicator beeped.

"You don't have time!" hissed the admiral.

But Will, never taking his eyes off the admiral, tapped it. "Riker here."

"Security alert, sir," came the deep voice of Worf. "An intruder was reported in your general vicinity. Have you seen him?"

Will Riker stared at his future self.

The admiral realized that everything was hinging on this moment. A word from Commander Riker would bring Worf and his people charging to the rescue. And the admiral had not had enough time to convince his younger self of the truth of his words.

Words.

His own words.

And in a very low voice, he said, "The future holds such promise . . . and just as I cannot imagine how I survived the past . . . without you . . ."

Will's eyes widened in shock, even as over his communicator Worf said, "Commander . . . what did you say?"

"Nothing," was the firm reply. "I haven't seen him. I'll meet you in a few minutes. I just . . . have to get dressed. Riker out."

There was a silence that, to both of them, seemed to stretch on for eternity. And then Will said, with slow understanding, "She died. In your past . . . my future . . . she died. And you've come back somehow to try and prevent it. You're . . . you're tampering with time . . . and the 'they' you're worried about are the people from your time—maybe scientists or, my God, Starfleet personnel—who might try and stop you."

"She wasn't supposed to die," said the admiral. "It was wrong. Wrong for her. Wrong for me, for everyone. And I'm here to prevent that wrong, and I don't give a damn what regulations say, and if you love her . . . if you're truly *Imzadi* . . . you won't give a damn either."

"But . . . but how am I supposed to believe you? How am I supposed to just . . . just take the future into my own hands. *Our* own hands?"

The admiral took a step toward him. "We do it every moment of our lives, kid. Every day we make our own future. But someone came back and decided to remake the future in their own image . . . and now I'm here to stop it."

"Unless someone stops you. Which means that someone isn't certain."

Admiral Riker grabbed Will Riker by his uniform front. Despite his age, his strength was almost undiminished and was fueled by anger. "Damn you, you sanctimonious clod! You think you know everything? You don't know a damn thing! You want certainty? This is a certainty, then—Deanna is going to die! She's going to writhe on the floor and beg you to do something, and all you're going to do is watch her suffer massive circulatory collapse and die! And it's not going to be until that moment, you purblind idiot, that you realize that she's the better part of you!"

"You're . . . it's wrong," Will said, but there was tremendous conflict in his eyes. "It's wrong to tamper with the past. . . . I can't believe that there's any circumstance under which I'd . . . I'd knowingly . . ."

"You think you can judge *me!*" said the admiral. "Remember what we wrote? 'And just as I cannot imagine how I survived the past without you . . . I cannot imagine a future without you.' Remember? Well, *I'm* the future without her, buddy boy, and I can tell you right now that it's not something you're going to relish." He shoved the vial into Will's palm. "It's going to happen, Riker! In just a few minutes now! Her life is going to end. You can save it! You have the power, right here, right now! Now are you going to stand there debating philosophies and moralities and rights and wrongs? Or are you going to deal with the genuine, real, here-and-now fact that Deanna's life is at stake and only you have a hope in hell of saving her. And if you don't save her, then hell is where you're going to be—forty years of hell! Of might-have-beens and what-ifs.

"Except for me, there was just the frustration that I should have done something, but didn't know what. For you, it's going to be the knowledge that you could have done something, but didn't. How much worse for you, Riker? When you call out with your mind, 'Imzadi,' and there's no one to respond, no part of your soul that acknowledges that the word has any meaning to anyone else, what will happen to you then? *God damn you,* Riker! When your heart's been cut out, how's it going to feel knowing that *you're the one who wielded the knife?"*

Will ripped away from him, his face ashen, his heart pounding.

"Deanna!" he screamed, and charged from his quarters.

Thirty-eight

Dann nibbled at Deanna's neck and began to work his way down. She sighed, a slow, languorous sigh. She was on the bed, wearing only the flimsiest of shifts. She started to push it down off her shoulders so that Dann's downward course would be unobstructed.

But still, something bothered her. "Dann . . . are you all right?"

He raised his head slightly. "Of course I am," he said reasonably. "Why wouldn't I be?"

"I don't know. I just sense . . . I mean . . ."

And suddenly she sat up, confused, a voice echoing in her head. "Will?" she said in bewilderment.

"What's wrong?" asked Dann, sitting up as well.

"It's . . . it's Will. Something's wrong . . . I sense . . . total panic. It's . . . something directed towards me, I don't . . ."

"Deanna, calm down," said Dann firmly, taking her by the shoulders. "He's probably just, well, jealous about us. That's what's giving him anxiety. He's probably even asleep and you're just . . . just tuning in to his dreams somehow. I know you two are close, but—"

"No!" She pushed him aside. "Something *is* wrong."

"Deanna . . ."

She got out of bed, adjusting the shift around her, and went over to her uniform, which was neatly hung nearby. She tapped the communicator on it and said, "Troi to Riker."

"Deanna!" came Riker's desperate shout. "Stay there! Don't move! I'll be there in a few seconds!"

She spun and faced Dann. "Did you hear that? He's terrified!"

"Yes," said Dann sadly. "Yes . . . I can't say I'm surprised."

Will hurtled down the corridor at warp speed. He skidded once and, to his panic, almost bobbled the vial and dropped it. But he recovered quickly and turned a corner.

His mind was racing furiously. He didn't know how or why any of this was happening, but there were two things of which he was completely, instinctively convinced—that he had confronted his future self, and that Deanna was going to die in the next few minutes.

He skidded to a halt outside her quarters and charged in. Deanna was seated on the bed, arguing with Dann, but when she saw Riker, she rose to her feet. "Will . . . ?"

He thrust the vial outward. "Drink this! Quickly!"

Dann came off the bed and stood between them. "What are you, crazy? She's not just going to drink some vial of unknown liquid because you told her to. Get out of here!"

"Deanna, you have to," said Riker. "Your life depends on it."

Deanna knew, of course, that Riker believed every word of what he was saying. But it didn't make her any less befuddled. "My *life?"*

"Out of my way!" Riker said to Dann, trying to push him aside.

"Like hell! Deanna, don't listen to him! He's trying to hurt you! He's jealous of me!"

Dann moved once again to block Riker, and this time Will grabbed him by the shoulders and tried to push him to one side. To his shock, Dann didn't budge. He was a head shorter and considerably slimmer than Riker, but he held his ground. Instead he grabbed Riker by the forearms and held him in a grip of iron.

"Deanna!" shouted Riker, and somehow, in his head, he heard a slow, steady ticking, like time slipping away from him, spiraling out of control. Everything seemed to slow down and distort as he twisted in Dann's grasp and flipped the vial onto the bed. It landed on the sheets, bounced once, and started to tumble to the floor. But Deanna's hand snatched out and grabbed it. She stared at it, trying to understand.

"Give me that!" shouted Dann, and her head snapped around in amazement at the desperation in his tone. With his free hand he lunged for the vial, but now Will Riker shifted his grip and spun on the ball of his foot. Dann was thrown across the room, crashing into furniture.

"Drink it!" Riker yelled at Deanna. "If you ever trusted me, if you ever loved me, *drink it!"*

Deanna needed no further urging. She pulled at the stopper.

It was stuck.

Dann came to his feet and with an animalistic roar sprang toward Deanna. Riker met his charge, braced himself, and the two of them went down in a tumble of arms and legs.

Riker rolled over, gaining the advantage, and pounded furiously on Dann's head. The blows didn't seem to have any effect, and Dann drove a knee up, shoving Riker off. But Riker didn't lose his grip on one of Dann's arms, and the Starfleet officer, even off balance, managed to send Dann crashing into the wall.

Deanna worked desperately at the stopper, kneading it with her fingers. It worked its way upward.

Dann began to transform.

He became larger, his body covered with thick brown fur, his hands shaping into claws.

Riker recognized his species immediately. It was a Chameloid. Shape-shifters, incredibly powerful, incredibly dangerous.

Deanna, her fingers still pushing on the stopper, stared at the man she had thought was Dann, her dark eyes registering her utter shock. And then, somewhere deep within her, she felt some sort of distant, burning sensation.

At that moment, the stopper popped off, rolling onto the bed.

"NO!" roared "Dann," and he made one final, desperate lunge. He shoved Riker aside, his fingers reaching for the vial, and then Riker snared his long, matted fur from behind and leaped on, wrapping his arms down and around the Chameloid's arms, and up around the creature's neck.

Deanna drank down the contents of the vial in one gulp.

The Chameloid howled in fury, trying to bat Riker off his back. "You idiot! Do you have any idea what you've done! *Do you?"*

Riker said nothing. Instead, all of his energy was being used to shove the creature's neck forward.

The Chameloid broke the grip, slamming Riker to the floor. Towering over him, the creature roared, "You selfish bastard! You've risked everything!"

"I've risked everything for Deanna before," Riker said defiantly, "and I'd do it again!"

"Well, I don't have that choice!" snapped the Chameloid.

He started toward Deanna, his hands outstretched . . .

And a phaser blast from behind sent the Chameloid to his knees.

Worf stood in the doorway, his phaser leveled. "One side, Commander," he said calmly. Immediately Riker leaped out of the way and Worf fired again. The phaser beam enveloped the Chameloid once again. He wailed in frustration, and then consciousness slipped from him and he pitched forward, right on top of Riker.

Worf helped roll the Chameloid off Riker, who sat up, rubbing his chest in pain. Then he looked to Deanna, who was making a similar motion of her own. "Deanna," he said urgently, "are you all right? Are—"

"I . . . I felt something. Some sort of . . . of burning pain in my chest . . . but now it's gone. Will . . . what's happened here? Who is . . . is that?" She pointed distastefully at the unconscious Chameloid. "Where did this vial come from? How did you know . . . ?"

Riker patted her hand with all the reassurance that he could muster at that moment. Then he said, "Worf . . . get our 'friend' here to the brig. Alert the captain, tell him to meet me outside my quarters. Emphasize that. *Outside* my quarters."

"Very well," said Worf, hauling the Chameloid over his shoulder. Two other security men had shown up by this point, but Worf clearly had matters in hand. "Am I correct in assuming that this is our intruder?"

Will looked up at him bleakly. "Worf, you don't know the half of it."

Worf grunted and headed off to the brig with the Chameloid. When he was gone, Riker rotated his arm, which had been banged up as he'd wrestled with the Chameloid.

Troi, for her part, merely looked at him with awe. "You saved my life, Will," she said quietly. "I was in danger, and you came charging in here—risked your life—and you saved me."

"Actually," said Riker, "not to sound boastful or anything—but it appears I went to even greater lengths than that to save you. You'd better get dressed and come with me. I don't think you're going to believe this unless you see it. I'll . . ." He cleared his throat, chucking a thumb toward the hallway. "I'll wait out here for you to put some clothes on."

"That's very decent of you, Commander."

She slid off the bed, stood on her toes, and kissed him.

"Thank you for saving me," she whispered in his ear.

He smiled tiredly. "All part of the service."

Thirty-nine

When Will and Deanna returned to his cabin, Picard was standing there looking extremely annoyed.

"All right, Number One," he said stiffly, arms folded. "I have complied with your wishes and stood here outside your cabin. I cannot say I like to be kept waiting."

"The counselor was just making herself look presentable," said Will.

"Presentable for whom?" demanded Picard.

"Yes, Commander," chimed in Troi. With the danger past, she was all business. "Whom exactly am I being made presentable for?"

For answer, Will walked into his cabin, hoping his future self had stayed put. It had potential to be a very embarrassing situation if—

He was gone.

Will stood in the middle of the cabin, looking around dismally. Troi and Picard followed him in, staring uncomprehendingly at the officer's obvious discomfiture.

"He was right here!" said Riker desperately.

"Number One," Picard told him, speaking slowly and deliberately, "who . . . *precisely* . . . was here?"

"Me."

It had been Will Riker's voice that had replied, but it was not the Will Riker that Picard was looking at. For an instant Picard thought that Riker was practicing ventriloquism or some such nonsense. But then, slowly, Picard realized that the voice had come from behind them.

He turned in time to see a gray-haired version of his second-in-command emerging from the bathroom. "I was here," he said. "Still am, actually. Which makes me con—"

He caught a glimpse of Deanna, who was standing just behind the younger Will Riker. Will stepped aside and gestured to her. "I did it," he said quietly, "or rather . . . we did it."

Picard had not yet fathomed what to say, much less what to make of the situation. At that precise moment, however, Picard could have been a million light-years away and Adm. William Riker would not have noticed.

Instead Riker was staring at Deanna Troi with a mixture of disbelief and shock. "Deanna . . . " he whispered.

She took a step toward him, stunned. "Will—?"

It was the fastest shift in emotion that Deanna had ever felt. An air of despair and doom had hung like a shroud over the man facing her . . . until he had set eyes on her. And suddenly it had been ripped away, just like that. How was it possible that one person—*one person*—could make that much difference in someone's life?

He approached her, reaching out to her. Picard and his Number One made no move, but merely watched in pure amazement.

The admiral brought his hands up to her face, hovered over it for an instant as if afraid to touch her. As if afraid that if he made any such movement, she would burst like a soap bubble and all of it, all of this moment, would just vanish.

But then he did touch her. Riker put his hands to her face, and they were shaking. "Oh . . . my God," he breathed.

It was like that moment in the Jalara Jungle, except now he was the one who was trembling. Deanna, for her part, reacted entirely on instinct, putting her arms around him and pulling him tightly against her.

His chest began to heave with pent-up emotion, and the old man began to sob. He no longer cared where he was, or who was watching. The ethics of his actions did not weigh on him. All that mattered was that she was there, and she was alive, and in his arms. Years of agony and guilt and second-guessing, washed away by the hot tears and first real emotion besides grief that he had experienced for decades.

And she heard his thoughts, and it was as startling as that first time had been. *Oh, God . . . Imzadi . . . I'm whole again,* echoed in her mind, the prayer of thanksgiving from a man who had given up on everything, especially himself. *I never knew . . . what I had until you were gone.*

"It's all right," she murmured, stroking his back. "It's all right."

He drew back from her to look her in the eyes, those eyes that had been closed in death for years. They were as bright and transcendent as he had remembered, and both of their faces were wet with tears. Whether hers was wet from his or she had generated her own, he couldn't tell. He also couldn't care.

Standing to one side, Comdr. Will Riker watched the reunion of two lovers and realized—insanely—that he was jealous.

"Worf to Riker."

Riker the elder had to rein in his impulse to answer, but instead nodded in the direction of Will. "I think it's for you."

Will tapped his communicator. "Yes?"

"We checked the cabin to which Ambassador Dann had been assigned and found him unconscious. Apparently the Chameloid had accosted Dann at some point earlier this evening and taken his place."

The admiral's head now turned, his attention switching to the matters at hand. He released his hold on Deanna and turned to Will, making a throat-cutting gesture. Will said, "Thank you, Mr. Worf. Make sure the Chameloid is secure. Riker out." Then he turned to his future self and said, "This Chameloid is one of 'them,' isn't he."

"I believe so," said the admiral. "You sure he's a Chameloid? Large? Brown hair and furry?" When Will nodded, Admiral Riker continued, "Well, unless I miss my guess, he's an officer named Blair. There was only one Chameloid on . . . on the ship, and Lieutenant Blair was it. I doubt . . . they could have gotten another one so quickly. It figures that he would assume the appearance of someone close to Deanna. If they anticipated my trying to save her, then the logical thing was to take on the aspect of whoever was with her at the key moment in time. Simplest way to keep an eye on her and make sure things progress smoothly."

"For all you knew," Will now said, *"I* could have been one of *them.* When you came here, you might have been walking into a trap."

"I know. That's why I mentioned the lines of poetry to you. I watched your reaction very carefully. That wasn't just to convince you that I'm you. It was also to convince me that you're me."

"I hate to break this up," Picard now said, stepping forward, "but I, who am unquestionably me, would be most grateful if either of you cared to tell either of me *what in hell is going on?"*

"Watch your tone with me, Captain," said the elder Riker with a half-serious smirk. "I have seniority, *and* I outrank you."

Picard was not someone who was easily flustered, but now he turned to his second-in-command with utter perplexity. "Number One—?" And there was a distinct tone of warning to his voice.

"Simply put, Captain," said Will, stepping forward and gesturing to the gray-haired man, "this is myself, from the future."

"I surmised that, Number One," said Picard tightly. "Now what the blazes is he doing here?"

"All right, Captain," the admiral told him. "To put this as succinctly, and as non-committally, as possible—Deanna's life was in danger. I came back through time to see her through that danger. And there are some people who would prefer that I didn't."

"Will . . . " began Picard.

Two Rikers said, "Yes?"

Despite the seriousness of the situation, Deanna had to make an effort not to laugh.

"Admiral," Picard started again, "Counselor Troi has been in danger before. We all have. Why was this threat so significant that it warranted your taking the extremely dangerous step of coming back through time?"

"She died," said the admiral, trying not to look at her. "But now she hasn't . . . except that I haven't returned to my own time. Which means . . ." And his voice darkened. "It means the danger to her isn't over yet."

Picard leaned against a bureau. "How . . . how did you come here?"

The admiral gave Riker a long, hard look. There seemed to be a great deal going through his mind, as if he were coming to a variety of decisions. "I can't tell you," he said finally.

Picard blinked. "Well, then . . . tell us why Counselor Troi was"—he found he couldn't say the word and settled for—"attacked. What happened as a consequence of it?"

"I can't tell you that, either."

"Oh, for God's sake!" said Picard in exasperation. "It seems just yesterday we went through this with Rasmussen—and he turned out to be from the past, for that matter!"

"I know," the admiral reminded him. "I was there."

"Well, then?"

The admiral placed the palms of his hands together. "Jean-Luc," he began, and noted the surprised expression of the *Enterprise* captain upon hearing his first name spoken by the man he still thought of as a subordinate. "Jean-Luc . . . you understand the tremendous risk I've taken by coming back here. You know, as well as I, the Starfleet regulations against any sort of interference with the time stream."

"Of course. But since you are here, and since you've already interfered . . ."

"In for a penny, in for a pound? Is that it?" The admiral smiled humorlessly. "I wish it were that simple. I came here for one reason and one reason only: to save Deanna. Violating those regulations—taking the responsibility for a universe on my shoulders—was the second most difficult thing I've ever done . . . the first being when I had to leave you behind to be killed by the Romulans."

The last time Will had seen Picard as white as he was now was back when he'd been transformed into a Borg. "I'm . . ." His voice was barely above a whisper. "I'm killed by the Romulans?"

"No, Jean-Luc. I made that up."

"You . . ." Picard looked at Will and Deanna, and then back to Riker. "You made that up? *Why?* Why would you joke about such a thing?"

"It wasn't a joke. It was to make a point. If I start talking about events—*any* events—beyond my immediate goal of saving Deanna, then I run the risk of saying the wrong thing. The slightest slip could end up changing the time stream beyond what I've already committed to. Making the initial decision was already enough of playing God for me. I'm not prepared, under any circumstance, to expand on it. What if I accidentally talk about someone on this ship—you, Worf, Beverly—in the past tense? Let slip that people I know now aren't around forty years from now. Then they get to spend the next forty years, every time they run into any sort of difficult situation, wondering, 'Is this it? Is this what results in my death?' Or the other way around. What if I tell you, Jean-Luc, that in my time, you're running Starfleet? That could result in your becoming overly confident. You could go into dangerous scenarios thinking that you'll definitely get out of them because, hell, you know you'll be around four decades hence. And as a result, you can get yourself, and everyone else, killed. Time is very malleable, Jean-Luc. And I'm just not going to mold the clay any further. I'm really very sorry."

The three younger officers looked at each other, and then Picard—drumming his fingers on the table—said, "If you don't tell us the bare facts we need to know in order to handle the situation . . . then Deanna could still die."

Riker looked up at her grimly. "I know that, Jean-Luc, but the first time, there was no warning. Now . . . forewarned is forearmed. That will have to do for you. And I still have a few tricks up my sleeve. I just can't show them to you, that's all."

Riker sat down and folded his arms in a manner that made it quite clear he was not going to say anything further.

Picard sighed. "Very well. I can't say that I'm overly pleased with the situation.

On the other hand . . . thanks to you . . . Counselor Troi is still alive. It would seem that I am going to have to hope that the instincts of the man whom I presently trust to be my second-in-command . . . are still present in the man who is also—at this moment in time—my superior officer."

Picard rose, and Riker stood with him. "I'll need some sort of modern-day Starfleet uniform . . . and preferably some sort of disguise, so I can move about."

"What you will need, Admiral, is some reading material to keep you busy. I have no interest in marching you around the ship—I think the fewer people who see you, the better. These quarters are going to serve as your personal brig. The doors will be sealed with an override that only I can command, and guards will be posted outside. You are going nowhere, Admiral."

"You can't do that!" said the admiral angrily. "There are things I can do that you can't! Things I know to watch out for."

"Maybe," said Picard. "Then again, maybe not. As you have made clear, time has already slipped into another stream. From here on in we are all of us improvising, Admiral, and to be blunt, I can tap-dance as well as you. You will stay safe and secure here so that I don't have to worry about a random time factor running about my ship. You, Counselor," he said to Deanna, "will go nowhere without Lieutenant Worf as a security escort."

"Won't he question why you've given him that full-time assignment if, as far as he knows, the danger is past?" said the admiral.

Picard, Will, and Troi looked at him in surprise.

He grimaced in chagrin. "What was I thinking? Of course he won't question: he's a Klingon. Forgive me. It's been a while since I dealt with . . ." He stopped. "Well . . . it's been a while. Captain . . . believe me, you're not pursuing the right course here. You've got to give me freedom to move."

"Number One," said Picard calmly, "kindly check him for weapons."

The first officer went to Riker, who stood absolutely still, glowering at Picard. Will took off him the phaser he'd taken from the guard, as well as another, much more diminutive phaser that he found hidden in his jacket. Will held it up and whistled. "Small. What'll they think of next?"

"You'll find out," the admiral informed him dryly. "Jean-Luc . . ."

"Save it, Admiral." Picard tapped his communicator and summoned two security guards to be stationed outside Riker's cabin. As they waited for the guards to arrive, no words were exchanged between the four of them . . . until finally Picard broke the silence and said, "Can you at least tell me . . . is there still a vessel named *Enterprise?"*

At that, Riker smiled slightly. "Is it important for you to know that?"

"I would like to."

"All right. The answer is yes," said Riker quietly. "And she carries the name as nobly as her forebearers did. You . . ." He paused and then said, "You see? I was either going to say that you *will* be proud of her, or that you *would* have been proud of her. Very easy to make mistakes. Like the one you're making by cooping me up in here."

"As with all mistakes, Admiral, we learn to live with them."

Riker looked at Deanna, his dry skin crinkling around the eyes. "Some of us never learn," he said in a bittersweet voice. "And some of us will move heaven and earth to change things for the better."

She looked down, her cheeks reddening slightly. The admiral picked up on it immediately. "I'm sorry. I'm embarrassing you . . . because I'm being so overt about how I feel for you, and you've gotten used to the nice, easy, comfortable relationship we developed while on the ship."

She bobbed her head. "Yes," she admitted.

The admiral turned and slapped Will on the chest. "You idiot," he admonished the surprised younger man. "You're choosing the tidy, easy path instead of the more difficult but ultimately more rewarding path. You aren't even smart enough to know when you have a good thing." The admiral made a noise of utter disgust and dropped down into a chair.

Picard, Will, and Troi slowly backed out of the quarters, leaving the sullen admiral to himself. Once in the corridor, they received the security guards, whom Picard instructed to stand outside and listen for signs of problems. If there were problems, they were to summon Captain Picard at once. They were not to enter under any circumstance. The guards nodded in obedience, if not in understanding, and then Picard issued an order to the computer to keep the doors sealed unless he himself should order them unsealed.

They moved away from the guards, who had taken up their position outside the doors. "I apologize, Captain," said Will. "And to you, too, Counselor."

Picard looked at him in surprise, as did Deanna. "Good heavens, Number One, why?"

"Because of his attitude."

"Yes, but he's not y—well, he *is* you, I suppose. But there are significant differences, Number One, not the least of which is years and experience. You shouldn't feel badly."

"Well . . . I do. Seeing someone who is, to all intents and purposes, *me,* acting that way . . ."

"I don't know," said Deanna with a shrug. "He didn't seem so bad to me."

"You're kidding," said Will. "I don't know . . . I mean . . . I know how much I owe him"—he looked at her—"for everything. But there was still something about him that just . . . just rubbed me the wrong way."

"But he's what you'll become, Number One," pointed out Picard. "You must have seen something of yourself in him."

"No," said Riker firmly. "Very, very little. To be honest, he reminded me of . . ." Then he stopped.

"Of who, Number One?"

Riker sighed. "He reminded me of my father."

Deanna chuckled, and Riker shot her a look.

"Yes, well," said Picard, trying to hide his own smile, "be that as it may . . . due to the delicate situation that we're in, we're going to keep this on a need-to-know basis. However . . . there is someone whom I feel that it's important to consult. Someone who should be able to afford some unique insight into our situation."

On the bridge, Data answered the signal on his communicator. "Commander Data here."

Over the comm unit came the familiar, clipped tone of Picard. "Mr. Data . . . I have a matter of some urgency to discuss with you. Please report to your quarters immediately."

"My quarters?" Data tilted his head in curiosity. "That is a rather unusual procedure, Captain."

"We're in a rather unusual situation, Mr. Data."

"Very well, Captain," said Data, standing. "I will be there directly."

Lieutenant Barclay was walking down the corridor, feeling disoriented, and he bumped shoulders with Data just as he passed the android officer's cabin. Data looked at him curiously. "Lieutenant . . . are you quite all right?"

"I'm . . . I'm fine, sir," said Barclay hollowly.

"Very well." Data turned and walked into his cabin.

Barclay sighed. He still didn't know what to make of his holodeck experience. Perhaps . . . perhaps he simply needed some regular, normal R&R. Not something holodeck-generated. Some real experience instead. Otherwise . . .

Well . . . was it possible that he was having difficulty separating fantasy from reality? Was he, in fact, totally losing touch with the world around him?

No, he thought. It couldn't be. It simply couldn't . . .

He turned a corner and bumped shoulders with Data.

Barclay stepped back, gasping in confusion. "But . . . but . . ."

Data stared at him, his yellow eyes glittering in curiosity. "Lieutenant, are you quite all right?"

With an insane sense of déjà vu, Barclay stammered out, "I'm . . . I'm fine, sir."

"Very well," said Data, taking him at his word and continuing on his way toward his cabin.

Barclay's head snapped back and forth like a yo-yo. Then he sagged against a wall and whimpered like a lost child.

Data entered his cabin and said, "Captain?"

The door closed behind him, but there was no sign of Picard. "Captain?" he said again.

He sensed a presence behind himself and he spun . . .

And a hand was already at his off-switch. He did not even manage to get a look at his assailant before he went limp.

The gold-skinned intruder lowered the insensate android onto the bed and then stepped back. Then he turned and studied his reflection in the mirror.

Perfect, of course. But then again, why shouldn't he be? He was, after all, the same individual. He hadn't aged a day. His body was the same, his brainpower undiminished. And his ability to mimic voices—in this case, Picard's—had been invaluable.

He tilted his head as a thought hit him. He had no recollection of this event ever occurring. But it had just happened in, effectively, his own past. How was it possible for something to have happened to him without his remembering it?

For that matter, how could Admiral Riker be acting as if the entire notion of saving Deanna Troi was just occurring to him? If he had gone back in time to his own past, then he should be aware of everything that had already happened. But unless he was engaging in a massive subterfuge for Data's benefit . . .

No. Data didn't think that was what was happening. The only thing that he could conceive of was that neither he nor Admiral Riker had any memory of the events because, to all intents and purposes, they hadn't happened yet. Right here, right now, was where they were shaping all that was to come.

Except all that was to come had already been shaped. Riker was trying to remold it to his own image. Data, on the other hand, had to try to preserve it.

Deanna Troi could not live to affect the peace conference . . . no matter what was required.

He removed the communicator from the unconscious Data's uniform, removed the one that he had taken from the same supplies room that he had stolen the uniform from that he was now wearing, and affixed Data's actual communicator to his uniform front. No point in leaving anything to chance.

He tapped the communicator. "Computer," he said briskly, "locate Counselor Deanna Troi."

For one moment he hoped that the computer would say, "Deanna Troi is in the morgue." That would have simplified things immensely.

Instead the computer said, "Deanna Troi is in her quarters."

Data nodded. Then he went to the unmoving form of Lieutenant Commander Data, made one small change to it as a safety precaution, and headed off to kill the ship's counselor.

Forty

Picard had gone straight from Riker's cabin to the Ten-Forward, and now he said in soft tones to Guinan, after telling her as much as he knew, "What do you think?"

"What do I think? I think it's possible," Guinan allowed.

"Would you know?" asked Picard. "If time had shifted around us . . . one way or the other . . . would you be aware of it? You've intimated in the past that you have a sensitivity for such things."

"A sensitivity, yes, but I'm not omniscient." She had just poured Picard a drink and slid it over to him. Now she stared at her reflection in the glass. "Look . . . I live day to day, same as you, Captain. Same as anyone. Now if there's a large enough disturbance in the space-time continuum . . . particularly when it has its origins in the past . . . I might be aware of it and be able to tell you that something's wrong. But if it's happening right here, right now"—she shook her head—"then I'm on the same roller coaster as you are, Captain. And all we can do is hold on."

He nodded. "For a moment I toyed with the notion of canceling the peace conference. After all, it would logically appear that an attempt on her life would be connected with the conference. Or I could have all the delegates questioned, or . . ." Then he shook his head in exasperation. "But now we enter the realm of temporal second-guessing. How far do I go, beyond guarding Deanna? If none of this had happened, then I would have no reason to take extraordinary measures. Which means that I really don't have any reason now."

"Best to let matters proceed then," said Guinan.

Again Picard nodded.

At that moment Data walked into the Ten-Forward. He looked around thoughtfully, then glanced up as Picard gestured for him to come over. Data took a place next to the captain, and politely nodded to Guinan.

"A question, Captain," said Data. "Why are Lieutenant Worf and three other security guards stationed around Counselor Troi's quarters?"

Picard glanced at Guinan and then lowered his glass. "I will tell *you,* Data, and will inform Commander Riker that you have been brought into our little circle of secrecy. But it is to go no further. Now the *official* reason is that an unknown assailant, presently in the brig, made an attempt on the counselor's life. That much is, in fact, true. However, it's quite a bit more involved than that . . ."

Data, naturally, knew precisely how involved it was.

He had gone to Troi's quarters, and when he had seen the guards there . . . including a scowling Worf studying every passerby with intense scrutiny . . . he knew he had a problem. It was, of course, perfectly likely that he could force his way past Worf and the others. They were not expecting a friendly face to turn on them, and he could probably down them before they could mount a serious defense. Deanna would have been dead before any help could have been summoned, and once that happened, the currents of time would have pulled him—and presumably, Riker and Blair—back to their own time.

But to attack her so overtly would have exposed that there was more than one Data waltzing around on the *Enterprise.* Or even worse . . . what if the present Data were unable to convince the others that he had not, in fact, simply gone berserk? In one scenario, they would have come to the realization that Data still existed in the future . . . and that knowledge could have serious consequences. On the other hand, if they simply decided that their own Data had become unreliable, or even dangerous, they might conclude that the only reasonable course of action was to deactivate or dismantle him. If they did that . . .

Then what?

Would he, the Data of the future, then cease to exist? And if he didn't exist, then who would go back to stop Admiral Riker? But if he didn't exist to come back to try to stop Admiral Riker, then how could he possibly kill Deanna Troi and set in motion the events that could get himself shut off? And who . . . ?

It was this sort of self-involving confusion that had once prompted Geordi LaForge to declare, during one such discussion of a theoretical paradox, "This is precisely why time travel gives me nosebleeds."

Data didn't have a nosebleed. Data had a situation.

But one way to remedy that situation was to get himself "officially" brought into the information loop. Which was precisely what he was doing now.

And once he had that information, it was just a matter of determining the most effective way to proceed.

Forty-one

There had been one change of security guards since the captain ordered the guard. Worf, however, had remained. This did not surprise anyone. In similar situations, Worf had displayed stamina that was, quite simply, inhuman.

As a result, when Will Riker approached, Worf turned to him with just as fierce a protective glare as he had possessed since he'd first taken his post.

"No one has seen or spoken to Counselor Troi," Worf said, "except for a carefully supervised visit by Dr. Crusher."

Riker nodded approvingly. "Good. Despite everything that happened last night, she wanted to be fresh for the peace conference." He tapped his communicator. "Riker to Counselor Troi. Are you awake, Deanna?"

"Yes, Commander. Awake and ready to go."

"Good." He gestured for Worf and the others to follow, and they entered behind him. Worf observed that Riker was wearing a phaser. Silently he approved.

Deanna was standing there, looking radiant.

"How are you feeling today, Counselor?"

"Well," she said, extending her neck. "Actually I wound up sleeping in a slightly awkward position. My neck is a little stiff."

"Need me to get the kink out?"

"No." She smiled. "Actually . . . the pain isn't so bad. It reminds me that I'm alive."

Riker returned the smile. "I can think of more pleasurable ways to be reminded of being alive."

"Yes, Commander," she said dryly. "I'm sure you can. Well"—she slapped her thighs and rose—"to the peace conference, then."

They started down the hallway—Deanna, Worf, Riker, and the guards. They attracted curious glances as others walked past them in the corridor, and in a low voice Deanna asked, "Do I really require an entire entourage?"

"Just until we get to the conference room," said Riker. "We've shifted the location, however, to the high-security conference room. We've set up a low-level null field that will detect any sort of weapons. Once you're there you'll be safe, and Worf and the others can return to their duties."

"My duty," said Worf firmly, "is to ascertain the safety of all personnel."

"And you've done an excellent job, Worf," Deanna told him.

The Klingon merely grunted.

"Are you sure you're all right?" Riker asked her.

Deanna nodded. "Right after you posted the guards, Beverly came down to check me over."

"Yes, so I heard. 'Carefully supervised.' "

"Her instruments didn't detect anything wrong with me. And yet I felt something . . . or at least, for a few moments, I had. That burning sensation I mentioned. But then it vanished. I can only assume that whatever was in that vial did whatever it was supposed to do. I truly owe a great debt to . . . both of you."

"I know," said Will. "We both do. I was thinking about it last night . . . and maybe I was a little hard on him. I mean, it took real guts to do what he did. I don't know if I could have done it."

She patted him on the arm. "Don't worry, Commander. I suspect the answer is yes . . . but hopefully you'll never have to find out."

In the quarters of Commander Riker, Adm. William Riker crouched in a corner and pulled at the heel of his boot.

He had kept a careful eye on his chronometer and now said, "Computer . . . locate Deanna Troi."

The communications function for the cabin had been deliberately disabled by Commander Riker. Wisely, he had anticipated the possibility that his older self might try to take advantage of their natural voice similarities and use that function to summon help from some unknowing individual. But the locator function still worked just fine.

"Deanna Troi is on deck twenty-three," replied the computer.

"Probable destination?"

The computer did not hesitate. "The Sindareen peace conference is scheduled for conference room twenty-three-D. Deanna Troi is among the personnel scheduled to attend the conference. She is presently one hundred and fifty meters from the conference room and moving towards it. The likelihood that her destination is the conference room is approximately—"

"Never mind. I get the idea."

He twisted the heel of his boot and it came clean off. Holding his palm under it, he upended it.

A miniature phaser fell into his palm.

He nodded approvingly and snapped the heel back in place.

As he did so, he prayed that he had done the right thing in withholding the information that he had. He could have told them so easily that the Sindareen were being duplicitous. Flushing that knowledge out into the open might have ended all of this . . . especially if it was, in fact, the Sindareen who were somehow behind the whole thing.

But he had spoken the truth to Picard. He was indeed treading on very shaky ground and was not at all sure just how far he should go in giving them information. Should he tell them about the Sindareen? Should he tell them about the fact that perhaps Data himself—Data from the future—might be wandering the ship? Certainly if he had been Data, that's what he would have done: gone back himself. Who knew the ship better? Who could blend in more effectively than someone who was already supposed to be there?

He couldn't just tell them all these things. Where would it end? Worse . . . what would it begin?

But he could take action himself . . . actions without explaining them. Be Deanna's guardian angel. Her knight, her cowboy riding to the rescue.

Her Imzadi.

First, though . . . he had to get out of there.

He went over to the far wall. He knew that the officer in the adjoining cabin was already on duty, so this was definitely the preferred exit route.

He held the phaser close up to the wall and set it for as low and quiet a setting as he could. He couldn't risk giving the guards any sort of warning at all.

He pressed down on the trigger device and a pencil-thin beam of light emerged from the miniature phaser. Forcing himself to be patient, Riker proceeded to cut a hole in the wall.

The ship's security system, programmed to recognize 398 different weapons, did not recognize the futuristic phaser for what it was. Therefore, it identified the weapon as the closest analogue in its system, a hand-held arc welder—just as the admiral knew the computer would do. Hardly a weapon, the welder was not something that required any sort of security alert. Riker continued his work undisturbed.

* * *

When Will and Deanna entered the conference room, they saw that Picard and the delegates from the Cordians, the Luss, and the Byfrexians were already there. Only the Sindareen had yet to arrive.

Dann was sitting next to the Luss ambassador, and he had a profoundly befuddled expression on his face. His inquiries as to how in hell he had come to be unconscious in his cabin had not really been answered by anyone. When he saw Deanna, he started to rise, his entire face a question. But Deanna silently gestured for him to sit back down, somehow putting across that she'd speak to him later about it.

Will turned to Worf and the other guards and said in a low voice, "All right . . . we'll be okay for now."

"If you are certain," said Worf slowly.

"Yes," said Riker, and he patted his phaser. "I have the only working weapon in the room—it's keyed into the safe code of the null field. I'll sit next to her and make sure no one gets near her. All this attention . . . it's disconcerting to her. We'll be fine."

"Very well," Worf said. "But summon me instantly at the first sign of trouble."

It sounded remarkably like an order, which was not particularly appropriate for a lieutenant to issue a commander. But Will took it in stride. "Yes, sir."

If Worf picked up on the amused sarcasm, he gave no sign. Instead he grunted again and then turned and exited the room.

"I see the Sindareen are not yet with us," observed Picard as Riker and Troi settled into their seats.

"Perhaps we should start without them," suggested the Cordian ambassador. "After all, the Sindareen peace initiative will probably go far more smoothly without the Sindareen actually being involved." This produced a small chuckle from around the table.

"I think we'll wait for them," said Picard good-humoredly. "After all . . . it would be the polite thing to do."

Data sat on the bridge, watching the home planet of the Sindareen turning beneath them.

The turbolift door opened and Worf emerged. Data waited until the Klingon had taken his station before rising and saying, "I have something I must attend to, Mr. Worf. You have the conn."

He walked out before Worf could say anything. Mentally, the Klingon shrugged. Whatever Data had to take care of, certainly it was none of his concern.

Lieutenant Barclay, deciding that the entire previous night had been one, long bad dream—overstimulation of the imagination—stepped out of the shower, dried himself off, and got dressed for duty.

The two security guards outside Riker's quarters took no notice when the door to the adjoining quarters hissed open.

As a result, they never had a chance to react before the phaser beam, now set to stun, cut loose from the miniature weapon in the hand of Admiral Riker. Instantly, they both fell to the ground, unconscious.

Riker bent over them, glancing around quickly and breathing a sigh of relief that no one was coming. He grabbed each of them by one wrist and, moving as quickly as he could and cursing the achiness of his aging muscles, backed up and dragged them into the cabin from which he'd just exited.

He left them lying on the floor, next to the large piece of wall that he had cut out and pushed through into this cabin. He knew that the phaser blast would have knocked them both out for at least an hour.

When he reemerged from the cabin, he was wearing the uniform of one of the guards. Although there was nothing he could do about his obvious resemblance to the *Enterprise*'s second-in-command, at least he could make himself a bit less noticeable as he moved through the corridors.

He had a little bit of time. He hoped that would be all he needed.

Data, he thought desperately, *if you are here . . . where would you be? What would you be up to? Would you really be so coldhearted as to kill Deanna . . . and if so, how would you go about it?*

Data stood on the turbolift as it whisked him to his destination. He had worked out what needed to be done and was reasonably certain that he could succeed.

He would leave some confusion in his wake. But confusion could easily be dealt with. There would be nothing absolutely incriminating.

And Deanna would be dead.

The Sindareen entered the conference room. "Our apologies," said Ambassador Nici. "We were unaware that the switch had been made to this conference room."

Eza was staring at Troi with a most peculiar expression on his face. And Deanna started to feel the first tickle to her mind of something . . . something that she was starting to place . . .

That vague feeling that she had encountered once before . . . when she had been the captive, years ago, of a Sindareen raider.

In the corridor, Admiral Riker suddenly skidded to a halt.

"Of course," he whispered.

He turned and barreled down the corridor.

Data stepped off the turbolift and abruptly a voice called, "Data!"

Geordi LaForge came up to him quickly. "I'm glad I happened to run into you. We've been getting some weird variants in the warp field fluctuations."

"Now is not a good time, Geordi." Data started down the hallway.

Geordi stopped him, looking at him with concern. "Data, are you okay?"

"Functioning perfectly. We can discuss the field fluctuations at a later date, Geordi. For the moment, I have other things to attend to."

"But it's really odd. The time-space capacitors seem to be reacting to . . . well, to nothing that I can detect."

"Later." Data's voice was firm. He turned and walked off, leaving a very puzzled chief engineer behind him.

Will Riker studied the ambassadors around the table. Everyone seemed perfectly calm. Everything seemed friendly . . . or at least polite.

He looked to Deanna. A faint, puzzled expression was on her face that he knew quite well. She was concentrating, trying to pick the threads of emotions out of the air and weave them into something that she could examine and make pronouncements on.

He thought of giving her a gentle nudge, to ask her what was happening . . . but then decided against it. When she was ready to tell him, she would.

Lieutenant Barclay checked his morning duty log, saw nothing particularly unusual, glanced in the mirror once more, approved of his hairstyle, and walked out of his quarters whistling and ready for a far more sane day.

He walked past Lieutenant Commander Data, who barely afforded him a glance. "Good morning, sir."

"Good morning, Barclay. You look much more relaxed today," said Data, and kept on going. Barclay, still whistling aimlessly, headed for the turbolift.

Admiral Riker dashed into Data's quarters and moaned softly.

Data was lying, unmoving, on the bed. From his skewed position, it was clear that he had been shut off and tossed there like a sack of wheat.

And to make matters worse . . . his head was gone.

Riker allotted sixty seconds to locate it before he went after the future Data himself. It would have been nice to have the strength of the present Data as backup . . . but he would make do if he had to.

He always had in the past . . .

. . . or future . . .

. . . or whatever.

The door to the conference room hissed open, and Data stepped in. Picard looked up at Data questioningly.

"A private matter, sir, for Counselor Troi."

"Very well," said a slightly puzzled Picard.

Troi rose, as did Will. With Data, they stepped over to one of the corners of the room.

"You are aware that the captain has filled me in on the present situation," Data said softly. When Riker and Troi nodded, he continued, "I have some rather bad news. Admiral Riker . . . your future self . . . seems to have suffered some sort of massive heart attack. Dr. Crusher says he's barely stabilized and"—he turned to Troi—"he's calling for you, Counselor."

Deanna frowned. "I . . . I don't feel him in that sort of distress."

"He's barely conscious, Counselor. Perhaps that affects your empathic abilities . . . or perhaps the proximity of our own Commander Riker deters your ability to focus on the other. I took the liberty of coming in person, rather than using communicators. In the event that unauthorized individuals are somehow tapping into our comm systems . . ."

"Yes, good thinking, Mr. Data," said Riker.

"I'd better go to him," Deanna said worriedly.

"I'll go, too," Riker added.

"Are you certain you wish to do that, Commander?" Data asked. "Watching yourself die . . . I'd think it would be difficult for you."

Deanna turned to Riker. "He's right, Will. Please . . . I don't want to put you through that. Data's with me. I'll be fine. Honestly . . . if you ask me, I think you're being overconcerned. The danger is probably over."

Data nodded in agreement.

Forty-two

With three seconds to spare in his self-imposed countdown, Admiral Riker found Data's head. It had been wrapped carefully in a sheet and shoved into the back of the closet . . . just inconvenient enough to serve as a delay, but not so dangerous that it would actually endanger the future existence of the android called Data.

Riker activated the head as soon as he had pulled it free from the cloth. Data blinked and looked around. Then he stared up into the face of his liberator.

"I assume you are not the person who put me into this predicament."

"No, Data. You did this all to yourself."

"You appear to be Commander Riker . . . but significantly aged."

"Come on," said Riker, getting to his feet. "Can you operate your body from here?"

With a cybernetic impulse from Data's positronic brain, his body lurched off the bed like something from an old horror film.

"Good," Riker snapped. "I'll fill you in on the way. Come on, let's go!"

"Be certain to face me forward so that I can see where I am going," Data cautioned him.

Riker bolted into the corridor and started down the hallway, Data's head tucked under one arm. Behind him at a rapid jog came Data's body.

"Would you care to apprise me of what is happening?" asked Data.

Riker was ready for this. He knew that if he told Data the truth, or even part of the truth, he might have a bigger problem than when he started. If this Data decided that the future Data's mission was a sound one, then he might very well have two androids trying to kill Deanna. That he did not need.

So he lied through his teeth.

"I'm Will Riker, all right, but from another dimension. We're pursuing the individual you know as Lore. He crossed over into our universe, killed Deanna Troi there for reasons that we do not know, and now has returned to this dimension and is intent on performing the same murderous act. We have no idea why he's doing these things."

"Neither do I," Data said, "but Lore has been known to behave in an irrational manner. He must be stopped. Shall we warn Counselor Troi via communicator?"

"No. Lore might be monitoring the frequencies. Our best hope is to catch him by surprise."

Commander Will Riker sat down again as Data and Troi walked out of the conference room together. Picard leaned over to him and said, "Number One?"

In a low voice, Will said, "My future self is . . . very ill. Data says he's calling for Deanna. She's going to him."

Picard studied Riker to make sure that his second-in-command was dealing with this news. But Riker's face was inscrutable . . . in fact, he seemed lost in thought.

* * *

Deanna Troi looked worriedly at Data as he stepped to one side when they emerged from the conference room and said, "After you, Counselor." She started down the corridor, Data a foot or two behind her.

Barclay stepped out of the turbolift . . . and stopped breathing.

The Riker from the holodeck pushed past him and onto the lift . . . which was impossible. Under his arm he'd tucked the head of Lieutenant Commander Data . . . which was also impossible since Barclay had just left Data on another deck. He turned, staring at the bizarre sight in utter shock, and then was rudely shoved out of the way by what appeared to be a headless body, which joined the other two . . . or maybe it was one and a half . . . in the turbolift.

"Hope you're keeping your nose clean, Barclay," Riker warned him.

"Good morning, Barclay," said Data's head. "You look much more relaxed today."

Then the turbolift hissed shut.

"Thank you, sir," was all Barclay managed to say, before he mercifully passed out.

Deanna Troi and her escort started down the hallway. Data had already determined how he would pin the blame on Lore, thus leaving his own time line unaffected. Now he studied her long neck, trying to decide what would be the most painless method of disposing of her. For some reason, now that the moment would shortly be at hand . . . he felt . . .

Reluctant.

But his duty was clear.

In the conference room, Riker suddenly jumped as if someone had jammed a rod into his back.

He had done so right as Nici began to make her opening remarks, and she looked at him with stern disapproval.

"Commander?" said Picard.

"Data said he's calling for her." He turned to face Picard and looked as if he'd seen a ghost.

Picard was at a loss, but he saw the consternation of his first officer. "I know, Number One. You told me th—"

Riker's voice became louder. "You don't understand, Captain! That's *exactly* what Data said. 'He's calling.' He said 'he's.' Several times! *He used contractions!"*

"But Data doesn't use—"

Immediately both officers were on their feet, but Riker was nearer the exit. The ambassadors were babbling in utter confusion as Riker bolted out the door.

He saw them, just turning the corner of the corridor.

As if from a separation of years, he shouted, *"Deanna! It's a trap!"*

Troi spun, his words and his mind reaching out to her and warning her.

Data, aware that he had been found out, drew back his fist, and Troi saw it just as she turned. He stepped forward and drove his fist straight toward her face.

With a cry of alarm, Deanna dropped back. Data's fist whistled bare inches from her face and smashed into a wall, going in with such force that his arm penetrated up to his elbow.

Deanna tried to run, but Data lashed out with one of his feet and tripped her up. She fell with a cry, and Will charged forward, bringing his phaser up.

With the hand that had already entered the wall, Data ripped out a huge chunk and hurled it directly at Riker. Riker dodged it, and as the twisted metal thudded to the ground in back of him, Riker fired the phaser.

Data moved with blinding speed and grabbed at the phaser that Riker was holding. Taking a desperate gamble, knowing that he couldn't match Data's superior strength, Riker relaxed his grip and instead shot his hand out toward Data's off-switch.

It wasn't there.

"I had it disconnected, Commander," said Data, sounding almost apologetic. "It became a nuisance." Data's fingers wrapped around the phaser and squeezed, and Riker had to release his grip or risk his hand getting crushed along with it.

Data dropped the twisted metal to the ground, then picked up Riker and hurled him against the far wall. Riker crashed into it and slumped to the ground, dazed.

Picard came from nowhere, hurtling through the air and grabbing Data from behind. Data reached around, grabbing the captain's arm and twisting it around and back. Picard cried out, but that didn't stop him from slamming his free hand up into Data's face. The resulting injury was severe . . . but not for Data. Picard, however, sprained his hand.

"I'm doing this for you, Captain," said Data, sounding almost remorseful. "If I had any choice, I'd do anything else." And he lifted Picard completely off his feet, about to hurl him into the ambassadors who were flooding into the hallway. They fell back, trying to get out of the way.

And Will Riker, pushing off from the wall, charged and tackled Data around the legs. It knocked the android off balance, and he lost his grip on Picard, who tumbled down on top of him.

"Stop it!" Deanna was shouting. *"Stop it!"*

Picard and Riker each grabbed an arm, trying to pin Data. It didn't work. With his superior strength, Data twisted around, lifting Riker clear and crushing him against Picard. Data started to get to his feet.

All the ambassadors were shouting at once.

Data was turning his attention to Deanna.

Riker, indomitable, was grabbing at Data's leg, trying to slow him down. Picard, using the wall for support, was pulling himself to his feet.

Everywhere there was confusion, chaos, raw emotions running rampant . . .

And that was when Deanna Troi pointed at the Sindareen delegation.

"They're deceiving us!" she cried out.

Time froze.

"It's a lie!" said Nici with amazing calm.

"No," said Deanna, her voice building in intensity. "No, it's not a lie."

"Shut up," Eza now said, looking to Nici. "Make her shut up."

"I sense that you want him"—she pointed at Data—"to succeed. You . . . you did not come here in good faith. I sense duplicity . . . lies, cheats, anything to stall for time for the Sindareen."

"This is madness," Nici snarled, louder and angrier.

But Deanna ignored her, whirling on Eza. "And you! You want me dead! You'd do anything to see me dead. You . . . you tried! You tried to kill me! Put something in the drink . . . I sense your emotions, homicidal, murderous."

The air around them seemed to be shifting, coming to life somehow. There was a crackling of energy that seemed to come from nowhere . . .

And Eza howled, *"You empathic bitch! You've ruined everything!"*

From his sleeve he produced a small phaser, smaller than almost anyone had ever seen.

He had a clear shot at Deanna. He wasn't going to miss.

And suddenly, arcing through the air over Deanna's head, came a tumbling, golden object. It struck Eza squarely in the chest, knocking him backward. The phaser fired but the shot went wide, striking the ceiling over Deanna's head.

The golden object skittered across the floor and rolled up to Deanna's feet. She looked down in astonishment at Data's face. "I suggest you drop to the floor, Counselor."

Deanna was still staring in confusion at Data's head, presenting a perfect target. A split second later, Data's body slammed into her from behind, knocking her to the floor next to Data's profusely apologizing head. However, his apologies were drowned out by the phaser beam that crackled over them. It enveloped Eza, staggering him, and he screeched in protest.

Adm. William T. Riker advanced on him slowly, inexorably, the power blasting out of his phaser. "Stay down, Deanna. It still takes a lot of phaser power to put these bastards down for the count."

"Bastards!" shrieked Nici in indignation. "Captain Picard, I object to being described in—"

"Be quiet!" snapped Picard.

Eza writhed in the power of the phaser. He lost his grip on his own phaser and it tumbled to the floor, but so consumed with fury was he that he still tried to make headway against the blast.

"You're from my time, aren't you," said the admiral, progressing relentlessly. "That's the only place you could have gotten that weapon. You're from the time stream that was . . . and will be again. You decided that this point in time was the turning point for your people—was the downfall of your race—and you decided to come back and change it to your liking. Kill the woman who blew the whistle on your people. And in one reality, you got away with it. But not in my reality, you murderer. Not in *my* reality! Because you picked the *wrong focal point!"*

Around Eza the scream of the phaser merged with the howling of the air, and he was knocked completely off his feet, thrown against the wall like a straw in a hurricane. He sagged to the floor, unconscious and helpless.

And then the air around them was roaring. Roaring with far-off winds that seemed to call from another time and place, from an infinity of maybes. A coruscating, sparkling whirlpool of color and light.

Eza was starting to dematerialize, his very molecules being drawn into the vortex around them.

And Will Riker suddenly lost his grip on Data. For a panicked moment he thought that the android had slipped loose and was going to make one final, desperate lunge for Deanna. But he realized his error immediately. Data was starting to fade. Will's hands were passing through him.

Deanna whirled to face the admiral.

He, too, was being drawn off. The color seemed to be fading from him, as if being yanked away.

"Deanna!" he called to her, reaching out.

Heedless of the danger to herself, Deanna Troi stretched out her hand to the man who had crossed decades, remodeled the universe, all for her.

Her hand passed right through him, as if he were a ghost. The ghost of things yet to come.

His body started to flatten out, twisting from three dimensions to two and then one.

"I'm sorry!" she cried out to him. "I tried . . . to touch you one last time."

He smiled, his body disappearing like the Cheshire cat's. His voice sounded distant as he said, "Don't be. Maybe it won't be the last time. Besides . . . who really cares about all this physical touching. Not young Deanna Troi. It's the spiritual that's important . . . that's forever . . ."

And then, with a final roar and burst of wind that swept over everyone in the corridor . . .

He was gone.

Forty-three

"Come in," said Deanna as the tone at her door chimed.

Riker entered, his hands behind his back. He stopped as the door closed behind him. "Are you okay?"

She shut off the computer screen she was studying, folded her hands, and said, "Why shouldn't I be okay?"

"Well . . . you went through a lot."

"We both did," she reminded him. "But that was twenty-four hours ago. I bounce back quickly, given time."

"Given time."

He walked slowly toward her. "I thought you'd be interested . . . the Chameloid disappeared about the same time as . . . the others."

"I assumed as much," she said quietly.

"The Sindareen ambassador has been sent packing. She's not particularly happy about it. The peace initiative has fallen apart, and the experts predict that it's just a matter of time now before the entire Sindareen civilization collapses. There's already talk about how the Federation might come in to pick up the pieces if that happens."

"That would be very humane."

"Oh, and Data has his head together . . . so to speak. It turns out that I . . . that the admiral told him that this other Data—the one who tried to kill you—was actually Lore."

"And was it?"

Riker paused. "I don't know," he said slowly. "I know Data believes it to be. I think he is far more . . . satisfied . . . with the notion that it was Lore than he would be with the concept that there would be a circumstance in which he'd try to murder you."

"We have no idea what influences will shape Data over the next forty years," she said slowly. "For all we know, given a set of circumstances where the life of one woman is weighed against the reality that he knows . . . he might very well decide that that woman is dispensable."

"Even if the woman is you?"

"Even if. And frankly . . . I'd understand his decision."

"Yes . . . but maybe he wouldn't understand. That's a hell of a thing for him to have to live with. So maybe it would be better if we . . ."

"Kept it between ourselves?"

He nodded.

"Consider it kept." She leaned back. "So . . . did you come here to discuss everything except what you really want to discuss?"

"And what might that be?"

"Us."

He let out a slow breath. She waited for him to speak.

"I don't know what's going to happen with us," he said. "I saw what my life was like without you . . . saw what I developed into. I can't say I like it very much. But . . . that was when you had been pulled from my life completely. We could continue in the way that we are now, and as long as you're there to be friend, confidant . . . soul mate . . . things could work out well for both of us."

"I see what you're saying," Deanna said slowly. "Of course, on the other hand, if we become . . . or go back to being . . . lovers . . . things could work out even better for us."

"Or worse," he pointed out.

"Or worse," she acknowledged.

He shook his head. "I feel so ridiculous. Do we really have to wait forty years until we're ready to take a chance on the two of us?"

"No, Will"—she smiled—"we just have to wait until we're ready. It might take forty years. Or who knows? It might take forty days. We have to wait and see. But at least we have a chance. It's up to us how we use it."

He nodded and then said, "Oh . . . by the way . . . I made something for you. It's only an approximation, of course, based on my memories . . . memories which were filled, at the time, with the sight of a particularly nubile young maid of honor and her magnificent figure."

Her face colored slightly. "Will, what are you talking about?"

He brought his hand from behind his back. In it was a thin, white, gauze headband.

She stared at it, uncomprehendingly at first. But then she understood. "That's . . . that's like the one Chandra wore!"

"So I *did* make it close enough so that it's recognizable. Good. Um . . . if you wouldn't mind turning your head . . ."

She angled her head around and he looped it around and back, pulling her hair through. She stood and presented herself for inspection. "How does it look?"

"As beautiful as the woman wearing it."

She felt her emotions turning to melted butter, and she went to him. He enveloped her in his arms, and their lips came together. . . .

And for a long moment, all the confusion and complexity of their lives fell away, and they were once again the young man and woman hungering for each other; the couple shyly learning about one another and exploring the things that each of them lacked and each of them provided; the new lovers in the jungle, intoxicated with their environment and each other; she was the woman whose life he'd saved, and he was the man whose life she had made.

And they had all the time in the universe. . . .

THE BEGINNING
OF THE
END

Forty-four

Mary Mac watched in astonishment as four people emerged from the swirling vortex of the Guardian of Forever: Admiral Riker, Commodore Data, Lieutenant Blair, and one more form that tumbled forward, clearly unconscious.

She went to them, rolling the body over to get a better look and confirm what she had thought. "This . . . this is Mar Loc!"

Data looked at her, his head tilted. "The scientist whom you said had departed?"

She nodded in silent amazement.

And then the Guardian spoke, in that vast and all-encompassing way that it had: **"All is . . . as it was."**

Data turned to face the Guardian. "You mean that Admiral Riker did indeed restore the time line to its original form?"

"All is as it was," repeated the portal.

And now Blair stepped forward, his long fur swirling. "For crying out loud," he shouted, "if you knew that time had been tampered with in the first place, and you knew that the admiral's actions were correct . . . then why in hell didn't you *tell* us that?!"

With utter serenity, the Guardian replied, **"You did not ask."**

There was dead silence, except for the howling of the wind, for about ten seconds. And then Blair managed to get out, "We didn't *ask?"*

Riker started to laugh.

"We didn't ask!" Blair sounded positively outraged. "You mean everything we went through, all the difficult decisions we had to make, all the . . . *we didn't ask!"*

"We didn't," said Data in quiet amazement. "That was very foolish of me. In my determination to uphold the Starfleet imperative of noninterference with time, I . . ."

And Riker, who had managed to calm himself down sufficiently, said, "What you did, Data, is forget the very first *duty* of Starfleet . . . something that I started thinking about when I was spending time with Capt. Wesley Crusher, and remembering the hard lesson he learned back in his Academy days. The duty that supersedes all the imperatives and directives . . ."

"That we must always seek the truth," said Data.

"Right. And the truth," said Riker, hauling the unconscious Mar Loc, a.k.a. Eza, to his feet, "is that this little sleaze decided to make his people's life better. Mary Mac . . . have you had any unexplained bruises in recent weeks?"

"Why . . . why yes," she said, looking at Data. "Remember, Commodore? I had a round bruise on my upper arm."

"A spray-hypo mark," said Riker. "Press down too hard, you leave one. One night while you were asleep, he must have shot you up with something to make sure you stayed asleep—or perhaps even something that induced sleepwalking. He brought you out to the Guardian, used you in your sleeping state to open the force field, returned you to where you were sleeping, stepped into the Guardian . . ."

"And the rest is history," said Blair.

Riker smiled. "Not anymore."

Moments later, Mary Mac had enlisted Blair's aid in dragging the unconscious Mar Loc away, vowing that when she got through with her report to the Federation science council, Mar Loc was going to be sent somewhere where time could truly be appreciated . . . an Orion prison (for his crimes against Mary Mac), where life was so difficult that days tended to pass like years.

"I want you to understand, Admiral," Data said slowly as they stared into the glowing arch of the Guardian of Forever, "that I am truly sorry for my actions."

"It's all right, Data. On the face of it . . . what you did, or tried to do, was correct."

"Curious . . . in my efforts to kill Deanna Troi, I made several mistakes. I did not intend to, but I did. They were almost *clumsy* in nature."

"Perhaps, Data, you did it on purpose. Perhaps you wanted to be stopped."

Data looked at Riker with curiosity. "Is that possible?"

"Of course it's possible. One of the key things about being human, Data . . . is that you don't always know why you do the things you do."

"How very odd. I must admit . . . I did feel somewhat like Brutus."

"Ah, but Brutus, remember, was an honorable man," pointed out Riker. "The important thing is that it's all worked out for the best."

"Has it?"

Riker looked at Data speculatively. "What do you mean?"

Data gestured around them. "While we are on this planet, Admiral, in the heart of the temporal vortex . . . we are untouched by whatever changes might have been made by your reparations. When Mar Loc originally altered time, we—and our memories—were simply altered with it. We had no awareness that anything was different. Now, however, we were at the center of the change. Although you were the architect of the restoration, the actual changes were made without us being a part of them in the here and now. When we leave this world . . . there is no certainty as to what will happen to us. Our memories may shift to accommodate the new time stream. Or we may retain our memories, but find ourselves in a strange new environment. There is even a remote possibility that we may simply blink out of existence, if we do not exist as entities in this time stream."

"I don't think that's going to happen. And you know why, Data? Because I meant what I said earlier. I think that this thing"—Riker pointed to the Guardian—"is God's window. And I don't think that God would have let us in through his window if he didn't intend for us to live in his house."

"That's very spiritual, Admiral."

"I didn't use to be a spiritual person, but I had a good teacher."

Riker gazed up at the swirling skies, the vast colored streaks and the miasma of temporal rifts that formed the heavens above the Forever World.

Distracted, he said, "I really don't know what else there is to say, Data, except . . ."

"Let's get the hell out of here?" suggested Data.

Not looking away from the skies, Riker simply nodded. "I think that probably covers it," he said, but he wasn't paying attention.

And he realized that in the sky's swirling and whirlpool shape, he saw a painting he'd seen a lifetime ago. . . .

"We're going to face a new and different universe, Admiral. Are you not at all afraid?"

There were reds and purples, and then, in the midst of that vast mixture of cosmic existence, Riker saw a face. . . .

"No, Data," he said quietly. "I'm not afraid at all. I think it's going to work out just fine."

And he called out, as he had called out in hopelessness and despair for year upon year of desolation.

And the answer came.

Whether it was from within him, or whether it came from somewhere out there in the galaxy, from someone who was the better part of all that he was, he couldn't be sure.

But it was there just the same. Tears came to his eyes as he heard, in his head, the words that he had waited half a lifetime to hear. Sweet and musical, in a voice filled with promise.

And the words were:

Welcome home . . . Imzadi . . .

TRIANGLE:
IMZADI II

The events take place during 2371,
just after the U.S.S. Enterprise NCC-1701-D
was destroyed in a crash landing, to 2374,
when Commander Worf was assigned to
Deep Space 9.

NOW

After the scream, he had more or less been numb.

He had held the body of his beloved Jadzia Dax, his wife, in his arms, and he had howled the Klingon death scream. Even though she had not been truly Klingon, in many ways she had attended to the teachings and standards of his race with more diligence than he had.

And now he had shut down.

Jadzia was dead. It had been so futile, so pointless, and above all, so sudden. They had just been speaking of having a child, just that very day, and just like that, she was gone.

Once upon a time, the Klingons had had gods. But then they had killed the gods because they were too much trouble. As a result, Klingons knew that once one was put into the universe, one was on one's own. There was no looking to a god or gods for answers, for none were ever going to be forthcoming. There was no court of higher appeal for the unfairness of life, there were no prayers to be served up asking for personal gain, support, or understanding. At this particular moment, Worf wished with all his heart that there were gods once again. . . .

He stood in his . . .

. . . their . . .

. . . his . . . quarters . . . preparing for the funeral. And yes, oh yes, he desperately wanted the gods back again . . . so that he could find a Klingon god, wrap his fingers around the god's throat, and demand whatever explanations there were to be provided before he crushed the deity's windpipe and slaughtered all the bastards personally this time.

In their quarters, he growled to himself. And what he growled was:

"I did everything right."

It was an incomprehensible statement for someone who was not sharing Worf's thoughts. The burly Klingon, serving in a permanent position on Deep Space 9, was speaking to no one in particular. It was simply a general address to the universe at large.

"I did everything right," he said again, and couldn't comprehend why things had turned out the way they had. It just wasn't right or fair.

"I tried to change . . . tried to learn . . . and grow . . . do everything they taught me . . . and it made no difference. IT MADE NO DIFFERENCE!" Losing control completely, Worf swept his hands across the fairly stark furnishings of their quarters.

All her things were there. Scents and makeup, souvenirs, irreplaceable knickknacks representing a life that had spanned decades. For Jadzia Dax was a gestalt being, a combination of a humanoid host and a worm-like symbiont called a Trill. When a Trill began a new life, contact with the old was strictly forbidden. Worf was suddenly—just like that—part of Jadzia Dax's past. He had no idea what was going to happen. Whether the Trill would return in another body, whether the new incarnation of Dax would still love him, whether he would love her . . .

. . . her?

. . . him? That would be *all* he needed.

And the pain, the anger, the rage he was feeling was unprecedented for him.

His impulse, barely restrained, was to rage, to strike out at anyone and anything, to vent the fury that was sweeping through him like something palpable.

The fact was that he had never felt like this before. But it wasn't as if this were the first time he had ever faced loss.

First and foremost, there had been his parents, torn from him at a young age during the raid on the Klingon outpost of Khitomer. They had died beneath the hammering of a Romulan assault, and Worf himself had been buried alive beneath a ton of rubble. Many were the nights he had lain awake, staring at the ceiling in the home of his adopted parents, and his line of thinking was always the same: First he would blame his parents for leaving him, and then he would blame himself for surviving them. It was an attitude he had grown out of, more or less . . . indeed, even as an adult, there was the occasional sleepless night and flicker of condemnation directed in one of several different directions.

But it wasn't the same as losing Jadzia.

Then there was K'Ehleyr. The Klingon emissary with whom Worf had had an on-again, off-again romantic relationship that had resulted, rather unexpectedly, in the conception of a son, Alexander. But K'Ehleyr had been killed by Duras; Worf had held her dying body in his arms and mourned her loss. He had then embarked on a tempestuous relationship with his son, who even now served the Klingon Empire to the best of his abilities. K'Ehleyr, who had seemed in every way a match for him. Whom he had even proposed to, although she had declined the offer.

But it wasn't the same as losing Jadzia.

And then there had been Deanna. . . .

"Deanna," he grunted. The very recollection of the name was enough to rekindle a burning anger within him. He remembered the last time he had encountered Deanna Troi, ship's counselor of the *Enterprise,* and William Riker, the first officer, during the Borg assault on Earth. The *Defiant* had been badly wounded and Worf had been one of the crewmen evacuated. His first impulse once he had been brought aboard the *Enterprise* was to stay down in sickbay, but his pride and sense of duty would not allow it. So he had insisted on being brought up to the bridge, even though the prospect of looking at Riker and Troi, of seeing them together, was almost more than he could tolerate.

He had not shown it, of course. That would have been unprofessional, and childish, and weak. And Riker didn't make it easier. Knowing the bad blood, the anger between them, Riker had made some poorly thought-out comments, passing for what he had considered to be humor. Upon learning that the *Defiant* was damaged but salvageable, he had noted, "Tough little ship." Worf had promptly glared at him, growling, "Little?"

As if that hadn't been enough, when Picard had assigned Worf to tactical, Riker had drifted over to him and inquired innocently, "You do remember how to fire phasers?" If they had not been in the middle of an emergency situation, Worf might have responded with anger. Realizing that his attempts to lighten the situation had backfired spectacularly, Riker had grinned, shaken his head, and put up his hands in a "Just kidding" manner. Fortunately enough, as far as Worf was concerned, subsequent events resulted in his having very little interaction with Riker and Troi for the remainder of their involvement with the Borg, and once the emergency was over, Worf couldn't get back to Deep Space 9 fast enough. Apparently, despite the time Worf had spent with the clerics at the monastery on Boreth, the anger still burned within him far more fiercely than he had realized.

It could have been so different. . . .

The thought came to his mind, unbidden, but once it was there he could not rid himself of it. If matters had not gone so wrong with Deanna, if he had not lost her, if they had married, if it had not been for Riker, and the kidnapping, and Deanna's damned mother, and the byzantine plot hatched with the intent of wiping out millions of innocents . . .

It was as if all the fates in the galaxy had conspired to find a way to totally destroy the intended relationship between Worf and Deanna Troi.

It was Troi's fault . . .

Lwaxana's fault . . .

Riker's fault . . .

. . . the Romulans' fault . . . the universes' fault . . . the fault of those damned gods who were supposed to keep their noses out of everything . . . it was . . .

. . . it was . . .

He stared into a mirror, gazing at himself, as if he could peer straight into his own soul.

"Does it matter?" he finally asked himself. "I am still alone . . . in any event . . ."

But it did matter. It mattered to him, to his determination to try and make sense out of the senselessness of it all.

And Worf, suddenly feeling bereft of strength, sank down into a nearby chair. It had been one of Jadzia's favorites; her scent still clung to it. He breathed deeply of her . . .

. . . and thought of times past . . .

THEN

One

Riker had no warning before the shock prod tapped him in the small of the back. Immediately he died, temporarily, from the waist down. He hated the occasions when it happened, the feeling of total helplessness. The knowledge that the fall was inevitable was more grueling and hurtful to him than the fall itself.

He hit the ground hard, as he always did on such occasions. He dropped his ore breaker in the hopes of cushioning some of the fall with his hands, and he was partly successful—but only partly, as the base of his hands crunched into the hard ground. He felt the jolt all the way up his elbows, and he gasped low in his throat. Then he braced himself for the inevitable kick. It came just as he had expected, a sharp blow to the stomach. In his first days in captivity, that had always been the worst, those stomach blows. Over time, however, he had learned to anticipate them, and he was able to condition himself against them. Just before the impact, he consciously tightened the muscles of his stomach so that a good deal of the impact was blunted. In his fantasies, his gut became so unassailable that his tormentor wound up breaking his ankle.

It was a very nice fantasy.

"Get up, Riker," said his captor, and he was kicked again. This time he didn't let out so much as a grunt, and the lack of response on his part seemed to incite his tormentor all the more. "Well?"

And Riker managed to get out, "Please, sir . . . I want . . . some more . . ."

The guard stared down at him in utter confusion. "All right . . . if that's your true desire . . ." He was about to kick Riker a third time, and then a sharp voice stayed the blow.

"That's enough," it said.

The Cardassian jailer lowered his foot and turned his attention to the individual who had spoken. The jailer, whose name was Mudak, was a beefy fellow, but anyone thinking him fat would have been in for a rude shock. Any excess on his frame was pure muscle, and when he moved it was with speed that was blinding. Mudak could be standing two feet away, his hands at his side, and you could suddenly be knocked on your back before you had the slightest awareness that a punch was coming.

He was also tall, and his eyes were the most striking thing about him. They were dark and pitiless; one would get more sympathy from a black hole than from those eyes. When Riker looked into those eyes, they reminded him of a shark's. They regarded him, and the other prisoners, with an air that clearly indicated that he didn't care whether they lived or died.

Mudak looked at the individual who had interrupted his sport. It was a Romulan, a head taller than Mudak, with graying hair and a darkly imperious look. In truth, the Romulan had no more status in this place of torment than did Riker. It was as if, in his manner and deportment, he was not interested in acknowledging his relatively low status in the grand scheme of things. From his attitude, it would have been unlikely that any bystander would have realized that Mudak was the jailer and the Romulan the prisoner.

Yet despite the Cardassian's ostensible authority over the Romulan, Mudak did not seem inclined to press the point. Instead he said, with a level voice that bordered on malevolence, "This is none of your affair, Saket."

Saket looked from the fallen Riker to Mudak. "It is now, Mudak. And you will leave this human alone."

"He was moving too slowly," Mudak retorted. "He was daydreaming."

Saket took a step closer so that he was almost in Mudak's face. "Leave him his dreams, Mudak. In the final analysis, what else have we in this place?'

Mudak considered this for a moment, and then he laughed low in his throat. It was an eerie noise, as if he were exercising muscles that were nearly atrophied from disuse. In a low voice he rumbled, "Someday, Saket, you will lose your usefulness to my superiors. And on that final day, you will pay for your arrogance."

"We all pay on the final day, Mudak," Saket said imperturbably. "Jailors and jailed alike; we all pay then."

Mudak's hands idly twisted on the shaft of the shock prod, as if contemplating shoving it down Saket's throat or into an even more inconvenient bodily orifice. But apparently he thought better of it. Instead he lightly tapped the now-deactivated end of the prod against his forehead in a sardonic salute and moved off. Saket then crouched next to the fallen Riker. "You should be able to feel something in your legs by now. He had the prod on one of the lower settings."

"I thought as much," grunted Riker. "This time around it was just agonizing instead of incredibly agonizing."

"You see? Your sense of humor returns already."

Saket stood, got a firm grip under Riker's arms, and hauled him to his feet. For a moment, Riker felt practically nothing beneath him, and Saket had to move him around bodily to try and get some sense of motion going. "One leg after the other," intoned Saket, "that's it, lad."

Under Saket's urging, Riker forced himself to move his legs and started to feel growing strength with every step. "Keep going," urged Saket, helping Riker move in a small circle. Within minutes, Riker was walking about in a manner fairly close to his normal strength and stride. "Come, Riker . . . let us go for a walk, you and I." And with that, the two of them made their slow way across the compound. "Were you out of your mind just before? Saying you wanted more?"

"It was . . . it was a quote . . . from a book, actually . . . about orphans, *Oliver Twist.* Author's name was Dickens . . . I felt it appropriate . . . since in a way I don't have a mother or father . . . I'm just sort of . . . of here . . ."

"You're babbling, Riker."

"No, I'm fine . . . truly. Dickens . . . great author . . . you should read him . . . *Bleak House* . . . story of my life . . . *Tale of Two Cities* . . . about two men who look alike, and one sacrifices himself for the other . . . never realized when I was reading him as a boy . . . how much resonance . . . he'd have for me . . ."

"Whatever you say, Riker," Saket said, shaking his head.

"Saket," Riker said, "we haven't known each other long. But we're friends . . . you can feel free to call me Thomas. Or Tom, if you prefer."

"Actually, I prefer Riker," replied Saket. "Always have. Stronger-sounding name. Sounds more pleasingly harsh to the ear."

"Guess it really doesn't matter," Riker admitted. "As long as you continue to call me 'friend.' "

They trudged past one of the central deutronium-processing centers, and Tom Riker was impressed—not for the first time—over the carefully crafted futility that filled the day-to-day existence in the Cardassian labor camp of Lazon II.

Tom Riker, the bizarre and perfect duplicate of William Riker who had been created through a strange transporter accident during a rescue operation at a station on Nervala IV. The fact that there had been a second Riker running around had been disconcerting enough to the original item. But after an abortive career in Starfleet, Tom Riker—taking his new name from his (their) middle name—had wound up joining the revolutionary group called the Maquis and endeavored to steal the starship *Defiant.* The result had been his incarceration on Lazon II.

Lazon II was a fairly desolate world, and the vast majority of it was uninhabitable. One section had been terraformed into someplace where humanoids could survive, and that was the section in which Tom Riker, Saket, and about fifty or sixty-odd enemies of the Cardassian state were currently living out their life sentences. It wasn't that the sentences they had been given were actually called life sentences. There was usually some limit, around twenty or thirty years. Unfortunately, the mortality rate on Lazon II was quite high. Sentencing to Lazon II therefore became a *de facto* death sentence.

Lazon II had never actually been intended as a work camp. Originally Lazon II had been of particular interest to the Cardassians since the planet was rich in deutronium ore. Processed deutronium had been a popular fuel for various Cardassian weapons systems and some earlier models of their war vessels. Since the Cardassians had already depleted the deutronium supplies on such worlds as Preplanus, the discovery of a sizable deutronium store on Lazon II had been greeted with much enthusiasm. The terraforming project on Lazon II had begun rather promptly . . .

. . . and then tapered off. There had been new advances in Cardassian technology during the intervening time, and deutronium as an energy source now served a minor need at best. Most of the weaponry and such that had utilized deutronium had become obsolete.

It was at that point that Lazon II was developed into a penal colony and hard-labor camp. And it was a masterful way in which they did it, because hard labor was bad enough. But hard labor for no real purpose was far worse. The prison populace of Lazon II would spend day after endless day working in weather that was either sweltering or else bitter cold. That was all at the control of the Cardassian wardens of the place, a convenient perk thanks to the terraforming equivalent that governed their little slice of the galaxy. The work consisted of taking massive chunks of deutronium ore and using handheld ore crackers to break the ore down into small, manageable pieces. The pieces were then hand-fed into blazing hot refineries that were antiquated beyond belief. It was the equivalent of embarking on interplanetary travel with the only speed available to you being impulse drive, knowing full well that faster-than-light capability existed for everyone else but you. Piles of deutronium that could be processed in minutes using modern facilities instead took days, even weeks. The processing was dangerous, to boot, as the ancient machinery tended to break down in spectacular fashion, usually killing one or two operators before the latest malfunction was locked down and contained. And once the deutronium was processed, it then sat, stockpiled, in Cardassian warehouse facilities, for the supply of deutronium far outstripped the demand. In short, all of the effort that the prisoners of Lazon II went to was a colossal waste of time. This the prisoners knew all too well. This was designed to help morale disintegrate, and it was quite effective.

They passed the fearsome twin towers that were the defense grids of Lazon II. There was a forcefield in place that covered the compound, but that was only one of the protective systems. Riker looked up as light glinted off the muzzles of the massive pulse-blasters, capable of inflicting cataclysmic damage on any potentially attacking vessels. There was also a sensor scrambler: a rather insidious device that made it impossible for any ships to lock on, via transporter, to anyone in particular on the planet's surface, whether it be via communicator or sensor readings. For instance, there was one Andorian on Lazon II. Under ordinary circumstances, an Andorian rescue vessel could take a stab at pounding the forcefield into oblivion, and then beam the target up to the ship while safely out of range of the blasters. Not so with the scrambler: They would have to come down and actually get their intended "rescuee," and by that point the blasters would reduce the attacking vessel into scrap.

Since transporters were therefore ineffectual on Lazon II, entrances to and exits from the facility were made entirely via shuttles and assorted small craft, which were housed at a landing field not far away. But the field was heavily guarded . . .

. . . although lately Riker noticed that there were fewer guards than usual. It seemed to him that there had been cutbacks on Lazon II, as if Cardassian forces were being stretched to deal with situations elsewhere. He might have been imagining it, but he didn't think so. Still, with all the protections that the facility carried, what difference did a few less men make?

The small, shabby hut that Riker and Saket shared with five other inmates—all of whom were on work detail at that moment—barely provided any sort of shelter. There were cracks in it that allowed the cold wind to blast through when the jailors were of a mind to torment them with harsh winds. When it was hot, the hut managed somehow to contain all the heat, turning the place into the equivalent of a blast furnace. All the huts were like that.

Today happened to be one of the cold days, although Riker wasn't sure how much of it was the air and how much was simply his lessened resistance to harsh climate at that particular moment.

"How long do you think they'll leave us alone in here?" Riker asked grimly.

"Long enough to catch our breath, get our bearings," Saket replied. He regarded Tom Riker thoughtfully. "Tell me, Riker . . . when you first came here, you seemed rather pleased with your situation. You stole a Federation ship, am I right?"

"The *Defiant.*" He nodded. "I intended to use it against the Cardassians."

"Because you had joined the Maquis. Correct?"

Once more Riker nodded.

"And when your plan did not pan out, the Cardassians intended to execute you, but instead you caught a stroke of luck and wound up"—and he gestured widely—"at this lovely facility instead."

"It seemed a lucky break at the time," Riker said ruefully. He was rubbing his thighs, trying to make sure that normal circulation had been fully restored.

Saket chuckled, or at least made what passed for a Romulan chuckle. Romulans were not particularly renowned for being the most mirthful of people. "Better, Riker, that they had killed you then and there. Better by far."

"I'm going to get off of here." Riker nodded firmly, although whether it was because he truly believed it or was simply trying to convince himself of it was difficult to tell. "Believe me, Saket, I am not going to end my life on this ball of rock. That much I know. I was meant for better things."

"And those things would be . . . ?"

"Better." He regarded Saket with open curiosity for a long moment. He had found it most odd that he had developed a close relationship with the Romulan. Riker had always been of the opinion that Romulans were largely duplicitous, fundamentally cowardly, and nonconfrontational except in those instances where the odds were so skewed on their side that there was no possibility of failure.

Saket, however, seemed a different story altogether. There was a dignity about him, a self-possession, even a nobility. Perhaps the thing that Riker found most refreshing was Saket's honesty. Saket seemed to have little to no patience for many of the Romulans in the modern empire. He told Riker with all earnestness that he felt as if the Romulan Empire had taken a wrong turn somewhere in its development. He particularly seemed to blame the Klingons for the modern-day situation.

"Our alliance had an effect on both our races," Saket once told Riker. "We learned from each other; unfortunately the mutual education was not an equitable one. We were a better, stronger, more decent race before we allied with the Klingons. An entire generation of our leadership grew up during the alliance, and learned from the Klingons their thieving ways, their duplicity and fundamental lack of trustworthiness. The Klingons, on the other hand, saw the way in which other races regarded us. Saw how our honor, our strategy and breeding elevated us in the eyes of others. And so they mimicked those attributes in order to raise themselves up to other races, discarding us once they had stripped us of our weaponry and our very character. They are parasites, Riker, parasites, and mark my words: They will destroy your Federation in the same way that they brought us down. If you trust them, then you are fools. I should know, because we trusted them and were no less foolish."

Riker wasn't entirely sure how much of Saket's argument he bought, but he certainly found him intriguing enough to listen to. Saket, for his part, seemed to appreciate the audience.

Most of the numbness seemed to be gone from Riker's legs. As he rose, he looked at Saket curiously and said, not for the first time, "How do you do it?"

"Do what?" Saket asked with raised eyebrow.

"Why are you an untouchable? I've seen it, we've all seen it. The guards never lay a hand on you, much less a prod. You tell them exactly what you think without any concern about your personal safety. They glower at you, they resent you . . . but they do nothing against you. How do you do it? What's your secret?"

"I am beloved," Saket told him.

"No one is that beloved, particularly to the Cardassians."

Saket appeared to contemplate Riker for a time. Then he looked right and left, as if wanting to make sure that no one was nearby, overhearing their discussion. Then he leaned forward and said very softly, "I know things."

"You know things?" This was not exactly the clear answer that Riker was hoping for. "What sort of things?"

"Things that they wish to know. Things about the rulers of the Romulan Empire. Things, for that matter, about key people in the Cardassian Empire as well." He smiled thinly. "I am a spy, Riker. I have been much of my life, and I know a great many things. That makes me a bit of a resource to them."

"Really. Well, I don't know if I know a great many things . . . but one of the things I do know is that the Cardassians are fabled for their ability to extract information. They're rather accomplished at it; some might even say they revel in it."

"That is very true. Their reputation is earned, not exaggerated."

"Then why," Riker asked reasonably, "have they not done so to you?"

"We have . . . an understanding, the Cardassians and I. Every so often, I will answer questions for them, give them key bits of information . . . most of it having to do with their own people. They are very suspicious of one another, you see. That will be the key to their eventual downfall, I should like to think. In exchange for that, I still do not have my freedom . . . but my captivity is—by Cardassian standards—not a particular hardship. Notice I do none of the truly difficult or undesirable tasks on Lazon Two. That, I fear, is left to the less gifted individuals such as yourself."

Riker shook his head. "I still don't understand, though. Why aren't they trying to force out of your head every scrap of knowledge you have?"

"Because, Riker, I have traveled many places and learned some intriguing things in my life. And one of those . . ." He smiled, which always looked odd on Romulans due to their distinctively Vulcanesque appearance. ". . . One of those is how to die."

"You mean with honor?" Riker clearly didn't get it.

"I mean"—and Saket leaned forward, his fingers interlaced— "I can end my life . . . with a thought."

Riker didn't quite know how to take that. "Well, we can all of us do that, Saket."

"No, you do not understand. Even within your own, human race, there are techniques, meditative skills, in which the practitioner can place himself into such a deeply meditative state that his heart slows down to near-undetectability."

"Yes, I know."

"In my case," continued Saket, "I can stop my heart . . . shut myself down . . . and die, if I so choose. My captors are quite aware of this, particularly when I demonstrated it for them."

"You . . . died . . . ?"

"Almost. I allowed myself to be resuscitated. It was an object lesson for them. The Cardassians can sometimes be reasonable, you see, Riker. Dead, I would be of no use to them. If they endeavor to torture me, I will simply end my life by sheer will alone. So I aid them in small ways that do no disservice to the Romulan Empire, and I wait patiently in the meantime for my day of liberation."

"But then why are you still here? You could threaten to kill yourself if they don't let you go."

Saket looked at him with slight pity, as if surprised that Riker should have to ask such an obvious question. "If I am free, then I am of no use to them. Indeed, I might even be a harm. They would rather have me alive than dead, but they would also rather have me dead than liberated. I am a prisoner of my own talent."

"I see. So you have a sort of detente worked out."

"In a manner of speaking, yes. How long it will last, it is difficult to say. It is possible that some day the Cardassians might lose their patience, or a change in the power structure might—"

The door to the hut banged open and Mudak was standing there, his lower lip curled into an impatient snarl. "Your legs will have recovered by now," he said sharply. "Why are you still in here?"

"No particular reason," Saket said. "We will be with you right away, Mudak."

"Right away. How charming." Mudak's face tightened a moment, and then he turned away and closed the door behind him.

"You're pushing him, Saket," Riker said worriedly. "Sooner or later . . ."

"Sooner or later, he will break," Saket said, the irony clearly not lost on him. "That, Riker, is my fondest hope."

"Why, Saket?"

"Why is that my fondest hope?" But from Riker's tone of voice, he sensed that wasn't what Riker was asking about.

"No. Why me. Sometimes I feel as if you've made me your personal project. You approached me . . . befriended me, if the term 'friend' can be applied . . ."

"And you wish to know why." Saket shrugged. "I've wondered that myself, Riker. I'm not entirely sure. I get feelings about people sometimes. A sense that they will be important somehow in the grand scheme of things. Perhaps it's because you are the only Federation man here. That alone is enough to make you stand out. And if Starfleet abandoned you to the degree that you're on your own, here in the heart of darkness . . . that alone is enough to recommend you to me as a possible ally."

"Starfleet didn't abandon me," Riker said sharply. "I abandoned the Fleet. I . . ."

"Why? You've never truly spoken of it in detail, and I did not wish to push. But why . . . ?"

Riker stared at nothing and shivered at the chill air blowing more harshly through the crack in the structure. "I'm the road not taken."

"Pardon?" He arched a confused eyebrow.

"There's a religion on Kanubus Three," said Riker after a moment, "that advocates total hedonism."

"Doesn't sound so terrible to me," Saket said, smiling, not pretending to understand where Riker was going with it.

"They do whatever they wish," Riker told him, "whenever they wish, and attach no importance to anything, because they have embraced the concept of the multiverse. They believe that nothing matters, because whatever decision you may make that takes you in one direction, in another universe you decide something that takes you in another direction entirely. Well . . . I'm sort of a self-contained alternate universe. In one aspect of this reality, I went in one direction. I became the ideal Starfleet officer, dedicated and unwavering. And since I already did that . . . I felt as if, to make my own way in life, I had to become something else. I couldn't let my existence simply be a rehash." He looked at Saket's blank expression and couldn't keep a smile off his face. "You have absolutely no idea what I'm talking about, do you?"

"About yourself? No. Not a clue," Saket admitted. "But I do know of alternate universes. I know all too well. I know of a woman, in fact, whose very existence hinges on an alternate universe. She was . . . is, I should say . . . very dear to me."

"Now *I* have no idea what *you're* talking about," said Riker. "How could someone owe their existence to an alternate universe?"

"It's rather . . . complicated. A tale for another time. Come. Even I don't desire to push Mudak's mood too far at this point." Riker nodded and followed Saket out.

And it was not too long after that that all hell broke loose, Saket died, and Tom Riker found himself staring down the barrel of a phaser with only a twitchy trigger finger between him and instant death. . . .

Two

"Nice landing."

The first million times or so—and that was only the mildest of exaggerations, as far as she was concerned—that Deanna Troi had heard that comment, she had felt more than a little annoyed. She had never purported to be helm material even under the best of circumstances, and having as her first experience an *Enterprise* that was crippled and already on a spiraling collision course with the surface of Veridian III was not exactly a fair test of a novice's abilities. Given some time, a stable situation, and ample practice, the ship's counselor had no doubt that she could easily have whipped herself into shape as a credible conn officer. Instead she'd been thrust into a situation where even the most experienced hand on the helm would have been unable to prevent the *Enterprise* 1701-D from tumbling to her doom.

As the battered and beleagured crew set up temporary stations on Veridian III, awaiting rescue, Deanna had walked among them, trying to allay their worries, assuring them that help would be on the way, and helping many of the civilians—particularly the younger children—deal with the fact that their home, the only home that many of them had ever known, had just tumbled from the sky like a wounded sparrow after an assault by a Klingon Bird-of-Prey. The bulk of the ship had exploded thanks to a warp-core breach, and the saucer section had plummeted through the atmosphere of Veridian III, Troi's decidedly unsteady hand at the helm, skipping across the planet's surface like a huge discus hurled by a gigantic Greek Olympian. The seemingly endless crash landing had, in fact, ended, and Troi felt it her job to see to the mental health of the crew members as best she could.

They seemed remarkably resilient . . . particularly considering the number of them that kept saying the same thing to her:

"Nice landing."

This time it was Lieutenant Sheligo. Tall and gaunt, with some burn marks on his face from the crash that had not yet been attended to, Sheligo had practically bent his lanky frame in half to scrunch up on the ground with his wife and child. At that moment, he was idly stroking the hair of his still-trembling three-year-old, and he glanced up at Troi with a wan expression as he said it.

Troi had long since stopped taking it personally, or as some sort of criticism or commentary on her "inadequacy." She had come to realize that, rather than a critique, it was a method of irreverent congratulations. The shaken crewmen still couldn't quite believe that they had managed to survive the last fiery moments of the great starship's demise. Commenting on her piloting skills was a way of laughing off the nearness of their deaths. They weren't attacking her. They were thanking her.

At least, that was what she chose to believe.

And she said to Sheligo the same thing she'd started saying to everyone else who felt obliged to comment on the narrowness of their escape: "We walked away from it."

"That we did," agreed Sheligo, and gave her a thumbs-up gesture. It was, after all, a sensible philosophy that had existed since, very likely, the Wright brothers had their first crash. Any landing that one could walk away from was a good one.

She noticed Geordi La Forge approaching, and she smiled to him, nodding in greeting. La Forge asked her jauntily, "Get a souvenir?"

Deanna paused in her steps. "Pardon?"

"A souvenir." He reached behind him and held up a piece of metal. It was blackened and scuffed; she thought it was from the ship's hull, but she couldn't be sure. "Everyone's getting them. There's certainly enough to go around. Lost a huge section of the underbelly in the skid. Pieces scattered all over the trench we left behind us."

"Got any spares, Commander?" inquired Sheligo.

"Sure," said Geordi. He reached into a satchel that he had slung around his shoulder and extracted a rounded piece. He flipped it to Sheligo, who caught it easily on the fly.

"It seems a bit . . . morbid," allowed Troi. "Don't you think?"

Sheligo turned the metal over in his hand, studying it. His little daughter stopped her trembling momentarily as her attention was caught by the sun's reflection off the shard. He didn't even appear to hear Deanna's questions.

"Morbid?" said Geordi. "Why?"

"Well . . . what happened here, it was . . . most unfortunate," she pointed out, picking the words as delicately as she could. "It was somewhat traumatic for all concerned. Aren't you at all worried, Lieutenant," she said to Sheligo, "that your daughter might find it a distressing reminder of what happened? And Geordi . . . you were the chief engineer. Won't you find it upsetting to have a piece of the vessel that is no more?"

"Counselor," Geordi replied easily, "are you kidding? This"—and he held up the piece of metal—"this is a good-luck charm. This is a reminder of a ship that held together and saved us all. A ship that I'm going to have fond memories of, no matter what her fate was. And a reminder, I guess, that—above all—she was still just a ship. A thing of metal and parts. But we're still alive, and that's a great way to be."

"Certainly beats the alternative," Sheligo commented.

At that, Deanna had to smile. "You know what, Geordi?" she said in even, good humor. "Sometimes I think that you missed your calling. Have you given thought to the joys of being a ship's counselor?"

"I'll take it under advisement. If you'll excuse me . . ." he said as he headed off. Then he called over his shoulder, "Oh! Counselor!"

"Yes, Geordi?"

He grinned and gave a thumbs-up gesture. "Nice landing."

She bowed slightly in an acceptance of the compliment that was both grudging and amused.

As she walked, she became more aware of the warmth of the sun upon her. Had they not happened to crash, uncontrolled, on this world, it might have made a credible location for shore leave. It was certainly pleasant enough, temperate and enjoyable. Would that the circumstances had been different.

No one else seemed to be in especially dire straits at that moment insofar as trauma counseling was concerned. She shouldn't have been surprised, really. These crewmen of the former *Enterprise,* they were determined, hardy stock, and at present the fact that they were still breathing (or whatever was their preferred means of air circulation) was enough to see them through. Later on would come the delayed effects of survivor shock. There could be trembling, or sudden, startled screams in the middle of the night. Many of them, particularly the younger ones, would never be able to look upon a starship with the same sense of security that had always served them so well. They would always know that the protective shell between them and the unforgiving vacuum of space was much more fragile than they had previously thought. Oh, they'd known it intellectually, of course. But knowing it in one's head was one thing. Knowing it because one's heart was thudding with fear as one was scrambling to questionable safety in the ship's saucer section while the rest of the vessel was on a countdown to doom . . . well, that was something very different.

And it wasn't going to be her problem.

That was a hard realization for her. No one knew what was going to happen next. Obviously they would be reassigned. The question was, where were they going to be reassigned to? It was most unlikely that the entire crew complement of a thousand would simply be kept together, cooling their collective heels, until such time as Starfleet had a ship they could serve on as a unit. They would most likely be split up, sent off to whatever vessels most immediately required their presence. She'd spoken ever-so-briefly with Captain Jean-Luc Picard, and he had seemed confident that another *Enterprise* would be commissioned. But he had no idea when or where, of course.

The officers might . . . *might* . . . be kept as a group. There was no guarantee of that, but on the other hand, a captain with the weight of authority and long, proud history that Picard carried with him would very likely be able to get his wishes met. If he wanted to keep his command crew intact, he might well be able to do it. But there was no way that he was going to be able to keep a thousand people locked up, idle, while awaiting a new command.

She knew them, Deanna Troi did. Over the course of seven years, she had come to know each and every person on the *Enterprise.* Knew them with a familiarity and casual, emotional intimacy that she had never thought possible. There had been all manner of reactions from various crewpeople in their encounters with her. Some had approached her openly and eagerly, others had felt uncomfortable dealing with an empath who could sense and assess their innermost emotions. But one by one, they had all grown comfortable. Somehow it simply didn't seem fair that, after all this time, she was going to lose her large and extended family.

She felt a slight choke in her throat and realized just how much all of this was upsetting her. Attuned to her unconscious needs, her body was already responding to the overwhelming emotion that was beginning to course through her. She was walking with quick, steady strides and was rapidly leaving behind the most crowded section of the temporary, makeshift encampment. She was distancing herself from the others so that they would not see her so disconcerted and at odds with herself.

She was, after all, supposed to be the source of strength, the emotional bulwark for the crew. There were some with whom she herself could relax, and by whom the counselor could herself be counseled. But Dr. Beverly Crusher was busy attending to all too many patients, Commander Will Riker was busy overseeing what might be salvageable from the wreckage of the *Enterprise* aside from pieces of scrap metal, and Worf . . .

Worf was . . .

. . . well . . . he was . . . he was so . . . *Worf.*

She sagged against a tree and her breast trembled slightly as she steadied herself. What she was wrestling with at that moment was weakness. That was how Worf would see it. Who could blame him? To a degree, that's how she saw it herself. And if there was one thing that Worf in specific and Klingons in general had a problem with, it was weakness.

Deanna had told herself that her relationship with Worf was a blessing to her for precisely that purpose. Associating with him gave her an increased sense of inner strength and determination. That was an extremely positive trait, and one that she was more than happy to acquire. It was not that she didn't already consider herself a strong woman. But she never had to worry about lapsing into melancholy, or depression, or self-doubt, because if there was one thing that Worf valued above all, it was strength. She did not desire to show weakness to Worf, and in so doing, made herself stronger.

Except . . .

You're not being yourself.

That nagging doubt was already beginning to gnaw at her, and she did not particularly appreciate it. She wanted to dismiss it out of hand. The fact was that couples—and she and Worf most definitely were a couple—always learned from each other. Learned and grew, taking the better part of each other (and occasionally the worse part) as their own. Worf's Klingon stoicism, his unflappability, and his sheer, raw, powerful personality were all of benefit to Deanna Troi, and she valued their time together.

So why was it that there was just the slightest inkling of . . . doubt?

No. She shook it off. No, there was no doubt. She and Worf had come too far, worked too hard as a couple, to begin having second thoughts. They just . . . just felt right together. Yes, that was it. They felt right. And if there was one thing that Deanna Troi knew, it was feelings.

Except your own?

She had no idea what this annoying little voice was that persisted in making snide add-on comments and undercutting her confidence, but she couldn't wait for this most annoying individual to go very far away and leave her to her indisputable happiness with . . .

"Worf?"

The last utter question came not as a result of her musing over the name of her beloved, but rather from what sounded like a rather familiar sound. It was a low, slightly animal growl. And in the depth of that animal growl, there was a word or two that sounded distinctly Klingonese. To be specific, they were Klingon profanities, which Deanna recognized all too readily and all too well.

And she was sensing something as well. Her empathic powers were anything but consistent; there were some races so alien to her that she was not able to get a reading off them at all. But Klingons were definitely not among that group. Their emotions were so close to the surface that she could have had a frontal lobotomy and still been able to read the average Klingon from half a mile away.

In this instance, what she was sensing was pain. Pure, agonizing, gut-wrenching pain. Not only that, but she also sensed an almost single-minded determination to ignore that same pain, to push it away as far as possible.

"Worf?" she called again. The voice had come from a patch of the forest nearby that was particularly dense. She was having trouble seeing. "Worf?" she said once more.

She heard another muttered Klingon profanity, and this time she recognized the origin of the throat that uttered it, if not the literal meaning. It was definitely not the Klingon security chief who was hiding somewhere within the shielding depths of the forest. Rather, it was his young son.

"Alexander!" she called.

"Go away," came back the tight snarl.

"Alex—!"

"I said go away!" came his voice again, filled with both agony and impatience. "What part of 'go away' didn't you hear?"

For just a moment she considered heeding the youth's pleadings, but then she promptly rejected the notion. Clearly Alexander was in distress, and she would do him no favors by ignoring whatever it was that the lad was going through. She started to push her way through the brush.

"Dammit, Deanna!" Alexander protested, but after that he fell silent, as if realizing that his protests weren't getting through to her and it would be less than dignified for him to keep repeating instructions that weren't being heeded.

The area was heavily shaded, and it took Deanna's eyes a moment to readjust. There was a sharp, tangy aroma from the trees that she found positively invigorating. But whatever benefits she might have garnered from the pleasantness of her surroundings quickly evaporated when she saw the dire straits that Alexander was in.

She could tell by the way in which his leg was twisted at an odd angle that the limb was broken. His trousers had a streak of blood across the upper thigh. He had stripped off the right sleeve of his shirt and was endeavoring to bind the break . . . to create, with the help of a nearby sturdy branch, a sort of makeshift splint.

Alexander had grown in recent months. Indeed, his development had been nothing short of astounding. Worf had sanguinely claimed that that was fairly standard for young Klingon males. Once they reached a certain age in the maturation process, they underwent a growth spurt that covered, within one year, the amount of development that would normally consume two to three years or more in a human male. It was as if, once a young Klingon survived the normal travails of extreme youth—thereby proving himself worthy of survival—the body then hastened development so that the Klingon would be less vulnerable, and for a shorter period.

At that particular moment, though, Alexander—who by Earth standards was bordering on adolescence—looked all too vulnerable. He was just reluctant to show it.

"What happened?" she gasped.

"I got trampled," grumbled Alexander.

"Trampled?"

"When people are running for their lives," Alexander observed, "they tend to run over whatever's in their way . . . particularly anyone shorter than they are. Don't worry, I'm taking care of it."

" 'Taking care of it'? Alexander, you need medical attention. And your father . . ."

"My father," grunted Alexander, "was busy. Hold on a moment."

"What are you going to—?"

He had taken a firm grip on his upper leg, and then Alexander gritted his teeth and suddenly twisted the leg around. He tried to hold back the yell of pain, but was only able to contain it for a moment before a howl erupted from his lips. Deanna, her empathy on full boil, gasped in sympathetic pain. When he made the abrupt movement, she could actually hear the sound of the bone snapping into place.

His eyes rolled back into the top of his head, and for a moment she thought that Alexander was going to faint. But then his eyes became twin orbs of glistening steel and he willed himself to remain conscious. "Do not," he said between gritted teeth, "ask me if I'm all right."

"Are you—" The question came so naturally to her that she had to bite off the inquiry in midsentence. She tried her best to ignore her own roiling emotions as she said in as authoritative a voice as she could, "We have to get you to your father."

"I told you, he was busy. Much too busy to worry about me."

"Alexander, that's unfair."

"Yes, I know."

"He was on the bridge! He couldn't abandon his post—"

"His post." Alexander made no effort to hide his contempt. "The ship had a warp-core breach. People were running everywhere. He made no effort to look for me, no effort to make sure that I was safe. I know why. It's perfectly obvious why."

"Oh?"

"He didn't care whether I was safe or not."

"Alexander," she sighed, "that's absurd. Your father cares about you. Is this why you crawled off here with your injured leg? To punish him somehow? To prove something?"

"This," he informed her, "is the Klingon way. If a warrior is injured . . . he tends to it himself. If he can stand, if he can fight, then he deserves to continue. If he cannot tend to himself, then he becomes a burden on others, a drain on resources."

"Your father taught you that?"

"Of course."

"Fine. Then let me teach you something. A very old saying, and it's not Betazoid. It's an Earth saying. You remember Earth, where your grandparents live."

"Of course I remember," Alexander said with impatience. "I lived there for a year, after all. They were . . . they were good people . . . for humans," he amended quickly.

"Yes, well, the Earth saying is that no man is an island. Do you know what that means?"

Alexander was busy affixing his leg to the makeshift splint and barely seemed to be listening. "Beyond the obvious, that no man is an island any more than he is a rock or a bush or a continent . . . not really, no."

"It means," she said patiently, "that we all need each other. That none of us is completely self-sufficient."

He looked up at her. "And it was an Earthman who said this."

"Yes. The quote in full," and she paused, pulling it from her memory, "is 'No man is an island, entire of itself; every man is a piece of the continent, a part of the main; if a clod be washed away by the sea, Europe is the less, as well as if a promontory were, as well as if a manor of thy friends or of thine own were; any man's death diminishes me, because I am involved in mankind; and therefore never send to know for whom the bell tolls; it tolls for thee.' "

"Done?" asked Alexander.

"Yes!" Troi said in surprise. "John Donne!"

"Who's John?" Alexander clearly looked confused.

"John?"

"It doesn't matter. I don't care if this 'John' is done. I was asking if you're done."

"Oh." She didn't know whether to be amused or abashed. "Yes . . ."

"Good." He lay back, resting his head on the ground. "Then I'd appreciate it if you'd go away and let me lie here with my leg throbbing in peace."

"No. I'm going to summon help."

"Deanna!"

"What do you expect me to do, Alexander? Let you lie here? If I go off to get help, you might crawl off somewhere else and hide some more. I do not feel like taking that chance."

"Well, I'm not going to lie here like an invalid." With an impatient hiss of breath between his teeth, Alexander grabbed a tree and began to haul himself up. "All right, fine. You win. Let's go."

"You can't . . ."

"Do not," Alexander said sharply, "make me ask you for help."

She hesitated, and then sighed. She hauled him upward, pulling him up so that his arms rested around her shoulders. Despite his growth, she was amazed by how light he was.

He leaned heavily on his good leg, taking almost no weight onto the injured limb but instead hobbling along rather adroitly with the aid of Troi. "You know something, Deanna," he said as they made their way back toward the main body of the forced encampment, "I knew that an Earthman said that, rather than a Klingon. A Klingon would never say that he was not an island, or that another's death diminishes him."

"No?"

"No. Because we believe that, aside from serving your companion in a war situation, we are all on our own, from birth to death, and whatever we gain or obtain for ourselves is purely through our own devising and dependent upon our own wits. As for death diminishing each other . . . Klingons kill in self-defense, in war, or in glory. To slay another is to insure either honor for another, or continued survival for one's self. Diminished? We are emboldened."

"Thank you for sharing that, Alexander," Deanna said with carefully hidden irony. "Just hearing that makes me feel much better."

"Oh, and by the way, Deanna . . ."

"Yes?"

"Nice landing."

Worf's eyes narrowed as he scanned the horizon, and then he aimed his tricorder in the direction that he was looking. After a moment, he nodded in satisfaction at the results of the search. For a moment he had thought he had caught movement of some sort, but a tricorder scan revealed that, in fact, it was simply shadows lengthening against the setting Veridian sun. He tapped his combadge. "Worf to captain."

"Picard here. Report, Mr. Worf," came the brisk reply of the erstwhile commander of the *Enterprise.*

"A thorough perimeter search shows no sign of hostile life. I do not believe any member of the crew is in danger from attack by any native life-form."

"That's good to hear, Mr. Worf. Now let's just hope that the Duras sisters didn't manage to get off a message to any allies who might come seeking revenge for their rather violent demise."

"That would be . . . most unfortunate," Worf rumbled after a moment's thought.

"Indeed. Let us be wary."

"Always."

"Picard out."

The moment that the signal cut off, however, Worf's combadge signaled again. He tapped it and said, "Worf here."

"Worf . . . this is Deanna. I'm with Alexander . . . he's been injured."

"Injured?" Worf's perpetual frown deepened. "Where is he? Where are you?"

"Heading back to the encampment. Coming over the northern ridge."

"I will meet you en route." Worf was already starting to move, but his voice maintained an even quality that did not betray the speed with which he was going. He might have been continuing to stand still for all the exertion one would have detected in his tone. "What is the nature of the injury?"

"His leg. He broke it, I believe. I've already alerted Beverly and she's on her way to meet us."

"Why did you not simply wait for assistance?" he demanded.

"Stubborn Klingon pride," she said with a trace of sarcasm. "Something I think you may have a passing familiarity with."

But Worf didn't seem to notice the ironic tone in her voice. "Yes. Of course. I shall get there as quickly as possible. Make certain the boy does not injure himself any further."

There was a brief pause as if she was considering how to respond to that. "I'll see what I can do," she finally replied.

Worf hurried through the encampment. Various crew members nodded to him or greeted him as he went past, but he didn't pay them any mind. His thoughts and concerns were entirely upon Alexander.

Where had the boy gotten himself off to? Why had he not contacted his father? Concern was writ large all over Worf's face . . .

. . . and then he began to slow as he comprehended.

Of course. Klingon pride, just as Deanna had said.

His heart began to swell with that selfsame pride as all of the reasons for Alexander's actions immediately became clear to him. He completely comprehended what it was that the boy had set out to do, and the last thing that Worf wanted was to say or do anything to detract from his son's obvious desire to prove his mettle. So by the time he drew within sight range of Alexander and Deanna, gone was the concern, gone was the urgency in his bearing. Instead he was walking with a brisk stride that was distance-consuming but, at the same time, unhurried.

Beverly Crusher was there, running a scanner over his leg. "It's a clean break," Worf heard her say. "You're lucky in that respect. What were you thinking, running off like that?"

"Klingons do not run," Alexander replied stiffly.

"They hobble with dignity," Deanna archly corrected Crusher. This response actually drew a fleeting smile from Alexander, although he quickly hid it again.

Crusher glanced up at Worf, who had drawn within range but had yet to say anything. "If I had sickbay," she said, "I could fix this fairly easily. Cellular regenerator could knit the bone without any problem. As it is, we'll have to wait until we get aboard a vessel with a more fully equipped setup. I'll arrange for it, make a notation to have him beamed directly to the first available sickbay."

"How do his field dressings measure up?" Worf demanded, sounding more like a drill sergeant than a concerned father.

"I just finished inspecting them. It seems he did a rather serviceable job."

Worf grunted.

"Was that a grunt of approval, Father?" asked Alexander. "Or does just 'serviceable' not measure up?"

Beverly looked from one to the other and suddenly decided that her interests would best be served if she was elsewhere. To that end, she quickly made herself scarce.

"You sound upset," Worf said flatly. "Are you upset with me?"

Alexander's jaw twitched but he said nothing. After a moment's hesitation, Deanna said, "Alexander feels . . . whether rightly or wrongly . . . that you were not concerned about his welfare during the ship's crash."

"Not concerned?" His eyes widened. "On what do you base that?"

"On the fact that you didn't ask after me," Alexander said. "That you didn't make any effort to make sure that I made it to the saucer section before the separation. That you didn't try to find me since the crash."

"How do you know that I made no effort?" demanded Worf. "Do you expect that I would go running from one person to the next, asking if they had seen you? I have, in fact, been endeavoring to spot you. Where were you?"

"He was in the woods, nursing his broken leg," Deanna informed him.

"Where he could not easily be seen," pointed out Worf. "This is nonsense, Alexander."

Alexander paused, as if trying to find exactly the right way to phrase it. "When . . . when everyone was running . . . trying to get to the saucer section . . . I saw parents. So many of them, officers and civilians alike . . . calling out for each other, finding each other, making sure that their children and spouses were all right. Did you come looking for me, Father? Answer me honestly. If you simply couldn't locate me in all the turmoil, that's . . . that's not so bad. But did you leave the bridge to look for me?"

"No," Worf said immediately. "I would not abandon my post. Nor would I insult you by looking for you."

"Insult me?" Alexander couldn't quite believe it. "Showing you cared about me . . . would be an insult . . . ?"

"Alexander," Worf said, clearly looking annoyed that something so self-evident to him required explanation. "You have participated in emergency drills on the *Enterprise*. You are familiar with what needs to be done in an evacuation scenario, are you not?"

"Yes."

"You are no longer a child. No longer a newling who requires constant maintenance. You are a young Klingon now, rapidly approaching the day when you will be warrior stock. For me to abandon my post and run about, attempting to find you and oversee you during an evacuation process in which you have been thoroughly schooled, would be to imply that I had no faith in you. That I did not believe you were fully capable of conducting yourself in an adult and professional manner befitting not only my son, but a Klingon. I trusted you to go where you needed to go, and be where you were required to be. I would not dream of insulting you by treating you in a manner that suggested you were incapable of tending to yourself. Is that what you want? That I should insult you in this way?"

Alexander looked down. "No, Father."

"Good. Enough of this nonsense, then."

And at that, Deanna said sharply and firmly, "It's not nonsense, Worf."

He glanced at her in confusion. "What?"

She opened her mouth to speak again, but then closed it. Instead she walked quickly to Worf and took him a few steps away from Alexander so that they could speak in relative privacy. In a low voice, she said, "Whether you agree with it or not . . . even though you yourself believe that you were operating from motives of only the purest respect . . . Alexander still felt slighted. He still felt as if you didn't care whether he lived or died. That is a very powerful emotion, Worf, and simply to brush it off as 'nonsense' is to diminish Alexander's sense of self-worth."

"Am I to apologize for not babying him?" demanded Worf. "He went off into the woods in order to tend to his own injury, did he not?"

"Yes."

"That is the Klingon way," he told her. "He has learned well. On a starship in which there are exactly two Klingons and he is surrounded by humans, I consider it nothing short of miraculous that in a time of stress, he acted properly. Would you have me backslide in my training of him now by making me fuss over him like a . . ."

"I'm not proposing to 'make' you do anything," Deanna said calmly. "It is clear, however, that you are very proud of your son. All I am saying is that there are ways in which to make that clear . . . and ways to do so in a manner that will acknowledge your son's concerns and lay them to rest without making him feel as if he's a fool simply for feeling that way."

"I did not . . ."

He wasn't able to finish the sentence, because she simply looked at him in that way that was both patient and stern. The wheels in his mind turned and he sighed. "Oh . . . very well," he growled.

"You can do it," she said confidently. "I know that you can."

He walked back to Alexander and stood over him, his arms folded. "I want you to know," he said slowly, "that I am very proud of the way that you have conducted yourself this day. You bring honor to yourself . . . and to me. I regret that the price for that conduct was a belief, on your part, that your survival was of secondary importance to me. You are, and always will be, of primary concern to me, Alexander. I would prefer that you never forget that, and know that I take utmost pride in you, and in your accomplishments." He paused a moment, ran what he had just said through his mind for review, and nodded. Then he turned to Troi. "How was that?"

She stood there, arms folded, amusement in her dark eyes. It was clear that she was waiting for him to add something, and he knew perfectly well what it was. The knowledge did not sit particularly well with him.

"You can do it," she prompted.

He growled, cleared his throat, and added—apparently under some small mental protest—"And . . . I love you." It was more muttered than anything, coming out as, "And . . . I uvu," which was not exactly inspiring. It was, however, apparently sufficient for Alexander, who nodded in acknowledgment of the sentiment.

"I love you too, Father," he replied.

"Of course you do," Worf said stiffly. "I knew that."

Then, to the surprise of the two Klingons, there was a musical, lilting laughter from near them. It was almost as if they had forgotten that Deanna was present. "What is so funny?" demanded Worf.

"The two of you," she said. "The body language, so stiff, so formal," and she squared her jaw in imitation. "Worf, Alexander . . . you have to maintain your sense of love for each other. Your familiarity. Your sense of fun!"

"We have crash-landed on a strange world and my son's leg is broken," Worf reminded her. "This would not particularly be the time to dwell on matters of 'fun.' "

"It's just that . . ." She sighed. "It seems an eternity ago that the two of you were dressing up as cowboys. Alexander, you're so much taller, and Worf, you're so much more serious. . . ."

"I do not know that I agree with that assessment. . . ."

Smiling, she placed a hand lovingly on his face. "Worf . . . remember your promotion ceremony the other day? I practically had to drag you, kicking and screaming, to the holodeck."

"I neither kicked nor screamed," Worf informed her archly. "Had I done so, not you nor a hundred Betazoids could have gotten me there."

"That would be the ceremony you wouldn't let me come to?" Alexander asked his father pointedly. "The one where you said it was a lot of adults acting foolishly, and you didn't want to expose me to it?"

He looked from Alexander to Troi, who was smirking in a knowing manner, and then back to Alexander. "I do not recall phrasing it in quite that manner."

"It wasn't especially flattering, however you phrased it," Alexander said.

"Worf, we can discuss it later. . . ."

"No," said Worf, suddenly feeling challenged, particularly thanks to the way that Alexander was looking at him. He turned to face Deanna and said, "What are you saying?"

"Worf, honestly, it—"

"Spell. It. Out." There was an edge to his voice that hadn't been there before.

"Well, it . . ." She cast about for the right words, and then shrugged and decided simply to go with whatever occurred to her. "You . . . tend to create shields around yourself. You don't let down your guard easily. And because of that, people—Alexander, in this case—tend to magnify everything you say and do. They get little to no feedback from you as to how you truly feel or what you're thinking. As a consequence, they tend to fill in the blanks themselves. This can lead to misinterpretation, hurt feelings . . . that sort of thing."

"Of course I am guarded. I am Klingon. If we do not have our guards up, we leave ourselves vulnerable to attack."

"Only in a war."

"Life," Worf intoned, as if it had been drilled into him, "is a war."

"No," Deanna shot back with surprising vehemence. "Life is life. War is the loss of life. And I think you know the difference, Worf . . . better than any other Klingon." Then, as if caught off guard at the stridency of her own reaction, she softened her voice and said, "And I can think of no Klingon better suited to teach that to Alexander than his father . . . provided, of course, that you come to believe that."

"I believe that you believe it." He paused a moment and then said, "May I speak to you in private a moment, Counselor?"

Deanna glanced over to Alexander, but he shrugged indifferently. "Don't worry about me. I won't run away," he said with bleak humor. "Not that I could even if I wanted to. . . ."

"All right," she said, and she walked off with Worf. Alexander watched them go and tried to figure out just what might be on his father's mind.

Deanna was doing much the same thing. Worf's thoughts seemed in a turmoil, which was somewhat surprising. More often than not, his emotions were as straightforward as a tossed spear. Also, when Worf walked he usually did so with such long strides that Deanna had to scurry slightly to keep up. This time, however, he automatically walked slowly enough that she had no trouble pacing him. That alone was enough to surprise her.

When they'd distanced themselves from Alexander, although he was still within visual range, Worf faced her and said, "Do you really feel that I have been . . . distant? Guarded?"

"I wouldn't say so if I didn't think it," she replied. "I didn't mean it as a criticism, really, Worf. More of an observation that you can simply take as you will."

"Be that as it may, I find it disturbing that you would feel that way. I have been endeavoring to be more . . ." He hesitated, as if he were about to utter a profanity against his will and finally managed to eject the word. ". . . vulnerable."

"I've noticed. You've practically developed a soft, squooshy center."

"I am serious, Deanna."

"I'm sorry," she said, physically wiping the smile off her face. "I shouldn't joke."

"I have been trying because of Alexander . . . and because of you . . . but it has not been easy. Sometimes"—he presented his back to her so that she could not see the clear frustration in his face—"I envy Data. In order to develop his personality, he merely has to place a new chip in his head and he immediately has the entire range of human emotions."

"A situation that has been very difficult for him," Troi immediately pointed out. "Nothing worth having is ever easy, Worf."

"Concepts such as leaving oneself open to hurt, physically or emotionally . . . or even humor . . . these are not simple things to grasp. Not for me. I have strode two worlds for so many years, you would think it would be second nature for me. But it is not. Nothing is second nature, since I have never fully decided upon what my first nature is."

"Klingon by nature, human by nurture," Deanna observed. "I don't envy you, Worf."

"No. But you help me. For that . . . I thank you," he said. As she had earlier, this time he touched her face and she was surprised at the gentleness of it. It was a stark contrast to the roughness of his hand.

"You have such a sensitive touch," she told him.

"Of course. Most Klingons do. It enables us to properly search out pressure points, to stop the blood flow and disable or kill an . . ." His voice trailed off as he saw her expression, her skin paling slightly, the darkness in her eyes suddenly looking much wider. "That was . . . the wrong thing to say, wasn't it?"

"It's okay." She patted him on the upper shoulder. "Fortunately enough, when one is romantically involved with a Klingon, one learns to have a sense of humor."

"I have a sense of humor as well," Worf told her. "It is simply . . . dissimilar from yours."

"Really. How dissimilar?"

"Well . . ." He gave it a moment's thought. "There was a time I attended an exhibition of proficiency with the *bat'leth,*" he said, referring to the curved, formidable Klingon sword, "being given by K'Plok, one of the foremost *bat'leth* experts in the Klingon Empire. Unfortunately, K'Plok had a cold on the scheduled day, but no self-respecting Klingon would cancel an obligation simply over a minor illness. In any event, as he was demonstrating the famed overhead reverse thrust, he sneezed and accidentally cut off his own head."

"Oh, my God," gasped Deanna. "What did you do?"

"We laughed. It was the single longest, most sustained laughter in the history of the empire. K'Plok was immortalized as the greatest comedian ever known to Klingons. In fact, his name was officially changed to K'Plop in our annals, in commemoration of the sound his head made when it struck the—"

She held up a hand. "I . . . get the picture, Worf. And did you truly think that was . . . funny?"

"If I did not think that, would I have kept the head when it ricocheted and flew into my lap?"

At that, Deanna visibly blanched. "You . . . you didn't . . ."

He paused only a moment, and then said, "That was a joke, Deanna."

She let out a sigh of relief that even resulted in a small chuckle at the realization that he'd fooled her.

"You see?" he pointed out triumphantly. "I do have a sense of humor. I made you laugh."

"Yes, you did." She hugged him affectionately. "Go be with your son now. I think he could use your company."

"You are very likely right . . . as you often are."

Worf headed off toward Alexander and, as he did so, made a mental note to send word to the Klingon homeworld, where many of his most treasured effects were in storage, and arrange for the prompt disposal of the head of K'Plop before Deanna found out. The Klingon Comedy Museum had been after him to donate it for years anyway, since they had an understandable dearth of displays.

He passed Beverly Crusher, who was talking to Data. Data appeared to be asking Crusher whether or not she had happened to see his cat in all of the confusion. Worf found it strange that, with everything that had happened, Data was remotely concerned about some animal. He called out, "Data . . ."

"Yes?" Data turned his attention to Worf as Beverly glanced over her shoulder at him.

"Remember the other day? When you pushed the doctor into the water?"

"Yes."

He stabbed a finger at Data. "That was funny. Damned funny. And do not let anyone else tell you otherwise." With that, he walked off, leaving a slightly confused Data and a rather teed-off Beverly Crusher.

The lake looked remarkably inviting.

The air was uncommonly warm. Deanna felt remarkably grungy, what with the crash landing (but at least they'd landed, dammit!) and her own overall sense of exhaustion. She had been ministering to the needs of the crew for some time. Rescue vessels were reportedly on their way, but—and it was vanity, she hated to admit it—she was reaching a point where she felt self-conscious just having people looking at her. She felt so disgusting, so . . .

"Yucch." She studied her reflection in the water and shook her head, discouraged. She picked up a few palmsful of water and splashed them on her face, but all she managed to do was take the dirt smears on her face and transform them into larger dirt smears. Meantime she became aware that there were no sounds nearby. Everyone was quiet, tended to. She wasn't particularly needed at that moment, and she was reasonably sure the area was secluded. Then again, it wasn't as if Deanna

Troi were the most modest individual in the galaxy in any event. Even if she was discovered paddling around, well . . . she had certainly attended her share of Betazoid marriages, during which the bride, the groom, and all the guests traditionally go naked. In fact, she had met William T. Riker, second-in-command of the *Enterprise,* at one of those exact functions.

And the water, to her surprise, was actually fairly warm. There was probably an underground spring somewhere helping to heat it up.

"Oh, why not?" she said to no one in particular. Within a minute, her uniform lay in a crumpled heap on the shore and Deanna was paddling through the water with quick, sure strokes. The moment that she submerged, she felt revitalized. She burst from the water, throwing her head back, droplets spraying the air, and she laughed joyously, just happy to be alive.

She sensed that she was not alone before she saw him. But the moment she sensed it, she knew who it was.

"Counselor," came the amused voice of William Riker, "I believe that you're ever-so-slightly out of uniform."

She dove beneath the surface again, turning around under water and coming back up facing the direction from which the voice had originated. She rubbed the water from her eyes and saw Riker seated on a large rock overlooking the lake. He was grinning widely and had her uniform neatly folded in his lap.

"You should try it yourself, Will," she suggested with merriment twinkling in her eye. "The water truly is wonderful."

"Oh . . . I don't think so. Thanks all the same."

At the far end of the lake, water cascaded down via a rather impressive-looking waterfall. As Troi backstroked in a most relaxed manner, she called out, "Does any of this remind you of anything?"

He looked around a moment, trying to think what she might be getting at, and then he laughed as he realized. "The Janaran Falls, in the Jalara jungle back on Betazed. How could I forget? It was after I'd rescued you from the Sindareen raiders, and we were heading back to the rendezvous point. Trip should have taken us three days, even though we were on foot. Took us five."

"Well, we kept getting . . . distracted," Troi said teasingly. "And we spent most of our last day at the falls."

"I don't know about you, but in my case, it was because I wasn't particularly anxious to leave."

"I felt the same way. Gods, we were so young, Will. We knew nothing about anything." She floated in place, treading water. "It seemed like we had all the time in the world. Who knew it would be the last time we'd see each other for so many years."

"Well . . . technically, it wasn't," Riker reminded her. "Unfortunately, everything that happened after that was . . . well . . ."

She winced, remembering. After they'd been picked up from the jungle, the young Deanna—under pressure from her mother—had broken off her involvement with Riker. The sudden turnaround in the relationship had hit Riker hard, and unfortunately for the both of them, he had done something typically male: knocked back a few drinks and fallen into bed with a rather nubile and willing young woman. And Troi, who had only hours before defiantly declared her independence from her mother's suffocating demands, had found the two of them together, and stormed off, hurt and angry. Had Riker remained on Betazed, they might have had the time to try and straighten things out. But such was not to be the case, as Riker had received his new shipboard assignment. There had been a fleeting reunion at a Betazed art museum before Riker had left, but it had been all too brief and unsatisfying. Once aboard his new ship, Riker had sent her a message, asking her to meet him on Risa some weeks later so they could take one last shot at salvaging their relationship. But the rendezvous was never kept . . . and they had lost touch until their unexpected reunion on the *Enterprise* years later.

"Funny that you remember that so clearly," she said. "Tom didn't."

"Tom? Oh." He got that frown then that usually crossed his face whenever the name of Tom Riker was brought up. Even though he was another person . . . he was also the same person. It was something that Riker didn't particularly like to dwell upon. "Did you have to bring him up?" asked Riker. "I mean, things were going so . . ." He paused and forced a smile. ". . . swimmingly."

"I'm sorry, Will," Deanna said, aware that she'd made him feel uncomfortable. "I didn't mean to . . ."

"It's all right," he told her, waving it off. "So Tom didn't remember anything that happened after the Janaran Falls?"

"Oh, I assume he did. When he said nothing of it, though, I chose not to point it out. It seemed . . . inappropriate, somehow. Perhaps even a little sad. It was likely a deliberate effort on his part not to dwell on it as well. He had a good deal of time on his own down on Nervala Four, and he claimed to have spent much of it thinking about me."

"I have no doubt," Riker said with raised eyebrow.

"So he probably idealized our relationship; chose to focus on the positive and pleasant memories rather than the . . ."

"Tragic conclusion?"

He said it with a good deal of humor, but there was something more to his tone that Deanna sensed very clearly. Plus, if there was any individual for whom she had an instant intuition for what he was thinking, it was . . .

". . . Worf?"

She blinked herself back to attention, realizing that the warm water and her own ponderings had prompted her to mentally drift. Riker had been saying something, and the last word was the name of the ship's resident Klingon officer. "I'm sorry . . . ?" she asked, admitting tacitly her distracted state.

"I was endeavoring," he sighed, "to make a ham-handed change in the conversation. So I was asking how things are going between you and Worf."

"Oh. Fine. Very well."

"I understand," and suddenly he was grinning in a devilish manner, "that Klingons read and write poetry during . . ."

"Will!" Her face flushed slightly although she was, at the same time, slightly amused. "I don't see that as any of your business. Unless, of course," she added after a moment's hesitation, "you feel your own abilities as a poet are being threatened. We were just talking about the falls. You wrote the poem there, remember? *The* poem."

He put his face in his hands. "Good lord, I'm never going to live that down. It was so awful. . . ."

"You keep saying that! It was not awful. It was beautiful." Her gaze softened at the recollection. " 'I hold you close to me . . .' "

"You still remember the first line?"

"The first line?" And without hesitation, she recited:

"I hold you close to me.
Feel the breath of you, and the wonder of you
And remember a time
Without you
But only as one would remember
A bleak and distant nightmare
And you shudder against me in your sleep
Do you share the memory with me of dark times past?
And you smile
Do you share the memory of times to come?
The future holds such promise
And just as I cannot imagine how I survived the past
Without you
I cannot imagine a future
Without you."

Riker stared at her in wonderment, shaking his head slowly. "I can't believe it. I can't believe you remember every line. I feel as if I wrote it a lifetime ago."

"In many ways . . . you did. I, uhm . . . I think I'd best be getting out now."

"Shall I turn around?"

"That would be the considerate course of action."

"All right." Riker got to his feet and turned completely around in a circle, so that he was facing her again just as she was about to emerge from the water. He grinned lopsidedly.

"You're a riot, Commander," Deanna said with just a touch of scold in her voice. And then, boldly, she emerged from the water.

Immediately Riker turned away, placing her uniform on the ground behind him. "My, my, Commander . . . becoming shy in your old age?" Deanna's voice floated to him. "It's not as if I have anything you haven't seen before."

"True. But it's just a matter of . . . of decorum," he said after a moment of searching for the right word. "After all, you and Worf are a couple now, and I . . . well, it's just . . . it wouldn't be appropriate for me to be ogling you."

" 'Ogling'? Are you saying the sight of me naked would contain some prurient interest to you? Would be stimulating in some manner?"

"No, I'm not saying that at all," he briskly and rather ineffectively lied. And he had the sick feeling that she saw through the lie since, of course, attempting to dissemble with an empath was generally an exercise in futility. "I can . . ." He cleared this throat, which was problematic considering that at the moment he felt as if there was too much blood in it. "I can admire your . . . figure . . . in the same way that I would admire any naturally crafted work of art."

"Why Commander, you flatterer!"

"I have my moments. The point is . . ." He heard the rustling of her clothing as she dressed, and endeavored to block it out. Searching for the right angle to come at it, he said, "I would just feel intrusive, that's all."

"I notice that you didn't feel so intrusive that you refused to sit by while I bathed."

"Old times' sake," he said quickly. "I admit, this place reminded me a bit of the Jalara jungle. I succumbed to nostalgia; hardly a capital offense. Besides, the bottom line is . . . how do you think Worf would feel if I started rhapsodizing about your body?"

"That's a good point," she admitted. "You can turn around now, Commander. And this time, one hundred and eighty degrees should suffice."

He did as she said. She was busy shaking out her hair, which was already beginning to dry in the warmth of the air and sun. Her uniform was still a bit ragged, but at least she was looking refreshed. "Your concern over Worf's sensibilities is very commendable, Will. But I am a bit concerned about yours."

"Mine? Deanna, we've been through this . . ."

"I know, Will. We've been through . . . a good deal. And I . . ." She hesitated, looking down. Very softly, she said, "Sometimes I think that we spend so much time telling each other that our relationship won't . . . shouldn't . . . be rekindled . . . that it's . . ."

"What?" he gently prompted her after a moment. He went to her, took her hands firmly in his. "What are you saying?"

She looked up at him with eyes that were deep pools in which he could have paddled forever. "Do we keep saying these things . . . because we believe it . . . or because we want to believe it? Because if we face the alternative, then we face the fact that we've wasted years that we could have been together."

It was a simple, casual, and calm observation, but it struck deeply into Riker's heart. Suddenly his lips felt very dry.

"Ow," said Deanna, and Riker realized that he was, all unawares, squeezing her hands far too tightly.

Quickly he released his hold on her and turned away from her. He straightened his jacket in unconscious imitation of a gesture he'd seen Picard make so many times. "Deanna . . . at this point, there's really nothing to discuss beyond simple friendship, because there are other considerations. Worf, in particular, who is as decent and honest a man as I've ever known . . . who will love you and protect you . . . anything that I might say which would lead us down a different path would have an effect on him, and on Alexander, who I know absolutely adores you. I can't operate without taking others into consideration."

" 'No man is an island,' " Deanna quoted ruefully.

"Donne."

"For the moment," she said.

He frowned, not understanding, and then the puzzlement cleared. "I mean John Donne. He wrote that poem."

"So he did." Deanna laughed. "I'm sorry, I was . . . never mind." Then her expression drew serious. "Will . . . I'm just . . . feeling a bit confused at the moment. Conflicted. You're saying one thing, you're saying another, and I sense that there's more, that . . ."

"Deanna . . . in many ways . . . I will always love you. Just . . . I'm not . . ."

His combadge beeped. Never before had he felt so relieved at that sound. He tapped the badge and said briskly, "Riker here."

"The rescue vessels are approaching, Number One," came the crisp voice of the captain of the *Enterprise* . . . or, more precisely, of what was left of the

Enterprise. "If you desire to have a final look around, now would be the time."

"I appreciate the suggestion, Captain . . . more than you know. Riker out." He turned to Deanna and said, "We should really go."

"Will . . ."

"Deanna . . ." His instinct was to reach for her shoulders, to look her squarely in the eyes, but he realized that—for whatever reason—he couldn't do it. So he said simply, "There's nothing that we're going to say to each other now that we haven't said before. The bottom line is, you're happy with Worf now. You love him, don't you?"

"I . . . yes. Yes, I . . . I do . . ."

"That's it, then." With that, he turned and headed back toward the wreckage of the fallen *Enterprise.*

But that's not it! Deanna wanted to shout after him. Whatever her feelings for Worf, whatever she and Riker said their feelings were for each other, she still felt as if there was much that was being left unsaid. It was a singularly frustrating state of mind for her. Here she was, the ship's counselor, ostensibly trained in helping others sort out their feelings. And yet for herself, for her own feelings, there was nothing but confusion and frustration. How was it that she could and should know everyone else's minds, but she couldn't know where her own mind was? Finally, she fell back on the word that summarized the bafflement of women throughout the ages. "Men," she sighed, and then added for good measure, "They're all alike."

Three

Worf was helping to oversee the orderly beaming up of the *Enterprise* crewmen to their respective ships. Everything was proceeding in a straightforward fashion, exactly as he would have expected it to. Some were heading to the saucer section in a final attempt to salvage belongings and, in a few cases, simply to try to find something to bring along as a reminder.

He was also rather pleased—although naturally he would never have admitted it—that Alexander had refused to go on ahead of him. The young Klingon was remaining determinedly by his father's side as others of the crew made their way to the beam-up sites.

"Why are people going in groups, Father?" Alexander asked as he watched people assemble at the sites. "The rescue ships could just bring people up from wherever they're standing."

"True. But this way close friends and families, of course, were able to stay together rather than be split up between ships and have to wait for a subsequent reunion," Worf explained.

"Oh."

Alexander sounded very distracted when he said it. It was surprising how much hidden meaning a one-syllable word—"Oh"—could carry with it.

"Is there something on your mind, Alexander?"

"No," Alexander quickly replied.

Worf made the impatient grunting noise that Alexander recognized only too well. "Alexander . . . you know that I have little patience with trying to extract information. With a hot light and an agonizer stick, I could easily rip your concerns from your screaming throat. That is not, however, good parenting . . . so I am told." As always, he spoke with such a grim mien that it was difficult for Alexander to tell just how serious he was. He certainly *sounded* serious. "In any event," continued Worf, "obfuscation is not the Klingon way."

"And do we only do things if they are the Klingon way?"

"What do you mean?"

Alexander looked off in the direction of the fallen saucer section. Worf had seen Deanna Troi head in there a few minutes earlier. Her hair had looked slightly damp, which he'd considered a bit odd, but beyond that she seemed rather peaceful, even happy. That was how she always seemed, in fact. That alone made her almost the polar opposite of him.

"Deanna is not very . . . Klingon," Alexander said. Apparently he'd seen her, too.

"That is true. She is as 'un-Klingon' as one could be and still be sentient."

"Why do you love her, Father?"

Worf bristled. "It is . . . not appropriate that we discuss these things."

"Not appropriate? Father . . . we've discussed war from every possible angle. We've discussed honor, tradition, combat tactics. I know how to kill someone fourteen different ways with my bare hands . . . at least, in theory. But how to love someone . . . especially someone so different . . ." He gestured helplessly.

Worf looked at the urgency in his son's eyes. "These are . . . these are not matters that come easily to me in terms of discussion, Alexander."

"I know that. Believe me, I know."

Alexander turned away from his father then and went back to watching the families gathering for rescue. Worf watched them, too, and he found himself studying them closely, as if he were an anthropologist observing the activities of another species. In a way, that was rather appropriate. He was another species, after all, and humanity was a race that he was still striving mightily to understand.

He watched the families. He watched the parents helping the children along, watched the mothers singing songs with the sons, the fathers carrying their little girls riding on their shoulders. He saw a set of parents dangling their giggling three-year-old between them, swinging the child like a pendulum, and the child let out a squeal of glee.

He knew that he and Alexander were a family, just as equal to and legitimate as any other family unit aboard the *Enterprise.* There were all manner of families besides the rather simplistic mother, father, child . . .

And yet . . .

And yet . . . in that very simplicity, there was a sort of elegance. Worf and Alexander as a family didn't seem wrong . . . and yet, a mother and father and child seemed so . . . so *right.*

"I envy them," Alexander said.

It was as if he had been reading his father's mind, as if he'd been completely keyed in to what Worf was thinking. Nevertheless, it was Worf's nature to be cautious and less than forthcoming. So, guardedly, he said, "Envy them? In what way?"

"Well, look at them! Look how happy they are."

"Are you not happy, Alexander?"

A dozen emotions seemed to play across Alexander's face all at once. It was as if he had no clear idea how to answer the question. Then, finally, he simply nodded and said, "Yes, Father. I am happy."

"But you could be happier."

"Which of us couldn't?" Alexander asked reasonably. He hesitated and then, summoning the nerve to return to his earlier line of questioning, he said, "It is just that . . . you've spoken to me in the past of my mother. K'Ehleyr was a warrior."

"A magnificent warrior." He felt his chest swelling with inexplicable pride just thinking about her. Then he stopped and looked at Alexander in confusion. "You speak as if you did not know her." When his son did not respond immediately, Worf prompted, "Alexander?"

"I am . . ." It seemed to Worf that Alexander appeared to be struggling, forcing the words from him. "I am . . . forgetting things. I cannot recall her voice as clearly as I did. She had a way of looking at me when she was very angry, and another when she was very loving, and I can't quite . . . see them. It's as if it's blurry."

"You are seeing it through the haze of time," Worf said regretfully. "Time tends to blur memories. Especially considering you were so young when you had them."

"What if I forget her completely?"

"You will not. I am sure of that."

"Well, I'm glad you're sure, Father. I'm not. So why Deanna?"

The sudden shift in topic, or angle back to an earlier topic, caught Worf off guard for a moment. "What?"

"Deanna. Even those memories I do have of my mother . . . they're so dissimilar from Deanna Troi. Why would you find yourself drawn to someone who is so different from K'Ehleyr? Is it deliberate?"

"Deliberate?" Worf's face darkened. "Are you implying that I did not have genuine feelings for your mother? Or that I am trying to forget her by becoming involved with someone who is her antithesis?"

"I'm saying . . ." Alexander began to look frustrated. "I don't know what I'm saying! I have everything all mixed up in my head, and I don't know what to say first! I can't . . . I can't choose, I can't . . ."

The boy was practically trembling in bafflement, trying to articulate all of the feelings that were tumbling around in him. Worf found himself easily able to sympathize. "Alexander . . . you have been through much. I understand. Believe it or not . . . I do." Worf was accustomed to standing, oftentimes rather stiffly, but now he actually sat next to his son, trying his best to look relaxed. "They are very different, your mother and Deanna. Very different. But different is not automatically bad or inferior."

"That's not always what you've told me, though."

"What do you mean?"

"Well . . . when you speak of the Klingon way of doing things . . . you talk about it with such pride, and so forcefully. You make it seem so obvious that the Klingon way is the best way."

"It is the best way . . ."

"You see?"

"For Klingons."

"But you were raised by humans, Father. And I lived with them, too, for a while. Are you telling me that everything they taught you, and me . . . was inferior? Was wrong?"

Worf's mouth opened for a moment, and then closed. His eyes narrowed, and for a second Alexander suddenly thought that he was in a world of trouble. But then, to his surprise, Worf looked down and slowly shook his head. When he looked up again, there was a hint of amusement in his eyes.

"Alexander," he told him, "do not be concerned that you are going to forget your mother. In many respects, you *are* your mother. If we sparred physically, I would invariably be the victor. But Kahless help me if we were involved in a battle of wits or an argument, because your mother was merciless and I never, *ever,* won."

"Mother told me she had beaten you in combat at arms on a couple of occasions."

"Well," Worf sniffed pridefully, "I would not wish to defame your mother's memory by implying that she was less than honest. Let us simply say that she remembers matters differently than I."

"All right, Father. And . . . it's okay. I understand why you have trouble discussing all this."

"Do you?"

"Love is . . . well, it's not a trait that we Klingons embrace, especially."

"You do not think so?"

"Well . . . no. I mean . . . it is one of the gentlest emotions, and we are many things, Father, but gentle we most certainly are not."

"Alexander," Worf said as he leaned forward, suddenly struck with the notion of how to explain it. "I have taught you that, in combat situations, you must approach different foes in different ways. A Romulan fights differently than a Klingon, a Klingon differently than a Tellarite, and so on. Have I not?"

"Yes, Father."

"It is different forms of combat but, nonetheless, it is still a battle. Just approached in varying manners. Correct?"

"Yes, Father," Alexander said again.

"Well . . . my feelings for K'Ehleyr and Deanna are much the same. In both cases, it is love. It is just in different ways."

"So love," Alexander began to comprehend, "is very much like war . . . except that no one tries to kill each other."

"Actually," Worf admitted, "there are many instances where love results in war . . . in romantic triangles that turn deadly . . . and even in death as angry lovers or jealous suitors turn against each other with fatal results."

"If that's the case . . . why, then . . . we Klingons can, and should, be the greatest lovers in the galaxy!"

Worf patted him on the back. "At last . . . you understand."

"But Father . . . you've had me read so many books on the Klingon way . . . and I've seen nothing on love and its link with war and death."

After considering that for a moment, Worf said, "I suggest you read the works of Shakespeare . . . preferably in the original Klingon. You will find *Romeo and Juliet,* in particular, most instructive. Warring houses, murder, suicide . . . I tell you, Alexander . . . it makes you proud to be a Klingon."

The search had been successful.

Deanna had come upon Data as he was making a last-ditch effort to locate his missing pet. Even though she felt there was little hope, she had agreed to aid the android. To her surprise, they had actually managed to find the feline that Data had mysteriously dubbed "Spot." As he held the animal close, Deanna said in amusement, "Another family reunited."

Then, to her astonishment, she felt something empathically from Data.

It surprised her completely, because the emotionless android had always been unreadable. From an empathic point of view, he might as well have been a black hole. But now that he was operating with a chip that provided him with human feelings, she was sensing an entire range of emotions rippling out from him. It was as if, in a way, he had literally just sprung into existence for her. "Data? Are . . . you all right?"

Data was sobbing uncontrollably as he held the cat tight. "I am uncertain, Counselor. I am happy to see Spot . . . yet I am crying. Perhaps the chip is malfunctioning."

She smiled. "I think it's working perfectly."

"Hello, Spot," Data said cheerfully as they made their way out of the ship's wreckage and toward one of the rendezvous points. Since both his hands were occupied with the cat, he did the best he could wiping the tears away from his eyes with his elbows. "I do not understand, Counselor. Why would I cry . . . if I am happy?"

"Tears are a natural reaction to all strong emotions, Data, not just grief. It's triggered by extremes. Happiness, love, anger . . . any of those can prompt tears."

"So it is somewhat all-purpose, then."

"That's correct."

"Then how do you know which emotion is prompting the outburst? And how do others know?"

"Trust me: You'll know. And so will they."

Riker caught a glimpse of Deanna and Data as they made their way out to the rendezvous point. He noticed that Data was carrying his cat and made a mental note that the final missing crewman—Spot—had been located. Another trauma avoided.

At that particular moment, Riker was walking out onto the remains of the bridge with Captain Jean-Luc Picard. For one morbid moment, Riker considered suggesting that Picard take his beloved fish—who had not survived the crash—and feed them to Spot so that they wouldn't go to waste. But a better impulse prevented him from doing so.

Having just recovered his photo album, Picard was waxing philosophical about mortality and legacies. "What we leave behind is not as important as how we've lived. After all, Number One, we're only mortal."

"Speak for yourself, sir," Riker said proudly. "I plan to live forever."

Riker then drifted over toward the command chair, which lay damaged and unusable. "I always thought I'd get a shot at this chair one day," he sighed.

He waited for Picard to say, *You want it? It's all yours. Take it as a souvenir. It will go wonderfully with your carpeting.* But the good captain was a bit too serious-minded an individual to be quite so flippant about something so important to him. Instead he said, "Perhaps you still will. Somehow, I doubt that this will be the last ship to carry the name *Enterprise.*" He tapped his combadge and said, "Picard to *Farragut.* Two to beam up."

Within moments, they had dematerialized and then reappeared aboard the *Farragut.* What followed then was the standard battery of debriefings, meetings, and preliminary investigations that were SOP where the destruction of a starship and loss of command was involved. Riker was utterly confident that Picard, naturally, would have no problems and come off from the incident spotlessly. He was less sanguine about himself; after all, he was the one who had been in command when the ship had crashed.

To that end, Riker met with Geordi La Forge in the temporary quarters he'd been given aboard the *Farragut*. They went over the final hours of the *Enterprise* minute by minute, trying to determine if there was anything that anyone could have done to prevent the great ship's destruction. The conclusion they reached was that, in fact, the answer was no.

It was not a conclusion that Riker was especially happy about. He shook his head in frustration and said, "I still feel that there should have been something . . . *something* I could have done. . . ."

"Don't do that to yourself, Commander, I'm telling you," Geordi said. "There's absolutely no point to it. Once the warp-core breach began, I couldn't stop it. And I was right down there. What could you, up on the bridge, have been expected to do?"

"I don't know, Geordi. Perhaps the events leading up to it could have been avoided—"

"Commander . . . you'll make yourself crazy if you keep thinking that. Don't go looking for someone to blame." With a ragged grin, he added, "That's Starfleet's job."

"Thanks, Geordi. I feel *so* much better now."

"You know what'll make you feel so much better? Trip to Ten-Forward. It's not as nice as the *Enterprise*'s, of course . . . but it'll take the sting off."

"You, Mr. La Forge, have got yourself a deal." He slapped his knees briskly and rose.

"Commander . . . pardon my asking, but . . . is everything okay? I mean, aside from the obvious problems, that is."

"Yes. Why?"

"Well, you . . . you sound distracted, that's all."

"I do?" He shrugged. "Deanna why I would be. Come on, let's have that drink."

"Pardon? What did you say?" Geordi was looking at him with a tilted head and a most peculiar frown.

"I said, 'Come on, let's have that drink.' "

"No, before that."

"I . . ." Riker looked confused. "Geordi, I wasn't expecting a quiz. . . ."

"You said, 'Deanna why I would be.' "

"What? What's that supposed to mean?"

"I don't know, Commander! *You* said it."

"No, I didn't." He frowned, and then his face cleared. "Oh. I said, 'Don't know why I would be.' "

But Geordi shook his head with certainty. "No, you said, 'Deanna why I would be.' "

"Geordi, don't be ridiculous! It doesn't make sense! It's not even a sentence! Subject, verb, object. Simple way to compose a sentence. 'Deanna why I would be' doesn't *mean* anything."

"Maybe it does to you," suggested Geordi.

Riker let out a long, frustrated sigh. "Geordi . . . let's go. I think you need that drink more than I do."

* * *

Deanna sat in the *Farragut*'s lounge, looking out at the stars as they hurtled past, and for the first time in a long time she felt adrift. She was now faced with the inescapable: The time with her extended family was ticking down. It bothered her that it bothered her. She was, after all, a Starfleet professional. She went where she was told, and served the needs of Starfleet to the best of her ability. For that matter, as a counselor, she was obligated to maintain a professional detachment at all times. She should not be letting herself get so close to the crew of the *Enterprise* that it would hurt when she left them. Yet that was precisely what had occurred. She had let them get too close, let them get to her, get under her skin. There was something to be said for that, she supposed. It was a measure of her compassion and her empathy. But now there was going to be a price for that empathy.

There was irony to it as well, for she realized that they would very likely not be dwelling on her as much as she would be on them. To all of them, she was simply one individual. But she had come to think of them as one great whole. Her crew. Her people. It was the height of egocentricity, she decided, to become as possessive as all that. It was inappropriate, and not in their best interest, and it sure as hell wasn't in her best interest.

She had to detach herself. Had to separate, had to be alone with herself . . .

"May I join you?"

She turned in her seat and looked up at Worf standing behind her. "You should not," he continued, "be seated in that fashion."

"What fashion?"

"With your back to the door. It is wise to have a clear view of the door at all times, in the event that there is an unexpected threat."

"You'll protect me, Worf," she said with exaggerated breathlessness, as if she were the heroine of some romantic melodrama.

Worf didn't so much as crack a smile. "Of course I will," he said matter-of-factly. He stepped around to the other side of the table and sat down opposite her.

"How is Alexander?"

"He is resting comfortably. I am appreciative of the aid that you extended to him. I shall not forget it."

"It was nothing."

"No . . . it was most definitely something." He leaned forward, his scowl deepening. "There is a matter I need to discuss with you."

She quickly discerned that it was something of a very grave nature. One didn't need to be an empath to figure it out; his overall demeanor was more than enough to signal to her that there were very dire matters waiting to be discussed. Was there more to Alexander's condition than Worf had been willing to admit? Or was there some political crisis with the Klingons that would need to be attended to? "What is it, Worf?" she asked worriedly.

"It has to do with . . . an arrangement."

"An arrangement?" She was lost. "You mean, like . . . a flower arrangement?"

"No. An arrangement having to do with us."

"Oh." She was no closer to understanding what he was talking about than she had been when he first sat down. "What did you have in mind?"

"It has to do with life and war."

"It does?" Her eyebrows were so high in puzzlement that they were bumping up against her hairline. "Does this have to do with a last will?"

"No . . . not that at all. Deanna . . ." He interlaced his fingers, and the depth of his glowering was Deanna's tip-off that he was thinking extremely hard. ". . . life is very much like a war. It has to be approached with planning and strategy. You have to anticipate that which may be thrown into your path, make optimum use of your resources and . . . most importantly . . . you must have solid allies and a firm army at your back."

"All right," she said slowly. "I'm with you so far. I don't especially pretend to understand where this is going, but I'm with you."

"I consider you a most valuable ally. You . . . you anticipate my concerns. You understand my strategies. You support me . . . even if you feel that my plans are wrong-headed or inappropriate. But you are not afraid to let your sentiments be known if you feel that I am acting in a counterproductive manner. I do not intimidate you."

"It takes all my self-control," Deanna said. "Normally one look of disapproval from you makes me weak at the knees and I just want to crawl under a chair and expire."

For a moment he was rather pleased to hear it, but then he said after due consideration, "You were being ironic."

"Actually it was more like sarcastic, but ironic is close enough."

She laughed softly, and he noted that her shoulders shook slightly as she did so. He realized that even the most casual movement of her body seemed like poetry to him.

"Worf"—and she placed a slender hand on his—"what is this about?"

"Alexander likes you."

"I like him, too," she said. "He doesn't have it easy. He's trying to stride two cultures, and I know from personal experience how difficult that can be. You should be proud of him."

"I am. And I believe that you have been a very positive influence on him. You listen to him."

"So do you."

Worf shook his head. "Not always. Not at first, certainly. You taught me how. You taught me to realize when he was not saying what was on his mind, rather than accepting his words at face value. You taught me to probe. And even now . . . it takes me tremendous effort to listen patiently to the boy. Frequently I find myself frustrated. But you do it so effortlessly. He knows that. I believe that is part of why he feels so affectionately toward you."

"As I do with him. And with his father," she added.

"Indeed. And how his father . . . that is to say, how I . . . feel about you." He growled angrily to himself. "I am doing this very badly."

"Doing what? We're having a very nice conversation about feelings. I know that's not necessarily the thing you're most comfortable discussing, but I'm proud of you for the effort. It's sincerely made."

"It is not simply a matter of discussing things. It is . . ."

"War?" she prompted.

"Yes. That is right. And I would like to . . ." He searched for the right words. "I wish to formalize our alliance."

She stared at him for a long moment, completely clueless as to what he could possibly be talking about. And then it hit her like a ten-ton anvil. Her eyes went wide, her jaw slack. "Worf, are you . . . are you asking me to . . . ?"

"If you laugh . . ." Worf cautioned her.

"No! No, I . . . I wouldn't think of laughing! I'm . . . I just, I don't know what to say. . . ."

"The preferred response to a marriage proposal is 'Yes.' "

She sat back in her seat as if rocked. "A marriage proposal. Worf, I . . . I won't lie to you. I never could lie to you, really. I love you, you know that, and I think you love me. . . ."

"Yes." He didn't sound particularly loving. It was more matter-of-fact. But it was enough that he'd said it.

"Still, for all that . . . Worf . . . may I ask what prompted this?"

"More self-examination?"

"If you hope to be married to me, you'd better get used to it."

"A valid point." He still had one hand tightly wrapped in hers. The other he drummed thoughtfully on the table. "I have been observing families . . . seen what they have to offer one another. Mother, father, child . . . I consider it a reasonable and intelligent situation. Not the only viable one, but it may very well be the ideal one. We complement each other well, Deanna. We function well as a team. And Alexander deserves . . ." He took a deep breath. ". . . he deserves better than for me to be his sole influence."

"Oh, Worf . . . don't sell yourself short. . . ."

"I do not. In fact, quite the opposite. I have a rather high opinion of my abilities as an officer and as an individual. I have my failings, Deanna, but false modesty is not one of them."

"Yes, so I've noticed."

"More sarcasm. It does not suit you."

"Sorry." She kept her lips pursed and a determinedly serious expression on her face.

"It is my opinion that whatever qualities I have are due to the exposure I had to a multiplicity of backgrounds. The galaxy is too small for isolationism. The more Alexander knows, the better he will be able to serve others and himself. And I . . ."

"Yes? What about you? Thus far we've spoken almost entirely about Alexander. What about you, Worf?"

"I . . . do not wish to be without you. Deanna," he said, looking her levelly in the eyes, "I know that I am not exactly the sort of mate that the average Betazoid dreams of. Has nightmares of, perhaps, but does not dream of. But I am stronger with you than without you, and I would like to think you feel the same way about me."

"I do feel that way, Worf. But it's such a major commitment . . . and everything is so much in flux right now . . ."

"Precisely my point. At a time when matters are in flux, that is the moment when security should be grabbed. A security that we can offer one another . . . and, together, offer Alexander."

"I . . ."

"I do not need an immediate answer," Worf told her, "but it would be preferable. For I know that an answer given now would be one given by your heart . . . and I would find that much easier to accept, no matter what the answer was, than one that required overintellectualization."

What he said struck a chord. She remembered when she had first met Will Riker, years ago, and how he had accused her at the time of overanalyzing things to death. Of being incapable of acting on impulse or with emotion, which was peculiar considering that she was someone who was supposed to understand emotion so thoroughly. . . .

Riker.

My God, she thought, *I'm in the middle of a marriage proposal . . . and I'm still thinking about Will.*

This was madness. All the time that they had spent together on the *Enterprise,* all the back-and-forth, and the suggestions, and the one step forward, two step back . . . all of it, really, amounted to nothing except pleasant memories of a relationship that had long ago cooled. Yet she realized, with startling clarity, that she was still holding on to it in some measure, deep down, for one of the simplest and most obvious of reasons:

Imzadi.

They were Imzadi.

They were Imzadi, and they were supposed to be together.

But life, as an Earth musician had said several centuries earlier, was what happened to you while you were making other plans. Life for Riker and Troi had taken them in other directions, and although there had been some dalliances and some rekindling here and there, the fire had never been fanned once more into full blaze.

With Worf, though, love burned very hot indeed. Worf did nothing in half measures, and although he had obvious trouble discussing things such as feelings, he nonetheless loved her with the type of all-consuming passion that she had once thought Riker felt for her, and she for him. The very thought of it made her heart pound, made her realize just how much she was missing.

And he was right. They were about to be cut adrift. Who knew where Starfleet would send them? Who knew if they would be reunited or sent in different directions? Requests could be put in, strings could be pulled, but in the final analysis no one knew anything for sure. Deanna had felt as if everything was slipping through her fingers, and here was an opportunity being given her to have something permanent, something real.

It's crazy, an inner voice cautioned her. *Marry for the right reasons, not because you're scared of being alone.*

But she was not afraid of solitude, of that she was quite positive. Being on her own, being alone with her thoughts . . . these were not things that held any trepidation for Deanna Troi. She was an independent, secure, self-sufficient woman. She had nothing to prove.

Why marry Worf?

She loved him, and he loved her. And she loved Alexander, too, or at least was reasonably sure she did. They had good chemistry, he was dependable and brave and would willingly lay down his life for her, although heaven forbid it would ever come to that; it was simply an indicator of the depth of his feelings for her. From a purely social growth point of view, he was an up-and-coming officer in Starfleet. They would be able to be assigned to the same ship.

Why not marry Worf?

It might still be too soon, the relationship too young.

But she had known him for so long. He wasn't a stranger. He wasn't . . .

Imzadi . . .

The word came unbidden to her once more, and with almost physical effort she pushed it away.

"Yes." She didn't say it so much as blurt it out, and a look of surprise crossed her face.

"Did . . . did you say, 'Yes'?" Worf asked, leaning forward and tilting his head slightly as if he needed to hear her better.

"I . . . I did, yes." Now that she had made the reply, she instantly felt as if a weight had been lifted from her. "Yes. Yes, Worf . . . I will marry you. . . ."

Worf leaped to his feet, slapping the table with enthusiasm, and shouting, "Yes! She said yes! We are engaged!"

And that was when Worf saw Commander Riker.

Riker was at a table halfway across the room. He was half standing, clearly in the act of rising from the table at which Geordi La Forge was also sitting. And he had frozen in position, his face completely inscrutable.

It was at that moment that Worf abruptly realized, at the most rudimentary of levels, that his engagement might well be the most short-lived on record.

As La Forge and Riker approached the Ten-Forward, Geordi could tell that something seemed to be preying on the first officer's mind. Geordi wasn't exactly sure whether it was his place to broach the observation. He fully respected William Riker as an officer and as a man, and he certainly didn't mind sitting down at one of their frequent poker games with the usual suspects. But he had never exactly been, well, "pals" with Riker. Shipmates, colleagues, yes. But they'd never really been all that tight.

Under most circumstances, Riker was a curious mixture of outgoing and conservative. He never lost sight of the responsibilities that his position entailed, but there was a clear devilish streak in him that always seemed to be hovering just below the surface. Geordi wasn't detecting any of that, however. Instead there seemed an air of near melancholy hanging over him. As they walked down the corridor of the *Farragut,* they'd pass assorted displaced *Enterprise* crewmen, and even individuals who had served with Riker in the past. In all instances, Riker would nod or say a few polite words. He unfailingly acknowledged everyone's presence. But his heart and his mind didn't seem truly engaged, even as he made small talk with all and sundry.

Finally, Geordi said, "It really wasn't your fault, Commander."

"Hmm?" Riker seemed to be in a world of his own. With effort he focused on Geordi. "What? Oh. The *Enterprise,* yes, well . . . I suppose you're right. I'll probably be replaying everything in my mind for years to come, but hopefully I'll come to that conclusion, sooner or later."

"Better sooner than later." He paused. "That's not it, though, is it?"

"What 'it' are you referring to, Geordi?"

"Look, I hope I'm not being out of line here . . . but you seem as if you've got a couple of iron weights tied to your shoulders."

"I'm just busy trying to plan for the future, Geordi, that's all. There's going to be a lot to deal with in terms of the crashed vessel . . . the reassignments . . . it's going to be difficult not looking at your face every day in engineering. Or the poker games where I could easily make a week's pay in just a few hours. That's a lot of loss to cope with."

When he had spoken, it was with a bit of the old pop and semi-teasing in his voice, but it seemed more of an effort than usual. Geordi wasn't at all sure what to make of it all.

They reached the doors to Ten-Forward and Riker gestured for Geordi to go in first. Geordi nodded appreciatively and preceded Riker in. There was a table to one side that a couple of crewmen were just leaving, so Geordi promptly claimed it and Riker sat down across from him, straddling the chair as was his custom. He held up two fingers to the bartender, and very shortly two glasses of synthehol found their way to the table.

"Oh!" Geordi said, pointing across the way. "There's Worf and Counselor Troi. They seem to be looking pretty cozy."

Riker turned around in his seat to glance in their direction. Worf was speaking and Deanna was leaning forward, completely involved in what Worf was saying, whatever that might have been.

Geordi, however, wasn't paying attention so much to Troi and Worf as he was to Riker. He tilted his head slightly, like a curious canine, and then slowly he let out a long, drawn-out "Ohhhhh. I get it now."

"You get it?"

"Yes, sir, I do."

"Well, good for you, Mr. La Forge," Riker said with affable confusion. "Now would you mind cluing me in as well?"

"I shouldn't have to. You're the one who gave it to me."

"Gave what to you?" Riker shook his head in frustration. "Geordi, I have no idea what you're talking about."

"Oh really. That's odd. You're the one whose respiration and heartbeat both jumped the moment you saw Worf and Counselor Troi together." He tapped the VISOR sagely. "You can fool me, Commander, and maybe you can even fool yourself . . . but you can't fool this."

Riker interlaced his fingers and leaned forward. He was the picture of controlled calm, at least to anyone who wasn't possessed of a VISOR that was practically capable of dissecting him at a molecular level. "If my heart goes pit-a-pat when I see Deanna and Worf together, *Mr.* La Forge, it's only because I am so pleased to see Deanna having some much-deserved happiness."

Instantly Geordi knew that Riker was lying through his teeth. His VISOR wasn't always one-hundred-percent dependable when serving as a lie detector, and when it came to encountering people for the first time who might be trying to hide something, Geordi's abilities as a truth barometer were sorely lacking. But when it came to people he knew extremely well, Geordi could make assessment of veracity that bordered on supernatural accuracy. In this instance, the abrupt jump in Riker's body readings was so clear to La Forge that it was the equivalent of a sighted man watching the words "I'm lying" appear in blazing letters on Riker's forehead.

But Geordi didn't exactly feel comfortable about confronting Riker with absolute knowledge of Riker's prevarication, and so he mustered his formidable poker face and said, "All right, Commander. That's nice to hear."

Riker kept a level gaze for a long moment, and then slowly he sighed. "Is it that obvious?" he asked after a time.

Inwardly, Geordi was relieved at Riker's response. He had certainly not wanted to offend Riker . . . or, even worse, cause him personal upset over stirring up matters that were painful to him. "Not to most folks," Geordi replied. "But I'm not most folks."

"No, Mr. La Forge, I dare say you're not." Riker looked over his shoulder at Troi and Worf, and then pointedly made an effort to look anywhere else.

Geordi leaned forward and lowered his voice, as if he were concerned that people might be eavesdropping. No one was, of course, but somehow it was the sort of conversation that lent itself to quiet discourse. "But I don't get it, sir. I thought you had given your blessing to their getting involved."

"I did."

"And I thought that you and the counselor weren't . . ." He wagged two fingers and then crossed them as if bringing them together.

"We aren't."

"Then what's the problem?"

"I don't know what the problem is."

Geordi took another deep swig of the synthehol. Its "intoxicating" powers were entirely voluntary. That was part of the beauty of it. It enabled the imbiber to "relax" himself sufficiently so that he could surrender to the giddy effects of the synthetic alcohol, but if an emergency presented itself, the drinker could instantly toss aside any feeling of inebriation and rise to whatever emergency presented itself. In this instance, Geordi allowed the most relaxing aspects of the liquor to sway him, emboldening his approach to Riker. "Or maybe you do," Geordi said challengingly, "and you just don't want to admit it."

"And that problem would be?" Riker didn't seem drunk at all. Clearly he preferred it that way.

"That maybe you still have strong feelings for her. You see the two of them together and it suddenly makes you say, 'Wait a minute . . . I'm letting her get away. What am I, crazy?' "

Very slowly, Riker nodded. "There is something to be said for that," he admitted.

Geordi was almost surprised at his own perspicacity. "There is?"

"It's just . . ." He rapped his knuckles on the tabletop thoughtfully. "I've had some tough scrapes before, Geordi. Some nasty bang-ups. But I've never had a ship go bust out from under me as the *Enterprise* did. Never had a landing quite like that one. I kept waiting for Captain Picard to say, 'I give you the ship for five minutes and look what happens!' Fortunately he didn't."

"Or at least he was polite enough not to say it," Geordi said helpfully.

"Not a problem. I would have blamed it on Deanna's steering." The offhand, wry comment provided some tension-relieving laughter, but only for a moment, and Riker wound up not looking any less apprehensive than he had before. "The *Enterprise* was more than my home, Geordi, and certainly more than simply where I went to work every day. It was a symbol not only of past adventures that we've all had together, but a symbol of times to come. Of stability. Earlier today I told Captain Picard that I'd always hoped to have a shot at the command chair. That ship was my living promise of the future. Not alive as an object, of course, but I'd imbued it with all my hopes and dreams and aspirations, something I didn't even quite realize until after she was gone. And now"—and he snapped his fingers so sharply that it sounded like a ricochet—"no promise. No future. No ship. The loss of the ship drove home for me just how transitory everything is." He swirled the liquid in his glass and stared idly at it. "And here I've been acting as if a future for Deanna and myself was something I could always get back to whenever I felt like it. I thought that the *Enterprise* would be forever, but obviously she wasn't. On Betazed I thought Deanna and I would be forever, but it didn't work out for a number of reasons. I've just begun reassessing my priorities, that's all."

"And are you going to do anything about it?"

He glanced in the direction of Deanna and Worf. "I don't think it's my place to," he said quietly.

"If not yours, then whose?"

"Perhaps no one's, Geordi," he said levelly. "I had my chance. More chances than any reasonable supreme being would willingly allow. People have met, married, and had children in the time that I've been playing Hamlet in regards to my feelings for Deanna."

"To be or not to be."

"That is the question." He laughed low in his throat. "Funny. All of my training in Starfleet had been to make decisions, and I can do it. Do it in a heartbeat. When the captain had been taken over by the Borg, transformed into Locutus, and he threatened the well-being of the *Enterprise,* I ordered that he be fired upon without a second thought. Snap judgment, the kind I'd been trained for, for years. No hesitation, no doubt. But when it comes to my personal life—and one woman, in particular . . ." He shrugged.

"Believe me, Commander, I know exactly how you feel. My track record with the opposite sex isn't exactly something to write home about. So I'm not the best person to be giving advice to anyone when it comes to that. Still, if you're comparing your respective decision-making abilities, there's one thing that occurs to me."

"And that would be . . . ?"

"Well . . ." Geordi shifted in his chair. "We were discussing earlier the measures we took to try and save the *Enterprise* from crashing and burning. Me, I'm satisfied that I did everything I could. I'll face any Starfleet board of inquiry with confidence, because that's what I truly believe. I'm fairly certain that you don't believe that you did everything you could, and knowing you—no offense—but you'll probably get up there and willingly take responsibility for the entire thing. I have no doubt, though, that eventually you'll be cleared, even over your own protests. Would you call that a fair assessment of the situation?"

"A tad cynical, but fair," Riker admitted.

"Okay. But let's say there was another board of inquiry. A board that investigated 'affairs of the heart,' for lack of a better phrase. If they put you in the hot seat and said, 'Riker, have you done everything you could about your relationship with Deanna Troi—truly explored every option, even completely admitted to yourself the depths of your feelings for her'—what would you say to them? Would your conscience be clear? And if it wasn't, do you think that they'd clear you in this instance, or would it be a much closer call?"

Riker began to tap a finger, just one, on the tabletop. He was doing it rapidly and then it began to slow as his thoughts appeared to coalesce.

"I see your point," he said after what seemed an eternity.

"Good."

"But the question becomes, am I just going to see it? Or am I actually going to do something about it?"

"That, Commander, I couldn't begin to tell you," La Forge replied. "I'm not running around inside your head, and frankly, I can see a whole lot of things . . . but even my VISOR doesn't let me see the future."

Riker took his glass of synthehol and tossed back half of it, as if steeling himself. "I am very likely," he said slowly, "about to make a bigger idiot of myself than I have in my entire career."

"You're going to talk to her."

"I'm going to talk to her, yes. And if this doesn't work out, or if I look like a complete fool, then at least I know who to blame it on."

"Me?"

"Precisely." But Riker was grinning widely, and it seemed to La Forge as if, suddenly, Riker had had a weight lifted from him. He was about to take action after ages of vacillation. He would no longer be Hamlet when it came to his personal life. Instead he would be a man of action, seizing the moment. "Because you know what, Geordi? Maybe the *Enterprise* did wind up going down in flames. But, dammit, she fought the good fight and she's got nothing to be ashamed of. If I never get to command her, the least I can do is live up to her example."

"That's the attitude to have, sir," Geordi said encouragingly.

"I'm going to go over there . . . I'm going to ask Mr. Worf to excuse us . . . and then Deanna and I are going to have a little talk. Actually, probably a big talk."

"Be kind to Worf, Commander. He's the innocent bystander in all this."

"Yes, he is," Riker said regretfully. "He had the courage to speak his mind and make his move while I just stood on the sidelines and let it happen. Still . . . he'll understand. At least I hope he will. Wish me luck, Geordi."

"Luck, Commander."

Riker began to rise from his seat, and that was when he heard a bang on the table from the direction of Deanna and Worf.

"Yes!" Worf crowed. "She said yes! We are engaged!"

Riker froze in midelevation. It was as if his entire universe had suddenly telescoped down to those few seconds. He had his drink still firmly in his hand. He felt Geordi's level gaze upon him, glanced from the corner of his eye, and saw the stricken expression on Geordi's face.

But his attention was truly on Worf and Troi, and then Worf caught his eye. Judging by the surprised look on Worf's face, the Klingon hadn't known he was there all this time.

Worf was perpetually one of the most confident of beings, but at that moment, Worf's eternal self-certainty suddenly appeared in jeopardy. Had he seen something in Riker's demeanor that betrayed his feelings? Had he known why it was that Riker was getting up from the table?

Sensing Worf's discomfiture, Deanna turned in her seat to see where he was looking, and her gaze locked with Riker's. It was as if they were looking at each other over a vast expanse of years. All of it . . . all of the potential emotion and confrontation . . . hung there for no more than a second or two. And then, as if it were all intended as one smooth motion, Riker fully rose to standing and raised his glass. His face split into a grin even as his heart split in half. "Let me be the first," he called out in a rock-steady voice, "to raise a toast to the happy couple and wish you congratulations!"

"Congratulations!" echoed the rest of the populace of the *Farragut* lounge. Shouts of "Hear, hear" and "To the happy couple" rebounded throughout the lounge.

Geordi felt that Riker's mental discipline was amazing. At that moment his mind might have been in a complete turmoil, and had that been the case, Deanna Troi would have known immediately. Geordi was positive of that, which meant that Riker was covering everything that was going through his mind, forcing instead only positive emotions to rise to the surface like cream. He smiled again, raised his glass once more, and then slowly lowered himself back down to his seat while Worf and Troi accepted the congratulations of everyone else sitting nearby.

Riker saw Geordi's stricken expression but simply shrugged as if it was all meaningless in the final analysis. "My fault," he said lightly. "I told you to wish me luck. I forgot to specify what kind."

"Commander . . ." Geordi didn't know what to say. He felt awful, even culpable, as if he'd helped to set Riker up for a fall.

As if sensing what Geordi was thinking, Riker waved it off dismissively. "Don't you worry about it, Geordi. When you play Hamlet long enough, sooner or later someone who is willing to make the decision is going to get the girl."

"Didn't the girl die in *Hamlet?"*

"It was Shakespearean tragedy. Naturally everyone died. People only lived if it was a comedy. He wasn't much for blending comedy with drama. He was more of an all-or-nothing kind of guy. I can sympathize, I suppose. Be willing to give your all . . . or wind up with nothing."

Suddenly he looked as if the sounds of congratulations in the background were a bit much for him. He rose from the table once more, keeping his back carefully to Worf and Troi. "If you'll excuse me, Geordi . . ."

Still feeling guilty, Geordi asked, "You want company, Commander?"

"No, thank you, Geordi. I think I'll be turning in for the night."

"For the night? Commander, it's not even twenty hundred hours. Look . . . maybe we can swing by the holodeck . . ."

"Geordi," he said as he smiled sadly and shook his head. "It'll be all right. *I'll* be all right. Granted, I lost a ship and a woman all in one day, but if we're going to be philosophical about it, then she and I were just . . . two ships, passing in the night. I just need to hit the sack right now, that's all. To sleep . . ." He looked over his shoulder one final time, to see Deanna laughing and smiling and shaking the hands of those around her. ". . . perchance to dream."

Four

Tom Riker was dreaming of freedom when everything went insane.

It had been a very pleasant dream. A dream of a woman, with dark eyes and hair that cascaded around her shoulders. A woman who had taught him of feelings and then slipped away as fate had sent them spiraling in different directions. And for just a brief moment, ever so brief, he had had her once more . . . and then lost her . . . but now she was back in the recesses of his dreaming mind . . . and he would never lose her again . . . he was holding her, covering her mouth with kisses, and they were free . . . free to plan a life together . . . free to . . .

The blast startled him awake, as it did the other prisoners. The others were still looking around in befuddlement, but Riker had already come to full wakefulness. He was on the floor in a crouch, looking around, squinting, trying to adjust to the light or lack thereof.

There was another explosion from nearby, and the ground of Lazon II rumbled.

It was some sort of heavy-duty weapons pounding from overhead. Riker didn't immediately recognize it, but Saket—on the floor nearby—immediately did. "That's Romulan weaponry."

"Are you sure?" Tom Riker asked.

"Positive. I'd know that blast echo in my sleep."

Riker didn't bother to point out that he had, in fact, practically done so. Once more the ground trembled. "Friends of yours?" Riker asked.

"I would say so, yes. Can't say that it's unexpected, either."

The pounding continued from overhead as the unseen, but not unknown, attacker continued to assail the force shield. But then Riker realized that the rumbling beneath them was not coordinated with the assault from overhead. It was nearly impossible to hear over the ruckus of the other prisoners shouting and the weapons fire from overhead. Riker drew his face near Saket's and shouted, and fortunately the Romulan's ears were designed to hear under even the most grueling of circumstances.

"Something's wrong!" Riker bellowed over the din. "The shooting from overhead . . . it's separate from the ground shaking!"

"What?!" Saket listened a moment to the assault, felt the trembling of the ground, and his eyes widened as he realized the truth of what Riker was saying.

The door to the hut flew open, and Mudak was standing in it. He had a blaster in one hand and he was leaning against the doorframe with the other as he shouted, "Everyone stay in here! No one is to move! Don't consider for one moment trying to escape! Anyone who does make such an attempt will be severely punished for his troubles, I promise you that!" If there was any trace of panic in Mudak, it was not on display. He acted with the certainty of someone who was confident that his forces would prevail. For all the concern he showed, the attack might just as well have been a routine drill.

For whatever reason, Mudak looked directly at Riker and Saket. It was as if he was particularly concerned about them. Perhaps he was endeavoring to freeze them in place with an ominous stare. Then he turned and bolted.

The prisoners were all on the floor, looking worriedly overhead at the source of the assault. And then one of the prisoners, a Tellarite named Redonyem, snorted out in a gravelly voice, "I say we take our chances outside! This place isn't a blast shelter! If they get through and this hut collapses, we're all dead!"

"You think we're any better off out there?" shot back Z'yk, an Orion.

"Yes!" The Tellarite had pulled himself up from his crouched position and stalked the interior of the hut, looking more and more like a wild animal, his hair skewed, his arms gesticulating widely. "This could be our chance to get off this rock! I have five mates, nineteen children, and a career as an arms dealer I want to get back to! And if you think I'm going to spend my last moments quaking in here, waiting for death from above, when there's a landing field with an opportunity for freedom not far from here, then you are sadly mistaken!"

"He's right," Saket said abruptly. "Redonyem is right. I say we get out of here, now!"

There was something about the firmness and certainty in Saket's voice that seemed to make up the minds of the half-dozen prisoners who were huddling for safety. They took a collective deep breath and then bolted for the door, Redonyem leading the way.

The instant they emerged from the door, a Cardassian blaster whined and struck Redonyem. It hit him with such force that it literally somersaulted him, sending him smashing back into Saket, who was directly behind him.

A Cardassian guard was standing not far away. He had clearly been on his way to someplace else—a battle station, perhaps—when he had noticed the prisoners making a break for it. He waved his hand weapon threateningly and shouted, "Back inside! Back inside!" From high overhead, they could glimpse the blasts from the Romulan intruder—numbers unknown—coruscating against the shield. For the moment it seemed to be holding, and the pulse-blaster cannons were ready to pick up the slack in the unlikely event that the force shield fell.

Redonyem sagged against Saket, and a bestial snarl erupted from deep in his throat. There was a large blackened area in his upper chest from the effects of the blaster, but he didn't seem willing to acknowledge it. Instead Redonyem steeled himself for a moment and then charged. The guard brought his weapon up to fire again, and at that moment Saket grabbed up a small piece of debris that had tumbled loose from the roof of the hut. Riker watched as Saket hurled it with remarkable accuracy, and it struck the guard full in the face. The Cardassian staggered, his shot going wide, and then Redonyem crashed into him and disarmed the guard through the simple expedient of yanking off his entire arm. The Cardassian went down with a howl, more in shock than anything since the immensity of the pain wouldn't kick in for some minutes yet, and Redonyem howled in triumph, holding the arm over his head and shaking it defiantly like a bloody trophy. Another Cardassian guard, coming around the corner at high speed, came upon the grisly scene and froze. It was only a momentary hesitation, but it was more than enough time for Redonyem to step forward, swing the arm around, and cave in the side of the unfortunate guard's head. Then he grabbed up the weapons from the two fallen guards. The maimed one was screaming so loudly that it got on Redonyem's nerves, and he kicked the guard fiercely in the head, silencing him.

Z'yk, the Orion, approached the fallen guards and looked up at Redonyem with a wolfish smile. "Find me a knife," he said. "I have an idea."

The compound was sprawled over ten square miles, and so it was that the group of escaping prisoners was nowhere near a Romulan attack vessel when it made its way into the camp. This was actually fortunate since, if they had been, they might very likely have been killed instantly due to the unorthodox nature of the vessel's entrance.

Mudak, unfortunately, happened to be much nearer and, as a result, nearly lost his life. As he raced across the compound, heading toward the defense tower, he suddenly became fully aware that the ground was not simply vibrating in response to the pounding from overhead. Instead it seemed to be responding to something coming from underneath. What had occurred to Riker and Saket some minutes before now finally registered on Mudak, who, to be fair, might have realized it sooner were he not distracted by the assault from above. Then again, that was the entire purpose of the aerial attack: to draw attention from the true means of assailing the compound.

The ground began to buckle only ten feet away from him. The vibrations knocked Mudak off his feet and he fell heavily onto his back. He kept a firm hand on his weapon, but even as he did so he scrambled backward, pulling himself along on his elbows as he watched with sheer incredulity an assault plan that was breathtaking in its simplicity.

Dirt and debris exploded upward, fountaining, geysering as if someone had set off a depth charge. Mudak, realizing that he couldn't get away in time, curled up defensively in a ball, tucking his head down and in, as dirt rained upon him. The dirt storm effectively buried him, obscuring him from casual view. He was, however, able to keep enough of the soil away from his face that he could clearly see what was happening.

From out of the hole emerged a vessel such as Mudak had never seen, but he was quickly able to discern its purpose. It was a core driver, a normally land-bound vessel that was used in—ironically, considering the circumstances—terraforming. On particularly hostile worlds, it enabled colonists to fashion subterranean storage and even, in a pinch, residential facilities. It was equipped with a series of rotating proto-dischargers, arranged in a large wheel on the front of the vehicle. As the wheel spun, the dischargers literally dissolved the dirt in a widening circle while at the same time hardening the resulting tunnel by reinforcing its molecular structure to nearly diamond-hard durability. Passages, even caves, could be carved out in a matter of minutes.

But this was no ordinary core driver. Someone had taken it and, through resourcefulness that bordered on the diabolical, mounted the entire thing on a warp sled. The vehicle, now spaceworthy but too small to be detected by any early-warning device, had made its own approach to the planet, simply entered the planet's surface at a point that was unprotected by the force shield, and burrowed underneath the shielding. The shielding didn't extend below the compound on Lazon II; it ended at the surface level. It was an oversight of which the Romulans (according to Saket) had taken full advantage.

Lazon II was at that point officially a madhouse. The explosions from beneath had completely unnerved others of the prisoners, and now everyone was running amok. Guards had no idea where to concentrate their efforts: on the intruder, or on the would-be escapees.

"Form ranks!" shouted a senior guard. The guards who were within earshot heard him and lined up, forming an extremely makeshift firing squad. The only question was where to aim. The senior guard immediately settled the matter by shouting, "Squad One, quell the prisoner uprising. Squad Two, fire on the intruders!"

Squad One had considerably more success as they opened fire on the fleeing prisoners. Two were killed instantly, far more sustained terrible wounds.

The core driver, for its part, trembled under the assault. It was not a combat vehicle, and its hull was simply not designed to take that kind of abuse, even from handheld weaponry. The vehicle shuddered and veered, its warp-sled propulsion system hammered. The driver had, for a few moments, been in the air, but a renewed attack flipped the entire vehicle over. Beneath the dirt, Mudak saw it coming his way. His breath caught as it rolled across the ground, and he braced himself for the impact, anticipating it running right over him and flattening him.

Instead, at the last second—as if Mudak were leading a charmed life—the wreckage took one final flip and sailed right over him. It slammed to the ground several feet beyond him, tumbling end over end and leaving a thick smoking trail behind it.

The guards let out a roar of triumph. Mudak had, by that point, managed to dig himself out. His sudden appearance caught a number of the others by surprise as he pushed free of the debris and stumbled toward the core driver. The skid along the ground had ripped open the cockpit, and Mudak—who, miraculously, was still holding his weapon firmly—brought it up and aimed it squarely at the control seat of the core driver.

It was empty.

Mudak rubbed dirt from his face as if improving his vision might put someone in the way of his weapon. Other guards assembled around him, and they likewise stared uncomprehendingly. "Well . . . well, where is—?" one of them said.

Mudak's gaze caught a blinking panel on the vehicle. He recognized the auto-drive mechanism that had been attached, enabling the core driver to either be placed on autopilot or be operated by remote control. . . .

Suddenly Mudak understood. "The hole!" he shouted, whirling towards the point of entry. "Fire on it! Close it up! Hurry—!"

It was too late.

The Romulan fighter craft exploded out of the hole that the core driver had created. As was common for other Romulan vessels, it had birdlike markings, but it was leaner and more vicious looking than its larger warbird cousins. Starfleet intelligence reports had classified it as a "Peregrine." And as opposed to the core driver, which had moved like a pig since its warp sled was useless in a confined area, the Romulan fighter was equipped for rapid-fire maneuvers and pinpoint turns. That quickly became evident as the Peregrine angled around and headed fearlessly toward the defense grid.

The pulse-blasters immediately came on line, their sensor-locking systems targeting the Peregrine. The cannons opened fire, and conventional wisdom said that the Peregrine didn't have a prayer.

The pilot of the Peregrine, however, apparently didn't know that. The ship weaved and darted about, the air exploding around it. Once or twice the cannons came close to nailing it, but only close. The Peregrine's own weaponry came on line and returned fire, pummeling the defense grid. The massive tower trembled, cracks appearing in its foundation. The grid wasn't designed to withstand a direct assault—not only was the force shield supposed to provide the first line of defense, but there was no way that a ship was supposed to get close enough to have a direct impact with weapons fire.

It seemed, however, that no one had informed the pilot of the Peregrine of those facts. The ship swooped down and around, dodging through the hail of fire around it and continuing to blast the towers.

And then the Cardassians got lucky. A ground-fire team, headed up by Mudak, manage to clip the Peregrine, knocking out its rear stabilizers. The Peregrine spun on its axis, and Mudak fully anticipated that it would crash at any moment. As it turned out, he was wrong. Through a feat of piloting that defied description, the Peregrine managed to hold its course steady even as it spiraled in a manner that would have spelled instant death for anyone else. It lurched for one moment toward the ground and then gained altitude and held on to its target . . . namely the defense grid of Lazon II.

"It's going to hit!" shouted Mudak, and from both the words and tone of his voice there was no necessity for going into the details of what that meant. The pulse-blasters struck the fast-moving Peregrine, and the rear section of the fighter transformed into a rapidly building ball of flame. But it was too little, too late, for there was no time for the blasters to accomplish anything else. The Peregrine was upon them.

A split instant before the small ship collided with the defense grid towers, anyone with exceptionally sharp eyes would have noticed what appeared to be a small figure bailing out of the cockpit. The canopy had been jettisoned and the pilot—and, it appeared, sole crewman—was ejected into the air, barely clearing the area before the Peregrine smashed into the defense grid. The explosion was deafening, and a ball of fire immediately enveloped the lower half of the tower and licked its way eagerly up the rest of the structure. It set off a series of smaller explosions which rapidly built in intensity, the ground shaking all the more violently. Within seconds the entire defense grid erupted, sending a column of thick black smoke spiraling skyward.

By this time the compound was in complete disarray, people running in all directions. Mudak was never quite sure how he found himself flat on the ground. All he knew was that a tremendous blast of heat had picked him up and thrown him off his feet, sending him sprawling on his back many yards away. His world seemed to be filled with nothing but running feet. He had no idea which way to look.

To his amazement he was still holding on to his weapon. It was as if his fingers had developed a life of their own, a life that cried out in anger for vengeance over this indignity inflicted upon Lazon II. He spit out a large chunk of dirt, since apparently the force of the impact had driven his face directly into the ground. He felt a distant throbbing in his head, and touched the side of his face in order to realize that there was a large patch of wetness on his skin. With an almost amused attitude, he looked at the discoloration on his fingers and saw the blood on it, wondered whose it was, and then realized it was his own. He did not, however, choose to let it bother him, for he had larger concerns at that moment.

Then, from the corner of his eye, he saw movement. It stood out for him because, all around him, everyone else was running there and about as if they were madpeople. But this individual was moving with caution and a canny awareness of her surroundings. She was emerging from just behind the wreckage, moving in a sort of half-crouch that made her a fairly small target but did nothing to slow her down. She had short blond hair, and elegantly tapering eyebrows and ears. She was dressed mostly in black, with a tunic of silver that picked up the flickering of flame from the burning tower and almost made her look like a being of pure elemental fire. There was blackness smeared on her face, and for a moment he thought it was camouflage makeup before he realized that, no, it was soot from the fire and possibly from the crash.

It took him a moment to fully grasp who it was that he was seeing. It was the pilot of the Romulan Peregrine which had demolished Lazon II's defense grid. Suddenly Mudak could think of nothing that was more important to him than tracking down that pilot and killing her where she stood. She had not spotted him, and that was all the incentive he needed to go after her.

From her attitude, it seemed to Mudak as if she were looking for someone. It became a top priority for Mudak, therefore, to make damned sure that she didn't find whoever that someone was. Smoke was hanging thick in the air and she seemed to disappear into it. Mudak staggered to his feet, waited for the world to stop tilting around him, and then moved off in pursuit.

Some distance away, Saket slowed in his running as he caught sight of the amazing precision flying of the Peregrine. It took him no time at all to realize who was at the helm of the ship, and then he smiled and shook his head in amazement. Clearly she had not lost her knack for pinpoint maneuvering.

"I knew you'd come," he said, and then he turned to Riker and said again, "I knew she'd come."

But Riker was nowhere to be seen, and Saket realized that Riker had become separated from him in the confusion.

Suddenly there was a massive explosion. Saket's head whipped around just in time to see the Peregrine enveloped in a fireball of such intensity that he could feel the heat even where he was standing. His momentarily elevated spirits sank as he realized he might have just seen the death of one of his best and most beloved pupils. He shook his head in grim denial. "No," he said firmly, "no, she can't be dead. I don't believe it."

He even started to take a step toward the blast. Smoke was starting to waft in their direction, and then Redonyem appeared out of nowhere and grabbed Saket by the upper elbow. "Wrong way, old man," said Redonyem. His color didn't look particularly good; his skin tone was distinctly pink, and that wasn't the best shade for a Tellarite. Nonetheless he said grimly, "We're heading this way."

"But—" began Saket.

"Look," Redonyem growled sharply. He had one of his blood-covered, meaty hands firmly over the large burn mark on his torso. "We don't have time to play. You interceded once for me with the guards, and I pay my debts. Come now or stay behind, either way, it's your decision, but make it now."

Saket hesitated only a moment, and then he followed the Tellarite toward possible freedom, unknowing of what had happened to either Riker or the female who had flown so boldly.

Mudak ran as fast as he could, climbing over rubble and vaulting over cracks in the very ground beneath him. He was certain that the Romulan woman was unaware that she was being pursued by him, and he didn't want to get off a shot and miss, because that would warn her that she was being followed and he would lose the element of surprise. Considering everything that was going on around them, it might have been the only trump card he had.

He was all too aware of the complete vulnerability of Lazon II. The forcefield was demolished. Whatever other ships were up there, ready to inflict damage on the helpless world, would be able to take their stab at the beleaguered prison planet. They were very likely on their way even then, larger Romulan ships descending from on high like scavenging birds of prey.

"I thought they were our damned allies," he growled. After all, hadn't that been why Lazon II was at a low ebb in terms of ready troops? Because many Cardassian troops and their vessels had been enlisted as part of a Cardassian/Romulan mutual endeavor to obliterate the Founders? So what were Romulans doing now, attacking Lazon II? Had it all been part of some sort of massive scam on the part of the Romulans? At that point in time, there was nothing that Mudak would put past them.

She had stopped. It seemed as if she was trying to get her bearings. It was the perfect opportunity, and Mudak brought his weapon up and aimed it squarely at her. For a moment he couldn't help but admire her from afar. She had a look about her that seemed almost animalistic, like a lithe stalking creature that was on the scent of prey. It was a clichéd sentiment, but he couldn't help but feel regret that he had not encountered her under more pleasant circumstances, because he was certain that she would be one wild ride.

None of this, however, deterred him from preparing to blow her brains out.

He had a clear shot and could not miss. She was unaware that she was a target and, with any luck, she would be dead before she ever realized it.

He squeezed the trigger on his blaster and the weapon belched out its destructive force.

It ripped through thin air.

For at the exact moment he had fired, the Romulan woman had suddenly been beamed out. It had been pure coincidence; she'd had no idea that she was targeted. She had simply called for one of the unseen Romulan vessels overhead—which could now beam people to and from the surface—to get her out of there. For just a moment she realized, belatedly, the peril she had been in as she reacted to the blaster beam bisecting her. But the transporter beams had already taken hold of her, reducing her to little more than rapidly disappearing molecules.

Mudak spat out a curse.

It did not take a genius to figure out the purpose of this entire invasion. They were trying to stage some sort of breakout, most likely of Saket. If that was the case, and they hadn't already managed to locate him, then Mudak was running out of time. Even if Lazon II was in flames around him, he would be damned if he allowed them to succeed in the goal of their mission.

Mudak knew every inch of the facility, and even in these less-than-ideal circumstances, he knew the way to the landing port. He dashed there as quickly as he reasonably could, circumventing pockets of fighting as he focused on the larger concern. He drew within range of the field and looked for some signs of life in the guard bunker. Not spotting any, he immediately determined that one of two things had happened: Either they had abandoned their post (not impossible, but not likely) or they had been overcome by a group of prisoners, particularly Saket (not impossible and far more likely).

Mudak slowed ever so slightly in order to give himself a fraction more reaction time. Even at that reduced speed he still covered distance with remarkable speed. His hair was hanging raggedly around his face, and thick beads of sweat were collecting in the bone ridges of his face. His breath was ragged in his chest because of the heat caused by the explosions, but not only did none of that stop him . . . it was in fact all forgotten when he spotted three forms in the haze making their way toward one of the vessels in the landing port.

He did not hesitate, nor did he give them the slightest chance for surrender. Instead he opened fire. He had it set on full power, because he was simply not in the mood to fool around.

The first blast caught the Tellarite, Redonyem, squarely in the upper back. It was a killing blast, but Redonyem did not die immediately. It was the second major hit he'd taken in the course of the day, and still he refused to die. Mudak, however, had promptly dismissed Redonyem from his immediate concerns because he was already firing on Saket. Saket was in a half-turn, spinning about to see what it was that now threatened them, and if Mudak's second blast had hit him squarely, Saket would have been dead before he hit the ground.

It was Redonyem who inadvertently saved him. Redonyem was staggering about, clutching at his chest, touching awful things that he didn't want to think about and trying to shove them back into his chest cavity. When Mudak fired on Saket, Redonyem unknowingly stepped between the two. The blast ripped a gaping hole through Redonyem, blood and innards exploding from within him, and the blast continued through the Tellarite and struck Saket squarely in the side. However, Redonyem had absorbed the brunt of the blast, albeit unintentionally, and he collapsed upon Saket, his body weight now a dead mass that drove Saket to the ground.

Z'yk, the Orion, turned and saw Mudak advancing. For a moment he considered trying to get off a shot with the weapon he had in his hand, but Mudak already had him targeted and was coming straight toward him, weapon unwavering. And Z'yk knew that by the time he had a bead on Mudak, Mudak would already have killed him. So Z'yk did the only thing he could: He dropped his weapon, put his hands over his head, and called out "I surrender!" loudly enough to be heard over the cries of panic that drifted in from not too far away.

Mudak nodded in acceptance of the offer and then blew Z'yk's head off. Z'yk's headless body stood there a moment, arms still raised, and then the body collapsed.

He surveyed the scene of the carnage for a moment, nodding in approval, and then he saw Saket stirring beneath the fallen body of Redonyem. It was only at that moment that Mudak realized that Saket was still alive. He kept the weapon aimed squarely at the Romulan as he called out, "Stand up."

"C-can't," Saket said. His voice was barely audible.

Mudak craned his neck slightly and then nodded approvingly. "Ah. I did kill you. I see it's just going to take a little longer. I wonder . . . should I end it now? Or should I let your suffering continue? Which would be more appropriate? Which would you prefer, Saket? Die slowly, or die quickly? Which do you think I should provide you?"

Even though Saket was in immense pain, he was not about to give Mudak the satisfaction of seeing that reflected on his face. Instead he kept his expression carefully neutral as he said, "How nice that you are finally, if belatedly, asking prisoners what sort of treatment they'd like to receive." It was everything that he could do to keep the agony out of his voice.

"When I think," growled Mudak, "of all the times I held my tongue because of your 'connections,' of all the special treatment you received . . ." He smiled thinly. "Perhaps it's appropriate that, in the final analysis, all you are is just another prisoner shot while trying to escape." He brought his weapon up and aimed it squarely at Saket's face. "Good-bye, Saket."

He saw the sudden movement to his right at the last moment. Instantly Mudak swung his weapon around, firing as he went, cutting a swath through the air.

Tom Riker, anticipating it, was already below it. He hit the ground in a shoulder roll and came up with his boots firmly planted in Mudak's stomach. Mudak staggered backward but managed to keep his footing. Riker, not even so much as slowing down, as if powered by nothing but pure anger, came to his feet and slammed into Mudak's midsection like a runaway shuttlecraft. He drove forward with such force that he lifted Mudak completely off his feet and the two of them went down in a tangle of arms and legs. Riker managed to pull himself clear and he swung a fist around, catching Mudak squarely on the point of his jaw. It was not the best of ways to strike a Cardassian; Riker felt one of his knuckles break on the hard bone.

Nonetheless, Mudak was momentarily stunned, and it was all the time that Riker needed to pry the weapon from Mudak's hand. He aimed it squarely into the Cardassian jailer's face, and when Mudak's eyes managed to refocus, he looked up at the weapon and then gave a look that bored straight into the back of Riker's head.

"You had best kill me," Mudak warned him. "Because if you do not, I swear I will find you."

Riker's gaze flickered for a moment, as if he was strongly considering it. Then he abruptly brought the butt of the weapon around and knocked Mudak cold.

The Cardassian's head slumped to one side and he lapsed into unconsciousness.

Riker didn't even afford him a second glance, but instead quickly crossed over to Saket and hauled him to his feet. It was obvious that the others were done for, and when he took a close look at Saket's wound, he had a fairly strong suspicion that Saket didn't have much of a prayer either.

Nor did Saket have any illusions as to his own longevity. "Good . . . timing there, Riker . . ." he said, and his voice sounded raspy.

"I was pinned down by some falling rubble," Riker said. "Sorry I didn't get here sooner. . . ."

"Soon enough . . . to help me die . . . where I wish . . . die free . . ."

"You're not going to die," Riker told him flatly, and he started hauling him toward the nearby shuttle.

"Die . . . free," Saket said as if Riker hadn't spoken. "That's the . . . important thing . . . didn't want to die here . . . no place to die . . ."

Riker was about to tell him once more that he wasn't going to die, but he knew that Saket was too intelligent to be lied to. Besides, Riker needed to save his breath to haul the two of them to the shuttle. The ground rumbled once more, and Riker caught flashes of phaser fire from overhead. Something big was in orbit around them. Indicating "up" with a quick tilt of his head, Riker said, "Friends of yours?"

But Saket wasn't listening. It was as if he was slipping off into his own world. He just kept saying, "Free . . . free . . ." over and over again. Riker saw the blood spreading faster across Saket's chest. He thought about stopping and applying some sort of first aid, but he quickly realized that it would be like trying to bail out a sinking ocean liner using a straw. No matter what he did, it wasn't going to even begin to be enough.

They made it to the shuttle and Riker practically stumbled in with Saket. It was not an especially large vehicle, but they didn't need all that much to get off the unpleasant rock called Lazon II. Riker quickly scanned the instrumentation; it was all Cardassian, but it was nothing he couldn't handle. His fingers flew over the controls and the shuttle rumbled to life around them. Ideally the prepping for a shuttlecraft was a two-man operation, but Saket didn't appear to be in shape to help with anything at that moment. Instead he was murmuring something, and Riker couldn't quite make out what he was saying. He dropped into the pilot's seat next to Saket as he made the final preparations for liftoff.

"I knew . . . her mother," he was saying softly, almost as if in a dream. "She was remarkable. No one quite like her. She had pride that they could never break in her . . . gods know they tried. We actually became . . . friends . . . I never would have expected that . . . on her deathbed . . . promised I'd watch for her daughter . . ."

The shuttle jostled under them as Riker fired up the engines. It was far from his smoothest liftoff, but then again the circumstances were hardly ideal. The shuttle lurched to the right and then Riker managed to even it off. The tossing about seemed to get Saket's attention. He began talking directly to Riker, but in that same distracted manner. "You know what she said to me, Riker . . . ?"

"What?" Riker wasn't paying all that much attention. Instead he was focused on the guards who, even at that moment, were charging into the landing field. They were pointing in his general direction and Riker knew that they'd run out of time. He opened up the thrusters to full faster than he should have, which ran the risk of shutting down the entire engine. He did not see himself as having much choice in the matter, though. The shuttle angled upward, blasts from ground fire below exploding around it.

"She said . . . she had no regrets. That once upon a time . . . she had died . . . but this time, she had gotten a second chance. That she was grateful for it all. That at least her death . . . meant something . . . instead of dying uselessly as she had before. I never quite understood what she was talking about."

Riker didn't know what Saket was going on about, nor did he care. The shuttle jumped upward, gaining speed with every moment. They hurtled upward, faster and faster, the ground fire ceasing as they drew out of range of the hand weapons.

"Although she did say . . . she missed the *Enterprise* . . ."

This comment was enough to immediately catch Riker's attention. He looked around at Saket and said, "The *Enterprise?* The *Starship Enterprise?"*

But Saket had stopped speaking. The only indication that he was still alive was the faint glitter in his eyes. He seemed amused, as if something tremendously funny had occurred to him in what was likely to be his last moments.

With a final thrust of its engines, the shuttle broke free of the planet's gravity. As unwelcoming, as cruel as the cold vacuum of space could be, for one moment Riker couldn't help but feel as if he had returned home.

The rear scanners gave him a picture of the world on which he'd been imprisoned. From space, it looked so unassuming, so similar to hundreds of other worlds. There was nothing to distinguish it for Riker except the knowledge of what had gone on there and the resolution that he would never allow himself to return to a hellhole like that again.

"Riker . . ." Saket said quietly, as if he were speaking from very far away. " . . . you have been . . . a good friend. I have . . . appreciated your company . . ."

"Stop talking in the damned past tense" was Riker's sharp reply. "Stop acting as if you're going anywhere. Not on my watch, you're . . ."

Suddenly the ship was jolted. "Are we . . . hit . . . ?" Saket asked. Although he asked the question, he only seemed mildly interested in the response.

"That would have been more localized. This shook the entire vessel. I think that we've just been grabbed by a tractor beam."

His ability to scan the area was greatly hampered by the different look of the Cardassian technology. He'd been able to discern such systems as the thrusters and impulse drive, but more than that was a matter of trial and error. He was about to try and figure out how to initiate a full sensor sweep when the question was answered for him as space began to shimmer in front of him. It was a phenomenon he knew all too well.

"A Romulan warbird decloaking directly ahead," Riker told him.

"Oh no . . . Romulans . . ." Saket replied with dry sarcasm. "Whatever will we do . . ."

"It's easy for you to be sarcastic. You're not the human in the shuttle, Saket . . ."

There was no response.

"Saket," he said again and twisted around in his seat. For a moment he was absolutely positive that Saket was dead, and then he saw the Romulan's chest rise ever so slightly. When it fell without the accompaniment of a death rattle, Riker said urgently, "Just hold on . . . hold on . . ."

"Free . . ." whispered Saket.

And then they dematerialized.

* * *

The Romulan transporter room faded into existence around Riker and he looked around with an almost detached curiosity. The lighting was far more harsh than in a Federation starship transporter room. The walls were gunmetal gray, and the floor was made of an unyielding grating that gave off a loud clacking as the booted feet of the Romulans entered the room in short order. There were about half a dozen of them, all with weapons drawn, as if they expected Riker to try and make some sort of break for it.

But Riker was too busy to think about any of that, because at that moment Saket—who was so weakened that he was incapable of standing up—sagged toward Riker. Instinctively Tom Riker caught him, supporting his full weight. Saket looked up at him with what seemed, to Riker, to be apology in his eyes.

Then another Romulan entered, a blond female with a gaze of piercing intensity. She was dressed in a flight suit, which would have indicated that she was of lower rank, a mere pilot. But the other Romulans parted to make way for her.

She took one look at Riker and made no effort to keep the astonishment from her face. "Riker?" she said.

He didn't nod or reply, but simply stared at her. He had absolutely no idea who she was, but clearly she knew him.

She looked from Riker to Saket and then back to Riker. "Help Saket. Get him to medical," she snapped out. Immediately several of the Romulans stepped forward and took the injured Romulan in their care. One of them, clearly a higher-ranking one, turned to face the woman and, indicating Riker, said, "What about this one?"

She smiled in a manner that could only be described as wolfen.

"Kill him," she said.

Five

Worf was somewhat amazed at just how much muscle power his mother packed.

When Helena Rozhenko opened the door of her modest farmhouse in Minsk, she let out a girlish squeal of delight that did not remotely seem to match her exterior as she saw Worf standing in the doorway. She threw her arms around him before he was able to get a word out, and as courageous as the Klingon was, he had to admit he felt *safer* in the elderly woman's embrace. "Sergey!" she cried out, summoning her husband. "Worf, why didn't you tell us you were coming . . . ?"

"I preferred to maintain the element of surprise."

She laughed. "Trust you, Worf, to turn even a simple visit into a military strategy. Sergey! Where is that man? Oh, and you brought company!" She glanced at Deanna and extended a hand. "Hello. Helena Rozhenko. I'm Worf's mother . . . adopted," she added with a laugh, "in case you didn't remember we met once before, but so fleetingly . . ."

"Even if we hadn't met, I'd know you. He's spoken of you many a time." Deanna shook Helena's firm hand. "In case *you* don't recall . . . Deanna Troi. Ship's counselor . . . well . . . when I have a ship."

"A Betazoid, correct? I could tell. Every Betazoid I've ever met has that same air of serenity about them as you do. And who's this?" Helena turned and looked at the young Klingon standing just behind Deanna and Worf. "Is this a friend of Alex . . . and . . . er's . . . ?" Her voice trailed as she spoke the rest of the name, her eyes widening in amazement. "Alexander?" she whispered.

"Hello, Grandmother."

"My God," she murmured. "Let me look at you." As opposed to the embrace she had given Worf, she held Alexander by either shoulder and stared at him in open astonishment. "You look a foot, a foot and a half taller. I'd forgotten. Good lord, I'd forgotten how it is with young Klingons. Your father did the same thing. We almost went bankrupt keeping him in shoes and clothing."

"It was not that bad," Worf rumbled humorlessly.

"Worf!" came a roar from a big bear of a man, with thick gray beard and boisterous attitude. Sergey Rozhenko strode toward them and much of the same round of introductions reoccurred. Helena, in the meantime, had already hustled into the kitchen and prepared tea and assorted small sandwiches for everyone. She did it so quickly that Worf would have sworn that she had everything prepared just on the off chance that guests should happen to stop by.

They went into the comfortable living room, furnished in rich brown textures and solid old-style furniture. Sergey walked with one great arm around Worf's shoulder and the other around Deanna's.

"So how long are you planning to be with us? You're staying. Tell us you're going to be staying." He raised his voice as if Worf had been contradicting him rather than simply walking and listening. "After all, whatever else you may have to do, what's more important than seeing your parents?" demanded Sergey with mock outrage, although he tossed a wink in Deanna's direction to underscore the tongue-in-cheek nature of his comment.

They sat on the couches, Helena bustling in moments later with the food and drink. There was a dark bottle on the tray and she said proudly, "Cognac, to celebrate." She glanced at Alexander and said to Worf, "Is he old enough, do you think . . . ?"

"He has Klingon biology," Worf said. "He could very likely outdrink most adult human males. Still, I was wondering . . . would you have any prune juice around?"

Sergey and Helena smiled at each other. "Of course, prune juice," Sergey said. "I remember."

"Prune juice is a true warrior's drink. Ideal to consume when you go to fight."

"No, we don't have any, Worf. Next time, you give us some notice, I'll make sure we have it," Helena apologized. "So what are you doing back here? We were worried, your father and I."

"We heard there was some sort of trouble with the *Enterprise.*"

"That is something of an understatement. In point of fact, the secondary hull was destroyed from a warp-core breach, and we crashed the saucer section on a planet's surface."

"Deanna was at helm," Alexander put in.

Sergey looked at Deanna appraisingly. "Nice landing," he said.

Deanna put her face in her hands.

In broad strokes, Worf proceeded to lay out for his parents everything that had happened. Since Sergey was formerly a Starfleet man himself, specializing in warp fields—and Helena, by association, had learned rather a great deal about such matters—they were able to fully understand and appreciate everything that the crew of the *Enterprise* had gone through. "There is a court of inquiry being held in San Francisco, at Starfleet Headquarters, later this week, investigating the conduct of both Captain Picard and Commander Riker."

"I think it's most unfair," Deanna put in. "The captain wasn't even there, and there was nothing that Will Riker could have done . . ."

Sergey shook his head and waved dismissively. "Do not concern yourself with it, young lady," he advised. "It is standard procedure for Starfleet when a ship is destroyed."

"I know."

"I wouldn't worry about it if I were you."

"Yes, the captain has said much the same thing. Deanna and I have already been debriefed by Starfleet, so our presence is no longer required."

"We offered to stay around for moral support, but both the commander and captain insisted that it wouldn't be necessary," Deanna said. Helena wasn't sure, but it seemed to her as if Deanna was less than comfortable over that decision. Worf, for his part, simply nodded, apparently unperturbed.

"So you're going to be staying with us for a while, then?" asked Helena. She had poured cognac into glasses for each of the guests and gently set them in front of each of them, including half a glass for Alexander.

"Just for the night," Deanna said. "We're scheduled on a transport to Betazed tomorrow, to visit my mother."

"That's nice," Sergey said. "Taking the time to go visit the families. Nowadays, people are so spread out, it's so easy to lose touch with one another. . . ."

But Helena was regarding the two of them with new suspicion, her eyes narrowing. "Worf, Deanna . . . it sounds to me like you're taking each other home to meet your respective parents. Like you're a couple."

"What?" Sergey looked at his wife, then back at Deanna and Worf and laughed. "Helena, where do you get these notions? They're friends, shipmates. Worf would have told us ages ago if he'd . . ."

He looked back to his adopted son and saw the stony expression on Worf's face, and the genuine amusement in Deanna's. As if to settle the matter, Deanna reached over, took Worf's hand, and interlaced her fingers with his.

"I am . . . an idiot," said Sergey.

"No, Father, you are right . . . I should have told you earlier. . . ."

"You shouldn't have had to. I would have realized if I'd had the brains of a turtle, or even your mother."

"I choose to take that as a compliment," Helena said archly. She spoke with a teasing tone, but she was watching Deanna keenly, as if sizing her up.

Deanna was all too aware of the scrutiny, but told herself that it was a natural attitude for Helena to have. After all, their relationship had been dropped squarely into the laps of Worf's parents, and it was natural that they would be concerned about it.

"So how did all this come about, Worf?" asked Sergey.

"Well," Worf said, taking a deep breath, "I was on my way back from a *bat'leth* competition on Forcas Three, aboard the shuttlecraft *Curie*. During my return, I passed near a quantum fissure in space, causing a breakdown in the barrier between quantum realities. As a result, I was thrown into a state of flux, passing from one reality to another. In one of those realities, I was married to Deanna. My state of quantum flux resulted in at least two hundred and eighty-five thousand alternate realities merging. Fortunately enough, I was able to use the *Curie* to create a broad-spectrum warp field to seal the quantum fissure and return me to my original reality. As a result of that sequence of events, I began to consider the not unpleasant prospect of Deanna as a mate."

There was a long moment of silence as Sergey and Helena digested that nugget of information.

"Amazing," said Sergey slowly. "Because the exact same thing happened to me and that's how I started dating your mother."

"Sergey . . ."

"What are the odds, I ask you?"

"Sergey!"

"Well, what do you expect me to say?!" Sergey demanded. "Why can't I ever get a nice, normal answer out of him! Other men, they notice the woman's eyes, or they're set up on a blind date, or they meet in some cute way. No, not our son! He has to be in a state of quantum flux! Deanna"—he turned to her pleadingly—"you tell me . . . how did all this come about?"

"I'd say the catalyst was very likely Alexander," said Deanna affectionately, pausing a moment to pat Alexander's smooth hair. "I helped ease the difficulties of Alexander settling into shipboard life, and Worf and I just formed a sort of bond that drew us closer together."

"Now, that's an answer!" Sergey said in relief. "No quantum fluxes, no two hundred thousand realities . . ."

"That is two hundred and eighty-five thousand," Worf reminded him.

"I stand corrected."

"Actually, Deanna is being somewhat tactful," Worf admitted. "I was, in fact, not an especially good father. I have never excelled in . . ." He almost choked on the word and forced it out as if it were a stuck chicken bone. ". . . feelings. But it quickly became apparent that, in order to be a proper father, one should have some reasonable touch for one's feelings."

"No one ever told my father that," muttered Sergey.

His wife gave him an extremely scolding look. "Sergey! You should know better! Speaking ill of the dead . . ."

"Dead is dead. What am I going to do? Hurt his feelings?"

"The point is, as Deanna worked to bring Alexander and myself closer together as father and son, I discovered her continued presence was not displeasing."

"High praise indeed," deadpanned Helena.

"One thing led to another and now . . ." Again, he hesitated.

This time, it was Alexander who stepped in. "They're engaged," he said.

There was stunned silence for a moment. Then a smile split wide Helena's face. *"Wonderful!"* she cried out. She rose quickly from the couch, took Deanna's face in her hands, and kissed either cheek. "I'm so happy for you! Sergey, aren't you happy for them?"

Sergey clearly hadn't quite managed to digest the information. "Engaged? To be married?"

"That is generally how it is done," Worf said.

"That's . . . wonderful," he said slowly. Instead of rising, he slid forward on the couch, extended a hand, and shook Worf's firmly. "Your mother and I could not be happier for you."

"Do you have a date set?" asked Helena.

"Not at the moment. We are waiting for an estimate from Starfleet as to reassignment."

"Oh, Starfleet can go hang," Helena said dismissively. "You make your plans, and let them work around you. You have to prioritize. And it's so sweet that you wanted to tell us in person."

"Yes, very sweet," echoed Sergey.

"And that's why you're heading off to Betazed after this . . . to tell Deanna's mother. I'm sure she'll be as thrilled as I am."

"I'm really looking forward to meeting her," said Sergey.

"No, you are not," Worf said darkly.

"Worf!" Deanna looked at him in surprise. She placed her hands on her hips and looked at him with mild annoyance. "What is that supposed to mean?"

"It simply means that your mother can be . . . daunting."

"Don't you worry about that, Worf," Helena assured him. "I know we'll all get along just fine. Oh, Worf . . ." She sighed. "I never would have said anything about it, and I never would have wanted to pressure you on it . . . but I think this is the best thing for you."

"You do?"

"Absolutely. Alexander could use a . . . well, darling"—and she turned to Alexander—"I don't, for a second, mean to imply that Deanna here, as wonderful as I'm sure she is, could possibly be a replacement for your mother. But a young boy needs positive female influences. I think that's the way it should be. And if your poor mother, God rest her soul, can't be with you, then at least you should have good, solid female role models. Like what I tried to be for you, and what I'm sure Deanna can and will be. A family. A true family." She rustled Deanna's hair affectionately. "I always wanted a daughter. Worf knows I love him, but he knows I always wanted a girl."

"That's why he grew his hair long enough to be a girl's hair," Sergey commented.

Helena's abashed "Sergey!" overlapped with Worf's stern "Father . . . !"

"Well, look how long it is . . ."

"You promised, Sergey—!"

"I promised, I promised. Like it would hurt him to get a haircut?"

Worf turned to Deanna and rumbled, "I retract the sentiment. I think my father and your mother are going to get along quite well."

Will Riker did not even try to stifle the chuckle that rose within him as Deanna related the details of her get-together with the Rozhenkos. The apartment he was residing in had been provided him by Starfleet during his stay in San Francisco. It was not particularly elaborate in its furnishings, but Riker wasn't really looking for much beyond functional, so he was content. Outside his window, the lights of the Golden Gate Bridge glittered in the evening air in what Riker could only think of as a pathetic imitation of the stars. "A haircut, huh."

"It was rather amusing."

"And you leave for Betazed tomorrow?"

"That's right." She nodded. "His mother seemed determined to teach me how to cook every single one of Worf's favorite dishes when he was growing up. Then later, Worf told me not to be concerned about it; that in point of fact, he never really liked anything his mother made. It wasn't her fault; how could she be expected to start turning out food suitable for Klingon taste?"

"And he never said anything to her?"

"Not to this day. Worf can be rather stoic."

"Yes, I've noticed."

"And the hearing?" Deanna asked. Riker knew her well enough to know that she was clearly worried about it, but was trying to act as if she weren't. "I know you said you weren't concerned about it, Will, but we can still come back. . . ."

He shrugged. "Well, Admiral Jellico is going to be running it. . . ."

"Jellico." She made no effort to hide the distaste in her expression. "Talk about bad luck of the draw."

"No, actually the captain and I expected it. If there was anyone who was going to be drawn to the scent of blood in the water, it would be Jellico. But even though he's chairing the hearing, he's only one of three ranking officers who will be overseeing the investigation. Truly, I don't think there's going to be any problems, and even if there were, there's nothing that you and Worf being there would contribute. We have the ship's log, which we salvaged from the crash, we have Geordi to discuss the technical aspects of the meltdown . . . it'll be fine, Deanna."

The door to Riker's apartment chimed. "Hold on a moment," he said to Deanna on the screen, and then he turned and called, "Come."

The door hissed open and Picard was standing there. It was a sign of the captain's strict adherence to decorum that he remained at the threshold, not presuming to enter. "Will, do you have a moment?"

"Absolutely, sir." Riker half rose from his chair in acknowledgment and then sat again as Picard nodded and walked in. Both Riker and Picard were wearing off-duty civilian clothes. For Riker, it felt as if they were both in pajamas. "Just talking with Deanna."

"Counselor." Picard inclined his head in greeting.

"Oh, Captain . . . there was something that Worf and I had wanted to ask you. This is as good a time as any, I suppose."

Picard nodded, smiling and waiting.

"We were wondering—that is, Worf and I were wondering—if, when we do marry, you would perform the ceremony . . . ideally on whatever the new ship they assign us to is."

For some reason, Picard found himself casting a glance in Riker's direction. But Riker was simply beaming, like a proud father, not seeming the least bit perturbed by the concept. Picard wasn't entirely sure why he had suddenly chosen to look at Riker at that moment. It had been something instinctive. Quickly he looked back to the screen, hoping that his shift in gaze had been so swift that she hadn't even noticed. "Of course, Counselor," he said. "I'd be honored."

"Thank you, Captain. I'll tell Worf. He'll be ecstatic."

"An ecstatic Worf. Now, there's something that's tough to picture."

They chatted for a few more moments, Deanna repeating much of what she had told Riker for Picard's benefit, and Picard being likewise amused by the image of Worf being castigated by his father for the length of his hair. Finally they signed off and Riker turned to face Picard. "What can I do for you, Captain?" he asked.

"Well . . . I had come to chat with you about what we can expect in terms of questions from the admirals named to the panel. I know there's no love lost between you and Jellico, but I wanted to go into more detail with you about admirals Gray and

Trebor. Still, I was wondering if there was something you might wish to discuss first."

"Discuss, sir?" asked Riker, his head inclined slightly and showing polite puzzlement.

"Will . . ." Picard cleared his throat and then smiled in an avuncular manner. "Will . . . I may be many things, but I am most definitely not a fool. Worf and Deanna's engagement . . . their request for me to perform the ceremony . . . it must be having an effect on you."

"It's flattering to know that everyone is concerned about me . . ." began Riker.

"Everyone?"

"Well . . . Geordi and I had a discussion," Riker admitted. "But I'll tell you the same thing I told him: Deanna and I had our chance together. We chose to remain simply good friends. And if she is going to be happy with Worf, then I'm happy for her. There's really nothing more to it than that."

"There always is." Picard paused a moment, and then said with a smile, "Did I ever tell you about Maggie?"

"Maggie, sir?"

"She and I went to the Academy together. I thought nothing could possibly distract me from my goals and career, but when Maggie and I saw each other . . . it was like lightning just connecting the two of us. My feelings for her made any previous relationship pale in comparison. It was as if they had been mere dalliances before her. The universe of possibilities which represented my future suddenly seemed to expand to include one more that had never been there before. And she felt the same way about me, I know it. For each of us, we were the first to touch each other's souls."

"Imzadi," Riker said softly.

"Pardon?"

"Nothing. Sorry to interrupt. You were saying . . . ?"

"Yes, well . . . Maggie and I made plans. We were going to serve together, we were going to be together always. We were willing to put aside our egos: If one of us became captain first, the other would willingly serve as first officer. It seemed that nothing could keep us apart, such was the intensity of our dedication for each other." He paused and then sighed. "But something did happen."

"What was that, sir?"

"Life, Will." He smiled. "Life. You plan for things, try to grab hold of your destiny and conform it to your desires, but you never quite manage to get a firm grasp on it. It always manages to slip away from you."

"Meaning no disrespect, sir . . ."

"Will, we're not in my ready room or on the bridge of a starship. It's just you and me, in an apartment on Earth. State your mind."

"Well, sir . . . what's the point you're trying to make?"

"The point is, you never stop trying. Resign yourself to the fact that you cannot control fate, but don't resign yourself to fate itself. Never stop fighting, never stop trying."

"And you think that's what I did with Deanna."

"I believe so, yes. It's what I did with Maggie. And I regret it to this day. Regrets are a terrible thing to have, Will. A terrible thing."

It was something that Riker knew all too well, for he had stared squarely into the face of regret. There had been a time when an incarnation of Riker from the future had used the Guardian of Forever to come back in time. In that Riker's reality, Deanna Troi had died forty years previously, and he had never gotten over it. Eventually he had come to the conclusion that Deanna had been murdered and, using the Guardian, had come back in time to try and avert that calamity. Riker had come face-to-face with his future self, and had never forgotten the look of torment in his eyes. "I'm your future without her, buddy boy," the Riker-to-come had growled at him, and it had been a truly frightening sight to behold. It wasn't the gray hair and gray beard, or even the wrinkles that Riker had found so daunting in his future incarnation. It was instead the sheer, burning fury in the eyes of a man who carried with him hatred for, quite possibly, the entire universe, for depriving him of the future that he clearly felt was his by right.

The immediate goal had been accomplished that time. Deanna's life had been saved, and ideally Admiral Riker had returned to a future more to his liking. But whether Riker and Deanna were going to wind up a couple was left unresolved. If there was anything worse than knowing one's future, it was knowing what it might be and not being sure how to attend to it.

"A terrible thing," echoed Riker. But then he brought himself to full attention and said firmly, "Captain, it's not the same thing. I simply know that I'm just not capable of giving Deanna the things she wants or needs."

"Really." Picard shook his head. "Will, do you know what your problem is?"

"No, sir, but I suspect you're about to tell me."

"Your problem is that if you are convinced that something can be done, then you will find a way to do it. You are unstoppable in that regard. By the same token, if you decide that something cannot be done, then nothing on heaven or Earth will get you to do it. You are governed entirely by self-fulfilling prophecy."

"Captain . . . I'm not alone in this matter. Deanna feels the same way that I do. She wants to remain simply friends. How am I supposed to conjure up feelings within her that she doesn't possess? Through sheer force of will?"

"Well, that *is* your name."

At that, Riker laughed. "You've got me there, Captain. But what would you have me do, sir? After the hearing, would you have me jump the first transport to Betazed? Burst in on them at Lwaxana Troi's house, tell Deanna that we should be a couple . . . ?"

"Is that how you feel?"

"No!"

"Then I suppose this entire conversation is moot," Picard observed.

"That's right, sir."

"All right, then. I beg your pardon for bringing it up."

"Don't worry about it, sir." With slow strides, Riker went to the window and leaned against it, looking out once more at the bridge. "By the way . . . whatever happened to Maggie? Do you ever see her?"

"From time to time. I'm seeing her tomorrow, as a matter of fact."

Riker turned and looked at him with raised eyebrow. "A date?"

"In a manner of speaking. She's one of the three admirals at the inquiry tomorrow."

Riker rubbed the bridge of his nose with his thumb and forefinger as if suddenly in great pain. "Just out of morbid curiosity, sir, and not wanting to pry: Who precisely broke it off with whom?"

"I say I did, she says she did."

"A request, then: For the duration of the investigation, can we go with her interpretation?"

"You read my mind, Number One. You read my mind."

There was a small porch in the back of the Rozhenkos' farmhouse. It was a chill night, and as a barechested Worf stood on the porch and gazed up at the full moon, his nostrils flared ever so slightly. He leaned on the porch railing, gripping it firmly, apparently oblivious to the crispness in the air.

"Nice night, isn't it."

Worf had heard him coming, but since his approach was silent, Worf had not said anything just in case his father had wanted his presence not to be known. "Lovely night, Father," Worf replied.

"Having trouble sleeping?"

"I simply find the night . . . alluring," Worf said. He took in the air deeply, his muscles stretching tautly over his rib cage. "I did not realize how much I had missed it."

Sergey was wearing a robe over his pajamas as he sauntered over to his son's side. "Do you remember the night you went hunting?" he asked.

Worf turned and looked at him with a puzzled expression. "Hunting . . . ?"

"One night, early on . . . back when we had the farm on Gault, when you first came to us . . . you came outside on a night much like this one, stripped off your clothes, and barreled off into the darkness. When we finally found you the next day, you were curled up in the woods. You were shivering slightly, you had a contented smile on your face . . . and there was blood encrusted on the edges of your mouth."

Worf shook his head. "I seem to have . . . vague recollections of it at most."

"Word spread rather quickly. It's somewhat difficult to cover up such a thing. The neighbors protested; they were afraid of you. It was a very difficult time for us. Very difficult."

"I do not think I appreciated the hardship on you at the time. Perhaps to this day I cannot fully appreciate it." He hesitated a moment and then asked, "Do you . . . regret it?"

Worf was mildly disconcerted when Sergey didn't answer immediately. When he did reply, it was in a rather roundabout manner.

"You have to understand the difference between your mother and me," Sergey began. "When I found you on Khitomer, battered and pathetic under that pile of rubble . . . my decision to bring you back to Gault, to adopt you, was made on the spur of the moment. That's the way I am. I don't think things out the way I should. I act on impulse . . . which is appropriate for a warp-field specialist, no?" He laughed at his own joke, but when he saw that Worf wasn't likewise laughing, he trailed off and cleared his throat. "Now, your mother . . . she was always the rational one. I told her about you, and she said, 'Sergey, do you have any idea what you're getting us into? Do you?' "

"Are you saying . . . she did not want me?" Worf asked slowly.

"Of course she wanted you. That's not the point. She wanted you . . . but she was fully aware of the consequences of our actions. She's very methodical, very reasonable. She thinks out everything and makes her choices based on what seems to be the most sensible course of action."

"Father . . . I do not mean to sound impertinent . . . but why are you telling me this?"

"Because you take after her in many ways. You have enough impulsiveness as it is from your Klingon heritage. But from your mother, you learned how to size up a situation, to make a reasoned choice. She taught you how to act from your brain instead of your heart. You see what I'm getting at?"

Worf nodded, then stopped. "No," he admitted.

Sergey had been looking out at the night, but now he turned to face his son. "This girl, she seems lovely. Intelligent, smart, calm. Your mother adores her, I can tell you that."

"And you do not?"

"I think she's great! I just . . ." He gestured vaguely. "When I pictured the type of woman I thought you'd wind up with, somehow she was never what I was expecting. No offense."

"None taken. You are not the first person to make that observation, Father. We are . . . opposites . . . in many ways. On the other hand, it certainly gives us a good deal to talk about."

Sergey grunted noncommittally. "Worf . . . why are you marrying this girl?"

"She has a name, Father. I would appreciate if you used it."

Unperturbed at the mild rebuke from his son, Sergey said, "Why are you marrying Deanna?"

"Because . . . she completes me, Father. She is a valuable addition. She integrates smoothly into the framework of the unit."

"Son, you make her sound like a warp coil. Or a weapon. Do you love this gir—Deanna?"

"Would I be marrying her if I did not?"

"Worf . . ." He paused, trying to find the words. "Worf . . . in the old days, in the very old days . . . matches weren't made from love. They were put together by a matchmaker, and any one of a dozen reasons might be deemed reasonable for making a match. It came from here," and he tapped his head, "and not from here," and he touched his heart.

"Father, we are discussing a decision that relates to the entirety of one's life. It should come from both sources, should it not?"

"I just . . ."

"Father," and he folded his arms in what could best be described as a defensive posture. "I love Deanna. If I did not, I would not marry her, despite all the other 'logical' reasons to do so. I did not come here seeking your blessing. However, I would be most appreciative if I received it."

Sergey looked into the eyes of his adopted son. So many times, he had found those cold eyes unreadable. Life among humans had never been easy, and Worf had been hurt time and again . . . first by the natural cruelty of children, and then by the far more insidious cruelty of adults who feared the burly Klingon as if he were a walking pile of explosives in their midst. But Worf would have considered it the height of humiliation to let any of that pain show through, and he became very adept at hiding it.

This time, though, Worf had let his guard down ever so slightly. It was all there in his eyes, the need for his father's approval. When Worf had taken on the formidable challenge of being the first Klingon in Starfleet, he had done so partly to emulate

Sergey. In taking on a wife, and endeavoring to do right by his child, Sergey realized that Worf was once more following Sergey's example, albeit perhaps unconsciously.

Sergey had reservations, serious reservations. It was Worf's life, however, and Worf wasn't asking for his opinion on Deanna (a lovely girl) or on how it would affect Alexander (he clearly was happy with her) or . . .

The more Sergey thought about it, the more it seemed to make sense. His instinct, upon which he had operated for so many years, told him that it was a mistake. That they were simply *too* different. But Sergey was hardly the expert on affairs of the heart. After all, he hadn't had to make decisions regarding a mate in nearly half a century, so it wasn't as if he were in practice.

His son needed him. That was the bottom line. His son needed the approval of his father, and he had no earthly reason to withhold it.

"Of course you have my blessing, Worf," he said. "You know that. Mine, and your mother's. I didn't want you think that I . . ."

"It is all right, Father." And then, to Sergey's surprise, the edges of Worf's mouth began to twitch. Slowly they pulled taut and then up, and Worf presented that rarest of phenomena: his smile. Not the feral cross between a grin and snarl that sometimes adorned his face when combat beckoned. This was a sincere, almost human smile. "I know that we are an unusual match, and I know that you have my best interests at heart."

"I'm relieved that you understand, Worf." He shivered slightly in the cold air. "Come, son. Getting a little cold for these old bones. How about if we go inside and I make you some warm milk, the way I used to."

"Father . . . you never made me warm milk."

"Never?"

Worf cast his thoughts back. "You did, however, give me vodka from time to time."

"Well, then . . ." He clapped his son on the shoulder. "Let's see what we can do to accommodate you. You have the vodka, I'll have the milk. Somehow, I think, that's appropriate."

Six

"Kill him."

The first syllable was barely out of the female Romulan's mouth when Tom Riker moved.

As tired as he was, as exhausted as he was, it didn't slow him in the slightest as he lunged before any of the Romulan guards could fire at him. The one thing he had going for him was that they were in relatively confined quarters. They couldn't all simply start shooting, since they would be as likely to hit one another as him. It was the only advantage he had going for him, and it really wasn't all that much of one. That alone was discouraging enough, but he wasn't about to let it slow him down.

It was a valiant effort. His initial charge took him into the midsection of the nearest Romulan, who let out a gasp of air as he staggered back, carried by Riker's weight and sheer manic energy. The woman blinked in surprise, as if amazed over the pure bravado and yet utter futility in which Riker indulged during what were certain to be his last moments. Riker shoved the Romulan guard away and lashed out with one foot to the crotch of the nearest standing Romulan. The guard doubled over, and for just the slightest of moments Riker actually seemed as if he might have a chance. A chance of what, exactly, he wasn't completely sure. He had no idea where to run, no clue to whom he could turn to garner an ally. But first thing was most definitely first: If he didn't get out of there and survive, he didn't have a hope in hell.

A sudden movement from one guard caught his eye. He turned to deal with the immediate threat, and as a consequence didn't see the butt of the Romulan disruptor that was being brought down with customary Romulan fierceness on his skull. Stars exploded behind his eyes, and Riker sank to one knee. He reached out as if trying to find an invisible support on which he could haul himself up. A second blow to the head finished off any hope of that avenue as Riker slid to the floor. He felt a wave of nausea gripping him. He now had a new plan: He wanted to live long enough to vomit onto someone's boots. That seemed all that he was capable of at that moment, but at least it had the merit of making a political statement.

That was when a loud, stern voice said, "Leave him alone!"

Riker couldn't quite believe the origin of the voice. In fighting through the haze that descended around his skull, he was able to see that the female Romulan was likewise surprised. She was looking at Saket, who had been about to leave when the scuffle in the transporter room broke out.

"Leave him alone," Saket repeated, every word clearly an effort. "He . . . saved my life, Sela. I owe him. So do you. If not for him, your rescue would have been in vain."

"But . . ."

"Don't 'but' me, Sela. I've known you too long. I knew your mother and she . . ."

Then Saket's knees began to buckle under him completely. The Romulans who were supporting him were frozen in place, clearly uncertain of what to do. "Get him out of here, now!" the woman whom he had called "Sela" ordered. Saket was promptly hauled away, faint protests still audible from his lips.

Riker didn't see any of it, because he was on his hands and knees, the world still whirling around him. A pair of booted feet slowly stepped into his narrow view of his environment, and he wondered if these were going to be the lucky boots onto which he was going to be heaving.

"What are you doing here, Riker?"

The angry and contemptuous question cut straight through him.

She knows me? Riker thought wonderingly, and then instantly it became clear to him. She knew Will Riker, his counterpart and identical twin. From the tone of voice, she'd had dealings with him that had not gone especially well for her. The logical thing to do would be to tell her that he was, in fact, not Will Riker at all, but rather Tom Riker. Tom Riker . . .

. . . Will Riker's identical and genetically impossible-to-differentiate twin created by a one-in-a-million transporter accident.

Oh yeah. That was going to fly.

That was exactly the thing to do when surrounded by a hostile enemy—put forward a preposterous story that would very likely be greeted with utter contempt. He could hear the reaction in his mind: *You expect us to believe that? Are you insane? What sort of fools do you take us for?* And that would immediately be followed by more kicking, more beatings, his head caved in and him, Riker, reduced to a state where he was either too pathetic to bother keeping alive, or such a mess that death would be preferable and they wouldn't oblige him just to be bastards.

But he didn't know what else to say.

So he said nothing. He just crouched there on the floor, trying to battle through the wave of nausea sweeping over him without succumbing to it.

"The strong, silent type. How very typical," said Sela. She hesitated a moment, weighing his fate, and then said briskly, "Lock him up. We'll deal with him later."

Well, that was certainly an improvement over "Kill him." He hadn't vomited, and he was about to be held prisoner by the Romulans, whose treatment of prisoners was legendary for its cruelty.

It looked like this was turning out to be his lucky day.

Sela stood by Saket's side, holding his hand tightly as the older Romulan lay on the table in medical. The Romulan medical facilities were not terrific to start with; the basic philosophy of the Romulans was survival of the fittest, and those who were too injured to survive were generally allowed to die as a matter of course. But Saket's was a very different situation, at least as far as Sela was concerned. She looked to the medical officer, who simply shook his head. There wasn't a damned thing that he could do. The damage was too extensive. By rights, Saket truly had no business being alive in the first place.

"I saw you flying that fighter," Saket whispered. Despite her keen hearing, Sela still had to lean forward to hear everything he was saying. "It was you, wasn't it."

"I wouldn't let anyone else handle it," Sela said. "My people all said I was crazy."

"You are. I have always known that about you. Sometimes I think that was my main contribution to your teachings." He coughed more and more violently, and then seemed to pull himself together through sheer force of will.

"Lie still, Saket . . ."

"And die . . . quietly . . . ? No . . ." He shook his head.

"Saket . . . where did you hide it?" she asked. "Tell me where. Do you have it on you? Is it back on Lazon Two?"

Saket didn't seem to hear her. Instead his mind was elsewhere. "Riker . . . he is a good man . . . to have on your side . . . I was . . . cultivating him for you . . . knew you'd come for me . . . he is . . . my final legacy . . . to you . . ."

"Use him how?" demanded Sela. "For the plan? We needed . . . need . . . you. We don't need him. . . ."

"No . . . we don't . . . but think how much . . . more effective . . ."

Slowly the truth of what he was saying began to dawn on her. "Yes . . . yes, it would be, wouldn't it . . ."

"You begin to see . . . always were . . . a quick pupil . . . you and Riker . . . good . . . good team . . . good couple . . ."

Despite the seriousness of the situation, Sela had to stifle an urge to laugh. "Good *couple?* Little late in your life to start a new career as matchmaker, wouldn't you say, Saket?"

Saket said nothing.

She called his name again, shook him slightly. Even as she did, though, she knew. Knew beyond any question that he was gone.

Sentiment began to wash over her, like a tide choked with pollutants. She shoved the feelings away. They were anathema to her; she had no time for them.

"He didn't tell us where it was," said the medical officer, a heavyset Romulan named Tok. "He was in too much pain . . . he could not focus on what was important."

"Either that," Sela said thoughtfully, "or he was certain we could find it without his help, and wanted to use his remaining strength to deal with other matters . . ."

"Such as Riker?"

"Such as, yes." She turned on her heel and headed for the exit.

"What about Saket?" asked Tok.

"Run a complete sensor sweep over him. Take him apart organ by organ, if you have to. If the sample is on him . . . I want it."

With that, Sela took her leave of the medical facility, leaving Tok to his work.

As she headed down the corridor, she walked rigidly, looking neither left nor right, as if she had no care for anyone around her. Outwardly she exuded complete calm and control. Inwardly she was a raging torrent. Saket was gone. The sample was still missing. And she had Will Riker in her possession.

What was she going to do with him?

That was something she was going to have to determine, and the little chat she was about to have with him would help her decide one way or the other.

Three times Riker had endeavored to sit up and each time the nausea had hit him. But the fourth time he had actually managed to pull himself together sufficiently to sit up without any ill effects. "And now, for my next trick . . ." he had muttered before steeling himself sufficiently to stand up. This he managed to do, leaning against the stark metal wall, drawing in a few deep breaths, and finally walking slowly around the perimeter of the Romulan lockup. It didn't take long to get the feeling for his surroundings: Six steps in any direction pretty much covered it. There was a hard-surfaced, horizontal board which served as the only piece of furniture in the place—couch and bed, all rolled into one. If he needed to relieve himself, or vomit up some of the unpalatable food they gave him, he was escorted under armed guard to a facility down the hall and then promptly brought back. That was the entirety of his existence.

There was a forcefield, naturally, barring his exit, and a guard firmly in place. The guard wasn't even deigning to look in Riker's direction, which was more or less fine with Riker. It wasn't as if he was feeling particularly chatty at that moment anyway.

He heard brisk footsteps coming his way, and wondered whether this was going to be the Romulan execution squad or whoever it was that was going to be sent to finish him off. Or perhaps they would torture him first for information. Now, wouldn't that be a little slice of heaven.

Tom reasoned that the window of opportunity had closed for him to inform his captors of who he truly was . . . although he still had serious doubts that such an endeavor would have met with the slightest bit of success. The Romulans were a prickly people, and they were just as likely to think that he was trying to make fools of them as anything else. Besides, the one chance he might have for survival was if they thought he knew more than he did, or was of more value than he truly was.

There was also the question of ransom. It was entirely possible that they might try to barter something in exchange for him, operating under the belief that they had in their possession the legendary Commander William Riker. Will Riker might indeed be a useful bargaining chip. Tom Riker, on the other hand, was useless.

That was a hard fact for Tom to deal with, but there it was. Tom Riker was someone whose capture and possible death in captivity was of no weight to anyone. He was already a disgraced traitor. Who in Starfleet would possibly put themselves on the line for him? He was a freak of nature, a transporter malfunction with a soul . . . someone else's soul. He had nothing. No freedom, no honor, not even the single most fundamental property possessed by every living being, sentient or otherwise, in the known galaxy: uniqueness. Out there, roaming free in the galaxy, was someone who was in every way identical, except when it came to career and regard by his peers; in those matters, he was far superior.

And Tom Riker, in trying to carve out his own niche in the galaxy, had paid for it dearly. Life in a Cardassian labor camp, and that was under a sentence that had been commuted.

Better that they had killed me, he thought bleakly.

It was while he was in this dark mood that Sela came to him.

She stood on the other side of the forcefield, regarding him for a moment as he sat on his uncomfortable piece of furniture. Then she nodded to the guard, who deactivated the forcefield. She stepped through, stood there with her arms folded, and waited.

Tom said nothing.

Nor did Sela.

They stood there in that way, in silence, for ten minutes. Then Sela turned on her heel and walked out without so much as a word having been exchanged.

The same thing happened the next day, the exact same thing happened, except this time it was for twenty minutes.

The day after that, thirty.

Still there was not a word spoken between the two of them. It had become an almost perverse test of will. She would stand there, and he would sit on the bed/seat, and that would be the extent of their interaction. If they had been telepaths, it might have made some sense. As it was, even the guard seemed mystified. Every time Sela departed the cell, he would look at her questioningly, but she didn't even return his glance.

During the third visit, as Sela was preparing to leave, Tom decided to amuse himself. Just as she began to turn away, Riker winked at her. She looked back at him, but his face was impassive once more. Not so much as a crack in the stone-faced façade that he had carefully crafted for himself. She hesitated ever so briefly, and then walked out once more.

When she came back the fourth time, it was with a proposal.

"We found it."

Truthfully, it had not taken Tok all that long. He had found it within twelve hours after beginning the autopsy, and he was mentally kicking himself for it having taken as long as it did.

Pieces of Saket lay scattered about the autopsy room, but Sela's attention was upon the eye that stared up (unblinkingly, of course) at her. "His left eye, to be precise," said Tok proudly. "It was a phenomenal construct, fabricated from actual living tissue. Designed to elude detection by even the most advanced of techniques. Fully functional, and indistinguishable from his living eye. You'd never know which one was the fake."

"In his eye," Sela said wonderingly.

Tok nodded eagerly and, using his medical tools, gently turned the eye over. Using a scalpel, he set the harmonics within to vibrate at a certain frequency that was apparently encoded into the eye's microcircuitry. Within moments there was a very soft, barely audible "click" and then the back of the eye opened. Ever so delicately, Tok removed a chip which glistened silver, except for one area which was dark blue.

"Is that it?" asked Sela. She tried to keep her voice calm and neutral, but there was clear excitement in her tone.

"I believe so. Yes . . . definitely. The circuitry of the chip keeps the chemical sample in a sort of stasis: inert and harmless."

"He did it." There was envy and awe in her voice. She looked in the direction of his heart, which sat by itself on a silver tray. "Saket, you old bastard, you actually did it. You found it. I didn't think it was possible . . . but if anyone could do it, you could." She considered eating the heart out of a sense of respect to Saket, but decided that it probably wasn't the appropriate time for such actions.

She cast a glance over her shoulder as if somehow she could actually see the Cardassians, their homeworld or their prison, from the Romulan warbird's medical facility. "How long will it take you to synthesize it?" she asked Tok without looking at him. "Synthesize it . . . and test it."

"I have no way to know, Sela," Tok said apologetically. "There are simply too many unknowns. Since I don't know what the compound consists of, I cannot say for sure what will be required to synthesize it . . . and whether it works or not has to be completely computer simulated. Unless, of course," he added, "you're volunteering to test it yourself."

"Don't be snide, Tok, unless you'd like me to pick you as someone upon whom we can try it . . . out . . ."

Her voice trailed off as she looked thoughtfully into the air.

Sela was oftentimes a mystery for Tok, but this time he thought he had an idea what she was thinking about. "Riker?" he guessed. "You're thinking that we test it on Riker?"

She glared at him in a way that indicated he had totally missed, once again, what she was considering. "You think too small, Tok. No, we're not going to test it on Riker. That would be an extraordinary waste of material. Take the time you need, Tok. We're in no hurry. No one is going anywhere. As for Riker . . . I have other thoughts in regards to him."

She had found him a most curious case. When she had first walked up to him while he was in captivity, she had had no idea that they were going to have so much difficulty just getting beyond initial contact. But somehow she had just expected that Riker was going to commence the festivities. That he was going to threaten, or cajole, or plead, or bluster . . . something, anything that would be oh-so-typical for the arrogant second-in-command of the *Enterprise.*

Instead there was nothing. Perhaps he was trying to show her that he held her in such disdain that he had no desire to talk to her . . . or else it was a massive show of bravado . . . or else he really just didn't give a damn. All of those options seemed rife with their own possibilities.

But she realized she wasn't going to get anywhere if matters continued as they were. So she was going to have to do something to move them to the next level, since it was becoming obvious that Riker wasn't about to.

* * *

"Saket is dead . . . in case you were wondering."

He almost jumped when she spoke, since it was the first time she had done so. But he very quickly regained his outward impassiveness.

"I was wondering, yes. Thank you for telling me." He paused and then added matter-of-factly, "I considered him a friend. My condolences to you, for whatever your relationship may have been to him."

"So how did you wind up there?"

"There? Where?"

"In a Cardassian labor camp, fool," Sela said testily. She was leaning in what appeared to be a leisurely fashion against one of the walls of Riker's cell. But Riker had the feeling that she was, in fact, battle-ready. If he made the slightest wrong move, she'd be ready to take him apart. At least, she probably presumed she could. Whether she really would be able to accomplish that feat was another matter, although considering Riker's condition after all these months, he wouldn't have wanted to bet against her.

He also noticed another Romulan standing in the corridor in a manner that was clearly supposed to suggest that he had no particular reason for being there. He was taller than the average Romulan, with a high forehead and uncommonly dark eyes that swam against a rather pale face. When the Romulan appeared to notice that he had caught Riker's attention, he moved off slightly to remove himself from Riker's field of vision, but Riker was certain he was still there. And whoever this Romulan was, not for a moment did Riker buy that he was there purely by happenstance. Romulans were far too methodical a people. Every word out of their mouths was carefully measured, and every action they took was done with meticulous planning. The pasty-faced Romulan hadn't been there before, and now he was. There was definitely a purpose for it.

Curiously, Riker was surprised to find that he didn't give too much a damn about what it was. Sela was the one to watch out for. To that end, he focused his thoughts purely on the conversation at hand, not letting himself wander off into mental byways. It was not difficult for him to do. Many years ago, Deanna had spent long hours teaching him the mental discipline that the Betazoids had honed to such a fine art. Riker was hardly a telepath, although he was able to communicate with Troi mentally when the circumstances were right . . . and even then it was a haphazard proposition. However, Riker's mental focus was second to none; when he was zeroed in on something, nothing could distract him. There was no way he was going to allow Sela to trick him into revealing something that he didn't want her to know. The trick was to be guarded, so the wrong thing didn't get said, but not to appear as if he were being guarded so that Sela wouldn't suspect if he was being less than candid.

"I was on a mission," Riker said. "A mission that would have been a major strike at the Cardassians."

"On behalf of Starfleet and the Federation?" she asked.

He tried to sound grimly humorous. "Let's just say they didn't disapprove." That much was true. At the time that Tom Riker had switched his allegiance to the Maquis—the underground terrorist group that had declared a private war on the Cardassians in defiance of Federation treaties—Starfleet had no awareness that he was not at his new post on the *Starship Gandhi.* Therefore, of course, they did not disapprove.

Sela nodded slowly. "Ah. Let me guess: Good luck to you, Riker, and if it doesn't go well, don't expect us to help you."

He said nothing. He figured it would benefit him more to keep his mouth shut and allow Sela to put forward the suppositions. That was even easier than trying to be careful with what he said.

"And the Cardassians caught you at it."

"That they did."

"And the Federation did nothing to help you?"

"That they did not."

"But of course," said Sela, walking with an odd little swagger, "if you had it to do over, you'd do the exact same thing. Because you are dedicated to your beloved Starfleet, aren't you, Riker?"

"Isn't this the point where you're supposed to be shining hot lights on me and breaking down my loyalty?"

She considered his level gaze, and a small smile actually played along the corners of her mouth. "Is that what you want me to do?"

Once more he said nothing.

"Is that what it would take," she continued, "to sever your allegiance to Starfleet?"

He'd known a question such as this one would likely be coming. He didn't hesitate, instead speaking with calm, deliberate candor. "The truth is," he said slowly, "that I've had time to reflect a good deal on my life. And if I had it to do over again . . . there's a lot I'd do differently."

"Really. Anything having to do with . . . oh . . . Deanna?"

This seemingly innocuous, offhand comment caught Riker momentarily offguard. Tom looked up at her, startled. He made no attempt to hide his confusion. "How did you know . . . ?"

"You talk in your sleep. Did no one ever tell you that? Two nights ago during your stay here, you murmured the name 'Deanna.' Muttered it somewhat; we had a bit of trouble understanding you at first. Would that be Deanna Troi, by any chance?"

This time he didn't ask how she knew, even in an abortive way. But she supplied the answer anyway: "One should always have a basic knowledge of who one's enemies are. She caused quite a bit of embarrassment to our intelligence service, the Tal Shiar. We captured a dissident not too long ago and he told us a number of tales in hopes of his life being spared. One of them was of one Deanna Troi of the *Starship Enterprise*—your vessel, as I recall—who passed herself off as a member of the Tal Shiar and helped M'ret and several top aides to escape their alleged persecution at the hands of our government. Oh yes, Deanna Troi made quite an impression on us, I assure you. So"—and she folded her arms and regarded him in an amused, even faintly smug manner—"are you enamored of her? Is that the case? Your concerns about her—"

"Are my concerns alone," Riker said sharply . . . so sharply, in fact, that the guard outside the door automatically took a defensive stance as if he was expecting trouble. Riker reined himself in and then said with impressive calm, "She wasn't what I was referring to."

"What, then?"

This was it. He took a deep breath and said, "I owe nothing to Starfleet. I've had to watch others no more deserving than I get all the breaks in life, while I was treated as if I was nothing special. I've been dealt one lousy hand after another, and if I never have anything to do with Starfleet again, I really couldn't give a damn."

He had said it all in one breath, as if he couldn't wait to get it out of his system. When he stopped speaking he simply glared at her for a few moments. "Is that what you wanted to hear?" he finally asked her.

"I wanted to hear the truth."

"You did."

She walked toward him with that same swagger that she effected so well. With each step she would hesitate just a moment before placing her foot down, as if trying to sense whether there might be a mine or some such device planted in the floor. "Are you saying . . . that you would not be opposed to a bit of payback to the Federation? That you feel as if you owe them nothing?"

"Oh, I know I owe them nothing. If there's one thing I've learned, it's that I have to make my own way in this galaxy. I have to be my own man, whatever it takes, and I certainly can't be that if I stick with Starfleet."

She nodded, looking quite noncommittal. He wondered what was going through her head, but she was inscrutable.

"And if you could strike back at Starfleet," she said abruptly, "and at the Federation by doing something that would hurt their interests . . . would you?"

"Depends," he said.

"Mmm." She nodded again, but this time she looked approving. "Good response. If you had simply said 'Yes,' I would know that you are lying, or desperate to say anything in order to endear yourself to me, regardless of its veracity. You are a man of annoyingly deep-rooted morality, Riker, that much I know. Most of your ilk are, even the disaffected ones such as yourself. Do you know what the parameters of those 'depends' might be?"

"I couldn't say for sure. I suppose I'd know it when I saw it."

"Would you draw the line at killing?"

He didn't hesitate in his response. "I've killed when I had to. I'd kill again. If I'd had my way, the mission that landed me in prison would have resulted in a hell of a lot of dead Cardassians had I managed to accomplish that."

"Could you kill Picard?"

For some reason, Riker rose from his "couch," as if the mere mention of Picard required that he stand at something vaguely approximating attention. "If I had to," he said after a moment. "I'd rather not . . . he see . . . he's a decent enough man." Mentally he kicked himself, since he'd almost slipped by saying, "He seems a decent enough man." Phrasing such as that might very well have tipped her off, or at least given her suspicions. Recovering quickly, he added, "I don't feel any overwhelming loyalty to him. Sometimes I feel as if I hardly know the man."

She seemed to take all this in. And then, without a word, she turned and walked out. As she passed the guard, she nodded slightly and he activated the forcefield once more.

Riker sat back down on his uncomfortable couch. Well, that had gone about as well as could be expected.

Sela was up to something, of that much he was certain. Saket had spoken any number of times of his favorite student, his greatest pupil, but he'd never mentioned her name. Riker chalked that up to discretion that was practically ground into Saket. But he'd certainly described this mystery pupil in sufficient detail that

Riker felt as if he knew her. It had since become clear to Riker that this Sela was that pupil, and more, that Sela had had dealings with Picard, Will Riker, and the *Enterprise.*

Furthermore, he was positive that she would not have staged the breakout if she hadn't had some sort of plan in place. And if that was the case, then it was imperative that Tom Riker get himself involved in it. Of course, if it was an attack or plan that was aimed at the Cardassians, he would zealously participate with a clear conscience. On the other hand, if it was indeed a mission that was directed at the Federation, then he would have to do everything he could to stop it.

Wouldn't he?

That dark thought crossed his mind for the briefest of moments, and then Tom Riker brushed it away with determination. Of course he would stop it if it was going to harm Starfleet or the Federation in some way. There was no question about it.

And he spent the rest of the day, and well into the night, convincing himself of that.

Sela sat in her quarters, drumming her fingers impatiently on her desk. Then there was a chime at her door. "Come," she said.

The door hissed open and the tall, rather pale Romulan who had been hovering in the corridor outside the lockup entered. He inclined his head slightly in greeting. Sela, for her part, did not seem particularly interested in cordialities. "Well?" she asked.

The Romulan she was addressing was named Kressn, and he was an empath.

It was a matter of some curiosity that Romulans, an offshoot race of the Vulcans, possessed none of the formidable mind powers that their parent race displayed with such facility. No one was entirely certain why that should be the case. Some felt it a matter of mere genetics, but that did not seem a satisfactory answer. For others it came down more to a matter of societal upbringing.

In their distant past, the Vulcans had been a bloodthirsty, savage, and warlike race. While the Vulcans, in order to save themselves lest they obliterate their entire race through endless bloodshed, had transformed themselves into paragons of logic, the Romulans had taken another direction entirely. They retained much of the aggressiveness and desire for conquest that had nearly brought their forebears to utter ruin. Since they had never become what anyone could possibly think of as a contemplative race, they had never found the inner strength of mind that the Vulcans had, nor had they managed to unlock the potential for telepathic abilities that afforded the Vulcans the ability to mind-meld.

Nonetheless, it could not reasonably be argued that there wasn't some genetic predisposition for mind powers. They couldn't have come from nowhere. That being the case, the potential for mental abilities must have existed equally in both the Romulans and Vulcans. Whereas the Vulcans had made the most of their potential, the Romulans had allowed that same potential in themselves to wither and die . . . possibly because their contact with the Vulcans had been severed more than a millennium earlier, at the time of Surak. Not being present for the Great Voyage of Discovery that the Vulcans had embarked upon, the Romulans simply didn't know, as a race, what they could do. Once they had become aware, however, when they had embarked on a campaign of war against the Federation a century earlier, there had been a movement afoot to try and play a sort of mental "catch-up" game with their cousins.

It had not been overwhelmingly successful thus far. There had been, however, a few small triumphs here and there. One of those triumphs happened to be Kressn. Tested at a young age and found to have definite psi potential, Kressn had been taken from his parents and handed over to the Tal Shiar. In his training over the years, Kressn had been found to have three major strengths: First, he was a gifted empath, capable of discerning the truth or falsehood of a subject's statements, as well as a range of other emotions; second, he had a knack for infiltration. It took a great deal of his concentration, but under the proper circumstances, he was capable of masking his presence from others in a room, much like old Earth ninjas or the fabled phantom people of Qu'uan. He would simply "convince" an onlooker to look in a direction other than that where Kressn happened to be. There was limited use to this ability: He wasn't capable of using his empathic abilities during such times, since retaining his "cloak," as he liked to call it, required all his concentration. Furthermore, if it was a very crowded room, sooner or later someone would bump into him and—at that point—not help but notice him. And if there was a surveillance camera, he was more or less dead.

And third, he was that rather rare breed, a projecting empath, capable of investing key emotions in individuals and "pushing" those emotions where he desired them to go.

In short, Kressn had his uses and his functions, which Sela had found out first-hand.

"Well?" she said again. Sometimes Kressn, seemingly off in his own world, did not answer without repeated prompting.

"He is holding something back . . . of that much I am certain. Are you positive he is who you think he is?"

"Of course he is." She rose from behind the table and circled the room. "Besides the fact that I know him on sight, Saket referred to him as Riker. And when I first encountered the *Enterprise,* I did full intelligence workups on all her senior officers. Riker was an only child. And I ran a full scan on his molecular structure from our own transporter records. It's fully human, meaning he's not a shapeshifter. So unless he somehow managed to pull a twin brother out of thin air within the last couple of years, that's William Riker."

"Very well. But he's still holding something back."

"Aren't we all," Sela remarked dryly.

"Perhaps." Kressn's tone lowered to something approaching conspiratorial. "Perhaps his presence there was some sort of trap. An attempt to infiltrate our operation."

It was clear from her general demeanor that she wasn't especially accepting of that notion. "You're asking me to believe that Starfleet consigned one of its top officers to a Cardassian hard-labor camp, in the hope that perhaps he could become friendly with a Romulan—a Romulan whom I have known my entire life and has an uncanny knack for seeing through duplicity—and then, on the off chance that the Romulan was rescued, Riker would be able to survive the assault and manage to save the Romulan's life so that maybe, just maybe, his new captors won't kill him? Is that the tortured logic you're asking me to accept, Kressn?"

"I am simply asking you to accept that all is not necessarily what it seems with the prisoner."

"Very well," Sela said impatiently. "Consider it a given. Putting that fact aside . . . what about the things he did say. Was he telling the truth?"

"He certainly believed what he was saying. It was definitely the truth as he believed it. However, his thoughts are finely tuned."

"Meaning what? That he's a telepath?"

"No. No, nothing quite that refined. But he has had training in mental disciplines that exceed anything Starfleet is currently offering. What it does mean is that if he had something he wished to keep hidden, he might very well be able to do so in such a way that nothing short of a deep probe would be able to dig it out."

"Can you do it?"

He shook his head. "Beyond my capabilities, I'm afraid. We have technology that could extract the information, but he might very well put up such a fight that whatever's left of him when we're through would be useless."

"We're going in circles here, Kressn," Sela said impatiently. "Give me your final assessment. Give me something I can work with."

"Very well. He is, without question, an angry and disillusioned man. He does not feel any particular attachment to Starfleet. If he feels anything for anyone, it would be for this Deanna person you mentioned. Your bringing her name up definitely provoked a mental spike from him. His feelings for her are exceedingly raw."

"Saket always told me that raw materials are the most useful, since they can be molded into so many different things," Sela said. She leaned back against her desk, stroking her chin thoughtfully. "Anything else?"

"Yes." Kressn cleared his throat and said, with what sounded like mild annoyance, "He finds you rather attractive."

"Does he?" She smirked at that. "Well, if there was any question as to whether he's really William Riker, that certainly resolved it. It was part of his psych profile when I first researched him: He considers himself quite the ladies' man. Apparently a number of ladies share that assessment."

"And would you be one of them?"

She looked at him, her gaze hardening. "You overstep yourself, Kressn."

He bowed slightly.

"These are different times, Kressn." She moved back around her desk. "Different times call for different measures. Tell me, Kressn . . . if we brought William Riker into our plan, and it was he who was responsible for the death of an entire race . . . how do you think that would reflect on Starfleet and the Federation?"

"You do not need to ask me that," he told her mildly. "You already know the answer."

"Yesss." She smiled. "And I think it an option that we would most definitely be benefited in exploring. I think that William Riker and I will be able to be of tremendous use to one another."

"I have no doubt, Sela," Kressn said. "I have no doubt at all."

Seven

Deanna had wanted to surprise her mother, but that had proven somewhat problematic. The moment that she had arrived on the transport to Betazed, she had been spotted by a longtime friend of the family, Silvan, who relayed the information telepathically to another friend, and so on down the line. Betazoids for the most part had telepathy of limited range, but with the advent of something as momentus as Deanna Troi's return to Betazed, the news followed a brisk chain of telepathic ricochets so that the news arrived at Lwaxana Troi's doorstep within approximately forty-five seconds of Deanna's having set foot on her homeworld. As a consequence, Lwaxana had a good deal of time to prepare for her daughter's arrival.

Immediately she contacted 135 guests in preparation for a banquet to honor her daughter's visit. She also let several very eligible Betazoid bachelors be aware of the fact that her wayward daughter had returned and that she was, you know, not getting any younger. Certainly the passage of time had done nothing to diminish her daughter's good looks, fine figure, and other assets that—on the whole—made her a superb catch, and the fact that she had gone unsnagged for this long only worked in a gentleman's favor, because at this point Deanna must be starting to realize that time and matrimony wait for no one, not even a Daughter of the Fifth House. In short, there was every possibility that she might be a lot less choosy these days, and that was to everyone's advantage.

And, of course, anyone who married Deanna would have the deep honor of having the famed Lwaxana Troi for a mother-in-law.

As she broadcast this, Lwaxana had the strangest feeling. It was the sound, in her head, of telepathic doors slamming. She wasn't entirely sure why that would be, but she was willing to shrug it off as not being of very much consequence.

It should be noted that when Silvan sent out the original thought-cast about Lwaxana, he had noticed that Deanna seemed engaged in lively and pleasant conversation with what appeared to be a Klingon father and son traveling together. This in and of itself did not appear particularly significant, however, and as a result Silvan did not happen to pass that along in the message. This was a pity, as it might have given Lwaxana at least some measure of warning. As a result, she had none. So when she greeted her wandering daughter in the grand foyer of *casa* Troi, she was not at all prepared for what was about to happen.

Mr. Homn, Lwaxana's towering manservant, stepped to one side as Lwaxana almost stampeded over him to get to her daughter. "Little One!" she said out loud, knowing that for some bizarre reason Deanna found it extremely off-putting to speak purely through the mind. "Did you tell me you were coming? Did I forget?" She draped an arm around Deanna's shoulders and strolled with her into the main sitting room, tugging her as if she were afraid that Deanna was going to bolt at any moment. "I know, I know, I'm getting on in years. You might have told me that you were coming for a visit and I simply forgot."

"Mother, you know better than that," Deanna gently scolded her. "You forget nothing. Your mind is as sharp as it ever was."

Lwaxana laughed, sounding surprisingly girlish considering that her girlish years were long gone. "There are some people," she said, as if sharing a naughty secret, "who would say that that isn't much of a compliment."

"We pity those people," Deanna deadpanned.

"Mr. Homn, some tea . . . Earl Gray, piping hot. Jean-Luc got me addicted to the stuff," she told Deanna, looking a bit embarrassed, "and now I just don't know what to do. It's not easy to come by here on Betazed, although I do have my methods and a rather long reach. Come, sit on the—"

Then Lwaxana suddenly stopped her cheerful burbling and stared at her daughter as if Deanna had grown a nose in the middle of her forehead. She folded her arms and, acquiring a slightly worried demeanor, said, "All right, Little One. What is it you're nervous about telling me?"

"Mother!" Deanna made no effort to hide her annoyance, not that it would have helped if she had tried. "You know I hate that! I hate when you skim the thoughts off the top of my mind! I want to tell you something, surprise you, and you won't even let me get to it in my own way and time."

"All right." Lwaxana looked as if she were making a physical effort to haul something unseen back into her head. "All right. Go ahead. Tell me."

"You . . . should be happy about it, actually," Deanna said. "Something's, well . . . something's come up, and I know that it's something that's been important to you for quite some time. . . ."

Lwaxana clapped her hands together, her dark eyes going wide with excitement. "You're getting married!"

"Mother! For heaven's sake—!"

"I didn't peek!" Lwaxana drew herself up as if her honor were being questioned, squaring her shoulders and looking at her daughter as if daring her to try and accuse her otherwise. "Deanna, I'm not stupid. I figured it out from the things you just said! At least, I believe I did. Did I? Figure it out, I mean?"

At that, Deanna couldn't hold back a laugh. Lwaxana Troi was not exactly one of the more staid individuals one could hope to meet, even under normal circumstances. Well, these circumstances were far from normal. Not wanting to keep her mother in suspense anymore, Deanna said, "Yes, Mother, you figured it out. I'm engaged to be married."

Lwaxana promptly slapped her lightly across the face.

Deanna was momentarily startled, and could feel a faint stinging sensation in her cheek, as much from surprise as anything else. But then Lwaxana immediately leaned forward and kissed the other cheek, and then Deanna remembered.

"The slap to remind you of the pain of married life," Lwaxana said, "and the kiss to remind you that, with love, all can be solved. Congratulations, Little One."

"Fortunately I remembered the tradition after you whacked me," Deanna said, rubbing the sore spot. "Next time give me a little bit of warning, though, all right?"

"Oh, don't complain. You're an engaged woman now, so don't whine about a little pain. So," and she took Deanna's hands in hers and sat them both on the luxurious couch. It was a bright orange with green diagonal stripes. Deanna had hated the couch since her youth. She'd once offered to buy it off her mother, just so she could man the transporter and disassemble the thing one molecule at a time. But her mother had been less than cooperative and wouldn't part with it. "So . . . have you and Riker set a date?"

"What?" asked Deanna in puzzlement.

"Riker. You and Will Riker. Your fiancé. I know it's Riker; you were thinking of him when you told me you were engaged. Oh, I'm sorry, I know I shouldn't pry, but it's a bad habit I'm trying to kick. . . ."

"Mother, I wasn't thinking about Will."

"Yes, you were. He was uppermost in your thoughts. . . ."

"That's because I have other thoughts occupying the deeper layers."

Lwaxana seemed utterly confused. "Are you saying . . . you're not marrying Riker?"

"You sound disappointed. I didn't know you felt so strongly about him as a husband for me . . ."

"Well, you are Imzadi, after all, and you've been together for all this time, and you hadn't written to me and told me that you'd gotten involved with someone new. . . ."

"Mother, I'm not obligated to fill you in on it every time I'm 'involved with someone new,' am I?"

"No, of course not." Lwaxana regarded her with open curiosity. "Although now that we're on the subject, how many men have you been involved with over the past years?"

"None," Deanna deadpanned. "I've been with no men in all these years. In fact, I never even really had sex with Will, not ever. I am, in fact, a virgin."

"You certainly know what a mother wants to hear," Lwaxana told her, smiling, her eyes twinkling in amusement. "Seriously, Deanna . . . if not Riker, then who? Not Jean-Luc!" She suddenly seemed stunned.

"No, Mother."

"That nice engineering fellow with the large hair clip on his face?"

"His name is Geordi, it's called a VISOR, and no, it's not him."

"Well, I doubt it's the android. . . ." She paused a moment to glance at Deanna for confirmation as to this supposition. Deanna quietly shook her head. "Then who . . . ?" Suddenly she seemed aghast. "Deanna, don't tell me . . . not . . . a non-com?!?"

"Have no fear, Mother. You needn't worry about becoming an outcast in polite society. He's not a noncommissioned officer." She took a deep breath, and then said, "Actually, it's . . . well . . . it's Worf."

Dead silence. Lwaxana just stared at her.

"Worf Rozhenko . . . the security guard," Deanna prompted. "We sat in a mud-bath together, remember?"

Still no reply.

"Has a young son named Alexander? Cute as a—"

Then Lwaxana started to laugh. This did not strike Deanna as being A Good Thing.

The laughter started out low and then began to grow, louder and louder, until she was shaking with such spasmodic contractions of her chest that Deanna was momentarily concerned that Lwaxana was literally going to die laughing. Only Lwaxana's formidable mental training was able to help her as she managed to pull herself together . . . unfortunately, only long enough for another peal of laughter to fill the mansion and, once more, it took time for her to recover her equilibrium.

"Oh, Deanna," she said at last, "you certainly know how to amuse your old mother. You and Mr. Woof . . . gods, child, for a moment there you had me going. Wheeww!" She sagged back in her chair, rubbing her ribs as if concerned that one might have snapped during her laughing fit.

"Mother, I'm not joking. . . ."

"No, of cooourse you're not." She patted Deanna affectionately on the arm.

"Mother, don't take that tone of voice with me. It's insulting to me. If you don't believe me, here," and suddenly she relaxed her guard, "let's just jump over the protests and the convincing and get right to it. Here. Look into my mind. Find out what you want, and then we'll talk."

Lwaxana didn't need a second invitation. Her body sagged a bit as she projected her formidable mind-reading abilities into Deanna's head. It took her only the briefest of moments to discern the information for which she was looking.

The moment she did, she went completely slack-jawed. Deanna didn't think that she'd ever seen her mother look quite that astonished.

"You're not serious," she said, but she was speaking from her surprised state of mind, because she was already more than aware that Deanna was not kidding in the least. "Deanna, what . . . what were you thinking? He's completely wrong for you. Certainly you must know that."

"May I remind you, Mother, that you didn't like Will Riker when I first brought him home."

"Nonsense. I adored him."

Deanna openly gaped at her mother. "Now *you're* the one who can't be serious, Mother! You threatened to bring him up on charges before Starfleet if he continued to be interested in me. Is that your definition of a ringing endorsement?"

"You were young and too easily swayed," Lwaxana said dismissively. "I was simply watching out for your own good. As an individual, though, I found him perfectly acceptable. Even charming in a rugged, tactless sort of way. I just didn't want you to make a mistake. . . ."

"And what's the excuse now, Mother? I'm quite a few years older than I was then. Are you still claiming that I'm still not sufficiently mature to know my own mind?"

"I'm just . . ." She tried to steady her hands as she gestured with them, since they were trembling with confusion and frustration. "I'm just saying that I've seen Mr. Woof in action . . ."

"Worf! His name is Worf!"

"Deanna Worf." Lwaxana shuddered at the notion.

"I wouldn't be Deanna Worf. If I chose to adapt to that Earth custom, I'd be Deanna Rozhenko."

"Oh, well that's just ever so much better. You'd trade Troi for Rozhenko? While you're at it, why don't you add another five syllables to 'Deanna'? And have you considered children? What would they look like? Half Betazoid, half Klingon? Half telepath, half warrior? They'd go around telling everyone what to think. They'd be at home nowhere in the galaxy."

"Congratulations, Mother," Deanna said dryly. "We haven't even taken any vows yet and you've already had us give birth to pariahs."

Lwaxana waved dismissively, like an imperious queen. "You're right, it's ridiculous to discuss this. I won't give permission for it."

"Permission?" Deanna was astounded at her mother's presumptuousness. "Mother . . . I came here to share happy news with you. But I did not come looking for your permission. Even if you 'forbid' it, I will still do as my heart tells me."

"Then your heart should be steering you to Will Riker."

Deanna put her face in her hands and moaned softly. "This from the woman who arranged a marriage for me when I was a child."

"Deanna." Lwaxana took her daughter's hand in hers. "I don't pretend that I haven't made mistakes in my time. More than my share, if truth be known. And I haven't . . . I haven't always done right by you. I know that, I admit it . . ."

"Mother, don't be so hard on yourself. . . ."

"But removed by a distance of years, I'm able to see not only my mistakes, but yours."

"How comforting it must be to be all-seeing."

Any trace of sarcasm in Deanna's voice was completely missed—or else simply and deliberately ignored—by Lwaxana. "Riker was your Imzadi, and you were his. I admit I was angry about it at the time, but it seems now, in retrospect, that you were destined to be a couple. You complemented each other in so many ways. When fate brought the two of you together again on the *Enterprise,* that wasn't coincidence. It couldn't have been. It was meant for you two to be together again."

"We . . . are just . . . friends," Deanna said patiently.

"Does Riker know about this . . . this engagement?"

"Yes. And he was the first to raise a glass in a toast to us."

Lwaxana shook her head, discouraged. "Then he is as foolish as you. Then again, I expected more from you."

"Mother, why are you so opposed to this . . . ?"

"Because . . ." She sighed. "Deanna . . . you're talking to a woman who has spent her entire life honing her emotions and feelings. They are, to me, a sort of natural resource. You should understand: You're an empath. To me, it just . . . it feels wrong. Feels so profoundly wrong that I can't even begin to articulate why."

"Well, don't you see, Mother? To me, it feels as right as it does wrong to you. So who's to say who's right?"

"I am."

Deanna almost laughed at that until she saw that Lwaxana was deadly serious. Suddenly she felt a small buzz of alarm. "Mother . . . what do you mean by that?"

"If you go through with this," Lwaxana said flatly, "then at your marriage, you will not be allowed to drink from the Sacred Chalice of Rixx."

Deanna was floored. It was as if her mother had hit her upside the head with a heated poker. "Mother!" she cried out as if stricken. "The women of the Fifth House have drunk from the Sacred Chalice at their weddings for over six centuries! Six centuries of tradition, Mother! That's when the chalice is passed down to its new holder!"

"That's a fairly dramatic reaction," Lwaxana said tartly, "from someone who once dismissed the Sacred Chalice as an old clay urn."

" 'Moldy old pot,' " Deanna corrected, sounding a bit chagrined. "It's what it symbolizes, Mother, no matter what it may actually be. Even your mother, although she disapproved of your marriage to my father, still passed on the Sacred Chalice in the time-honored manner. Would you be even more strict than she was?"

"I would do whatever I have to do," replied Lwaxana, "to make you realize the foolishness of this. Little One, he's so wrong for you. . . ."

"You said that Will Riker and I 'complemented' each other. Did you ever stop to consider, Mother, that perhaps Worf and I likewise complement each other?"

"It's a matter of extremes, Deanna. There's no middle ground, there's no . . ."

"How can you know that? You don't know him, not really. Although you certainly seemed to get on well enough with his son. As I recall, you adored Alexander."

"That's true enough," Lwaxana said slowly, even grudgingly. "He was the most soulful child. He seemed to be enduring a world of hurt with utter stoicism. I think I actually made some serious progress with him."

"If that's the case, then think how much progress I could make with him if I were like a mother to him. Or at least a continuous positive female influence on him."

"Taking care of the child on a temporary basis is one thing, Deanna. Becoming his full-time mother is something else again. I just . . ."

For a moment, Lwaxana seemed to be out of words, and Deanna used the opportunity to jump in. "Mother, at least give him, and us, a chance. Speak to Worf. Spend some real time with him and Alexander. Show a bit of faith in my judgment and realize that we truly are good for each other, Worf and I."

Lwaxana sighed heavily, as if expelling the weight of the world. "All right," she said finally. "Bring them here for dinner tonight. We'll have a nice, small, intimate little gathering, and discuss matters then."

"Thank you, Mother." She kissed Lwaxana on the cheek. "You won't regret it."

"I do already," Lwaxana said.

"A small, intimate little gathering?"

"That is what she said," Deanna told Worf. They were in a room at a nearby inn. Alexander had already found the mattress on his bed insufferably soft and, tired as he was from all the traveling, he had simply taken a blanket and dropped to sleep on the floor.

Worf was looking out a window at his view of the city. The clouds were pink and puffy in the sky. The city was a virtual tapestry of smoothly integrated buildings that were practically monuments to symmetry. It made him itch just to look at it.

"It's beautiful, isn't it," Deanna said, noticing that his gaze seemed captivated by it.

"Yes," Worf replied. Eager to change the subject, he said, "And your mother's reaction was . . . what? Is that all the two of you discussed? You told her of our engagement, and she invited us to dinner?"

"There may have been some chitchat in between, but that's more or less how it went."

Worf grunted. He didn't seem remotely convinced, which was understandable since Deanna was one of the worst liars he had ever known. Indeed, that may have been one of her more endearing qualities. "Were I your mother . . . I would not be pleased about this union."

"Worf! How could you say such a thing?"

"Look at me, Deanna. Put yourself in her position, and look at me not as a woman in love with me, but as a woman who would see me married to her daughter. I do not take it personally, but let us be realistic: Is a Klingon the ideal choice for a Betazoid son-in-law? For any son-in-law?"

She put a hand gently to his face. Not for the first time, she was amazed by the roughness of it. "You are my first choice, and that is all that matters."

He grunted again, and simply replied, "We shall see."

When they arrived at the mansion that evening, it was a mob scene.

It was not particularly loud or raucous. Indeed, it was amazingly quiet, for the house was packed with well over a hundred Betazoids. Deanna gaped in astonishment at the huge throng of people who were visible through the door opened by Mr. Homn. People she hadn't seen for years, major notables of Betazed, all were packed in. Mr. Homn barely afforded Worf a glance as he gestured for the Klingon to follow Deanna in. Alexander, staying close at his father's side, entered quickly, as if afraid the door would shut him out into the night.

"Mother!" Deanna called out. In comparison with the silence in the main foyer and every visible area, her voice was like thunder.

Lwaxana hustled across the foyer to her, her full-length puffy blue dress swirling about the floor, and light sparkling off a dazzling array of stones on a jeweled choker she wore around her throat. "Little One . . . Worf . . . Alexander . . . how wonderful to see you." She touched the choker. "It's new. Be honest . . . do you think it's too much? Does it stand out?"

"Absolutely," Worf said flatly. "When I saw you in the middle of this crowd, the first thought I had was 'Choker.' "

Lwaxana bobbed her head in appreciation, and then did a split second of a double take as she realized she wasn't entirely sure what he had just said. Recovering quickly, she said, "My apologies, children, for the unexpected crowd. . . ."

"You said a small, intimate gathering, Mother!"

"I know, Little One, and I forgot that I had arranged for a banquet here in your honor. The invitations had gone out, the food already prepared." She shrugged grandly, as if appealing to the universe to solve her problems. "What else was I supposed to do?"

"They're very quiet," Alexander noted.

"They're communing telepathically, for the most part. Does it bother you?"

"We can adapt," Worf said. "Correct, Alexander?"

"Yes, Father."

"Oh, no, you shouldn't have to . . ."

"That's correct, Mother," Deanna said icily. "They shouldn't."

Deanna!

A cry of pure joy sounded in her head and Deanna turned to see a slim blond woman, running toward her with her arms wide.

"Chandra!" Deanna cried out.

Deanna! Chandra replied directly into Deanna's head. She embraced her eagerly, then turned to Worf and thought, *And this is your fiancé?*

That's right, said Deanna as she informed Worf aloud, "Worf, this is Chandra, one of my best friends growing up. I was maid of honor at her wedding."

Worf nodded his head slightly in acknowledgment. "Hello."

"How did you know Worf was my fiancé?" Deanna asked.

"Are you joking? It's all over the city that you brought home a . . ." She stopped, turned, and smiled winningly at Worf. ". . . a . . . fiancé . . ."

Worf became painfully aware that he was rapidly becoming the center of attention. In the supernaturally quiet gathering, more and more Betazoids appeared to be glancing his way. He couldn't hear any of the conversation, of course, since it was all being conducted on a telepathic basis. But Worf had rather impressive peripheral vision, and he couldn't help but notice how people would glance quickly in his direction and then look away just as quickly.

It irked him to say the least.

"Deanna . . . perhaps Alexander and I would be best advised to return to the inn. . . ."

Upon hearing this pronouncement, Alexander's face immediately darkened in concern. "Is it something I did, Father?"

"No. No, it has nothing to do with you."

"Well, what then?"

"Yes, Mr. Woo . . . Worf, what could it be?" Lwaxana asked as she tousled Alexander's hair. "You know how much I adore spending time with you and, particularly, your son. Look, everything is set up." And indeed that was the case. Long tables had been put out, lined with an assortment of Betazoid delicacies. One would have thought that it required an army of servants to deal with the cooking, preparation, and setup. But instead there was just Mr. Homn, putting the finishing touches on the table and seemingly unperturbed at handling the massive undertaking, as near as anyone could tell, single-handedly. The room itself was rather opulent, with a glittering chandelier overhead that—very likely not coincidentally—matched Lwaxana's choker. Portraits of previous heads of the Fifth House lined the walls. It was easy to tell the order of ascension: Each painting was progressively larger. Not by much, each one perhaps no more than ten percent. But it was still evident when seen all together. The one of Lwaxana took up half a wall. Worf had a feeling that, when it came Deanna's turn, they'd have no choice but to paint a mural of her on the ceiling.

"This is clearly intended as a reunion for Deanna and her friends and associates," Worf observed. "We would seem . . . out of place."

There was a moment of silence, and it was Lwaxana who commented, very quietly, "If *you* say so, Mr. Worf."

"Father . . ." Alexander hesitated, clearly loath to say what was on his mind.

Worf looked down at him. "What?" he said with clear impatience.

"It's like . . . running away."

The words had the exact effect on Worf that one could have expected. He drew himself up, squaring his broad shoulders, and glowered. "This is not a matter of cowardice," he rumbled. "I am simply thinking of what is in Deanna's best interest. . . ."

"If that is the consideration," Deanna said, "then it is in my best interest, as far as I'm concerned, that you remain. Either that or"—and she cast a defiant look at her mother—"we will all leave."

"Oh, but that would be terrible,"said Lwaxana.

"Come, Worf . . . let's go." Clearly the decision was made, as far as Deanna was concerned. Since it was still largely silent in the room, eerily to Worf, like a morgue, her voice carried throughout the great dining room.

"Worf, please, stay . . . all of you." There was something akin to genuine pleading in Lwaxana's voice. Worf was not entirely sure just how she had been anticipating that this night would go, but he was positive that having Deanna simply walk out was not one of the options she had been strongly considering.

"Yes, of course we will stay," Worf said quickly.

Deanna turned to him. "Worf, we don't have to remain on my account. . . ."

"We will stay," he told her, "because it is the right thing to do."

"Thank you, Mr. Worf," Lwaxana said, and she even bowed slightly with apparently no hint of sarcasm. Then she turned and said loudly to the other guests, "My friends . . . out of respect for our guests tonight . . . I would ask that you converse out loud this evening. I would like them to feel as much at home as possible, in keeping with the Betazoid spirit of welcoming all who would join us."

There was a hesitation, as if everyone was self-conscious about being the first to open their mouths. But one after another they began to speak, and soon there was an undercurrent of polite conversation. Hardly a roar of noise; the Betazoids were too understated for that.

"More like the sort of sounds you're accustomed to at a social gathering, Mr. Worf?" Lwaxana asked.

"Most Klingon gatherings have the sound of bone striking bone scattered throughout," Worf replied. "However, I do not think it necessary to replicate that here."

The banquet was designed as purely a stand-up affair, with all of the food prepared as finger food so that the Betazoids would be able to more easily circulate around the room. Once she was convinced that Worf was truly comfortable in the surroundings, Deanna did not hesitate to begin serious mingling with her old friends. Lwaxana, meantime, had gravitated to Alexander and was making it a point to introduce the youngster around. At first Worf was a bit suspicious of it, but he quickly dismissed it from his mind. It was indisputable that, for whatever reason, Lwaxana had taken a shine to the lad. She had displayed it when she had met him on the *Enterprise* several years ago, and that attraction was resurging now.

But Worf was convinced that she was less than ecstatic about the prospect of the boy's father becoming a relation through marriage.

Worf was no fool. Despite Deanna's claims to the contrary, he knew where he stood with Lwaxana. He told himself that it was her problem rather than his, but he couldn't help but feel that that was simply too facile an answer.

He tried to stand off to the side, to remain inconspicuous, but Deanna saw him isolated and—believing that she was doing him a favor—pulled him along with her as she went from one cluster of people to another. With each group, it seemed to Worf that they were tripping over their words, trying to be polite but unaccustomed to verbalizing their thoughts, and certainly not used to dealing with Klingons.

An older man named Gart Xerx, who had introduced himself as Chandra's father, stood there with a drink in his hand and asked, "So what do you two talk about?"

"Talk . . . ?" Worf clearly found the question puzzling. "We talk about . . . all manner of subjects."

"Worf is extremely well read," Deanna said.

"Really? What sort of topics do you like to read about, Worf?"

"Strategy. Combat tactics. History. . . ."

"Ah, history. What sort of histories?"

"Warfare, for the most part."

Gart frowned in polite puzzlement. "And you find that . . . relaxing?"

"The purpose of reading is not to relax," Worf replied. "It is to learn. To learn and to plan for whatever situations may arise."

"But what about Klingon philosophies and such. Or do you have any?"

Worf immediately bristled and Gart took a step back, clearly startled by the intensity of the emotions he was feeling. "No offense intended," he said quickly.

"Worf . . ." Deanna said, putting a hand on his arm. As if her empathic abilities didn't already cue her to his mood, she could feel the muscles bunching up.

"Our philosophies," Worf said, "are as important and integral to our way of life as yours are to you. In many ways, we are the same."

"But . . . your way of life is war. Ours is of peace. They could not be more different. Or do you believe in peace as a way of life?"

"If Worf did not believe in the viability of peace as a way of life," Deanna told Gart, "then he certainly would not have chosen Starfleet as a place to spend his life."

"Is that why you chose Starfleet, Worf?" asked Gart.

And for the briefest of moments, Worf's mind flashed back to Khitomer. To being buried under rubble, sobbing and furious at the weakness implicit in his fear. In his mind's eye, he saw the rubble being pushed aside, saw the man who he would come to call father, saw the uniform that he wore and the round, metallic symbol on his uniform jacket . . . a symbol that would come to be synonymous with life, hope, and a second chance, one that he would covet as his own. . . .

But peace?

His desire for a life in Starfleet was born from an act of war. Peace never factored into it.

All this went through his mind in an instant, and the moment that it did, it was immediately known to Gart Xerx. "As I thought," he said politely, and he glanced at Deanna—not with any sort of triumph or smugness—but rather with a sort of detached sadness, as if to say, *How little you know of the truth.*

Worf felt anger bubbling within him. "A life dedicated only to peace is a pleasing fancy for children. Adults know better."

Gart's tone was not at all challenging or superior. If anything, he seemed mentally stimulated by the conversation. "Are you implying that we Betazoids are children? We have known only peace."

"Then you are ripe for conquest."

The quiet draped over the room as if a blanket of silence had been tossed upon it. Worf realized that, although he had been speaking out loud with Gart, Gart in turn was "multitasking," keeping a mental link with others as he engaged Worf in conversation. He might very well have been mentally chatting with others about utterly innocuous matters, but Worf's comment had immediately nailed the attention of everyone in the room.

"Is that a threat, Worf?" Gart asked.

"Gart! How could you—" Deanna began.

But Worf cut her off with a gesture. "No. Merely an observation. Peace . . ." He hesitated, trying to determine the best, least inflammatory way in which to put it. ". . . Peace can be . . . deceptive."

Mr. Homn appeared, as if by magic, and handed a drink to Worf. Worf took it and knocked back a swig automatically . . . and it registered on him, to his surprise, that it contained prune juice.

"Deceptive in what way?" asked Gart.

"At times of war, you know your enemy, you test his resources. In peace, you deceive yourself into believing there is no enemy. But there is. And your enemy prepares, while you delude yourself into thinking that the peace will be everlasting. It never is. Peace is a luxury purchased for a brief time through the efforts of war. Compassion, while praiseworthy, has been the downfall of a number of races who thought they had no enemies."

"And who would be our enemy?" Gart said in amusement, as if the very idea were beyond ludicrous.

"I do not know. But there is an enemy. There is always an enemy. That is the way of things."

"It is not," Gart Xerx said quietly, "our way."

"Then I pity you. For when an enemy does come, you will not be ready . . . and you will suffer all the more for it."

There followed another silence, and then Gart swirled the contents of his glass a bit and stared down into it as if hoping to find the secrets of the universe contained therein. "I believe I speak for all of us, Worf, in saying that we of Betazed do not feel as if we are in need of pity."

"I did not intend to insult," Worf said.

"Oh, you do not. Amuse, perhaps, but not insult."

The glass that Worf was holding shattered in his hand as he squeezed it reflexively. When he spoke, it was with waves of barely contained fury radiating from him, so suffocating and overwhelming that a number of Betazoids in proximity to him visibly flinched.

"AMUSE?" he practically roared.

"Worf, calm down!" Deanna said forcefully.

"I am not here for your amusement! You wished to know of Klingon philosophies, and I have told you. We believe in vigilance . . . in readiness. Our philosophy is one of strength, and that is what has enabled our people to survive for centuries while other races have vanished beneath the bootheels of conquerors."

"And here I thought," Gart shot back, showing a trace of annoyance for the first time, "that your people survived through the sufferance of the Federation and the Khitomer conference a century ago. A time when your race was weak and helpless, and the members of the Federation who were concerned over your barbaric ways—were they of a Klingon mindset—would have left you to die as a race, and thus have one less enemy with which to concern themselves. And for your information, Betazed was sitting on the Federation Council at the time. How fortunate for the Klingons that we believed in that praiseworthy compassion which, according to you, might yet be our downfall."

Worf was glowering so furiously that it seemed as if his eyes were about to leap from his skull. " 'Bar . . . baric . . . '?" he said with an unmistakable edge of danger.

Immediately Gart was contrite. "Perhaps that was the wrong word . . . and it was very long ago . . ."

"Barbaric!"

Deanna put a hand on his arm and said urgently, "Worf, perhaps it would be better if we left; we've had a long journey, and rest might be—"

"I think it best," he said in cold, measured tone, "if I departed. I do not believe I am welcome here."

"That's not true . . ."

He turned to her and for a moment . . . just a moment . . . there was a flicker of sadness in his eyes. "Trust me." He paused, then added, "Bring Alexander back to the inn when the party is over. We will talk then." And he walked quickly away, keeping his focus straight ahead of him, not looking at Alexander and, most particularly, not looking at Lwaxana Troi.

When Deanna and Alexander returned to the inn not too long after Worf's unceremonious exit, Alexander quickly retired to his own bedroom, not wanting to be present for the scene that he knew, beyond question, was to follow.

Deanna had half-expected to find Worf packing. Worf had half-expected that Deanna would simply drop Alexander off, turn on her heel, and head back to her mother's house. Both of them were inwardly pleased to see that their worst expectations had not been realized, but there was a long way to go when it came to finding a meeting of minds.

"Would you like to tell me what that was all about?" said Deanna, facing him with her hands planted firmly on her hips.

"A philosophical difference of opinion," he rumbled.

"The hell it was!" said Deanna with such vehemence that Worf's surprise was evident on his face. "You went in there spoiling for a fight!"

"I went in there expecting a small gathering, not an ambush."

"It was not an ambush, Worf!" she moaned, running her fingers through her hair in frustration. "Mother explained that—!"

"Are you taking her side?"

"I'm not taking anyone's side!"

"I would have hoped that you would take mine. That is the purpose of a marriage, is it not?"

"Worf, if you think the purpose of marriage is that the wife leaves her opinions at the doorstep and blindly follows her husband down whatever path he might randomly choose to take . . ."

"He called my people barbarians!" His fury was beginning to mount again.

Deanna, however, showed not the least signs of being intimidated. "And what did Klingons call other races? Races whom they considered weaker, or ripe for conquest? Terrans, Betazoids, Vulcans . . . are you saying there were no contemptuous nicknames for them bandied about in the places of power at the Klingon Empire? How clean have Klingon hands been, Worf? How clean are yours?"

The uncharacteristically harsh words from the normally calm counselor brought Worf to a halt. Deanna, for her part, immediately felt contrite . . . and then, to the surprise of both of them, she laughed softly. "What is so funny?" Worf asked testily.

"It must be beyond doubt that I love you. If I didn't, you couldn't possibly have gotten me as angry as you just did. I'm a professional counselor. I stay calm for a living. Only a loved one can get quite so under one's skin."

Worf shook his head. It seemed to Deanna that he was very far away, wrapped entirely in himself and whatever demons were eating at him.

"Worf . . ." And she sat next to him as he stared coldly into the air. "Worf . . . you seem so conflicted. Even frustrated. Can't you tell me what you're thinking?"

"It is not . . . easy . . ."

"The Worf that I know hasn't ever flinched from a challenge."

"I act . . . differently when I am with you. Perhaps the Worf you know is an illusion."

"Oh, Worf, I knew you for six years before we became involved as a couple. I think I've a fairly accurate assessment of your character. Please . . . tell me what's bothering you."

"He felt he was on display."

Both of their heads snapped around and they saw Lwaxana standing in the doorway. To Worf, it was nothing short of amazing that she had managed to make such a stealthy entrance. Indeed, it was somewhat alarming. Deanna was simply annoyed. "Mother . . ."

There had been any number of times where Lwaxana Troi had come across as a bit of a scatterbrain. Then there were other times when she was simply irritating, or amusing, or outrageous. But that was not the Lwaxana Troi they were seeing now. This was a woman who was accustomed to being attended to, listened to, and obeyed. Deanna didn't manage to get out another word, and Worf never even got started.

"Mr. Worf here went through much of his childhood feeling the outcast," Lwaxana said. Her dark eyes seemed to bore straight into the back of his skull.

"He lived in a world that prided itself on having outgrown racism, yet did not hesitate to ostracize him because of who he was, and the world did not grasp its hypocrisy. He insulated himself from that upon joining Starfleet, but the raw wounds of his childhood are present in him always. At the gathering this evening, he found himself not in the mind-set of Lieutenant Commander Worf, but instead with the injured ego of young Worf Rozhenko, reacting to every taunt, every harassment, every challenge to his very heritage that he faced as a youth. You were correct, Little One. He was spoiling for a fight, but only because he was simply seeking to repeat a pattern that was all too familiar to him from his childhood."

"Get out of my head," Worf said angrily.

"Well, it's a big head, there's enough room in there for everybody."

"Mother!"

"Oh, calm down, Little One, it was a joke." She leveled her gaze at Worf, and her expression seemed to soften ever so slightly. "Worf . . . for what it is worth . . . I do apologize for the mild fiasco this evening. I truly did intend for it to be just us. But when my absentmindedness and fate conspired to make it a large gathering, I thought that it might be easier rather than harder. That you would feel as if there was less pressure; you would just be a face in the crowd. I thought that the sizable gathering would be a blessing in disguise."

"It was a superb disguise," Worf noted.

"So . . . here is what we are going to do. Mr. Worf . . . do you still wish to marry my daughter?"

Almost to Worf's own surprise, he said without hesitation, "Yes." Even Deanna seemed startled by the speed and vehemence of his reply.

"Very well, then. In that case, Worf, to better understand us you will receive a full training in Betazed philosophy and harmony. You will plumb the very depths of our definitions of love and sacrifice. You need not necessarily subscribe to those beliefs, but at the very least, you will come to understand them and maybe—someday—embrace a few of them. I will handle your indoctrination into our principles myself."

"You? Mother, to begin with, I'm more qualified to—"

"You are too close to the situation, Little One, and besides, I am a Daughter of the Fifth House . . . holder of the Sacred Chalice of Rixx, and Heir to—"

"The Holy Rings of Betazed," Worf and Deanna intoned together.

Lwaxana appeared to take no notice of the sarcasm. "The point is, I can certainly impart upon Worf what he needs to know and do so in a dispassionate manner. Unless, of course, Worf feels it to be too much of a difficult undertaking . . ."

"Reverse psychology is hardly necessary," Worf informed her. He turned to Deanna and asked, "If I do as she requests . . ."

"I wasn't presenting it as a request," Lwaxana said.

He glanced at her and said flatly, "Yes. You were."

Lwaxana opened her mouth for a moment and then closed it again. "So I was," she said in a neutral tone.

"If I do this," he continued, "will it . . . please you?"

"Only if it will please you," replied Deanna.

"It will please me . . . but only if—"

The door to Alexander's room flew open, Alexander stuck his head out, and he fairly shouted, *"Will you just do it, Father, so you can get married and I can get some sleep?!"* And he slammed the door shut again.

The adults looked at each other.

"When do we start?" asked Worf.

Eight

Tom Riker was going out of his mind with boredom.

He had completely lost track of how long he had been cooped up in the brig of the Romulan warbird. Day passed into night with no clear delineation, which might have been as much by design as anything else. It was as if they were trying to destroy his internal rhythm, throw him off and thus make him more susceptible to . . .

. . . to what?

What were they planning to do to him? What the hell did they have in store? Had they seen through his charade somehow? Were they just trying to make him crazy out of pure Romulan sadism? What was their plan? *They have to have a plan,* he kept telling himself, *there must be a plan.* They wouldn't have mounted a raid to rescue Saket just out of nowhere. There had to be a reason for it, had to be something they wanted.

Except, since Saket was dead, there was the possibility that it was all moot. He might have been the key to whatever it was they wanted to do, and with him gone, the door was locked tight and the key was gone. In which case, they might just be busy trying to decide what would be the most painful way to dispose of Riker.

Then one day (night?) Riker heard the sound of marching feet. Since it was the first time that he'd detected such pronounced stomping, he could only surmise that it was being done for his benefit. They wanted him to know they were coming, probably to scare the hell out of him. But Tom Riker, at that point, was too tired and aggravated and just plain bored to feel anything more than impatience. He figured, *Let's just get it over with.*

The perpetual guard at his door stepped to one side as two more guards stepped into view. One of them reached up and shut off the field guarding the exit. Without a word, he gestured for Riker to emerge. For a moment, Tom considered the option of just folding his arms, crossing his legs, and refusing to budge. Try to provoke some sort of reaction from them. The thought gave him some small amount of satisfaction; on the other hand, the thought that it might prompt them to simply blow a hole in him the size of a sunspot prompted him to err on the side of discretion. As a result, Tom Riker stood and walked into the corridor.

They had not even bothered to draw their weapons. This was a bit of arrogant overconfidence that Riker couldn't help but feel the desire to test. One guard was in front of him, the other behind him. He stood there for a moment, poised on the balls of his feet, looking for all the world as if he were completely relaxed.

Then he made his move, darting toward the guard in front of him.

He actually managed to get three whole inches before the guard had his disruptor in his hand.

Riker had never seen a draw quite that fast. And he had the sneaking suspicion that, were he to turn around, he would see that the guard behind him likewise had a weapon trained on him. He risked a glance over his shoulder and, sure enough, he was looking down the barrel of a weapon. Without moving an inch, Riker casually took his outstretched hand and tried to move it, in a graceful manner, to the back of his neck, which he idly scratched. "You boys are jumpy," he observed, as if he had made no effort at all to attack them.

They didn't buy it. He knew they wouldn't. But they didn't seem to care particularly, either. Without further holdups on Riker's part, they walked down the corridors of the vessel. Very quickly Riker lost track of which hallway led into what. He had a feeling that that, likewise, was by intent. The last thing they wanted him to do was learn his way around the ship. But they wouldn't want simply to blindfold him, since that would make it too obvious that they were concerned that he could do them harm.

After what seemed the hundredth angle around yet another corner, they stopped in front of a door. It slid open and Riker, at their urging, entered. He looked around in confusion. It appeared to be a bathroom and dressing room, with a sonic shower in the corner, and a set of clean, pressed Romulan-style clothes draped over a chair. Fancy it most definitely was not, but it was definitely serviceable.

"What's this for?" he asked.

"You. Shower and then change clothes."

"Why?"

"Because you stink," the shorter of the two guards said reasonably. "Humans give off an odor that Romulans find distasteful. You are fairly reeking of it."

"Sorry. What with my being a prisoner and all, I probably sweated a bit more than I usually do."

Admittedly the attempt at humor was lame, but Riker felt that at the very least the guard could have tried to crack a smile. Such was not to be as he simply regarded Riker with an unsmiling face. When he was certain he had Riker's attention, he continued, "After you have cleaned yourself, you will put on those clothes and follow us."

"Where to?"

He should have known he wasn't going to get an answer, but rather just another cold stare. Knowing there was no point to fighting about or arguing over the matter, he stepped into the room and showered as quickly as he could . . . even though his impulse was to revel in it since it was the best he had felt in weeks. He dressed just as quickly and then stepped back out into the corridor. As near as he could tell, the guards had not moved so much as a centimeter from where they had been when he left them.

They went the rest of the way in silence, and then the guards halted in front of a set of doors. Clearly this was where they had been assigned to bring Tom. Riker wasn't sure what to expect when he walked in, although he was mentally prepared for anything, up to and including an abrupt barrage of phaser fire. For all he knew, this was the famed Romulan sense of humor about to display itself for his amusement.

Curiously, he was not expecting what he found.

There was a small table elegantly adorned, with a tall, thin candle flickering in the middle. It was the only source of light in the room. Food was laid out, not in abundance, but in sufficient quantity nonetheless and actually prepared to appear palatable. Seated on the far side of the table was Sela. She was still in uniform, but she had removed some of the armor pieces so that she appeared softer, if not exactly warm and cuddly. And she was actually smiling. For a moment, just a moment, Riker mistook her for someone else, so gentle were the lines in her face. Then he remembered that she was supposed to be a half-breed, born of an

Earthwoman named Tasha Yar and a Romulan noble. Riker found himself wishing that he had known Tasha Yar . . . and then had to remind himself that William Riker *had* known Tasha, and he would be well advised to remember that.

"Sit," she said, gesturing to the seat opposite her. Tom did so, his gaze never leaving her. She laughed, and it was a surprisingly musical noise. He had a feeling that she rarely did it. "You never take your eyes off me. Either you are utterly enamored of me, or else you are concerned that I'm going to slide a blade between your ribs."

"Let's just say a little bit of both."

"Fair enough. Eat." When she saw his hesitation, she reached over with a utensil, speared a piece of meat off his plate, and ate it. "See? No poison."

He pointed to another section of the plate and said, "That one."

She sighed. "You think I would eat off the 'safe' part and leave the rest to you. I may be part human, but I'm beginning to wonder if you may be part Romulan." She ate from the indicated section as well without hesitation. "Satisfied?"

"Of course, it could be a poison that works on humans and not Romulans."

"Perhaps. But as I just noted, I'm half human, so I would be at risk." She leaned forward, interlaced her fingers and rested her chin on them. She actually looked almost playful. "Riker, this is ridiculous. We have matters to discuss in which trust will be involved. If we can't even get past an entree, what is the point? Now eat the damned food or I'll blow you out an airlock, all right?"

Riker ate. In point of fact, the food wasn't too bad. A bit bland to his taste, but certainly palatable.

"Tell me about my mother."

The question caught him momentarily off guard. "You mean Tasha?"

She nodded. "I have hated her for many years, for betraying my father and leaving me. But . . ."

He might have been imagining it, but she actually seemed slightly to have let her guard down at the moment.

"I have . . . so few memories of her. She died when I was quite young. She . . . used to tell me stories. Fantasy stories. She spoke of giants, and magicians . . . and genies. Genies in a bottle where you would open the bottle and all your wishes would come true." She paused and then said, "I know, I know, it's very confusing . . . your records show that Tasha Yar died on some misbegotten planet somewhere, and yet she wound up on the bridge of the *Enterprise*-C as a lieutenant in Starfleet even though she'd really only been born a couple of years previously . . . I know all that, I understand that. Well . . . I think I understand it. That the Tasha you served with wasn't necessarily the same woman. But even so, there must have been some similarities. So . . . tell me what you know of her . . . knew of her . . ."

The problem was that Riker didn't know all that much about her. Will Riker did, of course, but not Tom. Then again, it didn't really matter if he kept it vague.

"She was . . . a superb officer. Brave. Dedicated. She was beautiful . . . and funny . . ."

"Funny?" Sela frowned. "I don't remember her ever being particularly . . . funny . . ."

"Well . . . considering what she'd been through . . . perhaps she wasn't feeling very humorous by the time she had you."

"No. No, I don't suppose she would have." She appeared thoughtful. "Tell me . . . something she did. Something you remember."

"She saved my life, on more than one occasion. There was this one time I remember . . ."

And he spun an entire story for her. He based it loosely on an actual event that had occurred earlier in his career, and he made a few substitutions . . . most notably, it had actually been Tom himself who had saved his commanding officer. But he inserted Tasha into the role of savior, himself into the role of the CO, and unspooled an exciting story of daring and sacrifice. Sela, like a woman suffering from drought, took it all in and seemed to absorb it into her soul.

He was making her happy.

It was a rather odd sensation.

"Tell me more," she said when he had finished his fabricated anecdote about her mother.

But Riker had finished the food in front of him, and he sensed that now was the time to try and push matters . . . now, when Sela seemed thoughtful and vulnerable.

"No."

She cocked an eyebrow, looking rather surprised at his abrupt change in tone. When she replied, her voice was silky, with an edge of danger to it. "No?"

"Why am I here? What is all this about? Are you planning to return me to the Cardassians . . . hold me for ransom . . . what? I could sit here all night rehashing old times and making you feel nice and nostalgic for your mother . . . but if it's all the same to you, I'd like to pretend we're two professionals who are capable of discussing whatever is on our mutual minds."

Very slowly, Sela brought her hands together and applauded in a steady and somewhat sarcastic manner. "Very nice display, Riker. Very nice. I'm trembling." Then she folded her hands on the table and leaned forward on her elbows, and Riker could see that he had gotten some sort of a reaction from her. Unfortunately, he wasn't entirely sure what it was, because it was as if she had draped a mask over her face and become completely unreadable. For a Romulan, she had the knack for Vulcan poker face.

"I could try to put this delicately, Riker, in order to spare myself some minor embarrassment. But I believe it best if we are straightforward with each other."

"That is generally preferable."

"I have fallen on what you would call 'hard times.' I have been an operative of the Romulan government for some years now, and I have had my share of successes. My failures, however, have been rather significant." As she cited each example, she tapped a finger on the table as if counting them out. "My attempt to reprogram your Mr. La Forge so that he would assassinate Klingon governor Vagh did not work out. Nor did my attempts to destabilize the Gowron regime by supporting the Duras family. However, my most significant failure was my thwarted attempt to invade Vulcan with Romulan forces. And the reason for these failures can always be traced back to the *Enterprise.* To your people, Riker, and to you. You have continually interfered with my endeavors, you have undercut my attempts to raise the Romulan Empire to its rightful place of power in the galaxy, and you have blocked me, time and again, from reaching my full potential and level within the Romulan power structure." She spread her hands wide and leaned back in her chair. "But am I bitter? Am I angry? Do I harbor resentment so sharp that it sticks within me like a perpetual dagger to my heart? Well? Do I?"

"Uhm . . . just guessing here, but . . . yes?"

"You bet your life I do," Sela confirmed. "The Romulan failure to conquer Vulcan was the worst. That was entirely my plan, from start to finish. Its bungling, and the subsequent loss of Romulan life, led my superiors to inform me that my services would no longer be required. In point of fact, I was likely scheduled for termination, since I had apparently—as the charming saying goes—outlived my usefulness. But I have my supporters. People who work under me and with me, or were loyal to my father and, by extension, to me. Through them and with them, I obtained the materials I needed to survive. I fled Romulus with the vessel you find yourself in now, plus several smaller ships that were stored in the hangar bay. You saw the single-person flier during the breakout, yes?"

"Yes, I did. Very impressive flying."

"Thank you," she said, and nodded in what appeared to be genuine appreciation . . . although with her it was hard to tell.

She rose from the other side of the table and slowly, very slowly, came around it. Riker noticed that she seemed to be swinging her hips a bit more than before. Was it his imagination, or was she moving in a deliberately provocative fashion?

And was it getting hotter in the room?

"The thing I remember most about my mother is that she would tell me stories of old Earth . . . especially about the warrior classes. She found the Japanese system of honor to be particularly intriguing, and passed that fascination on to me. At this point in my life, I am what might be referred to as a ronin . . . a masterless samurai. I have a great deal of anger burning within me, Riker . . . anger toward the *Enterprise* for failing my mother and abandoning her to the vagaries of the time stream . . . anger for the setbacks in my life that have prevented me from attaining the goals I've always felt I should have attained. What I have tried to do in my life is channel that anger toward purposes that would serve my career and the Romulan Star Empire. Having failed in that, I now seek redemption."

"And I'm to help you with that redemption, is that it?"

Slowly she nodded. She leaned forward and her voice was low and throaty, and he hadn't noticed it before but there was something almost intoxicating about her presence. "I sense in you a kindred spirit, Riker. You have been abandoned by the *Enterprise,* just as my mother was. You have given everything that you had to give to your government . . . only to have the government turn around and say, 'Not enough. We are sorry, but you simply have not done enough.' To know that your best was not only insufficient, but unappreciated."

"That," he said thoughtfully, "is certainly true enough."

She drew a finger across the line of his beard, tracing it. "I may have had some doubts about you at first, Riker, I freely admit that. But the most vital thing to remember is that Saket believed in you. I think he even liked you. And if you are good enough for Saket, then you are more than good enough for me. I believe that you can help me topple governments that I seek to disempower."

"You want me to help you disempower governments."

"That's right."

He tried not to laugh . . . but even more than that . . . he tried not to take it too seriously. Because he was starting to dwell on her words in a way that almost implied they made sense, held some appeal. They didn't, of course. They held no sway for him at all . . .

. . . except . . .

. . . except the Federation and Starfleet . . . really had left him out to dry, hadn't they? Maquis or not, he was Starfleet first and foremost. They could have done something to get him out of that hellhole, couldn't they? How long had they been intending to let him rot on Lazon? Forever? Probably. Yeah . . . probably.

With an effort, Riker fought to keep his senses on track. He had to remember the goal that he had set himself: to find out what Sela was up to, and figure out a way to thwart it. And in doing so . . .

In doing so . . . what?

Impress Starfleet? As if they cared about him. Still, that was another way that he and Sela were alike. Through sheer dogged determination, they were both trying to please the governments which had turned their respective backs upon them, in the same way that anxious children will do anything to try and please Mommy and Daddy.

He was not a child, though. He was William Riker . . .

No! He was Tom Riker . . .

But even as he thought that, he hated the reality of it. He was Will Riker, dammit. He was every bit as real and as vital and as deserving as the original—no, as the other—Will Riker.

Eight long years he had spent alone on Nervala IV. Eight long years.

One of the difficulties that mere mortals have trouble dealing with is the fact that life does indeed continue without them. But how much more galling for Tom Riker to learn that not only had everyone else's life gone on without him, but his had as well! And it was turning out so much better than his ever could. He would always be playing catch-up, always.

Better that he had died, alone and unknown, on Nervala IV. That was just more frustration that he felt himself lying at the figurative doorstep of the *Enterprise.*

"You can do yourself a favor, Riker," Sela almost purred. She was sitting quite close on the edge of the table, and she had an intoxicating scent to her. Riker had no idea whether she had applied it or it was a natural smell to her. He certainly didn't have the nerve to ask. "And it won't just be for yourself; it'll be for the Federation as well."

"Oh?" He shifted uncomfortably in his chair.

"That's right. You see, you feel as if your Federation has abandoned you. I know my empire has. But we can win back the admiration of both groups through the destruction of their mutual foe. . . ."

"The Cardassians?"

"Well, at the moment, the Cardassians are technically allies of the Romulans. Of course, my little raid doubtlessly didn't endear the Romulans to them, but my people will make the convincing argument that it was a rogue independent operator acting on her own. No, when I speak of mutual enemies"—she lowered her voice in obvious disdain—"I'm speaking of the Klingons and the Klingon Empire."

"The Klingons." Riker guffawed. "Sela, I know that you might be just a little out of touch, but last I looked, the Klingons and Federation were allies."

"The one who is out of touch is the Federation." She snorted disdainfully, wrinkling her nose in disgust. She had slid closer to him on the edge of the table, and one leg was swinging at the knee in a fashion that could best be described as "girlish." It was surprisingly fetching.

Eight years.

Eight years . . . by himself. With no company, no loved ones, no . . .

. . . no women.

It had been a long stretch, eight years. Riker had never anticipated living the celibate life of a monk. And yes, there had been the terribly brief reunion with Deanna, but circumstances had sped him through that get-together and there had been no one since then.

Riker had never had any problem obtaining bedmates when he had so desired. One yeoman had once commented that he should have the twinkle in his eye insured for a million credits. He seriously considered doing it just so he could name her as the beneficiary, just for laughs.

So eight years . . . going from feast to famine that totally and comprehensively . . .

He cleared his throat loudly, perhaps a bit too loudly, but he couldn't help it since it was feeling unnaturally closed up.

Sela, meantime, was still talking about Klingons.

"They are users," she said unequivocally. "They used the Romulans until it no longer served them, and then they allied with the Federation when their own resources were destroyed. Well, now other, powerful races have entered into the picture, haven't they. Powerful enemies, such as the Dominion and the Jem'Hadar. Inevitably, the Klingons will ally with them. It is their nature. They will ally themselves with the Dominion and shunt aside the Federation. Worse . . . they will turn against the Federation. The price of entry to join the galaxy-spanning club of the Dominion."

"You don't know that for certain . . ."

"Was it not a Terran . . . Santa Claus, I believe his name was . . . who said that those who do not listen to history are doomed to repeat it?"

Riker tried to cover his mouth and stifle a laugh. He was not one hundred percent successful. "I . . . I think you mean Santayana."

"Oh." Sela looked momentarily thrown, but then seemed to shrug it off mentally. "Well . . . the names are similar. I was close."

"Oh, definitely. They're practically interchangeable."

"The point is," she said forcefully, "that you can be instrumental in ending an alliance that should never have begun. Plus," and she smiled, "my plans involve a certain Klingon. One whose activities you must be all too well aware of."

For a moment Riker had absolutely no idea what she was talking about. The overheated effect that her presence was having on him abated slightly as he stared at her in confusion. "Who are you referring to?"

"Worf," she said flatly, and looked at him askance. "Are you saying you don't know? That their involvement was conducted without your knowledge?"

Worf. Worf from the *Enterprise.* Tom was with her that far, but her talking now about "involvement"? Riker was suddenly worried that he was approaching the outer reaches of his ability to carry off his masquerade. Trying to buy time, he said, "You've lost me. You've totally lost me."

"My oh my. I begin to understand." She reached over, took her chair by the back, and slid it behind herself. She sat so that she was face-to-face with Riker, their knees touching. She took her hands in his, and there was a look on her face that was genuinely sympathetic. "The heartlessness . . . the utter heartlessness . . . nothing could better underscore the pernicious Klingon mind-set . . ."

"What are you talking about?"

"Worf and your precious Deanna Troi, whom you talk about in your sleep—they are involved."

"In . . . involved?" The notion made his head swim. For years, when he had been stewing in his own juices alone on that godforsaken world, Deanna had been locked into his head, as if frozen in amber, and he had cherished the relationship that they had had. When he met up with her again on the *Enterprise,* it had seemed the perfect opportunity to make right that which he had botched the first time. He couldn't believe that she hadn't already been snatched up by someone, most particularly . . . well . . . himself.

And then what had he gone and done but blown it.

During his time in the work camp, he had dwelt on his actions since being rescued and, oddly enough, he regretted nothing—not even the actions that had cost him his freedom. Nothing . . . except the way that he had once again bungled his relationship with his Imzadi, with his Deanna. He had vowed that if he managed to get off the Cardassian rock that was his prison, he would somehow salvage the relationship.

In all those musings, it had never occurred to him that she might be taken because, after all, if fate had left her single for all that time, then certainly they were meant to be together.

And taken by . . . by Worf? By a Klingon warrior? What sort of madness was that? He was brutal where she was tender, bristling where she was smooth, rough where she was gentle . . .

Insanity . . .

He realized that Sela had kept talking, and with an effort he managed to refocus on what she was saying.

"—kept it secret while you were serving together," Sela was surmising, shaking her head in disbelief, "and then, once you were taken prisoner, they dropped the need for secrecy and flaunted their affair publicly."

"This . . . must be a mistake . . ."

"No mistake. I have . . . operatives . . . shall we say . . ."

"What are you talking about? Operatives where?"

She hesitated a moment, and then said, "All right. I may as well be candid. Our intelligence reports indicated that, in a full-blown war with the Dominion, Betazed would be a likely target for occupation by the Jem'Hadar. Both the Romulans and the Cardassians are keeping the planet under close surveillance, with a network of informants and such."

"So?"

"So, masterless samurai I may be, but I still have well-positioned sources in the Romulan intelligence-gathering network, at least. I hear of things. Once I knew of your interest in her, I checked into Deanna Troi's more recent activities just as a matter of course. It turns how she had just recently returned to Betazed . . . with her fiancé, Mr. Worf, in tow. Deanna's mother, Lwaxana Troi, held a rather large social gathering for her just the other day, in fact. A sort of welcome-home affair."

Riker looked as if he'd been smashed across the face with a brick. "Deanna . . . and Worf. No, he's . . . he's all wrong for her . . . how could he let this happen . . . ?"

"How could he let it happen?"

Riker's breath suddenly caught. He'd blown it, since of course he was referring to Will Riker, his counterpart.

But without hesitation, Sela replied, "He's a Klingon, Riker. That's my point.

He let it happen because he wanted it to happen. He cares nothing about loyalty or decency. As with all his kind, he wants what he can take because he is the stronger. He sees Deanna as a conquest; nothing more."

There was a pounding in Tom Riker's head then, a whirlpool of emotions swirling within him. Anger at Will Riker, fury with Worf, desire for Deanna tinted with a sense of betrayal, and a need . . .

. . . a need, like a living entity all its own. A need to love and be loved, a need to hold a woman in his arms, to reinforce his own desirability. A need to hurl himself into an abyss of passion and sensation, to release the emotion that was roiling within him . . .

It was as if Sela sensed that need. Her hand was at the base of his neck now, as if feeling the throb of his pulse. She seemed everywhere to him: in his mind, in his soul, and when she spoke again it was with her hot breath caressing the inside of his ear.

"You can have her again," she whispered. "You can take her from the brute . . . I can help you with that . . . I can help you with whatever you wish to do, for we are two of a kind . . . we are both the outcasts, the forgotten . . . we can help each other, Riker . . . we're good for each other . . . you have a need, don't you . . . don't you . . ."

And yet, with all the buildup in his mind, in his body, he didn't know that he would press his lips against hers until he actually did it. Had no idea that he would grab her with a fierceness that astounded even him, pulling her body up against his, feeling the hard shape of her beneath the clothing, the tautness of her flat stomach and lean muscles. He felt her gasp into his mouth and then she returned the ferocity of his kiss with an intensity of her own. . . .

Nine

Worf hadn't been completely certain what to expect upon his arrival at Lwaxana Troi's house, but the sight of Lwaxana in battle gear certainly wasn't it.

It was a fairly warm morning, as most were on Betazed. The grass was still wet from the dew, and Worf unaccountably felt a certain spring in his step. For no reason that he could really determine, he was filled with an odd faith that everything was going to work out. That confidence lasted up until the point that Lwaxana opened the door, at which point he decided that all bets were off.

The fact that she had answered the door herself rather than having Mr. Homn do it was surprising enough. But her garb and demeanor were nothing like what Worf was accustomed to. She was wearing no makeup, and her long hair was tied back with a cloth. She was wearing a formfitting, one-piece blue outfit, with heavy padding around the shoulders, upper chest, and upper arms, and hips. In either hand, she was holding a long staff, with what appeared to be lights at either end of each staff. The lights were not on, however.

In addition to her workout armor, she was also smiling. Worf wasn't quite certain which he found to be more disconcerting.

Worf decided to comment on the less obvious of the two unusual aspects of Lwaxana Troi that he was encountering. "Good morning, Mrs. Troi. You seem in a good mood today."

"Please, it's 'Lwaxana.' Let's not be so formal. And yes, as a matter of fact, I'm in a very good mood. Come in, come in," and she gestured for him to follow. He did so, allowing himself the briefest of moments to try and determine whether this was, in fact, Lwaxana Troi, or instead a rather brilliant imposter.

"The reason I'm in a good mood is that I just heard from Odo."

"Odo?" He frowned. "Security Chief Odo?"

"Oh, I should have realized you'd know of him. He's in the same line of work as you. He's a law enforcement officer on Deep Space Nine. Have you ever been there?"

"Yes, but I am not especially fond of space stations."

"Really?" She glanced over her shoulder at him. "Why not?"

"I do not like being aboard a stationary target."

"Worf, Worf, Worf," she sighed, "does everything with you have to be defined in military terms?"

"Yes."

"Well, at least you're honest. Anyway, Odo and I, we have a rather . . . special relationship. I just received a vid from him this morning. Would you like to see it?"

"No—"

"Then I'll tell you about it. 'Mrs. Troi,' " Lwaxana recited from memory, in a musical timbre, " 'I am in receipt of your latest communication. While I am certain that you considered your remarks to be flattering, I have to tell you that the desires you have expressed are misplaced and that our continued correspondence is going to prove increasingly uncomfortable for us both . . . particularly, it seems, for me.' We have a very special relationship, Odo and I," she said to Worf, back in her normal voice.

" 'Despite your impressions to the contrary, we have no relationship beyond friendship,' " Lwaxana continued, returning to her musical speech. " '. . . and at this point, at the risk of injured feelings, I must say that even that affiliation is becoming increasingly tenuous. Please . . . if you must continue this correspondence, do so in a more formal and strictly platonic manner . . . and preferably, with a message that consumes somewhat less time than . . .' " Lwaxana paused, remembering. " '. . . ninety-three minutes and eighteen seconds.' "

Finished, she turned to Worf and seemed unaccountably happy. "You may not have been able to tell from that, but that was positively tender compared to our earlier communiqués. He is definitely starting to come around. Isn't he marvelous?"

"His candor is admirable . . . albeit wasted," Worf observed. "What species is he?"

"I'm not entirely sure. I don't know if he knows, either. He is a shapeshifter, however. And a brilliant law-enforcement individual. If you're ever in a difficult situation, he's your man . . . well . . . he's your . . . whatever . . ." Then, as if she'd promptly dismissed him from her mind, she said, "All right . . . this way, Worf."

She guided him to an outdoor area with towering trees that provided a good deal of shade. There was a wide patio lined with colorful mosaics. Worf found his attention drawn to the mosaics for no reason that he could really discern. There was just something about them that captivated the eye. There was one section, however, that seemed to have been specially prepared. It was a rectangular area about twenty feet long and ten feet wide, and as opposed to the rest of the patio, it seemed to be composed of a spongy, rubbery material. Lwaxana stepped to the far end and indicated, with a wave of one of the staffs, that Worf should stand at the opposite end. He did so, getting the sick feeling that he knew where this was going.

"Why are you here, Worf?" asked Lwaxana. She was standing some feet away from him, and holding the two staffs in a relaxed position so that they were crisscrossing each other.

"I promised I would be."

"Are you happy about it?"

"That is irrelevant."

"Happiness is never irrelevant, Worf."

"Of course it is. Oftentimes, in fact. The first obligation of life is duty. Happiness is not a factor in that."

"But if you derive no happiness from it, then what's the point?" She seemed genuinely puzzled.

" 'Happiness,' if you insist upon the term, comes from knowing that one's duty has been fulfilled."

"But knowing it isn't enough. For example, it is the duty of a Daughter of the Fifth House to have a daughter of her own to carry on the traditions of the House. But if I were not happy about having Deanna . . . if I regarded motherhood simply as a fulfilled duty, and nothing beyond that, then what sort of mother would I be?"

"A Klingon mother."

She sighed and shook her head. "Worf . . . be honest with me. . . ."

"Have I a choice?"

"No," she said in a practical tone. "You think there's nothing you can learn from me, don't you."

He didn't reply.

"You think," she continued, "that because Betazoids love peace . . . and introspection . . . that we are weak."

"I would not marry Deanna if I thought Betazoids were weak."

"Perhaps. Or perhaps you simply regard her as the exception to the rule. Or perhaps you do see her as weak . . . and inferior . . . and therefore easy for you to control and no threat to your dominance."

"That is not true!" he bristled.

"All right," she said calmly. "But now let's see . . . if I can teach you a few things. Things about our philosophies, about our way of life. And maybe, just maybe . . . they'll be things you can apply to the way you live your life as not only the husband of a Betazoid, but as a Klingon." She tossed him one of the two staffs and he caught it effortlessly. Then she brought the remaining staff up to a horizontal position, resting it comfortably between the thumb and forefinger of each hand.

Worf gaped at her in undisguised astonishment. "Are you suggesting we fight?"

"You think Betazoid philosophies make us weak. Ripe for conquest. I want to show you otherwise. We were not always the thoughtful philosophers and sensitives that you know us as now. We had our wars, we had our violence. We learned the importance of growing beyond that. You will, too." She indicated the ends of the staffs. "This is a little game called B'thoon. The lights at the end of the staffs illuminate when they come into contact with your opponent. Moves can be to anywhere, but only a strike between the neck and waist counts as a point."

"I do not want to hurt you."

"Don't worry. You won't."

She spoke with surprising confidence. With a mental shrug, Worf took a stance, holding the rod out in front of him and endeavoring to look as challenged as he could considering his opponent was a middle-aged Betazoid woman.

Lwaxana let out a battle cry, whirled the staff in a dazzling spin, and came at him.

Worf's staff smacked her squarely in the stomach and lit up. Lwaxana hit the ground like a sack of rocks and lay there for a moment, gasping.

"Are you injured?" Worf asked. He extended a hand to help her up.

Lwaxana, all pride and wounded dignity, waved him off. She placed the bottom of the pole on the ground, pushed upward and got herself standing up. She took a deep breath and finally managed to say, "You're quick, Worf. I'll grant you that. And I'm just a little rusty. But I"—and she rallied her confidence—"was B'thoon champion of my graduating class. You won't catch me quite that easily again."

Once more she took a defensive stance, approaching him more cautiously this time. Worf didn't even move. He simply remained with his feet rooted to the ground, tracking her with a slight angling of his torso. She came in fast with a quick series of strikes aimed at the chest and arms. Worf blocked them without too serious an effort, ducked a swing of hers that went wide, and used the opportunity to angle his staff between her ankles and trip her up. Lwaxana's feet went out from under her, and she thudded to the ground. The spongy material absorbed much of the impact, but Lwaxana still looked jolted.

This is absurd, he thought.

Lwaxana got back to her feet a bit more slowly but no less determinedly. Her hair was somewhat askew and starting to get into her way. She pushed strands aside and readied herself. "Again."

"Lwaxana . . ."

"Now!"

Three, four quick exchanges, and this time he hit her just under the rib cage. It didn't knock her down, but the end of the staff lit up.

"Again," she said, her anger clearly building.

Again the staffs clacked together. This time Worf pivoted, dodging a full-bore charge by her, and struck her in the back just under the third vertebra. She spun around, and there was cold fury on her face. "I can do this," she declared.

"Lwaxana . . ."

"I can do this!"

She came at him again.

And again.

And again.

Each time he deflected her blows, or dodged them. A couple of times she came close to tagging him, but close was all she managed. Over and over he would nail her after a few exchanges, without working up any real exhaustion over it.

He kept waiting for Lwaxana to quit.

She wouldn't.

Her face, her clothes became soaked with sweat. Her breath became more tortured. Her movements slowed, each repetition more filled with effort than the one before. For Worf it became painful to watch. When she had fallen nearly three dozen times, Worf started to get genuinely concerned. It was not going to look good to Deanna if her fiancé killed his prospective mother-in-law. He was doing the best he could to control the severity of the impact with which the staff was striking her, but Worf was not accustomed to moderating the force of his blows. Klingons did not, as a rule, fight for the purpose of wounding.

So much perspiration was rolling off Lwaxana's brow that she was blinking furiously to keep it out of her eyes. Her hair was hanging, matted, around her face.

She tried to stand in one place as she planted herself for the next go-around, but she was wobbling. She took a moment to steady herself and Worf waited.

"Lwaxana . . . quitting is an option," he said.

There was a deep rasping in her throat, as if all the moisture in her body was on the outside and there was none left within. "You . . . first . . ." she said.

With that one sentence, that one defiant utterance, Worf understood what was at stake for her. She wasn't simply battling him. She was also fighting the memory of her own youth, of what she once was. Lwaxana Troi was a woman who thrived on self-esteem in the same way that others thrived on oxygen and light.

You first, she had said.

Well, that was all it would take, really. All Worf had to do was give in. Say that he'd had enough. Be the first one to back off.

He opened his mouth to say it . . .

. . . and the words stuck in his throat.

Quit? To hell with that. Lwaxana was battling demons of her youth. So what? Worf had to deal with that every day, and one didn't deal with that by giving up.

Slowly he shook his head and brought his staff up defensively again. Lwaxana grunted in acknowledgment that the battle was to continue. She licked her chapped lips, not doing much in the way of wetting them, and steeled herself for another attack.

In a surprising move, she swung at his legs. He vaulted over it, hit the ground rolling, blocked a return thrust by her, and hit her in the stomach again . . . lighter than the first time, but she still felt it. She bent over, staggering away from him, trying to regroup. And he heard her muttering something to herself, doing it so quietly that he was reasonably sure she didn't know he'd heard it.

"Just once," she was saying under her breath, "just once . . ."

Just once.

Well, that was really all it would take, wasn't it. The woman had her pride, but certainly she knew she was overmatched by this point. A pain in the ass Lwaxana Troi could be, but insane she most definitely was not. At this point, she was battling not with any hope of truly overcoming him or teaching him some profound lesson about just how tough Betazoids were. Instead she was fighting purely out of vanity. She couldn't withdraw from the field without managing to nail Worf at least once. He could even see the Lwaxana-skewed way that she would tell others of the battle: "There we were, a Klingon warrior and I, slugging it out with our B'thoon staffs, and suddenly, boom! Got him square in the chest!" Naturally she would leave out the three dozen or so strikes that he got her with first.

And it wasn't just for the retelling, either. If he let her get him once (without her realizing, of course, that he had allowed it) then it would go a long way toward restoring her sense of self-worth.

Just the one shot. Just the one.

Just throw one engagement. Move a hair too slowly, react a second less quickly, and she would tag him on the arm or somewhere, gain a point, and have a moral victory that would enable her to step back and announce, "Now we're done."

He saw her readying herself for another charge. She took two quick steps—or at least what passed for quick at that point—and then feinted a strike to the head. As feints went, it was fairly pathetic. She had telegraphed it; it was rather clear to Worf that what she was intending to do was reverse the direction of the staff and make her genuine attack to the chest, probably to the solar plexus. But all he had to do was be "fooled" by the feint. Bring his staff up, block it, and that would leave him open for Lwaxana to hit him.

All this went through his mind in a second.

Lwaxana's staff arced toward his head, and Worf made as if to block it. And then she reversed the staff and tried to strike him squarely in the chest.

The thrust came up several inches short of its target . . . the reason being that Worf's hand had snaked out and snared the staff about a foot from the end, away from the sensors so that it didn't register as a hit. Lwaxana's staff was held immobile by the Klingon's superior strength and then Worf shoved her staff right back at her. But he had overestimated his strength and the amount of resistance Lwaxana had left. The staff slid right through her sweat-soaked palms and struck her squarely in the forehead.

"Lwaxana!"

She stood there for a moment, wavering, her eyes blurring and then refocusing.

"Lwaxana, are you all right? Do you want to sit down?"

"Excellent idea, Pierre," Lwaxana announced. "The corn muffins look scrumptious today." And with that utter non sequitur, Lwaxana fell forward like a tree. If Worf hadn't caught her, she would have hit the ground face-first.

"So how are the lessons going?" asked Deanna, her face bright and smiling on the vidcom.

"As . . . well as can be expected," Worf replied, standing in the foyer of the Troi mansion.

"Do you feel you've learned anything?" She sounded almost playful with the question. Worf wondered just how playful Deanna would feel if she knew he'd nearly decapitated the Keeper of the Holy Rings of Betazed.

"Oh . . . yes."

"Like what?"

Desperate for an answer and looking for a way out, Worf fell back on possibly the oldest dodge in civilized history. "I . . . have to go . . . I hear your mother calling."

"I didn't." Deanna looked puzzled.

Worf tapped his head. "In here."

"Oh. Of course, how foolish. Well, I'm just glad to know the two of you are getting along. See you tonight. Love you." And she blinked off.

Shaking his head, Worf went to Lwaxana's bedroom, where she was lying with what appeared to be some sort of green liquid-encased compress on her head which Mr. Homn had just placed there. She had switched to a simple white shift, and Worf saw bruises lining her upper arms. He winced inwardly but said nothing as he wondered just how angry she was going to be.

Without turning her head, her gaze went in his direction, and to his surprise her expression actually softened to one of—well, not affection, but not overt hostility. If anything she seemed a little . . . sad, somehow. "Sit down, Worf."

He turned to look for a chair and was mildly startled to see that Mr. Homn was sliding one in behind him. He had not even realized the giant manservant had stepped away from the bed, so silently and effortlessly had he moved. Worf couldn't help but wonder just how much there was about Homn that he didn't know.

Worf sat with his back ramrod straight. He had absolutely no idea what to expect.

"Tell me . . . what you were thinking. Toward the end of our bout, I mean."

"Why do you ask?"

"Because I'm interested," she said matter-of-factly.

"No, I mean . . . why do you not just tell me what I was thinking?"

She made a soft, impatient clucking noise in the back of her throat as if annoyed that he had to ask. "Worf . . . believe it or not, I am capable of turning my abilities on and off. This is supposed to be about you. If I tell you what was on your mind, it becomes about me."

"Very well. It may hurt your feelings . . ."

"Hurt away," she said dryly.

"I felt . . . sorry for you. I thought you were pathetic."

"Good."

He blinked. "Good?"

"Yes. That's what I was going for. You don't seriously think I was under the impression that I could match you physically?"

"Well . . ." The question was clear on his face: What was the point of it all?

"What were your options? What were you considering, Worf? Faced with this pathetic, desperate old woman who seemed anxious to prove something to herself . . . what was going through your mind?"

"I . . . considered quitting."

"But you didn't."

"No. Then I considered allowing you to score a hit."

"And you didn't do that, either."

"No, I did not."

"Why?"

"Because . . . I felt it would do you a dishonor. That you deserved only my best effort."

"Oh, tribblefur," snapped Lwaxana.

Had Worf been a Delian Optistalk, his eyes would have lunged out of his head. *"What?"*

"You heard me. Your decisions, your combat tactics, had nothing at all to do with my 'honor.' You just couldn't stand to show anything that could possibly be interpreted as weakness. To quit, or to allow me to score would have threatened your Klingon pride."

"That is not true."

"It most certainly is. Here you had a helpless opponent. You could have withdrawn. But you refused, even though you had nothing to prove. Then, toward the end, I muttered, 'Just once,' just loudly enough for you to hear. You could have figured out a way to allow me to score, to salvage my 'pride.' But your own pride wouldn't allow it. You put yourself and your sense of duty above everything . . . in this instance, your duty to the Klingon code of honor, whether real or imagined. You couldn't allow a helpless woman even the most meager of triumphs against you because it would have been threatening to you. You had to fight; you couldn't refrain from it, could not justify it in your own mind no matter how much you tried. Your problem, Worf, is that you have too overpowering a sense of yourself."

Worf gaped at her. "With all respect, Lwaxana, when it comes to a sense of one's self, I do not believe I can begin to approach your own attitude. How many times have we heard your assorted titles bandied about with pride?"

She sat up, but too quickly, because clearly from her perspective the room was tilting dangerously. She lay back, keeping the compress against her head. "A valid enough point, Worf, as far as it goes. However, I am capable of putting aside myself. If I didn't . . . do you think I could have willingly subjected myself to our little sparring match earlier? It's not always easy, I admit, and as I get older I get more set in my ways. But I do have the ability to reach into myself . . . and cast myself aside."

"I do not understand."

This time she sat up a bit more carefully. Next to her bed was a large vase of cut flowers, and ever so gently she reached over and extracted one. It was large and fragrant, and had many petals of assorted colors. She removed the stem and cradled the bud itself in the palm of her hand. "To be Betazoid . . . is to be like this flower, Worf. Look at it. See the beauty of its shape? Its fragrance? See all the petals that surround it?"

He nodded.

Lwaxana then, one petal at a time, began to disassemble the flower. She did so very carefully, and each petal would be removed only to reveal another of a different color. When she spoke it was so softly that Worf had to strain to hear her.

"Each of these layers," she told him, "compose the flower. Just as we ourselves are composed of different layers and varying textures. Our experiences, our personal histories, our likes and dislikes, are all part of it. But you cannot let yourself define yourself by these trappings. They are merely aspects of you that the outside world is able to see. But if you strip it all away . . . what do you have?"

She held up her hand. It was empty. The petals lay scattered on the bed.

"You have . . . nothing," said Worf.

But she shook her head. "Wrong," she said with a smile. "The flower is still here. I can feel it in my palm . . . feel the texture of it, the slight weight. The fragrance of it stays with me. The core, the essence of it remains, even though it cannot be seen. You only believe in what you can see and touch, Worf. You believe in yourself. You have to be able to put yourself aside, to make yourself unimportant. Once you are nothing . . . then you can become something."

"That is double talk," he growled. "Klingon honor can neither be seen nor touched. I believe in that."

"You believe in it because it is results-oriented. It gives you things of substance. By attending to that code of ethics, the result is title, or properties, or higher rank, or makes you more desirable to the opposite sex, or at the very least minimizes the ways another Klingon can try to kill you since any number of ways would be dishonorable."

"I do not appreciate your cavalierly dismissing my way of life."

"I'm not dismissing it, Worf. I'm just giving it some thought rather than accepting it blindly. Have you ever done that?"

His jaw twitched slightly, the muscles flexing in annoyance.

"Why did you kill Duras? What was the purpose?"

The question caught him off-guard. "How do you know of that?"

"It was on your service record. I read up on you last night. Jean-Luc officially reprimanded you. So . . . what was the purpose?"

"He killed K'Ehleyr, Alexander's mother."

"That was the catalyst for your killing him. Not the purpose."

"I claimed the right of vengeance."

"And that was the excuse." She swung her legs around so that they were dangling off the bed. "Again, what was the purpose?"

"So that K'Ehleyr would be avenged," he said with growing impatience. He was becoming increasingly uncomfortable, even angry, with the line of discussion.

Lwaxana shook her head. "K'Ehleyr was dead, Worf. She was beyond Duras's ability to hurt or your ability to make her care."

"He framed my father as a traitor . . . deprived me of honor . . ."

"And with those offenses revealed, your father's name would have been cleared, your precious honor restored. So I ask again, what was the purpose of—"

Worf was on his feet with a roar that nearly shook the rafters, his hands balled into fists. *"Because I wanted him dead!"*

A hand slammed down on Worf's shoulder and, to the Klingon's astonishment, he was shoved forcibly back down into the chair. He craned his neck around to see Mr. Homn standing behind him. Worf couldn't believe it; Homn had done it with no apparent effort whatsoever. Very slowly, Mr. Homn shook his head from side to side in mild rebuke.

"You wanted him dead," Lwaxana said mildly, as if Worf hadn't blown his temper, "because his murder of K'Ehleyr compromised your sense of maleness . . . your ego, your pride. He had taken something away from you . . ."

"And from Alexander," Worf reminded her. Homn removed his hand from Worf's shoulder, apparently convinced that the Klingon had himself under control.

"If Alexander had never been born, would you still have killed Duras?"

"Yes," Worf admitted.

"So for his offenses . . . you had to take his life away from him. And it solved nothing. His sisters perpetuated the cycle of vengeance . . . a cycle which ended in the destruction of the *Enterprise* through the efforts of Duras's sisters. Innocent people died in that crash, Worf. Not many, thank heavens, but some. Innocent people who never knew K'Ehleyr, or cared about Klingon honor. People who were just going about their business and then they died . . . thanks to vengeance."

"That is a gross distortion of the facts."

"Is it?"

He rose, more carefully and unthreateningly this time. "I do not wish to discuss these matters any further. And I do not wish you to mention K'Ehleyr's name again."

For a long moment her dark eyes fixed on him, and then she lowered her gaze. "Very well," she said. "I apologize if I overstepped myself. I will see you tomorrow, Worf."

He nodded in acknowledgment and turned to leave. "Worf . . ." she called to him. He turned and looked back at her.

She was holding out her empty hand, palm up. "Would you like a flower?" she asked.

Worf sighed, shook his head, and walked out. Lwaxana raised her hand to her nose, inhaled deeply, saw the flower in her mind, and smiled in appreciation.

"So how did it go?" asked Deanna when Worf returned to the inn.

He considered the fact that he had battled hand to hand with Lwaxana, knocked her cold, had his entire system of honor brought into question, was manhandled with frightening ease by Mr. Homn, and offered a big handful of nothing as a parting gift.

"Actually," he said thoughtfully, "it went more or less as I expected."

Ten

William Riker hadn't realized that he was going to look in the mirror first thing that morning and that, in doing so, it was going to change his life. But that was what happened.

The investigation into the crash of the *Enterprise* 1701-D had gone about as well as it could have gone. Admiral Jellico was his usual charming self, leading the inquisition and asking most of the truly intense and combative questions. But Picard, doing most of the talking, managed to handle them with aplomb. After a day or so of deliberation, both Picard and Riker were cleared of any negligence and wrongdoing in the ship's demise.

After that had come the truly positive news. There was going to be a new *Enterprise,* designated the *Enterprise*-E. There had been some discussion about the possibility of simply starting over with a new registry number, but the ship had too much of a history about it. Indeed, it had been Picard who had argued most strenuously against redesignating her. "We owe it to the commanders of the earlier vessels . . . including, most notably, James T. Kirk," he had said, and he had spoken so forcefully about it that it was almost as if he were defending a personal friend. Consequently, the ship was indeed going to be designated "E."

Unfortunately, it was going to be a year before she was ready to go.

Picard was already guaranteed the captaincy, that much was a given. But then Picard had faced his toughest fight: keeping his command crew intact. There was any number of vessels and assignments available that were long-term, and the *Enterprise* officers were considered a highly valuable commodity. Keeping all of the assignments of Picard's key officers frozen so that they would be available for the new *Enterprise* when she was ready was considered by several key officials in Starfleet—including, most notably, Jellico once again—a tremendous waste of resources.

That had not daunted Picard, who had pulled every string he could and called in at least half a dozen favors accrued over the years. As a result, the assignments handed out to Picard's command crew were all short-term, most of them well within range of Earth or even planetside.

The only sticking point had been Riker.

There was a push to promote him. Enough was enough, it was felt. He had more than adequately proven his value in a command capacity, and it was time to assume a captaincy of his own. But as he had before, Riker had resisted the concept, citing the same reasons as he always had: There was no ship like the *Enterprise.* Anything else was going to be a step down. He was comfortable serving with Picard. More than that, in fact. "As long as there is an *Enterprise,* and Jean-Luc Picard is in the captain's seat," Riker had told Picard, "I would consider it an honor to serve as second-in-command." On that basis, Picard had pushed for—and gotten—Riker instated as his Number One. There was no reason for him to disbelieve Riker's sentiments. After all, he'd been saying it for years.

But this morning, after Riker had gotten out of bed, stretched, and trudged to the bathroom, he'd looked in the mirror and—for the first time—started to wonder.

What caused him to wonder was his beard.

For the first time he noticed truly pronounced gray hairs in it.

He frowned, tilting his head around, examining it from several different angles.

Yup. Definitely, gray hairs. It was odd that he hadn't noticed them before. He reached up, plucked one out and winced as he did so. But there were more of them, scattered throughout.

He brushed back his hair at his temples and saw a few telltale gray strands there as well. He was barechested at that moment, clad only in pajama bottoms, so he studied his chest hair. No gray there, thank goodness. Wasn't a hopeless cause, not yet.

It was funny. He'd never thought of himself as particularly vain before. But something about the encroaching gray bothered him more than he could comprehend. He could get it touched up, of course. That would be easy enough. It went against the grain, though, hiding something like that. Besides, all that would do was hide it. But it wouldn't stop it.

Why did it bother him so? Why?

He dwelled on it as he prepared breakfast, going through the various files that he'd been studying over the previous several nights. He'd been assigned a teaching slot at Starfleet Academy, lecturing in tactics and strategy. All things considered, it was a rather plum assignment. He was being given the opportunity to shape young minds, perhaps even save lives. After all, things that he taught today might be used to prevent disaster tomorrow.

But he kept coming back to the mirror.

And to his lack of desire for command, his wish to stay aboard the *Enterprise.* It gnawed at him, it bothered the hell out of him.

He tried to think of who he could talk to in order to try and get it all sorted out. His crewmates, his only real family, were scattered, busy with their own affairs. Besides, Riker wasn't really comfortable discussing his feelings and uncertainties with anyone . . . not even Picard, even after all this time, particularly when it came to questions about advancement, since Picard usually took any opportunity to say, in essence, "I will respect your wishes, Will, but damn, you should have your own ship."

There was only one person he could truly let down his guard with, of course, and that was Deanna.

Deanna, engaged to someone else.

Deanna, off to Betazed, with her fiancé.

Her fiancé . . .

"Her fiancé," he said out loud to nobody in particular, and he abruptly realized that he'd stopped his classroom preparation and had simply been staring across his living room for the last several minutes.

He pictured them, standing hand in hand. He wondered if she was showing him all the places that she had gone to with Riker. Places that had been Riker's and Troi's now would be Worf's and Troi's.

While Riker was sitting in a tastefully decorated apartment on Earth, was Deanna making love in the Jalara jungle with her fiancé? Was she responding to his touch the same way that she had to Riker's? Or better? Was she wondering why she had ever wasted time waiting for Will Riker to come around? Was all memory of the time and places they had shared on Betazed being supplanted or erased by the new experiences she was sharing with . . . him? With . . .

Riker couldn't even frame the Klingon's name in his mind.

"This is insane!" Will said. He rose from behind the table so quickly that he slammed his knee against the underside of it and winced in pain. "We're friends!

We're just friends! I want her to be happy, and she's happy with him, and that's all! That's it! We're done!"

He was speaking so loudly that the residents next door wondered who in the world he was arguing with.

"Why are you still here, Will?"

Riker was sitting in the captain's ready room, facing Picard. Picard, drinking a glass of prune juice, was looking at Riker with what appeared to be unveiled contempt. "You turned down a promotion. Why?"

"She's not the *Enterprise,"* Riker replied.

"So what? So bloody what? What sort of sentiment is that coming from Will Riker, one of the most ambitious men in Starfleet? This is nonsense, Will! Nonsense!"

Picard got up from behind the desk and skipped around it to Riker . . . and then smacked him upside the head. "Hey!" said Riker.

"I'm trying to get your attention, Will. Don't you understand what's going on? It's not about the *Enterprise!"*

"Yes, it is."

"No, it isn't."

"Yes, it is."

"Isn't."

"Is."

"Isn't isn't isn't."

"Captain, we're not getting anywhere like this!"

"Yes, we are."

"No, we're n—" Riker stopped, rubbing the bridge of his nose and wondering just what in the hell was going on.

Picard clonked him on the side of the head again. "Will you stop that!" Riker shouted.

"Business and pleasure, Will. Doesn't mix. Never did. Never has, never will . . . Will."

"Captain . . ."

Picard suddenly went behind his desk, picked up an apple, and tossed it with a fairly strong overarm throw. Riker tried to duck, but the apple tracked with him and it ricocheted off his temple. "What did you do that for?" he demanded.

"Isaac Newton. He understood things when an apple fell on him. I thought you might, too."

"Newton?"

"Yes," said Data. Riker wasn't entirely sure when Data had entered the room, or what he was doing there, or why he was wearing a mortarboard on his head. "Framer of theories of gravity, physics, and he also made a damned good fig cookie."

Riker had the distinct feeling that a headache was going to be forthcoming.

"Newtonian physics, Commander," continued Data while Picard played with a yo-yo. "Objects in motion tend to stay in motion, unless acted upon by an outside force."

"What's your point, Data?"

"Your career was in motion. It has been acted upon by an outside force."

"Oh really? And what would that be?"

Deanna walked in. She was naked. Riker noticed in a distant manner that he was as well.

He looked in a panic from Deanna to Data to Picard, and back to Deanna. "What . . . what do I do?"

Picard stabbed a finger toward Deanna with confidence and said, "Engage."

"En . . . engage?" He looked down into his hand and he was holding a shining diamond ring in his hand. It glittered with a fire as bright as a warp engine.

"Engage," Picard said firmly.

Riker turned to face Deanna. Worf, wearing full, bristling Klingon armor, was cradling her in his arms. Riker was frozen in place, incapable of saying anything. His voice, his emotions had all left him. Worf turned on his heel and headed out the door, the nude Deanna tossing off a cheerful wave as they exited.

"Nice going."

Picard and Data were gone. Seated behind Picard's desk was Admiral Riker . . . the older version of Riker from the future. Behind him, a grandfather clock was ticking away the years.

"Nice going, buddy boy," said the admiral.

"I . . ."

And a rage seemed to seize the admiral. He opened the grandfather clock, drew out a Klingon *bat'leth,* and swung the sword around in a vicious scythe straight toward Riker's neck. *"Nice bloody going!"* he howled, filled with fury that was ripped deep from within his soul, from his regrets, from every mistake that he had ever made.

Riker fell off the bed.

It was pitch black in the room, and it took Riker a few minutes to recover himself. He was gasping and twisted around in the sheets, his heart pounding against his chest. He felt as if he had gallons of sweat streaming from every pore. Even though the temperature was cool in his apartment, he still felt hot.

Usually, when Riker had dreams, he would awaken and sense the images flittering away to the far reaches of his subconscious. He never remembered them. This time, he did. Some of the exchanges were already blurring to him, but the general thrust was still very vivid and very potent.

And he understood. For perhaps the first time in his life . . . he understood.

It wasn't as if he'd had an overnight epiphany. It was the crystallization of years of thought, of hesitation, of uncertainty. Because the simple fact of the matter was that for years he had known exactly what he wanted and precisely where he wanted to be . . . and it had all gone straight out the window the moment that he found himself face-to-face with Deanna Troi on the bridge of the *Enterprise* when the words *Do you remember what I taught you,* Imzadi? echoed in his head, sent there by the woman he had spent years being absolutely positive that he had gotten over.

Oh, he had most definitely been Hamlet, standing there for years and wondering, prevaricating, trying to come to a decision and not sure what direction to take. Nothing less than the destruction of the *Enterprise* had been required to shake him from his mental lethargy. For if an object in motion tends to stay in motion, an object at rest likewise tends to stay at rest.

The object in motion had been his career. And it had stopped. And yes, all the reasons and rationalizations regarding the honor of serving aboard the *Enterprise* and all of that had been accurate as far as it went. But there was an element that he had not been dealing with, an object at rest—that object being his relationship with Deanna. One, he now believed, was intertwined with the other in a way that he had never fully comprehended.

He was in love with Deanna. Not as a friend, not as a former intimate. They were Imzadi. They had gotten into each other's souls, and not only had he never gotten her out of his, he had now come to the realization that he didn't want to.

It wasn't just the *Enterprise* herself that had a hold on him. It was Deanna herself, all unintentionally. If he'd gotten command of another vessel, he would have had to leave her behind. Either that, or force her to make a decision to come with him to his new post or stay with the *Enterprise.* He loved her too much to ask her to tear herself away from her extended *Enterprise* family, and he was still too damned vacillating on his own feelings about her to commit. And because of that vacillation, she was on Betazed at that very moment in the arms of Worf.

He felt ill, his stomach in a knot. He didn't know what to do.

No . . . Riker did know. It was just a matter of doing it. There were not immediate plans for a wedding, so he had a little time. Not infinite amounts, but a little.

He went to his vidcom and began to place a communiqué to Betazed . . . but then canceled it. Betazed was too far to allow instantaneous communication, which meant that he'd have to send a one-way. A one-way that said what? "Deanna, I love you, ditch Worf, get back here?" Besides, even if something instantaneous were possible, how could he do it? He had to be face-to-face with her, to touch her mind, and to see how she felt. After all, this was hardly just about him. There were her feelings to consider; she was the one who was engaged. She was the one who had moved on, and only Riker was left in neutral. It was entirely possible that she truly didn't love him anymore, that she didn't reciprocate the feelings he had finally realized he had. Plus there was Worf to contend with. Speaking one-to-one with Deanna would be going behind his back. He owed it to Worf to be frank with him, to be in his presence. It was, to be blunt, not a concept that Riker was in love with. "Hi, Worf, how you doing, I want your fiancée back, is that okay with you?" Oh, that was going to be just peachy.

But he had no choice. No choice whatsoever.

"You're not giving me much of a choice here, Commander," said Admiral Jellico.

It was the next morning. Riker had tried to fall back to sleep and had not been especially successful. When the morning sun played across his face, Riker finally gave up and got on the link with Jellico at Starfleet Headquarters. Jellico was admiral in charge of—among other things—personnel assignment. Riker would rather have gone to just about anyone else, up to and including Satan. Unfortunately for Riker, for what he was requesting, Jellico was the man to talk to.

"I regret that, sir, but it is rather important," Riker said.

"You want me to delay your assignment to the Academy so that you can go off and conduct personal business? Is that right?"

"That is correct, yes," said Riker for what seemed to him the umpteenth time.

"But you won't tell me what it is."

"I would rather not, sir."

"Because it's personal."

Riker fought down a smart-ass response. This was not the time to crack wise to a superior officer. "Yes, sir."

"This is not just any teaching assignment you've been selected for. Heavy emphasis is to be placed on tactics and strategy in dealing with the Borg. You are uniquely qualified. Only Shelby and Picard have more expertise: the former is unavailable, and it would just be too cruel to dredge up the hardships that Picard endured. We anticipate a year, two at most, before the Borg strike at Earth. We must be ready, and you *will* contribute." Jellico folded his hands on his desk. "Commander . . . as you know, I was strongly against the notion of keeping Picard's command crew in storage until such time that the new ship could be relaunched. Normally, that's my call to make. In this instance, I was overruled by highers up."

"Yes, sir, I know."

"I don't like making exceptions. Starfleet does not run on exceptions. It runs on discipline and uniformity of purpose. Not on certain captains and their crew being given preferential treatment and special dispensation. Are you reading me, Commander?"

Like a bad novel, you blowhard. "Yes, sir."

"That's the first thing. The second thing is, Riker, I don't particularly trust you."

"You don't 'trust' me, sir?" Now Riker was starting to get angry. "Sir, with all due respect . . ."

"There's that phrase again," muttered Jellico.

"I don't believe that my asking for a delay in my assignment gives you the right or the authority to question my loyalty to Starfleet."

"My rank gives me the authority, Commander. Your vagueness in your 'personal reasons' gives me the right. For that matter, I am still very disturbed over this business with your 'twin.' "

"What?" Riker stared at him. "Admiral, what are you talking ab—wait . . . you mean Tom? Last I heard, he was being assigned to the *Gandhi*."

"Ah." The syllable seemed to hang there for a moment, as if Jellico was suddenly uncomfortable. "Well . . . these events were quite recent, and with everything else going on, we hadn't yet informed you . . ."

"Informed me of what?"

"Your doppelgänger never reported for his assignment. He joined the Maquis, hijacked a starship, and tried to make a strike against the Cardassians. The last I heard, he was stewing in a Cardassian labor camp. I don't know much more than that; the Cardassians are never especially eager to share information with us, particularly when it comes to matters of internal security."

Riker was stunned. "Why wasn't I told at once? Why—"

"Believe it or not, Commander, when it comes to traitorous officers, Starfleet is only slightly more forthcoming than the Cardassians. It simply wasn't necessary for you to know."

And then the dime dropped for Riker. "Wait a minute. Admiral . . . are you saying that because Tom Riker joined the Maquis . . . my integrity, after all these years, is now called into question?"

For just a moment, Jellico seemed to backpedal. "No one is questioning it, Commander. However . . ."

"However what?"

"Well, it's clear that the potential for duplicity is present in you," Jellico told him, his voice becoming hard again. "It doesn't count against you, you understand. It's not as if Thomas Riker's deceit makes a mark on your record. But when it comes to your mysterious requests about—"

Completely fed up, Riker burst out with, "I need to talk to a woman about marrying me, all right, Admiral?"

Jellico blinked in surprise. "Oh. Any particular woman?"

"No, Admiral, I just figured I would grab the first likely candidate I ran across."

"Save the sarcasm, Commander." He paused and then said, in a slightly conciliatory tone, "I appreciate your candor."

"Thank you, sir," Riker said with a relieved breath.

"Request denied."

The breath caught in Riker's throat. "What?" he managed to get out.

"We all make sacrifices when it comes to our personal lives, Commander. That's one of the simple realities of Starfleet. If you don't believe me, go talk to the families of the crew of the *Voyager,* left in limbo and wondering if their loved ones are dead or not. You need to talk to a woman? That's what subspace radio is for. But I'm not about to rearrange the schedule of everyone else at the Academy just so that you can go off and engage in some frivolous adventure."

"I don't consider it frivolous, Admiral."

"Obviously. But I do. And I don't advise that you endeavor to go over my head on this, Commander, or go whining to your father figure, Picard. The goodwill afforded the crew of the *Enterprise* has been more than used up at this point. It will not reflect well on you or Picard if you start seeking out more personal favors."

"Very well, Admiral. Now you are leaving me no choice. I have no desire to leave anyone in the lurch, but if I have to seek a leave of absence . . ."

"By all means. If you want a leave of absence, that I will happily grant you."

That surprised the hell out of Riker. After being such a pain in the neck, for Jellico suddenly to be compromising . . . it was enough to make Riker start wondering if he'd misjudged him. "Oh! Well . . . thank you, sir . . ."

"Of course, the moment you begin your leave, your name is naturally moved to the bottom of the duty roster, and will stay there until such time that you return . . . at which point you then get to stand in line behind all the Starfleet personnel who didn't decide to take time off to pursue the course of true love."

"Meaning," Riker said tonelessly, "that I then lose out on my assignment to the new *Enterprise.*"

"Let's just say that it would be severely jeopardized. So . . . do we understand each other, Commander?"

"Oh, very plainly, Admiral. Very plainly."

"Good. So shall I inform the Academy that there will be a change in the current roster?"

Through gritted teeth, Riker said, "No, sir."

"They'll be so pleased. Jellico out."

Riker stared at the screen for a long while after Jellico's image disappeared. He saw his own reflection staring back . . . and the gray background of the screen gave him a distinctly older look.

"Time for Plan B," he said.

Roger Tang, former Starfleet sergeant and grizzled veteran of more battle campaigns than even he could remember, was busy cleaning glasses at his bar when he noticed a familiar reflection in the mirror on the wall behind him. The broad and beefy Tang squinted at first, racking his brains, and then he remembered. He pivoted on his one flesh-and-blood leg and called out, "Lieutenant! Didn't recognize you out of uniform."

Will Riker grinned and walked across the busy tavern. "Even officers get to be off duty every now and then, Tang."

He extended a hand and Tang shook it firmly. "It must be, what, a dozen years since Betazed?" asked Tang.

"At least." Riker grinned. "And it's Commander now."

"Commander! I'm impressed. Know what that means?"

"No. What?"

"Means I charge you twice as much for drinks. You can afford it."

Riker slid into a seat at the bar. "So how you feeling these days, Sarge?"

"Well as can be expected. Shouldn't complain, really. Over eleven thousand good people lost their lives at Wolf 359. Me, it was just a lost leg and a busted spine. And once upon a time, injuries like that get you a permanent bed and tubes up your nose. Look at me: Slower than I was, maybe, and got enough fake parts in me to supply a Swiss watch factory. But all in all, not a bad life, says I."

"You didn't have to leave Starfleet, you know. I always remember, when I was a lieutenant on Betazed, you told me the galaxy was divided into two types of cultures: Starfleet and everyone else."

"Yeah, I know," sighed Tang. "I loved it. But you know what, Commander? I'm a grunt. A scrapper. That's what makes me happy. The kinda hits I took, they don't let me keep doing what I love to do. If I'd been in the uniform and doing something else, behind a desk or something . . . I would've felt like I was just wearing a costume, y'know?"

"I understand."

"Hey, it's not like I was unprepared. I was always part owner of this place anyway. Just a silent partner. So . . . now I'm a loudmouth partner. Everyone's happy. So . . ." His eyes narrowed. "What can I do for you? Am I correct in assuming that you're not here just by happenstance?"

"You are indeed correct." Riker leaned forward, adopting a slightly conspiratorial tone. "It's my understanding that you have some holosuites here, in the back."

"Sure do. Why? You have a private party in mind?" grinned Tang.

"Not exactly. I have a bit of a delicate situation which I hope you can help me with."

"Is it legal?"

"Yes and no. It involves bending an order from Starfleet."

"I see." Tang pondered it a moment, then said, "Let me guess: A woman is involved, right?"

"How did you know?"

"Playing the odds, sir. Is it, by any chance, that curly-haired brunette from back on Betazed?"

Riker was dumbfounded. "Tang, you would put Sherlock Holmes to shame."

"Nothing amazing about it, sir. Remember, I saw you two bust up. But I could tell: You were meant for each other. And I figured at the time it would take you about a dozen years or so to realize it. Way I see it, you're right on schedule. So . . . let's discuss how I can offer a holosuite to guide the course of true love. Oh, by the way . . . have you booked passage to Betazed yet?"

"Uhm . . . no. I was handling one thing at a time."

"Ah. Well, if I can safely speculate for a moment that Starfleet isn't sanguine about your leaving planetside, you may want to depart under somewhat subtle conditions. I still have contacts that can arrange for that so that you can get there and back with no one being the wiser. Private carriers and such. Discreet and reliable. I can take care of that for you, if you want. No extra charge."

"You're a wonder, Tang."

Tang grinned in that lopsided way he had. "All part of the service, sir."

Eleven

One did not become leader of the Klingon High Council without learning to watch one's back. Gowron, the present holder of the title, was exploring the possibility of giving new definition to the term.

Gowron stood in the middle of the council chamber, turning his head to the right and then to the left, moving it quickly almost to the point of dizziness, and still couldn't quite believe what he was seeing. Standing nearby, his arms folded in smug satisfaction, was a rather small and harmless-looking Klingon named Duntis. Duntis, while growing up, had endured many taunts and threats to his life owing to his diminutive stature. He had more than made up for it, however, thanks to his gift for unique weapons and tools of espionage that he had developed for various heads of the High Council. In all the right circles of influence, Duntis was respected, Duntis was feared, and—most important for Duntis—he was rich.

"This is miraculous!" Gowron said in his customary growl, but in this instance it was a growl of grim satisfaction.

What Gowron was seeing was the area of the council chamber directly behind him. On his right eye, there was a microthin wafer of clear material that he had layered directly onto his eyeball, much like an Earth twentieth-century contact lens. But the lens was cybernetically linked with a tiny viewing scope which was pinned, like a common ornament, onto the back of Gowron's cloak. When Gowron closed his right eye for three seconds and then opened it, the motion served as the on/off activation for the lens and he was able to see whatever was in back of him. Duntis had been right about the one drawback: The device was going to take some getting used to. Gowron had to literally retrain his brain to perceive the images the lens was feeding him. As it was, it was blurred and distorted, and he was having trouble making anything out. But this was an inconvenience at best, and one that could be dealt with. Already, with practice, things were becoming clearer.

"You have outdone yourself, Duntis," Gowron commended him. "Assassins seeking to sneak up behind me will find Gowron more than ready to deal with them!" He thumped his fist on the back of a chair for good measure.

"I knew you'd be pleased, Great Gowron," Duntis cooed in his best sycophantic tone. "If you'd like, I can make more for the others in the council . . ."

Gowron looked at him as if he had lost his mind. "But then *they* could see *me* coming!"

Duntis winced in chagrin. "I'm sorry, Great Gowron. What was I thinking?"

Suddenly Gowron heard footsteps approaching. He kept his back deliberately to the sounds as an experiment, and strained to bring the image into as sharp focus as he mentally could. A moment later, a Klingon who walked with more than the normal degree of swagger appeared at the main entrance. His hair was cut more closely to the skull than most Klingons', though, and when he spoke it was in a voice that seemed suited to whispered conferences in the cover of night.

Without turning, Gowron said heartily, "K'hanq. Welcome home. It is good to see you once more."

If K'hanq was surprised by Gowron's ready identification of him despite the fact that he wasn't looking at him, he was too well trained to reveal it. "And you, Chancellor Gowron. Recognize my footfall, did you."

Gowron and Duntis shared a private smile before Gowron turned to face K'hanq. "That," boasted Gowron, "is how sharp these ears are. Although I do not hear nearly as much as you, K'hanq, nor in so many interesting places. Come. Sit and tell me what news. Duntis . . . you may go."

Duntis bowed slightly and then walked quickly away. Gowron knew that Duntis was already tallying up in his mind just how much his personal accounts would be supplemented by his latest achievement. That was fine as far as Gowron was concerned. As long as Duntis was kept satisfied by his reward for being in Gowron's service, Gowron never had to worry about Duntis providing convenient technology for any possible enemies of Gowron's. And there were enemies, of that Gowron was sure. Enemies everywhere, lurking in shadows, or strutting pridefully in the open.

And there was no one who was in a better position to keep Gowron informed than K'hanq. When it came to an operative skilled at gathering information, K'hanq was the most dependable source Gowron had. He had informants everywhere. If information was the coin of the Klingon realm, then K'hanq was one of its leading millionaires.

Gowron took care to keep him happy as well. Unfortunately, in this particular instance, K'hanq was not going to be keeping Gowron particularly happy.

"Keep in mind," K'hanq prefaced his comments, "that I am but the messenger."

"Ah. That is your way of telling me that I will not be pleased with what you have to say."

K'hanq nodded regretfully. "Your suspicions, it appears, are correct. The Romulans apparently are in the process of building an alliance with the Federation."

"Damn them!" snarled Gowron, his good mood already a thing of the past. He slammed a fist on the chair arm in frustration and nearly snapped the arm off. "Are they insane? Do they not know that the Romulans cannot be trusted? They endeavored to wipe out the Vulcans, for the love of Kahless! That hardly is a ringing endorsement!"

"Nevertheless, there is some rumbling that the Romulan Star Empire can be worked with. Ambassador Spock continues to advocate peace initiatives. . . ."

"Fool," muttered Gowron, but even he knew the significance of this. Spock was a legendary figure, and legends were notoriously influential, and irritating.

"Furthermore, Starfleet is pleased that the Romulans have loaned a cloaking device to the *Starship Defiant.* The Romulans, you see, are no happier about the Dominion and the Jem'Hadar than is the UFP. They represent a mutual enemy, and mutual enemies tend to breed allies."

"Are we not allies enough?" demanded Gowron.

K'hanq bared his teeth in annoyance. "We are perceived as unstable by some. A warrior race torn by civil war, unable to clean up after ourselves or solve any problems without the intervention of Starfleet officers such as Picard to guide us."

"They act as if we are but children!" Gowron bellowed.

"Not all of them," K'hanq hastened to emphasize. "The UFP does not speak with one voice in this case. There are those who respect the long-standing alliance . . . and certainly have no desire to see the Klingon Empire as enemies once again."

"That is wise of them."

"But there are others who see it differently. Who think that the Romulans represent the future. They do not trust us . . . nor do they trust the Romulans. And since they trust no one . . . they will deal with anyone."

"Insane." Gowron shook his head. "Simply insane. They must learn otherwise. They must see the error of their ways. No one knows the Romulans better than we. Were we not their allies? Do we not know their betraying ways? Their treacheries? We Klingons have not yet forgotten Khitomer. We have not forgotten the Romulan promises of loyalty that were tossed aside." He rose and began to pace. "Ironic, is it not, K'hanq? When we began our initial rapprochement with the Federation . . . that was when our alliance with the Romulans began to deteriorate. It was as if they were our allies simply because of our mutual antagonists, the Federation. Yet now they would switch sides. It is as if the Romulans need someone to hate before they can then work with someone else."

"And they most definitely hate us," said K'hanq.

"That is beyond question. So where does that leave us?"

"I regret that it leaves us on extremely uncertain ground. If the Federation comes to terms with the Romulans, and the Romulans launch hostilities against us . . ."

"What would the UFP do, do you think?"

"Well," K'hanq said thoughtfully, "if one can judge by past actions . . . there are three likely possibilities. The first is that they might attempt to mediate a settlement . . ."

"A settlement!" snorted Gowron disdainfully. "You mean some sort of compromise so that the Romulans could buy themselves more time to gather more strength against us!"

"The second is that they will simply stay neutral . . ."

"Allowing for an all-out war." This option clearly did not appeal to Gowron. "Not for a moment am I contemplating shrinking from a fight. I would welcome the opportunity to put those arrogant, pointy-eared bastards in their place. However, with all the recent civil stress and strife that have enveloped the empire, it would be akin to fighting a two-front war—from within and without. I would be less than enthused." He paused. "And the third possibility?"

"That the Romulans and Federation would ally against us."

There followed a long silence as the awesome challenge that represented hung in the air. K'hanq was unsure of what to expect from Gowron, for the Klingon leader's face was unreadable. And then his eyes sparkled with anticipation and he flashed a wolfen grin. "A fight like that . . . the Klingon Empire's last, hopeless stand against overwhelming and hopeless odds . . . gods, K'hanq . . . it would be glorious."

"It would at that, Gowron. Of course," he added as an afterthought, "it would also be suicide. And if none of us are left to tell the tale, what point in glory?"

"True," admitted Gowron. He gave it a bit more thought, and then said,

"K'hanq . . . I want you to find someone. For one of your talents, it should not be difficult."

"Who, Great One?"

"Worf."

"Worf, son of Mogh?"

"The very same."

"But why?" asked K'hanq. "He is in Starfleet."

"Precisely. But he is also beholden to me, K'hanq. I restored honor to his family, cleared the name of his father. If there is anyone who is trustworthy enough to tell me of how the Federation perceives matters . . . it is Worf."

"Once I have located him, do you desire to speak with him via subspace?"

Gowron snorted disdainfully at the very notion. "So that either Romulan or Federation spies can find a way to break through transmissions? Listen in on our conversations? I do not think so, K'hanq, no. No, bring him here."

"And if he will not come?"

Completely without warning, Gowron's temper flared. "I am Gowron!" he fairly roared. "Gowron, son of M'Rel! Leader of the High Council! If I say that Worf will come . . . then *he will come!* Is that clear?!"

"Yes, Gowron," K'hanq said quickly.

"Well? Do not just stand here. Go!"

K'hanq headed for the door. And as he did, Gowron . . . with his back to him . . . said, "And K'hanq . . . I will be watching you." K'hanq bowed slightly and left.

"He will come," Gowron said with confidence to the empty room. "He will come."

For no accountable reason . . . he felt a chill. The winds of war, perhaps, cutting to the bone. For the first time in a long time . . . Gowron felt old.

Twelve

Lwaxana had lost track of the days, as had Worf. But they knew one thing, beyond question:

Things were not getting easier.

"It's like slamming my head repeatedly against a rock!" Lwaxana had complained to Deanna at one point. "Except less fulfilling!"

"Mother, maybe you're going about this the wrong way. . . ."

"Little One, he has to understand! He has to be open to our ways!"

"And does it cut both ways, Mother? What if his Klingon relatives desire to enroll me in some sort of gladiatorial school?"

"Would you agree to do it?"

"Yes," said Deanna without hesitation.

"And would you give it your best effort?"

"Yes."

"Well, that's the point, dear. I don't think Worf is giving this his best effort. I think he's being stubborn and hardheaded, and if he really loved you—"

"Don't, Mother," Deanna had said, holding up a warning finger. "Don't put that sort of price on what's being done here. Worf has agreed to your tutelage on my behalf. If he is having trouble understanding, does the problem lie with the student or the teacher?"

Lwaxana had glowered at her and said nothing. For Lwaxana, saying nothing was an impressive feat all its own.

Worf looked at the painting with some confusion.

He had rendezvoused with Lwaxana, as promised, at a rather pleasant and scenic place. It was an overlook near Bacarba Lake, which was as flat and as blue as any body of water that Worf had ever seen.

"Glorious day, isn't it, Worf," Lwaxana had said when he had arrived. She was standing in front of an easel, wearing work clothes. She was busy applying paint in thick layers to the easel. "Not a cloud in the sky."

"Yes. That is preferable."

There was something in his tone that had caught her attention. "Why do you feel it's preferable?"

"Incoming ships are easy to spot. Reduces chances of a sneak attack, unless—of course—they have a cloaking device."

She sighed and shook her head. "Worf, I'll give you credit for one thing: You're consistent." She laid down her brush and gestured to the painting. "So . . . what do you think?"

He stared at it uncomprehendingly. The large easel was covered entirely with one color of red, top to bottom. The strokes were uniform, no variation at all. That was all it was, just . . . a big red easel.

"Very modern," he said judiciously. "A . . . sublime introspection."

"Hmm. You think? I just thought it was a big easel covered with red paint."

"Oh. Well . . . yes. It is."

"Then what were you just talking about?"

"I was being polite."

"Why Worf," said Lwaxana in mock astonishment, "you *are* capable of surprising me every once in a while."

"Is there a point to producing this . . . work?"

"Yes, there is. In fact, it's the subject of today's exercise. Sit down."

Once Worf had seated himself on the ground, he said, "Now what?"

"Now," Lwaxana told him, sitting next to him, "we're going to watch it."

"Watch it? Watch it do what?"

"Dry."

He couldn't quite believe he'd heard her properly. "You want me to sit here . . . and watch paint dry?"

"That's right."

He studied her carefully to see if there was some hint of humor in what she was saying, some slight endeavor on her part to be making a joke. She couldn't be serious. "For how long?"

"Until it's dry, of course. Otherwise it would be pointless."

"It is pointless in any event!"

"Worf," she sighed. She shifted around on the ground so that she could face him directly. "We're trying to deal in subtleties. That's what all this has been about."

"Subtleties? The sparring session? The underwater immersion for hours on end? The dozens of books you have had me read? The essays? The ten-mile barefoot hike? Having me try to chop down a tree with my teeth? I am still picking wood chips from my gums!"

"We have different definitions of subtlety."

Worf felt as if they had different definitions of reality altogether. "How is watching paint dry supposed to be of any use?"

"Worf . . . look at it." He looked. "Do you see how it is now? Wet? Glistening? Over the next hours, slowly that is going to fade, going to transform. The glistening will diminish, the paint will form its permanent bond with the easel. It will change before our very eyes. You build your starships, take them out into space, park them and have no trouble watching while a star is born or a star dies. But all you see are the big things, Worf. There are the little things as well. It is from those little things that true love blooms, you see. We may first be attracted to the big things about other people . . . the entire physical package, or the thunderbolt that hits us when we first look into their eyes. At first, love is wet and glistening and new. Over time, however, the love dries. You become bored looking at it . . . if you are in the wrong state of mind. But if you appreciate it properly . . . it can be a constant source of interest and amazement."

He stared at her blankly.

"So here is what we're going to do, Worf," she said, undaunted by his evident lack of enthusiasm. "We will watch the paint dry. And as we do, I want you to try and achieve two things. First, I want you actually to appreciate the simple and amazing process of the paint transforming from one state into the other. See it for the wonder that it is, and if you do not think that it is wonderful, then try to find a way to make it so. And second—since we'll have plenty of time—I want you to try and separate yourself from yourself. Do not think about other things you could be doing. Do not think about frustrations, or goals unachieved, or debates, or anything. Make this drying easel more important than you. Elevate it. Lose yourself in it, and ease yourself into a meditative state. See if one drop of paint looks different to you than another. See all the possibilities. Let yourself go, Worf. That's all I'm asking. Lose yourself . . ." She gestured to the easel. ". . . in that."

"I will . . . try," he growled.

They sat and stared at the easel.

Five minutes and seventeen seconds later, Worf said, "This is ridiculous."

"Worf . . ."

"The lesson is over." He rose and turned to face her. "I do not know what sort of elaborate game you are playing here, Lwaxana, and as of this point, I no longer care. I am a Klingon. Klingons do not sit around watching paint dry! There is no purpose to it except to waste more of my time than has already been wasted."

"Is that all you see of what we've been doing?" she asked, getting to her feet. She placed her hands on her hips. "Just wasting your valuable time? And don't you walk away from me!"

That was exactly what Worf was doing. "We are done with this absurdity."

"You don't love her, Worf. Not like Riker did."

The harsh words brought him up short. "What. Did. You. Say?"

"She deserves the best," Lwaxana said defiantly, not the least bit intimidated by his clearly building wrath. "Will and Deanna, they were Imzadi. They share a bond you can never have."

"What bond? What does 'Imzadi' mean? Is this another of your 'lessons'?"

She stared at him and he felt as if she were truly seeing him for the first time.

And she seemed, somehow, to deflate, ever so slightly, as if something had been taken away from within her. "No, Mr. Worf. The lessons are over. We're done. Here. Let me put it to you in a way you will understand."

And she went to the paint-covered easel, drew back her arm, and plunged her fist through it. The canvas ripped easily enough, and the entire easel tilted over. She caught the canvas before it fell, gripped it firmly, twisted at the waist, and then let fly with all her strength. As if on cue, a breeze caught up the easel and carried it down, down to the water far below. It landed there and floated for a moment, supported by the wood of the frame.

Lwaxana looked at her hands. Tinged with red paint as they were, they looked almost bloodstained. She gave him one last, disappointed look and then walked away, shaking her head. Worf remained behind, standing at the precipice, looking down at the ruined painting far below in the water. The tide was going out apparently, and slowly, ever so slowly, the ruined painting was carried away with it.

"Nice throw," he noted.

Deanna had just come back from the art museum and was burbling happily with Chandra over piping-hot glasses of *moog* when Worf walked in. He said nothing; just stood there and seethed. One did not have to be an empath to know that he was not particularly happy.

"Chandra, perhaps you'd better . . ." Deanna said.

". . . leave, yes, I was just thinking that," Chandra replied, overlapping her. With a hasty good-bye, she quickly exited the house, leaving Worf and Deanna alone.

"Where is Alexander?"

It wasn't the first thing she was anticipating that he would say, but she readily replied, "He wished to visit with my mother. They're very fond of each other, you know."

"Yes, I know."

"So I brought him over to the house. She wasn't home, but Mr. Homn was attending to him. I had the appointment with Chandra and I really didn't want to break it, otherwise I would have stayed with him. I didn't think there would be a problem with that. Is there?"

"No. No."

"Worf, what happened? I mean, clearly something did."

He paced a moment more before he could calm himself down sufficiently to frame his thoughts. "I know why she is doing this to me. But why are you doing it?"

"Doing what? I don't understand. . . ."

"Do you love me for who I am?"

"Absolutely. And I also love you for what you can b—"

"There," and he stabbed a finger at her. "There is the problem. We have different definitions of what I can be. Or should be. I am a Klingon, Deanna." He thudded his fist against his chest. "That is not a state of mind. That is who I am. If my adopted parents could not make me into a human, what makes you think you can make me into a Betazoid?"

"I'm not trying to turn you into a Betazoid, Worf, don't be absurd! Neither is my mother! We just wanted you to understand. Not become. Just understand . . ."

"Oh, I understand all too well. What is 'Imzadi'?"

She actually seemed to blanch when he said the word. "What?"

"What does that word mean? I am asking you a straightforward question. What means 'Imzadi'?"

"It's . . . a term of endearment. It means 'beloved.' "

But Worf shook his head, clearly refusing to believe it. "No. That is not all. Not from the way she said it. She gave it significance beyond a simple endearment."

"Worf, this is silly. Nothing is going to be accomplished by—"

"What does it mean!"

She was taken aback by what she saw in his eyes. There was a cold, burning fury. She wasn't intimidated, she didn't think he was going to hurt her. Instead the anger seemed directed inward, as if he was furious with himself over something that was eating at him. She drew herself up, steadied her chin, and said, "All right. It has a secondary and . . . deeper meaning."

"And that would be—?"

" 'The First.' "

"The First." It took a moment for him to understand, but then he did. His eyes widened. "Are you saying that Commander Riker . . . he was your . . ."

She nodded. "But it's more than that. It's not just the first person who captures your body. It's the first person who captures your . . . well . . . your soul."

"Your soul mate."

"I . . . wouldn't put it that way."

"But you would not deny it."

For a moment, it seemed as if tears were about to well up in Deanna's eyes. Tears of frustration, of upset over the hurt that she could see Worf was enduring . . . a hurt that he would never admit to, because he might consider it a sign of weakness. "Worf . . . what would you have me do? I can't go back and make myself not fall in love with Will, back when he was assigned here to Betazed. I can't alter the course of our relationship. I can't go back in time and reorder it to my liking."

Her comment touched a nerve in Worf . . . but he couldn't quite determine why. Instead he asked, "So . . . where does that leave us."

"It leaves us right where we were before, Worf! I love you. You love me, don't you?"

Slowly he nodded. "But," he said, "it can never be the same as what you had with William Riker, can it."

"So it won't be the same," she said tiredly. "It will be different. Not everyone loves everyone in the same way, Worf! You're not in competition with Will Riker."

"It seems to me that I am."

"I can't control how things seem to you, Worf. You just have to believe me that I'm not measuring you up against Will."

"Am I a better lover than he was?"

If Deanna paled before at the mention of the word "Imzadi," this time she went in the other direction, turning positively red. "Worf! Oh my God, I can't believe you asked that—! You don't hear me asking if I'm a better lover than Alexander's mother was!"

"Do you want to know?"

"No! I don't! Because unlike some people, I'm not in competition with a memory!"

"It is different."

"How?"

"Because she is dead . . . and he is not."

She saw the hurt in his eyes, the pained recollection of a wound that was clearly still raw in him. "I'm sorry," she whispered.

"It is . . . all right. I suppose . . . the question is irrelevant anyway. When I make love to you . . . I do so differently than I would with a Klingon woman."

"You . . . do?"

"Yes. I endeavor to use the techniques that a human male would use."

Deanna felt as if she had been experiencing an entire gamut of emotions. Minutes ago she had wanted to cry; now it was everything she could do not to laugh. "And you know these . . . how?"

"I . . ." He cleared his throat. "Researched it."

"Researched it? How?"

"I would rather not say."

"So tell me . . ." Deanna, trying to tease Worf away from his concerns, slunk across the room and draped her arms around his neck. ". . . would you be interested in making love to me . . . as you would to a Klingon woman?"

"No."

"Oh." The flatness of his turn-down startled her. Trying to recapture the mood, she said, "Why not?"

"Because it would likely either kill or incapacitate you."

Deanna's arms suddenly felt to her like two unmoving iron bars. "Oh," she said again.

"Riker, of course, never had that problem," Worf couldn't help but note.

Beginning to lose her patience, Deanna blew an annoyed puff of breath from between her round lips and said, "Worf . . . to love someone differently than someone else doesn't mean that you love them less. It's just that our relationship exists on a different level than what Will and I had. But the thing to remember is that you have one very significant advantage over Will."

"And that would be . . . ?"

"You're here. And he's not."

"I see. So you agreed to marry me . . . because I was convenient."

"No!" she cried out in frustration. "No, that's not it at all! I mean, are you marrying me because I'm convenient for you, because you know I can help you take care of Alexander?"

"No. Well . . ."

She waited for him to complete the sentence. He didn't. "Well . . . what?"

"There is . . . some element of that . . . I suppose," Worf admitted. "But that is part of seeing you as an ideal mate for a variety of factors. One factor is not inherently more important than another, correct?"

"Well . . ." She hesitated and then said, "Actually . . . I would think love is . . . wouldn't you? The more important, or most important, I mean."

"Yes. Of course."

They stared at each other uncertainly for a time, and then Worf said, "I . . . need some time to think, Deanna. Just a couple of hours to myself."

"Yes . . . yes, of course . . ."

"I will meet you at your mother's house, if that is acceptable. Perhaps then we may all . . . discuss matters."

"I would like that. And that is the Betazoid way, Worf: Talking out feelings. Coming to a meeting of minds. You see, you are learning."

"As you say," Worf replied, but he didn't sound completely convinced.

He walked for hours, from one end of the city to the other. Worf watched Betazoids in action, interacting with each other, laughing on occasion, enjoying themselves. But it was so quiet, so damned quiet. Worf had never realized before just how much general noise was created through the simple constant stream of chatter that most beings engaged in.

A Klingon city, on the other hand . . . the noise level! It was beyond belief. Perpetual shouting, howls of laughter or anger, explosive arguments that oftentimes seemed to be launched just to have something to argue about. Bone thudding bone as heads slammed together in reckless competition. It was as if Klingons thrived on noise for the purpose of reminding themselves that they were alive. If they could hear themselves, then they were there. Silence was reserved for the grave. Noise was for when you were alive and thriving on that life.

No wonder Betazoids had so much time to contemplate things. There was nothing in particular going on to distract them. The way things were around Worf, he could probably actually *hear* paint dry if he wanted to.

Why was he being so hard on himself? Why was he obsessing about Riker? Why couldn't he simply take Deanna's word that there was, indeed, no competition?

"You are going to ruin it," he warned himself. "You are going to ruin the best thing that ever happened to you simply because of your pride."

He was not in competition with Riker. It was foolish for him to think of it in those terms. He was not in competition because . . . because she had chosen him, that was why. So if there had been some sort of competition, it was over. He had won. He, Worf, had won.

There was still the matter of the Trois trying to make him over into something he was not. But after several hours of walking, he had the answer to that as well. He would indeed bring Deanna to Qo'noS, the Klingon homeworld, and have her undergo some rudimentary warrior rituals so she likewise could "understand." Yes. Yes, that would be most amusing. Deanna Troi, scaling the Flame Cliffs of Kutabi—blindfolded and with no gear. Deanna Troi, learning combat tactics and trying to defend herself in the ring against females half again her size (let alone males!).

He did not contemplate these matters out of a sense of vengeance, no. Far from it. If understanding was what it was all about, then understanding Deanna would have. And perhaps then, she would cease trying to change him in exchange for his not subjecting her to any of the assorted trials that the average Klingon was undergoing at the age of ten.

As he approached the Troi mansion, following a lovely path lined with exotic foliage, he was becoming increasingly satisfied with the way in which things were working out. Perhaps he had disappointed Lwaxana. But then again, he wasn't marrying Lwaxana. All he had to do was make Deanna happy, and that he was more than prepared to do.

Although, to be honest, he wished that he could have taken back his comment about killing her if he made love to her as if she were a Klingon woman. He could tell that hadn't gone over particularly well with her. Then again, he couldn't exactly blame her, now, could he.

As he approached the front door, the sun was just beginning to settle down upon the horizon. Long shadows cast themselves over the house, caressing it with darksome fingers. He knocked on the front door and waited for Mr. Homn to promptly open it, as he always did.

It didn't open.

Any other person might have taken a few moments to wonder what was going on. Where was Mr. Homn, why wasn't he answering it, he was usually so reliable, they must be busy, and so on.

Not Worf.

Immediately he went into a crouch, taking as a possibility that there was some sort of danger present. He reached for his phaser . . .

. . . and remembered he didn't have it.

Off-duty Starfleet personnel were not supposed to carry hand phasers with them. Worf was indeed off-duty, in civilian clothes, and had absolutely no reason to be toting small arms.

He was, however, a Klingon, and that was more than enough reason to be prepared for just about anything. Consequently, Worf reached into the tops of his boots and pulled out, from each one, a slim blade with a thin handle and notched end. Individually each of the blades was a nasty weapon, and could be yanked out instantly to deal with whatever emergency presented itself. Since he had a few moments before possibly launching himself into battle, it gave him the time he needed to connect the two blades together at the hilts. This presented him with a handgrip in the middle and blades extending from either side of his right hand. He cursed himself for not having more weaponry on him, but he was worried that it might have given Deanna the wrong impression if he'd gone to Betazed armed to the teeth. Besides, it was difficult to carry a *bat'leth* in the average suitcase.

He crept slowly around the perimeter of the mansion, alert to any possibility of enemy infiltration. Part of him was telling him that he was completely out of his mind, overreacting . . . that, in fact, he was trying to prove something, prove that danger lurked everywhere and only he, Worf, was genuinely prepared to deal with it.

There was a large picture window just ahead, and Worf crept toward it. Carefully, he looked in.

He had a clear view into the main foyer. There didn't seem to be anything amiss.

Then he spotted it: a pool of blood over at the far side.

His nostrils flared, and suddenly every battle-ready sense he had screamed at him that someone was right nearby. His head whipped around and he saw no one, but his blade swung around in a deadly arc nonetheless.

To his surprise, he heard a yelp of pain from what seemed to be thin air and then, inexplicably, a Romulan was suddenly there. He hadn't beamed in. He was just not there one moment, and present the next. He was tall, with a high forehead, pale skin, and dark eyes. Even if he hadn't simply popped in out of nowhere, something about his physical appearance would have been more than enough to tip Worf off that this was no ordinary Romulan. Of course, even the presence of an ordinary Romulan on Betazed was cause for concern.

The tall Romulan was nursing a cut on his upper arm. Thin green blood was trickling down it, the cloth hanging loose from where Worf had sliced him.

"The next one takes off your head. Who are you!" demanded Worf.

The Romulan's eyes seem to sink further into his head and then, just as suddenly, widen as if to consume the entirety of his face. And he spoke one word in a frighteningly raspy voice:

"Fear."

And suddenly Alexander was dead, and Deanna was dead, and Worf was old and weak and toothless, lying helplessly in his frailty as assassins stole toward him in the night, and all of the attendant anxiety of all those happenstances pounded through him and he was paralyzed, incapable of any sort of rational thought or developing any workable tactic. He had no idea where to go, what to do, he was overwhelmed, he—

"No!"

The paralysis should have lasted long enough for a direct attack to be made upon him, but Worf did not give them the opportunity. Rather than allowing him to be reduced to utter uselessness, Worf's training and mental conditioning drove him to action. He spun and lunged right toward the window, smashing through it. Glass rained everywhere as Worf took the impact with his shoulder and hit the floor in a forward roll.

Two Romulans came at him, one from either side. Neither of them were carrying disruptors, blasters, or any of the preferred means of lethally dispatching a foe. Instead they wielded shock prods, apparently hoping to numb him into unconsciousness. All they had to do was come into contact with his body.

Worf was not prepared to let them do that. Unfortunately, the fear was beginning to redouble itself in his mind, so neither was he prepared to fight at his best. But he had no choice.

One of the Romulans came in faster than the other. He was overanxious, lunging forward with the shock prod. Worf swept up with an inner arm block, driving the prod up and away from himself, and then jammed forward with the blade. It deflected off the chest armor that the Romulan was wearing, but still managed to do damage as it skidded up the metal and lodged in the underside of the Romulan's upper arm. The Romulan let out a howl and from the corner of his eye, Worf saw the other Romulan coming in quickly. He swung the knifed Romulan around, using him as a shield for a moment, and then shoved him bodily into the other Romulan. The two of them went down and the one who had been knifed dropped his prod. Worf immediately scooped it up, and what with wielding his double-bladed weapon in one hand and the prod in the other, he very much resembled someone with whom no reasonable individual would want to screw around.

"Father!"

Worf heard Alexander's alarmed scream from somewhere else in the house. "Alexander!" he shouted. "Where are—?!"

Then there was a crash in the great dining room adjacent to the living room. It was very likely a trap, but Worf had no choice. He barreled toward the dining room, his weapons extended. . . .

He rounded the corner, and at the far end was Deanna, pinned against the wall by a woman and for just a heartbeat, Worf thought that it was Tasha Yar, and then he realized . . .

"Sela! Release her! Now!"

And suddenly the house was alive with Romulans. The ceiling exploded and they dropped down from overhead, and the walls blasted inward as they crashed in from all sides. It was a trap, with Deanna as the bait and Worf, apparently, as the prize.

They were wielding shock prods, and clubs, and assorted blunt instruments, and they were upon him like hyenas on a lion. Worf, trained in all forms of Klingon combat, didn't use any of them. He hacked and slashed, slicing with the blade in one direction, sweeping with the shock prod in the other direction. The mass of foes who opposed him presented him with one great massive target of bodies. They were trying to overwhelm him through sheer force of numbers, and under other circumstances they might have succeeded.

But Worf was too thoroughly seized by pure battle fury. He roared, howled defiance, drowned out the shouts of the Romulans who were trying to bring him down. For there was more at stake here than just his life, or even the lives of Deanna and Alexander. He was fighting for his pride, for his honor. He had spent days on Betazed, and during that time he had come to feel—through no one's fault, really—that he was worthless and out of place. That he was a warrior in a land of peace that had no use for him. That he had nothing that he could offer to Deanna, that he was a walking freak show, something to be pitied or disdained or even feared. That the only way he was deserving of even staying on the same planet with Deanna was if he managed to change everything about the way he acted and thought and felt. He had been besieged with philosophies he did not agree with and concepts he could not understand.

But this . . . this he comprehended all too well. This was simple, straightforward. The smell of blood filled his lungs, the cries of those he managed to wound or cut down serenading him. His hair, previously tied back, had come loose and hung around him like a mane, accentuating the resemblance to a great beast beset by lesser predators.

Several shock prods managed to get through his guard, striking him on the shoulders, the chest, the legs. They should have stunned him. Instead they enraged him. Somewhere in the back of his mind he felt something trying to get in, trying to force cowardice upon him, but he blocked it out, so filled with a berserker rage was he.

A sustained shock charge numbed his right arm, and he dropped his blade. It didn't matter. He swung his momentarily deadened arm like a massive club of bone and sinew, knocking Romulans aside. He kicked, he bit, he clawed, he howled Klingon epithets and words of contempt. Above the melee he heard Sela shouting something about surrendering. It didn't really penetrate, though. Surrender and dishonor in front of Deanna was simply not an option. So battle-crazed was he that it literally didn't even occur to him that the cost of his refusal to give up could be Deanna's life.

One of the places through which the Romulans had made their entrance was a hole they had blasted in the wall. As Worf struggled, he saw Sela dragging Deanna, a disruptor to her head, through the hole. He shouted Deanna's name and then more Romulans blocked his vision of them.

With a bellow that sounded like that of a beast which had vanished in prehistory, Worf suddenly doubled over as the Romulans pushed in on him. For just a moment they thought they had him. They were mistaken. Worf gathered his strength, let out a war yell that would have done Kahless proud, and violently straightened up, knocking them back and giving him the moment he needed. He sprang clear of them and bolted for the hole.

Never had he felt so alive, so damned near invincible. It was more than just the adrenaline rush, or the berserker rage that had set upon him. It was the simple, clear, and irrefutable fact that he had been right all along. To be prepared for battle, to be the warrior at all times, was the correct way, the smart way, the Klingon way. Peace was a luxury that was purchased with violence. That was the truth, that was the reality. He was totally vindicated.

And he would be damned if he let Deanna die now that she knew he'd been right. As for Lwaxana, whose fate remained unknown to him, well . . . he'd rub her nose in it, as well. And that insufferable Gart Xerx, too.

He was able to indulge in the slightly vindictive little fantasies because he had never been more sure that he was going to triumph in battle than he was at that particular moment.

Just ahead of him, Sela had come to a halt. Worf smiled in grim amusement. How fitting that they should end up back here, of all places: the scenic precipice that overlooked the Bacarba Lake. Sela couldn't continue forward. She gripped Deanna firmly by the elbow, keeping the disruptor trained on her. Worf stopped short of them by ten feet and stood there in a semicrouch, balanced on the balls of his feet.

"You're not going to give up, are you, Mr. Worf," Sela said, sounding a bit impressed. "Why . . . I bet that if I threatened to blow your fiancée's pretty little head off . . . you still wouldn't surrender."

"You are not going to get away," Worf assured her.

Sela didn't seem concerned. Actually, she seemed bored. "In point of fact . . . I am. And I can still make use of Deanna here. You are clearly going to be too uncooperative, which is a shame. But I have a new philosophy, Worf: I try to constantly keep my plans adaptable. Too much structure makes it too easy for opponents to second-guess and counter me. So I try to handle things in a free-form manner. I wanted to make use of you. Your attitude precludes it, apparently, and I have no desire to waste further time with you. So . . ."

She brought the disruptor around and aimed it squarely at Worf.

He charged straight toward her, his head low, his arms pumping. He was still enveloped in his self-styled aura of invincibility, and was positive that—if he could make himself a moving target—she would miss.

And suddenly a fast-moving body came in quickly from the left and tackled him across the waist. Worf had a brief glimpse of his assailant, and he was so stunned that for a moment it completely disrupted his concentration.

It was Riker, legs pumping, able to use his momentum to actually lift the Klingon's feet clear off the ground. They hurtled forward, and Worf, with a bellow of betrayed fury, boxed Riker's ears with such ferocity that if he'd struck him any harder, he might well have smashed in both sides of his head.

"Will!" shouted Sela.

Riker tumbled forward, stunned, and lost his grip on Worf.

Worf had exactly two seconds to celebrate his triumph and then he abruptly realized that the ground was no longer beneath him. When Riker had fallen, he had dumped Worf right off the edge of the cliff.

Desperately, Worf lashed out with his one functioning hand, but he missed the edge of the cliff by a good two feet and then he was in free fall. He tumbled, end over end, and a scream wanted to rip its way from his throat but he wouldn't let it. He wouldn't give the Romulans or Riker (Riker!?) the satisfaction of hearing him.

Down he plummeted, down, and as he fell, the cumulative damage that he had sustained began to catch up with him. His joints seized up, he could barely breathe, the blood loss from several vicious gashes weakened him. By the time he hit the water, he was barely capable of movement. Under water, falling toward the bottom of the lake, the last thing he noticed, with morbid amusement, was the frame of the tattered painting lying nearby. Within moments the surface of the lake was still once more.

Thirteen

Deanna Troi left the suite at the inn, heading for her mother's house and wondering what conclusions Worf was going to come to during his time alone.

She was beginning to feel that they had done Worf a tremendous disservice. Their motivations, hers and her mother's, had been with the best of intentions. (At least, she thought Lwaxana was operating with the best of intentions; her comment about Riker and her bringing up of the term "Imzadi" was causing Deanna to wonder a bit.) But Worf seemed to regard their actions not as something to try and broaden his worldview, but rather as something to diminish him. To make him less than he was, rather than greater. How could he have come to that conclusion? If he knew that she loved him, if he believed in their relationship, then certainly he must have known that she would never to anything to hurt him.

Perhaps the problem lay in different definitions of what was hurting and helping. Perhaps . . .

"Imzadi."

She stopped in her tracks, not quite believing what she was hearing even though the voice was unmistakable. Slowly she turned to face him.

Riker was standing here, dressed in civilian clothes—a blue shirt, open at the neck, crisp black pants. He had a broad smile as if there was no one else in the universe he'd rather be looking at at that moment.

"Will!" She made no effort to hide her joy in seeing him. She went to him and threw her arms around him, hugging him soundly. "Will, what are you doing here? I heard that the board cleared both you and the captain! I knew it would! Is that why you've come, to celebrate? This is wonderful! Worf will be so pleased. . . ."

Then she stopped as she became aware that Worf might very well be anything but pleased. "How did you get here?" she asked, quickly changing the subject.

"Took a transport out here, arranged by . . . a friend, shall we say."

"So you actually came specifically here, to Betazed. It's not as if you were just passing through then . . ."

"I . . . needed to come and talk to you, Deanna," he said. He had one hand on her shoulder, and with the other he gently brushed away a thick black curl from the side of her face. "I've had a lot on my mind lately . . . and I've been doing a lot of thinking about us."

"I . . . have as well, Will." She gestured ahead of her. "I was heading up to Mother's house. Walk with me?"

"Anytime, anywhere," he said agreeably.

She tucked an arm through his elbow and they began to stroll. "So how is Worf?" Riker asked.

"He is . . . doing well. Our relationship has been having some . . . growing pains, shall we say. But it's nothing we can't handle."

"Isn't it?"

She looked up at him with confusion in her dark eyes. "What do you mean, Will?"

"Well, Deanna, you're newly engaged. This should be the happiest time of your life. Instead . . . and correct me if I'm reading it wrong . . . it sounds like you and Worf are having some problems."

"No problems that you shouldn't be familiar with, Will. Who knows better than you, after all, that life on Betazed can require a major broadening of one's horizons. I remember a certain young lieutenant who learned a few things while he was here."

"So do I," grinned Riker. But then his smile faded, and Deanna began to sense a great antipathy on his part. "Deanna . . ."

"Will . . . clearly you have something on your mind. Perhaps it would be best if you just said it. You've come rather far, after all, to do it."

"I know, I know. And all the way here, I kept rehearsing over and over what I was going to say. But now that I'm here, now that I'm faced with it . . ." He took a deep breath. "Deanna . . . I've been thinking about our relationship. About everything we meant to each other, and how I kept walking out on you . . ."

"It wasn't just you, Will. Don't take all the blame on yourself. There were things I could have done, could have said . . . but we made decisions, we had a friendship that we were content with . . ."

"Contentment." Riker shook his head with weary self-contempt. "A word that I once would have choked on. Nothing was ever enough for me. Nothing in my career track, nothing in my romantic life, nothing was ever, ever good enough. Contentment . . ." He shuddered. "I didn't know the meaning of it. So tell me . . . why was it that, of all things, I was supposed to be content with simply being friends with you?"

"We've been over it, Will. We had our careers, things never seemed to match up, we never both wanted the same thing at the same time. . . ."

"And we still don't . . ." After a significant pause, he added, ". . . or do we?"

"What do you mean?"

It was a slow, steady incline through lovely foliage as the path wended its way up to the Troi home. Riker had gradually been walking slower and slower, however, and when Deanna said that, he stopped. He continued looking straight ahead, as if trying to make out the future. "Did you decide to marry Worf . . . because he's what you want in a husband? Or was it to get a reaction out of me? To make me realize just how much you mean to me."

Deanna actually laughed at that. It wasn't derisive, but rather a laugh of almost affectionate amusement. "You know, Will, I would love to get a chart of the galaxy, as designed by you. There would be all the stars and planetary systems, and in the middle of the galaxy would be you, and everything would be revolving around you. And you'd have a big smile on your face because that's really the way I sometimes think you view reality. Will, I am actually capable of taking actions and making decisions without them directly relating to, or centering around, you."

"I know that, Deanna. But I have a feeling that this wasn't one of them. And if I'm right . . . if that is why you are planning to do this . . . then I want you to know that it worked."

"That it . . . Will, what do you mean . . . ?"

Before she could react, before she could do anything, Riker had taken her in his arms and brought her lips to his. On the one hand she had not expected it . . . and on the other, it seemed the most expected, the most natural thing in the world. The years fell away and she practically melted into him as the pure passion that he had for her seemed to flow out of him, nearly consuming her. All thoughts of Worf, of their life together, of her promise to him and all the things they had said to one another, were momentarily washed away and replaced by something pure and clean and . . . and right.

But only momentarily.

Deanna broke away from him, gasping slightly, her mind reeling and her thoughts in complete turmoil. She was beginning to feel as if she was never going to get solid ground beneath her feet. Between Worf's frustration and sense of competition with Riker, and now Will choosing this moment, of all moments, to declare himself . . . it was insane. Why couldn't she have a nice, normal engagement? For a moment she was tempted to dispense with the lot of them, find a Betazoid male, settle down, have a half-dozen children and hope that she never heard of William Riker, Worf, the Klingon Empire, or Starfleet ever again.

"Will . . . this is . . . this is all happening too quickly . . ."

"Too quickly?" He stared at her with incredulity. "Too quickly? Good lord, Deanna, I've been keeping my mouth shut for years, not saying anything for all this time. Having you there in front of me, not acting upon it. Too quickly? What's crazy is that I've taken this long."

"But I've made promises to Worf . . . I . . . we have an investment in that relationship, Will, I can't just toss it aside. . . ."

"How can that relationship compare to ours, Deanna?" There was something in his eyes, something that she had never seen before. A soulful pleading, a rawness of emotion. It was as if she was seeing a new side of him. "How can that compare to what we had?"

Lwaxana's house was visible from where they were standing. To Deanna, it almost seemed a safe haven, a neutral corner that she could retreat to, in order to collect herself and sort herself out. Deanna was hardly a little girl, depending upon her mother despite all the times that her mother called her "Little One," and yet at that moment she considered Lwaxana's near-presence to be the most comforting element of stability she had.

"Why do you hate me, Lwaxana?"

Lwaxana had been working on an elaborate three-dimensional puzzle with Alexander that would, when assembled, result in a dazzling representation of—well—Lwaxana's face. "A means of self-examination," she had called it, although Deanna had just sort of sighed when she saw the work in progress the other day and allowed a few stray thoughts about rampant ego to float from her head . . . deliberately, Lwaxana suspected.

But when Alexander asked his question, it so startled Lwaxana that she nearly knocked over the half-finished puzzle. "What? Alexander, why would you think such a thing?"

He stared at her unflinchingly. "Things I heard my father and Deanna saying."

"You heard them saying I hate you?"

"My father thinks you hate the Klingon way. I'm a Klingon. That's everything that I believe in . . . everything that makes me the way I am."

Lwaxana was stricken. There was clearly so much hurt in Alexander's voice. "Alexander, I don't hate the Klingon way. I don't."

"You think that my father and Deanna aren't right for each other."

She hesitated. The fact was, the boy was right, but she didn't want to just come out and say that. Besides, it wasn't exactly that simple. "Alexander . . . it's not that I don't think they're right for each other. It's just that . . . they're so different . . . and all I was trying to do was give your father some insight into the way that Deanna was raised. To make him realize what our philosophies are."

"No one can 'make' my father do anything," Alexander replied.

Well, that was it right there, wasn't it, Lwaxana realized. The lad had pretty much nailed it. "I'm not . . . trying to force something on him, Alexander. I just . . . Look, Alexander." She quickly changed the course of the discussion. "Whatever disagreements your father and I may have . . . however all of this relationship business works out . . . there's one thing that you have to believe: None of this has anything to do with you. My affections for you are unchanged. I think you're a wonderful boy . . . no. No, I take that back. I think you're a wonderful young man."

"Would you want to have a son like me?"

Lwaxana coughed to hide the smile on her face.

"Is something wrong?"

"No, Alexander. No, nothing's wrong. And to answer your question: Yes . . . yes, I would be proud to have a son like you. Although if you were my son, I'd probably encourage you to smile a bit more. But that would be all."

"You could love me the way I am?"

"Of course, Alexander."

"Well . . . if my father is to be your son-in-law . . . can't you love him the same way?"

For once in her life, Lwaxana had no idea what to say.

Deanna found that she was echoing the words she had said to Worf not too long ago. "Our relationship doesn't have to compare, Will. It's . . . different. That's all. It's just different."

"Different, but not better."

"I don't believe in comparing and contrasting in that—"

"Dammit, Deanna!" His temper flared for the first time. "In some ways, you're no different than you were years ago! Overintellectualizing everything instead of going with your gut! For someone who's supposed to be an empath, sometimes you can be so out of touch with your own feelings it's nothing short of amazing!"

"You don't have to be insulting, Will. . . ."

"I'm not . . ." With effort, he calmed himself. "I don't mean to be insulting, Deanna. I just . . . I had an image in my mind of how this was going to go, and it's not exactly . . . well . . ."

"Will, if there's one thing I've learned, it's that things don't always go the way they're supposed to."

"True enough. After all, if they did, you and Worf wouldn't be engaged."

"Will . . . what do you see happening here?"

He took her hands in his. "I see you realizing—as I have—that it's not too late for us. That we are meant to be together. That we can still make it all work. I know, I know, it's coming at a bad time. But I couldn't keep quiet any longer. I've had to reprioritize my life, and I want you to be a part of that, as I want to be a part of yours. And I want you to know that, no matter what happens, I love you as no one else can or will. Not Worf. Not anyone."

A dozen emotions vied for dominance in Deanna, her heart battling against her brain, her soul trying to sort it all out. "Come," she said suddenly, tugging on his hands.

"Come where?"

"To the house. Mother will want to see you."

"I . . . I don't think that'd be a good idea."

"Oh, why? You know she'd love to."

"She was never crazy about me," he said, shaking his head. "I don't think it'd be wise. . . ."

"Not crazy about you? Will, for heaven's sake, when Mother was in phase, she considered the possibility of you as a mate. Obviously you're not exactly repellent to her." She tilted her head in curiosity. "You look so surprised. . . ."

"I'm just . . . startled that you would bring that up, that's all. Actually, I guess that's part of the reason I'm uncomfortable about seeing her at the moment. Here I am, pleading my case with you. Considering my history with your mother, well . . . you know . . ."

"I . . . I suppose . . ." Deanna said uncertainly.

"I just need some more time with you . . . time to be alone, just the two of us, to talk things out . . . can you give me that, at least . . . ?"

"I . . ." She took a deep breath, with the distinct feeling that she was making a life decision. "All right, Will. I . . . I suppose I owe it to you . . . and to me . . . and to everything that we had . . ."

"Have."

". . . had together," she continued. "But I won't lie to Worf. I can't. You and I, we'll get together, and we'll talk and . . . and we'll see, we'll just see . . . but I'm going to tell Worf that that's what I'm doing."

"He's not going to be thrilled."

"He'll understand, I'm sure of it. He wouldn't want us to be married unless everyone's conscience was clear."

"All right." Riker looked less than enthused. "All right . . . I think you're making a mistake, but all right."

"Where do you want to go? There are some nice places in town. . . ."

"Actually . . . I know exactly where I want to go. There's only one place, really." He smiled, and he looked years younger. "The Janaran Falls."

"Oh, Will . . . I don't know . . ."

"The Janaran Falls, Deanna. It has to be there, don't you see? Everything that went wrong with the relationship . . . everything that I screwed up, and it was me, Imzadi, I admit it, it was me . . . happened after the Falls. We were happy there. It was the last time we saw each other, after all, and probably the best time."

Her hands tightened on his.

"Deanna . . . is something wrong . . . ?"

"The . . . last time we saw each other . . ."

"That's . . . that's right . . ." He looked confused. "Deanna . . . there is something wrong, isn't there. Is it something I said? I'm sorry, I just . . . I have such fond memories of that time. . . ."

"That last time."

"Right. Why do you keep saying that?"

Her jaw hardened, and her dark eyes became very cold. Then, without a word, she turned and started to head toward Lwaxana's house.

"Deanna! What's wrong? Come on, I'm entitled to know!"

She stopped some feet away from him. She was standing on an elevation of the incline and looked down at him in what seemed a most imperious fashion. "Oh, I think you already know."

"No, I don't!"

She was so angry that she didn't trust herself to verbalize. Instead a thought projection blew out from her with such force that it staggered Riker when it sounded in his head.

I think you do . . . Tom.

He tried to speak, but nothing came out.

"I will not meet you at the Janaran Falls," Deanna said loudly. "I don't know what your game is, or what you were hoping to accomplish. But you tried to fool me, to use me . . ."

"It's not like that, Deanna. . . ."

"It is exactly like that. I don't know what you're doing here, but your coming here was a mistake. I suggest you rectify it immediately by leaving, now."

"Deanna."

"Now!" With that, she walked stiffly away.

Except Riker wasn't about to let her get away that easily. He ran after her, grabbed her by the arm. "No, Deanna. I'm not going to let it end like this."

"It's already ended. I was foolish to listen to you at all. Go away."

"It's not that simple. Just say you'll meet me . . ."

"Go away! I never want to see you again!"

And then something seemed to ripple in the air to Deanna's right. She turned to look, but saw nothing . . . but she sensed it . . . sensed that something was there . . .

And then a Romulan appeared out of thin air. He was speaking into a comm link on his wrist. "She's not cooperating. Attack."

Deanna stepped back, confused and stunned. "What . . ."

Riker had a look of total despair on his face. His voice barely above a whisper, he said, "I'm sorry. . . ."

Just above them, in the cloudless skies, a Romulan warbird materialized.

"Oh my God," gasped out Deanna, and she tried to bolt for her mother's house. Intellectually, she knew it was pointless, that there was nowhere to run. But she did it anyway, as much to warn her mother and Alexander of the danger that had suddenly materialized at their very doorstep. Riker made no move to stop her. He didn't have to, for suddenly a squadron of Romulan soldiers materialized directly in front of Deanna, blocking her escape route. And squarely in the forefront of the squadron was Sela.

"Hello, Counselor," she said with a clear smirk. "I almost didn't recognize you, what with your not being disguised as a Romulan." Then amusement vanished from her face as she said brusquely to the others with her, "Take the house."

The Romulan warbird recloaked as the soldiers charged the home of Lwaxana Troi. As they did, Sela sidled up to Riker and ran a finger along the curve of his jaw. "So, Will . . . did you have a nice reunion?"

Deanna heard that and looked in confusion at Riker. And this time it was he who cast the thought into her head. And the thought was *If you say anything . . . we're both dead.*

She kept her mouth shut.

Kressn, the Romulan telepath, spearheaded the invasion force into the Troi home as the Romulans burst through the door and found Mr. Homn waiting for him.

He took no defensive posture, did not seem particularly disturbed over the fact that a squadron of Romulans was charging into the house. Assuming him to be no threat, they started to move right past him, at which point Mr. Homn picked up the nearest one as if he weighed nothing and threw him with full force against the nearest wall. The Romulan hit it so hard that he cracked the plaster and slid to the floor, leaving an imprint of himself behind.

"Get him!" shouted Kressn.

The Romulans aimed their disruptors at Mr. Homn. Disruptors had no variation settings in the way that phasers did. The only way to do less than lethal damage was to fire at extremities such as arms and legs, and even then the target could still die of shock. A blast to the head or vital areas was invariably fatal.

They aimed for the head and upper body, which generally contained most of the major organs. Considering Mr. Homn's size, one would have thought that they could not possibly miss.

One would have been in error. Mr. Homn darted like lightning between the opening salvo and lunged toward a nearby tapestry hanging on the wall. He ripped it down, turned, and hurled it toward the Romulans. The weight of the thing was formidable and when it landed upon them it flattened the lot of them.

"Mr. Homn, what in the world is going on?!" It was the strident voice of Lwaxana Troi, and she was heading into the main foyer, Alexander in tow.

It was a momentary distraction, but it was unfortunately enough. More Romulans poured through the door, and one of them got off a shot that caught Mr. Homn squarely in the chest. Lwaxana let out a shriek of horror as the blast cored through Homn, knocking him flat onto his back. Not a word emerged from his lips as he went down, hitting the floor hard and lying there, looking up at the ceiling, stunned but stoic. Blood pooled on the floor beneath him.

"Homn!" howled Lwaxana, and when she turned to look at the invaders, there was something very terrible in her eyes. Alexander, eager for the battle, started to charge forward, but Lwaxana held him back with one hand. "You bastards!" she shouted. "How dare you! *How dare you!"*

"Take her!" called Kressn.

The Romulans started to advance on her, and Lwaxana shouted at them.

In their heads.

When an ordinary person raises his or her voice at another, the result is simple irritation. When a telepath raises her voice—particularly as powerful and strident a telepath as Lwaxana Troi—it's another matter entirely, particularly when she is being driven by a combination of fear and complete moral outrage.

How dare you?!?

Lwaxana's voice blared in their minds like a massive horn ushering in doomsday. It was thunder in their heads, driving out every other thing they could possibly be thinking, indeed perhaps everything they had ever known. They staggered, putting their hands to their ears instinctively, except that it did them absolutely no good. The assault wasn't coming from outside their heads, but from inside.

How dare you do this! I am Lwaxana Troi, Daughter of the Fifth House . . .

They writhed in agony, falling to the floor, their weapons slipping out of their fingers.

Holder of the Sacred Chalice of Rixx, and Heir to the Holy Rings of Betazed! This is my home . . . these are my people . . . and you are not welcome here! Leave! Now!!

The Romulans wanted to shout that she should be stopped, that someone should shut her up, but they couldn't even put a coherent thought together. Fortunately for them, they didn't have to.

Kressn took all his strength, all his telepathy, all his ability to influence others, and in his mind gathered them into a large ball and hurled it with all his strength squarely into Lwaxana's brain.

Lwaxana was not a trained psi-warrior by any stretch of the imagination. She had never been in a true mindwar in her life, aside from the one time when she'd had a battle royale with Q . . . and even then, that wasn't exactly the same because her own abilities were supplemented with the power of the Q. In this case, she knew outrage, she had a tremendous sense of herself, and when she was angered, you simply did not want to get in her way. But she knew nothing of fighting a two-tiered mind battle. She was all offense, fueled by her moral fury, and so had no screens in place, no defensive capabilities.

Consequently, Kressn won.

She staggered under the shock of the retaliatory strike into her mind. Alexander cried out her name, but she didn't hear it. Instead she became as rigid as a board, her eyes wide and staring but not seeing, and she tumbled backward. Alexander, seeing her fall, caught her. "Lwaxana!" he said again, and suddenly Romulan hands were snatching him away from her. Lwaxana hit the floor and lay, immobile, next to Homn.

The Romulans who had been flattened slowly started to gather their wits about them. Kressn was on one knee, looking a bit haggard but otherwise all right.

"Mother!"

Deanna was horrified by the scene that greeted her when Sela prodded her forward through the door of the house. Her mother was immobile, Mr. Homn lay bleeding on the floor, and Alexander was being forcibly restrained by one of the soldiers. Suddenly Alexander sank his teeth into the hands of the man holding him and the Romulan lost his grip on him. Alexander slid loose and tried a desperate charge at Sela. He made it only a few feet, though, before another Romulan stepped forward and swung the butt end of a disruptor down and around. It stunned Alexander until they managed to restrain him once more.

A troop of Romulans was apparently trying to pull itself together, and the Romulan whom she had seen appear out of thin air appeared rattled. But they were all of no consequence to her.

Sela, for her apart, appeared rather annoyed. "What went on in here?" she asked impatiently. "I've trained you all myself. It doesn't reflect well on me when you have this much trouble dealing with an old woman, one giant, and a Klingon boy."

Deanna ran to her mother, knelt down, and looked deeply into Lwaxana's eyes. Whatever the Romulans had done to her, it was progressive, boring more and more deeply into Lwaxana's mind, like a fungus. *Mother* . . . she thought at her.

Something seemed to emerge from her mother's mind . . . a telepathic link, a bond that suffused Deanna, warmth and love reaching out as if to assure her that she was all right . . . nothing that could be articulated in words, but a connection such as Deanna had never known, forged by desperation and fear . . .

And Deanna was suddenly yanked away, the link broken with the force of cold water being dashed on her face. Sela was standing there, and she tucked the barrel of the disruptor under Deanna's chin. "Now . . . you're not going to make problems for us the way your mother did, are you?"

"She can't," Kressn said. "She's half human. She's not remotely the telepath her mother is. And . . . speaking of Mother . . . what should we do with her? With both of them?"

"Well, the big one is dead . . ."

"No, he's not."

Sure enough, Mr. Homn was still among the living. He wasn't moaning. Instead, incredibly, he had repositioned himself so that he was next to Lwaxana . . . and, operating as if from pure instinct as much as anything else, he had draped a protective arm over her and was looking at them defiantly. The wound was still very much in evidence, and there was a large pool of blood on the floor, but the bleeding had stopped.

"Now, that's impressive," said Sela. "We don't need a mental vegetable and a nearly dead man; the daughter and the boy will do. Kill these two."

"No!" shrieked Deanna.

The Romulans stepped forward, prepared to do as ordered, bringing their disruptors up and aiming them to finish the job.

That was when a firm voice rang out, loud and clear: "Weapons down. Sela . . . no."

It was a tone that was so obviously accustomed to command that the Romulans froze in the act. Sela, without even turning to look at the speaker, said, "This is none of your concern, Riker."

"Oh, yes it is," said Riker, crossing the room quickly and stepping around in front of Sela. "You asked me how far I would go, what I would be willing to do. What would I stop short of. Well, I stop short of this, Sela: being party to the cold-blooded murder of two helpless innocent people."

"Really." She snorted derisively. "You're a member of the Maquis, Riker. That's a terrorist organization. Do you truly believe that no harm has ever come to innocents during their activities? You took the *Defiant* and attacked Cardassian installations. Military targets, but there might well have been innocent people there: visitors, friends or family, simple maintenance people just trying to eke out a living. How many of them did you destroy, hmm? You don't really mean you won't be party to it. You just don't want to be involved with it when they wear the faces of people you know."

"Be that as it may . . . you hurt them, Sela, and I'm out."

"You're 'out'?" She raised one curved eyebrow. "Are you under the impression you can just pull out at any time?"

"Are you under the impression that you can stop me?" he replied tightly, his voice like a knife. "And do you think anything is going to be gained by both of us trying to find out?"

She appeared to consider the merits of the situation, and then she said to the others, "Get them out of sight. Move them upstairs."

"Shall we clean up the blood?" asked a Romulan.

"No. Leave it. The blood will upset him, make him aggressive and sloppy."

For a moment Deanna was confused, but then she understood. "Worf. You're laying a trap for Worf."

"That's right."

"But . . . I don't understand . . . why . . . why did you have to attack this house? Involve my mother and Homn, why . . ."

"Because," Sela said easily, "we wanted to have some fun."

Deanna couldn't believe what she had just heard. "Fun? *Fun?* You call all of this . . . chaos fun?"

"We all seek our amusements where we can, Deanna," Sela said. She had taken a step back to Riker's side, and then she suddenly wrapped an arm up and around the back of his head, drew it forward and kissed him with an almost violent enjoyment. Their faces drew apart, but she kept her teeth dug into his lower lip for an extended moment before releasing it. Then she cast a contemptuous glance at Deanna. "I take it we understand each other."

"Only too well," said Deanna, her eyes blazing as she looked at Riker. "Only too well."

Fourteen

The painting was exactly where Will Riker had remembered it being.

It hung on the wall of the Betazed museum of art, a canvas of concentric splashes of red, blue, green, white, black, and several colors that Riker still didn't recognize. A dozen years ago, Deanna and he had stood in front of it and she had tried to urge him to see something in it, to examine what it had suggested to him. At the time, all he had seen were paint swirls. Riker had never been much for abstract art. His feeling was that a painting should be of something recognizable. Otherwise he was always worried that somewhere out there, the artist was laughing at his admirers by simply splashing together whatever colors he felt like at random and calling it a painting.

But Riker had learned much during the intervening years, and when he gazed at the painting now, he relaxed his mind, let it wander. The curious thing to Riker was that, whenever he was willing to do that—let his thoughts simply run in free-floating directions rather than in nice, ordered headings—invariably they would always turn, sooner or later, to Deanna. One would have thought that consistent happenstance alone would have been sufficient to make him realize the depths of his feelings for her, but such had not been the case.

This time was no different than the other times, as the colors in the painting, in his mind, swirled and coalesced. And they seemed to form a face, smiling and loving, filling him with completion. As it happened, Riker felt connected not just to his past but to his future, as if he was standing at a crossroads in his life and seeing all the possibilities of his actions played out for him, here and now.

The face seemed to speak to him, and it was her face, it was her soul intertwined with his, and as if she were talking to him from every point in his existence, as if they had always been meant to be together and always would be, she said to Will Riker, *Welcome home . . . Imzadi . . .*

"Glad to be back," he murmured.

He closed his eyes, holding the image in his mind for a time longer, and then allowed it to dissipate. In doing so, he felt as if he was drawing it into every aspect of himself, fortifying his spirit for what was to come. It was not going to be easy, that much was certain. Will was going to have to talk to Deanna . . . talk to Worf . . . explain himself, make his case . . .

It was a daunting prospect.

He had already been on Betazed for a day or two. He had not come in through the normal spaceport, which was the required port of entry for standard commercial transports. His concern had been that, if he came through the main port of call and been ID'd as Will Riker, it might have set off bells in Jellico's office. But the transport pilot had been a friend of former Sergeant Tang's, and had been kind enough to bend the rules and drop him off a distance from the city. Unfortunately, to make sure that they were far enough away to avoid detection, he'd had to let Riker off quite a few miles from the city. But that had been okay, for Riker had found that he was anxious to give himself time to build up—of all things—his nerve. He knew he was going to have time; just before he had left, Deanna had dropped him a chatty vid in which she mentioned, among other things, that they had decided to extend their stay on Betazed. "Mother and Worf are getting to know each other," she had said perkily . . . or at least, it seemed as if she was trying to look perky. Riker didn't know whether to take that as a good sign or a bad one.

For all he knew, once he came to her, she would smile at him pityingly as she explained to him that it was over. And Worf . . . would look at him with pure contempt. He would be forever diminished in the Klingon's eyes for his weakness and uncertainty in waiting as long as he had. But then Will squared his shoulders, reinforcing his confidence. Whatever was going to happen would just have to happen. He'd live with the consequences of his actions.

Worst came to worst, he could always leave Starfleet and join a traveling circus.

He'd arrived on Betazed only a short time before. His first impulse had been to go straight to the Troi home, but he fought it. Instead he needed time to steel himself for what was to come, and had done so by visiting the museum. It had, after all, been the last place that he had seen Deanna before he embarked on a career that would take him away from her, only to wind up reuniting them. It was only fitting somehow that he return to the museum to pay his respects.

"Will!"

The voice sounded familiar but he couldn't immediately place it as he turned to see the speaker . . . and then he recognized her instantly. "Wendy! Wendy Roper! I don't believe it!"

The woman approaching him was small and slim, with her long black hair tied back in an elaborate braid. "Will Riker, you old sleaze!" she said in amazement. "When did you get so scruffy?"

"About eight years ago."

"Makes you look ancient."

"I feel ancient." He paused, thinking about the fact that the last time he had seen Wendy Roper, they had been naked together in his quarters, sleeping off a slightly (but only slightly) alcohol-supplemented assignation. Then Deanna, with whom he had thought he had broken up some hours before, showed up and discovered them together. The rest was history.

He shook his head. "I can't believe you're still here. I mean, you can't still be assigned here with your father . . ."

"Actually, Daddy left his job at the Federation Embassy about three years ago. And it's Wendy Berq, actually."

He looked at her in surprise. "Married?"

"That's usually the way."

"When?"

"Actually, about two years after you left. My husband is Betazoid . . . a teacher. That's why I stayed."

"My God . . ."

"But Will," she said urgently, her mood suddenly changing, "I heard about Deanna . . ."

"You did." He sighed.

"Is that why you're here?"

"In a way . . . it is. I mean . . . you know . . . in a way, I wanted it to happen to her . . ."

He didn't notice that Wendy was staring at him in clear astonishment. "What?"

"It's just, after all these years, she deserves something like that . . . in many ways, it couldn't happen to a better person . . ."

"Will, are you out of your mind?"

The intensity of her reaction caught him off guard. "Wha—? Wendy . . . what are you . . . ?"

"How can you say that? No one deserves to have something like that happen!"

"Wendy, what's the matter with you?" He gripped her arms, noticing that people were looking at them in confusion. "Get ahold of yourself."

"What's the matter with *me?* Will, I know that you and Deanna had a bad breakup, but it was a dozen years ago! You can't really think that after all this time, she deserves to have her home destroyed, her mother mentally brutalized, her—"

Will Riker went completely ashen.

"What . . ." he said slowly, "in heaven's name . . . are you talking about?"

Will ran through the hospital corridors so quickly that he nearly knocked over at least half a dozen people. Fortunately enough the Betazoids, being a fairly hypersensitive race, were adept enough to get the hell out of his way so that they didn't wind up with his footprints on their backs. Wendy ran behind him.

The news that Wendy had told him was simply beyond belief. Gart Xerx, whom Riker knew quite well, had stopped by the Troi household to visit on the spur of the moment and found the entire place a wreck. Destruction from above and the sides. Lwaxana and Homn, lying insensate in an upstairs room, Lwaxana in some sort of mental coma and Homn unconscious and having lost a ton of blood. No sign of Deanna, or Worf, or Alexander. No clue as to when any of it had happened. It was as if the galaxy had gone crazy.

"Excuse me," said one thin, gray-haired Betazoid woman, stepping deliberately in his way, "but you absolutely should not be running in—"

"Lwaxana . . . where is she . . . ?" he managed to gasp out. He had run ten blocks and up several flights of stairs, and was feeling a bit winded.

"Lwaxana? You mean Lwaxana Troi . . . Daughter of the Fifth House?"

"That's right."

The woman seemed taken aback. "I can take you to her. I'm her doctor. Come."

She turned and walked away. Will and Wendy fell into step behind her. They headed down the corridor, and Will could tell before they got there which room was very likely Lwaxana's. There were a number of people standing outside, most of them fairly tall and broad men, and they were wearing pale blue uniforms. Riker immediately recognized them as part of the Betazoid Peace Keepers force. The Peace Keepers were, for the most part, a figurehead force only, since crime was almost unknown on Betazed. Since all Betazoids were capable of mind-reading, getting away with any crime was virtually impossible. So outside races rarely bothered trying anything on Betazed, and the Betazoids themselves were—to all intents and purposes—above that sort of thing. All in all, the Peace Keepers' main function was to provide a nominally comforting presence to tourists and look good on a float during the annual Betazed Unity Parade. There was also a Starfleet security man, apparently connected to the embassy.

When they saw Riker coming, however, they stared at him with what appeared to be surprise. "You!" one of them said, and another called out, "He's here!"

"They know you?" Wendy asked.

"I've been back here from time to time, but I don't remember these guys in particular," Riker said in a low voice, and then he switched into "command mode," adopting the tone of voice that came so naturally to him when he was striding the bridge of a starship. "How is she, gentlemen? And Mr. Homn, what's his condition? I'm going to want to inform Starfleet of this immediately. Do we have any idea of the whereabouts of Deanna Troi? Or Mr. Worf, or his son? Or any clue as to the identity of the perpetrators of—"

A blunt object came down from behind Riker, catching him squarely in the back of the head and sending him to his knees. Wendy let out a shriek as Will pushed himself forward, trying to get distance between himself and whoever had just assaulted him, and staggered to his feet. He turned and saw, to his astonishment, a Cardassian. He was holding a shock prod, tapping it gently against his lower leg. He was tall, with the darkest and most pitiless eyes that Riker had ever seen in a sentient being. It had been the prod that he had used to slam Riker from behind, but it hadn't been activated. If it were, Riker would be immobile from the neck down.

"Who the hell are you?!" demanded Will.

"Are you going to pretend you don't remember me, Riker?" asked the Cardassian. "Your old friend, Mudak?"

"Remember you? I've never even met you! Will someone tell me what's going on?" He was rubbing the back of his aching neck.

"You should have finished off Homn when you had the chance, Riker. He regained consciousness for a time . . . long enough to tell us who was behind the attack. Romulans . . . and you."

"And . . . *me?* Are you insane? He's insane!" he said to Wendy.

Wendy turned to the Peace Keepers and said, "This is a mistake . . . Will Riker would never do something like th—"

"Will Riker?" Mudak laughed derisively. "This isn't Will Riker."

"What?" Wendy asked. "What do you mean, this isn't—"

"This is Thomas Riker, or at least that's what he calls himself," continued Mudak. "Terrorist. Member of the Maquis. Escapee from a Cardassian labor camp. And freak of nature . . . a walking accident, a duplicate created by a transporter mishap."

"No . . . I am Will Riker," Riker said, trying to fight down a rising sense of panic. "I didn't know that Tom had escaped . . . until recently, I didn't even know that he wasn't aboard the *Gandhi* . . ."

Wendy stared at him in astonishment. "You mean it's true? There's another . . . another you running around?"

"Yes," said Will, "but I'm not him. You," he said urgently to the Peace Keepers. "Look at my mind . . . you'll see that I'm Will Riker. . . ."

One of the Peace Keepers, the leader apparently, took a step forward and frowned momentarily. "He is Will Riker . . ."

"Of course he is!" said Mudak. "I explained that to you people when I first arrived! Timing worked against you, Riker. I've been tracking you ever since you escaped. Made you my pet project. I'd left word with key, discreet informants on certain worlds to be on the lookout for you, and when word of your involvement in this assault surfaced, I was here in no time. I didn't think you'd actually be foolish enough to return here. I've been waiting for Lwaxana Troi to recover so I could try and get more information from her, on the chance that she had scanned your mind and knew where you were going. But here you are. What were you doing, Riker? Coming back here to finish her off?"

"I am not . . . Tom Riker . . . I am Will Riker, now what do I have to do to make that clear to you? Lwaxana!" he suddenly raised his voice. "Lwaxana, I need to talk to you!"

The doctor was still there, and she was interposing herself between Riker and the entrance to Lwaxana's room. "You can't. Whatever happened to her, it left her in severe mental shock. She underwent some sort of psi attack. There may be memory loss . . . she's still not conscious, she has to build up her strength . . ."

"But she'll know me. More than anyone else could, except for Deanna, she'll know me . . . and maybe she can tell us where Deanna went, maybe—"

The Peace Keepers were gathering around her on either side, adding their bodies to the blockade. "I'm sorry," the doctor said firmly.

"All right, Riker, enough games," Mudak said, and with a click of a switch he activated his prod. "Please, I'm begging you . . . make this difficult. . . ."

"He might know where they are," one of the Peace Keepers pointed out.

"Their whereabouts are none of my concern," Mudak replied impatiently, "but if you wish to scan him on that matter, do it and be quick about it. I'm growing tired of these games."

Once more the Peace Keeper delved into Riker's thoughts. "He has no knowledge of their whereabouts. In fact, he has no recollection of, or knowledge of, what happened at all."

"You see?" Riker said.

But Mudak shook his head. "That proves nothing. The Troi woman had her mind tampered with; you said so yourself. They may have done a similar thing to him, in order to protect themselves, cover their tracks." He pointed the prod at Will. "I checked with Starfleet as soon as my contact passed the report on to me. Will Riker is still on Earth. I have that directly from one of their admirals who gave Will Riker his latest assignment. This is Tom Riker. He is my prisoner and he is coming with me now!" And over the startled gasps of the Peace Keepers, who were not remotely accustomed to even seeing the use of force, much less utilizing it themselves, Mudak lunged at Riker with the shock prod.

The prod came up a half foot shy of Riker's chest . . . because Wendy Roper had leaped onto Mudak's back, her fingers clawing at his face, and she was shouting, "Leave him alone!"

And Riker, who took the only opportunity open to him, turned and charged straight into the midst of the Peace Keepers. He slammed into them, knocking them aside as if they were weightless. It was not difficult; they were so stunned by the ferocity of his thoughts that they'd been momentarily paralyzed anyway.

Riker stumbled into the room, and the door hissed shut behind him. The open/close mechanism was to the right of the door, and Will quickly turned and ripped it out of the wall, decommissioning the door. He saw Lwaxana lying in a bed, motionless, staring upward at the ceiling with vacant eyes. "Lwaxana, it's me! It's Will! You have to come out of it!"

He ran to her, grabbed her by the shoulders. "Lwaxana!" he called her again, staring into her eyes, trying to pull her out of her stupor through sheer and unbridled determination. "Lwaxana, I have to help Deanna! I have to get to her! You may be the only one who can help! Come out of it, Lwaxana! Give me something to go on! Anything!"

Her eyes remained dark and opened, but there was nothing behind them.

"Lwaxana!"

In the corridor, an annoyed Mudak brought his shock prod up and touched Wendy's arm with it. Wendy shrieked, losing all sensation in the arm, and Mudak easily shoved her to the floor. Then he tried to get into the room, but the massed bodies of the Peace Keepers were blocking his way as they tried to pry open the door.

Inside, Riker was talking at Lwaxana with greater and greater urgency. "Lwaxana, it's me! It's Will! You know I wouldn't have tried to hurt you! You know I wasn't involved in any of this! I've got to find Deanna! I may be the only one who can do it! If Worf's with her, she might have a chance, but if Worf's dead, she's helpless! I've got to find her! I've got to!" He heard pounding at the door, the high-pitched whine of instruments prying at it. "Lwaxana! I've come all this way to get her! To get her back! But I'm going to wind up in a Cardassian prison camp unless you come around and help me!" His anger, his frustration began to build as there was still no sign of mental life in her eyes. "It can't end like this, Lwaxana! It can't! Not after everything we've been through! You owe it to her to help her! You owe it to me, to yourself! Lwaxana, I understand now! I finally understand! I have to help her! I have to! Because being stuck in a prison is nothing compared to not knowing where she is, knowing that she needs me, knowing that I'm not there for her! I have to be there for her! I have to, always! Always! *Dammit, Lwaxana! We are Imzadi, and I love her! Help me, dammit! Help me!"*

And suddenly Lwaxana's eyes focused on Riker. Focused with something that he hadn't seen before, an intensity, a determination . . .

. . . and abruptly Lwaxana was in his head . . .

. . . and Riker gasped as a flood of images overwhelmed him. Not just images . . . sensations, emotions, all pounding through him, filling him and overflowing . . .

. . . and there was Deanna, and she was everywhere, and he could see her, and the scent of her, and the sound of her voice was in his ears . . .

. . . and everything was amplified a thousand times, and there was the first brush of her lips against his . . .

. . . and the first time that their souls had touched . . .

. . . and the agony of their separation was so intense that it threatened to cleave him in two . . .

. . . and the joy of their reunion was so incredible that he began to sob . . .

. . . and there was a ripping noise of his universe being torn to shreds and then just as quickly being restructured with Deanna as its center, and how could he possibly have difficulty knowing where she was, because she was everywhere, in every pore, in every centimeter of his skin, in every aspect of his soul she was there . . .

The door to Lwaxana's room was suddenly torn open, and Mudak was the first one through. Riker didn't even see him and suddenly the shock prod slammed against the side of his head. The contact was so intense, so jolting, that Riker and Lwaxana both let out a scream. Lwaxana fell back onto her pillow, her eyes closing, her head lolling to one side.

Will was on the floor, trying to reorient himself, because everywhere there was Deanna, and he couldn't possibly be in any danger because she was there with him, one sensation tumbling over another, so that he made no effort at all to block the thrust of Mudak's boot as it slammed upward into his gut. Riker flipped completely over, lying on his back, gasping and, insanely, he was half-smiling as he whispered, "Deanna . . ." That was when Mudak kicked him a final time in the head and sent Riker spiraling into unconsciousness.

"Is the Daughter of the Fifth House all right?" asked one of the Peace Keepers urgently.

The doctor was doing a light scan and shaking her head in dismay. "Apparently she came to briefly, but now she's unconscious again. She overstrained herself, trying to fight him off."

"She is your concern, not mine," Mudak said as he hauled the insensate Riker to his feet. "I have my package; I'll be leaving now."

"The hell you will."

It had been Wendy Roper Berq who had spoken, and she was blocking his way. She was two heads shorter than he, but that didn't seem to matter to her. "I don't care what you say. That's Will Riker."

"You have no say in the matter, woman. Be glad I don't arrest you for interfering with the rightful recapturing of a Cardassian criminal."

"Save the threats, bone face," Wendy shot back. "I've got friends at the Federation Embassy. I already contacted them while you were busy smashing in the door. They've contacted the port and issued instructions that your ship is not to budge from there until we get, for ourselves, firsthand confirmation from Starfleet that Will Riker is back on Earth. And if he's not, then God help you, you crinkle-headed creep, because you just assaulted a Starfleet officer and I'm going to make it my personal mission to make sure that you're the one who's stuck in a prison camp until your idea of a good day is one where you can gum down your food without too much pain. Do we understand each other?"

Mudak stared at her impassively, and then said, "Former lover, I take it?"

"Drop dead."

He smiled humorlessly. "I assume that's a yes."

Fifteen

Admiral Jellico couldn't believe that he had just gotten yet another communiqué about the whereabouts of Commander William Riker. It seemed like just the other day that he'd been contacted by the Federation attaché in charge of Cardassian affairs. Jellico made it clear to him that he was not in the habit of discussing the whereabouts of Starfleet personnel with liaisons to the Cardassians, but when informed that Tom Riker had escaped from Lazon II, he reconsidered.

On that basis, Jellico judged that the situation warranted his at least informing the Attaché that Riker was Earthside. Of course, it wasn't as if Jellico trusted Will Riker either; naturally he had checked.

Yet now a message had come in from Betazed, from the embassy. Apparently Tom Riker had surfaced on Betazed, but he was insisting that he was, in fact, William Riker, and at least one person on Betazed believed him.

"Murphy," Jellico called to his aide in the front office, "put me through to Commander Riker's apartment, would you, please?"

"Yes, sir," came Murphy's voice from outside.

On Betazed, Gart Xerx walked into his office and was stunned to see Mudak sitting behind his desk, feet propped up. "What are you doing here?" hissed Gart.

"I thought we would have a chat, Gart," Mudak said, his dark eyes flashing with . . . amusement? Anger?

"We have nothing to chat about." Gart quickly tried to hustle Mudak away from his desk. "If someone should see you here . . ." He shuddered at the thought. "Go. Just go. Just . . ."

Mudak had risen from the chair, but now he lashed out with one powerful hand and grabbed Gart by the throat. He slammed him against the wall, and all the while his face remained impassive. One would have been hard-pressed to characterize him as someone who enjoyed his work. Gart pulled at Mudak's hand, trying to pry it loose, but Mudak wasn't releasing him. Instead he slowly started to push Gart up the wall, an inch at a time, Gart's feet dangling off the ground and air not getting through to his lungs.

"You have been very useful as an information peddler to Cardassia, Gart. My people and I have appreciated that." He angled his head as if examining a small bug. "However . . . it was our understanding that you were supposed to be working exclusively for us. You were not to deal with the Klingons . . . or the Romulans . . . or the Jem'Hadar . . . just us. An information peddler who can read minds and is unscrupulous enough to pass that information on is a valuable commodity. But part of that value is the exclusivity. If you learn of matters regarding other races and pass them on to us, that is useful. If, on the other hand, you learn things from us . . . and relay them to other customers . . . that is a bad thing. A very . . . bad thing. Do we understand each other?"

Gart managed to get out, "Ess . . . esss . . ."

"Is that a yes, Gart?"

Gart wasn't able to respond. Instead he was too busy gritting his teeth, his jaw looking like it was beginning to merge with the upper part of his skull.

Mudak opened his hand and Gart slid to the floor. He lay there for a moment, gasping.

"I believe I know," Mudak said conversationally, "what is going through your mind, Gart. You are hedging your bets, preparing for the future. You have looked at the way of the galaxy, seen the forces that are massing out there . . . and come to realize, despite any high-flown protestations to the contrary, that Betazed is a target. And if that should happen, if Betazed should fall to conquerors, why . . . you believe that if you were cooperative before the conquest happened, then you would receive favored status after the conquest. To that end, it seemed reasonable to me that you might be dealing with other parties as well."

"You . . . you suspect me . . . even though you have no proof?" Gart managed to get out, rubbing his throat in pain.

"I suspect you because you are pretentious and full of yourself, Gart, and you think that you are very, very clever. And you may indeed be clever. It might indeed be in your interest to deal with a multitude of 'exclusive' customers so that you have friends on all sides. But let me warn you of something, Gart," and Mudak knelt next to Gart, who was still seated on the floor, and tapped him at the base of his throat. "If this world is conquered, it doesn't matter who does it. It doesn't matter what happens to Cardassia, or if the entire Cardassian Empire falls. Through it all, one truth remains: If you double-deal, or betray anything that you learn from me or anyone else who has information that is useful and/or hurtful to Cardassia, then I swear I will come back here, Gart. I will find a way, even if every other Cardassian is dead. I will come back, I will find you . . . and I will kill you. Do we understand each other, Gart?"

Slowly Gart nodded.

Mudak rose and smiled thinly. "I'm pleased we had this chat then. I have arranged for the transfer of credits to your private account to cover your providing us with the information about Riker's whereabouts. As always, I know that we can count on your continued discretion . . . can we not?"

Gart nodded once more as Mudak said, "A pleasure doing business with you, as always," and walked out the door, to head over to the embassy and await word from Starfleet as to the identity of his captive.

Jellico continued to go through some routine duty-roster material until Murphy informed him, "Sir . . . got Commander Riker for you."

Turning to the screen on his wall, Jellico said, "Put him through." He leaned back in his chair, interlacing his fingers, and waited. A moment later, Riker's image appeared on the screen. He looked as if he had just been roused from a deep slumber, rubbing the sleep from his eyes, and Jellico remembered the time difference. At Riker's location, it was about one in the morning. "Commander," Jellico said briskly.

"Admiral. Didn't I just hear from you?"

"I'm afraid so, Commander. But I needed to verify your whereabouts."

"Admiral, with all respect, I wish I knew why you were so interested as to where I am at any given moment. Do you think I'm just going to run out of here at the first opportunity?"

"No, Commander. In point of fact, this has to do with Tom."

"I see."

"You'll probably be relieved to know that he's been apprehended on Betazed."

"I see," Riker said again.

"Or . . . perhaps you're not relieved," Jellico continued. "Perhaps you have a few . . . regrets? He is, after all, you. Or do you feel that he got what's coming to him?"

Riker put up his hands and shook his head. "I really would prefer not to get into this with you, Admiral. Whatever your opinion on the matter is, is fine with me."

"Well. Good to see you're finally beginning to treat superior officers with the proper respect, Commander. Enjoy your assignment shortly at the Academy. Jellico out." Riker blinked off the screen, and Jellico said to himself with growing confidence, "I didn't think he'd had the nerve to leave against orders. When all is said and done, Riker knows when to knuckle under. Murphy!" he called.

"Yes, sir."

"Send a message back to Betazed. Without providing information as to his whereabouts, assure them that Will Riker is with us. Tell them that we can verify Commander Riker's whereabouts, and we can personally assure them that he is nowhere near Betazed." He nodded to himself. "There. That should put an end to that problem once and for all."

Roger Tang had just been in the process of closing up his tavern for the night when the small computer console tucked neatly under his bar said, "Incoming call on private channel Riker Alpha."

"Origin?"

"Starfleet Planetary Headquarters, office Admiral Jellico."

"Good timing," murmured Tang. "Ten minutes later, I would've been out of here. Computer . . . activate holosuite B, run program Riker One Kiss-Up, and patch through call."

"Acknowledged," the computer said in its flat voice.

Deciding he needed some amusement, Tang then strolled over to the holosuite and stepped just inside the door. Inside the suite was a perfectly serviceable re-creation of Riker's apartment, and seated at his desk—looking appropriately bleary-eyed, since Tang had thought to work in a real-time coordination component—was "Riker."

It had been a fairly simple program to build, really. A holographic representation of Riker, designed to handle straightforward queries from interested parties . . . particularly Starfleet personnel. This Jellico, in particular, had been one that Riker had been especially keen about watching out for. So in addition to the straightforward program that passed for Riker's presence, Tang and Will had created an additional tweak to it that Tang had code-named "Kiss-Up." The problem was that, because Riker was in a hurry, there hadn't been a great deal of time to put together a holoprogram that would be adept enough to handle everything thrown at it. So Tang had rigged the holo-Riker with simple, failsafe responses. If holo-Riker was handed a piece of information that he was previously unaware of, he would just respond with "I see," "I understand," "All right," and other neutral phrases. If the Admiral began posing questions to him that were beyond the holo-Riker's ability to articulate reasonable responses to, then holo-Riker was programmed with half a dozen replies that were exactly the type of thing that Jellico would want to hear, ranging from noninflammatory to deferring to the admiral's thoughts on the matter. These phrases included, "I really would prefer not to get into this with you, Admiral," "Admiral, I think you've really said it best," "Whatever your opinion on the matter is, is fine with me," and "Who am I to argue?"

Of course, the fakery wouldn't hold up under close inspection. If Jellico or anyone else took the transmissions and relayed them to the Starfleet Transmission Analysis Section, they would be able to discern within a matter of minutes that they were talking to a hologram. Riker couldn't cover all the bases. But Tang had the sneaking suspicion that Jellico's own ego was their best defense. The admiral very likely simply wouldn't believe that Riker would take off against orders, and therefore would be satisfied with a cursory check as to Riker's whereabouts.

When the conversation was over and Jellico's image vanished from the screen, Tang called, "Computer, end program." The ersatz Riker and room interior disappeared, and Tang nodded with satisfaction. "Well, I just saved your butt again, Commander. Your secret remains safe, and I'll tell you, when you get back to Earth . . . you are going to owe me big time."

Sixteen

Worf could still see the water closing over his head. There was blackness everywhere, water filling up his lungs. He was thrusting out desperately in all directions, spinning in circles, darkness and cold everywhere.

Then he realized that he wasn't under water anymore. He was in the vacuum of space, just as helpless and confused, trying to remember how he had gotten there and desperately trying to figure out which way lay safety. The cold was cutting through to the bone. He felt completely paralyzed, hopelessness and despair settling in on him.

That was when he started to hear the beeping. In a distant way, he realized that he'd been hearing it for some time, but he had no idea for how long. After a moment, he recognized the sound: It was the beeping from some sort of medical monitor.

He did not even realize his eyes had been closed, and yet now he opened them.

A Klingon was looking down at him. It was not anyone he knew, and he wondered how in the world another Klingon had wound up in deep space with him. This new Klingon was clean-shaven, which in and of itself was something of an oddity. His hair was tied back on either side, and gray flecked his thick eyebrows.

Then, once piece at a time, Worf's awareness of his whereabouts began to stitch itself together. He was no longer under water, that much was obvious. Nor, clearly, was he in space. That still left him, however, with a lot of possibilities.

"Worf," said the Klingon. "The monitors indicate that you are conscious. Are you?"

"Yes," Worf said slowly. His voice sounded strange to him, as if he hadn't spoken in some time. He felt a strain in his vocal cords as well. "Yes . . . I am . . ."

"Good. In answer to the question that is probably next in your mind, I am Dr. Kwon, and you are in the personal medical facility of the leader of the High Council."

"Gowron?!" Worf tried to sit up, and it was at that point that he realized he had a medical scanner mounted across him, holding him in place.

"Yes, Gowron, at least for the moment," said Kwon. "Then again, such matters tend to change so quickly, it is hard to say for sure."

"Then I am on homeworld. How did I—"

"Get here? Gowron desired to see you, to speak to you about matters of some urgency. We were able to learn that you were on Betazed, and tracked you there . . . only to arrive just as you apparently were on the losing end of an altercation with some Romulans."

"Romulans . . ."

Then it all snapped back together for Worf. The fleeting images had been tumbling over themselves in his head, trying to sort themselves out, but now they came completely together for him once more. "Romulans! Yes! There was a battle, they—"

"They wounded you rather severely," Kwon said. "You sustained more damage than I think you were truly aware of at the time. When the ship dispatched by Gowron showed up, you had just tumbled into a lake and were sinking fast. We beamed you out of the lake, and were at that point more than prepared to attend to the Romulans as well. However, upon seeing our arrival the Romulans took the opportunity to depart the area as quickly as possible. Cloaked and vanished. Typical. Surprise attacks with uneven odds, those the Romulans are more than happy to engage in. But an equal fight with a prepared foe, and the Romulans would sooner leave such matters to others."

"So they got away?"

"The Klingon vessel attempted a pursuit, I understand, but the Romulans, well . . . you know their knack for stealth. They got away, I am afraid. Furthermore, you were in poor enough shape when you were fished out from the lake that it was felt putting you into stasis and getting you here as quickly as possible was the preferred course of action."

"Blast! What about Alexander? And Deanna? And—"

Kwon put up his hands in an endeavor to quiet Worf down. "I do not know anything about any of the matters you are asking about."

"I must go to see Gowron."

"You," Kwon said firmly, "are going to stay here until I feel that you are sufficiently strong enough to leave."

Worf sat up.

The fact that the scanner was atop him, theoretically holding him down, did not slow him in the least. It broke clear off the bed and fell, in several pieces, to the floor.

Nonplussed, Kwon promptly said, "I will inform Gowron that you will be right along."

"And those are my concerns, Worf."

Gowron, paranoid as always, had chosen a fairly secluded place for his meeting with Worf: They were in the middle of a desert.

Hardened ground stretched in every direction for as far as the eye could see. Worf, wearing a full set of Klingon leathers and armor, walked slowly next to Gowron, his hands draped behind his back and his hair loose and fluttering in the faint breeze that was rolling along the desert surface. Gowron had just explained to him the current status of the Federation's apparent budding alliance with the Romulans, as well as the other concerns that preyed upon him.

Before he had done that, however, he had given Worf detailed information as to what had occurred with the Romulans on Betazed. The information, supplied through K'hanq, was quite detailed and thorough. As Gowron told Worf of the disappearance of Deanna Troi and Alexander, and the capture of Tom Riker, he watched Worf's expression carefully to see just how he took the news. Worf, commendably, betrayed nothing in his face. "Good, Worf, good," he had observed. "A true warrior does not betray the impact that a loss has upon him, no matter what." Worf had simply nodded at the compliment and then listened patiently as Gowron had gone off on his own concerns about the future of the Klingon Empire.

When Gowron had finished, Worf said, "If those are indeed your concerns, Gowron . . . worries that the Federation will betray the empire . . . then your concerns are misplaced."

"Are they." He did not say it in what sounded like a questioning tone. He was still clearly very suspicious.

"The Federation is not in the habit of betraying its allies."

" 'Not in the habit,' Worf, simply means that it does not happen with frequency."

"It has never happened," Worf said flatly.

"Unprecedented is not the same thing as impossible. Would you agree?"

"On that point, yes. But I say again, it will not happen."

"I would very much like to believe you, Worf," sighed Gowron. "I simply wish I knew . . . that I could."

Pebbles and dirt were crunching under Worf's heavy footfall. But something in the way that Gowron had just said that suddenly suggested to Worf an implied questioning of Worf's integrity. He stopped in his tracks and said, "What do you mean by that?"

"Nothing."

"No. You did mean something by it. Clarify it."

"Worf . . . I tell you it was noth—"

"Clarify it *now.*"

Gowron had continued to walk even when Worf stopped, so when he halted in his tracks and turned to face Worf, he was several feet away. But the glare from him seemed to leap the distance. "You forget yourself, Worf," he said dangerously. "Do not confuse our familiarity with one another with the right to take liberties. I am still leader of the High Council. I am still Gowron. And you, Worf, had best watch your tone if you would prefer to continue using that insolent tongue of yours."

But Worf would not be cowed. "Did you intend, Gowron, to imply that I cannot be trusted." There was something in his voice that hinted that, High Council leader or not, if Gowron did not clarify and possibly apologize for this point, he was going to have a fight on his hands.

"Worf," he said slowly, "obviously I do not consider your ties to Starfleet, and the Federation, sufficient to challenge your loyalty to the Klingon Empire, the Klingon ethos, and the Klingon way. You have shown over the years that you are able to balance both . . . and indeed, when there is conflict between one and the other, you are fully capable of choosing the Klingon way." Worf, of course, knew that he was referring to Worf's slaying of Duras. "However," he continued, "marriage is something quite different."

"Marriage? You think that marriage to Deanna threatens my integrity?"

"I think it threatens your very essence, Worf. You proclaim your loyalty to Klingon ideals . . . yet your proposed wife, and the woman who would act as mother to your child, has philosophies that are as far from ours as they could possibly be."

"The first and foremost philosophy of the Federation—that which I have lived my life by—is the acceptance of all races as equals," Worf said. And, not without a sense of irony, he paraphrased words that had been said to him not very long ago.

"This is not a competition. Different is simply different, rather than one inherently better than the other."

"That is a very kind sentiment, Worf. I do not happen to believe it, but it is a very kind sentiment. You and a Betazoid . . ."

This reaction served only to anger Worf. "Perhaps," he said, "there are things we can teach each other."

"Superb notion, Worf. We can teach Deanna Troi how to fight, and she can teach us how to be captured."

Worf crossed the distance between himself and Gowron in what seemed little more than a single step. His face only inches from Gowron's, his eyes blazing with intensity, Worf said, "To voice disrespect for my fiancée . . . is to voice disrespect for me."

Gowron did not come close to looking upset or losing his cool. He simply stared at Worf for a time, and then replied in an unhurried tone, "No disrespect intended."

Worf took a step back, nodding and acknowledging it.

"However," continued Gowron, "the fact remains that you owe your status—your restored honor—to me, Worf. To me. And when I say to you that I believe a Klingon and a Betazoid is an inherently wrongheaded match, I expect you—at the very least—to consider my words. For if you were not to do so, then you would be treating me with disrespect. And that, Worf . . . could be very unwise."

"Your point is well made, Gowron."

The moment of hostility apparently having passed, Gowron clapped a hand on Worf's shoulder. It smacked down with a loud, leathery sound. "Stay with me for a time, Worf. Stay here on Qo'noS. There is no reason you cannot. Your vessel, the *Enterprise,* has been destroyed anyway. So you have no duty to hurry back to Picard. I believe, Worf, that you must recapture your Klingon roots. You must remember who you are."

"I must find my son and fiancée first," Worf replied. "I have no other choice."

"Starfleet has been alerted to the kidnapping. Certainly they are attending to it."

"They were taken from me. My fiancée, my son. They are mine. It is a matter of honor that I pursue their kidnappers myself."

Clearly Gowron was about to debate the point, but he saw in Worf's eyes that such an endeavor would be utterly fruitless. "Very well," sighed Gowron. "Do so for the sake of your son . . . as opposed to the proposed union which I do not approve."

"You are not required to approve it."

"I suspect the head of your house will not approve it, either," replied Gowron. "If she does not approve it, there will be no wedding, as you well know."

Worf bristled at the thought. "She would not refuse me."

"You, she would quite easily refuse. Me, however, she would not refuse." As Gowron said this he smirked slightly and ran a finger over his mustache.

"What are you saying, Gowron?"

"I am saying, Worf . . . that I can be more useful to you as an ally than as an enemy, as you well know. And I would be a more willing ally were I not concerned that, in becoming involved with this woman, you were in danger of turning your back on your heritage."

"I have lived with humans since an early age, Gowron," Worf said heatedly. "When the empire required me, I left Starfleet to answer the call. I raise my son in the Klingon way. Am I not sufficiently 'Klingon' for you? What more would you have of me?"

"It has not been easy for you, Worf," acknowledged Gowron. "You are to be commended for all that you are. But I am nonetheless concerned about what you will be. Perhaps these concerns are misplaced, perhaps not." He paused. "Tell me, Worf . . . what are the chances that Starfleet will provide you with a vessel with which you can attempt to track down your son and missing fiancée?"

"I . . . do not know," he admitted.

"And if you ask me for the same . . . ?"

He glowered at him. "You will help me . . . if you believe it will serve your own purpose in the future."

"You know me well, Worf. Perhaps too well. I will provide you with a long-range scout ship, armed with phaser cannons, in order to aid you in your endeavors. However . . ."

"However?"

"After you have accomplished your mission, for good or ill . . . you will return here, with your son—and fiancée, if you are so disposed—and remain until I am personally satisfied that the union does not pose a threat to either your resolve or your son's future as a member of the Klingon Empire. Agreed?"

Worf's first impulse was to argue, but he couldn't help but feel that every moment he might spend arguing was another moment wasted. He needed to go after Deanna and Alexander. He needed to rescue them, whatever it took.

"Agreed," he said. "And I would like you to agree to something as well."

"And that would be?"

"Inform Captain Picard of your concerns." As Gowron started to protest, Worf overspoke him. "You know that Picard can be trusted. He will be honest and direct with you; he always has been in the past. State your concerns to him. I suspect he may be able to put your mind at ease."

"All right, Worf," Gowron said reluctantly. "I will do as you suggest. Although I suspect that it will not do much to assuage my concerns. No matter what he may say to us . . . nothing can change the fact of the Federation's overtures to the Romulans. But let no one say that Gowron was unwilling to listen. So . . ." He brought the topic back to the matter of Worf's impending quest. "Where will you go first? Into Romulan territory? If you think you can simply head straight into the Neutral Zone undetected, you are mistaken. The scout ship does not come equipped with a cloaking device; it is too small, with nowhere near sufficient energy . . ."

"If it is necessary, I will find a way. First, however, I will question Tom Riker. You said the Cardassians have brought him to a labor camp?"

"Yes, on Lazon Two, according to our information. Apparently he had already been there and escaped. I imagine they questioned him and did not find him particularly cooperative."

"I will speak to him myself," Worf said coldly, shaking his head. "It is difficult for me to believe that Tom Riker would cooperate in such a venture. That he would have turned to the Maquis. He is a duplicate, down to the smallest detail, of William Riker . . . and Commander Riker is one of the most morally centered individuals I have ever known."

"Obviously this Tom Riker is not William Riker."

"Obviously," agreed Worf. "And I will learn what happened to Deanna and Alexander . . . if I have to break every bone in Tom Riker's body."

Seventeen

The room was completely without furnishings. There was only one source of light, in the ceiling, and it was not a particularly strong one. Much of the room remained shrouded in darkness.

Deanna sat just within the rim of light, feeling as if she were some sort of primitive creature, fearing the eyes that hovered in the darkness just beyond the light. In this instance, though, there was only one pair of eyes watching her from the dark, and she knew to whom they belonged.

Her body ached and she had no idea why. Some part of her felt as if she was in constant pain, but they had not really laid a hand on her since her captors had brought her to this place. Each time she awakened, it was with the feeling that she had not slept at all, even though she knew she had. And she felt . . . tormented. Physically, spiritually, it was as if someone had been at her nonstop.

And Will . . . she kept thinking of Will . . .

But he wasn't coming. He couldn't . . . he had no idea where they were, no . . .

She forcibly pried her mind away from those thoughts. "Alexander," she said softly, her legs tucked up under her chin, "how long are you going to sit there?"

There was no immediate reply, and then finally he said, "How long have we been here?"

"I don't know. I've really lost track of time. Now Vulcans . . . Vulcans can keep track of time. It's amazing. They have an internal clock that is like nothing that you've ever—"

"You do not need to make small talk in order to ease my worries," Alexander told her.

"Oh." A pause. "Are you worried?"

"No. I am angry. I am angry I did not do more. I let our captors take us and bring us here . . . wherever here is."

"You're just one person, Alexander, and a rather young one at that."

"When Kahless was half my age, he laid waste to half a continent, engaging in single combat with over three thousand foes, and he defeated them all."

"Really." She laughed softly. "Alexander, with all respect to Kahless . . . don't believe everything you read."

His eyes floated toward her and he emerged into the light. To her surprise, there was clear anger on his face. "Are you saying that Klingon history is filled with lies?"

"I am saying, Alexander, that history is written by the winners. I don't doubt that Kahless had great and tremendous victories. But sometimes, in the retelling, achievements get exaggerated. People like to embellish, it's only natural. Plus it can sometimes serve individual purposes, particularly if someone is trying to build themselves up. Inflating one's own accomplishments are not exactly unheard of in—"

"I think you are insulting Kahless the Unforgettable," Alexander told her. "Whether it is your intention or not, that's what I think you're doing."

"Alexander, I sincerely don't mean to make you feel that way. Tell me, though: Who was the first person who called Kahless 'the Unforgettable'?"

Alexander's annoyance seemed to waffle a bit. "Well . . ."

"Well what?" she prodded gently.

"I . . . seem to recall it was, uhm . . . Kahless. At his great battle rally on the

Mount of Despair, he said, 'I am Kahless the Unforgettable. Know my name and tremble in fear.' "

"Mm-hmm."

"But that proves nothing."

"All right."

They were silent for a time longer. Alexander had, unconsciously, adopted Deanna's legs-curled posture.

"My father isn't dead, you know."

"I know that," Deanna said with conviction. "It would take a lot more than that fall to stop your father."

"And Riker! How could he have joined the Romulans? I thought I knew him! I thought he was nice! It's because you and my father are engaged, isn't it?"

"Alexander . . ."

"That's it, I know it. He went insane with jealousy, that's all. That must be it."

"It is difficult to know what makes the human heart operate as it does," she told him. "We just have to . . . to try and understand . . ."

"No. We have to kill him. We have to kill all of them. If I get out of here . . . if I get a weapon in my hand . . . a thousand throats may be slit in a night by a running man."

"That may be, Alexander. But in the darkness of the night . . . sometimes the running man has trouble seeing who his friends are."

He looked at her uncomprehendingly. "I don't know what you mean."

"Neither do I," she admitted.

"Are we going to get out of here, do you think?"

"Yes. He'll find us."

"My father, you mean?"

Deanna didn't reply immediately. Because until she'd actually said it, she hadn't realized who it was that she had meant.

Somewhere out there was Will Riker, and her thoughts once more drifted back to him. In no way that she could account for, she had more of a sense of him than she had ever had before. He had not been far from her mind from the moment that they had been taken from the surface of Betazed. She had a belief in him, an unshakable confidence that he would come for her. She would drift in and out of sleep, and her dream would always be the same. She was always right where she was at that moment, there in the cell, lying in the middle of the light. The door would suddenly slide open, and there would be no sign of the guards. Light cascaded in from the corridor, backlighting a tall, powerful, and rugged figure standing there—a figure that seemed to glow with its own internal light of confidence. Then he would stride forward into Deanna's own pool of light, and it was as if the two light sources were joining. She would look up into Will's face, and yes, it was most definitely Will. Without a word he would reach down, pick her up, and cradle her in her arms. Deanna, the modern woman, Deanna the educated and intellectual counselor, dreaming of literally being swept away in the muscled arms of her Imzadi.

She sensed a pull toward him, deep within her mind. She felt as if she could reach out across light-years and touch him, as if he were right there . . . right there . . .

The door slid open and he was standing there.

Her spirit fell. She felt as if a shadow had been cast over her. She wondered how she could have been fooled by him, even for a moment. Granted, hindsight was always twenty/twenty, but even so . . . he simply felt wrong to her now. Perhaps it was because, deep down, she had so wanted his sentiments to be real . . .

But what did that say about her, then?

The fact that her thoughts remained in turmoil only survived to anger her even further, since he was the one who had set them into motion.

The Romulan guards were visible on either side of Tom Riker as he stood, unmoving, in the hallway. "I'd like to speak with you, Deanna, if that's all right."

"And if it isn't?"

"I'd like to speak with you anyway."

"And if I don't desire to?"

His voice floated into her head. *Deanna . . . you have to listen. . . .*

"Stop it," she said out loud and sharply. "I've been blocking you out on purpose. You have lost that privilege."

If he was chastened, or upset or chagrined, he didn't allow any of it to show. If there was one thing that he did have in common with Will Riker, it was that he was the consummate poker player. You couldn't tell what it was he had in his hand just by looking at his face.

It was also clear, however, that he wasn't about to walk away without her. With an annoyed sigh she got to her feet. Alexander was immediately at her side, and in a low voice he told her, "You don't have to go with him. I'll take him."

"No, Alexander . . . it'll be okay. Just stay here. I'll be back soon . . . won't I . . . Will."

Riker's face remained impassive, but he said, "You have my word."

"That means a lot," Alexander said sarcastically.

"Alexander," Deanna cautioned, not wanting to exacerbate the situation. Alexander looked as if he wanted to argue the point further, but abided by Deanna's obvious wishes and kept his silence. Deanna headed out the door and fell into step next to Tom Riker as the door closed them off from view.

They walked down the corridor in silence, Deanna not even looking at him. Even so, she had the sense that he was not taking his eyes off her.

The entire area seemed to have a makeshift quality to it. They were planetside, of that much Deanna was certain. Although in theory being on a starship should have been indistinguishable from being on a planet's surface, nonetheless—somehow—she could tell. There was a mustiness in the air that the internal air circulation couldn't quite filter out. Deanna had the feeling that they were in some sort of underground facility, something that had been carved out by hand phasers and thrown together with an on-the-fly construction capability.

"In here," Riker said, gesturing to one room. The doors slid open and Deanna walked in without the slightest hesitation. She didn't want to give any indication whatsoever that she was intimidated by the thought of being alone with him. Indeed, it was as if she wanted to try and project as much contempt for him as she could. He followed her, turned to the guards, and said, "We'll be fine, thank you." The doors hissed shut behind them.

The room was furnished ("decorated" would certainly not be the right word) very simply and very functionally. A bed, some dresser drawers, and that was all. Still, it seemed like a palace compared with what Deanna and Alexander had. Deanna stood there, arms folded, saying nothing.

"We have to talk," Tom said. "I had hoped to do it . . . well . . . in our heads . . ."

"I will never . . . let you in . . . again. Do we understand each other?"

"Perfectly." He took a deep breath and then, in so low a voice she could barely hear him, he said, "First . . . I want to thank you for not . . . betraying me."

"I felt there was enough betrayal for the one day, didn't you?"

"All right. All right, I had that coming."

She was silent for a time, and then her curiosity got the better of her when it seemed as if he wasn't volunteering any more information. "So how was the plan supposed to go?"

"I was . . ." He cleared his throat. "I was supposed to come to you . . . we'd talk . . . we would get together with Worf and Alexander . . . and then Sela and her people would show up and grab the four of us. They were then going to use you and Alexander as leverage to get Worf to do something for them."

"I see. But not you."

"We were . . . there was going to be a staged rescue attempt on my part. I was going to be 'knocked out,' taken out of the picture. All the pressure was going to be on Worf. He would have cooperated rather than let you and Alexander die. After all . . . he loves you."

"Yes. Yes, he does."

"And you love him."

"Yes, I do," she said defiantly. "And I would do anything for him. And I would never betray him. Not . . . ever. Do you understand the concept of loyalty? Do you? Because the man I once knew, the man I thought you were . . . he understood it."

He saw it in her eyes, saw the fury and contempt, and the simple unfairness of it caused a surge of anger in him. "Do you want to know what I understand?"

"No—"

"I understand," he steamrolled over her disinterest, "that the universe is more unfair than anyone could have given it credit for. I understand what it's like to live a life where the choices that you make make no difference. I understand what it's like not to be unique. I understand what it's like to know that, no matter what I do, I will never be the man . . . that I already am. And you can't know that. Oh, you could understand it if you wanted to. You're a damn empath, after all. You could understand anything if you put your mind to it. But I'm not worth even that, am I. I'm not entitled to the slightest bit of understanding from you, Miss Perfect, Miss Deanna Troi."

"Stop feeling sorry for yourself. It's beneath you."

"I love you . . . don't you understand that?"

"Oh, really. And what is Sela then? A happenstance? A diversion?"

"She's a kindred spirit. That's what she is. She has a ghost haunting her . . . her mother, and what she was to the Federation, just as I have my own personal spectre in . . . him. Neither of us, thanks to circumstances beyond our control, is possibly able to live up to the expectations built up for us by others. And so we chose our own lives, and made something for ourselves, and to hell with the expectations and demands of others."

To her surprise, Deanna actually felt tears of sadness stinging her eyes. She forced them back. "And is this the life you truly wanted? Being a felon? Hiding in some barren rock somewhere? Conspiring with Romulans to do . . . whatever it is that you're planning? What is it, anyway?"

"I'm . . . I don't know."

"You don't know? Or you just won't say?"

"I don't know. Sela said she didn't feel the need to tell me. And I didn't feel it wise to push."

"Incredible. I don't know you. The kind of man you've become . . . the William Riker I knew wouldn't have gone along with all this. He would have tried to stop it, he wouldn't have been satisfied with not knowing, he . . ."

And then something clicked in her head. She looked up at him. "Wait . . . I don't understand."

"What don't you understand?"

"The . . ."

"Never mind," he said sharply, cutting her off. "None of it matters. You made it clear when I was with you on Betazed that you didn't want to be with me. They were listening in . . . Kressn was there . . . and when they realized that you weren't going to be cooperative, they simply took matters into their own hands. So if you're looking for fault to be tossed around, you don't have to look any further than the mirror. If you had given me a chance, things might have gone differently. But no. No, I don't fit into your perfect universe. And you know what, Deanna? That's your loss. That is your damned loss."

He strode to the door and it opened automatically. Without waiting for her to follow, he said to the two Romulans who were standing nearby, "Take her back to the cell." Without another word, he stalked off.

Tom lay in Sela's bed, the Romulan woman curled up on his chest. He was staring at the ceiling. "You're rather quiet this evening," she said.

"Don't have much to say."

"That hasn't stopped you before."

"Oh. An insult." He affected a look of being hurt. "You know how to cut me, Sela."

"Yes. But I hope it won't be necessary." She rolled over, propping her head up with one hand, and idly fingered his chest hair. "I keep dwelling on how things went wrong on Betazed."

"It's my fault. I've already told you that. I completely misjudged her . . . thought there was still something there . . ."

"That's not what I was thinking about, actually," Sela said. She seemed to be appraising him, trying to dissect him with her eyes. "I was thinking about what happened at the cliffside."

"I told you . . . I thought he was going to get to you. I was trying to keep him away from you."

"I was armed. I had a clear shot at him."

"Perhaps. But I've seen him in action far more than you have, Sela," he reminded her. "Considering his state of mind, considering the speed with which he was moving, considering a thousand factors that all came together at that one moment . . . frankly, there was no guarantee that your disruptor shot would have been able to stop him. You had endangered his fiancée. If he'd gotten his hands on you, he could have snapped your neck in an instant. I was acting purely on instinct. I'm sorry if my desire to save you from harm was so overwhelming that it impeded our mission."

"Now, don't sound hurt," Sela scolded. "However, I'm thinking about how it worked out in the short term. Had you trusted me to stop him, we would have him here and the plan would proceed as intended."

"The plan that you still haven't told me," he reminded her.

As if he hadn't spoken, Sela continued, "But you knocked him off the cliff, sent him into the water. And thanks to the sudden appearance of the Klingons, he was lost to us. So if you were trying to thwart our plan without knowing what it was . . . that would have been the way to do it."

"Are you saying I'm in league with the Klingons, too? That I knew they were going to show up?"

"No. No, that would be a bit much. Still, it could have been simply a lucky coincidence. You could have been trying to buy time in hopes that some other opportunity might come along."

"You're saying you don't trust me." He sat up, shaking his head in disbelief. "You invite me into your bed, for God's sake. And you still don't trust me?"

Sela didn't seem particularly perturbed over his annoyance. In fact, she even seemed slightly playful. She ran her fingers across his bare thigh, causing a slight tremble through his body, and she said, "Trust is required for love, Riker. What we have is sex. Unless that is no longer satisfactory to you?"

Then she brought her mouth down on his as she slid her hand upward. He gasped into her mouth and they parted momentarily as he managed to say, "It's . . . more than satisfactory . . ."

"I'm glad to hear it," she said as she moved against him.

And for a little while, Tom Riker was able to toss aside his concerns about the unfairness of the universe, and bury himself deep within someone who—he truly did believe—was in many ways a kindred spirit. And when their passion was spent, and Tom felt exhaustion overwhelming him, as he slid into sleep he wondered—as he all too oftentimes did—what Will Riker was up to.

Knowing him, Tom mused, *if I'm lying next to a naked woman . . . he's probably lying next to three. . . .*

Eighteen

Will Riker lay on his bed, surrounded by men, for yet another night and once more didn't sleep.

The other men were not in the bed with him, of course. They were in their own beds, although that might have been too generous a term. They were the hard-mattressed bedlike things that were standard issue on Lazon II.

Will couldn't recall the last time he had slept soundly, or at all. He must have done so at some point. One simply couldn't stay awake for days on end. It just wasn't possible. Very likely, here and there, he had dozed. But at this point he was so disconnected from reality that time had ceased to have any meaning for him.

Mudak checked his surveillance cameras from his office and zoomed in on Riker, lying awake on his bed. He should have felt some degree of triumph over his recapture. Indeed, when he had first brought Riker off the vessel and dragged him through the main street of the penal colony, he had felt like a triumphant hunter. His superiors had noted, with utter deadpan, the battered look that Riker had about him after the voyage. "He tripped repeatedly" was the explanation that Mudak had given his superiors. They had snickered and told Mudak to watch Riker more carefully in the future. Mudak assured them that he would be giving Riker extra special attention.

And Mudak had more than done so. For now, with Riker having his reputation as escapee on his record, and with Saket no longer around to run interference, Mudak had been unstinting in his torment of Riker. From verbal abuse to shock prods to flat-out beatings, Mudak had unleashed upon Riker everything and anything that occurred to him.

And Riker hadn't seemed to notice.

This was, to put it mildly, annoying to Mudak. At least before when he had abused Riker, he could count on an angry glare, or harsh words back, or some show of defiance. But that wasn't happening anymore. Mudak would have liked to think that perhaps he had managed to break Riker's spirit altogether. That there was nothing left of the defiant prisoner that he had once been, the fight completely crushed. But that didn't seem to be the explanation either. Riker appeared to have spirit, all right. It was in another direction, though. He didn't seem to be aware that he was in a prison camp, or at least he didn't seem to care. No matter what Mudak did to him, it got no response beyond an occasional grunt of acknowledgment.

The processing chores of Lazon II were out of commission at the present time. Prisoners were still busy rebuilding the place from the damage that had been done during the Romulan attack. The prisoners were no more thrilled with Riker than anyone else; after all, he had apparently forged an alliance with the individuals who had wound up causing all the damage in the first place. So during the workday, anything they themselves could do to make his life miserable—trip him up, slam into him too hard, whatever—they were more than happy to do.

Riker didn't seem to notice that, either.

Mudak simply could not understand. It was as if Riker's mind was light-years away.

Deanna . . .

It was as if she were just beyond his reach. As sleepless hours piled one atop the other, as his body became more and more strained and stressed, he could almost touch her, sense her right ahead of him. He felt as if he had been blind for his entire life and at last his eyes were opened. How could he have spent all these years thinking he had had a real connection to her when, clearly, until now he had no true concept of what that was?

When he walked, he sensed her beside him. When he ate food, she was his sustenance, when he breathed, her scent intoxicated him. She was everywhere in general and somewhere in specific, and he knew her. . . .

Someone kicked his bed.

He was only vaguely aware of it, as he was only vaguely aware of most things, since his mind was not part of his trials on Lazon II. He slowly swiveled his gaze and saw Mudak standing over him.

"On your feet, Riker," growled Mudak. "You have a visitor."

"Deanna?" he whispered. Except somehow he knew it wasn't Deanna, it couldn't be, yes, it couldn't because she was so far away, so far . . . and yet he could feel her . . .

"No, not Deanna," Mudak said in disgust. He hauled Will to his feet. "There's a world outside your precious Deanna, you know."

"No. No . . . there's not," Will replied, but Mudak paid him no mind as he pulled him out of the dorm and toward the small, squat temporary building that housed his office.

Worf couldn't quite believe it when he saw Riker hauled into the office by Mudak and shoved unceremoniously into a chair. To a certain degree, he couldn't get past the fact that Tom was identical to Will. He felt as if he were seeing his longtime commander in such an abused condition, rather than a known traitor and felon. "I don't know what you hope to discover, Mr. Worf," Mudak said as he moved around his desk and took his place behind it. "The Betazoids already scanned his mind and said there was no knowledge of what transpired on the planet. I don't see why you think you'll have better luck."

"But you will allow me to question him?"

"Well . . ." Mudak smiled, his dark and merciless eyes almost glowing with an ebony light. "Considering the Klingon reputation for information extraction, my assumption had been that you were going to hurt him. Who am I to stand in the way of that?"

"Hopefully it will not come to that."

Mudak studied him curiously. "Really? Hmm. Are you sure you're a Klingon?"

"If that was meant as humor, I did not appreciate it," Worf said stiffly. He moved around Riker, looking him over. "Tom."

Riker didn't respond.

"Tom," he said again.

Slowly, ever so slowly, Riker looked up at him. There were bruises on his face, a cut just above his eye, and his lower lip looked swollen. "Worf? That you?"

"Yes, Tom."

"Will . . ." He coughed heavily, sounding as if he was trying to clear half a ton of debris out of his lungs. "I'm . . . I'm Will Riker . . ."

"You have been positively identified as Tom Riker," Worf said flatly. "Starfleet confirms that Will Riker is back on Earth. . . ."

"She's out there, Worf . . . wasting time here . . ." His voice drifted in and out. "We can . . . go get her . . . take you to her . . ."

The statement startled Worf. "It's a trick!" Mudak said, but Worf paid him no mind. Instead he crouched next to Riker and said, "You know where she is . . . ?"

"Where . . . no . . . don't know . . . but . . . feel her . . . take you . . ."

"This is nonsense," Mudak said. "You said it yourself, Worf: Starfleet reports him as back on Earth. . . ."

Riker shook his head with what appeared to be extreme effort. "Not . . . me . . . left . . . left holosuite . . . message . . . outsmarted myself . . ." His shoulders shook as if he were laughing, and then he coughed once more. "It's me, Worf . . . get me . . . get me out of here . . ."

"If you are Will Riker," Worf said, "then what happened to us on—"

"Oh, no you don't," Mudak said quickly. "No, you don't. You're not going to start asking him *Enterprise* trivia questions, the answers to which he could easily have found out from ships' logs or any of a hundred public sources. Or anecdotes that Will Riker might have shared with his other self back when Tom was aboard the *Enterprise.*"

"If this man is William Riker, I have to know it."

"This man is my prisoner, and there is no way that I am going to allow you to make a mockery of that. He got away from me. No one gets away from me," Mudak said, his voice beginning to rise above its normally quiet and controlled tone. "He is going to stay here until he rots."

"Even if he is not Tom Riker?"

"He is Tom Riker! There has been no mistake. I do not make mistakes, therefore none has been made."

"That is ridiculous."

"Really." Mudak took a step closer to Worf. "And tell me, Klingon . . . were I to stand here, let you ask questions, be 'satisfied' that he is your man and leave with him . . . how much of a fool would you consider me to be? After all, the Klingons and Romulans have a historic alliance. Perhaps it is being restored, and your presence here is an indicator of that."

"What are you saying?" Worf demanded, sounding rather dangerous.

"I am saying that if I were the Romulans who had broken Riker and Saket out . . . and the Klingons were my allies . . . I would simply ask for a well-known and somewhat respected Klingon to be sent to Lazon Two for the purpose of declaring that a mistake has been made and walking out with a Cardassian prisoner."

The atmosphere in the office seemed to crackle with energy, and then the tense silence was broken by Riker's voice as he said, "Worf . . . remember when . . . you announced your engagement . . . ?"

Worf looked at him. "Yes . . ."

"In Ten-Forward . . . you looked at Geordi and me . . . you saw me sitting there . . . you looked right in my eyes . . . when I raised a glass to you . . ." He paused and then, with a ferocity that Worf wouldn't have quite believed possible, he said, "What I really wanted to do . . . put my fist . . . down your throat . . ."

And then he passed out.

Without hesitation, Worf said to Mudak, "This is Will Riker. I want him freed at once."

"This is my prisoner," replied Mudak, "and you will take him over my dead body."

For a moment, Worf's hand drifted toward the phaser he had slung from his belt . . .

And Mudak's blaster was already in his hand. Worf hadn't even blinked, and so could scarcely believe what he had just seen. Mudak was conceivably the fastest draw he'd ever met. "And if you should get past me," Mudak continued, as if pulling the weapon on Worf had required no effort at all, "in case you have forgotten, there are half a dozen guards outside the door, and many more between you and the vessel that you landed nearby. Would you care to take on those odds, carrying an unconscious body?"

Ever so slowly, Worf lowered his hand. "I will be in touch with Starfleet," he informed him. "This does not end here."

"By all means, I eagerly anticipate hearing from you again. Good evening, Mr. Worf."

* * *

He drifted in and out of consciousness, and he could hear Deanna calling to him . . . and, oddly enough, he began to hear Lwaxana as well . . . he heard echoes of a future, and Lwaxana was screaming at him, *"You should have saved her! She asked you! She begged you!"*

Deanna

Go to her . . . you can do it . . .

Deanna

You can find her . . . I've given you that . . . go . . .

Deanna . . . Imzadi . . . help me . . .

The fierceness of the slap across his face brought him to wakefulness. He stared, bleary-eyed, up at Mudak. "Oh. Hi."

"Your Mr. Worf seems to have been rather convinced that you are, in fact, Will Riker." Mudak was slowly circling him, his hands behind his back. "Now I know that this is not the case. I know this. But I also know what else is going to happen. He is going to go back to Starfleet . . . and Starfleet will approach the Cardassian government . . . and there will be inquiries, and they will want to see you, and subject you to examination and deep-scan probes. And sooner or later, they may decide that, yes indeed, they believe you to be this William Riker. But this is a difficult proposition . . . because if you are indeed William Riker, which I assure you you are not, then that means that the reports of William Riker being back on Earth are false . . . and that Tom Riker, who indisputably helped with the assault on Betazed, is still running around free. So if they took you back, then the situation would result in my having no prisoner . . . a rather serious stain on my record . . . and Starfleet would have William Riker back.

"However," he continued, "if something were to happen to you . . . if there was no Tom Riker to be argued over and examined . . . that would be a different matter. If there were no William Riker on Earth, then that would simply be Starfleet's problem. Who knows? Perhaps he ran off to join the Maquis as did his duplicate. And Tom Riker would just be another dead prisoner. Case closed. I doubt my government would even pursue the matter much beyond the initial Starfleet inquiry. 'Tom Riker?' they would say. 'Tom Riker . . . ah yes, here's his file. Oh dear. We regret to inform you that Tom Riker is dead. Shot while trying to assault one of our top security people. Tragic shame, really. On to the next case.' "

Mudak nodded approvingly over the scenario that he had just described. "Yes. Yes, I like the sound of that quite a bit. Do you understand where I am going with all this, Tom?"

Riker began to drift off again.

"Very well. I see we're just going to have to end this clean, then." He pulled out his blaster and aimed it point blank at Will Riker's head. "Good-bye, Tom."

That was when he suddenly heard blaster fire out front. Mudak turned to head out and see what the problem was . . .

And the entire front of Mudak's office was caved in. The forward section of a Klingon scout ship smashed through with explosive impact, sending a shower of debris all over. Mudak tried to bring his phaser to bear, but it was too late as the front end of the ship ran him over, crushing his right arm and sending the blaster tumbling from his now useless hand. He went down, screaming, pinned under the vessel, pounding on it in futility with the left arm.

The entry port to the vessel irised open and Worf leaped out. Riker was lying on the floor, looking stunned, and Worf went to him and slung him over his shoulders. He headed back to the ship, stopping only long enough to look down at Mudak.

"You are going to need some new guards," he informed him.

Then he leaped into his ship, the door irising shut behind him. Moments later, with a roar, the Klingon vessel angled upward and shredded the ceiling of the office building like so much tissue paper. Within moments they were gone.

Deanna sat up so abruptly that Alexander's head tumbled off her stomach. He cracked his skull on the floor but otherwise was completely awake and alert. He looked at her in confusion. "What happened? What's wrong?"

She stared right through him . . . and there were tears of joy streaming down her face as she whispered, "I sense him . . . I feel him . . . oh, Alexander . . . I sense him as clearly as if he were right here . . . I didn't think it was possible . . ."

And with that she lay back down and went back to sleep, leaving a completely confused young Klingon to stare at her and wonder why, for the first time since they had been captured, Deanna Troi had a wide grin on her face.

Nineteen

Worf kept the scout ship moving briskly through warp space as Will Riker used the shower facilities in the rear of the vessel. They were cramped and rather spartan, which was more or less the way everything in a Klingon vessel was, but Riker didn't complain. After a few minutes, looking as if he actually had a grasp of where he was, Riker emerged. The clothing he had been wearing from the prison camp was torn and soiled, and so he had changed into a simple black tunic and pants from a storage chest in the back. For a Klingon, it was merely the base layer of clothing upon which they piled on their leathers, armor, and assorted accoutrements. For Will's purposes what he was wearing was sufficient, albeit a bit big on him. The boots, however, were hopelessly huge, so he didn't even bother with them.

"Are you all right, Commander?" Worf asked once Will dropped into a chair next to him.

Will nodded. "I've been better," he admitted. "Now that you're here, Mr. Worf . . . now that I'm off that place . . . it's becoming easier to focus my thoughts."

"You seemed rather distracted on Lazon Two."

"That, Mr. Worf, is putting it mildly." He leaned back in the chair, closing his eyes. "So how did you get on with Lwaxana?"

"Commander, with all respect, there must be better times to discuss this. Do you have a way of finding Deanna?"

"Lwaxana is quite a woman, isn't she."

"Yes, she is," Worf said impatiently. "But that is not relevant—"

"She can get into your head."

"True. But—"

"She got into mine."

"Commander." Worf's irritation was starting to grow beyond his ability to control. "We need to find—"

"Deanna, yes. And we'll do it because Lwaxana got into my head."

This brought Worf up short. "I . . . do not understand."

"Worf . . . Deanna and I, well . . . we had a sort of connection, forged when we first got together." Suddenly Riker seemed uncomfortable discussing it, but he steeled himself and kept going. "A link, if you will. She taught me certain disciplines . . . helped me with expanding my mind, so to speak. And we can . . . communicate without speaking. I'm sorry, this is very personal . . . I haven't spoken of it, really, and I'm not happy with talking about it now. But hell . . . you're practically family, right?"

It was a ragged attempt to lighten a difficult moment. It was greeted by a silent stare from Worf.

"Right. Anyway," continued Riker, "Lwaxana, she . . . also has a bond with Deanna. It comes from being mother and daughter . . . and she reinforced it just before Deanna was taken away. When I went to her in the hospital, Lwaxana . . . pushed the link into my mind. Took what was already there in me, and her, heightened it to the nth degree and downloaded it. She cross-wired Deanna and me, is the best—if somewhat inefficient—way that I can put it."

"Are you saying . . . you can read her mind? From here?"

"No. That would be simple. But I . . ." He closed his eyes once more, letting out a long, deep breath. "I can sense her. And I can bring us . . . to her . . ."

As Worf watched in silent disbelief, Riker's fingers rested upon the controls. He seemed to be reaching out, beyond the vessel, beyond himself.

When he was a young Klingon on Earth, there had been a young girl living next door to Worf who had some sort of ancient game she called a "Ouija board." Ostensibly it was devised for the purpose of communicating with the deceased. The girl would sit there for hours on end, her fingers resting on some sort of pointer, asking pointless questions and having her fingers "guided" by otherworldly spirits, providing answers by drifting the pointer from one letter to another. It seemed patently absurd to Worf. If the deceased were inclined to communicate via the living, why couldn't they simply take over someone's body and talk in a straightforward fashion?

But that was the closest analogue to what Worf was seeing now. It was as if Riker was channeling Deanna's spirit, and it was completely filling him, calling to him, like two halves of the same soul trying to rejoin. And as this happened, Will's fingers glided over the controls of the scout ship, setting coordinates. When he opened his eyes, he seemed rather surprised that he had actual headings laid in.

"Is that our course, sir?" asked Worf.

"It would appear so," replied Riker. He sighed. "Not exactly the most scientific way of going about it, is it, Mr. Worf."

" 'You will follow your heart . . . through space . . . and if it be ripped from your chest, you will follow the trail of blood . . .' "

Will turned and gaped at Worf. "Mr. Worf . . . that was borderline poetic."

"It actually is a poem. It is from *The Klingon Book of 300 Love Poems.*"

"Somehow I never saw Klingons as poets."

"When Klingon males read poetry to females during foreplay, they throw large objects."

"That would certainly be my reaction to that poem. No offense," he added hastily.

"I will try not to take any. Course locked in, sir."

Riker snapped off a quick point and said, "Engage."

The Klingon scout ship immediately headed off on its new course. As Worf monitored the systems, he asked, "How will we know when we are there?"

"We'll know," Riker said confidently.

"You mean you will know."

Riker nodded, trying to ignore the somewhat challenging tone of Worf's voice. But it wasn't possible when Worf persisted by saying, "Is that why you came to Betazed? To put your fist down my throat?"

Riker stared at him. "What?"

"On Lazon Two . . . you said that when Deanna and I announced our engagement . . . you envisioned yourself putting your fist down my throat."

"Worf, my brain was scrambled. Between what they did to me, and what Lwaxana had implanted . . . I was barely thinking straight. You can't believe everything I said while I was in that condition. . . ."

"If I had not believed it, you would still be there."

Will stared at him a moment, then looked away. "I didn't mean it," he said softly.

"You sounded most convincing."

"Well, I'm telling you, I didn't mean it."

"Then why were you on Betazed? Why did you come there?"

Riker stared out at the stars that were hurtling past. "I . . . wanted to visit," he said at last. "To wish you and Deanna well."

"Do not lie to me."

With an angry glare, Will turned to Worf and snapped, "You're still speaking to a superior officer, Mr. Worf. Watch it."

"I am speaking to a superior officer whom I rescued from a Cardassian prison planet because his going AWOL left Starfleet unable to vouch for him."

"Granted," Riker said after a moment, his expression softening slightly. "But I still don't appreciate your tone."

"We have larger problems than my tone, Commander. Why. Were you. On. Betazed."

"Because . . . I wanted to make sure that you really loved her. That's why. I was presumptuous enough to be concerned on her behalf. But I should never have tried to interfere. Perhaps the Prime Directive would be well applied to personal considerations as well."

"Is that the truth, Commander?"

"Yes, Mr. Worf," he sighed, "it is the truth. Are you satisfied?"

No, thought Worf.

"Yes," said Worf.

No words were exchanged for a time, and then Riker said, "I don't like this. We have no idea where we're going . . . and if we inform Starfleet of our whereabouts, they may think I'm the runaway Tom Riker. By the time we get everything straightened out, who knows what might have happened to Deanna and Alexander . . ."

"If they are not already dead," Worf said tonelessly.

"They're not" was Riker's confident reply. "At least *she's* not. I would know. And if she's okay, then the chances are that Alexander is, too. The point is, we can't afford any delays. We don't need to be intercepted by a starship. Between my either being a duplicate or AWOL, and you just having broken me out of Lazon Two, it's not a good time to have to bank on a stranger's good graces. On the other hand, we're heading into this with no backup, with no one knowing where we're going . . . not even the heading."

"We could try and communicate with the captain."

Riker shook his head. "We're too far away, and the comm system in this vessel is too weak. Anything we send out is going to be intercepted by a Starfleet vessel, and we may be worse off than when we started. Still, the captain is our best bet. . . ."

Worf's eyes narrowed. "Wait. Let me check our position." He did a quick scan, and then nodded. "Yes. I know of someone who can be trusted to get a confidential message to the captain."

"You do? Way out here? Are you sure he can be trusted?"

"I have it," Worf informed him, "on the highest authority."

Twenty

Jean-Luc Picard was extremely concerned.

When he had arrived on the Klingon homeworld, he had not been at all certain of what sort of reception to expect. The request to speak to Picard had come directly from Gowron, but Picard was uncertain as to the reason for it. Gowron had been uncharacteristically vague, and Starfleet had not been able to supply Picard with much in the way of details beyond the concept that Gowron was apparently bothered about something and wanted to deal directly with Picard.

What concerned Picard, at this particular moment, was the sound of combat. It didn't seem to bother the Klingons who were escorting him to the council chamber, but Picard was wondering if he was about to walk into the middle of yet another civil war.

He heard Gowron cry out loudly, and at that point Picard couldn't take it anymore. He hurried several steps ahead, pushed open the council doors . . .

. . . just in time to see Gowron swing a *bat'leth* with such speed that he could barely track its course. And the thrust was intercepted by Kahless the Unforgettable with his own *bat'leth.*

"What the devil—?" Picard called out.

"Not now, Picard!" called Gowron as he advanced on Kahless, who was giving ground, retreating before the rapidly whirling blade of Gowron. The chancellor of the High Council let out a triumphant laugh as the emperor and head of the Klingon spiritual community appeared on the brink of defeat. Gowron brought his blade down with what he hoped was going to be sufficient force to knock Kahless's weapon from his grasp.

And suddenly Kahless dropped his *bat'leth,* brought his hands around, and slapped them together on the descending blade. The move had been perfectly timed; he held the *bat'leth* immobile. A stunned expression crossed Gowron's face, and then Kahless ripped the *bat'leth* right out of Gowron's grasp. Before Gowron could move, Kahless whipped the curved blade around and brought it right to the base of Gowron's throat.

For a moment there was utter silence in the council chamber . . . and then Gowron let out a coarse laugh. "I almost had you! Admit it!"

"I let you think you almost had me," Kahless replied, lowering the *bat'leth.* "You will keep to your word."

"Of course I will keep to my word!" He turned to Picard. "You have just seen the emperor successfully negotiate a land deal for the Boreth monastery. As always, Emperor, a challenge doing business with you."

"And with you, Gowron." He lowered his voice and said, "In point of fact, you almost did have me . . . and if you repeat it, I will of course deny it utterly."

"Of course. Just as I will deny that, since childhood, I have fantasized what it would be like to hold my own against Kahless."

"It's good to see that the two of you have found a means of cooperating with each other successfully," said Picard. "As I recall, there was some friction initially. . . ."

"We all learn to adapt, Picard. You, Kahless . . . even I, when absolutely necessary. Kahless . . . I have matters to discuss with Picard. I am interested in your input."

Kahless nodded in deference to Gowron as the chancellor gestured for the three of them to retire to a conference room just off the main council chamber.

Picard was truly relieved to see the level of cooperation between Kahless and Gowron. When the legendary, and long-dead, Klingon leader had first made his return, Gowron had seen it as nothing less than a direct challenge to his authority. Eventually it had turned out that Kahless was, in fact, a clone of the original, created by the Klingon clerics of Boreth, but once the subterfuge was uncovered, Gowron had agreed to install Kahless as the emperor and spiritual leader.

"You see cooperation between us, Picard . . . between myself and Kahless," said Gowron, once they had settled down in the conference room.

"Yes, I do. As I said, it is most pleasing to me."

"You might say that we have had . . . incentive."

"Incentive?" Picard looked questioningly from one to the other. "And what might that incentive be?"

"We have shared concerns that are outside of the empire," said Kahless.

"And those would be?"

"You."

Picard blinked in polite confusion. "Me?"

"Not you specifically, Picard," amended Gowron. "The Klingon Empire has had no more consistent ally than you. If it were not for you, I feel safe in saying that . . . my ascension to chancellor would have been a bit more difficult."

No comment was forthcoming from Picard, but they both knew what he was thinking: If it hadn't been for Picard and the *Enterprise* stepping in at key times during the Klingon civil war and Gowron's struggle with the house of Duras, the odds were sensational that Gowron would never have gained control at all. Instead Picard simply asked for a clarification: "If not me in particular, than to what are you referring?"

"I am referring to the Federation's current flirtation with the Romulans."

Picard was not entirely unprepared for that. During his trip out to Qo'noS, he had had more than enough time to go over in his mind all the possibilities of things that might be disturbing Gowron. The recent Federation involvement with the Romulans, and acquisition of a cloaking device, was certainly foremost among them. "Ah," said Picard. "If that is all that is bothering you, Chancellor, I can assure you . . . our alliance with the Klingon Empire remains one of the centerpieces of our current state of peace."

"Current state of peace?" Gowron snorted. "Picard, are you looking at the same galaxy that I am? There is more consternation, more tumult nowadays than ever before. At times such as these, any alliance is in question."

"Not alliances forged with the Federation," Picard said firmly.

"You speak for the Federation, do you?" Kahless inquired.

"I'm simply a Starfleet captain. If you wanted a Federation negotiator, you could easily have sent for one. In point of fact, however . . . I do not see anything that requires negotiating. You are simply stating concerns, which you are more than entitled to do. Since you requested my presence, I would assume that—at this point—you feel more in the need of a friend for a sounding board, rather than someone to speak with you in an official capacity. Am I correct?"

"Quite correct," confirmed Gowron. "And as a friend . . . we can speak with you, friend to friend, and tell you what it is we desire."

Picard leaned forward, elbows on the table and wearing a look of patient amiability. "And what would that be? Friend to friend?"

"We desire that the Federation immediately cut off any talks with the Romulans," Gowron informed him. "That they return the cloaking device given them by the Romulan Star Empire. And that they make clear to the Romulans that there will be no further congress of any kind."

"The Romulans are not trustworthy and we, as allies of the Federation, feel threatened that they are being dealt with in any capacity," Kahless added. "Furthermore, we consider it not only an insult to our honor, but a threat to our internal security."

"We have not forgotten that the Romulans aided the Duras family in their attempts to overthrow me. You should not, either."

"Gowron . . . people who were once enemies can become allies," Picard said patiently. "I should not have to point that out, for if that were not the case, then obviously you and I would not be sitting here today."

"I agree," said Gowron. "And allies . . . can also become enemies. That is the status between the Klingon Empire and the Romulan Star Empire. And it is our opinion that the Romulans are manipulating the Federation for the purpose of continuing their vendetta against us . . . against the Vulcans . . . and, ultimately, against the Federation itself."

"A Federation that is apparently too foolish to realize that it is being played for a fool."

"I do not appreciate being thought of as a fool, Kahless. And Gowron . . . you have voiced your concern. I understand that. But there is simply no way that I can assure you that the Federation is going to break off its current contact with the Romulans. I admit, it is a dangerous galaxy out there. The Federation is at peace, but you are correct: It may very well not remain so. With that being the case, doesn't it make sense for us to have as many allies as possible?"

"The Federation's concerns are its own, and our concerns are ours," Gowron said. "And right now, our concern is the Federation and the Romulans. We do not approve of the direction that this relationship appears to be going. We do not wish it to continue."

"I take it," Picard said slowly, "that you are merely stating a concern?"

There was a long pause, and suddenly there was a knife in Kahless's hand. He swung it up, around, and down and it slammed point-first into the tabletop with a deafening thud. It quivered there long after Kahless removed his hand.

"Kahless," Gowron observed, "has something of a flair for the dramatic. He prefers to express himself with visual aids."

The symbolism of the knife in the table was not at all lost on Picard. "You are saying that you would sever relations with the Federation if we continue to seek improved relations with the Romulans?"

"There is no retaliation that we will rule out," Kahless replied, "up to and including a declaration of war."

Picard couldn't believe it. "Are you insane?"

"Far from it. I am the emperor, and the spiritual guide of my people. It would be an affront to our very spiritual core to think that the Romulans—the instigators, the assassins, the betrayers—are to be considered allies. For that is what we are speaking of, Picard. If the Federation is our ally, and the Romulans are the Federation's ally, then we are supposed to be allied with the Romulans. That is intolerable."

"And if the Romulans were to turn and attack us, the Federation would be split in its loyalty. We could not look to you for aid. Indeed, we might have to look upon you as an enemy. Perhaps better, then," said Gowron, "to declare war now and get right to it."

"Gowron . . . Kahless . . . you have stitched together an entire array of possibilities and are reacting to them before any of them have occurred."

"That, Picard, is how one avoids ambush and sneak attack. When one is a Klingon, that is how one stays alive."

"I appreciate that, Gowron. But I can tell you what will not be appreciated. You are, in essence, delivering an ultimatum to the Federation. The Federation, as a rule, does not generally respond well to ultimatums."

" 'Ultimatum,' " repeated Gowron. "Ultimatum is such a cold, passionless word."

"We prefer the term 'threat,' " said Kahless.

And the two Klingons smiled.

Which was definitely not a pleasant sight.

Picard had been given rather generous quarters by Gowron to reside in during his stay on Qo'noS. There was one thing that Picard was rather certain of: If he suddenly felt himself in need of a bladed weapon, he need look no farther than the nearest wall. Knives, and swords of every possible shape and size, seemed to be everywhere.

He had communicated the situation to Starfleet, and the response he had gotten back was exactly what he had suspected he was going to hear: Try and keep a lid on things. Federation resources were stretched thin enough as they were; the last thing they need was a flare-up with the Klingons. When Picard asked if there was any likelihood that a professional diplomat might be sent out to deal with the situation, the response he received was that they could think of no diplomat better qualified to deal with the situation than one Jean-Luc Picard, who—as happenstance would have it—already happened to be out there.

In truth, Picard wasn't exactly surprised. If a formal diplomatic team was sent to Qo'noS to discuss it, Federation mandate would require several member species as part of the group. That meant that a cross-section of Federation governments would be apprised of the Klingons' concerns, and what was at present simply a bit of Klingon angst over the current state of Federation affairs would immediately be elevated to the level of "sit-u-a-tion." And a "sit-u-a-tion" could morph into a "crisis" more quickly than anyone could give it credit for. "Crisis" led to "incident," "incident" to "confrontation," and from there . . .

Well . . . far better not to go there.

* * *

Some time later, there was a knock at Picard's door.

Picard glanced toward a book on the nightstand, then looked back at the door and said, "Come."

The door slid open and Picard blinked in surprise.

"Will!" he greeted him enthusiastically. "I didn't expect to see you here!"

And standing in the doorway, Riker replied, "That, Captain . . . makes two of us."

Twenty-one

Piloting the scout ship, Worf had been somewhat concerned as he watched Riker seated next to him. After their initial discussion, Riker had lapsed into not only silence, but a state of semi-sleep. This was somewhat frustrating to Worf, because he couldn't help but feel that Riker had been less than candid about his motivations for going to Betazed. But it might very well be that now was simply not the best time to discuss it anyway.

Riker had remained that way for hours. In a bleakly amused manner, Worf wondered just how long he would keep the ship going while waiting for Riker to make a further pronouncement as to Deanna's whereabouts. After all, at present heading and speed, they'd hit the edge of the galaxy in another fourteen years. He hoped that Riker might choose to speak up sometime before then.

The entire thing still made Worf uneasy. It had been his intent to conduct a thorough search . . . go to possible suppliers, individuals to whom Sela might have turned for supplies . . . endeavor to scan the area for warp signatures that could be traced, either from Lazon or Betazed. But this . . . this operating on the strength of a psychic connection that he couldn't even begin to understand . . . it bothered him tremendously.

Not only that, but he also had to admit to himself that he felt a certain degree of jealousy. Not enough that Riker and Troi shared their early relationship with one another, but now they had some sort of intense mental relationship that had been magnified by Lwaxana? Here, after Deanna had told him how he should not feel in competition with Riker, he now had to deal with the concept that Riker was closer with Deanna than ever. And he hadn't even worked for it! Lwaxana had just . . . just inserted it into his head. It hardly seemed fair.

Part of Worf's conscience told him that he shouldn't be concerned about such things. He should just be thankful that they might indeed have some means of tracking Deanna and Alexander that was quick and direct.

Nonetheless, he couldn't help it. And he could feel resentment of Riker building within him.

And then Riker abruptly sat up, his eyes wide. "Just ahead," he said. "Bring us out of warp, Mr. Worf."

"Taking us out of warp," Worf confirmed. In response to his powering down of the ship, space around them settled back to normal.

"Where are we?"

Worf looked at him in surprise. "You are the one leading us, Commander. I would have thought you knew to where."

"I'm linked to *her,* Worf, not to a starchart. Now where are we?"

"We are," he checked quickly, "in the Lintar system. Four planets, none habitable . . . although . . . Lintar Four does have a moon that has minimal . . ."

"That's it. I can feel it, just ahead."

He could feel it.

He could feel it.

Worf had a sudden, unreasonable urge to slam Riker's head against the front console while shouting. "Could you feel that?!" It was not worthy of him, he knew that. But he felt that way nonetheless, a surge of jealousy such as he had not thought possible. To a certain degree, it almost impressed him. It proved that he must really love Deanna.

Either that . . . or he felt threatened and angry that his property was being trespassed upon.

Moving at impulse, the scout ship approached the moon of Lintar IV. Will Riker was way forward on his seat, leaning on the control console, as if trying to push himself right through the front of the scout. Worf ran a quick sensor scan of the moon. "Sensors not providing us with any life readings thus far."

"They could be shielded. Would take a while longer to locate them."

"True. You are certain they are down there, though."

"Positive."

Worf pursed his lips thoughtfully. "I have a plan for how to locate them."

"Let's hear it."

"You guide the vessel to the planet's surface. There are two environment suits in storage in the rear of the vessel. We put the environment suits on, bring hand scanners for backup, and survey the surface of the moon. Once we have located the entrance into their lair, we sneak in, find Sela, capture her, use her in a hostage exchange to retrieve Alexander and Deanna, return to the scout ship, and leave the area after alerting Starfleet to their presence."

And suddenly the sensor array lit up. Directly in front of them, space seemed to shimmer, and then a Romulan warbird materialized directly in front of them, packing approximately twenty times the fire power possessed by the scout ship.

"Or we could surrender," suggested Will.

"That," admitted Worf, "would probably work also."

Tom Riker woke up and touched the other side of the bed, expecting to find the sleeping Sela. Instead it was empty, the sheet cold. She hadn't been there for a while. It was her absence that truly caused Tom to fully awaken as he sat up and rubbed his eyes in the darkness. Then the door slid open and he saw Sela standing there, fully dressed. Her arms were folded and she was regarding him with open curiosity. "Will," she said. "There's been an interesting development."

"Really," said Tom. He sat up, the covers still around him. "Have we finally determined what use we're going to put Deanna and Alexander to?"

"Actually, yes. Yes, I think we have. Get dressed and meet me at the interrogation room on level three."

"All right." There was something in her tone that he was less than enthused about, but he wasn't entirely sure what it was.

He dressed quickly and headed down to where Sela had instructed him to go. As he did so, he passed assorted Romulans and noticed that they seemed to be glancing at him oddly. He wondered what their problem was.

He entered the interrogation room. The room was actually divided into two sections. The area where Tom was entering was used for fairly straightforward, one-on-one questioning. Adjoining was a room, visible through a plexi shield, where questioning of a more intense nature, oftentimes requiring assorted medical equipment, was set up.

There were several Romulans there, including Kressn, to whom Tom had learned to take an intense dislike. For one thing, Tom had absolutely no idea how Kressn had managed to pull that little disappearing act of his, and Sela hadn't been forthcoming in telling him. Perhaps Kressn had some sort of personal cloaking device, but if that was the case, why didn't they all have them? Tom was certain that it was important, and he disliked missing that key piece of information.

Sela was there. And . . .

Tom came to a halt as he stood face-to-face with Will Riker. Next to Will was Worf, nodding grimly to himself.

"Isn't this cozy," Sela asked. "Most, most intriguing." She did a slow circle of the room. "We did a DNA scan on our new arrival here and matched him against yours, Will. He's an exact duplicate. Care to explain?"

"I would have thought he would have been more than happy to do it," said Tom.

"Oh, I'm sure he would. But we haven't asked him anything yet and he, being a good Starfleet officer, hasn't volunteered anything. So I'm asking you, Will: Who is this?"

Tom didn't hesitate.

"His name is Tom Riker," said Tom. "At least, that's what he calls himself." As he spoke, he watched Will's face, but Will kept his expression carefully neutral. Obviously Will, still uncertain about the situation, was allowing Tom to take the lead, at least for the moment. And Worf, good junior officer that he was, was looking to Will as to how to handle things.

In quick, broad strokes, Tom outlined the bizarre set of circumstances that had led to the creation of a second Riker. He only made one minor substitution and one omission: He claimed that the other was Tom when, in fact, the other was Will. And he stated that Tom Riker had been given the rank of lieutenant and assigned to the *Gandhi* . . . both of which were true enough. He did not make any mention, of course, of Tom—i.e., himself—having joined the Maquis. The concept of two Rikers going wrong might be too much to try and convince her of.

Gone wrong.

Odd . . . he had never thought of himself in those terms before. He had always been able to rationalize up one side and down the other why he had taken the actions that he had. But now, seeing the unrelenting and openly contemptuous gaze of Will Riker upon him, he felt . . .

. . . lost.

"Incredible," Sela said at last. She glanced at Kressn and Tom couldn't help but notice that Kressn, ever so slightly, nodded. "And he is Tom . . . and you are Will. Correct?"

"When you get right down to it, to be perfectly truthful . . . we're both Will Riker. One just calls himself something different for reference."

And again, damn . . . Kressn nodded. It was very subtle, but something that Sela could easily have seen out of the corner of her eye and made a mental note of. Somehow, Kressn was keeping her apprised as to truth and falsehood. Perhaps he was some sort of mind-reader or telepath. That would explain how he pulled his vanishing stunt; he convinced people that he wasn't there.

Which meant that Tom was now extremely vulnerable: If Sela asked for further clarification, there was no way that Tom was going to be able to dodge it.

Instead Sela turned to Will and said, "Is his description of the events on Nervala Four true?"

"Reasonably."

"My. What a curious universe we live in." And then, to his relief, Sela simply nodded, apparently satisfied with the responses she had gotten. "All right. This is most intriguing. We've gone from having no options . . . to several. Most, most useful. Gentlemen . . ." She stopped her circling directly in front of Worf and Will. "I'm going to offer you a deal."

"Klingons do not deal," Worf informed her.

"Nor do Starfleet officers," added Riker.

"I see. That being the case, do you mind telling me how you expected to get out of here? Were you going to shoot your way out? Or perhaps you thought you'd simply ask us to turn over the Betazoid and the Klingon child to you out of the goodness of our hearts."

"We have backup that will be here within the hour," Will informed her. "They'll be attuned to your warp signature and will easily be able to trace you. Nothing will be accomplished by holding us here. If you're wise, you'll pack up your people and get the hell out before Starfleet arrives."

As bluffs went, it wasn't bad. But Tom's heart sank as he saw Sela look once more to Kressn. Kressn very subtly shook his head and Sela turned back to Will with confidence. "We'll all wait together, I think. In fact . . . tell you what . . . I'm going to go on the assumption that that was a lie. That you're here on your own . . . although you obviously had your troubles getting here. Did someone beat you up and take your uniform, Tom?"

Will shrugged and said nothing. Tom mentally congratulated his counterpart for keeping his mouth shut.

"It doesn't matter," Sela continued. "Worf . . . Tom . . . here is what is going to happen. We want one of you to act as our agent in a small matter. It is a high-risk proposition and, possibly, a suicide mission. Nonetheless, it is necessary. We need you to attempt to assassinate Gowron."

Worf and Will looked at one another. "You tried something similar once . . . trying to reprogram Geordi's mind so that he would assassinate then-chancellor Vagh," Worf said.

"Apparently you weren't listening," Sela pointed out. "I didn't say you had to succeed in killing him. If you do, so much the better, but it's not required. You will attempt to poison him. You will use a bottle of Romulan ale which you will present to him, claiming you took it off a captured Romulan vessel. He will appreciate the irony of that, the smug bastard. He will trust you, of course . . . either Worf, whom he regards so highly, or you, Tom Riker, who will be able to pass easily for Will Riker, trusted second officer of the blessed Picard. Either way, you are to see that he drinks from it. One swig will make him deathly ill rather quickly. Two will likely be fatal. If they are unable to save him and he dies, that will obviously be the best situation . . . for us. If he survives, it will still come across as an obvious assassination attempt. Such obviousness can only be regarded as highest contempt on the part of the Federation. Not even a subtle attempt at assassination—instead, overt and unsubtle. As if daring the Klingons to do something about it."

"I see. And since it's quite likely a suicide mission," Will said, his gaze never leaving Tom, "naturally the original Riker wouldn't be willing to stick his neck out. Although I'm surprised, Sela," and he turned to her, "that you didn't try to rewire his mind, as you did with Geordi, and simply force him to do it."

"Actually, truth be known," and Sela smiled sweetly at Tom even as she addressed Will, "that was exactly what I was going to do. But he was so . . . pretty . . . and had his amusement value. I was in no rush; sooner or later, had I gotten bored with him, I could indeed have done just that. But now it won't be necessary. Everyone wins."

"Is that what you call it?" Worf sneered.

"Well . . . everyone who matters wins," she amended it. "If it puts your minds at ease, gentlemen . . . you would simply be hastening a situation that is deteriorating anyway. Gowron is already suspicious of the Federation due to the current talks being held with the Romulan government. Think of this as . . . an insurance policy."

"If you think," Worf told her, "that either of us would willingly poison Gowron . . . and damage the relationship between the Federation and the Klingon Empire . . . you are sadly mistaken."

"Mr. Worf speaks for both of us," said Riker.

"Does he. My, my, Will," she said to Tom, "it appears that your duplicate has more dedication to the Federation that you do."

"He can afford that luxury," Tom said grimly. "He hasn't been through what I have."

"Do you have any other excuses on hand for your behavior, or is that the extent of it?" Will said contemptuously. Tom met his gaze, although for some reason his impulse was to look away.

Sela slowly walked up to within a few feet of Worf and Will. "You understand that, if you refuse . . . there will be torture involved. However, if you agree to go . . . well, as I said, for whomever goes, it will be a suicide mission. But we will release Deanna, Alexander, and whichever of you is left behind. We have no reason to keep you. Oh, we'll erase your memory of our whereabouts, but other than that, you'll be intact."

"Nothing you can do to us is going to change our mind."

"Now, Mr. Riker . . . who said anything about torturing *you?*"

That was when they saw Deanna and Alexander hauled into the room on the other side of the plexi.

Both Rikers and Worf reacted with similar shock. In addition to the guards who were dragging Deanna and Alexander, there was another, fairly heavyset Romulan who seemed in the process of preparing a hypo.

When Deanna and Alexander saw Worf and Riker, their faces filled with momentary hope. Then they realized that their rescuers were as much captive as they. Tom saw Will and Worf looking utterly helpless and frustrated as they watched in impotent fury while the people they loved were strapped down to tables in the other side.

"Let them go!" Will said forcefully.

"Right, right, I know. The fleet. Backup. Last-minute rescue. This is just to have something to do while we wait, then. Tok . . . go ahead."

The heavyset Romulan whom she had addressed as Tok nodded, took the hypo he had prepared, and injected the contents into Deanna's arm. Then he reset it and did the same to Alexander.

"What are you doing? What did you do to them?" snarled Worf.

"Will," Sela said to Tom, "I must admit to being intrigued. I want to see if your duplicate has stronger feelings for Deanna Troi than you did. You see, gentlemen . . . and Worf . . . your loved ones have just been injected with poison. It is rather slow-acting. You're going to be able to watch them die, bit by bit, over the next few minutes. The antidote is close at hand and can easily be administered . . . if the terms are agreed to. By the way, you'll notice that it's soundproof in there. You can't hear them; the comm system is only one way. Don't worry, though, I'll attend to that. Tok . . . activate the two-way, if you would be so kind."

Tok nodded, stepping over a console. A moment later there was a click . . .

. . . and then began the longest minutes of Tom Riker's life.

For the poison that had been injected into the systems of Deanna Troi and Alexander was not some simple, painless toxin that slowly killed them. No, it ripped through their veins like liquid fire. Deanna cried out first; Alexander managed to hold out a little longer but, in short order, he too was moaning.

And their cries only increased in intensity.

Deanna's eyes were closed, and Tom immediately knew why. She didn't want to look at them . . . look to Will and Worf. She knew that they were helpless, that they were likely being asked to do something terrible, and that she and Alexander were being used as leverage. If she looked at them, if she let the pleading in her eyes show, it might unduly influence them, and she couldn't bear to do that to them. She would clearly rather die than put them in that position. Either that . . . or perhaps she just couldn't determine which of them she would look to for succor, and so looked at neither.

But Alexander . . . his eyes never left his father. Alexander was doing everything he could to repress the shouts of agony. He did not simply howl away; every so often, a scream would force itself out through his reluctant teeth, but for every one that he was unable to hold in, there were ten that he bit back. And Tom could see he was looking to his father . . . for help? For approval? He couldn't tell.

"Sela, is this necessary . . ." Tom began.

"Yes, Will, it is . . . unless you're going to volunteer to go," Sela replied. "Are you?"

Tom couldn't think, couldn't move. His mind was frozen. He had nothing to lose, really. Discredit the Federation . . . why not? Why not?

But . . . he had made a pledge to the Maquis. He had work yet to do. And . . . sacrifice himself . . . for what? For Deanna? He remembered the cold contempt that she'd had for him, the way she'd spoken to him. She had been all too ready to think of him as nothing but a traitor, even though he had tried to put across to her, as subtly as he could, that he'd actually been trying to thwart Sela's plan, to keep Worf out of it, to find a way where it could wind up just being him and Deanna, together. . . .

No, she'd made it all too clear. She was too good for the likes of him.

To hell with her.

She's dying . . . look at her . . . she's dying. . . .

He shut it out of his mind and forced himself to watch.

The cries of the victims grew in volume, Deanna's shrieks being louder, and even Alexander unable to hold back the agony as much as before.

"Time is ticking, gentlemen. They're not getting any healthier."

Deanna's skin was ashen, Alexander's not much better. Their eyes were glazing over, their bodies beginning to convulse.

"Well?" prompted Sela.

Will Riker looked as if his heart was being torn from him.

Worf was stoic. He turned to Sela and said flatly, "Death before dishonor. Deanna is Starfleet. My son is Klingon. They . . . will understand. If the situation were reversed . . . and I were in their place . . . they know I would rather die than see them suffer the humiliation of bowing to terrorists such as you. That . . ." He nodded grimly. ". . . is the Klingon way. A Klingon child . . . and a woman who would be the bride of a Klingon . . . understand that."

"I see," Sela said mildly. "Well then . . . Tom . . . it's up to you, then. You're the final arbiter of their fate. Will you cooperate? Or won't you?"

Alexander and Deanna were in their death throes. Within moments, even with the antidote, it would be too late. Deanna arched her back, seized with convulsions, and she let out a shriek that was the most hideous thing either Riker had ever heard.

And from the depths of his soul, Will Riker cried out, *"All right! I'll do it. I'll do what you want."*

"Tok!" Sela immediately called. Tok, for his part, had been prepared and immediately injected the antidote into both of them, first Troi and then Alexander. For a long moment—the longest moment in the lives of both Rikers—it didn't seem to have any effect. And then, slowly, the trembling which had taken over their bodies began to subside. The proper colors of their skin started to return.

"Heart . . . respiration . . . returning to respective norms," Tok announced calmly, checking his instruments. "The antidote worked . . . barely," he added with a slight tone of reproval. "Next time, Sela, try not to cut it quite that thin, if you please."

"It wasn't up to me," Sela replied, "but to them. Or rather . . . to Tom Riker here," and she nodded to Will. "You understand that, if you fail to cooperate . . . if you try some sort of trick . . . they will die."

"I . . . understand," said Will.

Tom Riker, for his part, didn't even know what he was feeling. Relief? Contempt for Will . . . or gratitude? Relief? What was it?

Will was unable to meet Worf's gaze. And as the two of them were ushered away, Tom had the feeling that all was definitely not going to be well between the two of them. Because Worf did not appear conflicted.

He was clearly and obviously angry.

Tom couldn't help but wonder why. Will had just saved not only Worf's fiancée, but his son. They and Worf, thanks to Will's sacrifice, were going to get away; Tom himself would see to that if Sela tried to renege on her promise. All in all, it had worked out rather badly for Will, but great for Worf.

What was the problem?

Twenty-two

"You call yourself a Starfleet officer!" Worf shouted.

Will and Worf had been tossed into a room together, apparently to wait while the Romulans scrounged up, somehow, a Starfleet uniform for him. There was nothing of particular interest in the room to look at. Will had found a door on one side against the wall, but when he had slid it open all he found was a closet with some uniforms stashed in it. Riker considered trying to don the uniforms and sneak out in disguise. But he didn't think he would pass for Romulan, and he was sure as hell positive that Worf didn't have a prayer of doing so.

So Riker leaned against a wall, trying to sort through his thoughts, and he didn't even bother glancing at Worf. "Not now, Worf."

"How could you agree to their demands!"

"I said not now, Lieutenant Commander," Will said with a far sharper tone.

"Not this time," Worf said hotly. "This time . . . no ranks . . . if you have the stomach for that."

Will's face grew flushed as he turned to face Worf. "All right," he said, in a slow, deliberate voice. "No ranks. Man to man . . . you watch yourself."

"What you did back there was wrong. Admit it."

"I had no choice."

"I see. You're going to say that this . . . empathic bond you've developed with Deanna forced you to do it."

But Will shook his head. "That bond, Worf . . . it was just a sort of . . . of locator device in my head. Emotionally it didn't make me any different . . . and it didn't cloud my judgment, I assure you."

"Then why . . . ?"

"I told you. I didn't have a choice."

"Meaning I did. Meaning you think I was wrong."

"You did what was right for you. I had to do what was right for me."

"What you should have done," snarled Worf, "was what was right for Starfleet! For the oath you took as an officer—!"

"Don't lecture me, Worf!" thundered Will. "I don't have to put up with it! I don't have to prove anything to you!"

"No. But you had to prove something to her."

"I wasn't trying to prove anything, Worf, I was trying to save her life. And in case it escaped your notice, I saved your son's life, as well."

"And do you expect his gratitude?" Worf demanded. "To die with honor is—"

"The Klingon way, yes, I know, believe me, I know. But did it occur to you that maybe, just maybe, there was an off chance that he wasn't ready to die simply because you had decided it was time for him to go."

"Do you think I did not want to save my own son!"

"I don't know, Worf! I've known you for almost half my adult life, and you're still as much of a mystery to me as you were when I first met you! I don't know what you want! I don't know what was going through your mind!"

"I wanted to save them," Worf said tightly. "But what is more important than life is the way that life is lived."

"And I wanted them to keep on living it, any way they could. And if you didn't, fine. I took the decision out of your hands, all right?" He spread his arms wide in a gesture indicating that he was fed up with the conversation. "If there's any dishonor here, it's on my head. The bottom line is, I bought us some time. Obviously I don't want to poison Gowron . . . but we needed time to think, time to—"

"You showed them that Starfleet officers can be pressured into turning against their oaths. Can be blackmailed. Do you think that it will end here? Even if they do let us go, which I very much doubt, they will know that they can make similar demands on others, endeavor to make other officers bend to their desires. And perhaps those other officers will not cave in as you did. In which case, you have doomed their innocent loved ones."

"I didn't . . . cave in . . ." Will said with forced calm. "I made a reasoned decision that—"

"You . . . caved . . . in. . . ."

"Would you have had me watch them die? Would you?"

"I was prepared to."

"Well, maybe they weren't prepared, Worf! Despite all your training of Alexander in the Klingon way, maybe he wasn't ready to throw his life away just to satisfy his father's definitions of honor. Did you consider that?"

Worf stepped in close to him. "I know why you did this."

"Enlighten me."

"You did this to make certain that you would always be between us. Between Deanna and me."

"That's ridiculous. . . ."

"You never stopped loving her. Admit it."

"Worf, now is not the ti—"

"There will not be another time! This will be said now! No more niceties! No more politeness dictated by rank! No more indecision on your part! I knew what I wanted with Deanna, I got it, and that sickens you, doesn't it. And when we announced our engagement, you were angry! Angry at yourself for years of wavering! Angry at me for stepping in when you would not do anything about it!"

"I did what was right for Deanna and me at the time, Worf! I can't fabricate emotions that weren't there and wish they were present when it was convenient for me!"

"They were always there, and that was the inconvenience," Worf shot back. "You could not muster yourself to take Deanna when she was yours, but you could not stand the thought of her being mine."

"If I couldn't stand the thought, then why didn't I say something at the time you two got together?"

"Because then you would have had to commit to her. And you are too selfish, too self-absorbed, to commit to anything except yourself. But I am not. I commit to the Klingon code of honor, to Deanna, and to our life together."

"Interesting order that you put those things in, Worf," Riker noted. He was moving now, unconsciously plotting a course like a matador guiding a bull. He and Worf were circling each other, their body language mirroring the pent-up anger of their words. "If you knew anything about love, you'd know that she comes first, always. Always."

"If you knew anything about honor, you would know that there are things more important than love. But then, you knew that. Except to you the things more important than love are your career and your own interests."

"If that's the case, then why am I putting my life on the line to save her?"

"I already told you: to make me look bad. To make certain that you are always uppermost in her thoughts. Admit it, that is what you want."

"You have no idea what I want."

"I know you fully—"

"You have no idea!" and suddenly it all burst out of him, a gushing torrent of emotion. "You had no idea what it was like, Worf! To see the two of you together, to see her in your arms! To see a true love light in her eyes, the kind that she once had for me, except she was looking at you! Every time, every damned time I saw you with her, it was like a knife in my heart. I never stopped loving her! Is that what you want to hear? I was coming to Betazed to tell her that. If it meant breaking you up, I was prepared for that, providing she still felt something for me! If she didn't, I wouldn't have blamed her. I made a command decision for years that we wouldn't be together. It was me, Worf, all me. You saw how quickly she got together with Tom, with only the slightest urging. She never stopped loving me, never. But me, I was second-in-command of the *Enterprise!* I had no time for distractions, for some sort of ongoing relationship! I couldn't give in to the emotions she stirred in me! And what if we did pursue it and, for whatever reason, it didn't work out? After all the years apart, who knew what kind of people we had become. So I forced myself to believe those emotions weren't there. And I did it so well that I convinced not only myself, but the woman who knows me better than anyone else. The one who is the better part of everything I am. I did it for her own good, for the good of both of us. And having made that decision, how could I stand in your way? How could I deny her happiness with you? It would have been wrong. It was what she wanted, it would have been wrong . . ."

"And am I supposed to feel sympathy for you?" Worf's fists were shaking with barely pent-up emotion.

"We're *Imzadi,* Worf. It means—"

"I know what it means. Lwaxana told me."

"Knowing it intellectually isn't enough. I don't expect you to understand."

"Because you believe I am stupid?"

"No!" shouted Riker, fed up with Worf's defensiveness. "Because you've never felt about anyone in your life the way I feel about Deanna! Not if you were willing to let her die! No matter how much I tried to force myself to think it was over because I wanted it to be so, the fact is that we are, now and forever, *Imzadi."*

"How dare you," Worf snapped. "How dare you tell me how I have and have not felt." He came in very close to Riker, barely inches away. "Do you think I did not know what the two of you meant to each other? Do you think I did not sense your ghost hovering between us whenever I was with her? That I did not feel as if I was constantly being measured up to you? That nothing I did was good enough? When we spoke, I always sensed that she was comparing my sentiments to yours. When we made love, I was always positive that she was thinking of you! Here I was willing to pursue the relationship that you were unwilling to give her. Afraid to give her—"

"I wasn't afraid—"

"You were! Afraid to share your life! Afraid to risk your precious career! Afraid to love someone more than you loved yourself! Do you think I was unafraid when I approached her, courted her? The risk of rejection, humiliation . . . it was overwhelming! But I pushed past that, went through it, because I believed that the prize was worth the risk! Yet still she remained attached to you, you who were unwilling to take any risk for her." Worf's voice escalated in volume until it was almost deafening. "Laying your life on the line now, that is easy for you! Entrap her love forever and then go off to die a hero's death, and leave me behind, painted as the one unwilling to sacrifice himself! When the fact is that you were too much the coward to be there for Deanna when she needed you, and too much the coward to be there for your duty when the Federation needed you!"

Riker hit him.

It was not one of the smarter moves Riker had ever made.

He hit him bone on bone, which was never a good move to begin with. His fist caught Worf squarely on the chin, promptly breaking one of Riker's knuckles. It landed with enough impact to knock Worf to the floor, and the combination of surprise and power behind the punch was enough to keep Worf down for a whole three seconds.

At which point Worf came up swinging.

Will backed up quickly, as Worf's first two roundhouses—driven more by fury than technique—missed him clean. While Worf was off-balance on the second one, Riker drove a knee up into Worf's gut. It doubled the Klingon over long enough for Riker to bring his hands together and double-slam a blow to the thick set of muscles in the base of Worf's neck. It was a move that Riker had used before, when he had been assigned to a Klingon vessel as part of an exchange program. It had worked rather well at the time against that particular opponent.

In this case, it didn't slow Worf down at all. It did succeed, however, in ticking him off.

Will Riker was suddenly airborne. Worf had grabbed his leg in one hand and his arm in the other, and when he straightened up, Riker was over his head and helpless. For one hideous moment Riker thought that Worf was going to make a wish and use Riker as the wishbone. Instead Worf pivoted and threw Riker. Riker meteored across the room and slammed into the far wall with the sound of a wet sack of potatoes. He slid to the ground, momentarily stunned, and then saw Worf charging toward him. He tried to muster the strength to get out of his way, but all he could manage was to try and crawl away, and then Worf had hauled him off his feet, his arm across Riker's throat, snarling in fury into his ear.

Riker dug his nails into Worf's hand. It was the only part of him that he could get close to, and the only tactic that he could think of.

Worf didn't let out a sound, other than a grunt. He tried to pull his hand free of Riker's but Riker held on as if his life depended on it—which it might very well have. Blood began to trickle from the point of penetration and finally Worf shoved Riker furiously away. Riker stumbled around but stayed on his feet.

Worf came at him and what followed was a dazzlingly fast flurry of blows. Riker stood his ground as Worf delivered one rapid-fire shot after another. Will blocked, moving entirely on instinct, faster than he ever had in his life. Worf growled in annoyance and then, for a moment, Worf got too close and his snarling face was near Riker's.

Riker tried to head-butt him, slamming his skull against Worf's.

If there was any move that Riker could have made that was less wise than having swung in the first place, it was that one.

The impact was audible from nearly three rooms away. Worf didn't give in the slightest, but Will stood there for a moment, the world swirling around him. And then, without Worf having to do another thing, Riker fell backward, crashing to the floor.

To his credit, Riker began to get back up again, even though he was starting to turn rather pale. Worf watched him, shaking his head.

Riker suddenly kicked him in the crotch.

Worf had been sure that Riker was virtually out for the count. The speed and ferocity of Riker's move caught Worf completely off-guard. The shot landed squarely and Worf sank to his knees. It was everything he could do not to moan.

Will staggered in place for a moment, about to try and press his advantage. Unfortunately he didn't have the opportunity, because suddenly he completely lost his ability to remain on his feet as a wave of nausea swept over him, courtesy of a delayed effect of the head-butting. Riker sank to the floor a few feet away from Worf, propping himself up with one hand and clearly trying not to vomit.

"H . . . had . . . enough . . ." he managed to get out.

"Was that . . . a question to me . . . or a . . . description of yourself . . ." Worf said between lungfuls of air.

At that moment, a squad of Romulans entered. They surveyed the damage that the two of them had done to each other, and Dr. Tok—who was carrying what appeared to be a medical kit—shook his head in annoyance. "Take this one," he pointed at Worf, "and stick him with his son and fiancée."

The Romulans did as they were told, while Tok knelt down opposite Riker. He pulled instruments from his kit and started working on Riker's face. "Hold still please," he said as the tools began to stimulate cellular growth in Will's skin.

"What are you doing?"

"Getting you fixed up. In case you're unaware of it, you came in here looking rather in bad shape to begin with. Your little brawl with the Klingon didn't do much for your complexion on top of that. Sela reasoned that sending you to the Klingon homeworld looking like you've been in a series of fights is hardly going to facilitate your passing yourself off as William Riker."

"Believe me," said Will, "that's the last person I'd want to be right now."

Worf was not entirely sure of the reaction he was going to get when he entered the room with Deanna and Alexander. So he was relieved when Deanna took one look at him, sighed, "Oh, Worf . . . thank God . . . ," and ran to embrace him. The warmth of her, the intensity of her arms around him . . . it all went a long way toward assuaging the serious concerns that he had been having. Deanna was, after all, the priority here. Although she was Starfleet, still she had been raised in the ways of Betazed. She might have had difficulty with the notion that Worf was prepared to sacrifice her rather than allow dishonor and dereliction of duty to hold sway. "I . . . I knew you were alive, even after I saw you take that fall . . . I knew it . . . and now you're here . . ."

"Everything will be all right," Worf assured.

"Yes, it will," Alexander spoke up. Then he paused and added, "Thanks to Riker."

There was silence in the room for a moment.

For a moment, Worf wanted to shout at his son. To dress him down, to verbally eviscerate him for taking that tone. But matters were difficult enough as it was. Now was the time for patience and understanding, the types of thing that Deanna had labored so mightily to teach him. To teach them both.

Before he could say anything, Deanna said to Alexander, "Alexander . . . what your father did . . . it was the right thing for him to do . . ."

"And Riker was wrong? You're saying it was wrong for us to live?"

"No . . . he . . . he also did . . . what was right for him . . ."

Inwardly, Worf shuddered at the fact that she was echoing Riker's own words. Was there anything that the two of them were not united upon? Was there any room for Worf in the equation at all?

"Alexander, I expected you to understand," Worf said. "Have I not taught you anything?"

"Oh, you taught me, Father," Alexander replied with quiet defiance. "You taught me just how important my life, and Deanna's life, is to you. And you've done it with such efficiency that I don't give a damn if I never see you again."

"Alexander!" Deanna said, shocked.

Under ordinary circumstances, there was every possibility that Worf would have blown his top by that point. But he was still feeling emotionally spent from his altercation with Riker. So instead patience ruled the moment. "You have to understand, Alexander . . . when you were dying, a part of me was dying with you. But everything that makes me who I am, everything that I believe to be important, dictated that I had no choice. My commitment to Starfleet, and the Federation, and the Klingon way of life, all required—"

Alexander walked slowly toward him, fists balled up, and he practically shouted, "It had nothing to do with Starfleet! Or the Federation! Or the Klingon way! It had to do with your own stubborn pride!"

"That is not true!" snapped back Worf. "I cared about doing my duty, first and foremost."

"Obviously you care about duty more than Deanna . . . or me . . . or anything."

"You do not understand."

"Oh, no . . . I understand. You've made it very clear," Alexander said to him. And then he turned and walked away from him, sitting with his back pointedly to his father.

Will looked in the mirror that had been provided him and was pleased to see that his face was well on the way to healing up. And he was wearing a Starfleet uniform, which, for some reason, made him feel more human again somehow.

The question was, had he betrayed that uniform by "knuckling under" to the Romulan demands?

The thought was repellent to him, but he had spoken the truth to Worf: He had simply felt as if he had no choice. The question wasn't how could he have saved them. The question was how could Worf not have. But he had been honest when he said that, in many ways, Worf remained a mystery to him. He just didn't understand the man.

Then again, considering the number of times that Riker didn't understand himself, it was probably a wash.

That was when he heard his own voice just outside the door.

"I want to have a few minutes alone with the prisoner," Tom Riker said. "It'll be all right, I assure you. Where's he going to go?" The guard who was on duty apparently agreed to Tom's request, because a moment later Tom was inside.

"Here to gloat?" asked Will.

"No," Tom replied calmly. He paused, gathering his thoughts. "Will . . . I know you don't think much of me . . ."

"Is this where I'm going to hear another lecture about how difficult it's been for you? Of the hand that you didn't get dealt. Are you going to try and rationalize away the fact that you're a traitor?"

"A traitor to whom, Will? A traitor to what?" Tom grinned raggedly. "I'm doing my duty, just as you are. But I have a different duty. So I became a member of the Maquis while you stayed with Starfleet. So what? *Someone* had to be the evil twin."

Will, to his own surprise, laughed at that. "I don't think of you as evil. Stupid, perhaps . . . and a traitor . . . but not evil."

"That's damned decent of you. We're no different, Will. I watched you stand there and throw away your Starfleet oath—risk interplanetary warfare—for the life of a single woman. How does that make you any less of a traitor?"

"It *is* different."

"The reasons may be different, but the result is exactly the same. Don't tell me it's not, we both know it is." He crouched down next to Will and lowered his voice. "You can fool Sela . . . but you can't fool us. Don't even bother trying to lie to me. I know what you're going to do. You'll try and pull some sort of double-cross, some sort of last-minute stunt. You're playing for time, and—unlike Worf—you don't mind lying or losing face or bending to the pressure. You just couldn't let her die."

"Really. Tell me this, then: If we're so much alike . . . how come you *could* let her die?"

Tom looked down. He actually appeared ashamed. "You know . . . when I first met you . . . and I saw that you had let Deanna just be there, part of your life but outside of your life all those years . . . I felt nothing but contempt for you. Perhaps some of that carried over to this day. But I think . . . to a degree . . . you are stronger than I ever could have been. Stronger because you resisted the impulse to pursue her, to reignite the relationship, even though you must have wanted to . . . just because you felt it was the right thing for her."

"Mr. Worf seems to feel that it was a sign of cowardice," Will said.

"From what I've seen of Mr. Worf, he would. You see, the thing that Worf hasn't learned yet is that just because you can do something doesn't always mean you should. He acts on impulse a good deal."

"Worf's impulse was to save Deanna and Alexander. He resisted it in the pursuit of a greater cause. I didn't. What does that make me?"

"Cagey," said Tom. "Because, as I said, I know that you wouldn't give in just like that. You must have something in mind."

Will was about to reply, but then he stopped. A look of caution crossed his face. "You must think I'm seriously stupid."

"No. No, I don't think that at all. Why would you think I do?"

"If I were planning something . . . if I was hoping to make a grandstand play . . . do you seriously think I would tell you?"

"Oh, of course. I'm the traitor."

"Yes. You are. You have no idea what it's like, Tom . . . to be ashamed of myself . . . and unable to do anything about it, because it's not myself . . . but it is."

"I suppose. After all, why would I have anything to be ashamed of when it comes to you, right? Will Riker, the great, Will Riker the wise. Will Riker who, even when he betrays his ideals, doesn't do it out of some nasty, dirty political cause. No, no. He does it . . ." He made a *thumpa-thumpa* gesture with his hands over his chest. ". . . for love." He paused and then said, "You know, Will . . . so many people ask themselves, if they had it to do over differently, would they? When the question had to do with your relationship with Deanna, you were probably the luckiest bastard in the galaxy. My existence gave you the opportunity to find that out. And the answer was, No, you wouldn't do it differently. How very gratifying."

"What's your point?"

"My point is . . . how do I get to find out? If I had something to do over again, would I do it differently? I don't get to have a convenient re-creation of me through a transporter accident. So if I want to find out if I'd do things differently . . . there's only one way to find out. I have to do it myself."

And before the full meaning of Tom's words managed to weigh on him, Will suddenly felt a pinch in his arm. He looked down and saw two, small dartlike objects nestled in his right biceps. Then his gaze swiveled over to Tom's hand, where a small weapon was held.

"Good night, Will," he said.

The world moved sideways around Will Riker. He tried to pull his head together, but he couldn't do it. A moment later he slumped over onto the floor.

"After all," Tom asked Will's insensate body, "how easy is it to betray one more person . . . when you've betrayed before?"

When the Romulans showed up, they saw only one Riker sitting in the middle of the room . . . the one with the Starfleet uniform.

"Where's Will Riker?" they asked.

"How do I know where he is. Am I my brother's keeper?" said Tom. "He said he had other matters that he needed to attend to. That's all I know. You want him so much, you go find him."

For all the seriousness of the moment, Tom was finding it somewhat amusing. For what seemed ages now, Tom Riker had been masquerading as Will Riker, hoping not to be found out. His impersonation had been so perfect that he had convinced the Romulans he was, in fact, Will Riker. Yet now he had to pass himself off as Tom Riker . . . which should have been simple, considering that he *was* Tom Riker, but even that was going to be slightly tricky since he had to remember to answer only to the name of Tom rather than Will . . . even though Will wasn't really his name . . . except it was.

His head started to hurt.

"Come on, then," one of the guards said, and they escorted Tom Riker down the hallway, leaving an unconscious Will Riker crunched up unseen in the closet.

Moments later, Tom was face-to-face with Sela. He looked for some hint of suspicion in her eyes, but there didn't seem to be any. "So, Tom . . . we understand each other?"

"Perfectly."

She presented him with the bottle of Romulan ale. "You are not to open it before you present it to Gowron. If he sees that it was tampered with—even by someone who is as theoretically trustworthy as you—he might have some trepidation about drinking from it."

"And we wouldn't want that."

"No," she said significantly. "We wouldn't."

"How am I going to get there?"

"We have a Federation runabout, which we captured some time ago. It will be more than sufficient. Once you arrive there, arrange for a meeting with Gowron and do what needs to be done. Believe me, I will know if you do not. And I will know if you seek help or try to betray us. We have eyes and ears there."

"What if something happens I can't control? Deanna, Worf, and Alexander shouldn't suffer if I try but fail."

"You're right. They shouldn't." Her voice turned hard. "So unless you intend to die in the attempt . . . I suggest you don't fail."

Twenty-three

"Will!" Picard said in amazement. "I didn't expect to see you here!"

And standing in the doorway, Riker replied, "That, Captain . . . makes two of us."

Slowly Tom Riker entered Picard's guest quarters, pretending to look around in as casual a fashion as he could. The fact was, his mind was racing fast and furiously.

This was it. Here was Jean-Luc Picard himself, capable of helping Tom Riker save the day.

When Tom had arrived on the Klingon homeworld, unannounced, he had gotten a fairly surprised greeting from the local officials. He had come up with an involved cover story explaining that he had journeyed to Qo'noS, purely on his own, as a gesture of friendship to let Gowron know that not everyone in Starfleet approved of the recent overtures to the Klingons. That would very likely appeal to Gowron's vanity. He would certainly welcome him on that basis.

Tom, however, did not have the opportunity to so much as open his mouth. For the first words that he was greeted with upon his arrival were "We assume you're here to join Picard."

Tom had done everything he could to cover his surprise. "Yes. Yes, that's correct." And the next thing he knew, he was being ushered into the presence not of Gowron, but of Picard. It left Tom in something of a lurch. There was now no politic way for him to inform Gowron that he wanted an audience, because the obvious question would be, why did he want to meet with Gowron separately? On the other hand, matters did become a bit easier. As it was, he was assured of seeing Gowron since, obviously, he was going to be meeting with Picard as well.

But even better . . . all he had to do was tell Picard the truth. Confide in him, tell him where the others were being held, and Picard could take it from there. He could contact Starfleet, they could send a rescue ship, and that would be that. It was perfect.

It was too perfect.

He didn't know whether he could trust Picard or not.

He didn't really know the man, not really. Will Riker knew him well enough, of course, but if Tom Riker was living proof of anything, it was that one cannot always trust the surface. Sela had taken pains to hold Picard up as trusted by the Klingons. Was that her expressing distaste for an opponent . . . or had he been turned by the Romulans? Or what if this wasn't even really Picard, but a shapeshifter of some kind, and the real Picard was gone? Was the fact that he was trusted by the Klingons something that she was boasting about because it worked to their advantage? Sela had said repeatedly that they had people there on Qo'noS, watching every move. Was that true . . . or was it simply something she was saying in order to make sure that Riker—any Riker—did as he was told to do?

But if Picard was on the Romulan side, then why in the world was someone else needed to try and poison Gowron? Well, that was obvious, of course. By having someone as key as Picard in their corner, it gave the Romulans a tremendous advantage not only in terms of their involvement with the Klingons, but in Starfleet itself. Tom could make the attempt on Gowron's life and Picard could easily claim that he knew nothing about it, that Riker had acted completely on his own. Picard's hands would remain clean.

Tom had absolutely no idea what to do. It was ironic: He was judging the entire world through his own perspective of skewed morality.

The thing was, he knew how to save Gowron.

And the fact was that the hostages should be able to save themselves. Because it was, in fact, William Riker who had been left behind in the Romulan outpost. But it wasn't William Riker who Sela thought was a traitor. Instead it was William Riker, the Starfleet officer, who—like Tom—would be in the odd position of having to impersonate himself. Sela trusted Will Riker—the Will Riker she knew, in any event. And because of that trust, Will would certainly have the opportunity to find a way to get them off of there. Hell, they might even be free already.

So he didn't have to trust Picard.

Except . . . he couldn't be one hundred percent sure that Will Riker could get Deanna, Worf, and Alexander off the Lintar moon. He needed to provide a fallback, but had to do so in such a way that, if Picard were a traitor—and Sela later found out about it—she wouldn't think that Tom had been dealing in less than good faith and had been planning to betray them from the get-go.

It was all very complicated. But Tom was becoming increasingly sure that he knew how to deal with it. The only downside was . . .

. . . it was going to cost him his life.

But he had come to regard that as a very small price to pay.

"Sit, Will! Please, sit," Picard said, gesturing for Tom to join him. Tom sauntered over to a chair, swung it around, and straddled it. "I must admit, I'm a bit confused. I thought Starfleet assigned you to the Academy for the interim."

"There was a last-minute rearrangement of schedules to accommodate another professor," Tom said easily. "It turned out he was available now, but not later. So they flip-flopped us. Actually, I start six months from now."

"Good heavens. All that time on your hands."

"It is daunting, sir."

"What brings you out here, of all places?"

"To be perfectly honest, sir . . . as you say, with all that time on my hands, I had nothing else to do. Starfleet said this is where you were. I figured I'd come join you. Spend some time together without having to worry about the day-to-day business of running the *Enterprise*."

"Well, that's a splendid idea, Will, but I admit to being a bit surprised. Starfleet led me to believe that they were going to be keeping my whereabouts rather quiet."

"I can be persuasive, sir."

"I've always known that about you, Number One."

They chatted for a while about things of varying consequence. All the while,

Tom wished desperately that he could see into the man's head, know whether this was some sort of elaborate ruse or whether Picard was genuinely a trustworthy individual. It was truly disturbing to Tom that his own actions had rendered him so unable and unwilling to trust others. Indeed, it was the first thing that he had ever felt truly disconcerted about in regards to his joining the Maquis. As they chatted, Tom noticed—of all things—a book lying on what appeared to be Picard's nightstand. "A paper book, Captain? Don't see those very often."

"I've always been a fan of such antique objects. You know that, Number One."

"Yes. Yes, of course I do, sir. Do you mind—?" He picked it up and made no effort to hide his surprise. *"A Christmas Carol?"*

"What can I say? I have a fatal weakness for Dickens."

"So do I, actually. Funny. I was just discussing that with someone not too long ago."

"Oh? Do I know him?"

Tom thought of Saket and wondered how differently things would have gone for him if Saket had not died. "No," Tom said after a moment. "No . . . I don't think so." Quickly trying to change his tone, he said, "Why *A Christmas Carol,* of all things?"

"It deals with themes I find attractive. Redemption. The thought that no soul is so completely beyond hope that he cannot turn things around for himself. In some ways, it doesn't matter what you did in the past. Only what you do in the future."

"Of course the past matters, Captain. Why else would there be punishment? Otherwise every day would be a clean slate." He put the book down.

"Hopefully, Number One, someday as the human races continues to develop . . . the very fact of the wrongdoing will be sufficient punishment, so that—yes—we can have a clean slate every day. Why, what's your favorite Dickens work?"

"A Tale of Two Cities. One man . . . identical to another . . . sacrificing himself so that those who are important to him have a second chance at life and happiness."

He thought of what he had done to that point . . .

. . . and thought of what he intended to do tomorrow . . .

. . . and he murmured, " 'It is far, far better thing that I do, than I have ever done; it is a far, far better rest that I go to . . . than I have ever known.' "

"Are you all right, Number One?"

"Quite all right, sir."

"Very well. If it's all the same to you, Will . . . I think I'll turn in early tonight. My discussions with Gowron and Kahless thus far have been less than exemplary. I'm hoping that tomorrow might be better. Who knows? Perhaps with you here as well, we can be twice as convincing."

"That," Riker smiled, "is certainly my plan."

They were scheduled to meet with Gowron, Kahless, and whomever else at fifteen hundred hours the next day, Gowron apparently having other business to attend to before he could meet with them.

Riker sat in his guest quarters, the bottle of Romulan ale nearby. There was a computer screen in front of him. He said, "Computer . . ."

"Working," came a harsh, guttural voice. He wasn't sure why he had expected anything else, considering where he was.

"Computer . . . I am about to record a message. It . . ."

Riker stopped. He thought he had heard a noise, something rather odd and liquid, as if there was a leak somewhere. He turned in his chair and looked behind him, checking to see if something was dripping. Nothing. Place was completely dry. Weapons and such up on the wall, the same as in Picard's quarters. Uncomfortable furniture. Nothing out of the ordinary.

He turned back to his computer. "This message is to be delivered to Jean-Luc Picard tomorrow at precisely sixteen hundred hours. Alert him that a message is waiting for him via his combadge. Is that understood?"

"Understood."

"Message as follows." He paused a moment and then said, "Captain . . . I am not William Riker. I am Thomas Riker. It is my mission to poison Chancellor Gowron tomorrow. The reasons are . . . my own. I intend to carry out this mission. But I want you to be informed that the . . . real . . ." The word had stuck in his throat. ". . . William Riker . . . along with Deanna Troi, Worf, and Worf's son, Alexander, are being held captive on the moon of Lintar Four. Please dispatch a vessel to retrieve them as quickly as possible. This is Tom Riker . . . out."

He leaned back, rubbing his eyes and feeling exhausted. There was so much he had wanted to say, so many explanations to give. But he hadn't dared risk it, just in case Picard was in fact a traitor. That way, if Sela did see the message, she wouldn't for a moment think that Tom hadn't been giving it his all . . . and, ideally, wouldn't take revenge on the others because of it.

The universe would go back to having one, and only one, William Thomas Riker. And that was probably for the best.

With that in mind, and knowing that this was to be the last day of his very odd life, Tom Riker went to bed and—to his surprise—slept soundly.

When Will Riker came to in the closet, dressed in the clothes that he had seen Tom Riker wearing not all that long ago, he thought for a moment that he had completely lost his mind. But Will was no dummy, and within moments he had figured out exactly what had happened. He couldn't believe it, but he had figured it out, just as Tom had suspected he would.

Will emerged from his room to find no Romulan guards standing there. This was too perfect. He smoothed his shirt and looked around, trying to decide the best course of action. Obviously the first priority was to get Deanna, Worf, and Alexander the hell off this place. He wasn't quite sure how he was going to accomplish it, but he was reasonably sure he could do it.

He walked down the corridor, his arms moving in a relaxed and easy rhythm, and then he saw Sela coming toward him from the other direction, accompanied by several Romulan guards. "Where did you get off to, Will?" she asked, walking up to him and putting her hands on her hips.

"Just feeling a little . . . worn out," he said.

"Now, Riker," she said, touching his chin affectionately. "Are you implying that I'm the one who wore you out?"

"I wasn't going to say that." He grinned.

"Oh, good." And then she turned to the guards and said, "Take him."

Before Riker could move so much as an inch, the guards were on him from all sides. "What are you doing?!" he shouted as they dragged him down the hallway. Sela followed, looking amused at his confusion.

Moments later they had brought him to the cell where Worf, Deanna, and

Alexander were being held. Without a second's hesitation, they shoved him in with the others. He thudded to the floor.

"You can pick him up," Sela said. "I know he's dressed like mine . . . but he's yours."

"What?" said a confused Deanna.

As if explaining to an idiot, Sela said patiently, "That's Will Riker. But he's not my Will Riker. He's yours. The one who almost got his head handed to him by your beloved Klingon over there."

"What?" Deanna said again, not comprehending any more than she did before.

Sela let out an impatient sigh as Riker got to his feet. "The man who was here before, representing himself as Will Riker . . . the man whom we rescued from a Cardassian prison colony . . . was actually Tom Riker. This man . . . who apparently decided to go along with the charade when he and you first arrived here . . . is Will Riker."

"You knew all along," said an astounded Deanna.

"Not all along. Not when I first . . . acquired him. But I'm not stupid. I did further checking, discovered that one Lieutenant Tom Riker had been sentenced to Lazon Two. Did still more checking and discovered his origins. Intelligence-gathering happens to be one of my specialties, Deanna."

"But then why did you let the masquerade continue?"

"Because I felt that he would be useful to me. In the short term, I found him . . . amusing. Although on our first 'date,' Kressn was kind enough to 'push' him in my direction. Oddly, he didn't need any extra urging after that. In the long term I intended to use him all along for my plan with Qo'noS. When you entered the picture, I simply adapted it to accommodate your presence. I didn't truly expect Worf to agree to cooperate. Believe me, I know the Klingon mind-set all too well. One Riker or the other, in the end, it makes no difference to me."

Something Sela had said earlier suddenly dawned on Deanna. She looked at Worf and said, "You and Will had a fight?"

"It was a disagreement," Worf said stonily.

Riker snorted and then turned back to Sela. "So at the moment . . . you've allowed your lover to take my place, to very likely go to his death . . . in order to have him poison Gowron. And you don't care about it."

To his surprise, Sela laughed.

"Poison Gowron? Is that all your imagination can handle? This has never been about simply poisoning Gowron."

Riker looked at her in confusion, as did the others. "Then what—?"

"Tom Riker thinks that he's carrying a bottle of poisoned ale. He's not. He's carrying a carefully prepared airborne virus, genetically engineered and crafted, developed by a little-known race called the Redeemers, who reside primarily in Thallonian space, and obtained for me by an old friend and mentor named Saket. The moment that he opens the bottle, in Gowron's presence, the virus will erupt from the bottle. The genie"—she smiled as if at some private joke—"will emerge and fulfill all my wishes. It will kill Gowron and everyone else in the council chamber. It will then spread throughout the immediate area and, by my estimates, obliterate every Klingon on the face of their homeworld within thirty-six hours."

Worf gasped audibly. Even the stoic Klingon seemed horrified by the scope of what Sela was discussing so calmly.

"Now, of course, the Klingon Empire is far-reaching. Not all of the Klingons will die. But I assure you, they will know who to blame. I will personally make sure of that. So you see, Tom gets to sacrifice himself on your behalf . . . you three I will set free, into a galaxy where what remains of the Klingon Empire will be eager to annihilate anyone or anything having to do with Starfleet, including counselors and Klingons in uniform . . . and I get my fondest desire. Everybody wins."

When Tom Riker and Jean-Luc Picard were escorted into the council chamber, Tom's heart fell as he saw that the entire council was there, along with Gowron and Kahless himself.

Terrific.

"Riker!" growled Gowron. "This is an unexpected . . . pleasure. What are you doing here?"

Riker stepped forward, the bottle of Romulan ale in his hand. "I'm here to add my sentiments to those expressed by Captain Picard . . . and to present a further token of esteem which I think you may find amusing."

He hold it up for Gowron to see. Gowron uttered a curt laugh. "Romulan ale!" This engendered further laughter from the other Klingons in the council. "Where did you get it?"

"Off a captured Romulan ship. It was the commander's private stock, I believe."

This prompted another round of guffaws and cheers, and several Klingons thudded their fists on their armrests in approval.

Gowron stepped down to receive the bottle. He took it from Riker, looking the bottle over . . .

. . . and then Riker said loudly, "What did you say, Chancellor?"

Gowron looked up at him in mild confusion.

Before he could get a word out, Riker cut him off, with clear anger in his voice. "I am hurt, Chancellor! I bring you this gift . . . and you would imply such a thing?"

"What did you say, Gowron?" demanded Kahless.

Gowron turned to Kahless, clearly befuddled. "I said—"

Before he could get the word "nothing" out, Riker jumped in once again. "He said, 'It's probably poison!' "

Immediately there was an outcry from the Klingons, shouts of surprise. Riker caught Picard's surprised look from the corner of his eye.

Gowron stood there, dumbfounded.

"What would you suggest, Gowron?" demanded Riker. "What would put your mind at ease? Are you going to insist I drink it first?"

And for just a moment . . . just a brief moment . . . he made full and direct eye contact with Gowron, and put as much desperation and as much of an unspoken cue into his look as he could. He could try and bluff the thing the rest of the way through . . . but he prayed that Gowron picked up on it.

Gowron's eyes narrowed.

"Yes!" he suddenly said. "Yes, I insist. If you bring this gift so freely, then you should not have any problem having the first drink!"

"Gowron!" Kahless said reprovingly.

Gowron turned toward Kahless and shot back, "These are dangerous times, Kahless! One cannot be too careful! You should know that!" He looked back to

Tom Riker and said, "You first, Riker." He handed the bottle back to him. "Here. Open it. For all I know," he added, "it might explode when you do so."

And Tom Riker, convinced that he had managed to stave off an intergalactic incident . . . thought, *Good-bye, life. Good-bye, second chance. Good-bye everything that I ever wanted to, or hoped that I would be able to, accomplish. Good-bye, Deanna. Good-bye, Will . . . and for God's sake, don't screw our life up this time . . .*

. . . and he twisted the cork.

Twenty-four

Sela sat in the communications room, awaiting word from her sources on the Klingon homeworld.

She could not recall a time when she had been happier. She knew that, thanks to the distances involved, it would be some time before she heard about the occurrence of the actual event.

She envisioned the planet cluttered with Klingon corpses. Klingons, dead and dying, old and young, tangled together in heaps of rotting flesh. It was going to be her calling card, her ticket back into the good graces of her people. No longer would she be Sela the ronin. No longer would she be without any true ties to her people. No longer would she be a failure and, most important, no longer would she be a disgrace to the memory of her father.

Her mother, of course, could rot in hell. Weak woman, that's what she had been. If she'd any strength in her, she would have stayed alive.

"Sela . . ."

Nearby, a Romulan woman named Beji, who was on far-sweep sensor duty, suddenly turned in her seat. Her color had gone several shades of white.

"We have a problem," she said.

The bottle wouldn't open.

He pulled on the cork again and again, and was unable to pry it off. He looked up at Gowron, who was clearly completely lost at this point as to what in the world Riker was trying to do with all of this.

And suddenly the bottle began to twist and writhe in his grasp. Utterly confused, Riker dropped the bottle to the ground and stared at it in astonishment.

The bottle righted itself . . . and grew. It stretched, transforming, morphing, until it was as tall as Tom Riker himself. Then it filled out, becoming humanoid, becoming . . .

"Hello, Lieutenant Riker," said Odo.

Pandemonium had just set in at the moon of Lintar IV.

"It's a Federation starship!" Beji informed her. "And it's coming straight for us!"

"Are you sure?" she demanded.

"Positive!"

Sela's mind was in a whirl. They were too far off the beaten path for this to be a coincidence. There was no way that the starship was coming simply to check out colonization possibilities on one of the uncolonizable planets in the system. That's why they had chosen this particular area.

It was impossible. It couldn't have been the prisoners who alerted them. When they had first arrived, Sela had questioned them as to how they had found the hide-away, so as to know whether or not their security was threatened and a relocation necessary. Will Riker—the real one—had given them an involved and frankly improbable tale of a psychic link with Deanna Troi, which Sela had been prepared to dismiss out of hand until Kressn confirmed that Riker was telling the absolute truth. It was one of those instances where truth was remarkably stranger than fiction.

But that being the case, then how . . .

It didn't matter.

The Romulan warbird was in orbit around the moon and cloaked. But in order to transport anyone up, the warbird was going to have to decloak . . . and the moment that it did, the starship would be able to target it. In order to minimize the amount of time that the ship would be vulnerable, it was necessary to get everyone together in one place and bring them up at one time.

"The prisoners," she said in a tight fury. "Somehow they must have gotten word out! Let's go! Grab the prisoners, bring them to the transport center! All hands, rendezvous at the transport center! We've got to get out, now!"

Immediately half a dozen Romulans descended to the lower section to round up Worf, Deanna, Riker, and Alexander. At disruptor-point, and with Kressn overseeing the operation, they were brought out of the room in which they'd been imprisoned and were hurried down a corridor. Unfortunately, the extreme pressure of the situation, and the flat-out rushing by the Romulans, cost them dearly.

Because Alexander suddenly stuck out a foot and tripped one of the Romulans. He tumbled forward, banging into another, drawing the attention of a third . . .

. . . and that was all the opening that the Starfleet personnel needed.

Riker suddenly pivoted and lashed out with a fist, smashing the face of the nearest Romulan. It knocked him off balance and Riker grabbed his disruptor, turning and shooting down a second. Worf and Alexander, meantime, plowed into the nearest ones. Worf grabbed one by the arm, swung him around into a second while Alexander leaped onto the back of a third and tried to snap his neck. He lacked the muscle strength to do it, but he wrenched the Romulan's neck severely and caused him to fall in agony.

Kressn, stepping back from the chaos, unleashed a broad-based command of *"Terror"* into their minds. For a moment it stopped them, sending fear into their movements, chilling them to the bone. But Kressn was accustomed to dealing with one mind at a time. Over four, he was stretching his abilities . . . and he gave Deanna Troi the opening she needed. Deanna was, for the most part, an empath, but linked into her mind as he was, it gave her the opportunity to cut back at him. And with a fury born of indignation, she sent an enraged thought straight into Kressn's mind with such force that it practically blew off the back of his head as

YOU HURT MY MOTHER, YOU BASTARD!!

ripped through his mind. Worf, Alexander, and Riker also caught a bit of it. But the main recipient of her ire was Kressn, who staggered, numb for a moment, unable to move.

Worf and Riker swung at the same time, Worf to the head, Riker to the gut. The double impact nearly broke Kressn in half and he went down, unconscious before he hit the floor. For a moment Riker and Worf looked at each other . . .

. . . and then they looked away.

Worf grabbed up a fallen Romulan who was still conscious and snarled, "What is happening?"

"Federation starship! We're . . . we're evacuating!"

"Are we now," said Worf. He drew back a fist and with a quick gesture knocked the Romulan cold.

"Let's make sure as few get away as possible!" shouted Riker, and they quickly gathered the disruptors from the fallen Romulans. They started running, Riker and Worf on point, Alexander in the middle, Deanna taking up the rear.

It was like a shooting gallery.

They kept stumbling over groups of Romulans who were hurrying toward the transport center. Although the Starfleet team was outnumbered, they consistently had the element of surprise since at no time were the Romulans anticipating someone within the confines of their own hideaway opening fire on them. Romulans went down, crashing into each other, blown backward by the disruptor blasts. Riker and Worf aimed as carefully as they could, and their marksmanship was fairly consistent, resulting in a minimum of fatalities. What he lacked in accuracy, Alexander more than made up for in enthusiasm, although at one point he came close to blowing off his father's head.

Offensive weapons fire not being her strong suit, Deanna mostly felt their pain. Except once when a squad of Romulans, apparently alerted to their presence, actually managed to get the drop on them from behind, at which point Deanna ruthlessly mowed them down single-handedly. Worf and Riker gaped, and Deanna calmly blew imaginary smoke off the barrel of the disruptor.

Then, from just ahead, they heard the sound of transporter beams.

They charged forward, rounded a corner, and saw Sela and the remains of her people beaming out of existence. Worf got off a shot, but too late as it went straight through Sela without damaging her. Sela, for her part, saw that they were free and spat out something that was clearly a curse, albeit hard to make out over the whine of the beams. A moment later, they had vanished.

"Damn!" snapped Riker.

"Next time, Will," Deanna said in a tone that was meant to be comforting. But all it did was accentuate Riker's frustration.

And then, suddenly, they heard the sound of more transporter beams. Figures were beginning to materialize right where the Romulans had vanished only moments before.

"Looks like next time came sooner than we anticipated," Riker said. "Weapons, everyone!" They formed a firing squad, preparing to obliterate what appeared to be the returning Romulans.

And then the Starfleet personnel lowered their weapons as the new arrivals fully materialized. It was an away team from a starship, their phasers out and ready for trouble. When they saw who they were facing, their actions became a mirror image as they likewise lowered their weapons. The woman in charge of the away team stepped forward. She had short blond hair and an amused expression.

"Well well well, I should have known. Riker. I should have known if anyone would be in the middle of this mess, it would be you. Deanna, Worf." She nodded to each of them.

"Who's this?" asked Alexander in confusion.

She grinned. "Commander Elizabeth Shelby, kiddo. First officer, *Starship Excalibur,* Captain Korsmo commanding. You're now officially saved."

Twenty-five

"K'hanq! Excellent! Thank you for coming in answer to my summons."

K'hanq entered Gowron's private study, bowing slightly as he did so. "When Gowron summons, how can I do anything but respond."

Gowron gestured for him to sit. "Well, you startled me, I must admit. After the attempted assassination several days ago, you left the planet rather quickly."

"Of course, Chancellor. As one of your reliable sources of security information, I felt it imperative that I immediately investigate how such a thing could have happened."

"As it turns out," Gowron said, "I did some investigating on my own. It is a rather fascinating story, as near as I can determine. Shall we compare notes?"

"If you wish, Chanc—"

"I shall go first. It's most intriguing. Listen—

"Deanna Troi and Alexander, son of Worf, had been kidnapped by Romulans, led by a woman named Sela. Worf was determined to go in pursuit of them. That much I knew. What I did not know was that William Riker . . . the real one . . . was being held prisoner on a Cardassian penal world in a case of mistaken identity. Worf rescued him from the penal camp and together they set out for what they believed to be the hideout of the Romulans. They were concerned, however, lest they run into difficulties beyond their ability to handle. They desired to leave word with Picard as to their activities and the full scope of their situation, but for various reasons felt they could not contact Starfleet directly."

"Indeed," said K'hanq neutrally.

"Worf, however, recalled someone whom his future mother-in-law, Lwaxana Troi, had mentioned as being utterly dependable and discreet. A changeling named Odo, who is the resident head of law enforcement at the station which the Cardassians refer to as Terok Nor and Starfleet calls Deep Space Nine. They relayed as much as they knew at the time to Odo. Odo, in turn, tracked down Picard and came here to deliver the message in person. Seemed he was a bit concerned that any messages which would arrive on Qo'noS might be subject to scrutiny by Klingon authorities. A very suspicious individual, this Odo."

"Perhaps we should have him on staff?" suggest K'hanq.

"Perhaps indeed. So imagine the surprise of both Picard and Odo when they were informed that a man purporting to be William Riker had arrived. Well, Picard knew instantly that this was none other than Thomas Riker. He was curious as to Riker's intent, and engaged him in conversation, while the shapechanger hid on a nightstand, disguised—at Picard's request—as a copy of an old Earth novel entitled *A Christmas Carol.* Picard, you see, felt that this Riker was a troubled individual. He said he was hoping that he could—you should find this amusing—redeem the fellow.

"When Thomas Riker returned to his quarters, Odo followed him. The changeling slid under the door in his liquid form. For a moment, he thought that Riker had heard him, but by the time Riker turned around Odo had already assumed a disguise as a sword on the wall. Odo eavesdropped on Riker, listened to him record a message that was to be delivered to Picard after what Odo believed to be an assassination attempt on me. Since Riker seemed to be carrying no weapons on him, and kept looking at the bottle of Romulan ale, Odo surmised that that was the instrument of intended murder. After Riker retired, Odo reported back to Picard, having determined the missing officers' whereabouts from eavesdropping on Riker. Starfleet was informed so that a rescue ship could be dispatched. Odo rested himself for a time . . . and then took the place of the bottle himself. They were curious to see what Riker would do . . . but at the same time, they wanted to make certain that I did not come to harm. Most considerate of them, I think."

"Very much so."

"It turns out that Tom Riker had taken the place of Will Riker, whom the Romulans were trying to force to assassinate me . . . or, at least, so he thought. The bottle, when later scanned, turned out to contain . . . well, we won't go into that. In any event, Riker was unaware of that and was prepared to drink the poison himself, under guise of insistence from me. In that way he hoped to save me, and avoid any accusation of Federation complicity. Obviously, if he drank it himself, the argument would have been made that he did not know the contents. That it was all some sort of horrible mistake. It all became moot, of course, but still . . . amazingly brave on his part. Do you not think so?"

"Unquestionably so. What happened with the Federation vessel and the Romulans?"

"A number of the Romulans were captured, although Sela and some of her personnel still managed to escape."

"And Thomas Riker? Certainly the Cardassians wanted him back."

"Yes indeed, they did. But you know, it was the oddest thing. Just before the Cardassians arrived . . . Thomas Riker escaped."

K'hanq sat up, confused. "Escaped? How?"

"Apparently those who had been assigned to guard him were unaccountably lax. I have, of course, chastised them severely. Last Riker was seen, he was in his runabout fleeing the approaching Cardassians. It is possible they captured him . . . then again, there is a slim chance he got away. Oddly, no one seemed particularly upset about it . . . except the Cardassians, of course. But I think we can survive their wrath."

"Yes, of course."

"Interesting, isn't it, K'hanq. Even the Starfleet officers who are in disgrace . . . still have enough strength of character to honor alliances. It hardly answers all of my concerns . . . but nonetheless, it is something to think about, is it not?"

"Most definitely, Chancellor."

"So tell me." Gowron leaned forward. "Does my information match with yours?"

"It is, in fact, far more detailed than mine, Chancellor. I am abashed. Perhaps it should be you who is in the intelligence-gathering business."

"Perhaps," smiled Gowron. "Perhaps." Then he slapped his legs and stood. K'hanq did as well. "Go, K'hanq. Continue to keep your ear to the ground. Let us know what you hear."

"I will, Gowron."

As K'hanq was about to leave, Gowron turned to stare out the window of his sanctum and he said, in a sort of offhand manner, "By the way, K'hanq . . . I spoke to Worf in some detail as well. He told me something rather curious: that this Sela seemed to have detailed knowledge of the concerns I had expressed in regards to the Federation."

"Hmm," said K'hanq. His hand was already straying to his belt, where he had a small disruptor tucked away. "Well . . . that was hardly a secret, Chancellor. I wouldn't be concerned about—"

"It was a secret, K'hanq . . . at the point where Sela related the information. The only ones who knew were me . . . and you." Gowron had still not turned to face K'hanq. "The implication is rather clear . . . and unpleasant . . . ?"

"Yes. I see." K'hanq leveled his weapon at Gowron.

Gowron, however, already had his weapon in his hand and he shot backward at waist level. The disruptor blast caught K'hanq dead center, lifting him up and smashing him squarely into the wall. K'hanq hung there for a moment as if defying gravity, and then tumbled to the floor.

Gowron turned his head slightly so that the lens mounted on the back of his collar could properly pick up K'hanq's unmoving body.

"I know you see, K'hanq," said Gowron as if he were still alive. "But some of us see . . . more than others."

Twenty-six

When Lwaxana opened her eyes, Deanna was waiting for her.

"Ohhhh, Little One," she said, her voice just above a whisper. "Am I dreaming?"

"No."

"Would you tell me if I were?"

"Yes," Deanna assured her with a laugh.

"He came for you? He did?"

"Yes. Yes, he did. He said you helped. Thank you."

Lwaxana shrugged as she settled back more comfortably into the hospital bed. "All I did was build upon what you already taught him . . . and what you had together. The rest was entirely the two of you." Then she remembered and her eyes filled with tears. "Mr. Homn . . . he . . . is he . . ."

"He's fine, Mother. At least, he's going to be fine. I had no idea . . . there are mountains that are more vulnerable than he is. The doctors say he'll be up and around and mute in no time."

"That's good to hear. And me . . . ?"

"You're mending. Should be out of here about the same time as Mr. Homn, actually."

"Oh, thank God. I wouldn't want to have to worry about cooking."

"I'll take care of it, Mother. I'll take care of both of you. The captain has arranged for my staying here awhile."

"Ah, Jean-Luc. I knew I could count on him." Then she said, "Mr. Worf fought like a madman to protect you, didn't he."

"He did, yes."

She sighed. "I . . . suppose I could be wrong about him. Perhaps . . . well . . . it's miraculous, really. You have two men who love you. I think I'm rather jealous, when one gets down to it. How are you going to choose, Little One? Things can't stay as they are, they—"

"Mother . . ." She patted Lwaxana's hand. "Don't worry about it. The biggest problem people have is that they choke-hold life and don't let it happen. Everything will sort itself out if we just let it."

"I taught you that, didn't I. Many years ago."

"Yes, Mother."

Lwaxana closed her eyes and let out a contented sigh. "I'm a very wise woman."

"Yes, Mother."

When Deanna went to the inn, Worf was waiting for her.

She looked around. Everything of his was already packed. Her things were not. Worf was sitting very still in the middle of the room. At first he didn't even seem to notice her when she came in. She looked at him in curiosity and said, "Worf?"

"I was thinking about . . . when Admiral Riker came back from the future . . . to save you."

"Why were you thinking about that?"

For the first time there actually seemed to be a touch of resigned admiration in Worf's voice. "He reordered the universe for you. That was how much he loved you. And yet I . . . could not find it in myself to save you from Sela. . . ."

"Because of your honor. You did what was right for you."

"Alexander has . . . requested some time away from me. He desires to return to his grandparents. I have . . . given him permission to do so. He has already left. I would have thought he would understand, that I had taught him well. Obviously I did not. Is that the pupil's fault . . . or the teacher's?"

At first Deanna didn't believe it. Naturally Worf had no reason to lie, but nonetheless it was hard for her to grasp. But it was true; all of Alexander's things were gone. She just hadn't noticed it before.

"I . . . have been concerned that you do not love me as you do . . . Will Riker," Worf said slowly. "I realize now that my priorities have been . . . misplaced. My concern should have been . . . that I do not love you as he does. You deserve that measure of love, Deanna. And I deserve . . ."

"What? What? Nothing, Worf? Is that what you're going to say?" She took one of rough hands in hers. "You're tearing yourself up over this. It's not right."

"No . . . it is not. Nor can I hope to find peace in my current frame of mind. For you see . . . despite all of it . . . I still believe that I did the right thing and Riker the wrong. And yet I realize that what he did was right . . . but I cannot understand why. I must learn, Deanna. I cannot be him, nor should I want to be . . . but in a way I do . . . but it conflicts with what I have been taught."

"So . . . so what are you going to do?"

"Learn other things."

"You can learn them with me, Worf. We can learn together."

He looked at her bleakly. "I am doing this . . . for you, Deanna. It—we—will never work. Never. Deanna . . . look at me. I am nothing like you. Look . . . your eyes are tearing up. Mine are dry. They are always dry. I will never, truly, make you happy, nor you me. You and Riker belong together. The thought that you and I can never have that measure of love . . . that I am incapable of giving it to you . . . angers me. I must deal with this anger . . . with that which I lack . . . with all of it. I will be returning to Qo'noS shortly, to serve in whatever capacity Gowron needs me. But I will ask him to release me to the clerics of Boreth. I suspect he will do so, as in many ways it serves both our purposes. There I will study . . . and learn . . . and, very likely, stay."

"Stay." She felt infinitely sad. "And that is how you're going to deal with difficulty loving, Worf? By running away from it?"

And Worf stared at her in a way that she had never seen before. The Klingon warrior, who had fought battle after battle . . . who had thrown himself into all manner of physical punishment . . . who had taken pleasure in flaunting just how much pain he could take . . . said four words she never thought she would hear him say:

"It . . . hurts . . . too much."

It was as if he had spent every last bit of energy getting out that sentence. And then, everything that could possibly be said having been said, he gathered up his belongings and left the room. Deanna sat there, alone, staring at the emptiness, feeling as if all the energy in the room had left with him.

When Deanna went to the Troi mansion, Will Riker was waiting for her.

A cleaning crew had already been through and put much of the house back in order. The walls had been rebuilt and replastered. Most of the objets d'art and such had not been replaced, since that was awaiting Lwaxana's personal touch. Indeed, the only thing that seemed to have survived, miraculously, was a vase over in the corner. Riker had placed the vase on a table and was fiddling with it when she walked in. He smiled at her.

"Will! What are you doing here?" Then she brought herself up short, folded her arms and said, "Two pair."

"Four of a kind," Riker replied immediately.

She relaxed slightly. It was the new signal they had developed for each other, just on the off chance that there was the slightest reason to suspect that Thomas Riker had unexpectedly shown up. "So . . . so what are you doing here?"

"Well, I did bring a few things with me when I came by here the first time. I came planetside to get them . . . which I have." He indicated a satchel near him. "And I . . . wanted to find out how Lwaxana is. And Mr. Homn."

"She's fine. They're both going to be fine. What about Starfleet? Are you in trouble for . . . ?"

"Well, I'm hardly on Jellico's top ten list, but the fact that we helped to capture a number of known Romulan terrorists and busted up a conspiracy to commit genocide on the Klingons certainly weighed heavily enough in our favor that Starfleet is willing to overlook the little matter of my being AWOL."

"That's certainly a relief."

He took a deep breath and said, "Deanna . . . I've been doing a lot of thinking . . . about us."

"Really. Well . . . so have I."

"And I . . ."

"And I . . ."

They laughed, both having spoken at the same time. "Can I go first?" asked Will.

"Of course."

"Deanna . . . I should never have tried to come between you and Worf."

Her face fell. "What?"

"It was . . . it was wrong of me. Perhaps one of the most wrong things I've ever done. I had no right. Worf was correct when he said I had my chance. I did. I was angry at him for taking you away, and I had no reason to be because I let you get away. You and Worf should be with each other, and . . . I know that 'I'm sorry' doesn't begin to cover it. But . . . I'm sorry. And that's it, that's what I came here to say."

"Worf has gone off to a monastery."

He stared at her. "What?"

"He broke off the engagement. We're not getting married. He says"—she folded her arms—"that he can never love me to the depth and degree that you do."

"He said that?"

She nodded.

"I . . . see."

" 'I see'? Will," and Deanna almost had to laugh, "you went through heaven and hell to find me . . . even my own ex-fiancé says we're meant to be together, and the most you can muster is 'I see'?"

"I mean, I don't know how to react."

"Well . . . you could take me in your arms. You could hold me, kiss me, tell me you love me. Those are acceptable approaches. That's what you came here to do, wasn't it?"

"Yes, but . . ." He started to pace the room, looking more and more uncomfortable. "But it's not . . . it wouldn't be right somehow."

She looked at him as if he'd grown a third eye. "Wouldn't be 'right'?"

"Deanna . . . let's say that I say all that to you. And you tell me you love me, too. That you want the two of us to be together forever."

"I don't know if I would say that, but would that be so terrible if I did?"

"Well . . . yes . . ."

"Yes?" Deanna felt as if someone had just knocked her world forty-five degrees to starboard.

"Look at it from my point of view. . . ."

"I'm trying!"

"If I said and did all the things that I'd been thinking of doing . . . and you told me you loved me and so on . . . how would I know it's genuine? Worf just dumped you."

"I wouldn't say 'dumped'. . . "

"All right, he called off the engagement. He broke it off. That . . . that must be shattering to you. You're probably still in shock, still trying to deal with it."

"I'm dealing with it fine, Will. It's you I'm getting impatient with."

"But if I attempt to put together a relationship with you now, I won't really know if it's what you genuinely want . . . or whether you're just on the rebound from Worf and looking for any emotional port in a storm. It would be disrespectful to the relationship you just had with Worf. You're one big walking exposed nerve. . . ."

"I'm not an exposed anything!" Deanna said. "What I am is a woman who just had a fiancé step aside on behalf of a man who is now saying that he doesn't want me out of respect to the man who stepped aside for him! I'm starting to feel like a leper!"

"It's not like that, Deanna," and he took her in his arms, holding her tight and rocking her back and forth. She found herself melting into the warmth of him and moving with the swaying. "I . . . do love you. I do. You know that."

"And I love you, Will."

"I just think we should give it time."

She stopped rocking and took a step back to look up at him. "Time," she said, her voice flat.

"Yes, time. That's all. And during that time we'll be working toward a—"

"Time!?"

"Yes. Time until it feels right . . ."

And she stalked him. Riker backed up apprehensively. "Deanna . . ."

"You know what? The only time you seem to want me . . . is when you can't have me! But when I'm available, suddenly you run in the opposite direction!"

"That's not true," Riker protested, running in the opposite direction. He snagged his satchel and said, "I think what we should do is discuss this when you're less emotionally worked up. This is for your own good. . . ."

"I am sick of people doing things for my own good, and I can assure you, you have not even begun to see me get worked up."

"Wait . . . I know." He held up a cautioning figure and put on his most charming smile. "I know . . . what you like to hear." He cleared his throat, straightened his shoulders, and, sounding more romantic than he ever had, started to recite . . .

> "I hold you close to me.
> Feel the breath of you, and the wonder of you
> And remember a time
> Without you
> But only as one would remember
> a bleak and distant *whoa!!!"*

The last word was the result of Riker seeing that Deanna had suddenly grabbed up the vase that he had so carefully placed on the table. She swung it in a fast underhand arc and let fly. Riker barely dodged as the vase shattered against the wall next to him.

"I read you poetry and you throw breakable objects at me in response?" he asked in astonishment. "How could you—?"

"It felt right!" bellowed Deanna.

"I'll . . . I'll see you back on the *Enterprise* . . . okay . . . ?"

"Not if I see you first!"

Deanna flopped down onto the couch as she listened to Riker's hastily retreating footsteps. She shook her head and sighed.

"Either I'm going to marry him . . . or kill him," she said after a time. And then she realized that the two weren't necessarily mutually exclusive.

It made her feel a little better.

NOW

Worf awoke with a start . . . and looked for Jadzia.

She wasn't there. Her scent remained in the chair, but she was gone. It took a moment for that fact to sink in, and when it did, he felt more empty than ever.

Nothing. It had all been for nothing.

He rummaged around their . . .

. . . his . . .

. . . quarters a bit more . . . and then he found a picture. A picture of the two of them from their wedding day. Worf and Jadzia, smiling toward the camera. Happy. So happy.

For nothing.

It had made no difference at all.

He ran his fingers across her portrait . . .

And the portrait was wet.

He didn't realize the origin at first . . . and then he did. It was liquid, coming from his own eyes, dripping onto the picture.

And his mind suddenly went to the world of Soukara. The world where they were to meet the Cardassian informer, Lasaran . . . and Jadzia had become injured. Had he left her, had he completed the mission . . . she would have died, there on Soukara. Instead he had come back for her, abandoned the mission, tossed aside everything that he had ever learned about duty . . .

. . . for her.

. . . for Jadzia.

Because of what he had felt for her. Feelings that were beyond anything, he realized, that he had ever felt for Deanna.

More tears fell from his eyes and he moved the picture so it wouldn't become wet.

He was still Klingon. Honor was as important to him as ever. That had never lessened in him . . . and yet . . .

. . . and yet . . .

. . . his first duty had been to her. To them. To his wife, to his beloved.

And he knew, beyond any question, perhaps with greater clarity than he had ever known before, that he would have done anything for her. That had been the plan, that they were to be together, forever and ever. Nothing could ever separate them. But she had gone away, and he had not expected it. And his first impulse had been to close off everything, to retreat once more, to look back on their life together and say it had made no difference. No difference . . .

. . . but he was wrong.

It had made a difference. For he felt things now, depth of emotion, passion, and the ability to covet a loving relationship beyond anything that he would once have thought possible. The death of their union did not end that. Those feelings, once tapped, could not be denied. He could try, of course. He could try and push it away . . .

. . . but that would be wrong. Wrong for the legacy that she had left him, wrong for the man that he had always wanted to be and—thanks to her—now was.

He held the picture tight to him and allowed the tears to cascade down his cheeks. He did not sob out loud; that would have been too much. Instead the tears flowed in eerie silence, but it didn't matter.

It hurt . . . but he didn't mind. It was a good hurt, the kind that one can grow from and learn from if one chooses to.

If he loved again, it could never be as it was with her. Never.

For she had been his first.

The first to get into his heart and soul. He realized that now. The first that he would sacrifice anything for. He would have died for her. Now he had to live for her.

And love with another . . . would be different necessarily better or worse. Even though he had once said it to Alexander, only now did he truly understand. It was just different, and should be celebrated as such. And it would never diminish what they had. He would keep it close to his heart, tucked away, and even as he made his way through life, that first love would still always be there. Nothing could end that love . . . even the end of the lover herself.

For he would always have in his head that first time they saw each other . . . the first time they held hands, the first time they kissed, the first time that their bodies pressed against each other, flesh to flesh, and they joined in a perfect union that neither time, nor distance, nor even death itself could ever take away.

He could move on without her, but in a way, she would always be with him. A fragrant flower, gone, yet he still had the sense of her within him.

And it would not be for nothing as long as he remembered that.

He kissed the picture gently, and she smiled back at him. And a word came to him through the years . . . a word that belonged to neither his race, nor hers . . . and yet, somehow, it was a part of the heart and soul of all races.

He pressed the picture against his chest, and in a voice that was deep and resonant and filled with hope for the future, he said . . .

"Good journey . . . Imzadi . . ."

A Look Inside

Imzadi and *Triangle: Imzadi II*

with Peter A. David

Kevin Dilmore: Let's go to 1989 and *Strike Zone,* your first *Star Trek* novel.

Peter A. David: That was not my first foray into *Star Trek;* just into *Star Trek* novels. Predating that, depending on how far back you want to go. When I was fifteen or sixteen years old, I did some fanzine work. My first professional work for *Star Trek* was on the DC Comics run of *Star Trek* [in 1988]. The DC comic actually led to my getting the novel.

KD: Tell us about that.

PAD: What had happened was that the *Star Trek* comic license had lapsed. So the comic story that I was writing just went away. It caught me somewhat off guard, as I had started on a multiple-issue story line, which I was not able to finish. I got put together with Dave Stern, the editor [of the Pocket Books' *Star Trek* line] at the time, who was a big fan of my work on the *Star Trek* comics. We got together for lunch, and he said he'd like to talk to me about writing *Star Trek* novels. I said to him, "Well, there's one I would love to do. I started a story for the *Star Trek* comic book, and I'd love to write an original *Star Trek* novel that continues and finishes up the story from the comic." Dave said to me, "Okay, here's the problem. I am booked up for original *Star Trek* novels for the next three years. However, we've just started up a *'[Star Trek: The] Next Generation'* line, and we need books for that. If you can write a novel quickly, I can have you on the stands in six months." And I said, "Did I say original *Trek?* I meant to say *Next Generation."*

KD: Fast thinking.

PAD: I quickly took the entire story line that I originally intended to conclude as an original series story and converted it over into the *Next Generation.* I carried over one of the characters from the original comic book—and fortunately enough it was a Klingon, so I just aged him a bunch of years—and essentially told the same story but just dropped in the other characters. As a consequence, you might say that it was then very easily the longest continuing story in *Star Trek* because it jumped over the generations. That was the story that developed into *Strike Zone.*

KD: Did the story require a lot of rewriting?

PAD: I did, of course, do a lot of additional things to it to make it unique to the *Next Generation* universe. You can't just substitute Picard for Kirk and think you're going to tell the same story. I also wound up introducing an alien race in there called the Selelvians, who I continue to use to this day and actually are turning into somewhat of a threat to the Federation. So, you see, waste nothing.

KD: So, fast forward to 1991, when the concept of Imzadi was born. This was published as one of the first hardback novels for *Star Trek: The Next Generation,* so I assume that the first thought was to make it a big story, something that was quite an event.

PAD: Yes. This was an idea that was presented to me. Essentially, they came to me and asked whether I would be interested in telling the story that would be the history of the Riker-Troi relationship. That certainly sounded intriguing to me. The thing is, I didn't want it to be something just set in the past. I wanted to have some degree of resonance in "modern," if you'll pardon the expression, *Star Trek.* That's when it occurred to me to essentially do a story that would be a reverse of [the original *Star Trek* series episode] "City on the Edge of Forever." Instead of Kirk going back to set things right by allowing Edith Keeler to die, Riker was going to deliberately go back and change the world around him because he could not tolerate the notion that Deanna Troi had died.

KD: I see.

PAD: [Scriptwriter] Harlan Ellison's original concept had Kirk trying to save Edith Keeler. He loved her so much that he literally was willing to let the rest of the universe go down the chute to save this woman. That's an incredibly powerful concept. And indeed it winds up that it's Spock who has to make sure that Edith Keeler dies, because he is the one who is nonhuman and is therefore not restricted by such things as emotion. But the sentiment was, "No, no, Kirk is the hero. Kirk can't allow the entire universe to go down the chute for this one woman." I always thought it would be interesting to do a story where we do just that. I put Riker in the Kirk role, and that is exactly what he is prepared to do. He is so convinced that this is a universe not worth living in, that he is willing to risk having the whole thing go right down the pipe or whatever if it means getting Deanna back. Then you have Data in the Spock role, and that just seemed to me to have a great deal of potential in terms of drama. So that's what I went for.

KD: Were you nervous about meeting fan expectations when dealing with not only one of the linchpins of the *Next Generation* in the Riker-Troi relationship but also in bringing in the Guardian of Forever?

PAD: No, I wasn't nervous about it because I was really confident that I had written a strong story. The further I got into the story, the more I was convinced that I really had something that the fans were really going to respond to. And it's very rare that I have that kind of confidence. It's not like I write a book and say, "Oh, the fans are going to love this." Usually, I'm very, very uncertain as to what the fans will like, and I put the book out there and keep my fingers crossed. But I was pretty certain that *Imzadi* would strike a personal chord with the fans. There were points in the book where even I was getting choked up. The point in the book where the Riker from the future has come back to the *Enterprise* and he sees Deanna and he just starts to lose it . . . I was losing it when I was writing that scene just from the raw emotion of that sequence. In fiction, we're almost jaded by the notion that "Someone's dead? Well, they'll come back. They can always come back."

KD: Especially in *Star Trek.*

PAD: The thing is, the notion of thinking that somebody is dead—you buried him—and he is alive and here before you, the true, real emotion that that would provoke is just overwhelming, which is why I had Riker being overwhelmed by it.

KD: And particularly in this case, given the intensity of the mental link that the two share.

PAD: Exactly.

KD: What else was it about the nature of that particular relationship that drew you to the project aside from being able to tell an emotionally intense story?

PAD: The thing that is exciting about working on *Star Trek* is that you're really contributing to a growing mythos. You know? Here I thought was an opportunity to contribute something really major to the mythos. If I'm writing a story that is simply an original story of mine, people will read it and get involved into what happens to those characters. But the characters of the *Star Trek* universe are practically mythic. It is a rare opportunity to make a substantive contribution to something that is so much bigger than yourself. So I was really eager on that basis.

KD: And it is a story that the fans have embraced. I would imagine that if I questioned readers as to what is their favorite Peter David novel, *Imzadi* would figure among the top three for each person I asked.

PAD: There have been people who have held polls for favorite *Star Trek* novels, and *Imzadi* invariably places near or at the top every single time, which obviously I am very flattered about. As I said, I really was confident that I had something magical there, but for people to respond to it as they did, even I could not have dreamed that. There's one guy who took the poem that Riker wrote to Deanna and used it as his wedding vows. I mean, wow!

KD: That would be pretty humbling to me.

PAD: Yeah, I was amazed and flattered.

KD: What kind of intensity were you drawing on yourself when writing *Imzadi?* I noted in the foreword that you mentioned your wife.

PAD: To a very large degree, the book was a love letter to my then-wife. It was about the pure intensity and power of love and what it can make us do. And they always say "Write what you know."

KD: With Deanna being so in tune to emotion and sensitivity, do you think that makes her intrinsically a *Star Trek* character that embodies love?

PAD: It certainly puts her in a unique position to be able to understand it as well as what people will do on behalf of it.

KD: There were ramifications from Riker's actions in *Imzadi.*

PAD: Right, up to and including having Data trying to kill him.

KD: So five or six years pass, and you are given the opportunity to write a sequel to *Imzadi.* Was that daunting?

PAD: Well, daunting and annoying. You see, I didn't want the book to be a sequel to *Imzadi.* I very much felt that *Imzadi* should be a piece in and of itself, not to mention the fact that this new concept was about Worf and Troi. My attitude was that *Imzadi* was Riker and Troi. If it's Worf and Troi, it should be called something else. I really didn't like the idea of the "sequel." So the agreement we came to was that the title of the book would be *Triangle* and that it would say *Imzadi II* but in really small letters.

KD: [laughs] And on the cover of my copy of the book . . .

PAD: It has *Imzadi II* really huge and it has *Triangle* in really small letters, so little that I wondered why they bothered to put it on. So I don't like viewing it as a sequel to *Imzadi* because the books are so different.

KD: I think the books are radically different in tone and storytelling. But aren't the two relationships themselves radically different?

PAD: Well, yes. *Imzadi* was about the newness of relationships and the willingness to do anything and make any sacrifice on behalf of love. Whereas *Imzadi II* was about relationships ending. It was about loss and about the concept that love cannot conquer all. Why? Well, by that point, I was divorced. I was in the midst of a not-real-fun place in my life. Naturally, the person that I was while writing *Imzadi* no longer existed. I couldn't write the same paean to love that I did the first time out because first, it would have been inappropriate in terms of the subject matter. I still felt that Troi and Worf had no business being together. And the other thing was that just from my own state of mind, that's not where I was. To say nothing of the fact that I was not able to write the ending I wanted to write.

KD: I had picked that sentiment up from other interviews I have read. That surprised me. You had posited a logical extension of the story ending with Riker's marriage proposal to Troi.

PAD: I wanted to end *Imzadi II* with them getting engaged. It seemed logical to me. I really felt that's where the characters would be going. But the guidelines said I couldn't change the status quo. So I had to write an ending that was not exactly what I wanted to do. I wrote a story that ends with them not getting engaged. As a result, the entirety of the story involved failure—failure to commit, failure to succeed as a couple . . . failure, failure, failure. So that is kind of hard to compare that to *Imzadi,* which was about love conquering all.

KD: It sure is.

PAD: Many people said they didn't like the second one as much as they did the first, and I really can't blame them. I don't think it would have been an issue had the book not been called *Imzadi II.* But because it was, fans were expecting something that was going to push all of the same emotional buttons that *Imzadi* did, and it couldn't because of a variety of factors.

KD: Chief among those factors has to be the relationship between Worf and Troi, which you already said didn't ring true to you.

PAD: Not only did it not ring true to me, but we already knew from [*Star Trek:*] *Deep Space Nine* that it had failed. In *Imzadi,* I was telling the story of a relationship that had incredible importance to both of them, and you found yourself wondering whether Riker from the future was going to succeed in his quest. Everything was up in the air. In *Imzadi II,* you knew that Worf and Troi were not going to remain together because *Deep Space Nine* already told you that.

KD: And to top it all, there's Worf's ill-fated marriage to Jadzia.

PAD: You were dealing with a lot more "knowns," so it was trickier and ultimately less satisfying. I don't think it's a bad book by any stretch of the imagination, but compared to *Imzadi,* which is going to be inevitable when you call it *Imzadi II,* it's going to come up short. That's why I wish to this day that they had called it ANYTHING else.

KD: But you still look back kindly on both books despite your ending of *Imzadi II.*

PAD: There were some people who, I hope, were satisfied by the ending. It wasn't exactly the way I would have wanted to end it and, given the events of [*Star Trek:*] *Nemesis,* you just find yourself just gnashing your teeth. But that's the way the cookie crumbles.

KD: This is great perspective on your work, Peter. Thanks for your time.

PAD: Sure. Thank you.